APOLLODORUS

THE LIBRARY

II

122

APOLLODORUS

THE LIBRARY

WITH AN ENGLISH TRANSLATION BY

SIR JAMES GEORGE FRAZER,

F.B.A., F.R.S.

FELLOW OF TRINITY COLLEGE, CAMBRIDGE

IN TWO VOLUMES

II

LONDON

WILLIAM HEINEMANN LTD

CAMBRIDGE, MASSACHUSETTS

HARVARD UNIVERSITY PRESS

MCMLXX

American ISBN 0–674–99136–2
British ISBN 0 434 99122 8

First Printed 1921
Reprinted 1946, 1956, 1963, 1970

Printed in Great Britain

CONTENTS

APOLLODORUS

THE LIBRARY

ΑΠΟΛΛΟΔΩΡΟΥ

ΒΙΒΛΙΟΘΗΚΗ

Γ

X. Ἄτλαντος δὲ καὶ τῆς Ὠκεανοῦ Πληιόνης
ἐγένοντο θυγατέρες ἑπτὰ ἐν Κυλλήνῃ τῆς Ἀρκαδίας, αἱ Πληιάδες προσαγορευθεῖσαι, Ἀλκυόνη
Μερόπη Κελαινὼ Ἠλέκτρα Στερόπη Ταϋγέτη

---

[1] As to the Pleiades, see Aratus, *Phaenomena*, 254–268 ;
Eratosthenes, *Cataster.* 23 ; Quintus Smyrnaeus, *Postho-
merica*, xiii. 551 *sqq.*; Scholiast on Homer, *Il.* xviii. 486 ;
Scholiast on Pindar, *Nem.* ii. 10 (16) ; Scholiast on Apollonius
Rhodius, *Argon.* iii. 226 ; Hyginus, *Astronom.* ii. 21 ; *id. Fab.*
192 ; Ovid, *Fasti*, iii. 105, iv. 169–178 ; Servius on Virgil,
Georg. i. 138, and on *Aen.* i. 744 ; *Scholia in Caesaris Germanici Aratea*, p. 397, ed. F. Eyssenhardt (in his edition of
Martianus Capella) ; *Scriptores rerum mythicarum Latini*,
ed. G. H. Bode, vol. i. p. 73 (First Vatican Mythographer,
234). There was a general agreement among the ancients
as to the names of the seven Pleiades. Aratus, for example,
gives the same names as Apollodorus and in the same order.
However, with the exception of Maia, a different list of
names is given by the Scholiast on Theocritus (xiii. 25), who
tells us further, on the authority of Callimachus, that they
were the daughters of the queen of the Amazons. As their
father was commonly said to be Atlas, they were sometimes
called Atlantides (Apollodorus, below ; Diodorus Siculus, iii.
60. 4 ; compare Hesiod, *Works and Days*, 382). But there
was much diversity of opinion as to the origin of the name
Pleiades. Some derived it from the name of their mother

APOLLODORUS

THE LIBRARY

BOOK III.—*continued*

X. ATLAS and Pleione, daughter of Ocean, had
seven daughters called the Pleiades, born to them at
Cyllene in Arcadia, to wit: Alcyone, Merope, Celaeno,
Electra, Sterope, Taygete, and Maia.[1] Of these,

Pleione; but the most probable view appears to be that the
name comes from πλεῖν, "to sail," because in the Mediterranean area these stars were visible at night during the
summer, from the middle of May till the beginning of
November, which coincided with the sailing season in antiquity. This derivation of the name was recognized by some
of the ancients (Servius on Virgil, *Georg.* i. 138). With
regard to the number of the Pleiades, it was generally agreed
that there were seven of them, but that one was invisible, or
nearly so, to the human eye. Of this invisibility two explanations were given. Some thought that Electra, as the
mother of Dardanus, was so grieved at the fall of Troy that
she hid her face in her hands; the other was that Merope,
who had married a mere man, Sisyphus, was so ashamed of
her humble, though honest, lot by comparison with the
guilty splendour of her sisters, who were all of them para-
mours of gods, that she dared not show herself. These alternative and equally probable theories are stated, for example,
by Ovid and Hyginus. The cause of the promotion of the
maidens to the sky is said to have been that for seven or
even twelve years the hunter Orion pursued them with his
unwelcome attentions, till Zeus in pity removed pursuer and
pursued alike to heaven, there to shine as stars for ever and

Μαῖα. τούτων Στερόπην μὲν Οἰνόμαος ἔγημε,
Σίσυφος <δὲ>[1] Μερόπην. δυσὶ δὲ ἐμίχθη Ποσει-
δῶν, πρώτῃ μὲν Κελαινοῖ, ἐξ ἧς Λύκος ἐγένετο, ὃν
Ποσειδῶν ἐν μακάρων ᾤκισε[2] νήσοις, δευτέρᾳ δὲ
Ἀλκυόνῃ, ἣ θυγατέρα μὲν ἐτέκνωσεν Αἴθουσαν
τὴν Ἀπόλλωνι Ἐλευθῆρα τεκοῦσαν,[3] υἱοὺς δὲ
Ὑριέα καὶ Ὑπερήνορα. Ὑριέως μὲν οὖν καὶ
Κλονίης νύμφης Νυκτεὺς καὶ Λύκος, Νυκτέως δὲ
καὶ Πολυξοῦς Ἀντιόπη, Ἀντιόπης δὲ καὶ Διὸς
Ζῆθος καὶ Ἀμφίων. ταῖς δὲ λοιπαῖς Ἀτλαντίσι
Ζεὺς συνουσιάζει.

2   Μαῖα μὲν οὖν ἡ πρεσβυτάτη Διὶ συνελθοῦσα
ἐν ἄντρῳ τῆς Κυλλήνης Ἑρμῆν τίκτει. οὗτος ἐν
σπαργάνοις[4] ἐπὶ τοῦ λίκνου κείμενος, ἐκδὺς εἰς

---

[1] δὲ added by Bekker.   [2] ᾤκισε Faber : ᾤκησε A.
[3] The MSS (A) add καλλίστην, which is retained by
Westermann, Müller, and Bekker, but omitted by Hercher
and Wagner and regarded as a marginal gloss by Heyne.
[4] σπαργάνοις Heyne (conjecture), Bekker, Hercher : πρώτοις A, Heyne (in text), Westermann : στρωτοῖς Valckenar,
Müller : πρώτοις <σπαργάνοις> Wagner.

---

to continue the endless pursuit. The bashful or mournful
Pleiad, who hid her light, is identified by modern astrono-
mers with Celaeno, a star of almost the seventh magnitude,
which can be seen now, as in antiquity, in clear moonless
nights by persons endowed with unusually keen sight. See
A. von Humboldt, *Cosmos*, translated by E. Sabine, iii.
47 *sq.*
    [1] Compare Pausanias, v. 10. 6. According to another
account, Sterope or Asterope, as she is also called, was not the
wife but the mother of Oenomaus by the god Ares. See
Eratosthenes, *Cataster.* 23 ; Hyginus, *Astronom.* ii. 21 ; *id.*
Fab. 84 and 159 ; *Scriptores rerum mythicarum Latini*, ed.
G. H. Bode, vol. i. p. 73 (First Vatican Mythographer, 234).
    [2] See above. iii. 5. 5.

Sterope was married to Oenomaus,[1] and Merope to Sisyphus. And Poseidon had intercourse with two of them, first with Celaeno, by whom he had Lycus, whom Poseidon made to dwell in the Islands of the Blest, and second with Alcyone, who bore a daughter, Aethusa, the mother of Eleuther by Apollo, and two sons Hyrieus and Hyperenor. Hyrieus had Nycteus and Lycus by a nymph Clonia; and Nycteus had Antiope by Polyxo; and Antiope had Zethus and Amphion by Zeus.[2] And Zeus consorted with the other daughters of Atlas.

Maia, the eldest, as the fruit of her intercourse with Zeus, gave birth to Hermes in a cave of Cyllene.[3] He was laid in swaddling-bands on the winnowing fan,[4] but he slipped out and made his way to Pieria

[3] The following account of the birth and youthful exploits of Hermes is based, whether directly or indirectly, on the beautiful Homeric Hymn IV, *To Hermes*, though it differs from the hymn on a few minor points, as to which Apollodorus may have used other sources. Compare *The Homeric Hymns*, ed. T. W. Allen and E. E. Sikes, pp. 130 *sq.* Among the other literary sources to which Apollodorus may have had recourse was perhaps Sophocles's satyric play *Ichneutae* or *The Trackers*. See below.

[4] Compare the Homeric *Hymn to Hermes*, 21, 63, 150 *sq.*, 254, 290, 358; Sophocles, *Ichneutae*, 269 (*The Fragments of Sophocles*, ed. A. C. Pearson, ii. 258). So Dionysus at birth is said to have been laid on a winnowing-fan (Servius on Virgil, *Georg.* i. 166): hence he got the surname of "He of the Winnowing-fan" (Λικνίτης, Plutarch, *Isis et Osiris*, 35). These traditions as to the gods merely reflected an ancient Greek custom of placing new-born children in winnowing-fans "as an omen of wealth and fruitfulness" (πλοῦτον καὶ καρποὺς οἰωνιζόμενοι). See the Scholiast on Callimachus, *Hymn* I, 48 (*Callimachea*, ed. O. Schneider, i. 109). As to the symbolism of the custom, see W. Mannhardt, "Kind und Korn," *Mythologische Forschungen*, pp. 351–374; Miss J. E. Harrison, "Mystica Vannus Iacchi," *Journal of Hellenic*

APOLLODORUS

Πιερίαν παραγίνεται, καὶ κλέπτει βόας ἃς ἔνεμεν
Ἀπόλλων.¹ ἵνα δὲ μὴ φωραθείη ὑπὸ τῶν ἰχνῶν,

Studies, xxiii. (1903), pp. 292–324. The custom was not
confined to ancient Greece, but has been widely practised in
India and other parts of the east down to modern times.
The motives assigned or implied for it are various. Sometimes it seems to have been intended to ensure the wealth
and prosperity of the infant, sometimes to guard it against
the evil eye and other dangerous influences. See *Spirits of
the Corn and of the Wild*, i. 5–11. To quote a single example,
among the Brahuis of Baluchistan, "most good parents keep
their babe for the first six days in a *chaj*, or winnowing-basket,
that God may vouchsafe them full as many children as the
basket can hold grain . . . But some folk will have nothing to
do with a winnowing-basket ; it harbours epilepsy, they say,
though how or why I am at a loss to think. So they lay the
child in a sieve, that good luck may pour upon him as
abundantly as grain pours through a sieve" (Denys Bray,
The Life-History of a Brāhūī, London, 1913, p. 13). The
substitution of a corn-sieve for a winnowing-fan seems to be
common elsewhere.

¹ Compare *Homeric Hymn to Hermes*, 68 *sqq.*; Antoninus
Liberalis, *Transform.* 23 ; Ovid, *Metamorph.* ii. 680 *sqq.*
The theft of cattle by the infant Hermes was the subject of
Sophocles's satyric drama *Ichneutae* or *The Trackers*, of
which some considerable fragments have been discovered in
recent years. The scene of the play is laid on Mount Cyllene.
Apollo appears and complains of the loss of the cattle,
describes how he has come from Thessaly and through
Boeotia in search of them, and offers a reward to anyone
who will help him to find the missing beasts. The procla-
mation reaches the ears of Silenus, who hurries to the scene
of action and warmly proffers the services of himself and his
Satyrs in the search, only stipulating that the reward shall
take the solid shape of cash down. His offer being accepted,
the Satyrs at once open on the scent like sleuth-hounds and
soon discover confused tracks of cattle pointing in different
directions. But in the very heat of this discovery they are
startled by a strange sound, the like of which they had never
heard before. It is, in fact, the muffled sound of the lyre

6

and stole the kine which Apollo was herding.[1] And
lest he should be detected by the tracks, he put

played by the youthful Hermes in the cave. At this point
the nymph Cyllene issues from the cavern and upbraids the
wild creatures with the hubbub they are raising in the stillness of the green wooded hills. The Satyrs tender a humble
apology for their intrusion, but request to know the meaning
of the strange sounds that proceed from the bowels of the
earth. In compliance with their request the nymph explains
how Zeus had secretly begotten Hermes on Maia in the cave,
how she herself was acting temporarily as nurse to the child,
how the infant grew at an astonishing and even alarming
rate, and how, being detained in the cave by his father's
orders, he devoted his leisure hours to constructing out of a
dead beast a curious toy which emitted musical notes. Being
pressed for a fuller explanation she describes how Hermes
made the lyre out of a tortoise shell, how the instrument
was "his only balm of grief, his comforter," and how the
child was transported with delight at the ravishing sweet-
ness of the tones which spoke to him from the dead beast.
Unmoved by this touching description, the Satyrs at once
charge the precocious infant with having stolen the cattle.
His nurse indignantly repels the charge, stoutly declaring
that the poor child had inherited no propensity to thieving
either from its father or from its mother, and recommending
his accusers to go and look for the thief elsewhere, since at
their age, with their long beards and bald heads, they ought
to know better than to trump up such ridiculous accusations, for which they may yet have to smart. The nurse's
passionate defence of her little charge makes no more impression on the Satyrs than her previous encomium on his musical
talent : indeed their suspicions are quickened by her reference
to the hides which the infant prodigy had used in the construction of the lyre, and they unhesitatingly identify the
skins in question with those of the missing cattle. Strong in
this conviction, they refuse to budge till the culprit has been
made over to them. At this point the Greek text begins to
fail ; we can just catch a few disjointed fragments of a heated
dialogue between the nurse and the satyrs ; the words
"cows," "thief," "rascal," and so forth, occur with painful
iteration, then all is silence. See *The Fragments of Sophocles,*

ὑποδήματα τοῖς ποσὶ περιέθηκε, καὶ κομίσας εἰς
Πύλον τὰς μὲν λοιπὰς εἰς σπήλαιον ἀπέκρυψε,
δύο δὲ καταθύσας τὰς μὲν βύρσας πέτραις καθή-
λωσε, τῶν δὲ κρεῶν τὰ μὲν κατηνάλωσεν ἑψήσας
τὰ δὲ κατέκαυσε· καὶ ταχέως εἰς Κυλλήνην ᾤχετο.
καὶ εὑρίσκει πρὸ τοῦ ἄντρου νεμομένην χελώνην.
ταύτην ἐκκαθάρας, εἰς τὸ κύτος χορδὰς ἐντείνας
ἐξ ὧν ἔθυσε βοῶν καὶ ἐργασάμενος λύραν εὗρε
καὶ πλῆκτρον. Ἀπόλλων δὲ τὰς βόας ζητῶν εἰς
Πύλον ἀφικνεῖται, καὶ τοὺς κατοικοῦντας ἀνέκρι-
νεν. οἱ δὲ ἰδεῖν μὲν παῖδα ἐλαύνοντα ἔφασκον,
οὐκ ἔχειν δὲ εἰπεῖν ποῖ ποτε ἠλάθησαν διὰ τὸ μὴ
εὑρεῖν ἴχνος δύνασθαι. μαθὼν δὲ ἐκ τῆς μαντικῆς
τὸν κεκλοφότα πρὸς Μαῖαν εἰς Κυλλήνην παραγίνεται, καὶ τὸν Ἑρμῆν ᾐτιᾶτο. ἡ δὲ ἐπέδειξεν
αὐτὸν ἐν τοῖς σπαργάνοις. Ἀπόλλων δὲ αὐτὸν
πρὸς Δία κομίσας τὰς βόας ἀπῄτει. Διὸς δὲ
κελεύοντος ἀποδοῦναι ἠρνεῖτο. μὴ πείθων δὲ ἄγει
τὸν Ἀπόλλωνα εἰς Πύλον καὶ τὰς βόας ἀποδί-
δωσιν. ἀκούσας δὲ τῆς λύρας ὁ Ἀπόλλων ἀντι-
δίδωσι τὰς βόας. Ἑρμῆς δὲ ταύτας νέμων σύριγγα
πάλιν πηξάμενος ἐσύριζεν. Ἀπόλλων δὲ καὶ

---

ed. A. C. Pearson, vol. i. pp. 224–270. From this seemingly
simple piece of mild buffoonery Miss J. E. Harrison would
extract a ritual of serious and indeed solemn significance, of
which, however, she admits that the author of the play was
himself probably quite unconscious. See her learned essay in
Essays and Studies presented to William Ridgeway, ed. E.
C. Quiggin (Cambridge, 1913), pp. 136 *sqq.*

[1] In the *Homeric Hymn to Hermes* (115 *sqq.*) we are told
that Hermes roasted the flesh of two oxen and divided it
into twelve portions (for the twelve gods), but that in spite
of hunger he ate none of it himself.

8

shoes on their feet and brought them to Pylus, and hid the rest in a cave; but two he sacrificed and nailed the skins to rocks, while of the flesh he boiled and ate some,[1] and some he burned. And quickly he departed to Cyllene. And before the cave he found a tortoise browsing. He cleaned it out, strung the shell with chords made from the kine he had sacrificed, and having thus produced a lyre he invented also a plectrum.[2] But Apollo came to Pylus[3] in search of the kine, and he questioned the inhabitants. They said that they had seen a boy driving cattle, but could not say whither they had been driven, because they could find no track. Having discovered the thief by divination,[4] Apollo came to Maia at Cyllene and accused Hermes. But she showed him the child in his swaddling-bands. So Apollo brought him to Zeus, and claimed the kine; and when Zeus bade him restore them, Hermes denied that he had them, but not being believed he led Apollo to Pylus and restored the kine. Howbeit, when Apollo heard the lyre, he gave the kine in exchange for it. And while Hermes pastured them, he again made himself a shepherd's pipe and piped on it.[5] And

[2] Compare Sophocles, *Ichneutae*, 278 *sqq.* (*The Fragments of Sophocles*, ed. A. C. Pearson, ii. 259). In the *Homeric Hymn to Hermes*, 22 *sqq.*, the invention of the lyre by Hermes precedes his theft of the cattle.

[3] In the *Homeric Hymn to Hermes* (185 *sqq.*) it is to Onchestus in Boeotia, not to Pylus, that Apollo goes at first to inquire after the missing cattle.

[4] Compare the *Homeric Hymn to Hermes*, 213 *sq.*, where it is said that Apollo discovered Hermes to be the thief through observing a certain long-winged bird.

[5] Compare the *Homeric Hymn to Hermes*, 511 *sq.*, where, however, nothing is said about an attempt of Apollo to get the pipes from Hermes, or about an exchange of the pipes for

ταύτην βουλόμενος λαβεῖν, τὴν χρυσῆν ῥάβδον
ἐδίδου ἣν ἐκέκτητο βουκολῶν. ὁ δὲ καὶ ταύτην
λαβεῖν ἀντὶ τῆς σύριγγος ἤθελε καὶ τὴν μαντικὴν
ἐπελθεῖν· καὶ δοὺς διδάσκεται τὴν διὰ τῶν ψήφων
μαντικήν. Ζεὺς δὲ αὐτὸν κήρυκα ἑαυτοῦ καὶ θεῶν
ὑποχθονίων τίθησι.

3   Ταϋγέτη δὲ ἐκ Διὸς <ἐγέννησε>¹ Λακεδαίμονα,
ἀφ᾽ οὗ καὶ Λακεδαίμων ἡ χώρα καλεῖται. Λακεδαίμονος δὲ καὶ Σπάρτης τῆς Εὐρώτα, ὃς ἦν ἀπὸ
Λέλεγος αὐτόχθονος καὶ νύμφης νηίδος Κλεοχα-
ρείας, Ἀμύκλας καὶ Εὐρυδίκη, ἣν ἔγημεν Ἀκρίσιος.
Ἀμύκλα δὲ καὶ Διομήδης τῆς Λαπίθου Κυνόρτης
καὶ Ὑάκινθος. τοῦτον εἶναι τοῦ Ἀπόλλωνος ἐρώ-
μενον λέγουσιν, ὃν δίσκῳ βαλὼν ἄκων ἀπέκτεινε.

¹ ἐγέννησε conjecturally supplied by Hercher. A verb is
certainly wanted. It may have been ἔτεκε.

---

the golden wand. However, there is a lacuna in the hymn
after verse 526, and the missing passage may have contained
the exchange in question and the request of Hermes for the
gift of divination, both of which are mentioned by Apollodorus but omitted in the hymn as it stands at present. See
Allen and Sikes on the *Homeric Hymn to Hermes*, 526 *sq.*,
in their edition of the Homeric Hymns, p. 190.

¹ For the gift of the golden wand, see *Homeric Hymn to
Hermes*, 527 *sqq.*

² Compare the *Homeric Hymn to Hermes*, 552 *sqq.* The
reference is to the divining pebbles called *thriae*, which were
personified as three winged sisters who dwelt on Parnassus,
and are said to have been the nurses of Apollo. See Zenobius,
Cent. v. 75; Callimachus, *Hymn to Apollo*, 45, with the
Scholiast; *Etymologicum Magnum*, p. 455. 45, *s.v.* Θρία;
Hesychius, *s.v.* θριαί; *Anecdota Graeca*, ed. Im. Bekker, i.
265. 11, *s.v.* Θριάσιον πεδίον. According to one account, the
divining pebbles were an invention of Athena, which so dis-
gusted Apollo that Zeus caused that mode of divination to
fall into discredit, though it had been in high repute before;

wishing to get the pipe also, Apollo offered to give him the golden wand which he owned while he herded cattle.[1] But Hermes wished both to get the wand for the pipe and to acquire the art of divination. So he gave the pipe and learned the art of divining by pebbles.[2] And Zeus appointed him herald to himself and to the infernal gods.

Taygete had by Zeus a son Lacedaemon, after whom the country of Lacedaemon is called.[3] Lacedaemon and Sparta, daughter of Eurotas (who was a son of Lelex,[4] a son of the soil, by a Naiad nymph Cleocharia), had a son Amyclas and a daughter Eurydice, whom Acrisius married. Amyclas and Diomede, daughter of Lapithes, had sons, Cynortes and Hyacinth.[5] They say that this Hyacinth was beloved of Apollo and killed by him involuntarily with the

and Apollo vented his spite at the practitioners of a rival art by saying that "There be many that cast pebbles, but few prophets." See Zenobius, *l.c.*; Stephanus Byzantius, *s.v.* Θρία. This tradition may perhaps be accepted as evidence that in time the simple mode of divination by pebbles went out of fashion, being cast into the shade by the far more stately and imposing ritual of the frenzied prophetesses at Delphi, whose wild words were accepted as the very utterances of the deity. However, we are informed that in the temple at Delphi there were divining pebbles in a bowl on a tripod, and that when an inquirer applied to the oracle, the pebbles danced about in the bowl, while the inspired priestess prophesied. See Nonnus, in Westermann's *Mythographi Graeci*, Appendix Narrationum, No. 67, p. 384; Suidas, *s.v.* Πυθώ. As to Greek divination by pebbles, see A. Bouché-Leclercq, *Histoire de la Divination dans l'Antiquité*, i. 192, *sqq.*; and my note on Pausanias, vii. 25. 10 (vol. iv. pp. 172 *sqq.*).

[3] Compare Pausanias, iii. 1. 2; Scholiast on Euripides, *Orestes*, 626.

[4] According to Pausanias (iii. 1. 1), Eurotas was a son of Myles, who was a son of Lelex.

[5] Compare Pausanias, iii. 1. 3.

Κυνόρτου δὲ Περιήρης, ὃς γαμεῖ Γοργοφόνην
τὴν Περσέως, καθάπερ Στησίχορός φησι, καὶ
τίκτει Τυνδάρεων Ἰκάριον Ἀφαρέα Λεύκιππον.
Ἀφαρέως μὲν οὖν καὶ Ἀρήνης τῆς Οἰβάλου[1]
Λυγκεύς τε καὶ Ἴδας καὶ Πεῖσος· κατὰ πολλοὺς
δὲ Ἴδας ἐκ Ποσειδῶνος λέγεται. Λυγκεὺς δὲ
ὀξυδερκίᾳ διήνεγκεν, ὡς καὶ τὰ ὑπὸ γῆν θεωρεῖν.
Λευκίππου δὲ θυγατέρες ἐγένοντο Ἰλάειρα καὶ
Φοίβη· ταύτας ἁρπάσαντες ἔγημαν Διόσκουροι.
πρὸς δὲ ταύταις Ἀρσινόην ἐγέννησε. ταύτῃ μίγνυται Ἀπόλλων, ἡ δὲ Ἀσκληπιὸν γεννᾷ. τινὲς
δὲ Ἀσκληπιὸν οὐκ ἐξ Ἀρσινόης τῆς Λευκίππου
λέγουσιν, ἀλλ᾿ ἐκ Κορωνίδος τῆς Φλεγύου ἐν

---

¹ See above, i. 3. 3 ; Nicander, *Ther.* 901 *sqq.*, with the
Scholiast on *v.* 902 ; Pausanias, iii. 1. 3, iii. 19. 5 ; J. Tzetzes,
Chiliades, i. 241 *sqq.* ; Ovid, *Metamorph.* x. 161–219 ; Pliny,
Nat. Hist. xxi. 66; *Scriptores rerum mythicarum Latini*,
ed. G. H. Bode, vol. i. pp. 37, 135 *sq.* (First Vatican Mythographer, 117 ; Second Vatican Mythographer, 181). The
tomb of Hyacinth was shown at Amyclae under the great
image of Apollo ; a bronze door opened into the tomb, and
sacrifices were there offered to him as a hero. See Pausanias,
iii. 19. 3. Compare *Adonis, Attis, Osiris*, Third Edition,
i. 313 *sqq.*

² See above, i. 9. 5, where Apollodorus represents Perieres
as the son of Aeolus (compare i. 7. 3), though he adds that
many people regarded him as the son of Cynortas. See below
iii. 10. 4 note.

³ Compare Pindar, *Nem.* x. 62 (116) *sq.* ; Pausanias, iv.
2. 7 (who seems to have misunderstood the foregoing passage
of Pindar) ; Tzetzes, *Schol. on Lycophron*, 553 ; Hyginus,
Fab. 14, p. 42, ed. Bunte.

⁴ See below, iii. 11. 2.

cast of a quoit.[1] Cynortes had a son Perieres, who married Gorgophone, daughter of Perseus, as Stesichorus says, and she bore Tyndareus, Icarius, Aphareus, and Leucippus.[2] Aphareus and Arene, daughter of Oebalus, had sons Lynceus and Idas and Pisus; but according to many, Idas is said to have been gotten by Poseidon. Lynceus excelled in sharpness of sight, so that he could even see things under ground.[3] Leucippus had daughters, Hilaira and Phoebe: these the Dioscuri carried off and married.[4] Besides them Leucippus begat Arsinoe: with her Apollo had intercourse, and she bore Aesculapius. But some affirm that Aesculapius was not a son of Arsinoe, daughter of Leucippus, but that he was a son of Coronis, daughter of Phlegyas in Thessaly.[5]

[5] The ancients were divided with regard to the mother of Aesculapius, some maintaining that she was a Messenian woman Arsinoe, daughter of Leucippus, others that she was a Thessalian woman Coronis, daughter of Phlegyas. See the Scholiast on Pindar, *Pyth.* iii. 8 (14), who quotes authorities on both sides: amongst the champions of Arsinoe were Asclepiades and an Argive writer named Socrates. The claims of the Messenian Arsinoe were naturally supported by patriotic Messenians, who looked on the god and his sons as in a sense their fellow countrymen. See Pausanias, ii. 26. 3–7, iv. 3. 2, iv. 31. 12. Apollodorus apparently accepted the Messenian view. But on the other side a long array of authorities declared in favour of Coronis, and her claim to be the mother of the god had the powerful support of the priesthood of Aesculapius at Epidaurus, one of the principal seats of the worship of the healing god. See the *Homeric Hymn to Aesculapius*, xvi. 1 *sqq.*; Pindar, *Pyth.* iii. 8 (14) *sqq.*; Apollonius Rhodius, *Argonaut.* iv. 616 *sq.*; Diodorus Siculus, iv. 71. 1, v. 74. 6; Pausanias, ii. 26. 3–7; Hyginus, *Fab.* 202; *id. Astronom.* ii. 40; Servius, on Virgil, *Aen.* vi. 617; Lactantius Placidus, on Statius, *Theb.* iii. 506; *Scriptores rerum mythicarum Latini*, ed. G. H. Bode, vol. i. pp. 17 and 37 (First Vatican Mythographer, 46 and 115). Pausanias,

APOLLODORUS

Θεσσαλία. καί φασιν ἐρασθῆναι ταύτης Ἀπόλλωνα καὶ εὐθέως συνελθεῖν· τὴν δὲ¹ παρὰ τὴν
τοῦ πατρὸς γνώμην [ἑλομένην]² Ἰσχυϊ τῷ Και-
νέως ἀδελφῷ συνοικεῖν. Ἀπόλλων δὲ τὸν μὲν
ἀπαγγείλαντα κόρακα καταρᾶται, ὃν³ τέως λευ-
κὸν ὄντα ἐποίησε μέλανα, αὐτὴν δὲ ἀπέκτεινε.
καιομένης δὲ αὐτῆς⁴ ἁρπάσας τὸ βρέφος ἐκ τῆς
πυρᾶς πρὸς Χείρωνα τὸν Κένταυρον ἤνεγκε, παρ'

¹ τὴν δὲ Aegius, Heyne, Müller, Hercher, Wagner: τοῦ
δὲ A, Westermann, Bekker.
² ἑλομένην Heyne, Müller, Wagner: ἑλομένου A, Bekker:
ἐλωμένου Rᵃ: ἐρωμένου Sevinus, Westermann. Hercher
omits the word, perhaps rightly.
³ ὃν Faber. The MSS. read ὅς or ὡς.
⁴ αὐτῆς A, Heyne, Westermann, Müller, Bekker, Hercher; ταύτης RRᵃ, Wagner.

---

who expressly rejects the claim of Arsinoe, quotes in favour
of Coronis a Delphic oracle, which he regards as decisive:
for who should know the true mother of Aesculapius better
than his own father Apollo? The testimony of the deity
for once was quite unambiguous. It ran thus :—
"O born to be the world's great joy, Aesculapius,
   Offspring of love, whom Phlegyas' daughter, fair Coronis,
      bore to me
   In rugged Epidaurus."
See Pausanias, ii. 26. 7. In modern times the stones of Epidaurus, if we may say so, have risen up to testify to the truth
of this oracle. For in the course of the modern excavations
at the great Epidaurian sanctuary of Aesculapius there was
discovered a limestone tablet inscribed with a hymn in honour
of Apollo and Aesculapius, in which the family tree of the
junior god is set out with the utmost precision, and it entirely
confirms the Delphic oracle. The author of the hymn was a
certain native of Epidaurus, by name Isyllus, a man of such
scrupulous accuracy that before publishing his hymn he took
the precaution of submitting it to the fount of knowledge at
Delphi with an inquiry whether the god would sanction its

And they say that Apollo loved her and at once consorted with her, but that she, against her father's judgment, preferred and cohabited with Ischys, brother of Caeneus. Apollo cursed the raven that brought the tidings and made him black instead of white, as he had been before; but he killed Coronis. As she was burning, he snatched the babe from the pyre and brought it to Chiron, the centaur,[1] by

publication. The deity granted his permission in very cordial terms; hence we may look on the hymn as an authentic document bearing the *imprimatur* of the Delphic Apollo himself. In it the pedigree of Aesculapius is traced as follows: Father Zeus bestowed the hand of the Muse Erato on Malus in holy matrimony (ὁσίοισι γάμοις). The pair had a daughter Cleophema, who married Phlegyas, a native of Epidaurus; and Phlegyas had by her a daughter Aegla, otherwise known as Coronis, whom Phoebus of the golden bow beheld in the house of her grandfather Malus, and falling in love he got by her a child, Aesculapius. See Ἐφημερὶς ἀρχαιολογική, iii. (1885) coll. 65 *sqq.* ; H. Collitz and F. Bechtel, *Sammlung der griechischen Dialekt-Inschriften*, iii. 1, pp. 162 *sqq.*, No. 3342.

[1] The story how Coronis played her divine lover false and was killed by him, and how the god rescued his child from the burning pyre and carried him to Chiron, is told by Pindar, *Pyth.* iii. 8 (14) *sqq.* Compare the Scholia on this passage of Pindar, especially on *v.* 27 (48); Pausanias, ii. 26. 6 (according to whom it was Hermes, not Apollo, who snatched the child from the burning pyre); Hyginus, *Fab.* 202; *id. Astronom.* ii. 40; Lactantius Placidus, on Statius, *Theb.* iii. 506; *Scriptores rerum mythicarum Latini*, ed. G. H. Bode, vol. i. pp. 17, 37, and 118 (First Vatican Mythographer, 46 and 115; Second Vatican Mythographer, 128). All these writers, except Pindar and Pausanias, relate the story of the tell-tale raven and his punishment. The story is also told by Ovid (*Metamorph.* ii. 534 *sqq.*) and Antoninus Liberalis (*Transform.*, 20), but neither of them mentions Aesculapius. It was narrated by Pherecydes, who may have been the source from which the other writers drew their information. See Scholiast on Pindar, *Pyth.* iii. 34 (59). The name of the

APOLLODORUS

ᾧ¹ καὶ τὴν ἰατρικὴν καὶ τὴν κυνηγετικὴν τρεφό-
μενος ἐδιδάχθη. καὶ γενόμενος χειρουργικὸς καὶ
τὴν τέχνην ἀσκήσας ἐπὶ πολὺ οὐ μόνον ἐκώλυέ
τινας ἀποθνῄσκειν, ἀλλ᾽ ἀνήγειρε καὶ τοὺς ἀποθα-
νόντας· παρὰ γὰρ Ἀθηνᾶς λαβὼν τὸ ἐκ τῶν
φλεβῶν τῆς Γοργόνος ῥυὲν αἷμα, τῷ μὲν ἐκ τῶν
ἀριστερῶν ῥυέντι πρὸς φθορὰν ἀνθρώπων ἐχρῆτο,
τῷ δὲ ἐκ τῶν δεξιῶν πρὸς σωτηρίαν, καὶ διὰ
τούτου² τοὺς τεθνηκότας ἀνήγειρεν. [εὗρον³ δέ
τινας λεγομένους ἀναστῆναι ὑπ᾽ αὐτοῦ, Καπανέα
καὶ Λυκοῦργον, ὡς Στησίχορός φησιν <ἐν> Ἐρι-
φύλῃ, Ἱππόλυτον, ὡς ὁ τὰ Ναυπακτικὰ συγ-

¹ ᾧ A : οὗ Hercher, Wagner.
² διὰ τούτου A, Heyne, Westermann, Müller, Bekker,
Hercher : διὰ τοῦτο ES, Wagner (but wrongly, since διὰ with
the accusative is never used to express the instrument).
³ As Heyne pointed out, the following list of persons
raised from the dead by Aesculapius is probably a marginal
gloss which has crept into the text. Nowhere else does
Apollodorus speak of himself in the first person or indeed
make any reference to himself.

---

human lover of Coronis is given as Ischys, son of Elatus, by
Pindar and Pausanias in agreement with Apollodorus. But
Antoninus Liberalis calls him Alcyoneus ; Lactantius Placidus and the Second Vatican Mythographer call him Lycus ;
and the First Vatican Mythographer describes him (*Fab.* 115)
simply as the son of Elatus. As to the connexion of Coronis
with the raven or the crow in Greek legendary lore, see my
note on Pausanias, ii. 17. 11 (vol. iii. pp. 72 *sq.*). Compare
D'Arcy Wentworth Thompson, *Glossary of Greek Birds*, p. 93.

¹ Compare Zenobius, *Cent.* i. 18, who probably copied
Apollodorus. According to Euripides (*Ion*, 999 *sqq.*), Pallas
gave Erichthonius two drops of the Gorgon's blood, one of
them a deadly poison, the other a powerful medicine for the
healing of diseases.

² For other lists of dead men whom Aesculapius is said
to have restored to life, see Sextus Empiricus, p. 658, ed.

16

whom he was brought up and taught the arts of healing and hunting. And having become a surgeon, and carried the art to a great pitch, he not only prevented some from dying, but even raised up the dead; for he had received from Athena the blood that flowed from the veins of the Gorgon, and while he used the blood that flowed from the veins on the left side for the bane of mankind, he used the blood that flowed from the right side for salvation, and by that means he raised the dead.[1] I found some who are reported to have been raised by him,[2] to wit, Capaneus and Lycurgus,[3] as Stesichorus says in the *Eriphyle;* Hippolytus,[4] as the author of the *Nau-*

Bekker; Scholiast on Pindar, *Pyth.* iii. 54 (96); Scholiast on Euripides, *Alcestis*, 1. These two Scholiasts mention that according to Pherecydes the people who died at Delphi were raised from the dead by Aesculapius. To the list of dead men whom Aesculapius restored to life, Propertius adds Androgeus, son of Minos (ii. 1. 61 *sq.*).

[3] The resurrection of these two men by the power of Aesculapius is mentioned also, on the authority of Stesichorus, by the Scholiast on Euripides, *Alcestis*, 1, and the Scholiast on Pindar, *Pyth.* iii. 54 (96). Otherwise the event is apparently not noticed by ancient writers, and of the many legendary persons who bore the name of Lycurgus we do not know which is referred to. Heyne conjectured that the incident took place in the war of the Epigoni against Thebes, when Capaneus, one of the original Seven against Thebes, and Lycurgus, son of Pronax (as to whom see i. 9. 13) may have been restored to life by Aesculapius. This conjecture is confirmed by a passage of Sextus Empiricus (p. 658 ed. Bekker), where we read: "Stesichorus in his *Eriphyle* says that he (Aesculapius) raised up some of those who fell at Thebes."

[4] As to the restoration of Hippolytus to life by Aesculapius see Pindar, *Pyth.* iii. 54 (96) *sqq.*, with the Scholiast; Sextus Empiricus, p. 658, ed. Bekker (who quotes as his authority Staphylus in his book on the Arcadians); Scholiast on Euripides, *Alcestis*, 1 (who quotes Apollodorus as his authority);

APOLLODORUS

γράψας λέγει, Τυνδάρεων, ὥς φησι Πανύασις,[1]
Ὑμέναιον, ὡς οἱ Ὀρφικοὶ λέγουσι, Γλαῦκον τὸι
4 Μίνωος, ὡς Μελησαγόρας λέγει.] Ζεὺς δὲ φοβη-
θεὶς μὴ λαβόντες ἄνθρωποι θεραπείαν παρ' αὐτοῦ[2]
βοηθῶσιν ἀλλήλοις, ἐκεραύνωσεν αὐτόν. καὶ διὰ
τοῦτο ὀργισθεὶς Ἀπόλλων κτείνει Κύκλωπας τοὺς
τὸν κεραυνὸν Διὶ κατασκευάσαντας. Ζεὺς δὲ
ἐμέλλησε ῥίπτειν αὐτὸν εἰς Τάρταρον, δεηθείσης

---

[1] Πανύασις S, Heyne, Westermann, Müller, Bekker: Πανύασσις RR[a] C, Wagner. [2] αὐτοῦ ES: αὐτῶν A.

Eratosthenes, *Cataster.* 6; Hyginus, *Fab.* 49; *id. Astronom.* ii. 14; Lactantius Placidus, on Statius, *Theb.* v. 434, vi. 353 (375).   After his resurrection Hippolytus is said to have gone to dwell at Aricia, on the Alban Hills, near Rome, where he reigned as a king and dedicated a precinct to Diana. See Pausanias, ii. 27. 4; Virgil, *Aen.* vii. 761 *sqq.*, with the commentary of Servius; Ovid, *Fasti*, iii. 263 *sqq.*, vi. 735 *sqq.*; *id. Metamorph.* xv. 297 *sqq.*; Scholiast on Persius, *Sat.* vi. 56, pp. 347 *sq.*, ed. O. Jahn; Lactantius, *Divin. Inst.* i.17; *Scriptores rerum mythicarum Latini*, ed. G. H. Bode, vol. i. p. 118 (Second Vatican Mythographer, 128).   The silence of Apollodorus as to this well-known Italian legend, which was told to account for the famous priesthood of Diana at Aricia, like his complete silence as to Rome, which he never mentions, tends to show that Apollodorus either deliberately ignored the Roman empire or wrote at a time when there was but little intercourse between Greece and that part of Italy which was under Roman rule.

[1] For the raising of Tyndareus from the dead by Aesculapius see also Sextus Empiricus, p. 658, ed. Bekker; Scholiast on Euripides, *Alcestis*, 1 (both these writers cite Panyasis as their authority); Lucian, *De saltatione*, 45; Zenobius, *Cent.* i. 47; Pliny, *Nat. Hist.* xxix. 3.

[2] See above, iii. 3. 1.

[3] This account of the death of Aesculapius, the revenge of Apollo, and his servitude with Admetus is copied almost verbally by Zenobius, *Cent.* i. 18, but as usual without acknowledgment.   Compare Pherecydes, quoted by the

pactica reports; Tyndareus, as Panyasis says;[1] Hymenaeus, as the Orphics report; and Glaucus, son of Minos,[2] as Melesagoras relates. But Zeus, fearing that men might acquire the healing art from him and so come to the rescue of each other, smote him with a thunderbolt.[3] Angry on that account, Apollo slew the Cyclopes who had fashioned the thunderbolt for Zeus.[4] But Zeus would have hurled him to Tartarus;

Scholiast on Euripides, *Alcestis*, 1; Pindar, *Pyth.* iii. 54 (96) *sqq.*; Euripides, *Alcestis*, 1 *sqq.*, 123 *sqq.*; Diodorus Siculus, iv. 71. 1-3; Hyginus, *Fab.* 49; Servius, on Virgil, *Aen.* vii. 761; *Scriptores rerum mythicarum Latini*, ed. G. H. Bode, vol. i. p. 17 (First Vatican Mythographer, 46). According to Diodorus Siculus (*l.c.*) Aesculapius as a physician was so successful in his practice that the death-rate was perceptibly lowered, and Hades accused the doctor to Zeus of poaching on his preserves. The accusation angered Zeus, and he killed Aesculapius with a thunderbolt. According to Pherecydes, with whom Apollodorus agrees, the period of Apollo's servitude with Admetus was one year; according to Servius and the First Vatican Mythographer it was nine years. This suggests that the period may have been what was called a "great" or "eternal" year, which included eight ordinary years. See above, iii. 4. 2, with the note on ii. 5. 11. According to one account the motive for Apollo's servitude was his love for Admetus. See Callimachus, *Hymn to Apollo*, 45 *sqq.*; Scholiast on Euripides, *Alcestis*, 1, quoting Rhianus as his authority. Apollo is said to have served Branchus as well as Admetus (Philostratus, *Epist.* 57), and we have seen that he served Laomedon. See above, ii. 5. 9 note.

[4] According to Pherecydes, quoted by the Scholiast on Euripides, *Alcestis*, 1, it was not the Cyclopes but their sons whom Apollo slew. The passage of Pherecydes, as quoted by the Scholiast, runs as follows : "To him" (that is, to Admetus) "came Apollo, to serve him as a thrall for a year, at the command of Zeus, because Apollo had slain the sons of Brontes, of Steropes, and of Arges. He slew them out of spite at Zeus, because Zeus slew his son Aesculapius with a thunderbolt at Pytho; for by his remedies Aesculapius raised the dead."

APOLLODORUS

δὲ Λητοῦς ἐκέλευσεν αὐτὸν ἐνιαυτὸν ἀνδρὶ θητεῦ-
σαι. ὁ δὲ παραγενόμενος εἰς Φερὰς πρὸς Ἄδμητον
τὸν Φέρητος τούτῳ λατρεύων ἐποίμαινε, καὶ τὰς
θηλείας βόας πάσας διδυμοτόκους ἐποίησεν.

Εἰσὶ δὲ οἱ λέγοντες Ἀφαρέα μὲν καὶ Λεύκιππον
ἐκ Περιήρους γενέσθαι τοῦ Αἰόλου, Κυνόρτου δὲ
Περιήρην, τοῦ δὲ Οἴβαλον, Οἰβάλου δὲ καὶ νηίδος
νύμφης Βατείας Τυνδάρεων Ἱπποκόωντα Ἰκάριον.
5 Ἱπποκόωντος μὲν οὖν ἐγένοντο παῖδες Δορυ-
κλεὺς [1] Σκαῖος Ἐναροφόρος Εὐτείχης Βουκόλος

[1] Δορυκλεύς. Heyne conjectured Δορκεὺς (comparing Pausanias, iii. 15. 1 sq.), which is accepted by Bekker and Hercher.

---

[1] See Appendix, "Apollo and the Kine of Admetus."
[2] As to these genealogies see above, i. 7. 3, i. 9. 5, ii. 4. 5, iii. 10. 3 ; Pausanias, ii. 21. 7, iii. 1. 3 sq., iv. 2. 2 and 4 ; Tzetzes, *Schol. on Lycophron*, 284, 511. Pausanias consistently represents Perieres as the son of Aeolus, and this tradition had the support of Hesiod (quoted by Tzetzes, *Schol. on Lycophron*, 284). On the other hand Tzetzes represents Perieres as the son of Cynortes (*Schol. on Lycophron*, 511). Apollodorus here and elsewhere (i. 9. 5) mentions both traditions without deciding between them. In two passages (i. 7. 3, i. 9. 5) he asserts or implies that the father of Perieres was Aeolus ; in another passage (iii. 10. 3) he asserts that the father of Perieres was Cynortes. In the present passage he seems to say that according to one tradition there were two men of the name of Perieres : one of them was the son of Aeolus and father of Aphareus and Leucippus ; the other was the son of Cynortes and father of Oebalus, who married the nymph Batia and became by her the father of Tyndareus, Hippocoon, and Icarius. Pausanias says that Gorgophone, daughter of Perseus, first married Perieres and had by him two sons, Aphareus and Leucippus, and that after his death she married Oebalus, son of Cynortas (Cynortes), and had by him a son Tyndareus. See Pausanias, ii. 21. 7, iii. 1. 4, iv. 2. 4. Apollodorus, on the other hand, represents Perieres as the father not only of Aphareus and Leucippus, but also

however, at the intercession of Latona he ordered
him to serve as a thrall to a man for a year. So he
went to Admetus, son of Pheres, at Pherae, and served
him as a herdsman, and caused all the cows to drop
twins.[1]

But some say that Aphareus and Leucippus were
sons of Perieres, the son of Aeolus, and that Cynortes
begat Perieres, and that Perieres begat Oebalus, and
that Oebalus begat Tyndareus, Hippocoon, and Icarius
by a Naiad nymph Batia.[2]

Now Hippocoon had sons, to wit: Dorycleus,
Scaeus, Enarophorus, Eutiches, Bucolus, Lycaethus,

of Tyndareus and Icarius by Gorgophone, daughter of Perseus.
See above, i. 9. 5, iii. 10. 3. Tzetzes (*Schol. on Lycophron*,
511) agrees with him as to the sons, but makes Perieres the
son of Cynortas instead the son of Aeolus. Thus there were
two traditions as to the father of Tyndareus; according to
one, his father was Perieres, according to the other, he was
Oebalus. But the two traditions were agreed as to the mother
of Tyndareus, whom they represented as Gorgophone,
daughter of Perseus. According to another account, which
may have been intended to reconcile the discrepant traditions
as to the father of Tyndareus, Oebalus was the son of Perieres
and the father of Tyndareus, Icarius, Arene, and the bastard
Hippocoon, whom he had by Nicostrate. See Scholiast on
Euripides, *Orestes*, 457; Scholiast on Homer, *Il.* ii 581.
This account is mentioned, but apparently not accepted, by
Apollodorus in the present passage, though he says nothing
about the daughter Arene and the bastardy of Hippocoon.
If we accept this last version of the genealogy, Tyndareus
was descended both from Oebalus and Perieres, being the son
of Oebalus and the grandson of Perieres. In a recently dis-
covered fragment of the *Catalogues* of Hesiod, that poet calls
Tyndareus an Oebalid, implying that his father was Oebalus.
See *Griechische Dichterfragmente*, i., *Epische und elegische
Fragmente*, bearbeitet von W. Schubart und U. von Wilamowitz-Moellendorff (Berlin, 1907), p. 30, line 38 (*Berliner
Klassikertexte*, v. 1); *Hesiod*, ed. H. G. Evelyn-White, p.
194, Frag. 68, line 38 (*The Loeb Classical Library*).

APOLLODORUS

Λύκαιθος Τέβρος[1] Ἱππόθοος Εὔρυτος Ἱπποκο-
ρυστὴς Ἀλκίνους Ἄλκων. τούτους Ἱπποκόων
ἔχων παῖδας Ἰκάριον[2] καὶ Τυνδάρεων ἐξέβαλε
Λακεδαίμονος. οἱ δὲ φεύγουσι πρὸς Θέστιον, καὶ
συμμαχοῦσιν αὐτῷ πρὸς τοὺς ὁμόρους πόλεμον
ἔχοντι· καὶ γαμεῖ Τυνδάρεως Θεστίου θυγατέρα
Λήδαν. αὖθις δέ, ὅτε Ἡρακλῆς Ἱπποκόωντα καὶ
τοὺς τούτου παῖδας ἀπέκτεινε, κατέρχονται, καὶ
παραλαμβάνει Τυνδάρεως τὴν βασιλείαν.

6   Ἰκαρίου μὲν οὖν καὶ Περιβοίας νύμφης νηίδος
Θόας Δαμάσιππος Ἰμεύσιμος Ἀλήτης Περίλεως,
καὶ θυγάτηρ Πηνελόπη, ἣν ἔγημεν Ὀδυσσεύς·
Τυνδάρεω δὲ καὶ Λήδας Τιμάνδρα, ἣν Ἔχεμος
ἔγημε, καὶ Κλυταιμνήστρα, ἣν ἔγημεν Ἀγαμέμνων, ἔτι τε Φυλονόη, ἣν Ἄρτεμις ἀθάνατον
7   ἐποίησε. Διὸς δὲ Λήδᾳ συνελθόντος ὁμοιωθέντος
κύκνῳ, καὶ κατὰ τὴν αὐτὴν νύκτα Τυνδάρεω,[3]
Διὸς μὲν ἐγεννήθη Πολυδεύκης καὶ Ἑλένη, Τυνδάρεω δὲ Κάστωρ <καὶ Κλυταιμνήστρα>.[4] λέγουσι

[1] Σεβρός Pausanias, iii. 15. 1 sq.
[2] ἰκαρὶ R (Rᵃ): ἰκαρίωνα A, Heyne, Westermann, Müller,
Bekker, Hercher. For the form Ἰκάριος compare i. 9. 5.
[3] Τυνδάρεω RRᵃ: τυνδάρεως A.
[4] καὶ Κλυταιμνήστρα inserted conjecturally by Gale, Bekker, Hercher, and Wagner, approved by Heyne.

---

[1] As to the banishment of Tyndareus and his restoration
by Hercules, see Diodorus Siculus, iv. 33. 5 ; Pausanias, ii.
18. 7, iii. 1. 4 sq., iii. 21. 4 ; Scholiast on Euripides, Orestes,
457 ; Scholiast on Homer, Il. ii. 581. According to the
Scholiasts on Euripides and Homer (ll.cc.), Icarius joined
Hippocoon in driving his brother Tyndareus out of Sparta.
[2] See above, ii. 7. 3.
[3] According to the Scholiast on Homer (Od. xv. 16), the
wife of Icarius was Dorodoche, daughter of Ortilochus ; but

Tebrus, Hippothous, Eurytus, Hippocorystes, Alcinus, and Alcon. With the help of these sons Hippocoon expelled Icarius and Tyndareus from Lacedaemon.[1] They fled to Thestius and allied themselves with him in the war which he waged with his neighbours; and Tyndareus married Leda, daughter of Thestius. But afterwards, when Hercules slew Hippocoon and his sons,[2] they returned, and Tyndareus succeeded to the kingdom.

Icarius and Periboea, a Naiad nymph,[3] had five sons, Thoas, Damasippus, Imeusimus, Aletes, Perileos,[4] and a daughter Penelope, whom Ulysses married.[5] Tyndareus and Leda had daughters, to wit, Timandra, whom Echemus married,[6] and Clytaemnestra, whom Agamemnon married; also another daughter Phylonoe, whom Artemis made immortal. But Zeus in the form of a swan consorted with Leda, and on the same night Tyndareus cohabited with her; and she bore Pollux and Helen to Zeus, and Castor and Clytaemnestra to Tyndareus.[7] But some say that Helen

he adds that according to Pherecydes she was Asterodia, daughter of Eurypylus.

[4] Perileos (Perilaus), son of Icarius, is said to have accused the matricide Orestes at the court of the Areopagus. See Pausanias, viii. 34. 4.

[5] Compare Pausanias, iii. 12. 1, iii. 20. 10 *sq.* According to the former of these passages, Ulysses won her hand in a foot-race. As to races for brides, see iii. 9. 2, *Epitome* ii. 5, and note on i. 7. 8.   [6] Compare Pausanias, viii. 5. 1.

[7] Compare Euripides, *Helen*, 16 *sqq.*; Lucian, *Dial. deorum*, xx. 14; *id. Charidemus*, 7; Scholiast on Homer, *Od.* xi. 298; Hyginus, *Fab.* 77; *id. Astronom.* ii. 8; *Scriptores rerum mythicarum Latini*, ed. G. H. Bode, vol. i. pp. 27, 64, 119 *sq.*, 163 (First Vatican Mythographer, 78 and 204; Second Vatican Mythographer, 132; Third Vatican Mythographer, 3. 6). As the fruit of her intercourse with the swan, Leda is said to have laid an egg, which in the time of Pau-

δὲ ἔνιοι Νεμέσεως Ἑλένην εἶναι καὶ Διός. ταύτην
γὰρ τὴν Διὸς φεύγουσαν συνουσίαν εἰς χῆνα τὴν
μορφὴν μεταβαλεῖν, ὁμοιωθέντα δὲ καὶ Δία κύκνῳ
συνελθεῖν· τὴν δὲ ᾠὸν ἐκ τῆς συνουσίας ἀποτεκεῖν,
τοῦτο δὲ ἐν τοῖς ἄλσεσιν[1] εὑρόντα τινὰ ποιμένα
Λήδᾳ κομίσαντα δοῦναι, τὴν δὲ καταθεμένην εἰς
λάρνακα φυλάσσειν, καὶ χρόνῳ καθήκοντι γεννηθεῖσαν Ἑλένην ὡς ἐξ αὐτῆς θυγατέρα τρέφειν.
γενομένην δὲ αὐτὴν κάλλει διαπρεπῆ Θησεὺς
ἁρπάσας εἰς Ἀφίδνας[2] ἐκόμισε. Πολυδεύκης δὲ
καὶ Κάστωρ[3] ἐπιστρατεύσαντες, ἐν Ἅιδου Θησέως ὄντος, αἴρουσι τὴν πόλιν καὶ τὴν Ἑλένην
λαμβάνουσι, καὶ τὴν Θησέως μητέρα Αἴθραν

[1] ἄλσεσιν A: ἄλσεσιν S: ἔλεσιν L. Preller (Griechische
Mythologie³, ii. 110, note 5), Hercher (compare Tzetzes,
Schol. on Lycophron, 88, ἐν τῷ ἕλει).

[2] Ἀφίδνας SR (first hand): ἀθήνας R (second hand), A.

[3] Κάστωρ. Here SR add εἰς Ἀφίδνας or εἰς Ἀθήνας, as
above. The words are omitted by Bekker, Hercher, and
Wagner.

---

sanias was still to be seen hanging by ribbons from the roof
of the temple of Hilaira and Phoebe at Sparta. See Pausanias, iii. 16. 1. According to one account (First Vatican
Mythographer, 78), Castor, Pollux, and Helen all emerged
from a single egg; according to another account (First
Vatican Mythographer, 204), Leda laid two eggs, one of which
produced Castor and Pollux, and the other Clytaemnestra
and Helen. In heaven the twins Castor and Pollux had each,
if we may believe Lucian, half an egg on or above his head
in token of the way in which he had been hatched. See
Lucian, Dialog. deorum, xxvi. 1. For the distinction between
Pollux and Castor, the former being regarded as the son of
Zeus and the latter as the son of Tyndareus, see Pindar.
Nem. x. 79 (149) sq. According to Hesiod, both Pollux and
Castor were sons of Zeus. See Scholiast on Pindar, Nem.
x. 80 (150).

was a daughter of Nemesis and Zeus; for that she, flying from the arms of Zeus, changed herself into a goose, but Zeus in his turn took the likeness of a swan and so enjoyed her; and as the fruit of their loves she laid an egg, and a certain shepherd found it in the groves and brought and gave it to Leda; and she put it in a chest and kept it; and when Helen was hatched in due time, Leda brought her up as her own daughter.[1] And when she grew into a lovely woman, Theseus carried her off and brought her to Aphidnae.[2] But when Theseus was in Hades, Pollux and Castor marched against Aphidnae, took the city, got possession of Helen, and led Aethra, the

---

[1] With this variant story of the birth of Helen compare Tzetzes, *Schol. on Lycophron*, 88 (who may have followed Apollodorus); Eratosthenes, *Cataster.* 25; Pausanias, i. 33. 7 *sq.*; Scholiast on Callimachus, *Hymn to Artemis*, 232; Hyginus, *Astronom.* ii. 8. According to Eratosthenes and the Scholiast on Callimachus (*ll. cc.*), the meeting between Zeus and Nemesis, in the shape respectively of a swan and a goose, took place at Rhamnus in Attica, where Nemesis had a famous sanctuary, the marble ruins of which may still be seen in a beautiful situation beside the sea. The statue of the goddess at Rhamnus was wrought by the hand of Phidias, and on the base he represented Leda bringing the youthful Helen to her mother Nemesis. In modern times some of these marble reliefs have been found on the spot, but they are too fragmentary to admit of being identified. See Pausanias, i. 33. 2–8, with my commentary, vol. ii. pp. 455 *sqq.*

[2] As to the captivity of Helen at Aphidnae, and her rescue by her brothers Castor and Pollux, see Apollodorus, *Epitome*, i. 23; Herodotus, ix. 73; Strabo, ix. 1. 17, p. 396; Diodorus Siculus, iv. 63. 2–5; Plutarch, *Theseus*, 31 *sq.*; Pausanias, i. 17. 5, i. 41. 3, ii. 22. 6, iii. 18. 4 *sq.*, compare v. 19. 3; Tzetzes, *Schol. on Lycophron*, 503; Hyginus, *Fab* 79. The story was told by the historian Hellanicus (Scholiast on Homer, *Il.* iii. 144), and in part by the poet Alcman (Scholiast on Homer, *Il.* iii. 242).

8 ἄγουσιν αἰχμάλωτον. παρεγένοντο δὲ εἰς
Σπάρτην ἐπὶ τὸν Ἑλένης γάμον οἱ βασι
λεύοντες Ἑλλάδος. ἦσαν δὲ οἱ μνηστευόμενο
οἵδε· Ὀδυσσεὺς Λαέρτου, Διομήδης Τυδέως,
Ἀντίλοχος Νέστορος, Ἀγαπήνωρ Ἀγκαίου, Σθέ-
νελος Καπανέως, Ἀμφίμαχος ¹ Κτεάτου, Θάλπιος
Εὐρύτου, Μέγης Φυλέως, Ἀμφίλοχος Ἀμφιαράου,
Μενεσθεὺς Πετεώ, Σχεδίος <καὶ> Ἐπίστροφος
<Ἰφίτου>,² Πολύξενος Ἀγασθένους, Πηνέλεως
<Ἱππαλκίμου>, Λήϊτος <Ἀλέκτορος>,³ Αἴας
Ὀιλέως, Ἀσκάλαφος καὶ Ἰάλμενος Ἄρεος, Ἐλε-
φήνωρ Χαλκώδοντος, Εὔμηλος Ἀδμήτου, Πολυ-
ποίτης Πειρίθου, Λεοντεὺς Κορώνου, Ποδαλείριος
καὶ Μαχάων Ἀσκληπιοῦ, Φιλοκτήτης Ποίαντος,
Εὐρύπυλος Εὐαίμονος, Πρωτεσίλαος Ἰφίκλου,
Μενέλαος Ἀτρέως, Αἴας καὶ Τεῦκρος Τελαμῶνος,

¹ Ἀμφίμαχος Heyne: ἀμφίλοχος SA. The name Ἀμφίλοχος occurs below.
² Σχεδίος <καὶ> Ἐπίστροφος <Ἰφίτου> Palmer, Bekker,
Hercher, Wagner: Σχέδιος Ἐπιστρόφου A.
³ Πηνέλεως <Ἱππαλκίμου καὶ> Λήϊτος <Ἀλεκτρυόνος>
Heyne: Πηνέλεως <Ἱππαλκίμου>, Λήϊτος <Ἀλέκτορος>
Bekker.

¹ For another list of the suitors of Helen, see Hyginus,
Fab. 81. Hesiod in his Catalogues gave a list of the suitors
of Helen, and of this list considerable fragments have been
discovered in recent years. They include the names of
Menelaus, the two sons of Amphiaraus (Alcmaeon and
Amphilochus), Ulysses, Podarces, son of Iphiclus, Protesilaus,
son of Actor, < Menestheus >, son of Peteos, Ajax of Salamis,
Elephenor, son of Chalcodon, and Idomeneus, son of Minos.
Thus the list only partially agrees with that of Apollodorus,
for it comprises the names of Podarces and Idomeneus,
which are omitted by Apollodorus, who also mentions only
one son of Amphiaraus, namely Amphilochus. Hyginus

mother of Theseus, away captive. Now the kings
of Greece repaired to Sparta to win the hand of
Helen. The wooers were these:[1]—Ulysses, son of
Laertes; Diomedes, son of Tydeus; Antilochus, son
of Nestor; Agapenor, son of Ancaeus; Sthenelus,
son of Capaneus; Amphimachus, son of Cteatus;
Thalpius, son of Eurytus; Meges, son of Phyleus;
Amphilochus, son of Amphiaraus; Menestheus, son
of Peteos; Schedius and Epistrophus, sons of
Iphitus; Polyxenus, son of Agasthenes; Peneleos,
son of Hippalcimus; Leitus, son of Alector; Ajax,
son of Oileus; Ascalaphus and Ialmenus, sons of
Ares; Elephenor, son of Chalcodon; Eumelus, son
of Admetus; Polypoetes, son of Pirithous; Leonteus,
son of Coronus; Podalirius and Machaon, sons of
Aesculapius; Philoctetes, son of Poeas; Eurypylus,
son of Evaemon; Protesilaus, son of Iphiclus; Menelaus, son of Atreus; Ajax and Teucer, sons of

includes Idomeneus, but not Podarces, nor the sons of
Amphiaraus. In these recently discovered fragments Hesiod
does not confine himself to a bare list of names; he contrives
to hit off the different characters of the suitors by describing
the different manners of their wooing. Thus the canny and
thrifty Ulysses brought no wedding presents, because he was
quite sure he had no chance of winning the lady. On the
other hand, the bold Ajax was extremely liberal with his
offer of other people's property; he promised to give magnificent presents in the shape of sheep and oxen which he proposed to lift from the neighbouring coasts and islands.
Idomeneus sent nobody to woo the lady, but came himself,
trusting apparently to the strength of his personal attrac-
tions to win her heart and carry her home with him
a blooming bride. See *Griechische Dichterfragmente*, i.,
Epische und elegische Fragmente, bearbeitet von W. Schubart
und U. von Wilamowitz-Moellendorff (Berlin, 1907), pp. 28
sqq. (*Berliner Klassikertexte*, v. 1); *Hesiod*, ed. H. G.
Evelyn-White (London, 1914), pp. 192 *sqq.* (*The Loeb Classical Library*).

27

APOLLODORUS

9 Πάτροκλος Μενοιτίου. τούτων ὁρῶν τὸ πλῆθος
Τυνδάρεως ἐδεδοίκει μὴ <προ>κριθέντος[1] ἑνὸς
στασιάσωσιν οἱ λοιποί. ὑποσχομένου δὲ Ὀδυσσέως, ἐὰν συλλάβηται πρὸς τὸν Πηνελόπης αὐτῷ
γάμον, ὑποθήσεσθαι τρόπον τινὰ δι' οὗ μηδεμία
γενήσεται στάσις, ὡς ὑπέσχετο αὐτῷ συλλήψε-
σθαι ὁ Τυνδάρεως, πάντας εἶπεν ἐξορκίσαι τοὺς
μνηστῆρας βοηθήσειν, ἐὰν ὁ προκριθεὶς νυμφίος
ὑπὸ ἄλλου τινὸς ἀδικῆται περὶ τὸν γάμον. ἀκούσας
δὲ τοῦτο Τυνδάρεως τοὺς μνηστῆρας ἐξορκίζει, καὶ
Μενέλαον μὲν αὐτὸς αἱρεῖται νυμφίον, Ὀδυσσεῖ
δὲ παρὰ Ἰκαρίου μνηστεύεται Πηνελόπην.

XI. Μενέλαος μὲν οὖν ἐξ Ἑλένης Ἑρμιόνην
ἐγέννησε καὶ κατά τινας Νικόστρατον, ἐκ δούλης
<δὲ>[2] Πιερίδος, γένος Αἰτωλίδος, ἢ καθάπερ

---

[1] <προ>κριθέντος Faber, Heyne, Hercher: κριθέντος SA,
Westermann, Müller, Bekker, Wagner. Compare ὁ προκριθεὶς
a few lines below.
[2] δὲ inserted by Westermann, accepted by Bekker, Hercher, Wagner.

---

[1] Compare Hesiod, in *Epische und elegische Fragmente*,
ed. W. Schubart and U. von Wilamowitz-Moellendorff, p.
33; Hesiod, ed. H. G. Evelyn-White, p. 198; Euripides,
Iphig. in Aulis, 57 *sqq.*; Thucydides, i. 9; Pausanias, iii.
20. 9; Scholiast on Homer, *Il.* ii. 339; Tzetzes, *Schol. on
Lycophron*, 202. According to Pausanias (*l.c.*) the suitors
took the oath standing on the severed pieces of a horse. As
to the custom of standing on the pieces of a sacrificial victim
or passing between them at the making of solemn covenants,
see *Folk-lore in the Old Testament*, i. 392 *sqq.*
[2] Homer definitely affirms (*Od.* iv. 12–14; compare *Il.* iii.
174 *sq.*) that Helen had only one child, her daughter Hermione. But according to Hesiod, whose verses are quoted
by the Scholiast on Sophocles, *Electra*, 539, Helen afterwards
bore a son Nicostratus to Menelaus. Compare Scholiast on
Homer, *Od.* iv. 11, who tells us further that according to

Telamon; Patroclus, son of Menoetius. Seeing the multitude of them, Tyndareus feared that the preference of one might set the others quarrelling; but Ulysses promised that, if he would help him to win the hand of Penelope, he would suggest a way by which there would be no quarrel. And when Tyndareus promised to help him, Ulysses told him to exact an oath from all the suitors that they would defend the favoured bridegroom against any wrong that might be done him in respect of his marriage. On hearing that, Tyndareus put the suitors on their oath,[1] and while he chose Menelaus to be the bridegroom of Helen, he solicited Icarius to bestow Penelope on Ulysses.

XI. Now Menelaus had by Helen a daughter Hermione and, according to some, a son Nicostratus;[2] and by a female slave Pieris, an Aetolian,

more recent writers Helen had a son Corythus or Helenus by Alexander (Paris). According to Dictys Cretensis (*Bell. Trojan.* v 5), Helen had three sons by Alexander, namely, Bunomus, Corythus, and Idaeus, who were accidentally killed at Troy through the collapse of a vaulted roof. The Scholiast on Homer, *Il.* iii. 175, says that the Lacedaemonians worshipped two sons of Helen, to wit, Nicostratus and Aethiolas. He further mentions, on the authority of Ariaethus, that Helen had by Menelaus a son Maraphius, from whom the Persian family of the Maraphions was descended. See Dindorf's edition of the Scholia on the *Iliad*, vol. i. pp. 147 *sq.*, vol. iii. p. 171. According to one account, Helen had a daughter by Theseus before she was married to Menelaus; this daughter was Iphigenia; Helen entrusted her to her sister Clytaemnestra, who reared the child and passed her off on her husband Agamemnon as her own offspring. This account of the parentage of Iphigenia was supported by the authority of Stesichorus and other poets. See Pausanias, ii. 22. 6 *sq.*; Antoninus Liberalis, *Transform.* 27. Sophocles represents Menelaus as having two children before he sailed for Troy (*Electra*, 539 *sq.*).

'Ακουσίλαός φησι Τηρηίδος, Μεγαπένθη, ἐκ
Κνωσσίας δὲ νύμφης κατὰ Εὔμηλον Ξενόδαμον.

2   Τῶν δὲ ἐκ Λήδας γενομένων παίδων Κάστωρ
μὲν ἤσκει τὰ κατὰ πόλεμον, Πολυδεύκης δὲ
πυγμήν, καὶ διὰ τὴν ἀνδρείαν ἐκλήθησαν ἀμφό-
τεροι Διόσκουροι. βουλόμενοι δὲ γῆμαι τὰς
Λευκίππου θυγατέρας ἐκ Μεσσήνης ἁρπάσαντες
ἔγημαν· καὶ γίνεται μὲν Πολυδεύκους καὶ Φοίβης

---

[1] Compare Homer, *Od.* iv. 10–12.
[2] Compare Homer, *Il.* iii. 237 ; *Od.* xi. 300.
[3] That is, "striplings of Zeus."
[4] The usual tradition seems to have been that Idas and
Lynceus, the sons of Aphareus, were engaged to be married
to the daughters of Leucippus, who were their cousins, since
Aphareus and Leucippus were brothers (see above, iii. 10. 3).
They invited to their wedding Castor and Pollux, who were
cousins both to the bridegrooms and the brides, since Tyndareus, the human father of Castor and Pollux (see above,
iii. 10. 7), was a brother of Aphareus and Leucippus (see
above, iii. 10. 3). But at the wedding Castor and Pollux
carried off the brides, and being pursued by the bridegrooms,
Idas and Lynceus, they turned on their pursaers. In the
fight which ensued, Castor and Lynceus were slain, and Idas
was killed by Zeus with a thunderbolt. See Theocritus,
xxii. 137 *sqq.* ; Scholiast on Homer, *Il.* iii. 243 ; Scholiast on
Pindar, *Nem.* x. 60 (112) ; Tzetzes, *Schol. on Lycophron*, 546 ;
id. Chiliades, ii. 686 *sqq.* ; Hyginus, *Fab.* 80 ; Ovid, *Fasti*, v.
699 *sqq.* ; *Scriptores rerum mythicarum Latini*, ed. G. H.
Bode, vol. i. p. 27 (First Vatican Mythographer, 77). According to Apollodorus, however, the fight between the cousins
was occasioned by a quarrel arising over the division of some
cattle which they had lifted from Arcadia in a joint raid.
This seems to have been the version of the story which
Pindar followed ; for in his description of the fatal affray
between the cousins (*Nem.* x. 60 (112) *sqq.*) he speaks only of
anger about cattle as the motive that led Idas to attack
Castor. The rape of the daughters of Leucippus by Castor
and Pollux was a favourite subject in art. See Pausanias,
i. 18. 1, iii. 17. 3 iii. 18. 11, iv. 31. 9. The names of the

or, according to Acusilaus, by Tereis, he had a son
Megapenthes;[1] and by a nymph Cnossia, according
to Eumelus, he had a son Xenodamus.

Of the sons born to Leda Castor practised the art
of war, and Pollux the art of boxing;[2] and on account
of their manliness they were both called Dioscuri.[3]
And wishing to marry the daughters of Leucippus,
they carried them off from Messene and wedded
them;[4] and Pollux had Mnesileus by Phoebe, and

damsels, as we learn from Apollodorus, were Phoebe and
Hilaira. Compare Stephanus Byzantius, *s.v.* Ἄφιδνα; Propertius, i. 2. 15 *sq.*; Hyginus, *Fab.* 80. At Sparta they had
a sanctuary, in which young maidens officiated as priestesses
and were called Leucippides after the goddesses. See Pausanias, iii. 16. 1. From an obscure gloss of Hesychius (*s.v.*
πωλία) we may perhaps infer that these maiden priestesses,
like the goddesses, were two in number, and that they were
called "the colts of the Leucippides." Further, since the
name of Leucippus, the legendary father of the goddesses,
means simply "White Horse," it is tempting to suppose that
the Leucippides, like their priestesses, were spoken of and
perhaps conceived as white horses. More than that, Castor
and Pollux, who carried off these white-horse maidens, if we
may call them so, were not only constantly associated with
horses, but were themselves called White Horses (λευκόπωλοι)
by Pindar, *Pyth.* i. 66 (126) and "White Colts of Zeus" by
Euripides in a fragment of his lost play the *Antiope*. See
S. Wide, *Lakonische Kulte* (Leipsic, 1893), pp. 331 *sq.*;
A. B. Cook, *Zeus*, i. 442. These coincidences can hardly be
accidental. They point to the worship of a pair of brother
deities conceived as white horses, and married to a pair of
sister deities conceived as white mares, who were served by
a pair of maiden priestesses called White Colts, assisted
apparently by a boy priest or priests; for a Laconian inscription describes a certain youthful Marcus Aurelius Zeuxippus
as "priest of the Leucippides and neatherd (? βουαγόρ) of the
Tyndarids," that is, of Castor and Pollux. See P. Cauer,
*Delectus Inscriptionum Graecarum propter dialectum me-
morabilium*[2], p. 17, No. 36; H. Collitz und F. Bechtel,
Sammlung der griechischen Dialekt-Inschriften, iii. 2, pp.
40 *sq.*, No. 4499:

Μνησίλεως, Κάστορος δὲ καὶ Ἰλαείρας Ἀνώγων.
ἐλάσαντες δὲ ἐκ τῆς Ἀρκαδίας βοῶν λείαν μετὰ
τῶν Ἀφαρέως παίδων Ἴδα καὶ Λυγκέως, ἐπιτρέ-
πουσιν Ἴδᾳ διελεῖν·¹ ὁ δὲ τεμὼν βοῦν εἰς μέρη
τέσσαρα, τοῦ πρώτου καταφαγόντος εἶπε τῆς
λείας τὸ ἥμισυ ἔσεσθαι, καὶ τοῦ δευτέρου τὸ
λοιπόν. καὶ φθάσας κατηνάλωσε τὸ μέρος τὸ
ἴδιον πρῶτος² Ἴδας, καὶ τὸ τοῦ ἀδελφοῦ, καὶ
μετ᾽ ἐκείνου τὴν λείαν εἰς Μεσσήνην ἤλασε.
στρατεύσαντες δὲ ἐπὶ Μεσσήνην οἱ Διόσκουροι
τήν τε λείαν ἐκείνην καὶ πολλὴν ἄλλην συνε-
λαύνουσι. καὶ τὸν Ἴδαν ἐλόχων καὶ τὸν Λυγκέα.
Λυγκεὺς δὲ ἰδὼν Κάστορα ἐμήνυσεν Ἴδᾳ, κἀκεῖνος
αὐτὸν κτείνει. Πολυδεύκης δὲ ἐδίωξεν αὐτούς,
καὶ τὸν μὲν Λυγκέα κτείνει τὸ δόρυ προέμενος,
τὸν δὲ Ἴδαν διώκων, βληθεὶς ὑπ᾽ ἐκείνου πέτρᾳ
κατὰ τῆς κεφαλῆς, πίπτει σκοτωθείς. καὶ Ζεὺς
Ἴδαν κεραυνοῖ, Πολυδεύκην δὲ εἰς οὐρανὸν ἀνάγει.
μὴ δεχομένου δὲ Πολυδεύκους τὴν ἀθανασίαν
ὄντος νεκροῦ Κάστορος, Ζεὺς ἀμφοτέροις παρ᾽
ἡμέραν καὶ ἐν θεοῖς εἶναι καὶ ἐν θνητοῖς³ ἔδωκε.

¹ διελεῖν Commelinus : διελθεῖν A.
² πρῶτος RRᵃBV : πρῶτον LT.   Hercher omits the word.
³ θνητοῖς. Hercher conjectured νεκροῖς. Perhaps we
should read τεθνηκόσιν. We can hardly suppose that Apollodorus used θνητοὶ in the sense in which John Wilson Croker
used it and was scarified by Macaulay for so doing.

¹ Compare Homer, *Od.* xi. 298–304; Pindar, *Nem.* x. 55
(101) *sqq.*, 75 (141) *sqq.*; *id. Pyth.* xi. 61 (93) *sqq.*; Schol. on
Homer, *Od.* xi. 302 ; Lucian, *Dialog. deorum,* xxvi. ; Virgil,
Aen. vi. 121 *sq.* ; Hyginus, *Fab.* 80 ; *id. Astronom.* ii. 22 ;
Scriptores rerum mythicarum Latini, ed. G. H. Bode, vol. i.
p. 120 (Second Vatican Mythographer, 132). The last of

32

Castor had Anogon by Hilaira. And having driven booty of cattle from Arcadia, in company with Idas and Lynceus, sons of Aphareus, they allowed Idas to divide the spoil. He cut a cow in four and said that one half of the booty should be his who ate his share first, and that the rest should be his who ate his share second. And before they knew where they were, Idas had swallowed his own share first and likewise his brother's, and with him had driven off the captured cattle to Messene. But the Dioscuri marched against Messene, and drove away that cattle and much else besides. And they lay in wait for Idas and Lynceus. But Lynceus spied Castor and discovered him to Idas, who killed him. Pollux chased them and slew Lynceus by throwing his spear, but in pursuing Lynceus he was wounded in the head with a stone thrown by him, and fell down in a swoon. And Zeus smote Idas with a thunderbolt, but Pollux he carried up to heaven. Nevertheless, as Pollux refused to accept immortality while his brother Castor was dead, Zeus permitted them both to be every other day among the gods and among mortals.[1]

these writers explains the myth to mean that when the star of the one twin is setting, the star of the other is rising. It has been plausibly argued that in one of their aspects the twins were identified with the Morning and Evening Stars respectively, the immortal twin (Pollux) being conceived as the Morning Star, which is seen at dawn rising up in the sky till it is lost in the light of heaven, while the mortal twin (Castor) was identified with the Evening Star, which is seen at dusk sinking into its earthy bed. See J. G. Welcker, *Griechische Götterlehre*, i. 606 *sqq.*; J. Rendel Harris, *The Dioscuri in the Christian Legends* (London, 1903), pp. 11 *sqq.* It would seem that this view of the Spartan twins was favoured by the Spartans themselves, for after their great naval victory of Aegospotami, at which Castor and Pollux

μεταστάντων δὲ εἰς θεοὺς τῶν Διοσκούρων, Τυνδάρεως μεταπεμψάμενος Μενέλαον εἰς Σπάρτην
τούτῳ τὴν βασιλείαν παρέδωκεν.

XII. Ἠλέκτρας δὲ τῆς Ἄτλαντος καὶ Διὸς
Ἰασίων καὶ Δάρδανος ἐγένοντο. Ἰασίων μὲν οὖν
ἐρασθεὶς Δήμητρος καὶ θέλων καταισχῦναι τὴν
θεὸν κεραυνοῦται, Δάρδανος δὲ ἐπὶ τῷ θανάτῳ
τοῦ ἀδελφοῦ λυπούμενος, Σαμοθρᾴκην ἀπολιπὼν
εἰς τὴν ἀντίπερα ἤπειρον ἦλθε. ταύτης δὲ ἐβασίλευε Τεῦκρος ποταμοῦ Σκαμάνδρου καὶ νύμφης
Ἰδαίας· ἀφ' οὗ καὶ οἱ τὴν χώραν νεμόμενοι
Τεῦκροι προσηγορεύοντο. ὑποδεχθεὶς δὲ ὑπὸ τοῦ
βασιλέως, καὶ λαβὼν μέρος τῆς γῆς καὶ τὴν
ἐκείνου θυγατέρα Βάτειαν, Δάρδανον ἔκτισε πόλιν
τελευτήσαντος δὲ Τεύκρου [1] τὴν χώραν ἅπασαν
2 Δαρδανίαν ἐκάλεσε. γενομένων δὲ αὐτῷ παίδων

---

[1] τεύκρου S: τεῦκρος A.

---

were said to have appeared visibly in or hovering over the
Spartan fleet, the victors dedicated at Delphi the symbols of
their divine champions in the shape of two golden stars, which
shortly before the fatal battle of Leuctra fell down and disappeared, as if to announce that the star of Sparta's fortune
was about to set for ever. See Cicero, *De divinatione*, i. 34.
75, ii. 32. 68. The same interpretation of the twins would
accord well with their white horses (see the preceding note),
on which the starry brethren might be thought to ride through
the blue sky.

[1] This account of the parentage of Iasion had the authority
of Hellanicus (Scholiast on Homer, *Od.* v. 125). Compare
Diodorus Siculus, v. 48. 2.

[2] Compare Conon, *Narrat.* 21 ; Strabo, vii. p. 331, frag. 50,
ed. Meineke ; Hyginus, *Astronom.* ii. 4. A different turn is
given to the story by Homer, who represents the lovers
meeting in a thrice-ploughed field (*Od.* v. 125–128). To the

And when the Dioscuri were translated to the gods, Tyndareus sent for Menelaus to Sparta and handed over the kingdom to him.

XII. Electra, daughter of Atlas, had two sons, Iasion and Dardanus, by Zeus.[1] Now Iasion loved Demeter, and in an attempt to defile the goddess he was killed by a thunderbolt.[2] Grieved at his brother's death, Dardanus left Samothrace and came to the opposite mainland. That country was ruled by a king, Teucer, son of the river Scamander and of a nymph Idaea, and the inhabitants of the country were called Teucrians after Teucer. Being welcomed by the king, and having received a share of the land and the king's daughter Batia, he built a city Dardanus, and when Teucer died he called the whole country Dardania.[3] And he had sons born

same effect Hesiod (*Theog.* 969–974) says that the thrice-ploughed field where they met was in a fertile district of Crete, and that Wealth was born as the fruit of their love. Compare Diodorus Siculus, v. 77. 1 *sq.*; Hyginus, *Fab.* 270. The Scholiast on Homer, *Od.* v. 125, attempts to rationalize the myth by saying that Iasion was the only man who preserved seed-corn after the deluge.

[3] As to the migration of Dardanus from Samothrace to Asia and his foundation of Dardania or Dardanus, see Diodorus Siculus, v. 48. 2 *sq.*; Conon, *Narrat.* 21; Stephanus Byzantius, *s.v.* Δάρδανος; compare Homer, *Il.* xx. 215 *sqq.* According to one account he was driven from Samothrace by a flood and floated to the coast of the Troad on a raft. See Lycophron, *Cassandra*, 72 *sqq.*, with the scholia of Tzetzes; Scholia on Homer, *Il.* xx. 215. As to his marriage with Batia, daughter of Teucer, and his succession to the kingdom, compare Diodorus Siculus, iv. 75. 1. According to Stephanus Byzantius (*s.v.* Δάρδανες), Batia, the wife of Dardanus, was a daughter of Tros, not of Teucer.

APOLLODORUS

Ἴλου καὶ Ἐριχθονίου, Ἴλος μὲν ἄπαις ἀπέθανεν,
Ἐριχθόνιος δὲ διαδεξάμενος τὴν βασιλείαν, γήμας
Ἀστυόχην¹ τὴν Σιμόεντος, τεκνοῖ Τρῶα. οὗτος
παραλαβὼν τὴν βασιλείαν τὴν μὲν χώραν ἀφ'
ἑαυτοῦ Τροίαν ἐκάλεσε, καὶ γήμας Καλλιρρόην
τὴν Σκαμάνδρου γεννᾷ θυγατέρα μὲν Κλεοπάτραν,
παῖδας δὲ Ἴλον καὶ Ἀσσάρακον καὶ Γανυμήδην.
τοῦτον μὲν οὖν διὰ κάλλος ἀναρπάσας Ζεὺς δι'
ἀετοῦ θεῶν οἰνοχόον ἐν οὐρανῷ κατέστησεν· Ἀσ-
σαράκου δὲ καὶ Ἱερομνήμης τῆς Σιμόεντος Κάπυς,
τοῦ δὲ καὶ Θεμίστης τῆς Ἴλου Ἀγχίσης, ᾧ δι'
ἐρωτικὴν ἐπιθυμίαν Ἀφροδίτη συνελθοῦσα Αἰ-
νείαν ἐγέννησε καὶ Λύρον, ὃς ἄπαις ἀπέθανεν.
3 Ἴλος δὲ εἰς Φρυγίαν ἀφικόμενος καὶ καταλαβὼν
ὑπὸ τοῦ βασιλέως αὐτόθι τεθειμένον ἀγῶνα νικᾷ
πάλην· καὶ λαβὼν ἆθλον πεντήκοντα κόρους²
καὶ κόρας τὰς ἴσας, δόντος αὐτῷ τοῦ βασιλέως
κατὰ χρησμὸν καὶ βοῦν ποικίλην, καὶ φράσαντος

¹ Ἀστυόχην SRᵃ: ἀστρόχην A.
² κόρους S: κούρους A.

---

¹ Compare Tzetzes, *Schol. on Lycophron*, 29. As to
Erichthonius, son of Dardanus, see Homer, *Il.* xx. 219 *sqq.*;
Diodorus Siculus, iv. 75. 2. According to Dionysius of Halicarnassus (*Antiquit. Rom.*, i. 50. 3) the names of the two
sons whom Dardanus had by his wife Batia were Erichthonius
and Zacynthus.

² Compare Homer, *Il.* xx. 230, who does not mention th
mother of Tros. She is named Astyoche, daughter of Simoeis,
by Tzetzes (*Schol. on Lycophron*, 29) in agreement with
Apollodorus.

³ Compare Homer, *Il.* xx. 231 *sq.*; Diodorus Siculus, iv.
75. 3. The name of the wife of Tros is not mentioned by
Homer and Diodorus. She is called Callirrhoe, daughter of
Scamander, by Tzetzes (*Schol. on Lycophron*, 29) and the

to him, Ilus and Erichthonius, of whom Ilus died childless,[1] and Erichthonius succeeded to the kingdom and marrying Astyoche, daughter of Simoeis, begat Tros.[2] On succeeding to the kingdom, Tros called the country Troy after himself, and marrying Callirrhoe, daughter of Scamander, he begat a daughter Cleopatra, and sons, Ilus, Assaracus, and Ganymede.[3] This Ganymede, for the sake of his beauty, Zeus caught up on an eagle and appointed him cupbearer of the gods in heaven ; [4] and Assaracus had by his wife Hieromneme, daughter of Simoeis, a son Capys ; and Capys had by his wife Themiste, daughter of Ilus, a son Anchises, whom Aphrodite met in love's dalliance, and to whom she bore Aeneas[5] and Lyrus, who died childless. But Ilus went to Phrygia, and finding games held there by the king, he was victorious in wrestling. As a prize he received fifty youths and as many maidens, and the king, in obedience to an oracle, gave him also a dappled

---

Scholiast on Homer, *Il.* xx. 231, who refers to Hellanicus as his authority. See *Scholia Graeca in Homeri Iliadem Townleyana,* ed. E. Maass, vol. ii. p. 321.

[4] Compare Homer, *Il.* xx. 232-235 ; *Homeric Hymn to Aphrodite,* 202 *sqq.* These early versions of the myth do not mention the eagle as the agent which transported Ganymede to heaven. The bird figures conspicuously in later versions of the myth and its representation in art. Compare Lucian, *Dialog. deorum,* iv. 1 ; Virgil, *Aen.* v. 252 *sqq.*; Ovid, *Metamorph.* x. 155 *sqq.*; *Scriptores rerum mythicarum Latini,* ed. G. H. Bode, vol. i. pp. 56, 139, 162, 256 (First Vatican Mythographer, 184, Second Vatican Mythographer, 198, Third Vatican Mythographer, 3. 5 and 15. 11).

[5] Compare Homer, *Il.* xx. 239 *sq.* ; Diodorus Siculus, iv. 75. 5. Neither writer names the wives of Assaracus and Capys. As to the love of Aphrodite for Anchises, and the birth of Aeneas, see Homer, *Il.* ii. 819-821, v. 311-313 ; Hesiod, *Theog.* 1008-1010.

APOLLODORUS

ἐν ᾧπερ ἂν αὐτὴ κλιθῇ τόπῳ πόλιν κτίζειν, εἵπετο
τῇ βοΐ. ἡ δὲ ἀφικομένη ἐπὶ τὸν λεγόμενον τῆς
Φρυγίας Ἄτης λόφον κλίνεται· ἔνθα πόλιν κτίσας
Ἴλος ταύτην μὲν Ἴλιον ἐκάλεσε, τῷ δὲ Διὶ
σημεῖον εὐξάμενος αὐτῷ τι φανῆναι, μεθ' ἡμέραν
τὸ διιπετὲς παλλάδιον πρὸ τῆς σκηνῆς κείμενον
ἐθεάσατο. ἦν δὲ τῷ μεγέθει τρίπηχυ, τοῖς δὲ
ποσὶ συμβεβηκός, καὶ τῇ μὲν δεξιᾷ δόρυ διηρμένον[1] ἔχον τῇ δὲ ἑτέρᾳ ἠλακάτην καὶ ἄτρακτον.

---

[1] διηρμένον Heyne : διηρτημένον A, Tzetzes, *Schol. on Lycophron*, 355.

---

[1] This legend of the foundation of Ilium by Ilus is repeated
by Tzetzes, *Schol. on Lycophron*, 29. The site of Thebes
is said to have been chosen in obedience to a similar oracle.
See above, iii. 4. 1. Homer tells us (*Il.* xx. 215 *sqq.*) that
the foundation of Dardania on Mount Ida preceded the
foundation of Ilium in the plain. As to the hill of Ate, compare Stephanus Byzantius, *s.v.* Ἴλιον.

[2] As to the antique image of Pallas, known as the Palladium,
see Dionysius Halicarnasensis, *Antiquit. Rom.* i. 68 *sq.*, ii.
66 5 ; Conon, *Narrationes*, 34 ; Pausanias, i. 28. 9, ii. 23. 5 ;
Clement of Alexandria, *Protrept.* iv. 47, p. 42, ed. Potter ;
J. Malalas, *Chronogr.* v. pp. 108 *sq.*, ed. L. Dindorf ;
Tzetzes, *Schol. on Lycophron*, 355 ; Suidas, *s.v.* Παλλάδιον ;
Etymologicum Magnum, *s.v.* Παλλάδιον, p. 649. 50 ; Scholiast
on Homer, *Il.* vi. 311 ; Virgil, *Aen.* ii. 162 *sqq.* ; Ovid, *Fasti*,
vi. 417-436 ; *id. Metamorph.* xiii. 337-349 ; Silius Italicus,
Punic. xiii. 30 *sqq.* ; Dictys Cretensis, *Bell. Trojan.* v. 5 ;
Servius, on Virgil, *Aen.* ii. 166 ; *Scriptores rerum mythicarum Latini*, ed. G. H. Bode, vol. i. pp. 14 *sq.*, 45 (First
Vatican Mythographer, 40 and 142). The traditions concerning the Palladium which have come down to us are all
comparatively late, and they differ from each other on various
points ; but the most commonly received account seems to
have been that the image was a small wooden one, that it
had fallen from heaven, and that so long as it remained in
Troy the city could not be taken. The Greek tradition was

cow and bade him found a city wherever the animal
should lie down; so he followed the cow. And when
she was come to what was called the hill of the
Phrygian Ate, she lay down; there Ilus built a
city and called it Ilium.[1] And having prayed to
Zeus that a sign might be shown to him, he beheld
by day the Palladium, fallen from heaven, lying before his tent. It was three cubits in height, its feet
joined together; in its right hand it held a spear
aloft, and in the other hand a distaff and spindle.[2]

that the Palladium was stolen and carried off to the Greek
camp by Ulysses and Diomedes (see Apollodorus, *Epitome*,
v. 10 and 13), and that its capture by the Greeks ensured the
fall of Troy. The Roman tradition was that the image remained in Troy till the city was taken by the Greeks, when
Aeneas succeeded in rescuing it and conveying it away with
him to Italy, where it was finally deposited in the temple of
Vesta at Rome. These two traditions are clearly inconsistent
with each other, and the Roman tradition further conflicts
with the belief that the city which possessed the sacred image
could not be captured by an enemy. Hence in order to
maintain the genuineness of the image in the temple of Vesta,
patriotic Roman antiquaries were driven to various expedients.
They said, for example, that an exact copy of the Palladium
had been publicly exposed at Troy, while the true one was
carefully concealed in a sanctuary, and that the unsuspicious
Greeks had pounced on the spurious image, while the knowing
Aeneas smuggled away the genuine one packed up with
the rest of his sacred luggage (Dionysius Halicarnasensis,
Antiquit. Rom. i. 68 *sq.*). Or they affirmed that the thief Diomedes had been constrained to restore the stolen image to its
proper owners (First Vatican Mythographer, *ll.cc.*); or that,
warned by Athena in a dream, he afterwards made it over to
Aeneas in Italy (Silius Italicus, *l.c.*). But the Romans were
not the only people who claimed to possess the true Palladium;
the Argives maintained that it was with them (Pausanias, ii.
23. 5), and the Athenians asserted that it was to be seen in
their ancient court of justice which bore the very name of
Palladium. See Pausanias, i. 28. 8 *sq.*; Harpocration, *s.vv.*

APOLLODORUS

Ἱστορία δὲ[1] ἡ περὶ τοῦ παλλαδίου τοιάδε
φέρεται· φασὶ γεννηθεῖσαν τὴν Ἀθηνᾶν παρὰ
Τρίτωνι τρέφεσθαι, ᾧ θυγάτηρ ἦν Παλλάς· ἀμφο-
τέρας δὲ ἀσκούσας τὰ κατὰ πόλεμον εἰς φιλονεικίαν
ποτὲ προελθεῖν. μελλούσης δὲ πλήττειν τῆς Παλ-
λάδος τὸν Δία φοβηθέντα τὴν αἰγίδα προτεῖναι,[2]
τὴν δὲ εὐλαβηθεῖσαν ἀναβλέψαι, καὶ οὕτως ὑπὸ
τῆς Ἀθηνᾶς τρωθεῖσαν πεσεῖν. Ἀθηνᾶν δὲ περί-
λυπον ἐπ᾽ αὐτῇ γενομένην, ξόανον ἐκείνης ὅμοιον
κατασκευάσαι,[3] καὶ περιθεῖναι τοῖς στέρνοις ἣν
ἔδεισεν αἰγίδα, καὶ τιμᾶν ἱδρυσαμένην παρὰ τῷ
Διί. ὕστερον δὲ Ἠλέκτρας κατὰ[4] τὴν φθορὰν
τούτῳ προσφυγούσης, Δία ῥῖψαι[5] [μετ᾽ Ἄτης

[1] Heyne thought that the whole of this paragraph, relating
to the Palladium, has been interpolated from an ancient
author. It is omitted from the text by Hercher and
bracketed as spurious by Wagner.

[2] προτεῖναι Faber: προθεῖναι R: προσθεῖναι R[a]: προσθῆ-
ναι A.

[3] κατασκευάσαι R: κατασκευάσασα A.

[4] κατὰ SA: μετὰ Bekker.

[5] Δία ῥῖψαι Gale, Bekker, Wagner: διαρρίψαι SA, Tzetzes
Schol. on Lycophron, 355, Heyne, Westermann, Müller.

βουλεύσεως and ἐπὶ Παλλαδίῳ; Suidas, *s.v.* ἐπὶ Παλλαδίῳ;
Julius Pollux, viii. 118 *sq.* ; Scholiast on Aeschines, ii. 87,
p. 298, ed. Schultz; Bekker's *Anecdota Graeca*, i. p. 311,
lines 3 *sqq.* The most exact description of the appearance of
the Palladium is the one given by Apollodorus in the present
passage, which is quoted, with the author's name, by
Tzetzes (*Schol. on Lycophron*, 355). According to Dictys
Cretensis (*l.c.*), the image fell from heaven at the time when
Ilus was building the temple of Athena ; the structure was
nearly completed, but the roof was not yet on, so the Palladium dropped straight into its proper place in the sacred
edifice. Clement of Alexandria (*l.c.*) mentions a strange
opinion that the Palladium " was made out of the bones of
Pelops, just as the Olympian (image of Zeus was made) out

The story told about the Palladium is as follows:[1] They say that when Athena was born she was brought up by Triton,[2] who had a daughter Pallas; and that both girls practised the arts of war, but that once on a time they fell out; and when Pallas was about to strike a blow, Zeus in fear interposed the aegis, and Pallas, being startled, looked up, and so fell wounded by Athena. And being exceedingly grieved for her, Athena made a wooden image in her likeness, and wrapped the aegis, which she had feared, about the breast of it, and set it up beside Zeus and honoured it. But afterwards Electra, at the time of her violation,[3] took refuge at the image, and Zeus threw the Palladium along with Ate[4] into the Ilian

of other bones of an Indian beast," that is, out of ivory. Pherecydes discussed the subject of *palladia* in general; he described them as "shapes not made with hands," and derived the name from πάλλειν, which he considered to be equivalent to βάλλειν, "to throw, cast," because these objects were cast down from heaven. See Tzetzes, *Schol. on Lycophron*, 355; *Etymologicum Magnum*, *s.v.* Παλλάδιον, p. 649. 50. Apollodorus as usual confines himself to the Greek tradition; he completely ignores the Romans and their claim to possess the Palladium.

[1] The following account of the origin of the Palladium was regarded as an interpolation by Heyne, and his view has been accepted by Hercher and Wagner. But the passage was known to Tzetzes, who quotes it (*Schol. on Lycophron*, 355) immediately after his description of the image, which he expressly borrowed from Apollodorus.

[2] Apparently the god of the river Triton, which was commonly supposed to be in Libya, though some people identified it with a small stream in Boeotia See Herodotus, iv. 180; Pausanias, ix. 33. 7; Tzetzes, *Schol. on Lycophron*, 519; compare Scholiast on Apollonius Rhodius, *Argon.* i. 109.

[3] See above, iii. 12. 1.

[4] Homer tells (*Il.* xix. 126–131) how Zeus in anger swore that Ate should never again come to Olympus, and how he seized her by the head and flung her from heaven.

καὶ]¹ τὸ παλλάδιον εἰς τὴν Ἰλιάδα χώραν, Ἴλον
δὲ τούτῳ² ναὸν κατασκευάσαντα τιμᾶν. καὶ περὶ
μὲν τοῦ παλλαδίου ταῦτα λέγεται.

Ἶλος δὲ γήμας Εὐρυδίκην τὴν Ἀδράστου
Λαομέδοντα ἐγέννησεν, ὃς γαμεῖ Στρυμὼ τὴν
Σκαμάνδρου, κατὰ δέ τινας Πλακίαν τὴν Ὀτρέως,³
κατ᾽ ἐνίους δὲ Λευκίππην,⁴ καὶ τεκνοῖ παῖδας μὲν
Τιθωνὸν Λάμπον⁵ Κλυτίον Ἱκετάονα Ποδάρκην,
θυγατέρας δὲ Ἡσιόνην καὶ Κίλλαν καὶ Ἀστυόχην,
ἐκ δὲ νύμφης Καλύβης Βουκολίωνα.

4   Τιθωνὸν μὲν οὖν Ἠὼς ἁρπάσασα δι᾽ ἔρωτα εἰς
Αἰθιοπίαν κομίζει, κἀκεῖ συνελθοῦσα γεννᾷ παῖδας
5 Ἠμαθίωνα καὶ Μέμνονα. μετὰ δὲ τὸ αἱρεθῆναι

---

¹ μετ᾽ Ἄτης καί. Heyne was probably right in regarding
these words as an interpolation introduced by a scribe who
remembered that Ate was flung from heaven by Zeus
(Homer, *Il.* xix. 131 *sq.*). For Ἄτης, which is a conjecture
of Gale's, the MSS. (SA) read αὑτῆς, which is retained by
Müller, Bekker, and Wagner. The words μετ᾽ αὑτῆς καί are
not bracketed by Wagner.

² τούτῳ S: τούτου A, Tzetzes, *Schol. on Lycophron*, 355:
τοῦτο Heyne.   ³ Ὀτρέως Hercher: ἀτρέως A.

⁴ Λευκίππην Heyne (conjecture), Bekker, Hercher, Wagner: Λευκίππου A, Heyne (in text), Westermann, Müller.
The reading Λευκίππην is supported by Tzetzes, *Schol. on
Lycophron*, 18, who says that the mother of Priam (Podarces) was Leucippe.

⁵ Λάμπον R, Bekker, Hercher, Wagner (compare Homer,
Il. iii. 147, xix. 238): λάμπωνα A, Westermann, Müller.

---

¹ Compare Homer, *Il.* xx. 236. Homer does not mention
the mother of Laomedon. According to one Scholiast on the
passage she was Eurydice, daughter of Adrastus, as Apollodorus has it ; according to another she was Batia, daughter
of Teucer. But if the family tree recorded by Apollodorus
is correct, Batia could hardly have been the wife of Ilus,
since she was his great-grandmother.

country ; and Ilus built a temple for it, and honoured it. Such is the legend of the Palladium.

And Ilus married Eurydice, daughter of Adrastus, and begat Laomedon,[1] who married Strymo, daughter of Scamander ; but according to some his wife was Placia, daughter of Otreus, and according to others she was Leucippe ; and he begat five sons, Tithonus, Lampus, Clytius, Hicetaon, Podarces,[2] and three daughters, Hesione, Cilla, and Astyoche ; and by a nymph Calybe he had a son Bucolion.[3]

Now the Dawn snatched away Tithonus for love and brought him to Ethiopia, and there consorting with him she bore two sons, Emathion and Memnon.[4]

---

[2] Compare Homer, *Il.* xx. 237 *sq.*, with whom Apollodorus agrees as to Laomedon's five sons. Homer does not mention Laomedon's wife nor his daughters. According to a Scholiast on Homer, *Il.* iii. 250, his wife's name was Zeuxippe or Strymo ; for the former name he cites the authority of the poet Alcman, for the latter the authority of the historian Hellanicus. Apollodorus may have followed Hellanicus, though he was acquainted with other traditions. According to Tzetzes (*Schol. on Lycophron*, 18), Priam and Tithonus were sons of Laomedon by different mothers ; the mother of Priam was Leucippe, the mother of Tithonus was Strymo or Rhoeo, daughter of Scamander. The Scholiast on Homer, *Il.* xi. 1, speaks of Tithonus as a son of Laomedon by Strymo, daughter of Scamander.

[3] Compare Homer, *Il.* vi. 23 *sqq.*, who says that Bucolion was the eldest son of Laomedon, but illegitimate and one of twins.

[4] As to the love of Dawn (*Eos*) for Tithonus, see the *Homeric Hymn to Aphrodite*, 218 *sqq.*; Tzetzes, *Schol. on Lycophron*, 18 ; Scholiast on Homer, *Il.* xi. 1 ; Propertius, ii. 18. 7–18, ed. Butler. Homer speaks of Dawn (Aurora) rising from the bed of Tithonus (*Il.* xi. 1 *sq.*; *Od.* v. 1 *sq.*). According to the author of the Homeric hymn, Dawn obtained from Zeus for her lover the boon of immortality ; according to the Scholiast on Homer, it was Tithonus himself who asked and

43

Ἴλιον ὑπὸ Ἡρακλέους, ὡς μικρὸν πρόσθεν ἡμῖν
λέλεκται, ἐβασίλευσε Ποδάρκης ὁ κληθεὶς Πρί-
αμος· καὶ γαμεῖ πρώτην Ἀρίσβην τὴν Μέροπος,
ἐξ ἧς αὐτῷ παῖς Αἴσακος γίνεται, ὃς ἔγημεν
Ἀστερόπην[1] τὴν Κεβρῆνος θυγατέρα, ἣν πενθῶν
ἀποθανοῦσαν ἀπωρνεώθη. Πρίαμος δὲ Ἀρίσβην
ἐκδοὺς Ὑρτάκῳ δευτέραν ἔγημεν Ἑκάβην τὴν
Δύμαντος, ἢ ὥς τινές φασι Κισσέως, ἢ ὡς ἕτεροι
λέγουσι Σαγγαρίου ποταμοῦ καὶ Μετώπης. γεν-
νᾶται δὲ αὐτῇ[2] πρῶτος μὲν Ἕκτωρ· δευτέρου δὲ

---

[1] Ἀστερόπην Commelinus : στερόπην SA.
[2] αὐτῇ A, Heyne, Westermann, Müller, Bekker, Hercher :
αὐτῷ S. Wagner.

---

obtained the boon from the loving goddess. But the boon
turned to be a bane ; for neither he nor she had remembered
to ask for freedom from the infirmities of age. So when he
was old and white-headed and could not stir hand or foot, he
prayed for death as a release from his sufferings ; but die he
could not, for he was immortal. Hence the goddess in pity
either shut him up in his chamber and closed the shining
doors on him, leaving him to lisp and babble there eternally,
or she turned him into a grasshopper, the most musical of
insects, that she might have the joy of hearing her lover's
voice sounding for ever in her ears. The former and sadder
fate is vouched for by the hymn writer, the latter by the
Scholiast. Tzetzes perhaps lets us into the secret of the
transformation when he tells us (*l.c.*) that "the grasshoppers,
like the snakes, when they are old, slough their old age" (τὸ
γῆρας, literally "old age," but applied by the Greeks to the
cast skins of serpents). It is a widespread notion among
savages, which the ancestors of the Greeks apparently shared,
that creatures which cast their skins, thereby renew their
youth and live for ever. See *Folk-lore in the Old Testament*,
i. 66 *sqq.* The ancient Latins seem also to have cherished
the same illusion, for they applied the same name (*senecta* or
senectus) to old age and to the cast skins of serpents.

[1] See above, ii. 6. 4.

But after that Ilium was captured by Hercules, as we have related a little before,[1] Podarces, who was called Priam, came to the throne, and he married first Arisbe, daughter of Merops, by whom he had a son Aesacus, who married Asterope, daughter of Cebren, and when she died he mourned for her and was turned into a bird.[2] But Priam handed over Arisbe to Hyrtacus and married a second wife Hecuba, daughter of Dymas, or, as some say, of Cisseus, or, as others say, of the river Sangarius and Metope.[3] The first son born to her was Hector; and when a second

[2] Compare Tzetzes, *Schol. on Lycophron*, 224, who seems to follow Apollodorus. The bird into which the mourner was transformed appears to have been a species of diver. See Ovid, *Metamorph.* xi. 749-795; Servius, on Virgil, *Aen.* iv. 254, v. 128.

[3] According to Homer (*Il.* xvi. 718 *sq.*) Hecuba was a daughter of Dymas, "who dwelt in Phrygia by the streams of Sangarius." But Euripides (*Hecuba*, 3) represents her as a daughter of Cisseus, and herein he is followed by Virgil, (*Aen.* vii. 320, x. 705). The mythographers Hyginus and Tzetzes leave it an open question whether Hecuba was a daughter of Cisseus or of Dymas. See Hyginus, *Fab.* 91, 111, 249; Tzetzes, *Schol. on Lycophron, Introd.* p. 266, ed. Müller. Compare the Scholiast on Euripides, *Hecuba,* 3: "Pherecydes writes thus: And Priam, son of Laomedon, marries Hecuba, daughter of Dymas, son of Eioneus, son of Proteus, or of the river Sangarius, by a Naiad nymph Evagora. But some have recorded that Hecuba's mother was Glaucippe, daughter of Xanthus. But Nicander, in agreement with Euripides, says that Hecuba was a daughter of Cisseus." The Scholiast on Homer, *Il.* xvi. 718, says that according to Pherecydes the father of Hecuba was Dymas and her mother was a nymph Eunoe, but that according to Athenion her father was Cisseus and her mother Teleclia. Thus it would appear that after all we cannot answer with any confidence the question with which the emperor Tiberius loved to pose the grammarians of his time, "Who was Hecuba's mother?" See Suetonius, *Tiberius,* 70.

APOLLODORUS

γεννᾶσθαι μέλλοντος βρέφους ἔδοξεν Ἑκάβη καθ᾽
ὕπνους[1] δαλὸν τεκεῖν διάπυρον, τοῦτον δὲ πᾶσαν
ἐπινέμεσθαι τὴν πόλιν καὶ καίειν. μαθὼν δὲ
Πρίαμος παρ᾽ Ἑκάβης τὸν ὄνειρον, Αἴσακον τὸν
υἱὸν μετεπέμψατο·[2] ἦν γὰρ ὀνειροκρίτης παρὰ
τοῦ μητροπάτορος Μέροπος διδαχθείς. οὗτος
εἰπὼν τῆς πατρίδος γενέσθαι τὸν παῖδα ἀπώλειαν,
ἐκθεῖναι τὸ βρέφος ἐκέλευε. Πρίαμος δέ, ὡς ἐγεννήθη τὸ βρέφος, δίδωσιν ἐκθεῖναι οἰκέτῃ κομίσαντι[3] εἰς Ἴδην· ὁ δὲ οἰκέτης Ἀγέλαος ὠνομάζετο.
τὸ δὲ ἐκτεθὲν ὑπὸ τούτου βρέφος πένθ᾽ ἡμέρας
ὑπὸ ἄρκτου[4] ἐτράφη. ὁ δὲ σωζόμενον εὑρὼν ἀναιρεῖται, καὶ κομίσας ἐπὶ τῶν χωρίων ὡς ἴδιον παῖδα
ἔτρεφεν, ὀνομάσας Πάριν. γενόμενος δὲ νεανίσκος
καὶ πολλῶν διαφέρων κάλλει τε καὶ ῥώμῃ αὖθις
Ἀλέξανδρος προσωνομάσθη, λῃστὰς ἀμυνόμενος[5]
καὶ τοῖς ποιμνίοις ἀλεξήσας [, ὅπερ ἐστὶ βοηθή-
σας].[6] καὶ μετ᾽ οὐ πολὺ τοὺς γονέας ἀνεῦρε.

Μετὰ τοῦτον ἐγέννησεν Ἑκάβη θυγατέρας μὲν

[1] καθ᾽ ὕπνους SR : καθ᾽ ὕπαρ A.
[2] μετεπέμψατο S : κατεπέμψατο A.
[3] κομίσαντι SA, Wagner : κομίσοντι Heyne, Westermann, Müller, Bekker : κομιοῦντι Hercher.
[4] ἄρκτου SR : ἄρτου A.
[5] ἀμυνόμενος SA, Heyne, Westermann, Müller, Bekker, Wagner : ἀμυνάμενος Hercher.
[6] ὅπερ ἐστὶ βοηθήσας omitted as a gloss by Hercher and Wagner.

[1] For Hecuba's dream and the exposure of the infant Paris, see Pindar, pp. 544, 546, ed. Sandys ; Scholiast on Homer, *Il.* iii. 325 ; Tzetzes, *Schol. on Lycophron,* 86 ; Cicero, *De divinatione,* i. 21. 42 ; Hyginus, *Fab.* 91 ; *Scrip-*

babe was about to be born Hecuba dreamed she
had brought forth a firebrand, and that the fire
spread over the whole city and burned it.[1] When
Priam learned of the dream from Hecuba, he sent for
his son Aesacus, for he was an interpreter of dreams,
having been taught by his mother's father Merops.
He declared that the child was begotten to be the
ruin of his country and advised that the babe should
be exposed. When the babe was born Priam gave
it to a servant to take and expose on Ida; now the
servant was named Agelaus. Exposed by him, the
infant was nursed for five days by a bear; and, when
he found it safe, he took it up, carried it away, brought
it up as his own son on his farm, and named him
Paris. When he grew to be a young man, Paris
excelled many in beauty and strength, and was
afterwards surnamed Alexander, because he repelled
robbers and defended the flocks.[2] And not long
afterwards he discovered his parents.

After him Hecuba gave birth to daughters, Creusa,

tores rerum mythicarum Latini, ed. G. H. Bode, vol. i. p.
139 (Second Vatican Mythographer, 197). The dream is
alluded to, though not expressly mentioned, by Euripides
(*Troades*, 919 sqq.) and Virgil (*Aen.* vii. 319 sqq.). The warning given by the diviner Aesacus is recorded also by Tzetzes
(*Schol. on Lycophron*, 224), according to whom the sage
advised to put both mother and child to death. Euripides
(*Andromache*, 293 sqq.) represents Cassandra shrieking in a
prophetic frenzy to kill the ill-omened babe. The suckling
of the infant Paris for five days by a she-bear seems to be
mentioned only by Apollodorus.

[2] Apollodorus apparently derives the name Alexander from
ἀλέξω "to defend" and ἀνδρός, the genitive of "man." As the
verb was somewhat archaic, he explains it by the more familiar βοηθῶ, if indeed the explanation be not a marginal gloss.
See the Critical Note.

Κρέουσαν Λαοδίκην Πολυξένην Κασάνδραν, ᾗ
συνελθεῖν βουλόμενος Ἀπόλλων τὴν μαντικὴν
ὑπέσχετο διδάξειν. ἡ δὲ μαθοῦσα οὐ συνῆλθεν·
ὅθεν Ἀπόλλων ἀφείλετο τῆς μαντικῆς αὐτῆς τὸ
πείθειν. αὖθις δὲ παῖδας ἐγέννησε Δηίφοβον
Ἕλενον Πάμμονα Πολίτην Ἄντιφον Ἱππόνοον
Πολύδωρον Τρωίλον· τοῦτον ἐξ Ἀπόλλωνος λέγεται γεγεννηκέναι.

Ἐκ δὲ ἄλλων γυναικῶν Πριάμῳ παῖδες γίνον-
ται Μελάνιππος Γοργυθίων Φιλαίμων Ἱππόθοος
Γλαῦκος, Ἀγάθων Χερσιδάμας Εὐαγόρας Ἱππο-
δάμας Μήστωρ, Ἄτας Δόρυκλος Λυκάων Δρύοψ
Βίας, Χρομίος Ἀστύγονος Τελέστας Εὔανδρος
Κεβριόνης, Μύλιος [1] Ἀρχέμαχος Λαοδόκος Ἐχέ-
φρων Ἰδομενεύς, Ὑπερίων Ἀσκάνιος Δημοκόων
Ἄρητος Δηιοπίτης, Κλονίος Ἐχέμμων Ὑπείροχος
Αἰγεωνεὺς Λυσίθοος Πολυμέδων, θυγατέρες δὲ
Μέδουσα Μηδεσικάστη Λυσιμάχη Ἀριστοδήμη.

[1] Μύλιος R : μήλιος A. Wagner compares Stephanus
Byzantius, Μύλιοι (Μύλισιν ed. Westermann), ἔθνος Φρυγίας.
Ἑκαταῖος Ἀσίᾳ.

[1] Laodice is mentioned by Homer as the fairest of Priam's
daughters and the wife of Helicaon (*Iliad*, iii. 122 *sqq.*,
vi. 252).

[2] Compare Aeschylus, *Agamemnon*, 1202–1212; Hyginus,
Fab. 93; Servius, on Virgil, *Aen.* ii. 247; *Scriptores rerum
mythicarum Latini*, ed. G. H. Bode, vol. i. pp. 55, 139
(First Vatican Mythographer, 180; Second Vatican Mythographer, 196). According to Servius (*l.c.*), Apollo deprived
Cassandra of the power of persuading men of the truth of
her prophecies by spitting into her mouth. We have seen
that by a similar procedure Glaucus was robbed of the faculty
of divination. See above, iii. 3. 2. An entirely different
account of the way in which Cassandra and her twin brother

Laodice,[1] Polyxena, and Cassandra. Wishing to gain Cassandra's favours, Apollo promised to teach her the art of prophecy; she learned the art but refused her favours; hence Apollo deprived her prophecy of power to persuade.[2] Afterwards Hecuba bore sons,[3] Deiphobus, Helenus, Pammon, Polites, Antiphus, Hipponous, Polydorus, and Troilus : this last she is said to have had by Apollo.

By other women Priam had sons, to wit, Melanippus, Gorgythion, Philaemon, Hippothous, Glaucus, Agathon, Chersidamas, Evagoras, Hippodamas, Mestor, Atas, Doryclus, Lycaon, Dryops, Bias, Chromius, Astygonus, Telestas, Evander, Cebriones, Mylius, Archemachus, Laodocus, Echephron, Idomeneus, Hyperion, Ascanius, Democoon, Aretus, Deiopites, Clonius, Echemmon, Hypirochus, Aegeoneus, Lysithous, Polymedon; and daughters, to wit, Medusa, Medesicaste, Lysimache, and Aristodeme.

Helenus acquired the gift of prophecy is given by a Scholiast on Homer, *Il.* vii. 44. He says that when the festival in honour of the birth of the twins was being held in the sanctuary of the Thymbraean Apollo, the two children played with each other there and fell asleep in the temple. Meantime the parents and their friends, flushed with wine, had gone home, forgetting all about the twins whose birth had given occasion to the festivity. Next morning, when they were sober, they returned to the temple and found the sacred serpents purging with their tongues the organs of sense of the children. Frightened by the cry which the women raised at the strange sight, the serpents disappeared among the laurel boughs which lay beside the infants on the floor; but from that hour Cassandra and Helenus possessed the gift of prophecy. For this story the Scholiast refers to the authority of Anticlides. In like manner Melampus is said to have acquired the art of soothsaying through the action of serpents which licked his ears. See above, i. 9. 11.

[3] Compare Homer, *Il.* xxiv. 248 *sqq.* ; Hyginus, *Fab.* 90.

APOLLODORUS

6 Ἕκτωρ μὲν οὖν Ἀνδρομάχην τὴν Ἠετίωνος
γαμεῖ, Ἀλέξανδρος δὲ Οἰνώνην τὴν Κεβρῆνος τοῦ
ποταμοῦ θυγατέρα. αὕτη παρὰ Ῥέας τὴν μαντικὴν μαθοῦσα προέλεγεν Ἀλεξάνδρῳ μὴ πλεῖν ἐπὶ
Ἑλένην. μὴ πείθουσα δὲ εἶπεν, ἐὰν τρωθῇ, παραγενέσθαι πρὸς αὐτήν· μόνην [1] γὰρ θεραπεῦσαι
δύνασθαι. τὸν δὲ Ἑλένην ἐκ Σπάρτης ἁρπάσαι,
πολεμουμένης δὲ Τροίας τοξευθέντα ὑπὸ Φιλο-
κτήτου τόξοις Ἡρακλείοις πρὸς Οἰνώνην ἐπανελ-
θεῖν εἰς Ἴδην. ἡ δὲ μνησικακοῦσα θεραπεύσειν [2] οὐκ
ἔφη. Ἀλέξανδρος μὲν οὖν εἰς Τροίαν κομιζόμενος
ἐτελεύτα, Οἰνώνη δὲ μετανοήσασα τὰ πρὸς θεραπείαν φάρμακα ἔφερε, καὶ καταλαβοῦσα αὐτὸν
νεκρὸν ἑαυτὴν ἀνήρτησεν.

Ὁ δὲ Ἀσωπὸς ποταμὸς Ὠκεανοῦ καὶ Τηθύος,
ὡς δὲ Ἀκουσίλαος λέγει, Πηροῦς καὶ Ποσειδῶνος,
ὡς δέ τινες, Διὸς καὶ Εὐρυνόμης. τούτῳ Μετώπη
γημαμένη [3] (Λάδωνος δὲ τοῦ ποταμοῦ θυγάτηρ
αὕτη) δύο μὲν παῖδας ἐγέννησεν, Ἰσμηνὸν καὶ
Πελάγοντα, εἴκοσι δὲ θυγατέρας, ὧν μὲν [4] μίαν
Αἴγιναν ἥρπασε Ζεύς. ταύτην Ἀσωπὸς ζητῶν

[1] μόνην SR : μόνη A.
[2] θεραπεύσειν SR (compend.), Hercher, Wagner : θεραπεῦσαι A, Heyne, Westermann, Müller, Bekker.
[3] τούτῳ Μετώπη γημαμένη R (compend.), Wagner : οὗτος
Μετώπην γημάμενος A, Heyne, Westermann, Müller, Bekker :
οὗτος Μετώπην γήμας Hercher.
[4] μὲν omitted by Hercher, perhaps rightly.

---

[1] See Homer, Il. vi. 395 sqq., where it is said that Eetion
was king of Thebe in Cilicia.

50

Now Hector married Andromache, daughter of Eetion,[1] and Alexander married Oenone, daughter of the river Cebren.[2] She had learned from Rhea the art of prophecy, and warned Alexander not to sail to fetch Helen; but failing to persuade him, she told him to come to her if he were wounded, for she alone could heal him. When he had carried off Helen from Sparta and Troy was besieged, he was shot by Philoctetes with the bow of Hercules, and went back to Oenone on Ida. But she, nursing her grievance, refused to heal him. So Alexander was carried to Troy and died. But Oenone repented her, and brought the healing drugs; and finding him dead she hanged herself.

The Asopus river was a son of Ocean and Tethys, or, as Acusilaus says, of Pero and Poseidon, or, according to some, of Zeus and Eurynome. Him Metope, herself a daughter of the river Ladon, married and bore two sons, Ismenus and Pelagon, and twenty daughters, of whom one, Aegina, was carried off by Zeus.[3] In search of her Asopus came

[2] For the loves of Paris and Oenone, and their tragic end, compare Conon, *Narrat.* 23; Parthenius, *Narrat.* 4; Ovid, *Heroides,* v.

[3] As to the river-god Asopus and his family, see Diodorus Siculus, iv. 72. 1–5; Pausanias, ii. 5. 1 *sq.*, v. 22. 6. According to Diodorus, Asopus was a son of Ocean and Tethys; he married Metope, daughter of the Ladon, by whom he had two sons and twelve daughters. Asopus, the father of Aegina, is identified by Diodorus and Pausanias with the Phliasian or Sicyonian river of that name; but the patriotic Boeotian poet Pindar seems to claim the honour for the Boeotian Asopus (*Isthm.* viii. 16 (35) *sqq.*), and he is naturally supported by his Scholiast (on *v.* 17 (37) of that poem) as well as by Statius

APOLLODORUS

ἧκεν εἰς Κόρινθον, καὶ μανθάνει παρὰ Σισύφου
τὸν ἡρπακότα εἶναι Δία. Ζεὺς δὲ Ἀσωπὸν μὲν
κεραυνώσας διώκοντα πάλιν ἐπὶ τὰ οἰκεῖα ἀπέ-
πεμψε ῥεῖθρα (διὰ τοῦτο μέχρι καὶ νῦν ἐκ τῶν
τούτου ῥείθρων ἄνθρακες φέρονται), Αἴγιναν δὲ
κομίσας ¹ εἰς τὴν τότε Οἰνώνην λεγομένην νῆσον,
νῦν δὲ Αἴγιναν ἀπ᾽ ἐκείνης κληθεῖσαν, μίγνυται,
καὶ τεκνοῖ παῖδα ἐξ αὐτῆς Αἰακόν. τούτῳ Ζεὺς
ὄντι μόνῳ ἐν τῇ νήσῳ τοὺς μύρμηκας ἀνθρώπους
ἐποίησε. γαμεῖ δὲ Αἰακὸς Ἐνδηΐδα τὴν Σκείρωνος,
ἐξ ἧς αὐτῷ παῖδες ἐγένοντο Πηλεύς τε καὶ Τε-
λαμών. Φερεκύδης δέ φησι Τελαμῶνα φίλον, οὐκ
ἀδελφὸν Πηλέως εἶναι, ἀλλ᾽ Ἀκταίου παῖδα καὶ
Γλαύκης τῆς Κυχρέως. μίγνυται δὲ αὖθις Αἰακὸς

¹ κομίσας Hercher, Wagner : εἰσκομίσας A, Heyne, Westermann, Müller, Bekker.

(*Theb.* vii. 315 *sqq.*) and his Scholiast, Lactantius Placidus
(on *Theb.* vii. 424). The Phliasians even went so far as to
assert that their Asopus was the father of Thebe, who gave her
name to the Boeotian Thebes; but this view the Thebans
could not accept (Pausanias, ii. 5. 2).
    ¹ Compare above, i. 9. 3 ; Pausanias, ii. 5. 1.
    ² Compare Callimachus, *Hymn to Delos*, 78 ; Scholiast on
Apollonius Rhodius, *Argon.* i. 117.
    ³ According to Lactantius Placidus (on Statius, *Theb.* vii.
315), live coals were to be found in the Asopus, and Statius,
in his windy style (*Theb.* vii. 325 *sqq.*), talks of the "brave
river blowing ashes of thunderbolts and Aetnaean vapours
from its panting banks to the sky," which may be a poetical
description of river-mists. But both the poet and his dutiful
commentator here refer to the Boeotian Asopus, whereas
Apollodorus probably refers to the Phliasian river of that
name.
    ⁴ Compare Diodorus Siculus, iv. 72. 5 ; Pausanias, ii. 29. 2 ;
Hyginus, *Fab.* 52. As to Oenone, the ancient name of Aegina,
compare Pindar, *Nem.* iv. 46 (75), v. 16 (29), viii. 7 (12),

to Corinth, and learned from Sisyphus that the
ravisher was Zeus.[1] Asopus pursued him, but Zeus,
by hurling thunderbolts, sent him away back to his
own streams;[2] hence coals are fetched to this day
from the streams of that river.[3] And having conveyed Aegina to the island then named Oenone, but
now called Aegina after her, Zeus cohabited with her
and begot a son Aeacus on her.[4] As Aeacus was
alone in the island, Zeus made the ants into men for
him.[5] And Aeacus married Endeis, daughter of
Sciron, by whom he had two sons, Peleus and Telamon.[6] But Pherecydes says that Telamon was a
friend, not a brother of Peleus, he being a son of
Actaeus and Glauce, daughter of Cychreus.[7] After-

Isthm. v. 34 (44); Herodotus, viii. 46; Strabo, viii. 6. 16,
p. 375; Hyginus, *Fab.* 52. Another old name for Aegina
was Oenopia. See Pindar, *Nem.* viii. 21 (45); Ovid, *Metamorph.* vii. 472 *sqq.*

[5] As to the transformation of the ants into men see Hesiod,
quoted by the Scholiast on Pindar, *Nem.* iii. 13 (21), and by
Tzetzes, *Schol. on Lycophron*, 176; Scholiast on Homer,
Il. i. 180; Strabo, viii. 6. 16, p. 375; Hyginus, *Fab.* 52;
Ovid, *Metamorph.* vii. 614 *sqq.*; *Scriptores rerum mythicarum Latini*, ed. G. H. Bode, vol. i. pp. 23, 142 (First
Vatican Mythographer, 67; Second Vatican Mythographer,
204). The fable is clearly based on the false etymology which
derived the name Myrmidons from μύρμηκες, "ants." Strabo
(*l.c.*) attempted to rationalize the myth.

[6] Compare Plutarch, *Theseus*, 10; Pausanias, ii. 29. 9;
Scholiast on Euripides, *Andromache*, 687. According to
another account, Endeis, the mother of Telamon and Peleus,
was a daughter of Chiron. See Scholiast on Pindar, *Nem.* v.
7 (12); Scholiast on Homer, *Il.* xvi. 14; Hyginus, *Fab.* 14.

[7] This account of the parentage of Telamon, for which we
have the authority of the old writer Pherecydes (about 480
B.C.), is probably earlier than the one which represents him
as a son of Aeacus. According to it, Telamon was a native,
not of Aegina, but of Salamis, his mother Glauce being a

APOLLODORUS

Ψαμάθη τῇ Νηρέως εἰς φώκην[1] ἠλλαγμένη διὰ τὸ
μὴ βούλεσθαι συνελθεῖν, καὶ τεκνοῖ παῖδα Φῶκον.
Ἦν δὲ εὐσεβέστατος πάντων[2] Αἰακός. διὸ καὶ
τὴν Ἑλλάδα κατεχούσης ἀφορίας διὰ Πέλοπα,
ὅτι Στυμφάλῳ τῷ βασιλεῖ τῶν Ἀρκάδων πολεμῶν
καὶ τὴν Ἀρκαδίαν ἑλεῖν μὴ δυνάμενος, προσποιη-
σάμενος φιλίαν ἔκτεινεν αὐτὸν καὶ διέσπειρε μελίσας, χρησμοὶ[3] θεῶν ἔλεγον ἀπαλλαγήσεσθαι τῶν
ἐνεστώτων κακῶν τὴν Ἑλλάδα, ἐὰν Αἰακὸς ὑπὲρ
αὐτῆς εὐχὰς ποιήσηται ποιησαμένου δὲ εὐχὰς
Αἰακοῦ τῆς ἀκαρπίας ἡ Ἑλλὰς ἀπαλλάττεται.

---

[1] φώκην S, Bekker, Hercher, Wagner : φύκην ROR[a],
Heyne, Westermann, Müller : φύλην A.
[2] πάντων ES : ἁπάντων A.
[3] χρησμοὶ S : χρησμοὶ δὲ A.

---

daughter of Cychreus, king of Salamis (as to whom see below,
iii. 12. 7). It is certain that the later life of Telamon was
associated with Salamis, where, according to one account
(Diodorus Siculus, iv. 72. 7), he married Glauce, daughter of
Cychreus, king of Salamis. the very woman whom the other
and perhaps earlier version of the legend represented as his
mother. See Sir R. C. Jebb, *Sophocles, Ajax* (Cambridge,
1896), Introduction, § 4, pp. xvii *sq.*

[1] Compare Hesiod, *Theog.* 1003 *sqq.* ; Pindar, *Nem.* v. 12
(21) *sq.* ; Scholiast on Euripides, *Andromache*, 687, who
mentions the transformation of the sea-nymph into a seal.
The children of Phocus settled in Phocis and gave their name
to the country. See Pausanias, ii. 29. 2, x. 1. 1, x. 30. 4.
Thus we have an instance of a Greek people, the Phocians,
who traced their name and their lineage to an animal
ancestress. But it would be rash to infer that the seal was
the totem of the Phocians. There is no evidence that they
regarded the seal with any superstitious respect, though the
people of Phocaea, in Asia Minor, who were Phocians by
descent (Pausanias, vii. 3. 10)), put the figure of a seal on
their earliest coins. But this was probably no more than a
punning badge, like the rose of Rhodes and the wild celery

54

wards Aeacus cohabited with Psamathe, daughter of Nereus, who turned herself into a seal to avoid his embraces, and he begot a son Phocus.[1]

Now Aeacus was the most pious of men. Therefore, when Greece suffered from infertility on account of Pelops, because in a war with Stymphalus, king of the Arcadians, being unable to conquer Arcadia, he slew the king under a pretence of friendship, and scattered his mangled limbs, oracles of the gods declared that Greece would be rid of its present calamities if Aeacus would offer prayers on its behalf. So Aeacus did offer prayers, and Greece was delivered from the dearth.[2] Even after his death

(*selinon*) of Selinus. See George Macdonald, *Coin Types* (Glasgow, 1905), pp. 17, 41, 50.

[2] Compare Isocrates, *Evagoras*, 14 *sq.* ; Diodorus Siculus, iv. 61. 1 *sq.* ; Pausanias, ii. 29. 7 *sq.* ; Clement of Alexandria, *Strom.* vi. 3. 28, p. 753 ; Scholiast on Pindar, *Nem.* v. 9 (17). Tradition ran that a prolonged drought had withered up the fruits of the earth all over Greece, and that Aeacus, as the son of the sky-god Zeus, was deemed the person most naturally fitted to obtain from his heavenly father the rain so urgently needed by the parched earth and the dying corn. So the Greeks sent envoys to him to request that he would intercede with Zeus to save the crops and the people. " Complying with their petition, Aeacus ascended the Hellenic mountain and stretching out pure hands to heaven he called on the common god, and prayed him to take pity on afflicted Greece. And even while he prayed a loud clap of thunder pealed, and all the surrounding sky was overcast, and furious and continuous showers of rain burst out and flooded the whole land. Thus was exuberant fertility procured for the fruits of the earth by the prayers of Aeacus " (Clement of Alexandria, *l.c.*). In gratitude for this timely answer to his prayers Aeacus is said to have built a sanctuary of Zeus on Mount Panhellenius in Aegina (Pausanias, ii. 30. 4). No place could well be more appropriate for a temple of the rain-god ; for the sharp peak of Mount Panhellenius, the highest mountain of Aegina, is a conspicuous landmark viewed from

APOLLODORUS

τιμᾶται δὲ καὶ παρὰ Πλούτωνι τελευτήσας Αἰακός,
καὶ τὰς κλεῖς τοῦ "Αιδου φυλάττει.

Διαφέροντος δὲ ἐν τοῖς ἀγῶσι Φώκου, τοὺς
ἀδελφοὺς [1] Πηλέα καὶ Τελαμῶνα ἐπιβουλεῦσαι·
καὶ λαχὼν κλήρῳ Τελαμὼν συγγυμναζόμενον αὐτὸν βαλὼν δίσκῳ κατὰ τῆς κεφαλῆς κτείνει, καὶ
κομίσας μετὰ Πηλέως κρύπτει κατά τινος ὕλης.
φωραθέντος δὲ τοῦ φόνου φυγάδες ἀπὸ Αἰγίνης ὑπὸ
7 Αἰακοῦ ἐλαύνονται. καὶ Τελαμὼν μὲν εἰς Σαλα-

---

[1] ἀδελφούς <φασιν> Eberhard.

---

all the neighbouring coasts of the gulf, and in antiquity a
cloud settling on the mountain was regarded as a sign of rain
(Theophrastus, *De signis tempestat.* i. 24). According to
Apollodorus, the cause of the dearth had been a crime of
Pelops, who had treacherously murdered Stymphalus, king
of Arcadia, and scattered the fragments of his mangled body
abroad. This crime seems not to be mentioned by any other
ancient writer; but Diodorus Siculus in like manner traces
the calamity to a treacherous murder. He says (iv. 61. 1)
that to punish the Athenians for the assassination of his son
Androgeus, the Cretan king Minos prayed to Zeus that
Athens might be afflicted with drought and famine, and that
these evils soon spread over Attica and Greece. Similarly
Alcmaeon's matricide was believed to have entailed a failure
of the crops. See above, iii. 7. 5 with the note.
   [1] In some late Greek verses, inscribed on the tomb of a
religious sceptic at Rome, Aeacus is spoken of as the warder
or key-holder (κλειδοῦχος) of the infernal regions; but in the
same breath the poet assures us that these regions, with all
their inmates, were mere fables, and that of the dead there
remained no more than the bones and ashes. See *Corpus
Inscriptionum Graecarum*, vol. iii. p. 933, No. 6298; G.
Kaibel, *Epigrammata Graeca ex lapidibus conlecta* (Berlin,
1878), pp. 262 *sq.*, No. 646. Elsewhere Pluto himself was
represented in art holding in his hand the key of Hades.
See Pausanias, v. 20. 3. According to Isocrates (*Evagoras*,
15), Aeacus enjoyed the greatest honours after death, sitting

Aeacus is honoured in the abode of Pluto, and keeps the keys of Hades.[1]

As Phocus excelled in athletic sports, his brothers Peleus and Telamon plotted against him, and the lot falling on Telamon, he killed his brother in a match by throwing a quoit at his head, and with the help of Peleus carried the body and hid it in a wood. But the murder being detected, the two were driven fugitives from Aegina by Aeacus.[2] And Telamon

as assessor with Pluto and Proserpine. Plato represents him as judging the dead along with Minos, Rhadamanthys, and Triptolemus (*Apology*, 32, p. 41 A), it being his special duty to try the souls of those who came from Europe, while his colleague Rhadamanthys dealt with those that came from Asia (*Gorgias*, 79, p. 524 A); apparently no provision was made for African ghosts. Lucian depicts Aeacus playing a less dignified part in the lower world as a sort of ticket-collector or customhouse officer (τελώνης), whose business it was to examine the ghostly passengers on landing from the ferry-boat, count them, and see that they had paid the fare. See Lucian, *Cataplus*, 4, *Charon*, 2. Elsewhere he speaks of Aeacus as keeping the gate of Hades (*Dialog. Mort.* xx. 1).

[2] As to the murder of Phocus and the exile of Peleus and Telamon, see Diodorus Siculus, iv. 72. 6 *sq.* (who represents the death as accidental); Pausanias, ii. 29. 9 *sq.*; Scholia on Pindar, *Nem.* v. 14 (25); Scholia on Euripides, *Andromache*, 687 (quoting verses from the *Alcmaeonis*); Scholiast on Homer, *Il.* xvi. 14; Antoninus Liberalis, *Transform.* 38; Plutarch, *Parallela*, 25; Tzetzes, *Schol. on Lycophron*, 175 (vol. i. pp. 444, 447, ed. Müller); Hyginus, *Fab.* 14; Ovid, *Metamorph.* xi. 266 *sqq.*; Lactantius Placidus on Statius, *Theb.* ii. 113, vii. 344, xi. 281. Tradition differed on several points as to the murder. According to Apollodorus and Plutarch the murderer was Telamon; but according to what seems to have been the more generally accepted view he was Peleus. (So Diodorus, Pausanias, the Scholiast on Homer, one of the Scholiasts on Euripides, *l.c.*, Ovid, and in one passage Lactantius Placidus). If Pherecydes was right in denying any relationship between Telamon and Peleus,

57

APOLLODORUS

μίνα παραγίνεται πρὸς Κυχρέα τὸν <Ποσειδῶνος
καὶ>[1] Σαλαμῖνος τῆς Ἀσωποῦ. κτείνας δὲ ὄφιν
οὗτος ἀδικοῦντα τὴν νῆσον αὐτῆς[2] ἐβασίλευε, καὶ
τελευτῶν ἄπαις τὴν βασιλείαν παραδίδωσι Τελα-

[1] Ποσειδῶνος καὶ inserted by Aegius.

[2] αὐτῆς Heyne (conjecture): ἧς αὐτὸς Heyne (in text),
Westermann, Müller, Bekker, Hercher, Wagner, apparently following the MSS. Compare Tzetzes, *Schol. on
Lycophron*, 175 (vol. i. p. 444, ed. Müller), Κυχρεὺς γὰρ ὁ
Ποσειδῶνος καὶ Σαλαμῖνος τῆς Ἀσωποῦ κτείνας τὴν νῆσον
λυμαινόμενον ἐβασίλευσεν αὐτῆς, ἄπαις δὲ τελευτῶν τὴν βασιλείαν Τελαμῶνι κατέλειψε φυγόντι πρὸς αὐτόν. In writing
thus, Tzetzes probably had the present passage of Apollodorus before him. Accordingly in Apollodorus we should
perhaps read ἐβασίλευσε for ἐβασίλευε.

---

and in representing Telamon as a Salaminian rather than an
Aeginetan (see above), it becomes probable that in the original
tradition Peleus, not Telamon, was described as the murderer
of Phocus. Another version of the story was that both
brothers had a hand in the murder, Telamon having banged
him on the head with a quoit, while Peleus finished him off
with the stroke of an axe in the middle of his back. This
was the account given by the anonymous author of the old
epic *Alcmaeonis*; and the same division of labour between
the brothers was recognized by the Scholiast on Pindar and
Tzetzes, though according to them the quoit was handled by
Peleus and the cold steel by Telamon. Other writers (Antoninus Liberalis and Hyginus) lay the murder at the door
of both brothers without parcelling the guilt out exactly
between them. There seems to be a general agreement that
the crime was committed, or the accident happened, in the
course of a match at quoits; but Dorotheus (quoted by Plutarch, *l.c.*) alleged that the murder was perpetrated by
Telamon at a boar hunt, and this view seems to have been
accepted by Lactantius Placidus in one place (on Statius,
Theb. ii. 113), though in other places (on vii. 344 and xi. 281)
he speaks as if the brothers were equally guilty. But perhaps
this version of the story originated in a confusion of the
murder of Phocus with the subsequent homicide of Eurytion,

betook himself to Salamis, to the court of Cychreus, son of Poseidon and Salamis, daughter of Asopus. This Cychreus became king of Salamis through killing a snake which ravaged the island, and dying childless he bequeathed the kingdom to Telamon.[1]   And

---

which is said to have taken place at a boar-hunt, whether the hunting of the Calydonian boar or another. See below, iii. 13. 2 with the note. According to Pausanias the exiled Telamon afterwards returned and stood his trial, pleading his cause from the deck of a ship, because his father would not suffer him to set foot in the island. But being judged guilty by his stern sire he sailed away, to return to his native land no more. It may have been this verdict, delivered against his own son, which raised the reputation of Aeacus for rigid justice to the highest pitch, and won for him a place on the bench beside Minos and Rhadamanthys in the world of shades.

[1] Compare Diodorus Siculus, iv. 72. 4 ; Tzetzes, *Schol. on Lycophron*, 110, 175, 451. In the second of these passages (on *v.* 175, vol. i. p. 444, ed. Müller) Tzetzes agrees closely with Apollodorus and probably follows him. A somewhat different version of the legend was told by Hesiod. According to him the snake was reared by Cychreus, but expelled from Salamis by Eurylochus because of the ravages it committed in the island ; and after its expulsion it was received at Eleusis by Demeter, who made it one of her attendants. See Strabo, ix. 1. 9, p. 394. Others said that the snake was not a real snake, but a bad man nicknamed Snake on account of his cruelty, who was banished by Eurylochus and took refuge at Eleusis, where he was appointed to a minor office in the sanctuary of Demeter. See Stephanus Byzantius, *s.v.* Κυχρεῖος πάγος ; Eustathius, *Commentary on Dionysius Periegetes*, 507 (*Geographi Graeci Minores*, ed. C. Müller, vol. ii. p. 314). Cychreus was regarded as one of the guardian heroes of Salamis, where he was buried with his face to the west. Sacrifices were regularly offered at his grave, and when Solon desired to establish the claim of Athens to the possession of the island, he sailed across by night and sacrificed to the dead man at his grave. See Plutarch, *Solon*, 9. Cychreus was worshipped also at Athens

μῶνι. ὁ δὲ γαμεῖ Περίβοιαν[1] τὴν Ἀλκάθου[2] τοῦ
Πέλοπος· καὶ ποιησαμένου εὐχὰς Ἡρακλέους ἵνα
αὐτῷ παῖς ἄρρην γένηται, φανέντος δὲ μετὰ τὰς
εὐχὰς αἰετοῦ, τὸν γεννηθέντα ἐκάλεσεν Αἴαντα.
καὶ στρατευσάμενος ἐπὶ Τροίαν σὺν Ἡρακλεῖ
λαμβάνει γέρας Ἡσιόνην τὴν Λαομέδοντος θυγατέρα, ἐξ ἧς αὐτῷ γίνεται Τεῦκρος.

XIII. Πηλεὺς δὲ εἰς Φθίαν φυγὼν πρὸς Εὐρυτίωνα[3] τὸν Ἄκτορος ὑπ᾽ αὐτοῦ καθαίρεται, καὶ
λαμβάνει παρ᾽ αὐτοῦ τὴν θυγατέρα Ἀντιγόνην καὶ
τῆς χώρας τὴν τρίτην μοῖραν. καὶ γίνεται θυγάτηρ

---

[1] Περίβοιαν A : Ἡερίβοια, Scholiast on Homer, *Il.* xvi. 14 :
Ἐρίβοια Pindar, *Isthm.* vi. 45 (65), Diodorus Siculus, iv. 72. 7.
[2] Ἀλκάθου Aegius : ἀλκάνδρου A.
[3] Εὐρυτίωνα Aegius : Εὔρυτον A, Tzetzes, *Schol. on Lycophron*, 175 (vol. i. p. 445, ed. Müller). As to Εὐρυτίων, see
a few lines below.

(Plutarch, *Theseus*, 10). It is said that at the battle of Salamis a serpent appeared among the Greek ships, and God
announced to the Athenians that this serpent was the hero
Cychreus (Pausanias i. 36. 1). The story may preserve a
reminiscence of the belief that kings and heroes regularly
turn into serpents after death. The same belief possibly
explains the association of Erichthonius or Erechtheus and
Cecrops with serpents at Athens. See *The Dying God*,
pp. 86 *sq.* On account of this legendary serpent Lycophron
called Salamis the Dragon Isle (*Cassandra*, 110).

[1] Compare Xenophon, *Cyneget.* i. 9 ; Scholiast on Homer,
Il. xvi. 14. According to Diodorus Siculus (iv. 72. 7), Telamon
first married Glauce, daughter of Cychreus, king of Salamis,
and on her death he wedded the Athenian Eriboea, daughter
of Alcathous, by whom he had Ajax. Pindar also mentions
Eriboea as the wife of Telamon : see *Isthm.* vi. 45 (65).

[2] As to the prayer of Hercules and the appearance of the
eagle in answer to the prayer, see Pindar, *Isthm.* vi. 35
(51) *sqq.* ; Tzetzes, *Schol. on Lycophron*, 455–461. Pindar,
followed by Apollodorus and Tzetzes, derived the name Ajax

Telamon married Periboea, daughter of Alcathus,[1] son of Pelops, and called his son Ajax, because when Hercules had prayed that he might have a male child, an eagle appeared after the prayer.[2] And having gone with Hercules on his expedition against Troy, he received as a prize Hesione, daughter of Laomedon, by whom he had a son Teucer.[3]

XIII. Peleus fled to Phthia to the court of Eurytion, son of Actor, and was purified by him, and he received from him his daughter Antigone and the third part of the country.[4] And a daughter Polydora was born

from *aietos* "an eagle." A story ran that Hercules wrapt the infant Ajax in the lion's skin which he himself wore, and that Ajax was thus made invulnerable except in the armpit, where the quiver had hung, or, according to others, at the neck. Hence, in describing the suicide of the hero, Aeschylus told how, when he tried to run himself through the body, the sword doubled back in the shape of a bow, till some spirit showed the desperate man the fatal point to which to apply the trenchant blade. See Scholiast on Sophocles, *Ajax*, 833; Tzetzes, *Schol. on Lycophron*, 455–461; Scholiast on Homer, *Il.* xxiii. 821. Plato probably had this striking passage of the tragedy in his mind when he made Alcibiades speak of Socrates as more proof against vice than Ajax against steel (*Sympos.* 35, p. 219 E).

[3] See above, ii. 6. 4. As Hesione, the mother of Teucer, was not the lawful wife of Telamon, Homer speaks of Teucer as a bastard (*Il.* viii. 283 *sq.*, with the Scholiast on *v.* 284). According to another account, it was not Telamon but his brother Peleus who went with Hercules to the siege of Troy. The poets were not consistent on this point. Thus, while in two passages (*Nem.* iv. 25 (40) *sq.*; *Isthm.* vi. 27 (39) *sqq.*) Pindar assigns to Telamon the glory of the adventure, in another he transfers it to Peleus (quoted by the Scholiast on Euripides, *Andromache*, 796; Pindar, p. 604 ed. Sandys). Euripides was equally inconsistent. See his *Troades* 804 *sqq.* (Telamon), contrasted with his *Andromache*, 796 *sqq.* (Peleus).

[4] Compare Tzetzes, *Schol. on Lycophron*, 175 (vol. i. pp. 444 *sq.*, 447, ed. Müller); Antoninus Liberalis, *Transform.*

αὐτῷ Πολυδώρα, ἣν ἔγημε Βῶρος ὁ Περιήρους.
2 ἐντεῦθεν ἐπὶ τὴν θήραν τοῦ Καλυδωνίου κάπρου
μετ᾽ Εὐρυτίωνος ἐλθών, προέμενος ἐπὶ τὸν σὺν
ἀκόντιον Εὐρυτίωνος τυγχάνει καὶ κτείνει τοῦτον
ἄκων. πάλιν οὖν ἐκ Φθίας φυγὼν εἰς Ἰωλκὸν
πρὸς Ἄκαστον ἀφικνεῖται καὶ ὑπ᾽ αὐτοῦ καθαί-
3 ρεται. ἀγωνίζεται δὲ καὶ τὸν ἐπὶ Πελίᾳ[1] ἀγῶνα,
πρὸς Ἀταλάντην διαπαλαίσας. καὶ Ἀστυδάμεια
ἡ Ἀκάστου γυνή, Πηλέως ἐρασθεῖσα, περὶ συνουσίας προσέπεμψεν αὐτῷ λόγους. μὴ δυναμένη

---

[1] Πελίᾳ Aegius : μελίᾳ A.

---

38 ; Diodorus Siculus, iv. 72. 6 ; Scholiast on Aristophanes,
Clouds, 1063 ; Eustathius on Homer, *Il.* ii. 684, p. 321.
There are some discrepancies in these accounts. According to
Tzetzes and the Scholiast on Aristophanes, the man who
purified Peleus for the murder of Phocus was Eurytus (not
Eurytion), son of Actor. According to Antoninus Liberalis,
he was Eurytion, son of Irus. According to Diodorus, he
was Actor, king of the country, who died childless and left
the kingdom to Peleus. Eustathius agrees that the host of
Peleus was Actor, but says that he had a daughter Polymela,
whom he bestowed in marriage on Peleus along with the
kingdom. From Tzetzes (*l.c.*, pp. 444 *sq.*) we learn that the
purification of Peleus by Eurytus (Eurytion) was recorded by
Pherecydes, whom Apollodorus may here be following.

[1] See Homer, *Il.* xvi. 173–178, who says that Polydora,
daughter of Peleus, had a son Menesthius by the river
Sperchius, though the child was nominally fathered on
her human husband Borus, son of Perieres. Compare
Heliodorus, *Aethiop.* ii. 34. Hesiod also recognized Polydora as the daughter of Peleus (Scholiast on Homer,
Il. xvi. 175). Homer does not mention the mother of
Polydora, but according to Pherecydes she was Antigone,
daughter of Eurytion (Scholiast on Homer, *l.c.*). Hence it
is probable that here, as in so many places, Apollodorus
followed Pherecydes. According to Staphylus, in the third
book of his work on Thessaly, the wife of Peleus and mother

to him, who was wedded by Borus, son of Perieres.[1]
Thence he went with Eurytion to hunt the Calydonian
boar, but in throwing a dart at the hog he involuntarily struck and killed Eurytion. Therefore flying
again from Phthia he betook him to Acastus at Iolcus
and was purified by him.[2] And at the games celebrated in honour of Pelias he contended in wrestling
with Atalanta.[3] And Astydamia, wife of Acastus,
fell in love with Peleus, and sent him a proposal for
a meeting;[4] and when she could not prevail on him

of Polydora was Eurydice, daughter of Actor (Scholiast on
Homer, *l.c.*). A little later on (§ 4 of this chapter) Apollodorus
says that Peleus himself married Polydora, daughter of
Perieres, and that she had a son Menesthius by the river
Sperchius, though the child was nominally fathered on Peleus.
In this latter passage Apollodorus seems to have fallen into
confusion in describing Polydora as the wife of Peleus, though
in the present passage he had correctly described her as his
daughter. Compare Höfer, in W. H. Roscher, *Lexikon der
griech. und röm. Mythologie*, iii. 2641 *sq.*

[2] As to this involuntary homicide committed by Peleus
and his purification by Acastus, see above, i. 8. 2 ; Scholiast
on Aristophanes, *Clouds*, 1063 ; Antoninus Liberalis, *Transform.* 38 ; Tzetzes, *Schol. on Lycophron*, 175 (vol. i. p. 447,
ed. Müller). The Scholiast on Aristophanes calls the slain
man Eurytus, not Eurytion. Antoninus Liberalis and Tzetzes
describe him as Eurytion, son of Irus, not of Actor. They
do not mention the hunt of the Calydonian boar in particular,
but speak of a boar-hunt or a hunt in general.

[3] See above, iii. 9. 2.

[4] The following romantic story of the wicked wife, the
virtuous hero, and his miraculous rescue from the perils of
the forest, in which his treacherous host left him sleeping
alone and unarmed, is briefly alluded to by Pindar, *Nem.* iv.
54 (88) *sqq.*, v. 25 (46) *sqq.* It is told more explicitly by the
Scholiast on Pindar, *Nem.* iv. 54 (88) and 59 (95); the Scholiast on Aristophanes, *Clouds*, 1063 ; and the Scholiast on Apollonius Rhodius, *Argon.* i. 224. But the fullest and clearest
version of the tale is given by Apollodorus in the present

δὲ πεῖσαι, πρὸς τὴν γυναῖκα αὐτοῦ πέμψασα ἔφη
μέλλειν Πηλέα γαμεῖν Στερόπην τὴν Ἀκάστου
θυγατέρα· καὶ τοῦτο ἐκείνη ἀκούσασα ἀγχόνην
ἀνάπτει. Πηλέως δὲ πρὸς Ἄκαστον καταψεύδεται, λέγουσα ὑπ' αὐτοῦ περὶ συνουσίας πεπει-
ρᾶσθαι. Ἄκαστος [1] <δὲ>[2] ἀκούσας κτεῖναι μὲν ὃν
ἐκάθηρεν οὐκ ἠβουλήθη, ἄγει δὲ αὐτὸν ἐπὶ θήραν[3]
εἰς τὸ Πήλιον. ἔνθα ἁμίλλης περὶ θήρας γενομένης, Πηλεὺς μὲν ὧν ἐχειροῦτο θηρίων τὰς γλώσσας
τούτων ἐκτεμὼν[4] εἰς πήραν ἐτίθει, οἱ δὲ μετὰ
Ἀκάστου ταῦτα χειρούμενοι κατεγέλων ὡς μηδὲν
τεθηρακότος[5] τοῦ Πηλέως. ὁ δὲ τὰς γλώσσας
παρασχόμενος ὅσας εἶχεν ἐκείνοις, τοσαῦτα ἔφη
τεθηρευκέναι. ἀποκοιμηθέντος δὲ αὐτοῦ ἐν τῷ
Πηλίῳ, ἀπολιπὼν Ἄκαστος καὶ τὴν μάχαιραν ἐν
τῇ τῶν βοῶν κόπρῳ κρύψας ἐπανέρχεται. ὁ δὲ
ἐξαναστὰς καὶ ζητῶν τὴν μάχαιραν, ὑπὸ τῶν
Κενταύρων καταληφθεὶς ἔμελλεν ἀπόλλυσθαι,
σώζεται δὲ ὑπὸ Χείρωνος· οὗτος καὶ τὴν μάχαιραν
αὐτοῦ ἐκζητήσας δίδωσι.

[1] ἃ Ἄκαστος Emperius, Westermann, Bekker.
[2] δὲ inserted by Hercher.   [3] θήραν R: θήρας A.
[4] ἐκτεμὼν R[a], Hercher: ἐκτέμνων Heyne, Westermann,
Müller, Bekker, Wagner, apparently following most MSS.
[5] τεθηρακότος RR[a]B, Westermann, Wagner: τεθηρευ-
κότος C, Heyne, Müller, Bekker.

---

passage. Pindar calls the wicked wife Hippolyta or Hippolyta Cretheis, that is, Hippolyta daughter of Cretheus. His
Scholiast calls her Cretheis; the Scholiast on Apollonius
Rhodius calls her Cretheis or Hippolyte; and the Scholiast
on Aristophanes calls her first Hippolyte and afterwards
Astydamia. The sword of Peleus, which his faithless host
hid in the cows' dung while the hero lay sleeping in the
wood, was a magic sword wrought by the divine smith
Hephaestus and bestowed on Peleus by the pitying gods as a

she sent word to his wife that Peleus was about to marry Sterope, daughter of Acastus; on hearing which the wife of Peleus strung herself up. And the wife of Acastus falsely accused Peleus to her husband, alleging that he had attempted her virtue. On hearing that, Acastus would not kill the man whom he had purified, but took him to hunt on Pelion. There a contest taking place in regard to the hunt, Peleus cut out and put in his pouch the tongues of the animals that fell to him, while the party of Acastus bagged his game and derided him as if he had taken nothing. But he produced them the tongues, and said that he had taken just as many animals as he had tongues.[1] When he had fallen asleep on Pelion, Acastus deserted him, and hiding his sword in the cows' dung, returned. On arising and looking for his sword, Peleus was caught by the centaurs and would have perished, if he had not been saved by Chiron, who also restored him his sword, which he had sought and found.

reward for his chastity. With this wondrous brand the chaste hero, like a mediaeval knight, was everywhere victorious in the fight and successful in the chase. Compare Zenobius, *Cent.* v. 20. The episode of the hiding of the sword was told by Hesiod, some of whose verses on the subject are quoted by the Scholiast on Pindar, *Nem.* iv. 59 (95). The whole story of the adventures of Peleus in the house of Acastus and in the forest reads like a fairy tale, and we can hardly doubt that it contains elements of genuine folk-lore. These are well brought out by W. Mannhardt in his study of the story. See his *Antike Wald- und Feldkulte* (Berlin, 1877), pp. 49 *sqq.*

[1] In fairy tales the hero often cuts out the tongues of a seven-headed dragon or other fearsome beast, and produces them as evidence of his prowess. See W. Mannhardt, *Antike Wald- und Feldkulte*, pp. 53 *sqq.* ; *Spirits of the Corn and of the Wild*, ii. 269.

4 Γαμεῖ δὲ ὁ Πηλεὺς Πολυδώραν τὴν Περιήρους,
ἐξ ἧς αὐτῷ γίνεται Μενέσθιος ἐπίκλην, ὁ Σπερ-
5 χειοῦ τοῦ ποταμοῦ. αὖθις δὲ γαμεῖ Θέτιν τὴν
Νηρέως, περὶ ἧς τοῦ γάμου Ζεὺς καὶ Ποσειδῶν
ἤρισαν, Θέμιδος [1] δὲ θεσπιῳδούσης ἔσεσθαι τὸν
ἐκ ταύτης γεννηθέντα κρείττονα τοῦ πατρὸς ἀπέ-
σχοντο. ἔνιοι δέ φασι, Διὸς ὁρμῶντος ἐπὶ τὴν
ταύτης συνουσίαν, εἰρηκέναι Προμηθέα τὸν ἐκ
ταύτης αὐτῷ γεννηθέντα οὐρανοῦ δυναστεύσειν.[2]
τινὲς δὲ λέγουσι Θέτιν μὴ βουληθῆναι Διὶ συνελθεῖν ὡς [3] ὑπὸ Ἥρας τραφεῖσαν, Δία δὲ ὀργισθέντα
θνητῷ θέλειν αὐτὴν [4] συνοικίσαι.[5] Χείρωνος οὖν
ὑποθεμένου Πηλεῖ συλλαβεῖν καὶ κατασχεῖν [6]
αὐτὴν μεταμορφουμένην, ἐπιτηρήσας συναρπάζει,
γινομένην δὲ ὁτὲ μὲν πῦρ ὁτὲ δὲ ὕδωρ ὁτὲ δὲ θηρίον
οὐ πρότερον ἀνῆκε πρὶν ἢ τὴν ἀρχαίαν μορφὴν
εἶδεν ἀπολαβοῦσαν. γαμεῖ δὲ ἐν τῷ Πηλίῳ, κἀκεῖ

---

[1] Θέμιδος ER : Θέτιδος A (also as a first-hand correction
in E).   [2] δυναστεύσειν Gale : δυναστεύειν A.
[3] ὡς E, but apparently wanting in A.
[4] αὐτὴν E : αὐτῇ A.
[5] συνοικίσαι Staverenus : συνοικίσειν E : συνοικῆσαι A.
[6] κατασχεῖν ER : κατέχειν C.

---

[1] See above, note on iii. 13. 1.
[2] Compare Homer, *Il.* xviii. 83 *sqq.*, 432 *sqq.*; Pindar,
Nem. iv. 61 (100) *sqq.*; Euripides, *Iphigenia in Aul.* 701 *sqq.*,
1036 *sqq.*; Apollonius Rhodius, *Argon.* iv. 805 *sqq.*; Catullus,
lxiv.; *Scriptores rerum mythicarum Latini*, ed. G. H. Bode,
vol. i. pp. 65, 142 *sq.* (First Vatican Mythographer, 207, 208 ;
Second Vatican Mythographer, 205).
[3] See Pindar, *Isthm.* viii. 27 (58) *sqq.* ; Apollonius Rhodius,
Argon. iv. 790 *sqq.* ; Ovid, *Metamorph.* xi. 217 *sqq.*, who
attributes the prophecy to Proteus.   The present passage of
Apollodorus is quoted, with the author's name, by Tzetzes,
(*Schol. on Lycophron*, 178).

Peleus married Polydora, daughter of Perieres, by whom he had a putative son Menesthius, though in fact Menesthius was the son of the river Sperchius.[1] Afterwards he married Thetis, daughter of Nereus,[2] for whose hand Zeus and Poseidon had been rivals; but when Themis prophesied that the son born of Thetis would be mightier than his father, they withdrew.[3] But some say that when Zeus was bent on gratifying his passion for her, Prometheus declared that the son borne to him by her would be lord of heaven;[4] and others affirm that Thetis would not consort with Zeus because she had been brought up by Hera, and that Zeus in anger would marry her to a mortal.[5] Chiron, therefore, having advised Peleus to seize her and hold her fast in spite of her shape-shifting, he watched his chance and carried her off, and though she turned, now into fire, now into water, and now into a beast, he did not let her go till he saw that she had resumed her former shape.[6] And he married her on Pelion,

[4] Compare Aeschylus, *Prometheus*, 908 *sqq.*; Scholiast on Homer, *Il.* i. 519; Quintus Smyrnaeus, *Posthomerica*, v. 338 *sqq.*; Hyginus, *Fab.* 54; *id. Astronom.* ii. 15. According to Hyginus, Zeus released Prometheus from his fetters in gratitude for the warning which the sage had given him not to wed Thetis.

[5] Compare Apollonius Rhodius, *Argon.* iv. 790-798, a passage which Apollodorus seems here to have had in mind.

[6] As to the various shapes into which the reluctant Thetis turned herself in order to evade the grasp of her mortal lover, see Pindar, *Nem.* iv. 62 (101) *sqq.*; Scholiast on Pindar, *Nem.* iii. 35 (60), iv. 62 (101); Pausanias, v. 18. 5; Quintus Smyrnaeus, *Posthomerica*, iii. 618-624; Tzetzes, *Schol. on Lycophron*, 175, 178 (vol. i. pp. 446, 457, ed. Müller); Scholiast on Apollonius Rhodius, *Argon.* i. 582; Ovid, *Metamorph.* xi. 235 *sqq.* She is said to have changed into fire, water, wind, a tree, a bird, a tiger, a lion, a serpent, and a

APOLLODORUS

θεοὶ τὸν γάμον εὐωχούμενοι καθύμνησαν. καὶ
δίδωσι Χείρων Πηλεῖ δόρυ μείλινον, Ποσειδῶν δὲ
ἵππους Βαλίον καὶ Ξάνθον· ἀθάνατοι δὲ ἦσαν
οὗτοι.

6   Ὡς δὲ ἐγέννησε Θέτις ἐκ Πηλέως βρέφος, ἀθάνατον θέλουσα ποιῆσαι τοῦτο, κρύφα Πηλέως εἰς
τὸ πῦρ ἐγκρύβουσα[1] τῆς νυκτὸς ἔφθειρεν ὃ ἦν
αὐτῷ θνητὸν πατρῷον, μεθ᾽ ἡμέραν δὲ ἔχριεν
ἀμβροσίᾳ. Πηλεὺς δὲ ἐπιτηρήσας καὶ σπαίροντα

---

[1] ἐγκρύβουσα SA : ἐγκρύπτουσα Ε.

---

cuttle-fish. It was when she had assumed the form of a
cuttle-fish (*sepia*) that Peleus at last succeeded in seizing her
and holding her fast (Tzetzes, *ll.cc.*). With the transformations which Thetis underwent in order to escape from
the arms of her lover we may compare the transformations
which her father Nereus underwent in order to escape from
Hercules (above, ii. 5. 11), the transformations which the
river-god Achelous underwent in his tussle with the same
doughty hero (above, ii. 7. 5, note), and the transformations
which the sea-god Proteus underwent in order to give the
slip to Menelaus (Homer, *Od.* iv. 354 *sqq.*). All these stories
were appropriately told of water-spirits, their mutability
reflecting as it were the instability of the fickle, inconstant
element of which they were born. The place where Peleus
caught and mastered his sea-bride was believed to be the
south-eastern headland of Thessaly, which hence bore the
name of Sepia or the Cuttle-fish. The whole coast of the Cape
was sacred to Thetis and the other Nereids ; and after their
fleet had been wrecked on the headland, the Persians sacrificed to Thetis on the spot (Herodotus, vii. 191). See further,
Appendix, " The Marriage of Peleus and Thetis."
[1] The Muses sang at the wedding of Peleus and Thetis,
according to Pindar (*Pyth.* iii. 89 (159) *sqq.*). Catullus
describes the Fates singing on the same occasion, and he has
recorded their magic song (lxiv. 305 *sqq.*).
[2] Compare Homer, *Il.* xvi. 140–144, with the Scholiast on
v. 140, according to whom Chiron felled the ash-tree for the

and there the gods celebrated the marriage with feast and song.[1] And Chiron gave Peleus an ashen spear,[2] and Poseidon gave him horses, Balius and Xanthus, and these were immortal.[3]

When Thetis had got a babe by Peleus, she wished to make it immortal, and unknown to Peleus she used to hide it in the fire by night in order to destroy the mortal element which the child inherited from its father, but by day she anointed him with ambrosia.[4] But Peleus watched her, and, seeing the child

shaft, while Athena polished it, and Hephaestus wrought (the blade). For this account the Scholiast refers to the author of the epic *Cypria*.

[3] Compare Homer, *Il.* xvi. 148 *sqq.*

[4] This account of how Thetis attempted to render Achilles immortal, and how the attempt was frustrated by Peleus, is borrowed from Apollonius Rhodius, *Argon.* iv. 869 *sqq.* Compare Tzetzes, *Schol. on Lycophron*, 178 (vol. i. p. 458, ed. Müller). According to another legend, Thetis bore seven sons, of whom Achilles was the seventh; she destroyed the first six by throwing them into the fire or into a kettle of boiling water to see whether they were mortal or to make them immortal by consuming the merely mortal portion of their frame; and the seventh son, Achilles, would have perished in like manner, if his father Peleus had not snatched him from the fire at the moment when as yet only his ankle-bone was burnt. To supply this missing portion of his body, Peleus dug up the skeleton of the giant Damysus, the fleetest of all the giants, and, extracting from it the ankle-bone, fitted it neatly into the ankle of his little son Achilles, applying drugs which caused the new, or rather old, bone to coalesce perfectly with the rest. See Ptolemy Hephaestionis, vi. in Westermann's *Mythographi Graeci*, p. 195; Lycophron, *Cassandra*, 178 *sq.*, with scholium of Tzetzes on *v.* 178 (vol. i. pp. 455 *sq.*); Scholiast on Homer, *Il.* xvi. 37; Scholiast on Aristophanes, *Clouds*, 1068, p. 443, ed. Fr. Dübner; Scholiast on Apollonius Rhodius, *Argon.* iv. 816. A similar story is told of Demeter and the infant son of Celeus. See above, i. 5. 1, with the note.

τὸν παῖδα ἰδὼν ἐπὶ τοῦ πυρὸς ἐβόησε· καὶ Θέτις
κωλυθεῖσα τὴν προαίρεσιν τελειῶσαι, νήπιον τὸν
παῖδα ἀπολιποῦσα πρὸς Νηρηίδας ᾤχετο. κομίζει
δὲ τὸν παῖδα πρὸς Χείρωνα Πηλεύς. ὁ δὲ λαβὼν
αὐτὸν ἔτρεφε σπλάγχνοις λεόντων καὶ συῶν
ἀγρίων καὶ ἄρκτων μυελοῖς, καὶ ὠνόμασεν Ἀχιλλέα (πρότερον δὲ¹ ἦν ὄνομα αὐτῷ Λιγύρων) ὅτι
τὰ χείλη μαστοῖς οὐ προσήνεγκε.

7   Πηλεὺς δὲ μετὰ ταῦτα σὺν Ἰάσονι καὶ Διοσ-

¹ δὲ E : μὲν A.

---

¹ Compare Apollonius Rhodius, *Argon.* iv. 875 *sqq.*, who
says that when Thetis was interrupted by Peleus in her effort
to make Achilles immortal, she threw the infant screaming
on the floor, and rushing out of the house plunged angrily
into the sea, and never returned again. In the *Iliad* Homer
represents Thetis dwelling with her old father Nereus and
the sea-nymphs in the depths of the sea (*Il.* i. 357 *sqq.*, xviii.
35 *sqq.*, xxiv. 83 *sqq.*), while her forlorn husband dragged
out a miserable and solitary old age in the halls (*Il.* xviii.
434 *sq.*). Thus the poet would seem to have been acquainted
with the story of the quarrel and parting of the husband and
wife, though he nowhere alludes to it or to the painful misunderstanding which led to their separation. In this, as in
many other places, Homer passes over in silence features of
popular tradition which he either rejected as incredible or
deemed below the dignity of the epic. Yet if we are right in
classing the story of Peleus and Thetis with the similar tales
of the marriage of a man to a mermaid or other marine
creature, the narrative probably always ended in the usual
sad way by telling how, after living happily together for a
time, the two at last quarrelled and parted for ever.
² Compare Scholiast on Homer, *Il.* xvi. 37. According to
Statius (*Achill.* ii. 382 *sqq.*), Chiron fed the youthful Achilles
not on ordinary victuals, but on the flesh and marrows of lions.
Philostratus says that his nourishment consisted of honey-
combs and the marrows of fawns (*Heroica*, xx. 2), while the
author of the *Etymologicum Magnum* (*s.v.* Ἀχιλλεύς, p. 181)

writing on the fire, he cried out; and Thetis, thus
prevented from accomplishing her purpose, forsook
her infant son and departed to the Nereids.[1] Peleus
brought the child to Chiron, who received him and
fed him on the inwards of lions and wild swine and
the marrows of bears,[2] and named him Achilles, because he had not put his lips to the breast;[3] but
before that time his name was Ligyron.

After that Peleus, with Jason and the Dioscuri,

says that he was nurtured on the marrows of deer. Compare
Eustathius, on Homer, *Il.* i. 1, p. 14. The flesh and marrows
of lions, wild boars, and bears were no doubt supposed to
impart to the youthful hero who partook of them the strength
and courage of these animals, while the marrows of fawns or
deer may have been thought to ensure the fleetness of foot
for which he was afterwards so conspicuous. It is thus that
on the principle of sympathetic magic many races seek to
acquire the qualities of certain animals by eating their flesh
or drinking their blood; whereas they abstain from eating
the flesh of other animals lest they should, by partaking of it,
be infected with the undesirable qualities which these creatures are believed to possess. For example, in various African
tribes men eat the hearts of lions in order to become lion-
hearted, while others will not eat the flesh of tortoises lest
they should become slow-footed like these animals. See
Spirits of the Corn and of the Wild, ii. 138 *sqq.* On the same
principle the ancients believed that men could acquire the art
of divination by eating the hearts of ravens, moles, or hawks,
because these creatures were supposed to be endowed with
prophetic powers. See Porphyry, *De abstinentia,* ii. 48;
Pliny, *Nat. Hist.* xxx. 19. So Medea is said to have restored
the aged Aeson to youth by infusing into his veins a decoction
of the liver of a long-lived stag and of the head of a crow
that had survived nine generations of men. See Ovid, *Metamorph.* vii. 273 *sqq.*

[3] Apollodorus absurdly derives the name Achilles from
α (privative) and χείλη, "lips," so that the word would mean
"not lips." Compare *Etymologicum Magnum,* p. 181, *s.v.*
Ἀχιλλεύς; Eustathius, on Homer, *Il.* i. 1, p. 14.

κούροις ἐπόρθησεν Ἰωλκόν, καὶ Ἀστυδάμειαν τὴν
Ἀκάστου γυναῖκα φονεύει, καὶ διελὼν μεληδὸν
διήγαγε δι᾽ αὐτῆς τὸν στρατὸν εἰς τὴν πόλιν.

8 ʹΩς δὲ ἐγένετο ἐνναετὴς Ἀχιλλεύς, Κάλχαντος
λέγοντος οὐ δύνασθαι χωρὶς αὐτοῦ Τροίαν αἱρεθῆναι, Θέτις προειδυῖα ὅτι δεῖ στρατευόμενον
αὐτὸν ἀπολέσθαι, κρύψασα ἐσθῆτι γυναικείᾳ ὡς
παρθένον Λυκομήδει[1] παρέθετο. κἀκεῖ τρεφό-

---

[1] Λυκομήδει ES, apparently wanting in A.

---

[1] As to the wicked behaviour of Astydamia to Peleus, see
above, iii. 13. 3. But it is probable that the cutting of the
bad woman in pieces and marching between the pieces into
the city was more than a simple act of vengeance ; it may
have been a solemn sacrifice or purification designed to ensure
the safety of the army in the midst of a hostile people. In
Boeotia a form of public purification was to cut a dog in two
and pass between the pieces. See Plutarch, *Quaestiones
Romanae*, 111. A similar rite was observed at purifying a
Macedonian army. A dog was cut in two : the head and
fore part were placed on the right, the hinder part, with the
entrails, was placed on the left, and the troops in arms
marched between the pieces. See Livy, xli. 6 ; Quintus
Curtius, *De gestis Alexandri Magni*, x. 9. 28. For more
examples of similar rites, and an attempt to explain them,
see *Folk-lore in the Old Testament*, i. 391 *sqq.* To the
instances there cited may be added another. When the
Algerine pirates were at sea and in extreme danger, it was
their custom to sacrifice a sheep, cut off its head, extract its
entrails, and then throw them, together with the head, over-
board ; afterwards " with all the speed they can (without
skinning) they cut the body in two parts by the middle, and
then throw one part over the right side of the ship, and the
other over the left, into the sea, as a kind of propitiation."
See Joseph Pitts, *A true and faithful Account of the Religion
and Manners of the Mohammetans* (Exon. 1704), p. 14. As
to the capture of Iolcus by Peleus, see Pindar, *Nem.* iii. 34
(59), iv. 54 (89) *sq.* In the former of these passages Pindar
says that Peleus captured Iolcus single-handed ; but the

laid waste Iolcus; and he slaughtered Astydamia, wife of Acastus, and, having divided her limb from limb, he led the army through her into the city.[1]

When Achilles was nine years old, Calchas declared that Troy could not be taken without him; so Thetis, foreseeing that it was fated he should perish if he went to the war, disguised him in female garb and entrusted him as a maiden to Lycomedes.[2] Bred at

Scholiast on the passage affirms, on the authority of Phere- cydes, that he was accompanied by Jason and the Tyndarids (Castor and Pollux). As this statement tallies with the account given by Apollodorus, we may surmise that here, as often elsewhere, our author followed Pherecydes. According to the Scholiast on Apollonius Rhodius (*Argon.* i. 224), Peleus on his return to Iolcus put to death Acastus himself as well as his wicked wife.

[2] As to Achilles disguised as a girl at the court of Lyco- medes in Scyros, see Bion, ii. 5 *sqq.*; Philostratus Junior, *Imag.* 1; Scholiast on Homer, *Il.* ix. 668; Hyginus, *Fab.* 96; Statius, *Achill.* i. 207 *sqq.* The subject was painted by Polygnotus in a chamber at the entrance to the acropolis of Athens (Pausanias i. 22. 6). Euripides wrote a play called *The Scyrians* on the same theme. See *Tragicorum Grae- corum Fragmenta*, ed. Nauck[2], pp. 574 *sq.* Sophocles com- posed a tragedy under the same title, which has sometimes been thought to have dealt with the same subject, but more probably it was concerned with Neoptolemus in Scyros and the mission of Ulysses and Phoenix to carry him off to Troy. See *The Fragments of Sophocles*, ed. A. C. Pearson, vol. ii. pp. 191 *sqq.* The youthful Dionysus, like the youthful Achilles, is said to have been brought up as a maiden. See above, iii. 4. 3, with the note. One of the questions which the emperor Tiberius used solemnly to propound to the anti- quaries of his court was: What was the name of Achilles when he lived as a girl among girls? See Suetonius, *Tiberius*, 70. The question was solemnly answered by learned men in various ways: some said that the stripling's female name was Cercysera, others that it was Issa, and others that it was Pyrrha. See Ptolemy Hephaestionis, *Nov. Hist.* i. in Westermann's *Mythographi Graeci*, p. 183.

μενος τῇ Λυκομήδους θυγατρὶ Δηιδαμεία μίγνυται,
καὶ γίνεται παῖς Πύρρος αὐτῷ ὁ κληθεὶς Νεοπτόλεμος αὖθις. Ὀδυσσεὺς δὲ μηνυθέντα παρὰ
Λυκομήδει[1] ζητῶν Ἀχιλλέα, σάλπιγγι χρησά-
μενος εὗρε. καὶ τοῦτον τὸν τρόπον εἰς Τροίαν
ἦλθε.

Συνείπετο δὲ αὐτῷ Φοῖνιξ ὁ Ἀμύντορος. οὗτος
ὑπὸ τοῦ πατρὸς ἐτυφλώθη καταψευσαμένης
φθορὰν[2] Φθίας τῆς τοῦ πατρὸς παλλακῆς.[3]
Πηλεὺς δὲ αὐτὸν πρὸς Χείρωνα κομίσας, ὑπ'
ἐκείνου θεραπευθέντα τὰς ὄψεις βασιλέα κατέ-
στησε Δολόπων.

Συνείπετο δὲ καὶ Πάτροκλος ὁ Μενοιτίου καὶ

[1] Λυκομήδει ES R (compend.): λυκομήδου A.
[2] φθορὰν ES: φθορᾷ A.
[3] παλλακῆς ES, Scholiast on Plato, *Laws*, xi. p. 931B:
παλλακίδος A.

---

[1] The usual story was that the crafty Ulysses spread out
baskets and women's gear, mingled with arms, before the
disguised Achilles and his girlish companions in Scyros; and
that while the real girls pounced eagerly on the feminine
gauds, Achilles betrayed his sex by snatching at the arms.
See Philostratus Junior, *Imagines*, i; Scholiast on Homer,
Il. xix. 326; Ovid, *Metamorph.* xiii. 162 *sqq.* Apollodorus
tells us that Achilles was detected by the sound of a trumpet.
This is explained by Hyginus (*Fab.* 96), who says that while
Achilles was surveying the mingled trumpery and weapons,
Ulysses caused a bugle to sound and a clash of arms to be
heard, whereupon Achilles, imagining that an enemy was at
hand, tore off his maidenly attire and seized spear and shield.
Statius gives a similar account of the detection (*Achill.* ii.
167 *sqq.*).

[2] See Homer, *Il.* ix. 437–484, with the Scholiast on *v.* 448.
But Homer says nothing about the blinding of Phoenix by
his angry father or his cure by Chiron; and according to
Homer the accusation of having debauched his father's con-

74

his court, Achilles had an intrigue with Deidamia, daughter of Lycomedes, and a son Pyrrhus was born to him, who was afterwards called Neoptolemus. But the secret of Achilles was betrayed, and Ulysses, seeking him at the court of Lycomedes, discovered him by the blast of a trumpet.[1] And in that way Achilles went to Troy.

He was accompanied by Phoenix, son of Amyntor. This Phoenix had been blinded by his father on the strength of a false accusation of seduction preferred against him by his father's concubine Phthia. But Peleus brought him to Chiron, who restored his sight, and thereupon Peleus made him king of the Dolopians.[2]

Achilles was also accompanied by Patroclus, son of

cubine was not false but true, Phoenix having been instigated to the deed by his mother, who was jealous of the concubine. But variations from the Homeric narrative were introduced into the story by the tragedians who handled the theme (Scholiast on Homer, *l.c.*). Sophocles and Euripides both wrote tragedies on the subject under the same title of *Phoenix*; the tragedy of Euripides seems to have been famous. See *Tragicorum Graecorum Fragmenta*, ed. A. Nauck[2], pp. 286, 621 *sqq.*; *The Fragments of Sophocles*, ed. A. C. Pearson, vol. ii. pp. 320 *sqq.* The blinding of Phoenix by his father Amyntor is alluded to by a poet of the Greek anthology (*Anthol. Palat.* iii. 3). Both the poet and Apollodorus probably drew on Euripides, who from an allusion in Aristophanes (*Acharn.* 421) is known to have represented Phoenix as blind. Both the blinding and the healing of Phoenix are related by Tzetzes (*Schol. on Lycophron*, 421), who may have followed Apollodorus. According to the Scholiast on Homer (*l.c.*), the name of the concubine was Clytia; according to Tzetzes (*l.c.*), it was Clytia or Phthia. Apollodorus calls her Phthia. The Scholiast on Plato (*Laws*, xi. p. 931 B), gives a version of the story which agrees entirely with that of Apollodorus, and may have been copied from it. The healing of Phoenix's eyes by Chiron is mentioned by Propertius (ii. 1. 60).

APOLLODORUS

Σθενέλης τῆς Ἀκάστου ἢ Περιώπιδος τῆς Φέρητος, ἢ καθάπερ φησὶ Φιλοκράτης, Πολυμήλης τῆς Πηλέως. οὗτος ἐν Ὀποῦντι διενεχθεὶς ἐν παιδιᾷ περὶ ἀστραγάλων[1] παῖδα Κλειτώνυμον[2] τὸν Ἀμφιδάμαντος ἀπέκτεινε, καὶ φυγὼν μετὰ τοῦ πατρὸς παρὰ Πηλεῖ κατῴκει, καὶ Ἀχιλλέως ἐρώμενος γίνεται.[3] . . .

XIV. Κέκροψ αὐτόχθων, συμφυὲς ἔχων σῶμα ἀνδρὸς καὶ δράκοντος, τῆς Ἀττικῆς ἐβασίλευσε πρῶτος, καὶ τὴν γῆν πρότερον λεγομένην Ἀκτὴν ἀφ' ἑαυτοῦ Κεκροπίαν ὠνόμασεν. ἐπὶ τούτου, φασίν, ἔδοξε τοῖς θεοῖς πόλεις καταλαβέσθαι, ἐν

---

[1] ἐν παιδιᾷ περὶ ἀστραγάλων παίζων A, Westermann, Müller, Wagner. I follow Bekker in omitting παίζων, but Heyne may be right in proposing to strike out both ἐν παιδιᾷ and παίζων as independent glosses on περὶ ἀστραγάλων. Compare Scholiast on Homer, *Il.* xii. 1, περὶ ἀστραγάλων ὀργισθεὶς ἀπέκτεινεν. Hercher changed παίζων into παῖς ὤν, but the jingle παῖς ὤν παῖδα is not at all in the manner of Apollodorus.

[2] κλειτώνυμον RO : κλυτώνυμον A : κλεισώνυμος Pherecydes (quoted by Scholiast on Homer, *Il.* xxiii. 87), Philostephanus (quoted by Scholiast on Homer, *Il.* xvi. 14) : κλισώνυμος Hellanicus (quoted by Scholiast on Homer, *Il.* xii. 1).

[3] Heyne was probably right in marking a lacuna here.

---

[1] Compare Homer, *Il.* xi. 785 *sqq.* Homer does not mention the name of Patroclus's mother.

[2] See Homer, *Il.* xxiii. 84–90; compare Scholiast on Homer, *Il.* xii. 1; Strabo, ix. 4. 2, p. 425; Ovid, *Ex Ponto,* i. 3. 73 *sq.* The name of the slain lad was variously given as Clisonymus (Scholiast, *l.c.*) or Aeanes (Strabo and Scholiast, *ll.cc.*).

[3] According to the *Parian Chronicle* (*Marmor Parium,* lines 2–4), with which Apollodorus is in general agreement,

Menoetius[1] and Sthenele, daughter of Acastus; or
the mother of Patroclus was Periopis, daughter of
Pheres, or, as Philocrates says, she was Polymele,
daughter of Peleus. At Opus, in a quarrel over a
game of dice, Patroclus killed the boy Clitonymus,
son of Amphidamas, and flying with his father he
dwelt at the house of Peleus[2] and became a
minion of Achilles.

XIV. Cecrops, a son of the soil, with a body
compounded of man and serpent, was the first king
of Attica, and the country which was formerly called
Acte he named Cecropia after himself.[3] In his time,
they say, the gods resolved to take possession of

the first king of Attica was Cecrops, and the country was
named Cecropia after him, whereas it had formerly been
called Actice (*sic*) after an aboriginal named Actaeus. Pausanias (i. 2. 6) represents this Actaeus as the first king of
Attica, and says that Cecrops succeeded him on the throne
by marrying his daughter. But Pausanias, like Apollodorus (iii. 15. 5), distinguishes this first Cecrops from a
later Cecrops, son of Erechtheus (i. 5. 3). Apollodorus is
at one with Pausanias in saying that the first Cecrops
married the daughter of Actaeus, and he names her
Agraulus (see below, iii. 14. 2). Philochorus said, with
great probability, that there never was any such person as
Actaeus; according to him, Attica lay waste and depopu-
lated from the deluge in the time of Ogyges down to the
reign of Cecrops. See Eusebius, *Praeparatio Evangelii*, x. 10.
J. Tzetzes (*Chiliades*, v. 637) and Hyginus (*Fab.* 48) agree
in representing Cecrops as the first king of Attica; Hyginus
calls him a son of the earth. As to his double form, the
upper part of him being human and the lower part serpen-
tine, see Aristophanes, *Wasps*, 438, with the Scholiast;
Euripides, *Ion*, 1163 *sq.*; Tzetzes, *Schol. on Lycophron*,
111; *id. Chiliades*, v. 638 *sqq.*; Scholiast on Aristophanes,
Plutus, 773; Diodorus Siculus, i. 28. 7, who rationalizes the
fable after his usual fashion.

αἷς ἔμελλον ἔχειν τιμὰς ἰδίας ἕκαστος. ἦκεν οὖν
πρῶτος Ποσειδῶν ἐπὶ τὴν Ἀττικήν, καὶ πλήξας
τῇ τριαίνῃ κατὰ μέσην τὴν ἀκρόπολιν ἀπέφηνε
θάλασσαν, ἣν νῦν Ἐρεχθηίδα καλοῦσι. μετὰ δὲ
τοῦτον ἦκεν Ἀθηνᾶ, καὶ ποιησαμένη τῆς κατα-
λήψεως Κέκροπα μάρτυρα ἐφύτευσεν ἐλαίαν, ἣ
νῦν ἐν τῷ Πανδροσείῳ[1] δείκνυται. γενομένης δὲ
ἔριδος ἀμφοῖν περὶ τῆς χώρας, διαλύσας Ζεὺς

---

[1] Πανδροσείῳ Bekker : πανδροσίῳ EA.

---

[1] As to the contest between Poseidon and Athena for
possession of Attica, see Herodotus, viii. 55 ; Plutarch,
Themistocles, 19 ; Pausanias, i. 24. 5, i. 26. 5 ; Ovid, *Metamorph.* vi. 70 *sqq.* ; Hyginus, *Fab.* 164 ; Servius, on Virgil,
Georg. i. 12 ; Lactantius Placidus, on Statius, *Theb.* vii. 185 ;
Scriptores rerum mythicarum Latini, ed. G. H. Bode, vol. i.
pp. 1, 115 (First Vatican Mythographer, 2 ; Second Vatican
Mythographer, 119). A rationalistic explanation of the fable
was propounded by the eminent Roman antiquary Varro.
According to him, the olive-tree suddenly appeared in Attica,
and at the same time there was an eruption of water in
another part of the country. So king Cecrops sent to inquire
of Apollo at Delphi what these portents might signify. The
oracle answered that the olive and the water were the
symbols of Athena and Poseidon respectively, and that the
people of Attica were free to choose which of these deities
they would worship. Accordingly the question was submitted to a general assembly of the citizens and citizenesses ;
for in these days women had the vote as well as men. All
the men voted for the god, and all the women voted for the
goddess ; and as there was one more woman than there were
men, the goddess appeared at the head of the poll. Chagrined
at the loss of the election, the male candidate flooded the
country with the water of the sea, and to appease his wrath
it was decided to deprive women of the vote and to forbid
children to bear their mother's names for the future. See
Augustine, *De civitate Dei*, xviii. 9. The print of Poseidon's
trident on the rock of the acropolis at Athens was shown

cities in which each of them should receive his own peculiar worship. So Poseidon was the first that came to Attica, and with a blow of his trident on the middle of the acropolis, he produced a sea which they now call Erechtheis.[1] After him came Athena, and, having called on Cecrops to witness her act of taking possession, she planted an olive-tree, which is still shown in the Pandrosium.[2] But when the two strove for possession of the country, Zeus parted

down to late times. See Strabo, ix. 1. 16, p. 396; Pausanias, i. 26. 5. The "sea," which the god was supposed to have produced as evidence of his right to the country was also to be seen within the Erechtheum on the acropolis; Pausanias calls it a well of sea water, and says that, when the south wind blew, the well gave forth a sound of waves. See Herodotus, viii. 55; Pausanias, i. 26. 5, viii. 10. 4. According to the late Latin mythographers (see the references above), Poseidon produced a horse from the rock in support of his claim, and this version of the story seems to have been accepted by Virgil (*Georg.* i. 12 *sqq.*), but it is not countenanced by Greek writers. The Athenians said that the contest between Poseidon and Athena took place on the second of the month Boedromion, and hence they omitted that day from the calendar. See Plutarch, *De fraterno amore*, 11; *id. Quaest. Conviv.* ix. 6. The unlucky Poseidon also contested the possession of Argos with Hera, and when the judges gave a verdict against him and in favour of the goddess, he took his revenge, as in Attica, by flooding the country. See Pausanias, ii. 22. 4; compare *id.* ii. 15. 5; Polemo, *Greek History*, cited by the Scholiast on Aristides, vol. iii. p. 322, ed. G. Dindorf.

[2] The olive-tree seems to have survived down to the second century of our era. See Herodotus, viii. 55; Dionysius Halicarnasensis, *De Dinarcho Judicium*, 3; Pausanias, i. 27. 3; Cicero, *De legibus*, i. 1. 2; Hyginus, *Fab.* 164; Pliny, *Nat. Hist.* xvi. 240. Dionysius agrees with Apollodorus in representing the tree as growing in the Pandrosium, which is proved by inscriptions to have been an enclosure to the west of the Erechtheum. See my commentary on Pausanias, vol. ii. p. 337.

APOLLODORUS

κριτὰς ἔδωκεν,[1] οὐχ ὡς εἶπόν τινες, Κέκροπα κα
Κραναόν,[2] οὐδὲ Ἐρυσίχθονα, θεοὺς δὲ τοὺς δώδεκα.
καὶ τούτων δικαζόντων ἡ χώρα τῆς Ἀθηνᾶς
ἐκρίθη, Κέκροπος μαρτυρήσαντος ὅτι πρώτη[3] τὴν
ἐλαίαν ἐφύτευσεν. Ἀθηνᾶ μὲν οὖν ἀφ' ἑαυτῆς
τὴν πόλιν ἐκάλεσεν Ἀθήνας, Ποσειδῶν δὲ θυμῷ
ὀργισθεὶς τὸ Θριάσιον πεδίον ἐπέκλυσε καὶ τὴν
Ἀττικὴν ὕφαλον ἐποίησε.

2   Κέκροψ δὲ γήμας τὴν Ἀκταίου κόρην Ἄγραυλον παῖδα μὲν ἔσχεν Ἐρυσίχθονα, ὃς ἄτεκνος
μετήλλαξε, θυγατέρας δὲ Ἄγραυλον Ἔρσην
Πάνδροσον. Ἀγραύλου μὲν οὖν καὶ Ἄρεος Ἀλ-
κίππη γίνεται. ταύτην βιαζόμενος Ἁλιρρόθιος,
ὁ Ποσειδῶνος καὶ νύμφης Εὐρύτης, ὑπὸ Ἄρεος
φωραθεὶς κτείνεται. Ποσειδῶνος δὲ <εἰσάγοντος>
ἐν Ἀρείῳ πάγῳ κρίνεται δικαζόντων τῶν δώδεκα
θεῶν Ἄρης[4] καὶ ἀπολύεται.

---

[1] Ἀθηνᾷ καὶ Ποσειδῶνι κριτὰς δέδωκεν ὁ Ζεὺς E : Ἀθηνᾶν καὶ
Ποσειδῶνα διαλύσας Ζεὺς κριτὰς ἔδωκε A : Ἀθηνᾷ καὶ Ποσειδῶνι
διαλύσας Ζεὺς κριτὰς ἔδωκε Wagner. The words Ἀθηνᾷ καὶ
Ποσειδῶνι (or Ἀθηνᾶν καὶ Ποσειδῶνα) appear to be a gloss on
the preceding ἀμφοῖν, as Heyne perceived. Accordingly I
have omitted them with Hercher.

[2] Κραναὸν Aegius : δαναὸν A.

[3] πρώτη ER (compend.), Hercher, Wagner : πρῶτον A,
Heyne, Westermann, Müller, Bekker.

[4] Ποσειδῶνος δὲ <εἰσάγοντος> ἐν Ἀρείῳ πάγῳ κρίνεται δικαζόντων τῶν δώδεκα θεῶν Ἄρης Scaliger : Ποσειδῶν δὲ ἐν Ἀρείῳ
πάγῳ κρίνεται, δικαζόντων τῶν δώδεκα θεῶν, Ἄρει Heyne,
Westermann, Müller, Bekker, Hercher, Wagner. But the
construction κρίνεσθαί τινι in the sense of "bring a person to
trial" is impossible, and the abrupt change of nominative
from κρίνεται (Ποσειδῶν) to ἀπολύεται (Ἄρης) is very harsh, if
not intolerable. Scaliger's emendation certainly gives the
right sense and may be verbally correct also. The accidental omission of εἰσάγοντος would not be difficult. The
emendation is recorded, but not accepted, by Heyne.

them and appointed arbiters, not, as some have affirmed, Cecrops and Cranaus, nor yet Erysichthon, but the twelve gods.[1] And in accordance with their verdict the country was adjudged to Athena, because Cecrops bore witness that she had been the first to plant the olive. Athena, therefore, called the city Athens after herself, and Poseidon in hot anger flooded the Thriasian plain and laid Attica under the sea.[2]

Cecrops married Agraulus, daughter of Actaeus, and had a son Erysichthon, who departed this life childless; and Cecrops had daughters, Agraulus, Herse, and Pandrosus.[3] Agraulus had a daughter Alcippe by Ares. In attempting to violate Alcippe, Halirrhothius, son of Poseidon and a nymph Euryte, was detected and killed by Ares.[4] Impeached by Poseidon, Ares was tried in the Areopagus before the twelve gods, and was acquitted.[5]

[1] Compare Ovid, *Metamorph.* vi. 72 *sq.*

[2] As to this flood, see Varro, in Augustine, *De civitate Dei*, xviii. 9; Hyginus, *Fab.* 164. The Thriasian plain is the plain in which Eleusis stands. See Strabo, ix. i. 6, p. 392, ix. i. 13, p. 395.

[3] Compare Pausanias, i. 2. 6; Hyginus, *Fab.* 146; Ovid, *Metamorph.* ii. 737 *sqq.* All these writers call the first of the daughters Aglaurus instead of Agraulus, and the form Aglaurus is confirmed by inscriptions on two Greek vases (*Corpus Inscriptionum Graecarum*, vol. iv. p. 146, Nos. 7716, 7718).

[4] Compare Pausanias, i. 21. 4; Stephanus Byzantius and Suidas, *s.v.* Ἄρειος πάγος; Bekker's *Anecdota Graeca*, vol. i. p. 444, lines 8 *sqq.* From the three latter writers we learn that the story was told by the historians Philochorus and Hellanicus, whom Apollodorus may here be following.

[5] See Euripides, *Ion*, 1258 *sqq.*, *Iphigenia in Tauris*, 945 *sq.*; Demosthenes, xxiii. 66, p. 641; *Parian Chronicle* (*Marmor Parium*), lines 5 *sq.*; Pausanias, i. 28. 5; Scholiast on Euripides, *Orestes*, 1648, 1651. The name Areopagus was

3 Ἔρσης δὲ καὶ Ἑρμοῦ Κέφαλος, οὗ ἐρασθεῖσα
Ἠὼς ἥρπασε καὶ μιγεῖσα ἐν Συρίᾳ παῖδα ἐγέννησε
Τιθωνόν, οὗ παῖς ἐγένετο Φαέθων, τούτου δὲ
Ἀστύνοος, τοῦ δὲ Σάνδοκος,[1] ὃς ἐκ Συρίας ἐλθὼν
εἰς Κιλικίαν, πόλιν ἔκτισε Κελένδεριν, καὶ γήμας
Φαρνάκην[2] τὴν Μεγασσάρου τοῦ Ὑριέων βα-
σιλέως[3] ἐγέννησε Κινύραν.[4] οὗτος ἐν Κύπρῳ,

[1] Σάνδοκος RRᵃC: σάνδακος B.
[2] Φαρνάκη Muncker (on Antoninus Liberalis, *Transform.*
34, p. 277, ed. Koch, comparing Hesychius, *s.v.* Κινύρας·
Ἀπόλλωνος καὶ Φαρνάκης παῖς): θαινάκην RRᵃ: θανάκην A.
[3] τῶν Ὑριέων βασιλέως Bekker, Hercher, Wagner: τοῦ
συριων βασιλέως R: τῶν συριων βασιλέα A.
[4] Κινύραν R: κινύρας A.

---

commonly supposed to mean "the hill of Ares" and explained by the tradition that Ares was the first to be tried
for murder before the august tribunal. But more probably,
perhaps, the name meant "the hill of curses." See my note
on Pausanias. i. 28. 5 (vol. ii. pp. 363 *sq.*). For other legendary or mythical trials in the court of the Areopagus, see
below, iii. 15. 1, iii. 15. 9.

[1] See above, i. 9. 4, note, where Cephalus is said to have
been a son of Deion by Diomede; compare ii. 4. 7, iii. 15. 1.
Pausanias also calls Cephalus a son of Deion (i. 37. 6, x. 29. 6),
and so does Antoninus Liberalis (*Transform.* 41). The Scholiast on Homer (*Od.* xi. 321) calls his father Deioneus. Hyginus in two passages (*Fab.* 189, 270) describes Cephalus as
a son of Deion, and in another passage (*Fab.* 160) as a son of
Hermes (Mercury) by Creusa, daughter of Erechtheus.
Euripides tells how "Dawn with her lovely light once
snatched up Cephalus to the gods, all for love" (*Hippolytus*,
454 *sqq.*).

[2] According to Hesiod (*Theog.* 986 *sqq.*) and Pausanias
(i. 3. 1), Phaethon was a son of Cephalus and the Dawn or
Day. According to another and seemingly more usual
account the father of Phaethon was the Sun. See Diodorus
Siculus, v. 23; Pausanias, i. 4. 1, ii. 3. 2; Lucian, *Dialog.
deorum*, xxv. 1; J. Tzetzes, *Chiliades*, iv. 357 *sqq.*; Eustathius, on Homer, *Od.* xi. 325, p. 1689; Scholiast on Homer,

Herse had by Hermes a son Cephalus, whom Dawn loved and carried off,[1] and consorting with him in Syria bore a son Tithonus, who had a son Phaethon,[2] who had a son Astynous, who had a son Sandocus, who passed from Syria to Cilicia and founded a city Celenderis, and having married Pharnace, daughter of Megassares, king of Hyria, begat Cinyras.[3] This Cinyras in Cyprus, whither he had come with

---

[1] Od. xvii. 208 ; Ovid, *Metamorph*. ii. 19 *sqq*. ; Hyginus, *Fab*. 152, 156 ; Lactantius Placidus, on Statius, *Theb*. i. 221 ; *Scholia in Caesaris Germanici Aratea*, p. 421, ed. Fr. Eyssenhardt, in his edition of Martianus Capella ; *Scriptores rerum mythicarum Latini*, ed. G. H. Bode, vol. i. pp. 37, 93, 208 (First Vatican Mythographer, 118 ; Second Vatican Mythographer, 57 ; Third Vatican Mythographer, iii. 8. 14) ; Servius on Virgil, *Aen*. x. 189. The mother who bore him to the Sun is usually called Clymene (so Lucian, Tzetzes, Eustathius, Ovid, Hyginus, Lactantius Placidus, the Vatican mythographers, and Servius) ; but the Scholiast on Homer (*l.c.*) calls her Rhode, daughter of Asopus. Clymene herself, the mother of Phaethon, is said to have been a daughter of Ocean and Tethys (J. Tzetzes, *Chiliades*, iv. 359 ; Ovid, *Metamorph*. ii. 156) or of Iphys or Minyas (Eustathius, *l.c.*). Apollodorus passes over in silence the famous story how Phaethon borrowed the chariot of the Sun for a day, and driving too near the earth set it on fire, and how in his wild career he was struck dead by Zeus with a thunderbolt and fell into the river Eridanus, where his sisters mourned for him till they were turned into poplar trees, their tears being changed into drops of amber which exuded from the trees. The story is told at great length and with many picturesque details by Ovid (*Metamorph*. ii. 1 *sqq*.). Compare Lucretius, v. 396 *sqq*.; Diodorus Siculus, Lucian, the Scholiast on Homer, Hyginus, and the Latin Mythographers, *ll.cc.* Euripides wrote a tragedy on the subject, of which some considerable fragments survive. See *Tragicorum Graecorum Fragmenta*, ed. A. Nauck[2], pp 599 *sqq*. For some similar stories, see Appendix, "Phaethon and the Chariot of the Sun."

[3] According to Hyginus (*Fab*. 142), Cinyras was a son of Paphus.

APOLLODORUS

παραγενόμενος σὺν λαῷ, ἔκτισε Πάφον, γήμας δὲ
ἐκεῖ Μεθάρμην, κόρην Πυγμαλίωνος Κυπρίων
βασιλέως, Ὀξύπορον ἐγέννησε καὶ Ἄδωνιν, πρὸς
δὲ τούτοις θυγατέρας Ὀρσεδίκην <καὶ> Λαογόρην
καὶ Βραισίαν. αὗται δὲ διὰ μῆνιν Ἀφροδίτης
ἀλλοτρίοις ἀνδράσι συνευναζόμεναι τὸν βίον ἐν
4 Αἰγύπτῳ μετήλλαξαν. Ἄδωνις δὲ ἔτι παῖς ὢν
Ἀρτέμιδος χόλῳ πληγεὶς ἐν θήρᾳ¹ ὑπὸ συὸς
ἀπέθανεν. Ἡσίοδος δὲ αὐτὸν Φοίνικος καὶ Ἀλ-
φεσιβοίας λέγει, Πανύασις² δέ φησι Θείαντος

¹ θήρᾳ Heyne (conjecture), Hercher, Wagner: θήραι RRᵃ:
θήραις A, Heyne (in text), Westermann, Müller, Bekker.
² πανύασσος A.

¹ A different and apparently more prevalent tradition represented Adonis as the son of Cinyras by incestuous intercourse with his daughter Myrrha or Smyrna. See Scholiast
on Theocritus, i. 107 ; Plutarch, *Parallela*, 22 ; Antoninus
Liberalis, *Transform.* 34 (who, however, differs as to the
name of Smyrna's father) ; Ovid, *Metamorph.* x. 298 *sqq.* ;
Hyginus, *Fab.* 58, 164 ; Fulgentius, *Mytholog.* iii. 8 ; Lactantius Placidus, *Narrat. Fabul.* x. 9 ; Servius, on Virgil,
Ecl. x. 18, and on *Aen.* v. 72 ; *Scriptores rerum mythicarum
Latini*, ed. G. H. Bode, vol. i. p. 60 (First Vatican Mythographer, 200). Similar cases of incest with a daughter are
frequently reported of royal houses in antiquity. They perhaps originated in a rule of transmitting the crown through
women instead of through men ; for under such a rule a
widowed king would be under a strong temptation to marry
his own daughter as the only means of maintaining himself
legitimately on the throne after the death of his wife. See
Adonis, Attis, Osiris, 3rd ed., i. 43 *sq.* The legend of the
incestuous origin of Adonis is mentioned, on the authority
of Panyasis, by Apollodorus himself a little lower down.
² Compare Bion, *Idyl.* i. ; Cornutus, *Theologiae Graecae
Compendium*, 28 ; Plutarch, *Quaest. Conviv.* iv. 5. 3, § 8 ;
Athenaeus, ii. 80, p. 69ʙ ; Tzetzes, *Schol. on Lycophron*,

some people, founded Paphos; and having there married Metharme, daughter of Pygmalion, king of Cyprus, he begat Oxyporus and Adonis,[1] and besides them daughters, Orsedice, Laogore, and Braesia. These by reason of the wrath of Aphrodite cohabited with foreigners, and ended their life in Egypt. And Adonis, while still a boy, was wounded and killed in hunting by a boar through the anger of Artemis.[2] Hesiod, however, affirms that he was a son of Phoenix and Alphesiboea; and Panyasis says that he was a son

831; Aristides, *Apology*, ed. J. Rendel Harris (Cambridge, 1891), pp. 44, 106 *sq.*; Propertius, iii. 4 (5) 53 *sq.*, ed. F. A. Paley; Ovid, *Metamorph.* x. 710 *sqq.*; Hyginus, *Fab.* 248; Macrobius, *Saturnal.* i. 21. 4; Lactantius, *Divin. Inst.* i. 17; Firmicus Maternus, *De errore profanarum religionum*, 9; Augustine, *De civitate Dei*, vi. 7. There are some grounds for thinking that formerly Adonis and his Babylonian proto-type Tammuz were conceived in the form of a boar, and that the story of his death by a boar was only a misinterpretation of this older conception. See *Spirits of the Corn and of the Wild*, ii. 22 *sq.*; C. F. Burney, *The Book of Judges* (London, 1918), pp. xvii *sqq.*, who refers to "the brilliant discovery of Ball (*PSBA.* xvi. 1894, pp. 195 *sqq.*) that the Sumerian name of Tammuz, DUMU.ZI (Bab. *Du'ûzu, Dûzu*) is identical with the Turkish *dōmūz* 'pig,' and that there is thus an 'original identity of the god with the wild boar that slays him in the developed legend.'" W. Robertson Smith, as Professor Burney points out, had many years ago expressed the view that "the Cyprian Adonis was originally the Swine-god, and in this as in many other cases the sacred victim has been changed by false interpretation into the enemy of the god" (*Religion of the Semites*, New Edition, London, 1894, p. 411, note [4]). The view is confirmed by the observation that the worshippers of Adonis would seem to have abstained from eating swine's flesh. See W. W. Baudissin, *Adonis und Esmun* (Leipsic, 1911), p. 142, quoting *SS. Cyri et Joannis Miracula*, in Migne's *Patrologia Graeca*, lxxxvii. 3, col. 3624.

APOLLODORUS

βασιλέως Ἀσσυρίων, ὃς ἔσχε θυγατερα Σμύρναν.
αὕτη κατὰ μῆνιν Ἀφροδίτης (οὐ γὰρ αὐτὴν ἐτίμα)
ἴσχει τοῦ πατρὸς ἔρωτα, καὶ συνεργὸν λαβοῦσα
τὴν τροφὸν ἀγνοοῦντι τῷ πατρὶ νύκτας δώδεκα
συνευνάσθη. ὁ δὲ ὡς ᾔσθετο, σπασάμενος <τὸ>[1]
ξίφος ἐδίωκεν αὐτήν· ἡ δὲ περικαταλαμβανομένη
θεοῖς ηὔξατο ἀφανὴς γενέσθαι. θεοὶ δὲ κατοικτεί-
ραντες αὐτὴν εἰς δένδρον μετήλλαξαν, ὃ καλοῦσι
σμύρναν.[2] δεκαμηνιαίῳ δὲ ὕστερον χρόνῳ τοῦ
δένδρου ῥαγέντος γεννηθῆναι τὸν λεγόμενον Ἄδωνιν, ὃν Ἀφροδίτη διὰ κάλλος ἔτι νήπιον κρύφα
θεῶν εἰς λάρνακα κρύψασα Περσεφόνῃ παρί-
στατο. ἐκείνη δὲ ὡς ἐθεάσατο, οὐκ ἀπεδίδου.
κρίσεως δὲ ἐπὶ Διὸς γενομένης εἰς τρεῖς μοίρας
διῃρέθη ὁ ἐνιαυτός, καὶ μίαν μὲν παρ' ἑαυτῷ
μένειν τὸν Ἄδωνιν, μίαν δὲ παρὰ Περσεφόνῃ προσ-
έταξε, τὴν δὲ ἑτέραν παρ' Ἀφροδίτῃ· ὁ δὲ

[1] τὸ added by Hercher.
[2] σμύρναν Rᵃ: μύρναν B, μύρνας C.

[1] According to Antoninus Liberalis (*Transform.* 34),
Smyrna, the mother of Adonis, was a daughter of Belus by
a nymph Orithyia. Tzetzes mentions, but afterwards rejects,
the view that Myrrha, the mother of Adonis, was a daughter
of Thias (*Schol. on Lycophron*, 829, 831). Hyginus says that
Cinyras, the father of Adonis, was king of Assyria (*Fab.* 58).
This traditional connexion of Adonis with Assyria may well
be due to a well-founded belief that the religion of Adonis,
though best known to the Greeks in Syria and Cyprus, had
originated in Assyria or rather in Babylonia, where he was
worshipped under the name of Dumuzi or Tammuz. See
Adonis, Attis, Osiris, 3rd ed., i. 6 *sqq.*
[2] As to the transformation of the mother of Adonis into a
myrrh-tree, see Scholiast on Theocritus, i. 107 ; Plutarch,
Parallela, 22 ; Antoninus Liberalis, *Transform.* 34 ; Tzetzes,

86

of Thias, king of Assyria,[1] who had a daughter Smyrna. In consequence of the wrath of Aphrodite, for she did not honour the goddess, this Smyrna conceived a passion for her father, and with the complicity of her nurse she shared her father's bed without his knowledge for twelve nights. But when he was aware of it, he drew his sword and pursued her, and being overtaken she prayed to the gods that she might be invisible; so the gods in compassion turned her into the tree which they call *smyrna* (myrrh).[2] Ten months afterwards the tree burst and Adonis, as he is called, was born, whom for the sake of his beauty, while he was still an infant, Aphrodite hid in a chest unknown to the gods and entrusted to Persephone. But when Persephone beheld him, she would not give him back. The case being tried before Zeus, the year was divided into three parts, and the god ordained that Adonis should stay by himself for one part of the year, with Persephone for one part, and with Aphrodite for the remainder.[3]

Schol. on Lycophron, 829; Ovid, *Metamorph.* x. 476 *sqq.*; Hyginus, *Fab.* 58, 164; Fulgentius, *Mytholog.* iii. 8; Lactantius Placidus, *Narrat. Fabul.* x. 9; Servius, on Virgil, *Ecl.* x. 18 and *Aen.* v. 72; *Scriptores rerum mythicarum Latini*, ed. G. H. Bode, vol. i. p. 60 (First Vatican Mythographer, 200). The drops of gum which oozed from the myrrh-tree were thought to be the tears shed by the transformed Myrrha for her sad fate (Ovid, *l.c.* 500 *sqq.*).

[3] According to another version of the story, Aphrodite and Persephone referred their dispute about Adonis to the judgment of Zeus, and he appointed the Muse Calliope to act as arbitrator between them. She decided that Adonis should spend half the year with each of them; but the decision so enraged Aphrodite that in revenge she instigated the Thracian women to rend in pieces Calliope's son, the musician Orpheus. See Hyginus, *Astronom.* ii. 6. A Scholiast on Theocritus (*Id.* iii. 48) reports the common saying that the dead Adonis

Ἄδωνις ταύτῃ προσένειμε καὶ τὴν ἰδίαν μοῖραν.
ὕστερον δὲ θηρεύων Ἄδωνις ὑπὸ συὸς πληγεὶς
ἀπέθανε.

5 Κέκροπος δὲ ἀποθανόντος Κραναὸς <ἐβασί-
λευσεν>[1] αὐτόχθων ὤν, ἐφ' οὗ τὸν ἐπὶ Δευκαλίωνος λέγεται κατακλυσμὸν γενέσθαι. οὗτος
γήμας ἐκ Λακεδαίμονος Πεδιάδα τὴν Μύνητος[2]
ἐγέννησε Κρανάην καὶ Κραναίχμην καὶ Ἀτθίδα,
ἧς ἀποθανούσης ἔτι παρθένου τὴν χώραν Κραναὸς
Ἀτθίδα προσηγόρευσε.

6 Κραναὸν δὲ ἐκβαλὼν Ἀμφικτύων ἐβασίλευσε·
τοῦτον ἔνιοι μὲν Δευκαλίωνος, ἔνιοι δὲ αὐτόχθονα[3]
λέγουσι. βασιλεύσαντα δὲ αὐτὸν ἔτη[4] δώδεκα
Ἐριχθόνιος ἐκβάλλει. τοῦτον οἱ μὲν Ἡφαίστου
καὶ τῆς Κραναοῦ θυγατρὸς Ἀτθίδος εἶναι λέγουσιν, οἱ δὲ Ἡφαίστου καὶ Ἀθηνᾶς, οὕτως·
Ἀθηνᾶ παρεγένετο πρὸς Ἥφαιστον, ὅπλα κατασκευάσαι θέλουσα. ὁ δὲ ἐγκαταλελειμμένος[5] ὑπὸ
Ἀφροδίτης εἰς ἐπιθυμίαν ὤλισθε τῆς Ἀθηνᾶς,

---

[1] ἐβασίλευσεν conjecturally inserted by Gale.
[2] Μύνητος Bekker, Hercher, Wagner : μήνυτος A.
[3] αὐτόχθονα Rᵃ : αὐτόχθονος A.
[4] ἔτη L : ἐπὶ A.
[5] ἐγκαταλελειμμένος E : ἐγκαταλελεγμένος A.

---

spends six months of the year in the arms of Persephone, and
six months in the arms of Aphrodite; and he explains the
saying as a mythical description of the corn, which after
sowing is six months in the earth and six months above
ground.
    [1] Compare Pausanias, i. 2. 6.
    [2] According to the *Parian Chronicle* (lines 4–7), Deucalion
reigned at Lycorea on Mount Parnassus, and when the flood,
following on heavy rains, took place in that district, he fled
for safety to king Cranaus at Athens, where he founded a

However Adonis made over to Aphrodite his own share in addition; but afterwards in hunting he was gored and killed by a boar.

When Cecrops died, Cranaus came to the throne [1]; he was a son of the soil, and it was in his time that the flood in the age of Deucalion is said to have taken place.[2] He married a Lacedaemonian wife, Pedias, daughter of Mynes, and begat Cranae, Cranaechme, and Atthis; and when Atthis died a maid, Cranaus called the country Atthis.[3]

Cranaus was expelled by Amphictyon, who reigned in his stead;[4] some say that Amphictyon was a son of Deucalion, others that he was a son of the soil; and when he had reigned twelve years he was expelled by Erichthonius.[5] Some say that this Erichthonius was a son of Hephaestus and Atthis, daughter of Cranaus, and some that he was a son of Hephaestus and Athena, as follows: Athena came to Hephaestus, desirous of fashioning arms. But he, being forsaken by Aphrodite, fell in love with Athena, and began to pursue

sanctuary of Rainy Zeus and offered thank-offerings for his escape. Compare Eusebius, *Chronic.* vol. ii. p. 26, ed. A. Schoene. We have seen that, according to Apollodorus (iii. 8. 2), the flood happened in the reign of Nyctimus, king of Arcadia.

[3] Compare Pausanias, i. 2. 6; Eusebius, *Chronic.* vol. ii. p. 28, ed. A. Schoene.

[4] Compare the *Parian Chronicle*, lines 8–10; Pausanias, i. 2. 6; Eusebius, *Chronic.* vol. ii. p. 30, ed. A. Schoene. The Parian Chronicle represents Amphictyon as a son of Deucalion and as reigning, first at Thermopylae, and then at Athens; but it records nothing as to his revolt against Cranaus. Pausanias says that Amphictyon deposed Cranaus, although he had the daughter of Cranaus to wife. Eusebius says that Amphictyon was a son of Deucalion and son-in-law of Cranaus.

[5] Compare Pausanias, i. 2. 6.

καὶ διώκειν αὐτὴν ἤρξατο· ἡ δὲ ἔφευγεν. ὡς δὲ
ἐγγὺς αὐτῆς ἐγένετο πολλῇ ἀνάγκῃ (ἦν γὰρ
χωλός), ἐπειρᾶτο συνελθεῖν. ἡ δὲ ὡς σώφρων
καὶ παρθένος οὖσα οὐκ ἠνέσχετο· ὁ δὲ ἀπεσπέρ-
μηνεν εἰς τὸ σκέλος τῆς θεᾶς. ἐκείνη δὲ μυσα-
χθεῖσα ἐρίῳ ἀπομάξασα τὸν γόνον εἰς γῆν ἔρριψε.
φευγούσης δὲ αὐτῆς καὶ τῆς γονῆς εἰς γῆν
πεσούσης Ἐριχθόνιος γίνεται. τοῦτον Ἀθηνᾶ
κρύφα τῶν ἄλλων θεῶν ἔτρεφεν, ἀθάνατον θέλουσα ποιῆσαι· καὶ καταθεῖσα αὐτὸν εἰς κίστην
Πανδρόσῳ τῇ Κέκροπος παρακατέθετο, ἀπει-
ποῦσα τὴν κίστην ἀνοίγειν. αἱ δὲ ἀδελφαὶ τῆς
Πανδρόσου ἀνοίγουσιν ὑπὸ περιεργίας, καὶ θεῶν-
ται τῷ βρέφει παρεσπειραμένον δράκοντα· καὶ
ὡς μὲν ἔνιοι λέγουσιν, ὑπ' αὐτοῦ διεφθάρησαν
τοῦ δράκοντος, ὡς δὲ ἔνιοι, δι' ὀργὴν Ἀθηνᾶς
ἐμμανεῖς γενόμεναι κατὰ τῆς ἀκροπόλεως αὐτὰς
ἔρριψαν. ἐν δὲ τῷ τεμένει τραφεὶς Ἐριχθόνιος

---

[1] With this story of the birth of Erichthonius compare
Scholiast on Homer, *Il.* ii. 547 (who agrees to a great extent
verbally with Apollodorus) ; Euripides, *Ion*, 20 *sqq.*, 266 *sqq.*;
Eratosthenes, *Cataster.* 13 ; Nonnus, in Westermann's *Mythographi Graeci, Appendix Narrationum*, 3, pp. 359 *sq.*;
Tzetzes, *Schol. on Lycophron*, 111 ; Antigonus Carystius,
Histor. Mirab. 12 ; *Etymologicum Magnum, s.v.* Ἐρεχθεύς,
p. 371. 29 ; Hyginus, *Fab.* 166 ; *id. Astronom.* ii. 13 ; Servius, on Virgil, *Georg.* iii. 113 ; Fulgentius, *Mytholog.* ii. 14 ;
Lactantius, *Divin. Inst.* ii. 17 ; Augustine, *De civitate Dei*,
xviii. 12 ; *Scholia in Caesaris Germanici Aratea*, p. 394,
ed. Fr. Eyssenhardt (in his edition of Martianus Capella) ;
Scriptores rerum mythicarum Latini, ed. G. H. Bode, vol. i.
pp. 41, 86 *sq.*, 88 (First Vatican Mythographer, 128 ; Second
Vatican Mythographer, 37, 40). The story of the birth of
Erichthonius was told by Euripides, according to Eratosthenes (*l.c.*) and by Callimachus, according to the Scholiast on

her; but she fled. When he got near her with much
ado (for he was lame), he attempted to embrace her;
but she, being a chaste virgin, would not submit to
him, and he dropped his seed on the leg of the
goddess. In disgust, she wiped off the seed with
wool and threw it on the ground; and as she fled
and the seed fell on the ground, Erichthonius was
produced.[1] Him Athena brought up unknown to the
other gods, wishing to make him immortal; and having
put him in a chest, she committed it to Pandrosus,
daughter of Cecrops, forbidding her to open the chest.
But the sisters of Pandrosus opened it out of curiosity,
and beheld a serpent coiled about the babe; and, as
some say, they were destroyed by the serpent, but according to others they were driven mad by reason of
the anger of Athena and threw themselves down from
the acropolis.[2] Having been brought up by Athena

Homer (l.c.). Pausanias was plainly acquainted with the
fable, though he contents himself with saying that Erichthonius was reported to be a son of Hephaestus and Earth (i. 2. 6,
i. 14. 6). As C. G. Heyne long ago observed, the story is
clearly an etymological myth invented to explain the meaning
of the name Erichthonius, which some people derived from
ἔρις, "strife," and χθών, "the ground," while others derived
it from ἔριον, "wool," and χθών, "the ground." The former
derivation of eri in Erichthonius seems to have been the more
popular. Mythologists have perhaps not sufficiently reckoned
with the extent to which false etymology has been operative
in the creation of myths. "Disease of language" is one
source of myths, though it is very far from being the only
one.

[2] With this story of the discovery of Erichthonius in the
chest compare Euripides, Ion, 20 sqq., 266 sqq.; Pausanias,
i. 18. 2; Antigonus Carystius, Hist. Mirab. 12; Ovid, Metamorph. ii. 552 sqq.; Hyginus, Fab. 166; id. Astronom.
ii. 13; Fulgentius, Mytholog. ii. 14; Lactantius, Divin. Inst.
i. 17; Scriptores rerum mythicarum Latini, ed. G. H. Bode,
vol. i. pp. 41, 86 sq., 88 (First Vatican Mythographer, 128;

APOLLODORUS

ὑπ᾿ αὐτῆς Ἀθηνᾶς, ἐκβαλὼν Ἀμφικτύονα ἐβασίλευσεν Ἀθηνῶν, καὶ τὸ ἐν ἀκροπόλει ξόανον
τῆς Ἀθηνᾶς ἱδρύσατο, καὶ τῶν Παναθηναίων
τὴν ἑορτὴν συνεστήσατο, καὶ Πραξιθέαν[1] νηίδα

---

[1] Πραξιθέαν Heyne : πρασιθέαν A : Πασιθέαν Aegius. Tzetzes
calls her Φρασιθέα (Chiliades, i. 174, v. 671), but mentions
Πραξιθέα as the wife of Erechtheus and mother of Cecrops
(Chiliades, i. 177, v. 674).

Second Vatican Mythographer, 37, 40). Apollodorus apparently describes the infant Erichthonius in the chest as a purely
human babe with a serpent coiled about him. The serpent
was said to have been set by Athena to guard the infant ;
according to Euripides (Ion, 20 sqq.), there were two such
guardian serpents. But according to a common tradition
Erichthonius was serpent-footed, that is, his legs ended in
serpents. See Nonnus, in Westermann's Mythographi Graeci,
Appendix Narrationum, 3, p. 360 ; Etymologicum Magnum,
s.v. Ἐρεχθεύς, p. 371. 47 ; Hyginus, Fab. 166 ; Servius, on
Virgil, Aen. iii. 113 ; Scriptores rerum mythicarum Latini,
ed. G. H. Bode, vol. i. pp. 41, 87 (First Vatican Mythographer, 128, Second Vatican Mythographer 37). Indeed,
in one passage (Astronom. ii. 13) Hyginus affirms that
Erichthonius was born a serpent, and that when the
box was opened and the maidens saw the serpent in it,
they went mad and threw themselves from the acropolis,
while the serpent took refuge under the shield of Athena
and was reared by the goddess. This view of the identity
of Erichthonius with the serpent was recognized, if not
accepted, by Pausanias ; for in describing the famous statue
of the Virgin Athena on the acropolis of Athens, he notices
the serpent coiled at her feet behind the shield, and adds
that the serpent "may be Erichthonius" (i. 24. 7). The
sacred serpent which lived in the Erechtheum on the acropolis of Athens and was fed with honey-cakes once a month,
may have been Erichthonius himself in his original form of
a worshipful serpent. See Herodotus, viii. 41 ; Aristophanes,
Lysistrata, 758 sq., with the Scholiast ; Plutarch, Themistocles, 10 ; Philostratus, Imagines, ii. 17. 6 ; Hesychius, s.vv.
δράκαυλος and οἰκουρὸν ὄφιν ; Suidas, s.v. Δράκαυλος ; Etymo-

herself in the precinct,[1] Erichthonius expelled Amphictyon and became king of Athens; and he set up the wooden image of Athena in the acropolis,[2] and instituted the festival of the Panathenaea,[3] and

logicum Magnum, s.v. δράκαυλος, p. 287; Photius, Lexicon, s.v. οἰκουρὸν ὄφιν; Eustathius on Homer, Od. i. 357, p. 1422, lines 7 sqq. According to some, there were two such sacred serpents in the Erechtheum (Hesychius, s.v. οἰκουρὸν ὄφιν). When we remember that Cecrops, the ancestor of Erichthonius, was said, like his descendant, to be half-man, half-serpent (above, iii. 14. 1), we may conjecture that the old kings of Athens claimed kinship with the sacred serpents on the acropolis, into which they may have professed to transmigrate at death. Compare The Dying God, pp. 86 sq.; and my note on Pausanias, i. 18. 2 (vol. ii. pp. 168 sqq.). The Erechtheids, or descendants of Erechtheus, by whom are meant the Athenians in general, used to put golden serpents round the necks or bodies of their infants, nominally in memory of the serpents which guarded the infant Erichthonius, but probably in reality as amulets to protect the children. See Euripides, Ion, 20–26, 1426–1431. Erechtheus and Erichthonius may have been originally identical. See Scholiast on Homer, Il. ii. 547; Etymologicum Magnum, s.v. Ἐρεχθεύς, p. 371. 29; C. F. Clinton, Fasti Hellenici, vol. i. p. 61 note [n].

[1] "The precinct" is the Erechtheum on the acropolis of Athens. It was in the Erechtheum that the sacred serpent dwelt, which seems to have been originally identical with Erichthonius. See the preceding note.

[2] That is, the ancient image of Athena, made of olive-wood, which stood in the Erechtheum. See my note on Pausanias, i. 26. 6 (vol. ii. pp. 340 sq.).

[3] Compare the Parian Chronicle, line 18; Harpocration, s.v. Παναθήναια; Eratosthenes, Cataster. 13; Hyginus, Astronom. ii. 13, who says that Erichthonius competed at the games in a four-horse car. Indeed, Erichthonius was reputed to have invented the chariot, or, at all events, the four-horse chariot. See the Parian Chronicle, lines 18 and 21; Eusebius, Chronic. vol. ii. p. 32, ed. A. Schoene; Virgil, Georg. iii. 113 sq.; Fulgentius, Mytholog. ii. 14. According to some, he invented the chariot for the purpose of

νύμφην ἔγημεν, ἐξ ἧς αὐτῷ παῖς Πανδίων
ἐγεννήθη.

7 Ἐριχθονίου δὲ ἀποθανόντος καὶ ταφέντος ἐν
τῷ αὐτῷ¹ τεμένει τῆς Ἀθηνᾶς Πανδίων ἐβασίλευσεν, ἐφ' οὗ Δημήτηρ καὶ Διόνυσος εἰς τὴν
Ἀττικὴν ἦλθον. ἀλλὰ Δήμητρα μὲν Κελεὸς [εἰς

¹ τῷ αὐτῷ Scaliger, Wagner : τῷ ἁ Rᵃ : τῷ ἁ τῷ A.

---

concealing his serpent feet. See Servius, on Virgil, *Georg.*
iii. 113 ; *Scriptores rerum mythicarum Latini*, ed. G. H.
Bode, vol. i. pp. 41, 87 (First Vatican Mythographer, 127 ;
Second Vatican Mythographer, 37). The institution of the
Panathenaic festival was by some attributed to Theseus
(Plutarch, *Theseus*, 24), but the *Parian Chronicle* (line 18),
in agreement with Apollodorus, ascribes it to Erichthonius ;
and from Harpocration (*l.c.*) we learn that this ascription
was supported by the authority of the historians Hellanicus
and Androtion in their works on Attica. Here, therefore,
as usual, Apollodorus seems to have drawn on the best
sources.

¹ Compare Clement of Alexandria, *Protrept.* iii. 45, p. 39,
ed. Potter, who gives a list of legendary or mythical personages who were said to have been buried in sanctuaries or
temples. Amongst the instances which he cites are the
graves of Cinyras and his descendants in the sanctuary of
Aphrodite at Paphus, and the grave of Acrisius in the
temple of Athena on the acropolis of Larissa. To these
examples C. G. Heyne, commenting on the present passage
of Apollodorus, adds the tomb of Castor in a sanctuary at
Sparta (Pausanias, iii. 13. 1), the tomb of Hyacinth under
the image of Apollo at Amyclae (Pausanias, iii. 19. 3), and
the grave of Arcas in a temple of Hera at Mantinea (Pausanias, viii. 9. 3). "Arguing from these examples," says
Heyne, "some have tried to prove that the worship of the
gods sprang from the honours paid to buried mortals."

² Compare Pausanias, i. 5. 3, who distinguishes two kings
named Pandion, first, the son of Erichthonius, and, second,

married Praxithea, a Naiad nymph, by whom he had a son Pandion.

When Erichthonius died and was buried in the same precinct of Athena,[1] Pandion [2] became king, in whose time Demeter and Dionysus came to Attica.[3] But Demeter was welcomed by Celeus at Eleusis,[4] and

the son of Cecrops the Second. This distinction is accepted by Apollodorus (see below, iii. 15. 5), and it is supported by the *Parian Chronicle* (*Marmor Parium*, lines 22 and 30). Eusebius also recognizes Pandion the Second, but makes him a son of Erechtheus instead of a son of Cecrops the Second (*Chronic.* bk. i. vol. i. col. 185, ed. A. Schoene). But like Cecrops the Second, son of Erechtheus (below, iii. 15. 5), Pandion the Second is probably no more than a chronological stop-gap thrust into the broken framework of tradition by a comparatively late historian. Compare R. D. Hicks, in *Companion to Greek Studies,* ed. L. Whibley, 3rd. ed. (Cambridge, 1916), p. 76.

[3] Here Apollodorus differs from the *Parian Chronicle,* which dates the advent of Demeter, not in the reign of Pandion, but in the reign of his son Erechtheus (*Marmor Parium,* lines 23 *sq.*). To the reign of Erechtheus the *Parian Chronicle* also refers the first sowing of corn by Triptolemus in the Rharian plain at Eleusis, and the first celebration of the mysteries by Eumolpus at Eleusis (*Marmor Parium,* lines 23-29). Herein the *Parian Chronicle* seems to be in accord with the received Athenian tradition which dated the advent of Demeter, the beginning of agriculture, and the institution of the Eleusinian mysteries in the reign of Erechtheus. See Diodorus Siculus, i. 29. 1-3. On the other hand, the Parian Chronicler dates the discovery of iron on the Cretan Mount Ida in the reign of Pandion the First (*Marmor Parium,* lines 22 *sq.*). He says nothing of the coming of Dionysus to Attica. The advent of Demeter and Dionysus is a mythical expression for the first cultivation of corn and vines in Attica; these important discoveries Attic tradition referred to the reigns either of Pandion the First or of his son Erechtheus.

[4] See above, i. 5. 1.

95

APOLLODORUS

τὴν Ἐλευσῖνα]¹ ὑπεδέξατο, Διόνυσον δὲ Ἰκάριος·
ὃς² λαμβάνει παρ’ αὐτοῦ κλῆμα ἀμπέλου καὶ τὰ
περὶ τὴν οἰνοποιίαν μανθάνει. καὶ τὰς τοῦ θεοῦ
δωρήσασθαι θέλων χάριτας ἀνθρώποις, ἀφικνεῖται
πρός τινας ποιμένας, οἳ γευσάμενοι τοῦ ποτοῦ
καὶ χωρὶς ὕδατος δι’ ἡδονὴν ἀφειδῶς ἑλκύσαντες,
πεφαρμάχθαι νομίζοντες ἀπέκτειναν αὐτόν. μεθ’
ἡμέραν δὲ νοήσαντες³ ἔθαψαν αὐτόν. Ἠριγόνη
δὲ τῇ θυγατρὶ τὸν πατέρα μαστευούσῃ κύων
συνήθης ὄνομα Μαῖρα, ἣ τῷ Ἰκαρίῳ συνείπετο,
τὸν νεκρὸν ἐμήνυσε· κἀκείνη κατοδυραμένη⁴ τὸν
πατέρα ἑαυτὴν ἀνήρτησε.

¹ εἰς τὴν Ἐλευσῖνα. These words may be, as Heyne
thought, a gloss on εἰς τὴν Ἀττικήν. They are omitted by
Hercher. Wagner keeps them unbracketed.
² ὃς . . . μανθάνει E : καὶ . . . μανθάνων A.
³ νοήσαντες A : νήψαντες Valckenar.
⁴ κατοδυραμένη Hercher : κατοδυρομένη Heyne, Westermann, Müller, Bekker, Wagner.

---

¹ The implication is that their wassailing had taken place
by night. The Greek μεθ’ ἡμέραν regularly means "by day"
as opposed to "by night"; it is not to be translated "the
day after." See Herodotus, ii. 150, οὐ νυκτὸς ἀλλὰ μετ’ ἡμέρην
ποιεύμενον ; Plato, Phaedrus, p. 251 D, ἐμμανὴς οὖσα οὔτε νυκτὸς
δύναται καθεύδειν οὔτε μεθ’ ἡμέραν. Compare Apollodorus, i
9. 18, iii. 5. 6 (νύκτωρ καὶ μεθ’ ἡμέραν), iii. 12. 3, Epitome, iv. 5,
vii. 31 (μεθ’ ἡμέραν μὲν ὑφαίνουσα, νύκτωρ δὲ ἀναλύουσα).
² With this story of the first introduction of wine into
Attica, and its fatal consequences, compare Scholiast on
Homer, Il. xxii. 29 ; Aelian, Var. Hist. vii. 28 ; Nonnus,
Dionys. xlvii. 34–245 ; Hyginus, Fab. 130 ; id. Astronom.
ii. 4 ; Statius, Theb. xi. 644–647, with the comment of Lactantius Placidus on v. 644 ; Servius, on Virgil, Georg. ii.
389 ; Probus, on Virgil, Georg. ii. 385 ; Scriptores rerum
mythicarum Latini, ed. G. H. Bode, vol. i. pp. 6, 94 sq.
(First Vatican Mythographer, 19 ; Second Vatican Mythographer, 61). The Athenians celebrated a curious festival of

Dionysus by Icarius, who received from him a branch of a vine and learned the process of making wine. And wishing to bestow the god's boons on men, Icarius went to some shepherds, who, having tasted the beverage and quaffed it copiously without water for the pleasure of it, imagined that they were bewitched and killed him; but by day [1] they understood how it was and buried him. When his daughter Erigone was searching for her father, a domestic dog, named Maera, which had attended Icarius, discovered his dead body to her, and she bewailed her father and hanged herself.[2]

swinging, which was supposed to be an expiation for the death of Erigone, who had hanged herself on the same tree at the foot of which she had discovered the dead body of her father Icarius (Hyginus, *Astronom*. ii. 4). See Hesychius and *Etymologicum Magnum*, *s.v.* Αἰώρα; Athenaeus, xiv. 10, p. 618 EF; Festus, ed. C. O. Müller, p. 194, *s.v.* "Oscillantes." Compare *The Dying God*, pp. 281 *sqq*. However, some thought that the Erigone whose death was thus expiated was not the daughter of Icarius, but the daughter of Aegisthus, who accused Orestes at Athens of the murder of her father and hanged herself when he was acquitted (so *Etymologicum Magnum*, *l.c.*; compare Apollodorus, *Epitome*, vi. 25 with the note). Sophocles wrote a play *Erigone*, but it is doubtful to which of the two Erigones it referred. See *The Fragments of Sophocles*, ed. A. C. Pearson, vol. i. pp. 173 *sqq*. The home of Icarius was at Icaria (Stephanus Byzantius, *s.v.* Ἰκαρία). From the description of Statius (*l.c.*) we infer that the place was in the woods of Marathon, and in accordance with this description the site has been discovered in a beautiful wooded dell at the northern foot of the forest-clad slopes of Mount Pentelicus. The place is still appropriately named Dionysos. A rugged precipitous path leads down a wild romantic ravine from the deserted village of Rapentosa to the plain of Marathon situated at a great depth below. Among the inscriptions found on the spot several refer to the worship of Dionysus. See my commentary on Pausanias, vol. ii. pp. 461 *sqq*., compare p. 442.

8   Πανδίων δὲ γήμας Ζευξίππην τῆς μητρὸς τὴν
ἀδελφὴν θυγατέρας μὲν ἐτέκνωσε Πρόκνην καὶ
Φιλομήλαν, παῖδας δὲ διδύμους Ἐρεχθέα καὶ
Βούτην. πολέμου δὲ ἐνστάντος[1] πρὸς Λάβδακον
περὶ γῆς ὅρων ἐπεκαλέσατο βοηθὸν ἐκ Θράκης
Τηρέα τὸν Ἄρεος, καὶ τὸν πόλεμον σὺν αὐτῷ
κατορθώσας ἔδωκε Τηρεῖ πρὸς γάμον τὴν ἑαυτοῦ
θυγατέρα Πρόκνην. ὁ δὲ ἐκ ταύτης γεννήσας

---

[1] ἐνστάντος E : ἐξαναστάντος A, Heyne, Westermann,
Müller, Bekker, Hercher, Wagner. But such a use of
ἐξαναστὰς seems unparalleled, whereas ἐνστὰς is regularly
applied to war breaking out or threatening. See below iii.
15. 4, πολέμου ἐνστάντος πρὸς Ἀθηναίους : Isocrates, Or. v. 2,
τὸν πόλεμον τὸν ἐνστάντα σοὶ καὶ τῇ πόλει περὶ Ἀμφιπόλεω ;
Demosthenes, Or. xviii. 89, ὁ γὰρ τότε ἐνστὰς πόλεμος, and
139, οὐκέτ᾽ ἐν ἀμφισβητησίμῳ τὰ πράγματα ἦν, ἀλλ᾽ ἐνειστήκει
πόλεμος ; Polybius, i. 71 4, μείζονος γὰρ ἐνίστατο πολέμου
καταρχή.

---

[1] This tradition of marriage with a maternal aunt is remarkable. I do not remember to have met with another
instance of such a marriage in Greek legend.

[2] For the tragic story of Procne and Philomela, and their
transformation into birds, see Zenobius, Cent. iii. 14 (who, to
a certain extent, agrees verbally with Apollodorus) ; Conon,
Narrat. 31 ; Achilles Tatius, v. 3 and 5 ; J. Tzetzes, Chiliades, vii. 459 sqq. ; Pausanias, i. 5. 4, i. 41. 8 sq., x. 4. 8 sq. ;
Eustathius, on Homer, Od. xix. 518, p. 1875 ; Hyginus, Fab.
45 ; Ovid, Metamorph. vi. 426–674 ; Servius, on Virgil, Ecl.
vi. 78 ; Lactantius Placidus, on Statius, Theb. v. 120 ; Scriptores rerum mythicarum Latini, ed. G. H. Bode, vol. i. pp.
2 and 147 (First Vatican Mythographer, 8 ; Second Vatican
Mythographer, 217). On this theme Sophocles composed a
tragedy Tereus, from which most of the extant versions of
the story are believed to be derived. See The Fragments of
Sophocles, ed. A. C. Pearson, vol. ii. pp. 221 sqq. However,
the version of Hyginus differs from the rest in a number of
particulars. For example, he represents Tereus as transformed into a hawk instead of into a hoopoe ; but for this

Pandion married Zeuxippe, his mother's sister,[1] and begat two daughters, Procne and Philomela, and twin sons, Erechtheus and Butes. But war having broken out with Labdacus on a question of boundaries, he called in the help of Tereus, son of Ares, from Thrace, and having with his help brought the war to a successful close, he gave Tereus his own daughter Procne in marriage.[2] Tereus had by her a son Itys,

transformation he had the authority of Aeschylus (*Suppliants*, 60 *sqq.*). Tereus is commonly said to have been a Thracian, and the scene of the tragedy is sometimes laid in Thrace. Ovid, who adopts this account, appears to have associated the murder of Itys with the frenzied rites of the Bacchanals, for he says that the crime was perpetrated at the time when the Thracian women were celebrating the biennial festival (*sacra trieterica*) of Dionysus, and that the two women disguised themselves as Bacchanals. On the other hand, Thucydides (ii. 29) definitely affirms that Tereus dwelt in Daulia, a district of Phocis, and that the tragedy took place in that country; at the same time he tells us that the population of the district was then Thracian. In this he is followed by Strabo (ix. 3. 13, p. 423), Zenobius, Conon, Pausanias, and Nonnus (*Dionys.* iv. 320 *sqq.*). Thucydides supports his view by a reference to Greek poets, who called the nightingale the Daulian bird. The Megarians maintained that Tereus reigned at Pagae in Megaris, and they showed his grave in the form of a barrow, at which they sacrificed to him every year, using gravel in the sacrifice instead of barley groats (Pausanias, i. 41. 8 *sq.*). But no one who has seen the grey ruined walls and towers of Daulis, thickly mantled in ivy and holly-oak, on the summit of precipices that overhang a deep romantic glen at the foot of the towering slopes of Parnassus, will willingly consent to divest them of the legendary charm which Greek poetry and history have combined to throw over the lovely scene.

It is said that, after being turned into birds, Procne and Tereus continued to utter the same cries which they had emitted at the moment of their transformation; the nightingale still fled warbling plaintively the name of her dead son, *Itu! Itu!* while the hoopoe still pursued his cruel wife

παῖδα Ἴτυν, καὶ Φιλομήλας ἐρασθεὶς ἔφθειρε καὶ
ταύτην, [εἰπὼν τεθνάναι Πρόκνην,]¹ κρύπτων ἐπὶ
τῶν χωρίων. [αὖθις δὲ γήμας Φιλομήλαν συνηυνάζετο,]² καὶ τὴν γλῶσσαν ἐξέτεμεν αὐτῆς. ἡ δὲ
ὑφήνασα ἐν πέπλῳ γράμματα διὰ τούτων ἐμήνυσε
Πρόκνῃ τὰς ἰδίας συμφοράς. ἡ δὲ ἀναζητήσασα
τὴν ἀδελφὴν κτείνει τὸν παῖδα Ἴτυν, καὶ καθε-
ψήσασα Τηρεῖ δεῖπνον ἀγνοοῦντι παρατίθησι·³
καὶ μετὰ τῆς ἀδελφῆς διὰ τάχους⁴ ἔφυγε.⁵ Τηρεὺς
δὲ αἰσθόμενος, ἁρπάσας πέλεκυν ἐδίωκεν. αἱ δὲ ἐν
Δαυλίᾳ τῆς Φωκίδος γινόμεναι περικατάληπτοι
θεοῖς εὔχονται ἀπορνεωθῆναι, καὶ Πρόκνη μὲν
γίνεται ἀηδών, Φιλομήλα δὲ χελιδών· ἀπορνε-
οῦται δὲ καὶ Τηρεύς, καὶ γίνεται ἔποψ.

XV. Πανδίονος δὲ ἀποθανόντος οἱ παῖδες τὰ
πατρῷα ἐμερίσαντο, καὶ τὴν <μὲν>⁶ βασιλείαν
Ἐρεχθεὺς λαμβάνει, τὴν δὲ ἱερωσύνην τῆς Ἀθηνᾶς
καὶ τοῦ Ποσειδῶνος τοῦ Ἐρεχθέως⁷ Βούτης.

¹ εἰπὼν τεθνάναι Πρόκνην omitted by Hercher.
² αὖθις δὲ γήμας Φιλομήλαν συνηυνάζετο omitted by Hercher.
The narrative gains in clearness by the omission.
³ παρατίθησι Zenobius, Cent. iii. 14, Bekker, Hercher,
Wagner: προτίθησι EA, Heyne, Westermann, Müller.
⁴ διὰ τάχους E: διαταχέως A: διὰ ταχέος Müller: διὰ
ταχέων Westermann, Bekker, Hercher.
⁵ ἔφυγε EA: ἔφευγε Hercher.
⁶ μὲν inserted by Bekker.
⁷ Ἐρεχθέως Heyne (conjecture), Hercher, Wagner: Ἐριχθονίου A, Westermann, Müller, Bekker.

---

crying, Poo! poo! (ποῦ, ποῦ, "Where? Where?"). The
later Roman mythographers somewhat absurdly inverted the
transformation of the two sisters, making Procne the swallow
and the tongueless Philomela the songstress nightingale.

¹ Erechtheus is recognized as the son of Pandion by the
Parian Chronicle (Marmor Parium, lines 28 sq.), Eusebius

and having fallen in love with Philomela, he seduced
her also saying that Procne was dead, for he concealed her in the country. Afterwards he married
Philomela and bedded with her, and cut out her
tongue. But by weaving characters in a robe she
revealed thereby to Procne her own sorrows. And
having sought out her sister, Procne killed her son
Itys, boiled him, served him up for supper to the un-
witting Tereus, and fled with her sister in haste.
When Tereus was aware of what had happened, he
snatched up an axe and pursued them. And being
overtaken at Daulia in Phocis, they prayed the
gods to be turned into birds, and Procne became a
nightingale, and Philomela a swallow. And Tereus
also was changed into a bird and became a hoopoe.

XV. When Pandion died, his sons divided their
father's inheritance between them, and Erechtheus
got the kingdom,[1] and Butes got the priesthood
of Athena and Poseidon Erechtheus.[2] Erechtheus

(*Chronic.* vol. i. p. 186, ed. A. Schoene), Hyginus (*Fab.* 48),
and Ovid (*Metamorph.* vi. 675 *sqq.*). According to Ovid
(*l.c.*), Erechtheus had four sons and four daughters.

[2] Compare Harpocration, *s.v.* Βούτης, who tells us that the
families of the Butads and Eteobutads traced their origin to
this Butes. There was an altar dedicated to him as to a
hero in the Erechtheum on the acropolis of Athens (Pausanias, i. 26. 5). Compare J. Toepffer, *Attische Genealogie*
(Berlin, 1889), pp. 113 *sqq.* Erechtheus was identified with
Poseidon at Athens (Hesychius, *s.v.* Ἐρεχθεύς). The Athenians sacrificed to Erechtheus Poseidon (Athenagoras, *Suppli-
catio pro Christianis*, 1). His priesthood was called the
priesthood of Poseidon Erechtheus (Pseudo-Plutarch, x. *Orat.
Vit., Lycurgus*, 30, p. 1027, ed. Dübner ; *Corpus Inscriptionum Atticarum*, iii. No. 805 ; Dittenberger, *Sylloge Inscriptionum Graecarum* [3], No. 790). An inscription found at
the Erechtheum contains a dedication to Poseidon Erechtheus

γήμας δὲ Ἐρεχθεὺς Πραξιθέαν τὴν Φρασίμου
καὶ Διογενείας τῆς Κηφισοῦ, ἔσχε παῖδας Κέκροπα Πάνδωρον Μητίονα, θυγατέρας δὲ Πρόκριν
Κρέουσαν Χθονίαν Ὠρείθυιαν, ἣν ἥρπασε Βορέας.

Χθονίαν μὲν οὖν ἔγημε Βούτης, Κρέουσαν δὲ
Ξοῦθος, Πρόκριν δὲ Κέφαλος <ὁ> Δηιόνος. ἡ δὲ

(*Corpus Inscriptionum Atticarum*, i. No. 387). Hence we
may conclude with great probability that Heyne is right in
restoring Ἐρεχθέως for Ἐριχθονίου in the present passage of
Apollodorus. See the Critical Note.

[1] Orithyia is said to have been carried off by Boreas from
the banks of the Ilissus, where she was dancing or gathering
flowers with her playmates. An altar to Boreas marked the
spot. See below, iii. 15. 2; Plato, *Phaedrus*, p. 229 B C;
Pausanias, i. 19. 5; Apollonius Rhodius, *Argon.* i. 212 *sqq.*,
with the Scholiast on *v.* 212, from whom we learn that the
story was told by the poet Simonides and the early historian
Pherecydes. Compare Ovid, *Metamorph.* vi. 683 *sqq.* According to another account, Orithyia was seen and loved by
Boreas as she was carrying a basket in a procession, which
was winding up the slope of the acropolis to offer sacrifice to
Athena Polias, the Guardian of the City; the impetuous
lover whirled her away with him, invisible to the crowd
and to the guards that surrounded the royal maidens. See
Scholiast on Homer, *Od.* xiv. 533, who refers to Aculias as
his authority. A different tradition as to the parentage of
Orithyia appears to be implied by a vase-painting, which
represents Boreas carrying off Orithyia in the presence of
Cecrops, Erechtheus, Aglaurus, Herse, and Pandrosus, all of
whom are identified by inscriptions (*Corpus Inscriptionum
Graecarum*, vol. iv. p. 146, No. 7716). The painting is
interpreted most naturally by the supposition that in the
artist's opinion Aglaurus, Herse, and Pandrosus, the three
daughters of Cecrops (see above, iii. 14. 2), were the sisters
of Orithyia, and therefore that her father was Cecrops, and
not Erechtheus, as Apollodorus, following the ordinary Greek
tradition (Herodotus, vii. 189), assumes in the present passage. This inference is confirmed by an express statement
of the Scholiast on Apollonius Rhodius (*Argon.* i. 212) that

married Praxithea, daughter of Phrasimus by Diogenia, daughter of Cephisus, and had sons, to wit,
Cecrops, Pandorus, and Metion ; and daughters, to
wit, Procris, Creusa, Chthonia, and Orithyia, who was
carried off by Boreas.[1]

Chthonia was married to Butes,[2] Creusa to Xuthus,[3]
and Procris to Cephalus, son of Deion.[4] Bribed by

Cecrops was the father of Orithyia. As to the vase-painting
in question, see F. G. Welcker, *Antike Denkmäler*, iii. 144
sqq. ; A. Baumeister, *Denkmäler des klassischen Altertums*,
i. 351 *sqq.*

[2] This is the third instance of marriage or betrothal with
a niece, the daughter of a brother, which has met us in
Apollodorus. See above, ii. 4. 3, ii. 4. 5. So many references to such a marriage seem to indicate a former practice
of marrying a niece, the daughter of a brother.

[3] Compare Euripides, *Ion*, 57 *sqq.* ; Pausanias, vii. 1. 2,
where, however, Creusa is not named.

[4] The tragic story of Cephalus and Procris was told with
variations in detail by ancient writers. See Scholiast on
Homer, *Od.* xi. 321 ; Eustathius on Homer, *l.c.*, p. 1688 ;
Antoninus Liberalis, *Transform.* 41 ; J. Tzetzes, *Chiliades*,
i. 542 *sqq.* ; Hyginus, *Fab.* 189 ; Ovid, *Metamorph.* vii.
670–862 ; Servius, on Virgil, *Aen.* vi. 445 ; *Scriptores rerum
mythicarum Latini*, ed. G. H. Bode, vol. i. pp. 16 *sq.*, 147
(First Vatican Mythographer, 44 ; Second Vatican Mythographer, 216). Of these writers, Tzetzes closely follows
Apollodorus, whom he cites by name. They are the only
two authors who mention the intrigue of Procris with Pteleus
and the bribe of the golden crown. The story was told by
Pherecydes, as we learn from the Scholiast on Homer, *l.c.*,
who gives an abstract of the narrative. In it the test of his
wife's chastity is made by Cephalus himself in disguise ;
nothing is said of the flight of the abashed Procris to Minos,
and nothing of the love of Dawn (Aurora) for Cephalus,
which in several of the versions figures conspicuously, since
it is the jealous goddess who suggests to her human lover
the idea of tempting his wife to her fall. The episode of
Procris's flight to Minos is told with some differences of
detail by Antoninus Liberalis. As to the dog which Procris

λαβοῦσα χρυσοῦν στέφανον Πτελέοντι συνευνάζεται, καὶ φωραθεῖσα ὑπὸ Κεφάλου πρὸς Μίνωα
φεύγει. ὁ δὲ αὐτῆς ἐρᾷ καὶ πείθει συνελθεῖν. εἰ
δὲ συνέλθοι γυνὴ Μίνωι, ἀδύνατον ἦν αὐτὴν
σωθῆναι· Πασιφάη γάρ, ἐπειδὴ πολλαῖς Μίνως
συνηυνάζετο γυναιξίν, ἐφαρμάκευσεν αὐτόν, καὶ
ὁπότε ἄλλῃ συνηυνάζετο, εἰς τὰ ἄρθρα ἀφίει[1]
θηρία, καὶ οὕτως ἀπώλλυντο. ἔχοντος οὖν αὐτοῦ
κύνα ταχὺν <καὶ> ἀκόντιον ἰθυβόλον, ἐπὶ τούτοις
Πρόκρις, δοῦσα τὴν Κιρκαίαν πιεῖν ῥίζαν πρὸς τὸ
μηδὲν βλάψαι, συνευνάζεται. δείσασα δὲ αὖθις
τὴν Μίνωος γυναῖκα ἧκεν εἰς Ἀθήνας, καὶ διαλ-
λαγεῖσα Κεφάλῳ μετὰ τούτου παραγίνεται ἐπὶ
θήραν· ἦν γὰρ θηρευτική. διωκούσης δὲ αὐτῆς
ἐν τῇ λόχμῃ[2] ἀγνοήσας Κέφαλος ἀκοντίζει, καὶ
τυχὼν ἀποκτείνει Πρόκριν. καὶ κριθεὶς ἐν Ἀρείῳ
πάγῳ φυγὴν ἀίδιον καταδικάζεται.

2   Ὠρείθυιαν δὲ παίζουσαν[3] ἐπὶ Ἰλισσοῦ ποταμοῦ
ἁρπάσας Βορέας συνῆλθεν· ἡ δὲ γεννᾷ θυγατέρας
μὲν Κλεοπάτραν καὶ Χιόνην, υἱοὺς δὲ Ζήτην καὶ
Κάλαϊν πτερωτούς, οἳ πλέοντες σὺν Ἰάσονι καὶ

---

[1] ἀφίει Heyne (conjecture), Bekker, Hercher : ἐφίει, Westermann, Müller, Wagner, following apparently the MSS.
[2] λόχμῃ O : λόγχῃ A.
[3] παίζουσαν Staverenus, Hercher, Wagner (compare παίζουσαν in Plato, Phaedrus, p. 229 c; Pausanias, i. 29. 5;
Scholiast on Apollonius Rhodius, Argon. i. 212) : περῶσαν A,
Westermann, Bekker.

---

received from Minos, see above, ii. 7. 1. The animal's name
was Laelaps (Ovid, Metamorph. vii. 771 ; Hyginus, Fab.
189). According to Hyginus (l.c.), both the dog and the
dart which could never miss were bestowed on Procris by
Artemis (Diana). Sophocles wrote a tragedy Procris, of

a golden crown, Procris admitted Pteleon to her bed, and being detected by Cephalus she fled to Minos. But he fell in love with her and tried to seduce her. Now if any woman had intercourse with Minos, it was impossible for her to escape with life; for because Minos cohabited with many women, Pasiphae bewitched him, and whenever he took another woman to his bed, he discharged wild beasts at her joints, and so the women perished.[1] But Minos had a swift dog and a dart that flew straight; and in return for these gifts Procris shared his bed, having first given him the Circaean root to drink that he might not harm her. But afterwards, fearing the wife of Minos, she came to Athens and being reconciled to Cephalus she went forth with him to the chase; for she was fond of hunting. As she was in pursuit of game in the thicket, Cephalus, not knowing she was there, threw a dart, hit and killed Procris, and, being tried in the Areopagus, was condemned to perpetual banishment.[2]

While Orithyia was playing by the Ilissus river, Boreas carried her off and had intercourse with her; and she bore daughters, Cleopatra and Chione, and winged sons, Zetes and Calais. These sons sailed

which antiquity has bequeathed to us four words. See *The Fragments of Sophocles*, ed. A. C. Pearson, vol. ii. pp. 170 *sq.* The accidental killing of Procris by her husband was a familiar, indeed trite, tale in Greece (Pausanias, x. 29. 6).

[1] The danger which the women incurred, and the device by which Procris contrived to counteract it, are clearly explained by Antoninus Liberalis (*Transform.* 41). According to him, the animals which Minos discharged from his body were snakes, scorpions, and millipeds.

[2] Compare J. Tzetzes, *Chiliades*, i. 552. After the homicide of his wife, Cephalus is said to have dwelt as an exile in Thebes (Pausanias, i. 37. 6).

τὰς ἁρπυίας διώκοντες ἀπέθανον, ὡς δὲ Ἀκουσίλαος λέγει, περὶ Τῆνον ὑφ' Ἡρακλέους ἀπώλοντο.
3 Κλεοπάτραν δὲ ἔγημε Φινεύς, ᾧ γίνονται παῖδες
<ἐξ>¹ αὐτῆς Πλήξιππος καὶ Πανδίων. ἔχων δὲ
τούτους ἐκ Κλεοπάτρας παῖδας Ἰδαίαν ἐγάμει²
τὴν Δαρδάνου. κἀκείνη τῶν προγόνων πρὸς Φινέα
φθορὰν καταψεύδεται, καὶ πιστεύσας Φινεὺς
ἀμφοτέρους τυφλοῖ. παραπλέοντες δὲ οἱ Ἀργο-
ναῦται σὺν Βορέᾳ κολάζονται³ αὐτόν.
4 Χιόνη δὲ Ποσειδῶνι⁴ μίγνυται. ἡ δὲ κρύφα

----

¹ ἐξ inserted by Heyne.
² γαμεῖ Hercher.
³ κολάζουσιν Bekker (conjecture), Hercher.
⁴ Χιόνη δὲ Ποσειδῶν Hercher.

----

¹ See above, i. 9. 21; Apollonius Rhodius, *Argon.* i. 211
sqq., ii. 273 *sqq.*; Scholiast on Homer, *Od.* xiv. 533; Scholiast
on Sophocles, *Antigone*, 981; Hyginus, *Fab.* 14, pp. 42 *sq.*,
ed. Bunte; Ovid, *Metamorph.* vi. 711 *sqq.*; Servius, on
Virgil, *Aen.* iii. 209. According to Hyginus (*l.c.*), their wings
were attached to their feet, and their hair was sky-blue.
Elsewhere (*Fab.* 19) he describes them with wings on their
heads as well as on their feet. Ovid says that they were
twins, and that they did not develop wings until their beards
began to grow; according to him, the pinions sprouted from
their sides in the usual way.
² This is the version adopted by Apollonius Rhodius (*Argon.*
i. 1298–1308), who tells us that when Zetes and Calais were
returning from the funeral games of Pelias, Hercules killed
them in Tenos because they had persuaded the Argonauts to
leave him behind in Mysia; over their grave he heaped a
barrow, and on the barrow he set up two pillars, one of which
shook at every breath of the North Wind, the father of the
two dead men. The slaughter of Zetes and Calais by Hercules is mentioned by Hyginus (*Fab.* 14, p. 43, ed. Bunte).
³ See above, i. 9. 21. The story of Phineus and his sons is
related by the Scholiast on Sophocles (*Antigone*, 981), referring

with Jason[1] and met their end in chasing the Harpies; but according to Acusilaus, they were killed by Hercules in Tenos.[2] Cleopatra was married to Phineus, who had by her two sons, Plexippus and Pandion. When he had these sons by Cleopatra, he married Idaea, daughter of Dardanus. She falsely accused her stepsons to Phineus of corrupting her virtue, and Phineus, believing her, blinded them both.[3] But when the Argonauts sailed past with Boreas, they punished him.[4]

Chione had connexion with Poseidon, and having

to the present passage of Apollodorus as his authority. The tale was told by the ancients with many variations, some of which are noticed by the Scholiast on Sophocles (*l.c.*) According to Sophocles (*Antigone*, 969 *sqq.*), it was not their father Phineus, but their cruel stepmother, who blinded the two young men, using her shuttle as a dagger. The names both of the stepmother and of her stepsons are variously given by our authorities. See further Diodorus Siculus, iv. 43 *sq.*; Scholiast on Homer, *Od.* xii. 69 (who refers to Asclepiades as his authority); Scholiast on Apollonius Rhodius, *Argon.* ii. 178; Hyginus, *Fab.* 19; Servius, on Virgil, *Aen.* iii. 209; Scholiast on Ovid, *Ibis*, 265, 271; *Scriptores rerum mythicarum Latini*, ed. G. H. Bode, vol. i. pp. 9, 124 (First Vatican Mythographer, 27; Second Vatican Mythographer, 124). According to Phylarchus, Aesculapius restored the sight of the blinded youths for the sake of their mother Cleopatra, but was himself killed by Zeus with a thunderbolt for so doing. See Sextus Empiricus, *Adversus mathematicos*, i. 262, p. 658, ed. Bekker; compare Scholiast on Pindar, *Pyth.* iii. 54 (96); Scholiast on Euripides, *Alcestis*, 1. Both Aeschylus and Sophocles composed tragedies entitled *Phineus*. See *Tragicorum Graecorum Fragmenta*, ed. A. Nauck², pp. 83, 284 *sqq.*; *The Fragments of Sophocles*, ed. A. C. Pearson, vol. ii. pp. 311 *sqq.*

[4] Here Apollodorus departs from the usual tradition, followed by himself elsewhere (i. 9. 21), which affirmed that the Argonauts, instead of punishing Phineus, rendered him a great service by delivering him from the Harpies.

τοῦ πατρὸς Εὔμολπον τεκοῦσα, ἵνα μὴ γένηται
καταφανής, εἰς τὸν βυθὸν ῥίπτει τὸ παιδίον.
Ποσειδῶν δὲ ἀνελόμενος εἰς Αἰθιοπίαν κομίζει
καὶ δίδωσι Βενθεσικύμῃ τρέφειν, αὑτοῦ θυγατρὶ
καὶ Ἀμφιτρίτης. ὡς δὲ ἐτελειώθη,[1] ὁ Βενθεσι-
κύμης ἀνὴρ τὴν ἑτέραν αὐτῷ τῶν θυγατέρων
δίδωσιν. ὁ δὲ καὶ τὴν ἀδελφὴν τῆς γαμηθείσης
ἐπεχείρησε βιάζεσθαι, καὶ διὰ τοῦτο φυγαδευθεὶς
μετὰ Ἰσμάρου τοῦ παιδὸς πρὸς Τεγύριον ἧκε,
Θρᾳκῶν βασιλέα, ὃς αὑτοῦ τῷ παιδὶ τὴν θυγατέρα
συνῴκισεν.[2] ἐπιβουλεύων δὲ ὕστερον Τεγυρίῳ
καταφανὴς γίνεται, καὶ πρὸς Ἐλευσινίους φεύγει
καὶ φιλίαν ποιεῖται πρὸς αὐτούς. αὖθις δὲ Ἰσμάρου τελευτήσαντος μεταπεμφθεὶς ὑπὸ Τεγυρίου
παραγίνεται, καὶ τὴν πρὸ τοῦ μάχην διαλυσάμενος τὴν βασιλείαν παρέλαβε. καὶ πολέμου
ἐνστάντος πρὸς Ἀθηναίους τοῖς Ἐλευσινίοις,[3]
ἐπικληθεὶς ὑπὸ Ἐλευσινίων μετὰ πολλῆς συνε-

---

[1] After ἐτελειώθη some MSS. read ἔνδον or ἔνδον ἐν, which
Bekker changed into Ἔνδιος and Hercher into Ἔναλος. It
seems probable that the name of Benthesicyme's husband is
concealed under ἔνδον or ἔνδον ἐν.

[2] συνῴκισεν Rᵃ : συνῴκησεν A.

[3] τοῖς Ἐλευσινίοις Heyne, Westermann, Müller, Bekker,
Hercher, Wagner : καὶ Ἐλευσινίοις A.

---

[1] With this account of the parentage of Eumolpus, compare
Pausanias, i. 38. 2 ; Scholiast on Euripides, *Phoeniss.* 854 ;
Hyginus, *Fab.* 157. Isocrates (iv. 68) agrees with Apollodorus
in describing Eumolpus as a son of Poseidon, but does not
name his mother. On the other hand the *Parian Chronicle*
(*Marmor Parium*, lines 27 *sq.*) represents Eumolpus as a son
of Musaeus, and says that he founded the mysteries of Eleusis.
Apollodorus does not expressly attribute the institution of the

given birth to Eumolpus[1] unknown to her father, in order not to be detected, she flung the child into the deep. But Poseidon picked him up and conveyed him to Ethiopia, and gave him to Benthesicyme (a daughter of his own by Amphitrite) to bring up. When he was full grown, Benthesicyme's husband gave him one of his two daughters. But he tried to force his wife's sister, and being banished on that account, he went with his son Ismarus to Tegyrius, king of Thrace, who gave his daughter in marriage to Eumolpus's son. But being afterwards detected in a plot against Tegyrius, he fled to the Eleusinians and made friends with them. Later, on the death of Ismarus, he was sent for by Tegyrius and went, composed his old feud with him, and succeeded to the kingdom. And war having broken out between the Athenians and the Eleusinians, he was called in by the Eleusinians and fought on their side with a large

mysteries to Eumolpus, but perhaps he implies it. Compare ii. 5. 12. It seems to have been a common tradition that the mysteries of Eleusis were founded by the Thracian Eumolpus. See Plutarch, *De exilio*, 17; Lucian, *Demonax*, 34; Photius, *Lexicon*, *s.v.* Εὐμολπίδαι. But some people held that the Eumolpus who founded the mysteries was a different person from the Thracian Eumolpus; his mother, according to them, was Deiope, daughter of Triptolemus. Some of the ancients supposed that there were as many as three different legendary personages of the name of Eumolpus, and that the one who instituted the Eleusinian mysteries was descended in the fifth generation from the first Eumolpus. See Scholiast on Sophocles, *Oedipus Colon.* 1053; Photius, *Lexicon*, *s.v.* Εὐμολπίδαι. The story which Apollodorus here tells of the casting of Eumolpus into the sea, his rescue by Poseidon, and his upbringing in Ethiopia, appears not to be noticed by any other ancient writer.

μαχει Θρακῶν δυνάμεως. Ἐρεχθεῖ δὲ ὑπὲρ[1]
Ἀθηναίων νίκης χρωμένῳ ἔχρησεν ὁ θεὸς κατορ-
θώσειν τὸν πόλεμον, ἐὰν μίαν τῶν θυγατέρων
σφάξῃ. καὶ σφάξαντος αὐτοῦ τὴν νεωτάτην καὶ
αἱ λοιπαὶ ἑαυτὰς κατέσφαξαν· ἐπεποίηντο γάρ,
ὡς ἔφασάν τινες, συνωμοσίαν ἀλλήλαις συναπο-
λέσθαι. γενομένης δὲ μετὰ <τὴν>[2] σφαγὴν τῆς
5 μάχης Ἐρεχθεὺς μὲν ἀνεῖλεν Εὔμολπον, Ποσειδῶνος δὲ καὶ τὸν Ἐρεχθέα καὶ τὴν οἰκίαν αὐτοῦ κατα-
λύσαντος, Κέκροψ ὁ πρεσβύτατος τῶν Ἐρεχθέως
παίδων ἐβασίλευσεν, ὃς γήμας Μητιάδουσαν τὴν
Εὐπαλάμου παῖδα ἐτέκνωσε Πανδίονα. οὗτος
μετὰ Κέκροπα[3] βασιλεύων ὑπὸ τῶν Μητίονος

---

[1] ὑπὲρ A : περὶ Hercher.
[2] τὴν inserted by Bekker.
[3] Κέκροπα Heyne : κέκροπος A.

---

[1] As to the war between the Athenians and the Eleusinians,
see Pausanias, i. 5. 2, i. 27. 4, i. 31. 3, i. 36. 4, i. 38. 3, ii. 14.
2, vii. 1. 5, ix. 9. 1; Alcidamas, *Odyss.* 23, p. 182, ed. Blass;
Scholiast on Euripides, *Phoeniss.* 854; Aristides, *Or.* xiii.
vol. i. pp. 190 *sq.*, ed. Dindorf. Pausanias differs from
Apollodorus and our other authorities in saying that in the
battle it was not Eumolpus, but his son Ismarus or, as
Pausanias calls him, Immaradus who fell by the hand of
Erechtheus (i. 5. 2, i. 27. 4). According to Pausanias (i. 38.
3), Erechtheus was himself slain in the battle, but Eumolpus
survived it and was allowed to remain in Eleusis (ii. 14. 2).
Further, Pausanias relates that in the war with Eleusis the
Athenians offered the supreme command of their forces to the
exiled Ion, and that he accepted it (i. 31. 3, ii. 14. 2, vii. 1. 5);
and with this account Strabo (viii. 7. 1, p. 383) substantially
agrees. The war waged by Eumolpus on Athens is mentioned
by Plato (*Menexenus*, p. 239 B), Isocrates (iv. 68, xii. 193),
Demosthenes (lx. 8. p. 1391), and Plutarch (*Parallela*, 31).
According to Isocrates, Eumolpus claimed the kingdom of
Athens against Erechtheus on the ground that his father
Poseidon had gained possession of the country before Athena.

force of Thracians.[1] When Erechtheus inquired of
the oracle how the Athenians might be victorious,
the god answered that they would win the war if he
would slaughter one of his daughters; and when he
slaughtered his youngest, the others also slaughtered
themselves; for, as some said, they had taken an oath
among themselves to perish together.[2] In the battle
which took place after the slaughter, Erechtheus killed
Eumolpus. But Poseidon having destroyed Erechtheus [3] and his house, Cecrops, the eldest of the sons
of Erechtheus, succeeded to the throne.[4] He married
Metiadusa, daughter of Eupalamus, and begat Pandion. This Pandion, reigning after Cecrops, was

[2] Compare Lycurgus, *Contra Leocratem*, 98 *sq.*, ed. C.
Scheibe; Plutarch, *Parallela*, 20; Suidas, *s.v.* παρθένοι;
Apostolius, *Cent.* xiv. 7; Aristides, *Or.* xiii. vol. i. p. 191,
ed. Dindorf; Cicero, *Pro Sestio*, xxi. 48; *id. Tusculan.
Disput.* i. 48. 116; *id. De natura deorum*, iii. 19. 50; *id. De
finibus*, v. 22. 62; Hyginus, *Fab.* 46. According to Suidas
and Apostolius, out of the six daughters of Erechtheus only
the two eldest, Protogonia and Pandora, offered themselves
for the sacrifice. According to Euripides (*Ion*, 277-280), the
youngest of the sisters, Creusa, was spared because she was
an infant in arms. Aristides speaks of the sacrifice of one
daughter only. Cicero says (*De natura deorum*, iii. 19. 50)
that on account of this sacrifice Erechtheus and his daughters
were reckoned among the gods at Athens. "Sober," that is,
wineless, sacrifices were offered after their death to the
daughters of Erechtheus. See Scholiast on Sophocles,
Oedipus Coloneus, 100. The heroic sacrifice of the maidens
was celebrated by Euripides in his tragedy *Erechtheus*, from
which a long passage is quoted by Lycurgus (*op. cit.* 100).
See *Tragicorum Graecorum Fragmenta*, ed. A. Nauck², pp.
464 *sqq.*
[3] According to Hyginus (*Fab.* 46), Zeus killed Erechtheus
with a thunderbolt at the request of Poseidon, who was
enraged at the Athenians for killing his son Eumolpus.
[4] Compare Pausanias, i. 5. 3, vii. 1. 2.

υἱῶν κατὰ στάσιν ἐξεβλήθη, καὶ παραγενόμενος
εἰς Μέγαρα πρὸς Πύλαν τὴν ἐκείνου θυγατέρα
Πυλίαν[1] γαμεῖ. αὖθις <δὲ>[2] καὶ τῆς πόλεως
βασιλεὺς[3] καθίσταται· κτείνας γὰρ Πύλας τὸν
τοῦ πατρὸς ἀδελφὸν Βίαντα τὴν βασιλείαν δίδωσι
Πανδίονι, αὐτὸς δὲ εἰς Πελοπόννησον σὺν λαῷ
παραγενόμενος κτίζει πόλιν Πύλον.

Πανδίονι δὲ ἐν Μεγάροις ὄντι παῖδες ἐγένοντο
Αἰγεὺς Πάλλας Νῖσος Λύκος. ἔνιοι δὲ Αἰγέα
Σκυρίου εἶναι λέγουσιν, ὑποβληθῆναι δὲ ὑπὸ
6 Πανδίονος. μετὰ δὲ τὴν Πανδίονος τελευτὴν οἱ
παῖδες αὐτοῦ στρατεύσαντες ἐπ' Ἀθήνας ἐξέ-
βαλον τοὺς Μητιονίδας καὶ τὴν ἀρχὴν τετραχῇ
διεῖλον· εἶχε δὲ τὸ πᾶν κράτος Αἰγεύς. γαμεῖ δὲ
πρώτην[4] μὲν Μήταν τὴν Ὁπλῆτος, δευτέραν δὲ
Χαλκιόπην τὴν Ῥηξήνορος. ὡς δὲ οὐκ ἐγένετο
παῖς αὐτῷ, δεδοικὼς τοὺς ἀδελφοὺς εἰς Πυθίαν[5]

---

[1] Πυλίαν Faber, Bekker, Hercher, Wagner, preferred by
Heyne : πελίαν A, Westermann, Müller.
[2] δὲ conjectured by Heyne, accepted by Westermann,
Hercher, and Wagner.
[3] βασιλεὺς. The MSS. (A) add ὑπ' αὐτῆς, which is kept by
Westermann, Bekker, and Wagner, but altered into ὑπ'
αὐτοῦ by Müller. I have followed Hercher in omitting the
words as a gloss, which was the course preferred by Heyne.
[4] πρώτην Hercher, Wagner : πρῶτον AS.
[5] Πυθίαν a rare, if not unexampled, form of the old name
for Delphi. The usual form is Πυθώ, which is used by Apollodorus elsewhere (i. 4. 1) and should perhaps be restored
here.

---

[1] Compare Pausanias, i. 5. 3, who tells us that the tomb
of Pandion was in the land of Megara, on a bluff called the
bluff of Diver-bird Athena.

expelled by the sons of Metion in a sedition, and going to Pylas at Megara married his daughter Pylia.[1] And at a later time he was even appointed king of the city; for Pylas slew his father's brother Bias and gave the kingdom to Pandion, while he himself repaired to Peloponnese with a body of people and founded the city of Pylus.[2]

While Pandion was at Megara, he had sons born to him, to wit, Aegeus, Pallas, Nisus, and Lycus. But some say that Aegeus was a son of Scyrius, but was passed off by Pandion as his own.[3] After the death of Pandion his sons marched against Athens, expelled the Metionids, and divided the government in four; but Aegeus had the whole power.[4] The first wife whom he married was Meta, daughter of Hoples, and the second was Chalciope, daughter of Rhexenor.[5] As no child was born to him, he feared his brothers, and went to Pythia and consulted the

---

[2] Compare Pausanias, i. 39. 4, iv. 36. 1, vi. 22. 5, who variously names this Megarian king Pylas, Pylus, and Pylon.

[3] Compare Tzetzes, *Schol. on Lycophron*, 494, who may have copied Apollodorus. The sons of Pallas, the brother of Aegeus, alleged that Aegeus was not of the stock of the Erechtheids, since he was only an adopted son of Pandion. See Plutarch, *Theseus*, 13.

[4] Compare Pausanias i. 5. 4, i. 39. 4, according to whom Aegeus, as the eldest of the sons of Pandion, obtained the sovereignty of Attica, while his brother Nisus, relinquishing his claim to his elder brother, was invested with the kingdom of Megara. As to the fourfold partition of Attica among the sons of Pandion, about which the ancients were not agreed, see Strabo, ix. i. 6, p. 392; Scholiast on Aristophanes, *Lysistrata*, 58, and on *Wasps*, 1223.

[5] Compare Tzetzes, *Schol. on Lycophron*, 494, who may have copied Apollodorus.

ἦλθε καὶ περὶ παίδων γονῆς ἐμαντεύετο. ὁ δὲ
θεὸς ἔχρησεν αὐτῷ·

ἀσκοῦ τὸν προύχοντα ποδάονα,[1] φέρτατε λαῶν,
μὴ λύσῃς, πρὶν ἐς ἄκρον Ἀθηναίων ἀφίκηαι.

ἀπορῶν δὲ τὸν χρησμὸν ἀνῄει πάλιν εἰς Ἀθήνας.
7 καὶ Τροιζῆνα διοδεύων ἐπιξενοῦται Πιτθεῖ τῷ
Πέλοπος, ὃς τὸν χρησμὸν συνείς, μεθύσας αὐτὸν
τῇ θυγατρὶ συγκατέκλινεν Αἴθρᾳ. τῇ δὲ αὐτῇ
νυκτὶ καὶ Ποσειδῶν ἐπλησίασεν αὐτῇ. Αἰγεὺς
δὲ ἐντειλάμενος Αἴθρᾳ, ἐὰν ἄρρενα γεννήσῃ, τρέφειν, τίνος ἐστὶ μὴ λέγουσαν,[2] ἀπέλιπεν ὑπό τινα
πέτραν[3] μάχαιραν καὶ πέδιλα, εἰπών, ὅταν ὁ
παῖς δύνηται τὴν πέτραν ἀποκυλίσας ἀνελέσθαι
ταῦτα, τότε μετ᾽ αὐτῶν αὐτὸν ἀποπέμπειν.

Αὐτὸς δὲ ἧκεν εἰς Ἀθήνας, καὶ τὸν τῶν Παναθηναίων ἀγῶνα ἐπετέλει, ἐν ᾧ ὁ Μίνωος παῖς
Ἀνδρόγεως ἐνίκησε πάντας. τοῦτον Αἰγεὺς[4] ἐπὶ
τὸν Μαραθώνιον ἔπεμψε ταῦρον, ὑφ᾽ οὗ διεφθάρη.
ἔνιοι δὲ αὐτὸν λέγουσι πορευόμενον εἰς Θήβας[5]

---

[1] ποδάονα ES, Scholiast on Euripides, *Medea*, 679, Tzetzes,
Schol. on Lycophron, 494 (where, however, the MSS. seem
to vary), Heyne, Wagner: πόδα μέγα A, Plutarch, *Theseus*, 3,
Westermann, Müller, Bekker, Hercher. The form ποδάων
seems to be known only in these passages: elsewhere the
word occurs in the form ποδεών.

[2] τίνος ἐστὶ μὴ λέγουσαν ES : καὶ τίνος ἔσται μὴ λέγειν A.

[3] τινα πέτραν ESA, Westermann, Wagner: τινι πέτρᾳ
Heyne, Müller, Bekker, Hercher.

[4] Αἰγεὺς ES : ὁ ζεὺς A.

[5] Θήβας Meursius (compare Diodorus Siculus, iv, 60. 5;
Scholiast on Plato, *Minos*, p. 321 A) : ἀθήνας A.

---

[1] As to the oracle, the begetting of Theseus, and the
tokens of his human paternity, see Plutarch, *Theseus*, 3 and

oracle concerning the begetting of children. The
god answered him :—

"The bulging mouth of the wineskin, O best of men,
    Loose not until thou hast reached the height of
    Athens." [1]

Not knowing what to make of the oracle, he set
out on his return to Athens. And journeying by
way of Troezen, he lodged with Pittheus, son of
Pelops, who, understanding the oracle, made him
drunk and caused him to lie with his daughter Aethra.
But in the same night Poseidon also had connexion
with her. Now Aegeus charged Aethra that, if she
gave birth to a male child, she should rear it, without
telling whose it was ; and he left a sword and sandals
under a certain rock, saying that when the boy could
roll away the rock and take them up, she was then
to send him away with them.

But he himself came to Athens and celebrated
the games of the Panathenian festival, in which Androgeus, son of Minos, vanquished all comers. Him
Aegeus sent against the bull of Marathon, by which
he was destroyed. But some say that as he journeyed

6 ; Tzetzes, *Schol. on Lycophron*, 494 ; Hyginus, *Fab.* 37.
As to the tokens, compare Diodorus Siculus, iv. 59. 1 and 6 ;
Pausanias, i. 27. 8, ii. 32. 7. Theseus is said to have claimed
to be a son of Poseidon, because the god had consorted with
his mother ; and in proof of his marine descent he dived into
the sea and brought up a golden crown, the gift of Amphitrite, together with a golden ring which Minos had thrown
into the sea in order to test his claim to be a son of the sea-
god. See Bacchylides, xvi. (xvii.) 33 *sqq.* ; Pausanias, i.
17. 3 ; Hyginus, *Astronom.* ii. 5. The picturesque story was
painted by Micon in the sanctuary of Theseus at Athens
(Pausanias, *l.c.*), and is illustrated by some Greek vase-
paintings. See my commentary on Pausanias, vol. ii. pp.
157 *sq.*

ἐπὶ τὸν Λαΐου ἀγῶνα πρὸς τῶν ἀγωνιστῶν ἐνε-
δρευθέντα διὰ φθόνον ἀπολέσθαι. Μίνως δέ,
ἀγγελθέντος αὐτῷ τοῦ θανάτου,[1] θύων ἐν Πάρῳ
ταῖς χάρισι, τὸν μὲν στέφανον ἀπὸ τῆς κεφαλῆς
ἔρριψε καὶ τὸν αὐλὸν κατέσχε, τὴν δὲ θυσίαν
οὐδὲν ἧττον ἐπετέλεσεν· ὅθεν ἔτι καὶ δεῦρο χωρὶς
αὐλῶν καὶ στεφάνων ἐν Πάρῳ θύουσι ταῖς χάρισι.
8 μετ' οὐ πολὺ δὲ θαλασσοκρατῶν ἐπολέμησε
στόλῳ τὰς Ἀθήνας, καὶ Μέγαρα εἷλε Νίσου
βασιλεύοντος τοῦ Πανδίονος, καὶ Μεγαρέα τὸν
Ἱππομένους ἐξ Ὀγχηστοῦ Νίσῳ βοηθὸν ἐλθόντα
ἀπέκτεινεν. ἀπέθανε δὲ καὶ Νῖσος διὰ θυγατρὸς
προδοσίαν. ἔχοντι γὰρ αὐτῷ πορφυρέαν ἐν μέσῃ
τῇ κεφαλῇ τρίχα ταύτης ἀφαιρεθείσης ἦν χρησμὸς τελευτῆσαι·[2] ἡ δὲ θυγάτηρ αὐτοῦ Σκύλλα
ἐρασθεῖσα Μίνως ἐξεῖλε τὴν τρίχα. Μίνως[3] δὲ
Μεγάρων κρατήσας καὶ τὴν κόρην τῆς πρύμνης
τῶν ποδῶν ἐκδήσας ὑποβρύχιον ἐποίησε.

[1] ἀγγελθέντος αὐτῷ τοῦ θανάτου Wyttenbach (on Plutarch, *Praecepta sanit. tuend.*, 132 ᴇ, vol. ii., p. 154, Leipsic, 1821), Westermann, Bekker, Hercher, Wagner : ἐπαγγελθέντος αὐτῷ τοῦ θανάτου Heyne ; ἐπελθόντος αὐτοῦ θανάτου A, Müller.

[2] ἦν χρησμὸς τελευτῆσαι E : τελευτᾷ A (omitting ἦν χρησμὸς). [3] Μίνως E : μόνον A.

---

[1] This account of the murder of Androgeus is repeated almost verbally by the Scholiast on Plato, *Minos*, p. 321 ᴀ. Compare Diodorus Siculus, iv. 60. 4 *sq.* ; Zenobius, *Cent.* iv. 6 ; Scholiast on Homer, *Il.* xviii. 590. All these writers mention the distinction won by Androgeus in the athletic contests of the Panathenian festival as the ultimate ground of his undoing. Servius (on Virgil, *Aen.* vi. 14) and Lactantius Placidus (on Statius, *Achill.* 192) say that, as an eminent athlete who beat all competitors in the games, Androgeus was murdered at Athens by Athenian and Megarian conspirators. Pausanias (i. 27. 10) mentions the killing of Andro-

to Thebes to take part in the games in honour of
Laius, he was waylaid and murdered by the jealous
competitors.[1] But when the tidings of his death were
brought to Minos, as he was sacrificing to the Graces
in Paros, he threw away the garland from his head
and stopped the music of the flute, but nevertheless
completed the sacrifice; hence down to this day they
sacrifice to the Graces in Paros without flutes and
garlands. But not long afterwards, being master of
the sea, he attacked Athens with a fleet and captured
Megara, then ruled by king Nisus, son of Pandion,
and he slew Megareus, son of Hippomenes, who had
come from Onchestus to the help of Nisus.[2] Now
Nisus perished through his daughter's treachery.
For he had a purple hair on the middle of his head,
and an oracle ran that when it was pulled out he
should die; and his daughter Scylla fell in love with
Minos and pulled out the hair. But when Minos had
made himself master of Megara, he tied the damsel
by the feet to the stern of the ship and drowned her.[3]

geus by the Marathonian bull. According to Hyginus (*Fab.*
41), Androgeus was killed in battle during the war which his
father Minos waged with the Athenians.

[2] Compare Pausanias, i. 39. 5, who calls Megareus a son of
Poseidon, and says that Megara took its name from him.

[3] With this story of the death of Nisus through the
treachery of his daughter Scylla, compare Aeschylus,
Choephor. 612 *sqq.*; Pausanias, i. 19. 5, ii. 34. 7; Tzetzes,
Schol. on Lycophron, 650; Scholiast on Euripides, *Hippo-
lytus,* 1200; Propertius, iv. 19 (18) 21 *sqq.*; [Virgil,] *Ciris,*
378 *sqq.*; Hyginus, *Fab.* 198; Ovid, *Metamorph.* viii. 6 *sqq.*;
Servius, on Virgil, *Ecl.* vi. 74; Lactantius Placidus, on
Statius, *Theb.* i. 333, vii. 261; *Scriptores rerum mythicarum
Latini,* ed. G. H. Bode, vol. i. pp. 2, 116 (First Vatican
Mythographer, 3; Second Vatican Mythographer, 121). A
similar tale is told of Pterelaus and his daughter Comaetho.
See above, ii. 4. 5, ii. 4. 7.

Χρονιζομένου δὲ τοῦ πολέμου, μὴ δυνάμενος
ἑλεῖν Ἀθήνας εὔχεται Διὶ παρ᾽ Ἀθηναίων λαβεῖν
δίκας. γενομένου δὲ τῇ πόλει λιμοῦ τε καὶ λοιμοῦ.
τὸ μὲν πρῶτον κατὰ λόγιον Ἀθηναῖοι παλαιὸν
τὰς Ὑακίνθου κόρας, Ἀνθηίδα Αἰγληίδα Λυταίαν
Ὀρθαίαν, ἐπὶ τὸν Γεραίστου τοῦ Κύκλωπος τάφον
κατέσφαξαν· τούτων δὲ ὁ πατὴρ Ὑάκινθος ἐλθὼν
ἐκ Λακεδαίμονος Ἀθήνας κατῴκει. ὡς δὲ οὐδὲν
ὄφελος ἦν τοῦτο, ἐχρῶντο περὶ ἀπαλλαγῆς. ὁ
δὲ θεὸς ἀνεῖλεν [1] αὐτοῖς Μίνωι διδόναι δίκας ἃς
ἂν αὐτὸς αἱροῖτο.[2] πέμψαντες οὖν πρὸς Μίνωα
ἐπέτρεπον αἰτεῖν δίκας. Μίνως δὲ ἐκέλευσεν
αὐτοῖς κόρους [3] ἑπτὰ καὶ κόρας τὰς ἴσας χωρὶς
ὅπλων πέμπειν τῷ Μινωταύρῳ βοράν. ἦν δὲ

---

[1] ἀνεῖλεν Faber, Hercher, Wagner: ἀνεῖπεν Scholiast on
Plato, *Minos*, p. 321 A, Heyne, Westermann, Müller, Bekker:
ἀπεῖπεν A.

[2] αἱροῖτο E, Wagner: αἱρεῖται A, Heyne, Müller: αἱρῆται
Scholiast on Plato, *Minos*, p. 321 A, Westermann, Bekker,
Hercher.

[3] κόρους E, Scholiast on Plato, *Minos*, p. 321 A: κούρους A.

---

[1] Compare Diodorus Siculus, xvii. 15. 2; Hyginus, *Fab.*
238 (who seems to mention only one daughter; but the passage
is corrupt); Harpocration, *s.v.* Ὑακινθίδες, who says that the
daughters of Hyacinth the Lacedaemonian were known as the
Hyacinthides. The name of one of the daughters of Hyacinth
is said to have been Lusia (Stephanus Byzantius, *s.v.* Λουσία).
Some people, however, identified the Hyacinthides with the
daughters of Erechtheus, who were similarly sacrificed for
their country (above, iii. 15. 4). See Demosthenes, lx. 27, p.
1397; Suidas, *s.v.* παρθένοι. According to Phanodemus in the
fifth book of his *Atthis* (cited by Suidas, *l.c.*), the daughters
of Erechtheus were called Hyacinthides because they were
sacrificed at the hill named Hyacinth. Similarly, as Heyne
pointed out in his note on the present passage, the three
daughters of Leos, namely, Praxithea, Theope, and Eubule,

When the war lingered on and he could not take Athens, he prayed to Zeus that he might be avenged on the Athenians. And the city being visited with a famine and a pestilence, the Athenians at first, in obedience to an ancient oracle, slaughtered the daughters of Hyacinth, to wit, Antheis, Aegleis, Lytaea, and Orthaea, on the grave of Geraestus, the Cyclops; now Hyacinth, the father of the damsels, had come from Lacedaemon and dwelt in Athens.[1] But when this was of no avail, they inquired of the oracle how they could be delivered; and the god answered them that they should give Minos whatever satisfaction he might choose. So they sent to Minos and left it to him to claim satisfaction. And Minos ordered them to send seven youths and the same number of damsels without weapons to be fodder for the Minotaur.[2] Now the Minotaur was confined

are said to have sacrificed themselves voluntarily, or to have been freely sacrificed by their father, for the safety of Athens in obedience to an oracle. A precinct called the Leocorium was dedicated to their worship at Athens. See Aelian, *Var. Hist.* xii. 28; Demosthenes, lx. 28, p. 1398; Pausanias, i. 5. 2, with my note (vol. ii. p. 78); Apostolius, *Cent.* x. 53; Aristides, *Or.* xiii. vol. i. pp. 191 *sq.*, ed. Dindorf; Cicero, *De natura deorum*, iii. 19. 50. So, too, in Boeotia the two maiden daughters of Orion are said to have sacrificed themselves freely to deliver their country from a fatal pestilence or dearth, which according to an oracle of the Gortynian Apollo could be remedied only by the voluntary sacrifice of two virgins. See Antoninus Liberalis, *Transform.* 25; Ovid, *Metamorph.* xiii. 685–699. The frequency of such legends, among which the traditional sacrifice of Iphigenia at Aulis may be included, suggests that formerly the Greeks used actually to sacrifice maidens in great emergencies, such as plagues and prolonged droughts, when ordinary sacrifices had proved ineffectual.

[2] Compare Diodorus Siculus, iv. 61. 1–4; Plutarch, *Theseus*, 15; Pausanias, i. 27. 10; Scholiast on Plato, *Minos*, p. 321 A; Virgil, *Aen.* vi. 20 *sqq.*; Servius on Virgil, *Aen.* vi. 14; Hyginus, *Fab.* 41; Lactantius Placidus, on Statius, *Achill.* 192.

APOLLODORUS

οὗτος ἐν λαβυρίνθῳ καθειργμένος, ἐν ᾧ τὸν εἰσελ-
θόντα ἀδύνατον ἦν ἐξιέναι· πολυπλόκοις γὰρ
καμπαῖς τὴν ἀγνοουμένην ἔξοδον ἀπέκλειε. κατε-
σκευάκει δὲ αὐτὸν Δαίδαλος ὁ Εὐπαλάμου παῖς
τοῦ Μητίονος καὶ Ἀλκίππης. ἦν γὰρ[1] ἀρχι-
τέκτων ἄριστος καὶ πρῶτος ἀγαλμάτων εὑρετής.
οὗτος ἐξ Ἀθηνῶν ἔφυγεν, ἀπὸ τῆς ἀκροπόλεως
βαλὼν τὸν τῆς ἀδελφῆς [Πέρδικος][2] υἱὸν Τάλω,[3]
μαθητὴν ὄντα, δείσας μὴ διὰ τὴν εὐφυΐαν αὐτὸν
ὑπερβάλῃ· σιαγόνα γὰρ ὄφεως εὑρὼν ξύλον λεπ-

---

[1] ἦν γὰρ E : οὗτος ἦν SA.
[2] πέρδικος A : περδίκας E, Tzetzes, Chiliades, i. 493.
[3] Τάλω Diodorus Siculus, iv. 76. 4 : ἀτάλω AS (Rheinisches
Museum, xlvi. 1891, p. 618) : ἀττάλω Tzetzes, Chiliades, i.
493 : ἀτάλην E.

---

[1] As to the Minotaur and the Labyrinth, see above, iii. 1. 4.
[2] Compare J. Tzetzes, Chiliades, i. 490, and the Scholiast
on Plato, Ion, p. 121 A, both of whom name the father and
mother of Daedalus in agreement with Apollodorus. The
father of Daedalus is called Eupalamus also by Suidas (s.v.
Πέρδικος ἱερόν), the Scholiast on Plato (Republic, vii. p. 529
D), Hyginus (Fab. 39, 244, and 274), and Servius (on Virgil,
vi. 14). He is called Palamaon by Pausanias (ix. 3. 2), and
Metion, son of Eupalamus, son of Erechtheus, by Diodorus
Siculus (iv. 76. 1). Our oldest authority for the parentage of
Daedalus is Pherecydes, who says that the father of Daedalus
was Metion, son of Erechtheus, and that his mother was
Iphinoe (Scholiast on Sophocles, Oedipus Coloneus, 472) ; and
this tradition as to the father of Daedalus is supported by
Plato (Ion, 4, p. 533 A). According to Clidemus, cited by
Plutarch (Theseus, 19), Daedalus was a cousin of Theseus, his
mother being Merope, daughter of Erechtheus. On the whole,
tradition is in harmony with the statement of Pausanias (vii.
4. 5) " that Daedalus came of the royal house of Athens, the
Metionids." Compare J. Töpffer, Attische Genealogie, pp.
165 sqq. Through the clouds of fable which gathered round

in a labyrinth, in which he who entered could not find his way out; for many a winding turn shut off the secret outward way.[1] The labyrinth was constructed by Daedalus, whose father was Eupalamus, son of Metion, and whose mother was Alcippe;[2] for he was an excellent architect and the first inventor of images. He had fled from Athens, because he had thrown down from the acropolis Talos, the son of his sister Perdix;[3] for Talos was his pupil, and Daedalus feared that with his talents he might surpass himself, seeing that he had sawed a thin stick

his life and adventures we may dimly discern the figure of a vagabond artist as versatile as Leonardo da Vinci and as unscrupulous as Benvenuto Cellini.

[3] As to Daedalus's murder of his nephew, his trial, and flight, compare Diodorus Siculus, iv. 76. 4–7; Pausanias, i. 21. 4, i. 26. 4, vii. 4. 5; J. Tzetzes, *Chiliades*, i. 490 *sqq.*; Suidas and Photius, *Lexicon*, *s.v.* Πέρδικος ἱερόν; Apostolius, *Cent.* xiv. 17; Scholiast on Euripides, *Orestes*, 1648; Ovid, *Metamorph.* viii. 236–259; Hyginus, *Fab.* 39 and 244; Servius, on Virgil, *Georg.* i. 143 and on *Aen.* vi. 14; Isidore, *Orig.* xix. 19. 9. The name of the murdered nephew is commonly given as Talos, but according to Pausanias and Suidas (*ll.cc.*) it was Calos. On the other hand Sophocles, in his lost play *The Camicians* (cited by Suidas and Photius, *ll.cc.*) called him Perdix, that is, Partridge; and this name is accepted by Ovid, Hyginus, Servius, and Isidore. But according to a different tradition, here followed by Apollodorus, Perdix ("Partridge") was the name, not of the murdered nephew, but of his mother, the sister of Daedalus, who hanged herself in grief at the death of her son; the Athenians worshipped her and dedicated a sanctuary to her beside the acropolis (so Apostolius, Suidas, and Photius, *ll.cc.*). The grave of Talos or Calos was shown near the theatre, at the foot of the acropolis, probably on the spot where he was supposed to have fallen from the battlements (Pausanias, i. 21. 4). The trial of Daedalus before the Areopagus is mentioned by Diodorus Siculus and the Scholiast on Euripides (*ll.cc.*).

τὸν ἔπρισε. φωραθέντος δὲ τοῦ νεκροῦ κριθεὶς
ἐν Ἀρείῳ πάγῳ καὶ καταδικασθεὶς πρὸς Μίνωα
ἔφυγε. [κἀκεῖ¹ Πασιφάῃ ἐρασθείσῃ² τοῦ Ποσει-
δωνείου³ ταύρου συνήργησε⁴ τεχνησάμενος ξυλί-
νην βοῦν, καὶ τὸν λαβύρινθον κατεσκεύασεν, εἰς
ὃν κατὰ ἔτος Ἀθηναῖοι κόρους⁵ ἑπτὰ καὶ κόρας
τὰς ἴσας τῷ Μινωταύρῳ βορὰν ἔπεμπον.]

XVI. Θησεὺς δὲ γεννηθεὶς ἐξ Αἴθρας Αἰγεῖ
παῖς, ὡς ἐγένετο⁶ τέλειος, ἀπωσάμενος τὴν πέτραν
τὰ πέδιλα καὶ τὴν μάχαιραν ἀναιρεῖται, καὶ πεζὸς
ἠπείγετο εἰς τὰς Ἀθήνας. φρουρουμένην⁷ δὲ ὑπὸ
ἀνδρῶν κακούργων τὴν ὁδὸν ἡμέρωσε. πρῶτον
μὲν γὰρ Περιφήτην τὸν Ἡφαίστου καὶ Ἀντικλείας, ὃς ἀπὸ τῆς κορύνης ἣν ἐφόρει κορυνήτης
ἐπεκαλεῖτο, ἔκτεινεν ἐν Ἐπιδαύρῳ. πόδας δὲ
ἀσθενεῖς⁸ ἔχων οὗτος ἐφόρει κορύνην σιδηρᾶν,⁹
δι' ἧς τοὺς παριόντας ἔκτεινε. ταύτην ἀφελό-
2 μενος Θησεὺς ἐφόρει. δεύτερον δὲ κτείνει Σίνιν

¹ The passage enclosed in square brackets (κἀκεῖ Πασιφάης
. . . βορὰν ἔπεμπον) is found in ESA, but is probably an
interpolation, as Heyne observed. It is merely a repetition
of what the author has already said (iii. i. 4, iii. 15. 8).
² Πασιφάῃ ἐρασθείσῃ E: Πασιφάης ἐρασθείσης SA, Heyne,
Müller, Westermann, Bekker, Wagner.
³ Ποσειδωνείου E: Ποσειδῶνος Heyne, Müller, Westermann,
Bekker, Wagner, following apparently the other MSS.
⁴ συνήργησε E: συνήρτησε S: συνήρπασε A.
⁵ κόρους ES: κούρους A.   ⁶ ἐγένετο E: ἐγεννήθη SA.
⁷ φρουρουμένην . . . τὴν ὁδὸν E: φρουρουμένης . . . τῆς ὁδοῦ A.
⁸ ἀσθενεῖς A: βριαροὺς S.
⁹ σιδηρᾶν. In S there follow the words ἣν ἀπὸ τὸν Ἡφαίστου Περιφήτην ἔλαβεν.

¹ He is said to have improved the discovery by inventing
the iron saw in imitation of the teeth in a serpent's jawbone.
See Diodorus Siculus, iv. 76. 5; J. Tzetzes, *Chiliades*, i.

with a jawbone of a snake which he had found.[1]
But the corpse was discovered; Daedalus was tried in
the Areopagus, and being condemned fled to Minos.
And there Pasiphae having fallen in love with the
bull of Poseidon, Daedalus acted as her accomplice
by contriving a wooden cow, and he constructed the
labyrinth, to which the Athenians every year sent
seven youths and as many damsels to be fodder for
the Minotaur.

XVI. Aethra bore to Aegeus a son Theseus, and
when he was grown up, he pushed away the rock
and took up the sandals and the sword,[2] and hastened
on foot to Athens. And he cleared[3] the road, which
had been beset by evildoers. For first in Epidaurus
he slew Periphetes, son of Hephaestus and Anticlia,
who was surnamed the Clubman from the club which
he carried. For being crazy on his legs he carried
an iron club, with which he despatched the passers-
by. That club Theseus wrested from him and
continued to carry about.[4] Second, he killed Sinis,

---

494 *sqq.* Latin writers held that the invention was suggested
to him by the backbone of a fish. See Ovid, *Metamorph.*
viii. 244 *sqq.*; Hyginus, *Fab.* 274; Servius, on Virgil, *Aen.*
vi. 14; Isidore, *Orig.*, xix. 19. 9. According to these Latin
writers, the ingenious artist invented the compass also. As
to Talos or Perdix and his mechanical inventions, see A. B.
Cook, *Zeus*, i. 724 *sqq.*

[2] The tokens of paternity left by his human father Aegeus.
See above, iii. 15. 7.

[3] Literally, "tamed." As to the adventures of Theseus
on his road to Athens, see Bacchylides, xvii. (xviii.) 16 *sqq.*;
Diodorus Siculus, iv. 59; Plutarch, *Theseus*, 8 *sqq.*; Pausanias, i. 44. 8, ii. 1. 3 *sq.*; Scholiast on Lucian, *Jupiter
Tragoedus*, 21, pp. 64 *sq.*, ed. H. Rabe; Ovid, *Metamorph.*
vii. 433 *sqq.*; *id. Ibis*, 407 *sqq.*; Hyginus, *Fab.* 38.

[4] Compare Diodorus Siculus, iv. 59. 2; Plutarch, *Theseus*,
8. 1; Pausanias, ii. 1. 4; Ovid, *Metamorph.* vii. 436 *sq.*;

τὸν Πολυπήμονος καὶ Συλέας τῆς Κορίνθου. οὗτος
πιτυοκάμπτης ἐπεκαλεῖτο· οἰκῶν γὰρ τὸν Κορινθίων ἰσθμὸν ἠνάγκαζε τοὺς παριόντας πίτυς κάμ-
πτοντας ἀνέχεσθαι· οἱ δὲ διὰ τὴν ἀσθένειαν οὐκ
ἠδύναντο, ¹ καὶ ὑπὸ τῶν δένδρων ἀναρριπτούμενοι
πανωλέθρως ἀπώλλυντο. τούτῳ τῷ τρόπῳ καὶ
Θησεὺς Σίνιν ἀπέκτεινεν.

¹ ἠδύναντο. E and apparently A add κάμπτειν, which was
rightly rejected as a gloss by Heyne and omitted by Hercher. It is retained by Westermann, Bekker, and Wagner,
and bracketed by Müller.

Hyginus, *Fab.* 38. Periphetes dwelt in Epidaurus, which
Theseus had to traverse on his way from Troezen to the Isthmus of Corinth. No writer but Apollodorus mentions that
this malefactor was weak on his legs; the infirmity suggests
that he may have used his club as a crutch on which to hobble
along like a poor cripple, till he was within striking distance
of his unsuspecting victims, when he surprised them by
suddenly lunging out and felling them to the ground.
¹ Compare Bacchylides, xvii. (xviii.) 19 *sqq.*; Diodorus
Siculus, iv. 59. 3; Plutarch, *Theseus*, 8. 2; Pausanias, ii.
1. 4; Scholiast on Lucian, *Jupiter Tragoedus*, 21; Scholiast
on Pindar, *Isthm.*, *Argum.* p. 514, ed. Boeckh; Ovid,
Metamorph. vii. 440 *sqq.*; Hyginus, *Fab.* 38. Bacchylides,
the Scholiast on Pindar, and Hyginus call Sinis a son of
Poseidon (Neptune). The ancients are not agreed as to the
exact mode in which the ruffian Sinis despatched his victims.
According to Diodorus, Pausanias, and the Scholiast on
Pindar he bent two pine-trees to the ground, tied the extremities of his victim to both trees, and then let the trees go,
which, springing up and separating, tore the wretch's body
in two. This atrocious form of murder was at a later time
actually employed by the emperor Aurelian in a military exe-
cution. See Vopiscus, *Aurelian*, 7. 4. A Ruthenian pirate,
named Botho, is said to have put men to death in similar
fashion. See Saxo Grammaticus, *Historia Danica*, bk. vii.

son of Polypemon and Sylea, daughter of Corinthus. This Sinis was surnamed the Pine-bender; for inhabiting the Isthmus of Corinth he used to force the passers-by to keep bending pine-trees; but they were too weak to do so, and being tossed up by the trees they perished miserably. In that way also Theseus killed Sinis.[1]

vol. i. pp. 353 *sq.*, ed. P. E. Müller. According to Hyginus, Sinis, with the help of his victim, dragged down a pine-tree to the earth; then, when the man was struggling to keep the tree down, Sinis released it, and in the rebound the man was tossed up into the air and killed by falling heavily to the ground. Apollodorus seems to have contemplated a similar mode of death, except that he does not mention the co-operation of Sinis in bending the tree to the earth. According to the *Parian Chronicle* (*Marmor Parium*, lines 35 *sq.*) it was not on his journey from Troezen to Athens that Theseus killed Sinis, but at a later time, after he had come to the throne and united the whole of Attica under a single government; he then returned to the Isthmus of Corinth, killed Sinis, and celebrated the Isthmian games. This tradition seems to imply that Theseus held the games as a funeral honour paid to the dead man, or more probably as an expiation to appease the angry ghost of his victim. This implication is confirmed by the Scholiast on Pindar (*l.c.*), who says that according to some people Theseus held the Isthmian games in honour of Sinis, whom he had killed. Plutarch tells us (*l.c.*) that when Theseus had killed Sinis, the daughter of the dead man, by name Perigune, fled and hid herself in a bed of asparagus; that she bore a son Melanippus to Theseus, and that Melanippus had a son Ioxus, whose descendants, the Ioxids, both men and women, revered and honoured asparagus and would not burn it, because asparagus had once sheltered their ancestress. This hereditary respect shown by all the members of a family or clan for a particular species of plant is reminiscent of totemism, though it is not necessarily a proof of it.

EPITOME

APOLLODORI BIBLIOTHECA
EPITOMA

EX EPITOMA VATICANA ET FRAGMENTIS SABBAITICIS COMPOSITA[1]

E   I. Τρίτην ἔκτεινεν ἐν Κρομμυῶνι σῦν τὴν καλου-
μένην Φαιὰν ἀπὸ[2] τῆς θρεψάσης γραὸς αὐτήν·
ταύτην τινὲς Ἐχίδνης καὶ Τυφῶνος λέγουσι.
2 τέταρτον ἔκτεινε Σκείρωνα τὸν Κορίνθιον τοῦ
Πέλοπος, ὡς δὲ ἔνιοι Ποσειδῶνος. οὗτος ἐν τῇ
Μεγαρικῇ κατέχων τὰς ἀφ᾽ ἑαυτοῦ κληθείσας
πέτρας Σκειρωνίδας, ἠνάγκαζε τοὺς παριόντας
νίζειν αὐτοῦ τοὺς πόδας, καὶ νίζοντας εἰς τὸν
βυθὸν αὐτοὺς ἔρριπτε βορὰν ὑπερμεγέθει χελώνῃ.
3 Θησεὺς δὲ ἁρπάσας αὐτὸν τῶν ποδῶν ἔρριψεν
<εἰς τὴν θάλασσαν>.[3] πέμπτον ἔκτεινεν ἐν

---

[1] The passages derived from the Vatican and Sabbaitic manuscripts respectively are indicated in the margin by the letters E (= Vatican Epitome) and S (= Sabbaitic). The combination ES signifies that the passage is found in both manuscripts, though sometimes with variations, which are indicated in the Critical Notes. The point of transition from the one manuscript to the other, or from one to both, or from both to one, is marked by a vertical line in the Greek text.

[2] ἀπὸ Wagner: ὑπὸ E.

[3] εἰς τὴν θάλασσαν added by Wagner, comparing Scholiast on Euripides, *Hippolytus*, 979, ῥίψας εἰς θάλασσαν, and Pausanias, i. 44. 8, ἀφεθέντα ἐς θάλασσαν.

EPITOME OF *THE LIBRARY* OF APOLLODORUS

COMPOUNDED OF THE VATICAN EPITOME AND THE SABBAITIC FRAGMENTS

I. Third, he slew at Crommyon the sow that was called Phaea after the old woman who bred it;[1] that sow, some say, was the offspring of Echidna and Typhon. Fourth, he slew Sciron, the Corinthian, son of Pelops, or, as some say, of Poseidon. He in the Megarian territory held the rocks called after him Scironian, and compelled passers-by to wash his feet, and in the act of washing he kicked them into the deep to be the prey of a huge turtle. But Theseus seized him by the feet and threw him into the sea.[2]

---

[1] Compare Bacchylides, xvii. (xviii.) 23 *sq.*; Diodorus Siculus, iv. 59. 4 ; Plutarch, *Theseus*, 9 ; Pausanias, ii. l. 3 ; Hyginus, *Fab.* 38, who calls the animal a boar. Plutarch notices a rationalistic version of the story, which converted the sow Phaea into a female robber of that name. No ancient writer but Apollodorus mentions the old woman Phaea who nursed the sow, but she appears on vase-paintings which represent the slaughter of the sow by Theseus. See Baumeister, *Denkmäler des klassischen Altertums*, iii. pp. 1787 *sq.*, 1789, fig. 1873; Höfer, in W. H. Roscher, *Lexikon der griech. und röm. Mythologie*, ii. 1450 *sq.*

[2] Compare Bacchylides, xvii. (xviii.) 24 *sq.* ; Diodorus Siculus, iv. 59. 4 ; Plutarch, *Theseus*, 10 ; Pausanias, i. 44. 8 ; Scholiast on Euripides, *Hippolytus*, 979 ; Scholiast on Lucian, *Jupiter Tragoedus*, 21, p. 65, ed. H. Rabe ; Ovid, *Metamorph.*

Ἐλευσῖνι Κερκυόνα τὸν Βράγχου καὶ Ἀργιόπης
νύμφης. οὗτος ἠνάγκαζε τοὺς παριόντας παλαίειν
καὶ παλαίων ἀνῄρει· Θησεὺς δὲ αὐτὸν μετέωρον
4 ἀράμενος ἤρραξεν εἰς γῆν. ἔκτον ἀπέκτεινε Δαμά-
στην, ὃν ἔνιοι Πολυπήμονα λέγουσιν. οὗτος τὴν

---

vii. 443 *sqq.*; Hyginus, *Fab.* 38; Lactantius Placidus, on
Statius, *Theb.* i. 333; *Scriptores rerum mythicarum Latini*,
ed. G. H. Bode, vol. i. pp. 52, 117 (First Vatican Mythographer, 167; Second Vatican Mythographer, 127). Curiously
enough, the Second Vatican Mythographer attributes the
despatching of Sciron, not to Theseus, but to the artist Daedalus.
The Megarians, as we learn from Plutarch, indignantly
denied the defamatory reports current as to the character
and pursuits of their neighbour Sciron, whom they represented
as a most respectable man, the foe of robbers, the friend of
the virtuous, and connected by marriage with families of the
highest quality; but their efforts to whitewash the blackguard
appear to have been attended with little success. The
Scironian Rocks, to which Sciron was supposed to have given
his name, are a line of lofty cliffs rising sheer from the sea;
a narrow, crumbling ledge about half way up their face
afforded a perilous foothold, from which the adventurous
traveller looked down with horror on the foam of the
breakers far below. The dangers of the path were obviated
about the middle of the nineteenth century by the construction of a road and railway along the coast. See my note on
Pausanias, i. 44. 6 (vol. ii. pp. 546 *sqq.*).

[1] Compare Bacchylides, xvii. (xviii.) 26 *sq.*; Diodorus Siculus,
iv. 59. 5; Plutarch, *Theseus*, 11; Pausanias, i. 39. 3; Scholiast on Lucian, *Jupiter Tragoedus*, 21, p. 65, ed. H. Rabe;
Ovid, *Metamorph.* vii. 439; Hyginus, *Fab.* 38, who calls
Cercyon a son of Vulcan (Hephaestus). The place associated with the story, known as the wrestling-school of
Cercyon, was near Eleusis, on the road to Megara (Pausanias,
l.c.). The Scholiast on Lucian (*l.c.*) says that it was near
Eleutherae, but he is probably in error; for if the place were
near Eleutherae, it must have been on the road from Eleusis
to Thebes, which is not the road that Theseus would take on
his way from the Isthmus of Corinth to Athens.

Fifth, in Eleusis he slew Cercyon, son of Branchus and a nymph Argiope. This Cercyon compelled passers-by to wrestle, and in wrestling killed them. But Theseus lifted him up on high and dashed him to the ground.[1] Sixth, he slew Damastes, whom some call Polypemon.[2]

---

[2] More commonly known as Procrustes. See Bacchylides, xvii. (xviii.) 27 *sqq.*; Diodorus Siculus, iv. 59. 5; Plutarch, *Theseus*, 11; Pausanias, i. 38. 5; Scholiast on Euripides, *Hippolytus*, 977; Ovid, *Metamorph.* vii. 438; Hyginus, *Fab.* 38. Ancient authorities are not agreed as to the name of this malefactor. Apollodorus and Plutarch call him Damastes; but Apollodorus says that some people called him Polypemon, and this latter name is supported by Pausanias, who adds that he was surnamed Procrustes. Ovid in two passages (*Metam.* vii. 438, *Heroides*, ii. 69) calls him simply Procrustes, but in a third passage (*Ibis*, 407) he seems to speak of him as the son of Polypemon. The Scholiast on Euripides (*l.c.*) wrongly names him Sinis. The reference of Bacchylides to him is difficult of interpretation. Jebb translates the passage: "The mighty hammer of Polypemon has dropt from the hand of the Maimer [*Prokoptes*], who has met with a stronger than himself." Here Jebb understands *Prokoptes* to be another name for Procrustes, who received the hammer and learned the use of it from Polypemon, his predecessor, perhaps his father. But other translations and explanations have been proposed. See the note in Jebb's Appendix, pp. 490 *sq.*; W. H. Roscher, *Lexikon der griech. und röm. Mythologie*, iii. 2683, 2687 *sqq.* The hammer in question was the instrument with which Procrustes operated on the short men, beating them out till they fitted the long bed, as we learn from the Scholiast on Euripides as well as from Apollodorus; a hand-saw was probably the instrument with which he curtailed the length of the tall men. According to Apollodorus, with whom Hyginus agrees, Procrustes had two beds for the accommodation of his guests, a long one for the short men, and a short one for the long men. But according to Diodorus Siculus, with whom the Scholiast on Euripides agrees, he had only one bed for all comers, and adjusted his visitors to it with the hammer or the hand-saw according to circumstances.

οἴκησιν ἔχων παρ᾽ ὁδὸν ἐστόρεσε δύο κλίνας, μίαν μὲν μικράν, ἑτέραν δὲ μεγάλην, καὶ τοὺς παριόντας ἐπὶ ξένια[1] καλῶν τοὺς μὲν βραχεῖς ἐπὶ τῆς μεγάλης κατακλίνων σφύραις ἔτυπτεν, ἵν᾽ ἐξισωθῶσι[2] τῇ κλίνῃ,[3] τοὺς δὲ μεγάλους ἐπὶ τῆς μικρᾶς, καὶ τὰ ὑπερέχοντα τοῦ σώματος ἀπέπριζε.

Καθάρας οὖν Θησεὺς τὴν ὁδὸν ἧκεν εἰς ᾽Αθήνας.[4]

ES 5 | Μήδεια δὲ Αἰγεῖ τότε συνοικοῦσα[5] ἐπεβούλευσεν αὐτῷ, καὶ πείθει τὸν Αἰγέα φυλάττεσθαι ὡς ἐπίβουλον αὐτῷ.[6] Αἰγεὺς δὲ τὸν ἴδιον ἀγνοῶν παῖδα, δείσας[7] ἔπεμψεν ἐπὶ τὸν Μαραθώνιον ταῦρον.[8]

6 ὡς δὲ ἀνεῖλεν αὐτόν, παρὰ Μηδείας λαβὼν αὐθήμερον[9] προσήνεγκεν αὐτῷ φάρμακον. ὁ δὲ μέλλοντος αὐτῷ τοῦ ποτοῦ προσφέρεσθαι ἐδωρήσατο τῷ πατρὶ τὸ ξίφος, ὅπερ ἐπιγνοὺς Αἰγεὺς[10] τὴν κύλικα ἐξέρριψε τῶν χειρῶν αὐτοῦ. Θησεὺς δὲ

---

[1] ξένια Wagner : ξενίαν E. Compare iii. 8. 1.

[2] ἐξισωθῶσι Wagner : ἐξισωθῇ E.

[3] τῇ κλίνῃ Frazer : ταῖς κλίναις E, Wagner.

[4] καθάρας οὖν Θησεὺς τὴν ὁδὸν ἧκεν εἰς ᾽Αθήνας E. The whole opening passage, down to and inclusive of this sentence, is wanting in S, which substitutes the following : ἔκτεινε δὲ πάντας καὶ κατετροπώσατο τοὺς ἀντιπράττοντας ἥρωας καὶ πάντας τοὺς ληστρικὸν μετιόντας βίον. "And he slew all and put to flight the heroes that withstood him and all that pursued a robber life." But the verb κατατροπόομαι is late, the use of ἥρως is suspicious, and the whole sentence is probably an independent concoction of the abbreviator.

[5] συνοικοῦσα E : συνοικοῦσα ᾽Αθήναις S.

[6] αὐτῷ Frazer : αὐτοῦ ES, Wagner : αὐτόν Bücheler. For the dative, compare Plato, Symposium, p. 203 D, ἐπίβουλός ἐστι τοῖς καλοῖς.

[7] δείσας E : δείσας αὐτὸν ὡς βριαρὸν ὄντα S. The rare epic adjective βριαρὸς, "strong," seems to be rather a favourite with S, for he goes out of his way to apply it absurdly to the crazy legs of Periphetes. See Critical Note on iii. 16. 1.

He had his dwelling beside the road, and made up
two beds, one small and the other big; and offering
hospitality to the passers-by, he laid the short
men on the big bed and hammered them, to make
them fit the bed; but the tall men he laid on the
little bed and sawed off the portions of the body that
projected beyond it.

So, having cleared the road, Theseus came to
Athens. But Medea, being then wedded to Aegeus,
plotted against him [1] and persuaded Aegeus to beware
of him as a traitor. And Aegeus, not knowing his
own son, was afraid and sent him against the Marathonian bull. And when Theseus had killed it,
Aegeus presented to him a poison which he had
received the selfsame day from Medea. But just as
the draught was about to be administered to him,
he gave his father the sword, and on recognizing it
Aegeus dashed the cup from his hands.[2] And when

---

[1] That Theseus was sent against the Marathonian bull at
the instigation of Medea is affirmed also by the First Vatican
Mythographer. See *Scriptores rerum mythicarum Latini*,
ed. G. H. Bode, vol. i. p. 18, *Fab.* 48. Compare Plutarch,
Theseus, 14; Pausanias, i. 27. 10; Ovid, *Metamorph.* vii.
433 *sq.* As to Medea at Athens, see above, i. 9. 28.

[2] Compare Plutarch, *Theseus*, 12; Scholiast on Homer,
Il. xi. 741; Ovid, *Metamorph.* vii. 404-424. According to
Ovid, the poison by which Medea attempted the life of
Theseus was aconite, which she had brought with her from
Scythia. The incident seems to have been narrated by
Sophocles in his tragedy *Aegeus*. See *The Fragments of
Sophocles*, ed. A. C. Pearson, vol. i. pp. 15 *sq.*

---

[8] ἔπεμψεν ἐπὶ τὸν Μαραθώνιον ταῦρον E : ἐπὶ τὸν Μαραθώνιον
ἔπεμψε ταῦρον ἀναλωθῆναι ὑπ' αὐτοῦ S.
[9] αὐθήμερον S : αὐθημερινὸν E.
[10] ἐπιγνοὺς Αἰγεὺς E : Αἰγεὺς ἐπιγνοὺς S.

ἀναγνωρισθεὶς τῷ πατρὶ καὶ τὴν ἐπιβουλὴν μαθὼν
ἐξέβαλε τὴν Μήδειαν.

7 Καὶ εἰς τὸν τρίτον δασμὸν τῷ Μινωταύρῳ συγ-
E καταλέγεται¹ | ὡς δέ τινες λέγουσιν, ἑκὼν ἑαυτὸν
ἔδωκεν. ἐχούσης δὲ τῆς νεὼς μέλαν ἱστίον Αἰγεὺς
τῷ παιδὶ ἐνετείλατο, ἐὰν ὑποστρέφῃ ζῶν, λευκοῖς
ES 8 πετάσαι τὴν ναῦν ἱστίοις. | ὡς δὲ ἧκεν εἰς Κρήτην,²
Ἀριάδνη θυγάτηρ Μίνωος ἐρωτικῶς διατεθεῖσα
πρὸς αὐτὸν³ συμπράσσειν⁴ ἐπαγγέλλεται,⁵ ἐὰν
ὁμολογήσῃ γυναῖκα αὐτὴν ἕξειν ἀπαγαγὼν εἰς
Ἀθήνας. ὁμολογήσαντος δὲ σὺν ὅρκοις Θησέως
δεῖται Δαιδάλου μηνῦσαι τοῦ λαβυρίνθου τὴν
9 ἔξοδον. ὑποθεμένου δὲ ἐκείνου, λίνον εἰσιόντι
Θησεῖ δίδωσι· τοῦτο ἐξάψας Θησεὺς τῆς θύρας⁶
ἐφελκόμενος εἰσῄει. καταλαβὼν δὲ Μινώταυρον

¹ συγκαταλέγεται E : συγκαταλέγει βοράν S.
² ὡς δὲ ἧκεν εἰς Κρήτην E : ἐξέπλει δ᾿ εἰς Κρήτην καὶ ἧκεν S.
³ Ἀριάδνη θυγάτηρ Μίνωος ἐρωτικῶς διατεθεῖσα πρὸς αὐτὸν E :
Ἀριάδνη γοῦν ἡ Μίνωος θυγάτηρ ἐρωτικῶς τῷ Θησεῖ διατεθεῖσα S.
⁴ συμπράσσειν S : συμπεράσειν E.
⁵ ἐπαγγέλλεται E : ἐπαγγέλλεται πρὸς τὴν Μινωταύρου εἰσέ-
λευσιν λαβυρίνθου S.
⁶ Θησεὺς τῆς θύρας E : τῆς θύρας Θησεὺς S.

---

¹ Compare Plutarch, *Theseus*, 17; Eustathius, on Homer,
Od. xi. 320, p. 1688; Scholiast on Homer, *Od.* xi. 322, and on
Il. xviii. 590; Hyginus, *Fab.* 41; Lactantius Placidus, on
Statius, *Achill.* 192. The usual tradition seems to have been
that he volunteered for the dangerous service; but a Scholiast
on Homer (*Il.* xviii. 590) speaks as if the lot had fallen on
him with the other victims. According to Hellanicus, cited
by Plutarch (*l.c.*), the victims were not chosen by lot, but
Minos came to Athens and picked them for himself, and on
this particular occasion Theseus was the first on whom his
choice fell.
² As to the black and white sails, see Diodorus Siculus, :

Theseus was thus made known to his father and informed of the plot, he expelled Medea.

And he was numbered among those who were to be sent as the third tribute to the Minotaur; or, as some affirm, he offered himself voluntarily.[1] And as the ship had a black sail, Aegeus charged his son, if he returned alive, to spread white sails on the ship.[2] And when he came to Crete, Ariadne, daughter of Minos, being amorously disposed to him, offered to help him if he would agree to carry her away to Athens and have her to wife. Theseus having agreed on oath to do so, she besought Daedalus to disclose the way out of the labyrinth. And at his suggestion she gave Theseus a clue when he went in; Theseus fastened it to the door, and, drawing it after him, entered in.[3] And having found

61. 4; Plutarch, *Theseus*, 17 and 22; Pausanias, i. 22. 5; Catullus, lxiv. 215–245; Hyginus, *Fab.* 41 and 43; Servius, on Virgil, *Aen.* iii. 74. According to Simonides, quoted by Plutarch (*l.c.*), the sail that was to be the sign of safety was not white but scarlet, which, by contrast with the blue sea, would have caught the eye almost as easily as a white sail at a great distance.

[3] Compare Scholiast on Homer, *Od.* xi. 322, and on *Il.* xviii. 590; Eustathius, on Homer, *Od.* xi. 320, p. 1688; Diodorus Siculus, iv. 61. 4; Plutarch, *Theseus*, 19; Hyginus, *Fab.* 42; Servius, on Virgil, *Aen.* vi. 14, and on *Georg.* i. 222; Lactantius Placidus, on Statius, *Theb.* xii. 676; *Scriptores rerum mythicarum Latini*, ed. G. H. Bode, vol. i. pp. 16, 116 *sq.* (First Vatican Mythographer, 43; Second Vatican Mithographer, 124). The clearest description of the clue, with which the amorous Ariadne furnished Theseus, is given by the Scholiasts and Eustathius on Homer (*ll.cc.*). From them we learn that it was a ball of thread which Ariadne had begged of Daedalus for the use of her lover. He was to fasten one end of the thread to the lintel of the door on entering into the labyrinth, and holding the ball in his hand to unwind the skein while he penetrated deeper and deeper into

ἐν ἐσχάτῳ μέρει τοῦ λαβυρίνθου παίων πυγμαῖς
ἀπέκτεινεν,¹ ἐφελκόμενος δὲ τὸ λίνον πάλιν ἐξήει.
καὶ διὰ νυκτὸς μετὰ ᾿Αριάδνης καὶ τῶν παίδων
εἰς Νάξον ἀφικνεῖται. ἔνθα Διόνυσος ἐρασθεὶς
᾿Αριάδνης ἥρπασε, καὶ κομίσας εἰς Λῆμνον ἐμίγη.

S | καὶ γεννᾷ Θόαντα Στάφυλον Οἰνοπίωνα καὶ
Πεπάρηθον.²

E 10 | Λυπούμενος δὲ Θησεὺς ἐπ᾿᾿Αριάδνῃ καταπλέων
ἐπελάθετο πετάσαι τὴν ναῦν λευκοῖς ἱστίοις.
Αἰγεὺς δὲ ἀπὸ τῆς ἀκροπόλεως τὴν ναῦν ἰδὼν
ἔχουσαν μέλαν ἱστίον, Θησέα νομίσας ἀπολω-
ES 11 λέναι ῥίψας ἑαυτὸν μετήλλαξε. | Θησεὺς δὲ παρέ-

¹ ἀπέκτεινεν E : ἀπέκτεινεν αὐτόν S.
² Πεπάρηθον Bücheler : πάρηθον S.

---

the maze, till he found the Minotaur asleep in the inmost
recess ; then he was to catch the monster by the hair and
sacrifice him to Poseidon ; after which he was to retrace his
steps, gathering up the thread behind him as he went.
According to the Scholiast on the *Odyssey* (*l.c.*), the story
was told by Pherecydes, whom later authors may have
copied.
¹ That is, the boys and girls whom he had rescued from
the Minotaur.
² Compare Diodorus Siculus, iv. 61. 5 ; Plutarch, *Theseus*,
20 ; Pausanias, i. 20. 3, x. 29. 4 ; Scholiast on Apollonius
Rhodius, *Argon.* iii. 997 ; Scholiast on Theocritus, ii. 45 ;
Catullus, lxiv. 116 *sqq.* ; Ovid, *Heroides*, x. ; *id. Ars amat.*
i. 527 *sqq.* ; *id. Metamorph.* viii. 174 *sqq.* ; Hyginus, *Fab.* 43 ;
Servius, on Virgil, *Georg.* i. 222 ; *Scriptores rerum mythicarum
Latini*, ed. G. H. Bode, vol. i. pp. 116 *sq.* (Second Vatican
Mythographer, 124). Homer's account of the fate of Ariadne
is different. He says (*Od.* xi. 321–325) that when Theseus
was carrying off Ariadne from Crete to Athens she was
slain by Artemis in the island of Dia at the instigation of
Dionysus. Later writers, such as Diodorus Siculus, identified
Dia with Naxos, but it is rather "the little island, now

the Minotaur in the last part of the labyrinth, he
killed him by smiting him with his fists; and drawing
the clue after him made his way out again. And by
night he arrived with Ariadne and the children [1] at
Naxos. There Dionysus fell in love with Ariadne
and carried her off; [2] and having brought her to
Lemnos he enjoyed her, and begat Thoas, Staphylus,
Oenopion, and Peparethus. [3]

In his grief on account of Ariadne, Theseus forgot
to spread white sails on his ship when he stood for
port; and Aegeus, seeing from the acropolis the ship
with a black sail, supposed that Theseus had perished;
so he cast himself down and died. [4] But Theseus

Standia, just off Heraclaion, on the north coast of Crete.
Theseus would pass the island in sailing for Athens" (W. W.
Merry on Homer, *Od.* xi. 322). Apollodorus seems to be the
only extant ancient author who mentions that Dionysus
carried off Ariadne from Naxos to Lemnos and had intercourse with her there.

[3] Compare Scholiast on Apollonius Rhodius, *Argon.* iii.
997. Others said that Ariadne bore Staphylus and Oenopion
to Theseus (Plutarch, *Theseus,* 20).

[4] Compare Diodorus Siculus, iv. 61. 6 *sq.* ; Plutarch, *Theseus,* 22 ; Pausanias, i. 22. 5 ; Hyginus, *Fab.* 43 ; Servius, on
Virgil, *Aen.* iii. 74 ; *Scriptores rerum mythicarum Latini,*
ed. G. H. Bode, vol. i. p. 117 (Second Vatican Mythographer,
125). The three Latin writers say that Aegeus threw himself
into the sea, which was hence called the Aegean after him.
The Greek writers say that he cast himself down from the
rock of the acropolis. Pausanius describes the exact point
from which he fell, to wit the lofty bastion at the western
end of the acropolis, on which in after ages the elegant little
temple of Wingless Victory stood and still stands. It com-
mands a wonderful view over the ports of Athens and away
across the sea to Aegina and the coast of Peloponnese, looming
clear and blue through the diaphanous Attic air in the far
distance. A better look-out the old man could not have
chosen from which to watch, with straining eyes, for the
white or scarlet sail of his returning son.

S λαβε[1] τὴν Ἀθηναίων δυναστείαν, <καὶ>[2] | τοὺς
μὲν Πάλλαντος παῖδας πεντήκοντα τὸν ἀριθμὸν
ἀπέκτεινεν· ὁμοίως δὲ καὶ ὅσοι ἀντᾶραι ἤθελον
παρ' αὐτοῦ ἀπεκτάνθησαν, καὶ τὴν ἀρχὴν ἅπασαν
ἔσχε μόνος.

E 12 | Ὅτι Μίνως, αἰσθόμενος τοῦ φεύγειν τοὺς μετὰ
Θησέως, Δαίδαλον αἴτιον ἐν τῷ λαβυρίνθῳ μετὰ
τοῦ παιδὸς Ἰκάρου καθεῖρξεν, ὃς ἐγεγέννητο αὐτῷ
ἐκ δούλης Μίνωος Ναυκράτης. ὁ δὲ πτερὰ κατασκευάσας ἑαυτῷ καὶ τῷ παιδὶ ἀναπτάντι ἐνετείλατο μήτε εἰς ὕψος πέτεσθαι, μὴ τακείσης τῆς
κόλλης ὑπὸ τοῦ ἡλίου αἱ πτέρυγες λυθῶσι, μήτε
ἐγγὺς θαλάσσης, ἵνα μὴ τὰ πτερὰ ὑπὸ τῆς νοτί-
13 δος λυθῇ. Ἴκαρος δὲ ἀμελήσας τῶν τοῦ πατρὸς
ἐντολῶν ψυχαγωγούμενος ἀεὶ μετέωρος ἐφέρετο·
τακείσης δὲ τῆς κόλλης πεσὼν εἰς τὴν ἀπ' ἐκείνου
κληθεῖσαν Ἰκαρίαν θάλασσαν ἀπέθανε. <Δαί-

---

12 Zenobius, *Cent.* iv. 92:[3] Δαίδαλον γὰρ σὺν Ἰκάρῳ
τῷ παιδὶ καθεῖρξε Μίνως ἐν τῷ λαβυρίνθῳ, δι' ὅπερ εἰργά-
σατο μύσος ἐπὶ τῷ τῆς Πασιφάης ἔρωτι τῷ πρὸς τὸν
ταῦρον. ὁ δὲ πτερὰ κατασκευάσας ἑαυτῷ καὶ τῷ παιδὶ
ἐξῆλθε τοῦ λαβυρίνθου καὶ ἀναπτάμενος ἔφυγε σὺν Ἰκάρῳ.
13 Ἰκάρου μὲν οὖν μετεωρότερον φερομένου καὶ τῆς κόλλης
ὑπὸ τοῦ ἡλίου τακείσης, αἱ πτέρυγες διελύθησαν. καὶ
οὗτος μὲν εἰς τὸ ἀπ' ἐκείνου κληθὲν Ἰκάριον πέλαγος κατα-

[1] Θησεὺς δὲ παρέλαβε E: Θησεὺς παραλαβὼν S.
[2] καὶ τοὺς μὲν Frazer: τοὺς μὲν S, Wagner.
[3] The version of Zenobius, which is probably based on
that of Apollodorus, is here printed for comparison.

---

[1] Pallas was the brother of Aegeus (see above, iii. 15. 5);
hence his fifty sons were cousins to Theseus. So long as
Aegeus was childless, his nephews hoped to succeed to the

succeeded to the sovereignty of Athens, and killed the sons of Pallas, fifty in number;[1] likewise all who would oppose him were killed by him, and he got the whole government to himself.

On being apprized of the flight of Theseus and his company, Minos shut up the guilty Daedalus in the labyrinth, along with his son Icarus, who had been borne to Daedalus by Naucrate, a female slave of Minos. But Daedalus constructed wings for himself and his son, and enjoined his son, when he took to flight, neither to fly high, lest the glue should melt in the sun and the wings should drop off, nor to fly near the sea, lest the pinions should be detached by the damp. But the infatuated Icarus, disregarding his father's injunctions, soared ever higher, till, the glue melting, he fell into the sea called after him Icarian, and perished.[2] But Daedalus made his way safely to

throne; but when Theseus appeared from Troezen, claiming to be the king's son and his heir apparent, they were disappointed and objected to his succession, on the ground that he was a stranger and a foreigner. Accordingly, when Theseus succeeded to the crown, Pallas and his fifty sons rebelled against him, but were defeated and slain. See Plutarch, *Theseus*, 3 and 13; Pausanias, i. 22. 2, i. 28. 10; Scholiast on Euripides, *Hippolytus*, 35, who quotes from Philochorus a passage about the rebellion. In order to be purified from the guilt incurred by killing his cousins, Theseus went into banishment for a year along with his wife Phaedra. The place of their exile was Troezen, where Theseus had been born; and it was there that Phaedra saw and conceived a fatal passion for her stepson Hippolytus, and laid the plot of death. See Euripides, *Hippolytus*, 34 *sqq.*; Pausanias, i. 22. 2. According to a different tradition, Theseus was tried for murder before the court of the Delphinium at Athens, and was acquitted on the plea of justifiable homicide (Pausanias, i. 28. 10).

[2] Compare Strabo, xiv. 1. 19, p. 639; Lucian, *Gallus*, 23; Arrian, *Anabasis*, vii. 20. 5; Zenobius, *Cent.* iv. 92: J.

δαλος δὲ διασῴζεται εἰς Κάμικον τῆς Σικελίας.>[1]
14 Δαίδαλον δὲ ἐδίωκε Μίνως, καὶ καθ' ἑκάστην
χώραν ἐρευνῶν ἐκόμιζε κόχλον, καὶ πολὺν ἐπηγγέλλετο δώσειν μισθὸν τῷ διὰ τοῦ κοχλίου λίνον
διείραντι,[2] διὰ τούτου νομίζων εὑρήσειν Δαίδαλον.
ἐλθὼν δὲ εἰς Κάμικον τῆς Σικελίας παρὰ Κώκαλον,
παρ' ᾧ Δαίδαλος ἐκρύπτετο, δείκνυσι τὸν κοχλίαν.
ὁ δὲ λαβὼν ἐπηγγέλλετο διείρειν[3] καὶ Δαιδάλῳ
15 δίδωσιν· ὁ δὲ ἐξάψας μύρμηκος λίνον καὶ τρήσας
τὸν κοχλίαν εἴασε δι' αὐτοῦ διελθεῖν. λαβὼν δὲ
Μίνως τὸ λίνον διειρμένον[4] ᾔσθετο ὄντα παρ'
ἐκείνῳ Δαίδαλον, καὶ εὐθέως ἀπῄτει. Κώκαλος
δὲ ὑποσχόμενος ἐκδώσειν ἐξένισεν αὐτόν· ὁ δὲ

---

14 πίπτει, Δαίδαλος δὲ διασῴζεται. ὁ Μίνως οὖν ἐδίωκε
Δαίδαλον καὶ καθ' ἑκάστην χώραν ἐρευνῶν ἐκόμιζε κόχλον,
καὶ πολὺν ὑπισχνεῖτο δοῦναι μισθὸν τῷ διὰ τοῦ κοχλίου
λίνον διείραντι, διὰ τούτου νομίζων εὑρήσειν Δαίδαλον.
ἐλθὼν δὲ εἰς Κώκαλον, παρ' ᾧ Δαίδαλος ἐκρύπτετο,
δείκνυσι τὸν κοχλίαν. ὁ δὲ λαβὼν ἐπηγγέλλετο διείρειν
15 καὶ Δαιδάλῳ δίδωσιν· ὁ δὲ ἐξάψας μύρμηκος λίνον καὶ
τρήσας τὸν κοχλίαν εἴασε δι' αὐτοῦ διελθεῖν. λαβὼν δὲ
Μίνως τὸν λίνον διειρμένον ᾔσθετο εἶναι παρ' ἐκείνῳ τὸν
Δαίδαλον, καὶ εὐθέως ἀπῄτει· Κώκαλος δὲ ὑποσχόμενος
δώσειν ἐξένισεν αὐτόν. ὁ δὲ λουσάμενος ὑπὸ τῶν Κωκάλου
θυγατέρων ἀνῃρέθη ζέουσαν πίσσαν ἐπιχεαμένων αὐτῷ.

---

[1] Δαίδαλος δὲ διασῴζεται εἰς Κάμικον τῆς Σικελίας inserted by
Wagner from a comparison with Zenobius, *Cent.* iv. 92 and
Tzetzes, *Chiliades,* i. 506, Ὁ Δαίδαλος δ' εἰς Κάμινον (sic)
σῴζεται Σικελίας.
[2] διείραντι Valckenar : διείρξαντι E : διείξαντι Zenobius.
[3] διείρειν Valckenar : διείρξειν E : διείρξειν Zenobius.
[4] διειρμένον Valckenar : διειργμένον E : διειργασμένον Zenobius.

Camicus in Sicily. And Minos pursued Daedalus, and in every country that he searched he carried a spiral shell and promised to give a great reward to him who should pass a thread through the shell, believing that by that means he should discover Daedalus. And having come to Camicus in Sicily, to the court of Cocalus, with whom Daedalus was concealed, he showed the spiral shell. Cocalus took it, and promised to thread it, and gave it to Daedalus; and Daedalus fastened a thread to an ant, and, having bored a hole in the spiral shell, allowed the ant to pass through it. But when Minos found the thread passed through the shell, he perceived that Daedalus was with Cocalus, and at once demanded his surrender.[1] Cocalus promised to surrender him, and made an entertainment for

Tzetzes, *Chiliades*, i. 498 *sqq.*; Severus, *Narr.* 5, in Wester-mann's *Mythographi Graeci, Appendix Narrationum*, 32, p. 373; Scholiast on Homer, *Il.* ii. 145; Ovid, *Metamorph.* viii. 183-235; Hyginus, *Fab.* 40; *Scriptores rerum mythicarum Latini*, ed. G. H. Bode, vol. i. pp. 16 and 117 (First Vatican Mythographer, 43, Second Vatican Mythographer, 125). According to one account, Daedalus landed from his flight at Cumae, where he dedicated his wings to Apollo. See Virgil, *Aen.* vi. 14 *sqq.*; Juvenal, iii. 25. The myth of the flight of Daedalus and Icarus is rationalized by Diodorus Siculus (iv. 77. 5 *sq.*) and Pausanias (ix. 11. 4 *sq.*). According to Diodorus, the two were provided by Pasiphae with a ship in which they escaped, but in landing on a certain island Icarus fell into the sea and was drowned. According to Pausanias, father and son sailed in separate ships, scudding before the wind with sails, which Daedalus had just invented and spread for the first time to the sea breeze. The only writer besides Apollodorus who mentions the name of Icarus's mother is Tzetzes; he agrees with Apollodorus, whom he may have copied, in describing her as a slave woman named Naucrate.

[1] The story of the quaint device by which Minos detected Daedalus is repeated by Zenobius (*Cent.* iv. 92), who probably copied Apollodorus. See above, pp. 138, 140. The device was

λουσάμενος ὑπὸ τῶν Κωκάλου θυγατέρων ἔκλυτος
ἐγένετο.[1] ὡς δὲ ἔνιοί φασι, ζεστῷ καταχυθεὶς
\<ὕδατι\>[2] μετήλλαξεν.

ES 16 | Συστρατευσάμενος δὲ ἐπὶ Ἀμαζόνας Ἡρακλεῖ
S ἥρπασεν[3] Ἀντιόπην, ὡς δέ τινες Μελανίππην,
Σιμωνίδης δὲ Ἱππολύτην.[4] διὸ ἐστράτευσαν ἐπ'

[1] ἔκλυτος ἐγένετο. These words can hardly be right. The
required sense is given by Zenobius, ἀνηρέθη. Perhaps we
should read ἐν λουτροῖς ἀπέθανεν or ἀπώλετο. Compare Diodorus Siculus, iv. 79. 2, κατὰ τὸν λουτρῶνα ὠλίσθηκε καὶ πεσὼν
εἰς τὸ θερμὸν ὕδωρ ἐτελεύτησε. But see Exegetical Note.

[2] ζεστῷ καταχυθεὶς ὕδατι Wagner (comparing Scholiast
on Homer, Il. ii. 145, ἀποθνῄσκει καταχυθέντος αὐτοῦ ζεστοῦ
ὕδατος): ζεστῷ καταλυθεὶς Ε.

[3] συστρατευσάμενος δὲ ἐπὶ Ἀμαζόνας Ἡρακλεῖ ἥρπασεν S: ὅτι
Θησεὺς Ἡρακλεῖ συστρατευσάμενος ἐπὶ Ἀμαζόνας ἥρπασε Ε.

[4] Ἀντιόπην . . . Ἱππολύτην S: Γλαύκην τὴν καὶ Μελανίππην Ε.

---

mentioned by Sophocles in a lost play, *The Camicians*, in
which he dealt with the residence of Daedalus at the court
of Cocalus in Sicily. See Athenaeus, iii. 32, p. 86 OD; *The
Fragments of Sophocles*, ed. A. C. Pearson, ii. 3 *sqq*.

[1] Compare Zenobius, *Cent.* iv. 92; Diodorus Siculus, iv. 79.
2; J. Tzetzes, *Chiliades*, i. 508 *sq*.; Scholiast on Homer, *Il.*
ii. 145; Scholiast on Pindar, *Nem.* iv. 59 (95); Ovid, *Ibis*,
289 *sq*., with the Scholia. The account of Zenobius agrees
closely with that of Apollodorus, except that he makes the
daughters of Cocalus pour boiling pitch instead of boiling
water on the head of their royal guest. The other authorities
speak of boiling water. The Scholiast on Pindar informs us
that the ever ingenious Daedalus persuaded the princesses to
lead a pipe through the roof, which discharged a stream of
boiling water on Minos while he was disporting himself in the
bath. Other writers mention the agency of the daughters of
Cocalus in the murder of Minos, without describing the mode
of his taking off. See Pausanias, vii. 4. 6; Conon, *Narrat.*
25; Hyginus, *Fab.* 44. Herodotus contents himself with
saying (vii. 169 *sq*.) that Minos died a violent death at Camicus in Sicily, whither he had gone in search of Daedalus.
The Greek expression which I have translated " was undone "
(ἔκλυτος ἐγένετο) is peculiar. If the text is sound (see Critical

Minos; but after his bath Minos was undone by the daughters of Cocalus; some say, however, that he died through being drenched with boiling water.[1]

Theseus joined Hercules in his expedition against the Amazons and carried off Antiope, or, as some say, Melanippe; but Simonides calls her Hippolyte.[2]

Note), the words must be equivalent to $\dot{\epsilon}\xi\epsilon\lambda\acute{v}\theta\eta$, "was relaxed, unstrung, or unnerved." Compare Aristotle, *Problem* i. p. 862 b 2 *sq.*, ed. Bekker, $\kappa\alpha\tau\epsilon\psi\upsilon\gamma\mu\acute{\epsilon}\nu o\upsilon$ $\pi\alpha\nu\tau\delta s$ $\tauo\hat{\upsilon}$ $\sigma\acute{\omega}\mu\alpha\tau os$ $\kappa\alpha\grave{\iota}$ $\dot{\epsilon}\kappa\lambda\epsilon\lambda\upsilon\mu\acute{\epsilon}\nu o\upsilon$ $\pi\rho\delta s$ $\tauo\grave{\upsilon}s$ $\pi\acute{o}\nu o\upsilon s$. Aristotle also uses the adjective $\dot{\epsilon}\kappa\lambda\upsilon\tau os$ to express a supple, nerveless, or effeminate motion of the hands (*Physiog.* 3, p. 808 a 14) ; and he says that tame elephants were trained to strike wild elephants, $\ddot{\epsilon}\omega s$ $\ddot{a}\nu$ $\dot{\epsilon}\kappa\lambda\acute{\upsilon}\sigma\omega\sigma\iota\nu$ $(\alpha\dot{\upsilon}\tauo\acute{\upsilon}s)$, "until they relax or weaken them" (*Hist. anim.* ix. 1, p. 610 a 27, ed Bekker). Isocrates speaks of a mob $(\ddot{o}\chi\lambda os)$ $\pi\rho\delta s$ $\tau\grave{o}\nu$ $\pi\acute{o}\lambda\epsilon\mu o\nu$ $\dot{\epsilon}\kappa\lambda\epsilon\lambda\upsilon\mu\acute{\epsilon}\nu os$ (*Or.* iv. 150). The verb $\dot{\epsilon}\kappa\lambda\acute{\upsilon}\epsilon\iota\nu$ is used in the sense of making an end of something troublesome or burdensome (Sophocles, *Oedipus Tyrannus*, 35 *sq.* with Jebb's note) ; from which it might perhaps be extended to persons regarded as troublesome or burdensome. We may compare the parallel uses of the Latin *dissolvere*, as applied both to things (Horace, *Odes*, i. 9. 5, *dissolve frigus*) and to persons (Sallust, *Jugurtha*, 17, *plerosque senectus dissolvit*).

[2] As to Theseus and the Amazons, see Diodorus Siculus, iv. 28 ; Plutarch, *Theseus*, 26–28 ; Pausanias, i. 2. 1, i. 15. 2, i. 41. 7, ii. 32. 9, v. 11. 4 and 7 ; Zenobius, *Cent.* v. 33. The invasion of Attica by the Amazons in the time of Theseus is repeatedly referred to by Isocrates (*Or.* iv. 68 and 70, vi. 42, vii. 75, xii. 193). The Amazon whom Theseus married, and by whom he had Hippolytus, is commonly called Antiope (Plutarch, *Theseus*, 26, 28 ; Diodorus Siculus, iv. 28 ; Pausanias, i. 2. 1, i. 41. 7 ; Seneca, *Hippolytus*, 927 *sqq.*; Hyginus, *Fab.* 30). But according to Clidemus, in agreement with Simonides, her name was Hippolyte (Plutarch, *Theseus*, 27), and so she is called by Isocrates (*Or.* xii. 193). Pausanias says that Hippolyte was a sister of Antiope (i. 41. 7). Tzetzes expressly affirms that Antiope, and not Hippolyte, was the wife of Theseus and mother of Hippolytus (*Schol. on Lycophron*, 1329). The grave of Antiope was shown both at Athens and Megara (Pausanias, i. 2. 1, i. 41. 7).

'Αθήνας 'Αμαζόνες. καὶ στρατοπεδευσαμένας[1]
αὐτὰς περὶ τὸν "Αρειον πάγον Θησεὺς μετὰ 'Αθη-
ES ναίων ἐνίκησεν. | ἔχων δὲ[2] ἐκ τῆς 'Αμαζόνος παῖδα
17 Ἱππόλυτον, λαμβάνει μετὰ ταῦτα παρὰ Δευκαλί-
S ωνος Φαίδραν τὴν Μίνωος θυγατέρα, | ἧς ἐπιτε-
λουμένων τῶν γάμων 'Αμαζὼν ἡ προγαμηθεῖσα
Θησεῖ τοὺς συγκατακειμένους σὺν ταῖς μεθ' ἑαυτῆς
'Αμαζόσιν ἐπιστᾶσα σὺν ὅπλοις κτείνειν ἔμελλεν.
οἱ δὲ κλείσαντες διὰ τάχους τὰς θύρας ἀπέκτειναν
αὐτήν. τινὲς δὲ μαχομένην αὐτὴν ὑπὸ Θησέως
ES 18 λέγουσιν ἀποθανεῖν. | Φαίδρα δὲ γεννήσασα Θησεῖ
δύο παιδία 'Ακάμαντα καὶ Δημοφῶντα ἐρᾷ[3] τοῦ
ἐκ τῆς 'Αμαζόνος παιδὸς [ἤγουν τοῦ Ἱππολύτου][4]
καὶ δεῖται συνελθεῖν αὐτῇ.[5] ὁ δὲ μισῶν πάσας
γυναῖκας[6] τὴν συνουσίαν ἔφυγεν. ἡ δὲ Φαίδρα,
δείσασα μὴ τῷ πατρὶ διαβάλῃ, κατασχίσασα[7]
τὰς τοῦ θαλάμου θύρας καὶ τὰς ἐσθῆτας σπα-
19 ράξασα κατεψεύσατο Ἱππολύτου βίαν. Θησεὺς
δὲ πιστεύσας ηὔξατο Ποσειδῶνι Ἱππόλυτον δια-
φθαρῆναι· ὁ δέ, θέοντος αὐτοῦ ἐπὶ τοῦ ἅρματος[8]
καὶ παρὰ τῇ θαλάσσῃ ὀχουμένου, ταῦρον ἀνῆκεν
ἐκ τοῦ κλύδωνος. πτοηθέντων δὲ τῶν ἵππων κατηρ-

---

[1] στρατοπεδευσαμένας Bücheler: στρατευσαμένας S, Wagner.
[2] ἔχων δὲ . . . μετὰ ταῦτα S: ἐξ ἧς [scil. Γλαύκης] ἔσχε παῖδα
Ἱππόλυτον. τὴν πρότερον δὲ διαλυσάμενος ἔχθραν λαμβάνει E.
[3] Φαίδρα δὲ γεννήσασα Θησεῖ δύο παιδία 'Ακάμαντα καὶ Δημοφῶντα ἐρᾷ S: ἐξ ἧς [scil. Φαίδρας] γεννᾷ δύο παῖδας 'Ακάμαντα
καὶ Δημοφῶντα. Φαίδρα γοῦν ἐρᾷ E.
[4] τοῦ ἐκ τῆς 'Αμαζόνος παιδὸς ἤγουν τοῦ Ἱππολύτου E: Ἱππολύτου S.
[5] συνελθεῖν αὐτῇ E: συνελθεῖν S.
[6] πάσας γυναῖκας E: πάσας τὰς γυναῖκας S.
[7] κατασχίσασα S: κατασχοῦσα E.
[8] ἐπὶ τοῦ ἅρματος E: ἐπὶ ἅρματος S.

144

Wherefore the Amazons marched against Athens, and having taken up a position about the Areopagus[1] they were vanquished by the Athenians under Theseus. And though he had a son Hippolytus by the Amazon, Theseus afterwards received from Deucalion[2] in marriage Phaedra, daughter of Minos; and when her marriage was being celebrated, the Amazon that had before been married to him appeared in arms with her Amazons, and threatened to kill the assembled guests. But they hastily closed the doors and killed her. However, some say that she was slain in battle by Theseus. And Phaedra, after she had borne two children, Acamas and Demophon, to Theseus, fell in love with the son he had by the Amazon, to wit, Hippolytus, and besought him to lie with her. Howbeit, he fled from her embraces, because he hated all women. But Phaedra, fearing that he might accuse her to his father, cleft open the doors of her bedchamber, rent her garments, and falsely charged Hippolytus with an assault. Theseus believed her and prayed to Poseidon that Hippolytus might perish. So, when Hippolytus was riding in his chariot and driving beside the sea, Poseidon sent up a bull from the surf, and the horses were frightened, the chariot

[1] According to Diodorus Siculus (iv. 28. 2), the Amazons encamped at the place which was afterwards called the Amazonium. The topography of the battle seems to have been minutely described by the antiquarian Clidemus, according to whom the array of the Amazons extended from the Amazonium to the Pnyx, while the Athenians attacked them from the Museum Hill on one side and from Ardettus and the Lyceum on the other. See Plutarch, *Theseus*, 27.

[2] This Deucalion was a son of Minos and reigned after him; he was thus a brother of Phaedra. See above, iii. 1. 2; Diodorus Siculus, iv. 62. 1. He is not to be confounded with the more famous Deucalion in whose time the great flood took place. See above, i. 7. 2.

ράχθη[1] τὸ ἅρμα. ἐμπλακεὶς δὲ <ταῖς ἡνίαις>[2]
Ἱππόλυτος συρόμενος ἀπέθανε. γενομένου δὲ τοῦ
ἔρωτος περιφανοῦς ἑαυτὴν ἀνήρτησε Φαίδρα.

[1] κατηρράχθη E : κατεάχθη S.
[2] ταῖς ἡνίαις inserted by Wagner (comparing Scholiast on
Plato, *Laws*, xi. p. 931 B, ταῖς ἡνίαις ἐμπλακεὶς ἑλκόμενος
θνήσκει ; Euripides, *Hippolytus*, 1236, ἡνίαισιν ἐμπλακεὶς ;
Diodorus Siculus, iv. 62. 3 ; ἐμπλακὲν τοῖς ἱμᾶσιν ἑλκυσθῆναι).

[1] The guilty passion of Phaedra for her stepson Hippolytus
and the tragic end of the innocent youth, done to death by
the curses of his father Theseus, are the subject of two extant
tragedies, the *Hippolytus* of Euripides, and the *Hippolytus*
or *Phaedra* of Seneca. Compare also Diodorus Siculus, iv.
62 ; Pausanias, i. 22, 1 *sq.*, ii. 32. 1–4 ; Scholiast on Homer,
Od. xi. 321, citing Asclepiades as his authority ; Tzetzes,
Schol. on Lycophron, 1329 ; *id. Chiliades*, vi. 504 *sqq.* ;
Scholiast on Plato, *Laws*, xi. p. 931 B ; Ovid, *Metamorph.*
xv. 497 *sqq.* ; *id. Heroides*, iv. ; Hyginus, *Fab.* 47 ; Servius,
on Virgil, *Aen.* vi. 445, and vii. 761 ; *Scriptores rerum
mythicarum Latini*, ed. G. H. Bode, vol. i. pp. 17, 117 *sq.*
(First Vatican Mythographer, 46 ; Second Vatican Mythographer, 128). Sophocles composed a tragedy *Phaedra*,
of which some fragments remain, but little or nothing is
known of the plot. See *The Fragments of Sophocles*, ed. A.
C. Pearson, vol. ii. pp. 294 *sqq.* Euripides wrote two
tragedies on the same subject, both under the title of *Hippolytus* : it is the second which has come down to us. In the
first *Hippolytus* the poet, incensed at the misconduct of his
wife, painted the character and behaviour of Phaedra in
much darker colours than in the second, where he has
softened the portrait, representing the unhappy woman as
instigated by the revengeful Aphrodite, but resisting the
impulse of her fatal passion to the last, refusing to tell her
love to Hippolytus, and dying by her own hand rather than
endure the shame of its betrayal by a blabbing nurse. This
version of the story is evidently not the one here followed by
Apollodorus, according to whom Phaedra made criminal advances to her stepson. On the other hand the version of
Apollodorus agrees in this respect with that of the Scholiast
on Homer (*l.c.*) : both writers may have followed the first

dashed in pieces, and Hippolytus, entangled in the reins, was dragged to death. And when her passion was made public, Phaedra hanged herself.[1]

Hippolytus of Euripides. As to that lost play, of which some fragments have come down to us, see the life of Euripides in Westermann's *Vitarum Scriptores Graeci Minores,* p. 137; the Greek argument to the extant *Hippolytus* of Euripides (vol. i. p. 163, ed. Paley); *Tragicorum Graecorum Fragmenta,* ed. A. Nauck[2], pp. 491 *sqq.* Apollodorus says nothing as to the scene of the tragedy. Euripides in his extant play lays it at Troezen, whither Theseus had gone with Phaedra to be purified for the slaughter of the sons of Pallas (*Hippolytus,* 34 *sqq.*). Pausanias agrees with this account, and tells us that the graves of the unhappy pair were to be seen beside each other at Troezen, near a myrtle-tree, of which the pierced leaves still bore the print of Phaedra's brooch. The natural beauty of the spot is in keeping with the charm which the genius of Euripides has thrown over the romantic story of unhappy love and death. Of Troezen itself only a few insignificant ruins remain, over-grown with weeds and dispersed amid a wilderness of bushes. But hard by are luxuriant groves of lemon and orange with here and there tall cypresses towering like dark spires above them, while behind this belt of verdure rise wooded hills, and across the blue waters of the nearly landlocked bay lies Calauria, the sacred island of Poseidon, its peaks veiled in the sombre green of the pines.

A different place and time were assigned by Seneca to the tragedy. According to him, the events took place at Athens, and Phaedra conceived her passion for Hippolytus and made advances to him during the absence of her husband, who had gone down to the nether world with Pirithous and was there detained for four years (*Hippolytus,* 835 *sqq.*). Diodorus Siculus agrees with Euripides in laying the scene of the tragedy at Troezen, and he agrees with Apollodorus in saying that at the time when Phaedra fell in love with Hippolytus she was the mother of two sons, Acamas and Demophon, by Theseus. In his usual rationalistic vein Diodorus omits all mention of Poseidon and the sea-bull, and ascribes the accident which befell Hippolytus to the mental agitation he felt at his stepmother's calumny.

E 20 |῞Οτι ὁ ᾿Ιξίων ῞Ηρας ἐρασθεὶς ἐπεχείρει βιά-
ζεσθαι, καὶ προσαγγειλάσης τῆς ῞Ηρας γνῶναι
θέλων ὁ Ζεύς, εἰ οὕτως ἔχει τὸ πρᾶγμα, νεφέλην
ἐξεικάσας ῞Ηρᾳ παρέκλινεν αὐτῷ· καὶ καυχώμενον
ὡς ῞Ηρᾳ μιγέντα ἐνέδησε τροχῷ, ὑφ᾿ οὗ φερόμενος
διὰ πνευμάτων ἐν αἰθέρι ταύτην τίνει δίκην. νε-
φέλη δὲ ἐξ ᾿Ιξίονος ἐγέννησε Κένταυρον.

Z 21 <Συνεμάχησε δὲ[1] τῷ Πειρίθῳ Θησεύς, ὅτε
κατὰ τῶν Κενταύρων συνεστήσατο πόλεμον.

---

[1] Συνεμάχησε δὲ ... ὁ Θησεὺς αὐτῶν ἀνεῖλεν. This passage
is inserted from Zenobius, *Cent.* v. 33, who probably borrowed it from Apollodorus.

---

[1] Compare Pindar, *Pyth.* ii. 21 (39)–48 (88), with the Scholiast on *v.* 21 (39) ; Diodorus Siculus, iv. 69. 4 *sq.* ; Scholiast
on Euripides, *Phoenissae*, 1185 ; Scholiast on Homer, *Od.*
xxi. 303 ; Scholiast on Apollonius Rhodius, *Argon.* iii. 62 ;
Hyginus, *Fab.* 62 ; Servius, on Virgil, *Aen.* vi. 286 (who does
not mention the punishment of the wheel) ; Lactantius Placidus on Statius, *Theb.* iv. 539 ; *Scriptores rerum mythicarum Latini*, ed. G. H. Bode, vol. i. pp. 4, 110 *sq.* (First
Vatican Mythographer, 14 ; Second Vatican Mythographer,
106). J. Tzetzes flatly contradicts Pindar and substitutes a
dull rationalistic narrative for the poet's picturesque myth
(*Chiliades*, vii. 30 *sqq.*). According to some, the wheel of
Ixion was fiery (Scholiast on Euripides, *l.c.*) ; according to
the Vatican Mythographer it was entwined with snakes.
The fiery aspect of the wheel is supported by vase-paintings.
From this and other evidence Mr. A. B. Cook argues that the
flaming wheel launched through the air is a mythical expression for the Sun, and that Ixion himself "typifies a whole
series of human Ixions who in bygone ages were done to
death as effete embodiments of the sun-god." See his book
Zeus, i. 198–211.

[2] This passage concerning the fight of Theseus with the
centaurs at the marriage of Pirithous does not occur in our text

Ixion fell in love with Hera and attempted to force her; and when Hera reported it, Zeus, wishing to know if the thing were so, made a cloud in the likeness of Hera and laid it beside him; and when Ixion boasted that he had enjoyed the favours of Hera, Zeus bound him to a wheel, on which he is whirled by winds through the air; such is the penalty he pays. And the cloud, impregnated by Ixion, gave birth to Centaurus.[1]

And Theseus allied himself with Pirithous,[2] when he engaged in war against the centaurs. For when

of Apollodorus, but is conjecturally restored to it from Zenobius (*Cent.* v. 33), or rather from his interpolator, who frequently quotes passages of Apollodorus without acknowledgment. The restoration was first proposed by Professor C. Robert before the discovery of the *Epitome*; and it is adopted by R. Wagner in his edition of Apollodorus. See C. Robert, *De Apollodori Bibliotheca*, pp. 49 *sq.*; R. Wagner, *Epitoma Vaticana ex Apollodori Bibliotheca*, p. 147. As Pirithous was a son of Ixion (see above, i. 8. 2), the account of his marriage would follow naturally after the recital of his father's crime and punishment. As to the wedding of Pirithous, see further Diodorus Siculus, iv. 70. 3; Plutarch, *Theseus*, 30; Pausanias, v. 10. 8; Scholiast on Homer, *Od.* xxi. 295; Hyginus, *Fab.* 33; Ovid, *Metamorph.* xii. 210–535; Servius, on Virgil, *Aen.* vii. 304; *Scriptores rerum mythicarum Latini*, ed. G. H. Bode, vol. i. pp. 51, 111 (First Vatican Mythographer, 162; Second Vatican Mythographer, 108). The wife of Pirithous is called Deidamia by Plutarch, but Hippodamia by Diodorus Siculus, Hyginus, and the Second Vatican Mythographer, as well as by Homer (*Il.* ii. 742). Ovid calls her Hippodame. The scene of the battle of the Lapiths with the centaurs at the wedding of Pirithous was sculptured in the western gable of the temple of Zeus at Olympia; all the sculptures were discovered, in a more or less fragmentary state, by the Germans in their excavations of the sanctuary, and they are now exhibited in the museum at Olympia. See Pausanias, v. 10. 8, with my commentary (vol. iii. pp. 516 *sqq.*).

Πειρίθους γὰρ Ἱπποδάμειαν μνηστευόμενος εἱστία
Κενταύρους ὡς συγγενεῖς ὄντας αὐτῇ. ἀσυνήθως
δὲ ἔχοντες οἴνου ἀφειδῶς ἐμφορησάμενοι ἐμέθυον,
καὶ εἰσαγομένην τὴν νύμφην ἐπεχείρουν βιά-
ζεσθαι· ὁ δὲ Πειρίθους μετὰ Θησέως καθοπλισάμενος μάχην συνῆψε, καὶ πολλοὺς ὁ Θησεὺς
αὐτῶν¹ ἀνεῖλεν.>

E 22 |῞Οτι Καινεὺς πρότερον ἦν γυνή, συνελθόντος
δὲ αὐτῇ Ποσειδῶνος ᾐτήσατο ἀνὴρ γενέσθαι ἄτρω-
τος· διὸ καὶ ἐν τῇ πρὸς Κενταύρους μάχῃ τραυ-
μάτων καταφρονῶν πολλοὺς τῶν Κενταύρων
ἀπώλεσεν, οἱ δὲ λοιποί, περιστάντες αὐτῷ,
ἐλάταις τύπτοντες ἔχωσαν εἰς γῆν.

¹ αὐτῶν Wagner : ἀπ' αὐτῶν MSS. of Zenobius.

---

¹ As to Caeneus, his change of sex and his invulnerability,
see Apollonius Rhodius, *Argon.* i. 57–64, with the Scholiast
on *v.* 57 ; Scholiast on Homer, *Il.* i. 264 ; Plutarch, *Stoic.
absurd.* 1 ; *id. De profectibus in virtute,* 1 ; Lucian, *Gallus,*
19 ; *id. De saltatione,* 57 ; Apostolius, *Cent.* iv. 19 ; Palaephatus, *De incredib.* 11 ; Antoninus Liberalis, *Transform.* 17 ;
Virgil, *Aen.* vi. 448 *sq.* ; Ovid, *Metamorph.* xii. 459–532 ;
Hyginus, *Fab.* 14, pp. 39 *sq.*, ed. Bunte ; Servius, on Virgil,
Aen. vi. 448 ; Lactantius Placidus on Statius, *Achill.* 264 ;
Scriptores rerum mythicarum Latini, ed. G. H. Bode, vol. i.
pp. 49, 111 *sq.*, 189 (First Vatican Mythographer, 154; Second
Vatican Mythographer, 108 ; Third Vatican Mythographer,
6. 25). According to Servius and the Vatican Mythographers,
after his death Caeneus was changed back into a woman, thus
conforming to an observation of Plato or Aristotle that the sex
of a person generally changes at each transmigration of his
soul into a new body. Curiously enough, the Urabunna and
Waramunga tribes of Central Australia agree with Plato or
Aristotle on this point. They believe that the souls of the
dead transmigrate sooner or later into new bodies, and that
at each successive transmigration they change their sex. See
(Sir) Baldwin Spencer and F. J. Gillen, *The Northern Tribes
of Central Australia* (London, 1904), p. 148. According to

Pirithous wooed Hippodamia, he feasted the centaurs because they were her kinsmen. But being unaccustomed to wine, they made themselves drunk by swilling it greedily, and when the bride was brought in, they attempted to violate her. But Pirithous, fully armed, with Theseus, joined battle with them, and Theseus killed many of them.

Caeneus was formerly a woman, but after that Poseidon had intercourse with her, she asked to become an invulnerable man; wherefore in the battle with the centaurs he thought scorn of wounds and killed many of the centaurs; but the rest of them surrounded him and by striking him with fir-trees buried him in the earth.[1]

Ovid (*Metamorph.* xii. 524 *sqq.*), a bird with yellow wings was seen to rise from the heap of logs under which Caeneus was overwhelmed; and the seer Mopsus explained the bird to be Caeneus transformed into that creature. Another tradition about Caeneus was that he set up his spear in the middle of the market-place and ordered people to regard it as a god and to swear by it. He himself prayed and sacrificed to none of the gods, but only to his spear. It was this impiety that drew down on him the wrath of Zeus, who instigated the centaurs to overwhelm him. See the Scholiast on Homer, *Il.* i. 264; Scholiast on Apollonius Rhodius, *Argon.* i. 57. The whole story of the parentage of Caeneus, his impiety, his invulnerability, and the manner of his death, is told by the old prosewriter Acusilaus in a passage quoted by a Greek grammarian, of whose work some fragments, written on papyrus, were discovered some years ago at Oxyrhynchus in Egypt. See *The Oxyrhynchus Papyri*, part xiii. (London, 1919), pp. 133 *sq.* Apollodorus probably derived his account of Caeneus from Acusilaus, whom he often refers to (see Index). The fortunate discovery of this fragment of the ancient writer confirms our confidence in the excellence of the sources used by Apollodorus and in the fidelity with which he followed them. In his complete work he may have narrated the impiety of Caeneus in setting up his spear for worship, though the episode has been omitted in the *Epitome*.

23 "Ὅτι Θησεύς, Πειρίθῳ συνθέμενος Διὸς θυγατέρας γαμῆσαι, ἑαυτῷ μὲν ἐκ Σπάρτης μετ'
ἐκείνου ἥρπασεν Ἑλένην δωδεκαέτη οὖσαν, Πειρίθῳ δὲ μνηστευόμενος τὸν Περσεφόνης γάμον εἰς
Ἅιδου κάτεισι. καὶ Διόσκουροι μὲν μετὰ Λακεδαιμονίων καὶ Ἀρκάδων εἷλον Ἀθήνας καὶ
ἀπάγουσιν Ἑλένην καὶ μετὰ ταύτης Αἴθραν τὴν
Πιτθέως αἰχμάλωτον· Δημοφῶν δὲ καὶ Ἀκάμας
ἔφυγον. κατάγουσι δὲ καὶ Μενεσθέα καὶ τὴν ἀρχὴν
24 τῶν Ἀθηναίων διδόασι τούτῳ. Θησεὺς δὲ μετὰ
Πειρίθου παραγενόμενος εἰς Ἅιδου ἐξαπατᾶται,
καὶ <ὃς> ὡς [1] ξενίων μεταληψομένους πρῶτον ἐν
τῷ τῆς Λήθης εἶπε καθεσθῆναι θρόνῳ, ᾧ προσ-
φυέντες σπείραις δρακόντων κατείχοντο. Πειρίθους μὲν οὖν εἰς ἀίδιον [2] δεθεὶς ἔμεινε, Θησέα
δὲ Ἡρακλῆς ἀναγαγὼν ἔπεμψεν εἰς Ἀθήνας.
ἐκεῖθεν δὲ ὑπὸ Μενεσθέως ἐξελαθεὶς πρὸς Λυκο-

---

[1] ὃς ὡς Herwerden : ὡς E, Wagner.
[2] ἀίδιον Herwerden : Ἀιδωνέα E, Wagner.

---

[1] See above, iii. 10. 7, with the note. Diodorus Siculus (iv.
63. 2) says that Helen was ten years old when she was
carried off by Theseus and Pirithous.

[2] Compare Diodorus Siculus, iv. 63. 3 and 5 ; Plutarch,
Theseus, 32 and 34 ; Pausanias, i. 17. 5, ii. 22. 6. According
to these writers, it was not Athens but Aphidna (Aphidnae)
that was captured by the Dioscuri.

[3] Menestheus was one of the royal family of Athens, being
a son of Peteos, who was a son of Orneus, who was a son of
Erechtheus. See Plutarch, *Theseus*, 32 ; Pausanias, ii. 25. 6.
That he was restored and placed on the throne by Castor
and Pollux during the absence of Theseus is mentioned also
by Pausanias (i. 17. 6) and Aelian (*Var. Hist.* iv. 5). Compare Plutarch, *Theseus*, 32 *sq.*

[4] As to Theseus and Pirithous in hell, and the rescue of
Theseus by Hercules, see above, ii. 5. 12 with the note. The
great painter Polygnotus painted the two heroes seated in

Having made a compact with Pirithous that they would marry daughters of Zeus, Theseus, with the help of Pirithous, carried off Helen from Sparta for himself, when she was twelve years old,[1] and in the endeavour to win Persephone as a bride for Pirithous he went down to Hades. And the Dioscuri, with the Lacedaemonians and Arcadians, captured Athens and carried away Helen, and with her Aethra, daughter of Pittheus, into captivity;[2] but Demophon and Acamas fled. And the Dioscuri also brought back Menestheus from exile, and gave him the sovereignty of Athens.[3] But when Theseus arrived with Pirithous in Hades, he was beguiled; for, on the pretence that they were about to partake of good cheer, Hades bade them first be seated on the Chair of Forgetfulness, to which they grew and were held fast by coils of serpents. Pirithous, therefore, remained bound for ever, but Hercules brought Theseus up and sent him to Athens.[4] Thence he was driven by

chairs, Theseus holding his friend's sword and his own, while Pirithous gazed wistfully at the now useless blades, that had done such good service in the world of light and life. See Pausanias, x. 29. 9. No ancient author, however, except Apollodorus in the present passage, expressly mentions the Chair of Forgetfulness, though Horace seems to allude to it (*Odes*, iv. 7. 27 *sq.*), where he speaks of "the Lethaean bonds" which held fast Pirithous, and which his faithful friend was powerless to break. But when Apollodorus speaks of the heroes growing to their seats, he may be following the old poet Panyasis, who said that Theseus and Pirithous were not pinioned to their chairs, but that the rock growing to their flesh held them as in a vice (Pausanias *l.c.*). Indeed, Theseus stuck so fast that, on being wrenched away by Hercules, he left a piece of his person adhering to the rock, which, according to some people, was the reason why the Athenians ever afterwards were so remarkably spare in that part of their frame. See Suidas, *s.v.* Λίσποι; Scholiast on Aristophanes, *Knights*, 1368; compare Aulus Gellius, x. 16. 13.

μήδην ἦλθεν, ὃς αὐτὸν βάλλει κατὰ βαράθρων[1]
καὶ ἀποκτείνει.

II. Ὅτι ὁ Τάνταλος ἐν Ἅιδου[2] κολάζεται,
πέτρον ἔχων ὕπερθεν ἑαυτοῦ ἐπιφερόμενον, ἐν
λίμνῃ τε διατελῶν καὶ περὶ τοὺς ὤμους ἑκατέρωσε
δένδρα μετὰ καρπῶν ὁρῶν παρὰ τῇ λίμνῃ πεφυ-
κότα· τὸ μὲν οὖν ὕδωρ ψαύει αὐτοῦ τῶν γενύων,
καὶ ὅτε θέλοι σπάσασθαι τούτου ξηραίνεται,
τῶν δὲ καρπῶν ὁπότε βούλοιτο μεταλήψεσθαι
μετεωρίζονται[3] μέχρι νεφῶν ὑπ' ἀνέμων τὰ
δένδρα σὺν τοῖς καρποῖς. κολάζεσθαι δὲ αὐτὸν
οὕτως λέγουσί τινες, ὅτι τὰ τῶν θεῶν ἐξελάλησεν
ἀνθρώποις μυστήρια, καὶ ὅτι τῆς ἀμβροσίας τοῖς
ἡλικιώταις μετεδίδου.

2   Ὅτι Βροτέας κυνηγὸς ὢν τὴν Ἄρτεμιν οὐκ

---

[1] βαράθρων Wagner : βάθρων E.
[2] Ἅιδου Wagner : ἄδη E.
[3] μετεωρίζονται Wagner : μετεωρίζοντα E.

---

[1] Compare Plutarch, *Theseus*, 35 ; Pausanias, i. 17. 6 ;
Diodorus Siculus, iv. 62. 4.

[2] As to the punishment of Tantalus, see Homer, *Od.* xi.
582–592, who describes only the torments of hunger and
thirst, but says nothing about the overhanging stone. But
the stone is often mentioned by later writers. See Archilochus,
quoted by Plutarch, *Praecept. Ger. Reipub.* 6, and by the
Scholiast on Pindar, *Olymp.* i. 60 (97) ; Pindar, *Olymp.* i. 55
(87) *sqq.*, with the Scholia on *v.* 60 (97) ; *id. Isthm.* viii. 10
(21) ; Euripides, *Orestes*, 4–10 ; Plato, *Cratylus*, p. 395 D E ;
Hyperides, *Frag.* 176, ed. Blass ; Antipater, in *Anthologia
Palatina, Appendix Planudea*, iv. 131. 9 *sq.* ; Plutarch, *De
superstitione*, 11 ; Lucian, *Dial. Mort.* 17 ; Pausanias, x. 31.
10 ; Philostratus, *Vit. Apollon.* iii. 25 ; Apostolius, *Cent.* vii.
60, xvi. 9 ; Nonnus, *Narrat.* in Westermann's *Mythographi
Graeci, Appendix Narrationum*, 73, p. 386 ; Athenaeus, vii.
14, p. 281 B C ; Lucretius, iii. 980 *sq.* ; Cicero, *De finibus*, i.

Menestheus and went to Lycomedes, who threw him down an abyss and killed him.[1]

II. Tantalus is punished in Hades by having a stone impending over him, by being perpetually in a lake and seeing at his shoulders on either side trees with fruit growing beside the lake. The water touches his jaws, but when he would take a draught of it, the water dries up; and when he would partake of the fruits, the trees with the fruits are lifted by winds as high as the clouds. Some say that he is thus punished because he blabbed to men the mysteries of the gods, and because he attempted to share ambrosia with his fellows.[2]

Broteas, a hunter, did not honour Artemis, and

18. 60; *id. Tuscul. Disput.* iv. 16. 35; Horace, *Epod.* 17, 65 *sq.* and *Sat.* i. 1. 68 *sq.*; Ovid, *Metamorph.* iv. 458 *sq.*; Hyginus, *Fab.* 82. Ovid notices only the torments of hunger and thirst, and Lucian only the torment of thirst. According to another account, Tantalus lay buried under Mount Sipylus in Lydia, which had been his home in life, and on which his grave was shown down to late times (Pausanias, ii. 22. 3, v. 13. 7). The story ran that Zeus owned a valuable watchdog, which guarded his sanctuary in Crete; but Pandareus, the Milesian, stole the animal and entrusted it for safekeeping to Tantalus. So Zeus sent Hermes to the resetter to reclaim his property, but Tantalus impudently denied on oath that the creature was in his house or that he knew anything about it. Accordingly, to punish the perjured knave, the indignant Zeus piled Mount Sipylus on the top of him. See the Scholiast on Pindar, *Olymp.* i. 60 (97); Scholiast on Homer, *Od.* xix. 518, xx. 66. In his lost play *Tantalus* Sophocles seems to have introduced the theft of the dog, the errand of Hermes to recover the animal, and perhaps the burial of the thief under the mountain. See *The Fragments of Sophocles*, ed. A. C. Pearson, vol. ii. pp. 209 *sqq.*

ἐτίμα· ἔλεγε δέ, ὡς οὐδ᾽ <ἂν>¹ ὑπὸ πυρός τι
πάθοι· ἐμμανὴς οὖν γενόμενος ἔβαλεν εἰς πῦρ
ἑαυτόν.

3   Ὅτι Πέλοψ σφαγεὶς ἐν τῷ τῶν θεῶν ἐράνῳ
καὶ καθεψηθεὶς ὡραιότερος ἐν τῇ ἀναζωώσει γέ-
γονε, καὶ κάλλει διενεγκὼν Ποσειδῶνος ἐρώμενος
γίνεται, ὃς αὐτῷ δίδωσιν ἅρμα ὑπόπτερον· τοῦτο
καὶ διὰ θαλάσσης τρέχον τοὺς ἄξονας οὐχ ὑγραί-
4   νετο. τοῦ δὲ βασιλεύοντος Πίσης Οἰνομάου
θυγατέρα ἔχοντος Ἱπποδάμειαν, καὶ εἴτε αὐτῆς

---

¹ οὐδ᾽ ἂν Herwerden : οὐδ᾽ E, Wagner.

---

¹ This Broteas, mentioned by Apollodorus between Tantalus and Pelops, is probably the Broteas, son of Tantalus,
who was said to have carved the ancient rock-hewn image of
the Mother of the Gods which is still to be seen on the side of
Mount Sipylus, about three hundred feet above the plain.
See Pausanias, iii. 22. 4, with my note on v. 13. 7 (vol. iii.
pp. 553 *sq.*). Ovid mentions a certain Broteas, who from a
desire of death burned himself on a pyre (*Ibis*, 517 *sq.*), and
who is probably to be identified with the Broteas of Apollodorus, though the Scholiasts on Ovid describe him either as
a son of Jupiter (Zeus), or as a son of Vulcan (Hephaestus)
and Pallas (Athena), identical with Erichthonius. According
to one of the Scholiasts, Broteas, son of Zeus, was a very
wicked man, who was blinded by Zeus, and loathing his life
threw himself on a burning pyre. According to another of
the Scholiasts, Broteas, son of Hephaestus and Athena, was
despised for his ugliness, and this so preyed on his mind that
he preferred death by fire. See Ovid, *Ibis*, ed. R. Ellis,
p. 89. It seems not improbable that this legend contains a
reminiscence of a human sacrifice or suicide by fire, such as
occurs not infrequently in the traditions of western Asia. See
K. B. Stark, *Niobe und die Niobiden* (Leipsic, 1863), pp.
437 *sq.*; and for the Asiatic traditions of a human sacrifice
or suicide by fire, see *Adonis, Attis, Osiris*, Third Edition,
vol. i. pp. 172 *sqq.*
² The story was that at a banquet of the gods, to which he

said that even fire could not hurt him. So he went mad and threw himself into fire.[1]

Pelops, after being slaughtered and boiled at the banquet of the gods, was fairer than ever when he came to life again,[2] and on account of his surpassing beauty he became a minion of Poseidon, who gave him a winged chariot, such that even when it ran through the sea the axles were not wet.[3] Now Oenomaus, the king of Pisa, had a daughter Hippodamia,[4] and whether it was that he loved her, as some

had been invited, Tantalus served up the mangled limbs of his young son Pelops, which he had boiled in a kettle. But the murdered child was restored to life by being put back into the kettle and then drawn out of it, with an ivory shoulder to replace the shoulder of flesh which Demeter or, according to others, Thetis had unwittingly eaten. See Pindar, *Olymp.* i. 24 (37) *sqq.*, with the Scholia on *v.* 37; Lucian, *De saltatione*, 54; Tzetzes, *Schol. on Lycophron*, 152; Nonnus, *Narr.*, in Westermann's *Mythographi Graeci, Appendix Narrationum*, 57, p. 380; Servius, on Virgil, *Aen.* vi. 603, and on *Georg.* iii. 7; Hyginus, *Fab.* 83; *Scriptores rerum mythicarum Latini*, ed. G. H. Bode, vol. i. pp. 109, 186 (Second Vatican Mythographer, 102; Third Vatican Mythographer, vi. 21). The ivory shoulder of Pelops used afterwards to be exhibited at Elis (Pliny, *Nat. Hist.* xxviii. 34); but it was no longer to be seen in the time of Pausanias (Pausanias, i. 13. 6).

[3] Compare Pindar, *Olymp.* i. 37 (60) *sqq.*, 71 (114) *sqq.*; Tzetzes, *Schol. on Lycophron*, 156. Pindar describes how Pelops went to the shore of the sea and prayed to Poseidon to give him a swift chariot, and how the god came forth and bestowed on him a golden chariot with winged steeds. On the chest of Cypselus at Olympia the horses of Pelops in the chariot race were represented with wings (Pausanias, v. 17. 7).

[4] The following account of the wooing and winning of Hippodamia by Pelops is the fullest that has come down to us. Compare Pindar, *Olymp.* i. 67 (109) *sqq.*; Diodorus Siculus, iv. 73; Pausanias, v. 10. 6 *sq.*, v. 14. 6, v. 17. 7,

ἐρῶντος, ὥς τινες λέγουσιν, εἴτε χρησμὸν ἔχοντος
τελευτῆσαι ὑπὸ τοῦ γήμαντος αὐτήν, οὐδεὶς αὐτὴν
ἐλάμβανεν εἰς γυναῖκα· ὁ μὲν γὰρ πατὴρ οὐκ
ἔπειθεν αὐτῷ[1] συνελθεῖν, οἱ δὲ μνηστευόμενοι

[1] αὐτῷ Frazer : αὐτῇ E, Wagner. ἐπέτρεπεν οὐδενὶ αὐτῇ
Herwerden.

---

vi. 20. 17, vi. 21. 6-11, viii. 14. 10 *sq.* ; Scholiast on Homer,
Il. ii. 104 ; Scholiast on Pindar, *Olymp.* i. 71 (114) ; Scholiast
on Sophocles, *Electra*, 504 ; Scholiast on Euripides, *Orestes*,
982 and 990 ; Scholiast on Apollonius Rhodius, *Argon.* i.
752 ; Tzetzes, *Schol. on Lycophron*, 156 ; Hyginus, *Fab.* 84 ;
Servius, on Virgil, *Georg.* iii. 7, ed. Lion ; *Scriptores rerum
mythicarum Latini*, ed. G. H. Bode, vol. i. pp. 7, 125 (First
Vatican Mythographer, 21 ; Second Vatican Mythographer,
146). The story was told by Pherecydes, as we learn from
the Scholiasts on Sophocles and Apollonius Rhodius. (*ll. cc.*)
It was also the theme of two plays called *Oenomaus*, one of
them by Sophocles, and the other by Euripides. See *Tragicorum Graecorum Fragmenta*, ed. A. Nauck[2], pp. 233 *sqq.*,
539 *sqq.* ; *The Fragments of Sophocles*, ed. A. C. Pearson,
vol. ii. pp. 121 *sqq.* The versions of the story given by
Tzetzes and the Scholiast on Euripides (*Orestes*, 990) agree
closely with each other and with that of Apollodorus, which
they may have copied. They agree with him and with the
Scholiast on Pindar in alleging an incestuous passion of Oenomaus for his daughter as the reason why he was reluctant to
give her in marriage ; indeed they affirm that this was the
motive assigned for his conduct by the more accurate historians, though they also mention the oracle which warned him
that he would perish at the hands of his son-in-law. The fear
of this prediction being fulfilled is the motive generally alleged
by the extant writers of antiquity. Diodorus Siculus mentions
some particulars which are not noticed by other authors.
According to him, the goal of the race was the altar of Poseidon at Corinth, and the suitor was allowed a start ; for before
mounting his chariot Oenomaus sacrificed a ram to Zeus, and
while he was sacrificing the suitor drove off and made the best
of his way along the road, until Oenomaus, having completed
the sacrifice, was free to pursue and overtake him. The sacri-

say, or that he was warned by an oracle that he must die by the man that married her, no man got her to wife; for her father could not persuade her to cohabit with him, and her suitors were put by him to death.

fice was offered at a particular altar at Olympia, which some people called the altar of Hephaestus, and others the altar of Warlike Zeus (Pausanias, v. 14. 6). In the eastern gable of the temple of Zeus at Olympia the competitors with their chariots and charioteers were represented preparing for the race in the presence of an image of Zeus; among them were Hippodamia and her mother Sterope. These sculptures were found, more or less mutilated, by the Germans in their excavation of Olympia and are now exhibited in the local museum. See Pausanias, v. 10. 6 *sq.* with my commentary (vol. iii. pp. 504 *sqq.*). Curiously enough, the scene of the story is transposed by the Scholiast on Euripides (*Orestes*, 990), who affirms that Oenomaus reigned in Lesbos, though at the same time he says, in accordance with the usual tradition, that the goal of the race was the Isthmus of Corinth. The connexion of Oenomaus with Lesbos is to a certain extent countenanced by a story for which the authority cited is Theopompus. He related that when Pelops was on his way to Pisa (Olympia) to woo Hippodamia, his charioteer Cillus died in Lesbos, and that his ghost appeared to Pelops in a dream, lamenting his sad fate and begging to be accorded funeral honours. So Pelops burned the dead man's body, buried his ashes under a barrow, and founded a sanctuary of Cillaean Apollo close by. See the Scholiast on Homer, *Il.* i. 38 (where for ἐξερυπάρου τὸ εἴδωλον διὰ πυρός we should perhaps read ἐξεπύρου τὸ εἴδωλον διὰ πυρός, "he burned the body to ashes with fire," εἴδωλον being apparently used in the sense of "dead body"). Strabo describes the tomb of Cillus or Cillas, as he calls him, as a great mound beside the sanctuary of Cillaean Apollo, but he places the grave and the sanctuary, not in Lesbos, but on the opposite mainland, in the territory of Adramyttium, though he says that there was a Cillaeum also in Lesbos. See Strabo, xiii. l. 62 and 63, pp. 612, 613. Professor C. Robert holds that the original version of the legend of Oenomaus and Hippodamia belonged to Lesbos and not to Olympia. See his *Bild und Lied*, p. 187 note.

APOLLODORUS

5 ἀνῃροῦντο ὑπ' αὐτοῦ. ἔχων γὰρ ὅπλα τε καὶ
ἵππους παρὰ Ἄρεος ἆθλον ἐτίθει τοῖς μνηστῆρσι
τὸν γάμον, καὶ τὸν μνηστευόμενον ἔδει ἀναλα-
βόντα τὴν Ἱπποδάμειαν εἰς τὸ οἰκεῖον ἅρμα φεύγειν
ἄχρι τοῦ Κορινθίων ἰσθμοῦ, τὸν δὲ Οἰνόμαον
εὐθέως διώκειν καθωπλισμένον καὶ καταλαβόντα
κτείνειν· τὸν δὲ μὴ καταληφθέντα ἔχειν γυναῖκα
τὴν Ἱπποδάμειαν. καὶ τοῦτον τὸν τρόπον πολλοὺς
μνηστευομένους ἀπέκτεινεν, ὡς δέ τινες λέγουσι
δώδεκα· τὰς δὲ κεφαλὰς τῶν μνηστήρων ἐκτεμὼν [1]
τῇ οἰκίᾳ προσεπαττάλευε.

6 Παραγίνεται τοίνυν καὶ Πέλοψ ἐπὶ τὴν μνη-
στείαν· οὗ τὸ κάλλος ἰδοῦσα ἡ Ἱπποδάμεια ἔρωτα
ἔσχεν αὐτοῦ, καὶ πείθει Μυρτίλον τὸν Ἑρμοῦ
παῖδα συλλαβέσθαι αὐτῷ· ἦν δὲ Μυρτίλος [παρας
7 βάτης εἴτουν] ἡνίοχος Οἰνομάου. Μυρτίλος οὖν
ἐρῶν αὐτῆς καὶ βουλόμενος αὐτῇ χαρίσασθαι, ταῖς
χοινικίσι τῶν τροχῶν τοὺς ἥλους οὐκ ἐμβαλὼν
ἐποίησε τὸν Οἰνόμαον ἐν τῷ τρέχειν ἡττηθῆναι
καὶ ταῖς ἡνίαις συμπλακέντα συρόμενον ἀποθανεῖν,
κατὰ δέ τινας ἀναιρεθῆναι ὑπὸ τοῦ Πέλοπος· ὃ-

---

[1] ἐκτεμὼν Frazer : ἐκτέμνων E, Wagner.

---

[1] The number of the slain suitors was twelve according to
Tzetzes (*Schol. on Lycophron*, 156) and the Scholiast on Euripides (*Orestes*, 990); but it was thirteen according to Pindar
and his Scholiasts. See Pindar, *Olymp.* i. 79 (127) *sq.*, with
the Scholia on *v.* 79 (127), where the names of the suitors are
given. A still longer list of their names is given by Pausanias
(vi. 21. 7), who says that they were buried under a high
mound of earth, and that Pelops afterwards sacrificed to them
as to heroes every year.

[2] According to Hyginus (*Fab.* 84), when Pelops saw the
heads of the unsuccessful suitors nailed over the door, he

160

For he had arms and horses given him by Ares, and he offered as a prize to the suitors the hand of his daughter, and each suitor was bound to take up Hippodamia on his own chariot and flee as far as the Isthmus of Corinth, and Oenomaus straightway pursued him, in full armour, and if he overtook him he slew him; but if the suitor were not overtaken, he was to have Hippodamia to wife. And in this way he slew many suitors, some say twelve;[1] and he cut off the heads of the suitors and nailed them to his house.[2]

So Pelops also came a-wooing; and when Hippodamia saw his beauty, she conceived a passion for him, and persuaded Myrtilus, son of Hermes, to help him; for Myrtilus was charioteer to Oenomaus. Accordingly Myrtilus, being in love with her and wishing to gratify her, did not insert the linchpins in the boxes of the wheels,[3] and thus caused Oenomaus to lose the race and to be entangled in the reins and dragged to death; but according to some, he was killed by Pelops. And

began to repent of his temerity, and offered Myrtilus, the charioteer of Oenomaus, the half of the kingdom if he would help him in the race.

[3] According to another account, which had the support of Pherecydes, Myrtilus substituted linchpins of wax for linchpins of bronze. See Scholiast on Apollonius Rhodius, *Argon.* i. 752; Tzetzes, *Schol. on Lycophron,* 156; Scholiast on Euripides, *Orestes,* 998; Servius, on Virgil, *Georg.* iii. 7, ed. Lion, where for *cereis* we should read *cereis* (the text in Thilo and Hagen's edition of Servius is mutilated and omits the passage); *Scriptores rerum mythicarum Latini,* ed. G. H. Bode, vol. i. pp. 7, 125 (First Vatican Mythographer, 21; Second Vatican Mythographer, 146).

ἐν τῷ ἀποθνήσκειν κατηράσατο τῷ Μυρτίλῳ γνοὺς
τὴν ἐπιβουλήν, ἵνα ὑπὸ Πέλοπος ἀπόληται.

8   Λαβὼν οὖν Πέλοψ τὴν Ἱπποδάμειαν καὶ διερ-
χόμενος ἐν τόπῳ τινί, τὸν Μυρτίλον ἔχων μεθ᾽
ἑαυτοῦ, μικρὸν ἀναχωρεῖ κομίσων ὕδωρ διψώσῃ
τῇ γυναικί· Μυρτίλος δὲ ἐν τούτῳ βιάζειν αὐτὴν
ἐπεχείρει. μαθὼν δὲ τοῦτο παρ᾽ αὐτῆς [1] ὁ Πέλοψ
ῥίπτει τὸν Μυρτίλον περὶ Γεραιστὸν ἀκρωτήριον
εἰς τὸ ἀπ᾽ ἐκείνου κληθὲν Μυρτῷον πέλαγος· ὁ δὲ
ῥιπτούμενος ἀρὰς ἔθετο κατὰ τοῦ Πέλοπος γένους.

9   παραγενόμενος δὲ Πέλοψ ἐπ᾽ ὠκεανὸν καὶ ἁγνι-
σθεὶς ὑπὸ Ἡφαίστου, ἐπανελθὼν εἰς Πῖσαν τῆς
Ἤλιδος τὴν Οἰνομάου βασιλείαν λαμβάνει, χειρωσάμενος τὴν πρότερον Ἀπίαν καὶ Πελασγιῶτιν
λεγομένην, ἣν ἀφ᾽ ἑαυτοῦ Πελοπόννησον ἐκάλεσεν.

10   Ὅτι υἱοὶ Πέλοπος Πιτθεὺς Ἀτρεὺς Θυέστης
καὶ ἕτεροι· γυνὴ δὲ Ἀτρέως Ἀερόπη τοῦ Κατ-

---

[1] αὑτῆς Wagner : αὐτὴν E.

---

[1] Compare Tzetzes, *Schol. on Lycophron*, 156 ; Scholiast
on Homer, *Il.* ii. 104. The latter writer says, somewhat absurdly, that the incident took place when Pelops and Hippodamia were crossing the Aegean Sea, and that, Hippodamia
being athirst, Pelops dismounted from the chariot to look for
water in the desert.

[2] Compare Euripides, *Orestes*, 989 *sqq.*

[3] Compare Tzetzes, *Schol. on Lycophron*, 156 ; Scholiast
on Euripides, *Orestes*, 990.

[4] As to Apia, the old name of Peloponnese, see above, ii.
1. 1 ; Pausanias, ii. 5. 7 ; Stephanus Byzantius, *s.v.* Ἀπία.
The term Pelasgiotis seems not to occur elsewhere as a name
for Peloponnese. However, Euripides uses Pelasgia apparently as equivalent to Argolis (*Orestes*, 960).

[5] According to Pindar, Pelops had six sons by Hippodamia,
and three different lists of their names are given by the
Scholiasts on the passage. All the lists include the three

162

in dying he cursed Myrtilus, whose treachery he had
discovered, praying that he might perish by the hand
of Pelops.

Pelops, therefore, got Hippodamia; and on his
journey, in which he was accompanied by Myrtilus,
he came to a certain place, and withdrew a little to
fetch water for his wife, who was athirst; and in the
meantime Myrtilus tried to rape her.[1] But when
Pelops learned that from her, he threw Myrtilus into
the sea, called after him the Myrtoan Sea, at Cape
Geraestus[2]; and Myrtilus, as he was being thrown,
uttered curses against the house of Pelops. When
Pelops had reached the Ocean and been cleansed by
Hephaestus,[3] he returned to Pisa in Elis and
succeeded to the kingdom of Oenomaus, but not till
he had subjugated what was formerly called Apia
and Pelasgiotis, which he called Peloponnese after
himself.[4]

The sons of Pelops were Pittheus, Atreus, Thyestes,
and others.[5] Now the wife of Atreus was Aerope,

mentioned by Apollodorus. See Pindar, *Olymp.* i. 89 (144),
with the Scholia. Three sons, Hippalcimus, Atreus, and
Thyestes, are named by Hyginus (*Fab.* 84). Besides his legitimate sons Pelops is said to have had a bastard son Chrysippus, who was born to him before his marriage with Hippodamia. His fondness for this love-child excited the jealousy
of his wife, and at her instigation Atreus and Thyestes murdered Chrysippus by throwing him down a well. For this
crime Pelops cursed his two sons and banished them, and
Hippodamia fled to Argolis, but her bones were afterwards
brought back to Olympia. See Thucydides, i. 9; Pausanias,
vi. 20. 7; J. Tzetzes, *Chiliades*, i. 415 *sqq* ; Scholiast on
Homer, *Il.* ii. 105; Hyginus, *Fab.* 85. Euripides wrote a
tragedy *Chrysippus* on this subject. See *Tragicorum
Graecorum Fragmenta*, ed. A. Nauck[2], pp. 632 *sqq.* The
tragedy is alluded to by Cicero (*Tuscul. Disput.* iv. 33. 71).
As to Chrysippus, see also above, iii. 5. 5.

APOLLODORUS

ρέως,¹ ἥτις ἥρα Θυέστου. ὁ δὲ Ἀτρεὺς εὐξάμενός
ποτε τῶν αὐτοῦ² ποιμνίων, ὅπερ ἂν κάλλιστον
γένηται, τοῦτο θῦσαι Ἀρτέμιδι, λέγουσιν ἀρνὸς
φανείσης χρυσῆς ὅτι κατημέλησε τῆς εὐχῆς·
11 πνίξας δὲ αὐτὴν εἰς λάρνακα κατέθετο κἀκεῖ
ἐφύλασσε ταύτην· ἣν Ἀερόπη δίδωσι τῷ Θυέστῃ
μοιχευθεῖσα ὑπ' αὐτοῦ. χρησμοῦ γὰρ γεγονότος
τοῖς Μυκηναίοις ἑλέσθαι βασιλέα Πελοπίδην,
μετεπέμψαντο Ἀτρέα καὶ Θυέστην. λόγου δὲ
γενομένου περὶ τῆς βασιλείας ἐξεῖπε Θυέστης τῷ
πλήθει τὴν βασιλείαν δεῖν ἔχειν τὸν ἔχοντα τὴν
ἄρνα τὴν χρυσῆν· συνθεμένου δὲ τοῦ Ἀτρέως
12 δείξας ἐβασίλευσε. Ζεὺς δὲ Ἑρμῆν πέμπει πρὸς
Ἀτρέα καὶ λέγει συνθέσθαι πρὸς Θυέστην περὶ
τοῦ βασιλεῦσαι Ἀτρέα, εἰ τὴν ἐναντίαν ὁδεύσει
ὁ Ἥλιος· Θυέστου δὲ συνθεμένου τὴν δύσιν εἰς
ἀνατολὰς ὁ Ἥλιος ἐποιήσατο· ὅθεν ἐκμαρτυρή-
σαντος τοῦ δαίμονος τὴν Θυέστου πλεονεξίαν, τὴν
βασιλείαν Ἀτρεὺς παρέλαβε καὶ Θυέστην ἐφυ-
13 γάδευσεν. αἰσθόμενος δὲ τῆς μοιχείας ὕστερον

---

¹ Κατρέως Wagner: καστρέως E.
² αὐτοῦ Wagner: αὐτοῦ E.

---

¹ This story of the golden lamb, and of the appeal made to its
possession by the two brothers in the contest for the kingdom,
is told in substantially the same way by J. Tzetzes, *Chiliades*,
i. 425 *sqq.*; Scholiast on Homer, *Il.* ii. 106; Scholiast on
Euripides, *Orestes*, 811, 998. Tzetzes records the vow of Atreus
to sacrifice the best of his flock to Artemis, and he cites as
his authority Apollonius, which is almost certainly a mistake
for Apollodorus. Probably Tzetzes and the Scholiasts drew
on the present passage of Apollodorus, or rather on the
passage as it appeared in the unabridged text instead of in
the *Epitome* which is all that we now possess of the last

daughter of Catreus, and she loved Thyestes. And Atreus once vowed to sacrifice to Artemis the finest of his flocks; but when a golden lamb appeared, they say that he neglected to perform his vow, and having choked the lamb, he deposited it in a box and kept it there, and Aerope gave it to Thyestes, by whom she had been debauched. For the Mycenaeans had received an oracle which bade them choose a Pelopid for their king, and they had sent for Atreus and Thyestes. And when a discussion took place concerning the kingdom, Thyestes declared to the multitude that the kingdom ought to belong to him who owned the golden lamb, and when Atreus agreed, Thyestes produced the lamb and was made king. But Zeus sent Hermes to Atreus and told him to stipulate with Thyestes that Atreus should be king if the sun should go backward; and when Thyestes agreed, the sun set in the east; hence the deity having plainly attested the usurpation of Thyestes, Atreus got the kingdom and banished Thyestes.[1] But afterwards being apprized

---

part of the *Library*. Euripides told the story allusively in much the same way. See his *Electra*, 699 *sqq.*; *Orestes*, 996 *sqq.* Compare Plato, *Politicus*, 12, pp. 268 *sq.*; Pausanias, ii. 18. 1; Lucian, *De astrologia*, 12; Dio Chrysostom, *Or.* lxvi. vol. ii. p. 221, ed. L. Dindorf; Accius, quoted by Cicero, *De natura deorum*, iii. 27. 68; Seneca, *Thyestes*, 222–235; Lactantius Placidus, on Statius, *Theb.* iv. 306; *Scriptores rerum mythicarum Latini*, ed. G. H. Bode, vol. i. pp. 7, 125 *sq.* (First Vatican Mythographer, 22; Second Vatican Mythographer, 147). From these various accounts and allusions it would seem that in their dispute for the kingdom, which Atreus claimed in right of birth as the elder (J. Tzetzes, *Chiliades*, i. 426), it was agreed that he who could exhibit the greatest portent should be king. Atreus intended to produce the golden lamb, which had been born in

κήρυκα πέμψας ἐπὶ διαλλαγὰς αὐτὸν ἐκάλει· καὶ
ψευσάμενος εἶναι φίλος, παραγενομένου τοὺς παῖδας, οὓς εἶχεν ἐκ νηίδος νύμφης, Ἀγλαὸν [1] καὶ
Καλλιλέοντα καὶ Ὀρχομενόν, ἐπὶ τὸν Διὸς βωμὸν
καθεσθέντας ἱκέτας ἔσφαξε, καὶ μελίσας καὶ
καθεψήσας παρατίθησι Θυέστῃ χωρὶς τῶν ἄκρων,
ἐμφορηθέντι [2] δὲ δείκνυσι τὰ ἄκρα καὶ τῆς χώρας
14 αὐτὸν ἐκβάλλει. Θυέστης δὲ κατὰ πάντα τρόπον

[1] Ἀγλαὸν Wagner (comparing J. Tzetzes, *Chiliades*, i. 449,
τὸν Ἀγλαόν, Ὀρχομενόν, Κάλλαον): ἀγωδὸν E.
[2] ἐμφορηθέντι Frazer : ἐμφορηθέντα E, Wagner.

---

his flocks; but meanwhile the lamb had been given by his
treacherous wife Aerope to her paramour Thyestes, who produced it in evidence of his claim and was accordingly awarded
the crown. However, with the assistance of Zeus, the right-
ful claimant Atreus was able to exhibit a still greater portent,
which was the sun and the Pleiades retracing their course in
the sky and setting in the east instead of in the west. This
mighty marvel, attesting the divine approbation of Atreus,
clinched the dispute in his favour; he became king, and
banished his rival Thyestes. According to a different account,
which found favour with the Latin poets, the sun reversed
his course in the sky, not in order to demonstrate the right
of Atreus to the crown, but on the contrary to mark his disgust and horror at the king for murdering his nephews and
dishing up their mangled limbs to their father Thyestes at
table. See J. Tzetzes, *Chiliades*, i. 451; Statyllius Flaccus,
in *Anthologia Palatina*, ix. 98. 2; Hyginus, *Fab.* 88 and 258;
Ovid, *Tristia*, ii. 391 *sq.*; *id. Ars amat.* i. 327 *sqq.*; Seneca,
Thyestes, 776 *sqq.*; Martial, iii. 45. 1 *sq.* From the verses
of Statyllius Flaccus we may infer that this latter was the
interpretation put on the backward motion of the sun by
Sophocles in his tragedy *Atreus.* See *The Fragments of
Sophocles*, ed. A. C. Pearson, vol. i. p. 93. In later times
rationalists explained the old fable by saying that Atreus
was an astronomer who first calculated an eclipse, and so
threw his less scientific brother into the shade (Hyginus,

of the adultery, he sent a herald to Thyestes with a
proposal of accommodation; and when he had lured
Thyestes by a pretence of friendship, he slaughtered
the sons, Aglaus, Callileon, and Orchomenus, whom
Thyestes had by a Naiad nymph, though they had
sat down as suppliants on the altar of Zeus. And
having cut them limb from limb and boiled them, he
served them up to Thyestes without the extremities;
and when Thyestes had eaten heartily of them, he
showed him the extremities, and cast him out of the
country.[1] But seeking by all means to pay Atreus

Fab. 158; Servius, on Virgil, *Aen.* i. 568), or who first pointed
out that the sun appears to revolve in a direction contrary
to the motion of the stars. See Strabo, i. 2. 15, p. 23; Lucian,
De astrologia, 12. A fragment of Euripides appears to show
that he put in the mouth of Atreus this claim to astronomical
discovery. See *Tragicorum Graecorum Fragmenta,* ed. A.
Nauck[2], p. 639 (frag. 861). A still more grandiose explanation of the myth was given by Plato (*l.c.*), who adduced it,
with grave irony, as evidence that in alternate cycles of vast
duration the universe revolves in opposite directions, the
reversal of its motion at the end of each cycle being accompanied by a great destruction of animal life. This magnificent
theory was perhaps suggested to the philosopher by the spe-
culations of Empedocles, and it bears a resemblance not only
to the ancient Indian doctrine of successive epochs of creation
and destruction, but also to Herbert Spencer's view of the
great cosmic process as moving eternally in alternate and
measureless cycles of evolution and dissolution. See Sir
Charles Lyell, *Principles of Geology,* Twelfth Edition (London,
1875), i. 7, quoting the *Laws of Manu*; Herbert Spencer,
First Principles, Third Edition (London, 1875), pp. 536 *sq.*
Compare *Spirits of the Corn and of the Wild,* ii. 303 *sqq.*

[1] As to the famous, or infamous, Thyestean banquet, see
Aeschylus, *Agamemnon,* 1590 *sqq.*; Pausanias, ii. 18. 1; J.
Tzetzes, *Chiliades,* i. 447 *sqq.*; Hyginus, *Fab.* 88; Seneca,
Thyestes, 682 *sqq.*; Servius, on Virgil, *Aen.* i. 568, xi. 262;
Lactantius Placidus, on Statius, *Theb.* iv. 306; *Scriptores
rerum mythicarum Latini,* ed. G. H. Bode, vol. i. pp. 7, 126,

APOLLODORUS

ζητῶν Ἀτρέα μετελθεῖν ἐχρηστηριάζετο περὶ τούτου καὶ λαμβάνει χρησμόν, ὡς εἰ παῖδα γεννήσει
τῇ θυγατρὶ συνελθών. ποιεῖ οὖν ¹ οὕτω καὶ γεννᾷ
ἐκ τῆς θυγατρὸς Αἴγισθον,² ὃς ἀνδρωθεὶς καὶ
μαθών, ὅτι Θυέστου παῖς ἐστι, κτείνας Ἀτρέα
Θυέστῃ τὴν βασιλείαν ἀποκατέστησεν.

*   *   *   *   *   *   *   *

TZ 15 <Τὸν δ' Ἀγαμέμνονα ³ τροφὸς μετὰ τοῦ Μενελάου

¹ οὖν Frazer : γοῦν E, Wagner.
² Wagner marks a lacuna between θυγατρὸς and Αἴγισθον.
There seems to be none in the MS.
³ τὸν δ' Ἀγαμέμνονα . . . Μενέλαος Ἑλένην. These verses
are inserted from J. Tzetzes, *Chiliades*, i. 456–465, who may
have borrowed the substance of them from Apollodorus.

---

209 (First Vatican Mythographer, 22; Second Vatican Mythographer, 147 ; Third Vatican Mythographer, viii. 16). Sophocles wrote at least two tragedies on the fatal feud between the
brothers, one of them being called *Atreus* and the other
Thyestes. The plots of the plays are not certainly known, but
it is thought probable that in the former he dealt with the
cannibal banquet, and in the latter with the subsequent
adventures and crimes of Thyestes.   See *The Fragments of
Sophocles*, ed. A. C. Pearson, vol. i. pp. 91 *sqq*., 185 *sqq*.
Euripides also wrote a tragedy called *Thyestes*.   See *Tragicorum Graecorum Fragmenta*, ed. A. Nauck², pp. 480 *sqq*.
Tzetzes agrees with Apollodorus as to the names of the three
murdered sons of Thyestes, except that he calls one of them
Callaus instead of Callileon.   Only two, Tantalus and Plisthenes, are named by Seneca and Hyginus.
  ¹ The later history of Thyestes, including his incest with his
daughter Pelopia, is narrated much more fully by Hyginus
(*Fab.* 87 and 88), who is believed to have derived the story
from the *Thyestes* of Sophocles.   See *The Fragments of
Sophocles*, ed. A. C. Pearson, vol. i. pp. 185 *sqq*.   The incest
and the birth of Aegisthus, who is said to have received his

out, Thyestes inquired of the oracle on the subject, and received an answer that it could be done if he were to beget a son by intercourse with his own daughter. He did so accordingly, and begot Aegisthus by his daughter. And Aegisthus, when he was grown to manhood and had learned that he was a son of Thyestes, killed Atreus, and restored the kingdom to Thyestes.[1]

*   *   *   *   *   *   *   *

But[2] the nurse took Agamemnon and Menelaus

name because he was suckled by a goat, are told more briefly by Lactantius Placidus (on Statius, *Theb.* iv. 306) and the First and Second Vatican Mythographers (*Scriptores rerum mythicarum Latini*, ed. G. H. Bode, vol. i. pp. 7 *sq.*, 126). The incest is said to have been committed at Sicyon, where the father and daughter met by night without recognizing each other ; the recognition occurred at a later time by means of a sword which Pelopia had wrested from her ravisher, and with which, on coming to a knowledge of her relationship to him, she stabbed herself to death.

[2] The passage translated in this paragraph does not occur in our present text of Apollodorus, which is here defective. It is found in the *Chiliades* of J. Tzetzes (i. 456–465), who probably borrowed it from Apollodorus ; for in the preceding lines Tzetzes narrates the crimes of Atreus and Thyestes in agreement with Apollodorus and actually cites him as his authority, if, as seems nearly certain, we should read Apollodorus for Apollonius in his text (see above p. 164). The restoration of the passage to its present place in the text of Apollodorus is due to the German editor R. Wagner. Here after describing how Aegisthus had murdered Atreus and placed his own father Thyestes on the throne of Mycenae, Apollodorus tells us how the nurse of Atreus's two children, Agamemnon and Menelaus, saved the lives of her youthful charges by conveying them to Sicyon. The implied youthfulness of Agamemnon and Menelaus at the time of the death of their father Atreus is inconsistent with the narrative of Hyginus (*Fab.* 88), who tells how Atreus had sent his two sons abroad to find and arrest Thyestes.

ἄγει πρὸς Πολυφείδεα, κρατοῦντα Σικυῶνος,
ὃς πάλιν τούτους πέπομφε πρὸς Αἰτωλὸν Οἰνέα.
μετ᾽ οὐ πολὺ Τυνδάρεως τούτους κατάγει πάλιν,
οἳ τὸν Θυέστην μὲν αὐτὸν "Ηρας βωμῷ φυγόντα
ὁρκώσαντες διώκουσιν οἰκεῖν τὴν Κυθηρίαν.
οἱ δὲ Τυνδάρεω γαμβροὶ γίνονται θυγατράσιν,
ὁ Ἀγαμέμνων μὲν λαβὼν σύνευνον Κλυταιμνήστραν,
κτείνας αὐτῆς τὸν σύζυγον Τάνταλον τὸν Θυέστου
σὺν τέκνῳ πάνυ νεογνῷ, Μενέλαος Ἑλένην.>

S 16 | Ἀγαμέμνων δὲ βασιλεύει Μυκηναίων καὶ γαμεῖ
Τυνδάρεω θυγατέρα Κλυταιμνήστραν, τὸν πρότερον αὐτῆς ἄνδρα Τάνταλον Θυέστου σὺν τῷ
παιδὶ κτείνας,[1] καὶ γίνεται αὐτῷ παῖς μὲν Ὀρέστης, θυγατέρες δὲ Χρυσόθεμις Ἠλέκτρα Ἰφιγένεια.
Μενέλαος δὲ Ἑλένην γαμεῖ καὶ βασιλεύει Σπάρτης, Τυνδάρεω τὴν βασιλείαν δόντος αὐτῷ.

III. Αὖθις δὲ Ἑλένην Ἀλέξανδρος ἁρπάζει, ὥς
τινες λέγουσι κατὰ βούλησιν Διός, ἵνα Εὐρώπης
καὶ Ἀσίας εἰς πόλεμον ἐλθούσης[2] ἡ θυγάτηρ
αὐτοῦ ἔνδοξος γένηται, ἢ καθάπερ εἶπον ἄλλοι
2 ὅπως τὸ τῶν ἡμιθέων γένος ἀρθῇ. διὰ δὴ τούτων

---

[1] κτείνας Frazer (compare Euripides, *Iphigenia in Aulis*,
1150 ; Pausanias, ii. 18. 2, ii. 22. 2 *sq.*; J. Tzetzes, *Chiliades*
i. 464, quoted above): κτείναντος S, Wagner.
[2] ἐλθούσης S.   Perhaps we should read ἐλθουσῶν.

---

[1] Polyphides is said to have been the twenty-fourth king
of Sicyon and to have reigned at the time when Troy was
taken. See Eusebius, *Chronic.* vol. i. coll. 175, 176, ed.
A. Schoene.
[2] As to Tantalus, the first husband of Clytaemnestra, and
his murder by Agamemnon, see Euripides, *Iphigenia in*

to Polyphides, lord of Sicyon,[1] who again sent them to Oeneus, the Aetolian. Not long afterwards Tyndareus brought them back again, and they drove away Thyestes to dwell in Cytheria, after that they had taken an oath of him at the altar of Hera, to which he had fled. And they became the sons-in-law of Tyndareus by marrying his daughters, Agamemnon getting Clytaemnestra to wife, after he had slain her spouse Tantalus, the son of Thyestes, together with his newborn babe, while Menelaus got Helen.

And Agamemnon reigned over the Mycenaeans and married Clytaemnestra, daughter of Tyndareus, after slaying her former husband Tantalus, son of Thyestes, with his child.[2] And there were born to Agamemnon a son Orestes, and daughters, Chrysothemis, Electra, and Iphigenia.[3] And Menelaus married Helen and reigned over Sparta, Tyndareus having ceded the kingdom to him.[4]

III. But afterwards Alexander carried off Helen, as some say, because such was the will of Zeus, in order that his daughter might be famous for having embroiled Europe and Asia; or, as others have said, that the race of the demigods might be exalted. For

----

Aulis, 1148 *sqq.* ; Pausanias, ii. 18. 2, ii. 22. 2 *sq.* According to Pausanias, he was a son of Thyestes or of Broteas, and his bones were deposited in a large bronze vessel at Argos.

[3] In Homer (*Il.* ix. 142 *sqq.*) Agamemnon says that he has a son Orestes and three daughters, Chrysothemis, Laodice, and Iphianassa (Iphigenia), and he offers to give any one of his daughters in marriage to Achilles without a dowry, if only that doughty hero will forgive him and fight again for the Greeks against Troy. Electra, the daughter of Agamemnon, who figures so prominently in Greek tragedy, is unknown to Homer, and so is the sacrifice of Agamemnon's third daughter, Iphigenia.

[4] See above, iii. 11. 2.

ES μίαν αἰτίαν | μῆλον περὶ κάλλους Ἔρις ἐμβάλλει
Ἥρᾳ καὶ Ἀθηνᾷ καὶ Ἀφροδίτῃ, καὶ κελεύει Ζεὺς [1]
Ἑρμῆν εἰς Ἴδην πρὸς Ἀλέξανδρον ἄγειν, ἵνα ὑπ
ἐκείνου διακριθῶσι. αἱ δὲ ἐπαγγέλλονται δῶρα
δώσειν Ἀλεξάνδρῳ, Ἥρα μὲν πασῶν προκριθεῖσα
βασιλείαν πάντων,[2] Ἀθηνᾷ δὲ πολέμου νίκην,
Ἀφροδίτῃ δὲ γάμον Ἑλένης. ὁ δὲ [3] Ἀφροδίτην
προκρίνει καὶ πηξαμένου Φερέκλου ναῦς [4] εἰς Σπάρ-
3 την ἐκπλέει. ἐφ' ἡμέρας δ' ἐννέα ξενισθεὶς παρὰ
Μενελάῳ, τῇ δεκάτῃ πορευθέντος εἰς Κρήτην ἐκείνου κηδεῦσαι τὸν μητροπάτορα Κατρέα, πείθει
τὴν Ἑλένην ἀπαγαγεῖν σὺν ἑαυτῷ. ἡ δὲ ἐνναέτη

---

[1] Ζεὺς E, omitted in S.

[2] Ἥρα μὲν πασῶν προκριθεῖσα βασιλείαν πάντων E : Ἥρα μὲν
οὖν ἔφη προκριθεῖσα δώσειν αὐτῷ πάντων βασιλείαν S.

[3] ὁ δὲ Ἀφροδίτην . . . τῇ δεκάτῃ δὲ E : Ἀφροδίτην δὲ προκρίνας
πηξαμένου ναῦς Φερέκλου πλεύσας εἰς Σπάρτην ἐπὶ ἐννέα ἡμέρας
ξενίζεται παρὰ Μενελάου. τῇ δεκάτῃ δὲ S.

[4] ναῦς S : νῆας E. For the form ναῦς compare ii. 8. 2,
Epitome, iii. 9, 11, 12, 13, 14, 17, 31, iv. 4, v. 13, 22, vi. 29,
vii. 3, 4.

---

[1] As to the judgment of Paris (Alexander), see Homer, Il.
xxiv. 25 sqq.; Cypria, in Proclus, Chrestom. i. (Epicorum
Graecorum Fragmenta, ed. G. Kinkel, pp. 16 sq.; Hesiod,
etc., ed. H. G. Evelyn-White, pp 488, 490, in Loeb Classical
Library); Euripides, Troades, 924 sqq., Iphigenia in Aulis,
1290 sqq., Helen, 23 sqq., Andromache, 274 sqq.; Isocrates,
Helene, 41; Lucian, Dial. deorum, 20, Dial. marin. 5,
Tzetzes, Schol. on Lycophron, 93; Hyginus, Fab. 92; Ser-
vius, on Virgil, Aen. i. 27; Scriptores rerum mythicarum
Latini, ed. G. H. Bode, vol. i. pp. 65 sq., 142 sq. (First
Vatican Mythographer, 208; Second Vatican Mythographer,
205). The story ran that all the gods and goddesses, except
Strife, were invited to attend the marriage of Peleus and
Thetis, and that Strife, out of spite at being overlooked,
threw among the wedding guests a golden apple inscribed

one of these reasons Strife threw an apple as a prize
of beauty to be contended for by Hera, Athena, and
Aphrodite; and Zeus commanded Hermes to lead
them to Alexander on Ida in order to be judged by
him. And they promised to give Alexander gifts.
Hera said that if she were preferred to all women,
she would give him the kingdom over all men; and
Athena promised victory in war, and Aphrodite the
hand of Helen. And he decided in favour of
Aphrodite[1]; and sailed away to Sparta with ships
built by Phereclus.[2] For nine days he was entertained by Menelaus; but on the tenth day, Menelaus
having gone on a journey to Crete to perform the
obsequies of his mother's father Catreus, Alexander
persuaded Helen to go off[3] with him. And she

[1] with the words, "Let the fair one take it," or "The apple
for the fair." Three goddesses, Hera, Athena, and Aphrodite, contended for this prize of beauty, and Zeus referred
the disputants to the judgment of Paris. The intervention
of Strife was mentioned in the *Cypria* according to Proclus,
but without mention of the golden apple, which first appears
in late writers, such as Lucian and Hyginus. The offers made
by the three divine competitors to Paris are recorded with
substantial agreement by Euripides (*Troades*, 924 *sqq.*), Isocrates, Lucian, and Apollodorus. Hyginus is also in harmony
with them, if in his text we read *fortissimum* for the *for-
missimum* of the MSS., for which some editors wrongly read
formosissimum. The scene of the judgment of Paris was
represented on the throne of Apollo at Amyclae and on the
chest of Cypselus at Olympia (Pausanias, iii. 18. 12, v. 19. 5).

[2] Compare Homer, *Il.* v. 59 *sqq.*, from which we learn
that the shipbuilder was a son of Tecton, who was a son of
Harmon. The names of his father and grandfather indicate,
as Dr. Leaf observes, that the business had been carried on
in the family for three generations. Compare Tzetzes, *Schol.
on Lycophron*, 97.

[3] The Greek for "to go off" is ἀπαγαγεῖν, a rare use of
ἀπάγειν, which, however, occurs in the common phrase, ἄπαγε,
"Be off with you!"

Ἑρμιόνην καταλιποῦσα, ἐνθεμένη τὰ πλεῖστα τῶν
4 χρημάτων, ἀνάγεται τῆς νυκτὸς σὺν αὐτῷ. Ἥρα
δὲ αὐτοῖς ἐπιπέμπει χειμῶνα πολύν, ὑφ᾽ οὗ βια-
σθέντες προσίσχουσι Σιδῶνι. εὐλαβούμενος δὲ
Ἀλέξανδρος μὴ διωχθῇ, πολὺν διέτριψε χρόνον
ἐν Φοινίκῃ καὶ Κύπρῳ. ὡς δὲ ἀπήλπισε τὴν
5 δίωξιν, ἧκεν εἰς Τροίαν μετὰ Ἑλένης. ἔνιοι δέ
φασιν Ἑλένην μὲν ὑπὸ Ἑρμοῦ κατὰ βούλησιν
Διὸς κομισθῆναι κλαπεῖσαν¹ εἰς Αἴγυπτον καὶ
δοθεῖσαν Πρωτεῖ τῷ βασιλεῖ τῶν Αἰγυπτίων
φυλάττειν, Ἀλέξανδρον δὲ παραγενέσθαι εἰς Τροίαν
πεποιημένον ἐκ νεφῶν εἴδωλον Ἑλένης ἔχοντα.

¹ κλαπεῖσαν E : κατὰ πεῖσαν S.

---

[1] With this account of the hospitable reception of Paris in
Sparta, the departure of Menelaus for Crete, and the flight of
the guilty pair, compare Proclus, *Chrestom.* i., in *Epicorum
Graecorum Fragmenta*, ed. G. Kinkel, p. 17; J. Tzetzes,
Antehomerica, 96–134. As to the death of Catreus, the
maternal grandfather of Menelaus, see above, iii. 2. 1 *sq.*

[2] The voyage of Paris and Helen to Sidon was known to
Homer (*Il.* vi. 289 *sqq.*, with the Scholia on *v.* 291). It was
also recorded in the epic *Cypria*, according to Proclus, who
says that Paris captured the city (*Epicorum Graecorum Fragmenta*, ed. G. Kinkel, p. 18). Yet according to Herodotus
(ii. 117), the author of the *Cypria* described how Paris and
Helen sailed in three days from Sparta to Ilium with a fair
wind and a smooth sea. It seems therefore that Herodotus
and Proclus had different *texts* of the *Cypria* before them.
Dictys Cretensis tells how, driven by the winds to Cyprus,
Paris sailed with some ships to Sidon, where he was hospitably entertained by the king, but basely requited his
hospitality by treacherously murdering his host and plun-
dering the palace. In embarking with his booty on his ships,
he was attacked by the Sidonians, but, after a bloody fight
and the loss of two ships, he succeeded in beating off his
assailants and putting to sea with the rest of his vessels.
See Dictys Cretensis, *Bellum Trojanum*, i. 5.

abandoned Hermione, then nine years old, and putting most of the property on board, she set sail with him by night.[1] But Hera sent them a heavy storm which forced them to put in at Sidon. And fearing lest he should be pursued, Alexander spent much time in Phoenicia and Cyprus.[2] But when he thought that all chance of pursuit was over, he came to Troy with Helen. But some say that Hermes, in obedience to the will of Zeus, stole Helen and carried her to Egypt, and gave her to Proteus, king of the Egyptians, to guard, and that Alexander repaired to Troy with a phantom of Helen fashioned out of clouds.[3]

[3] Compare Euripides, *Helene*, 31–51, 582 *sqq.*, 669 *sqq.*, *Electra*, 1280 *sqq.* In the *Helene* the dramatist says that Hera, angry with Paris for preferring Aphrodite to her, fashioned a phantom Helen which he wedded, while the real Helen was transported by Hermes to Egypt and committed to the care of Proteus. In the *Electra* the poet says that it was Zeus who sent a phantom Helen to Troy, in order to stir up strife and provoke bloodshed among men. A different account is given by Herodotus (ii. 112–120). According to him, Paris carried the real Helen to Egypt, but there king Proteus, indignant at the crime of which Paris had been guilty, banished him from Egypt and detained Helen in safekeeping until her true husband, Menelaus, came and fetched her away. Compare Philostratus, *Vit. Apollon.* iv. 16; J. Tzetzes, *Antehomerica,* 147 *sqq.* Later writers accepted this view, adding that instead of the real Helen, whom he kept, Proteus conjured up by magic art a phantom Helen, which he gave to Paris to carry away with him to Troy. See Tzetzes, *Schol. on Lycophron*, 113; Servius, on Virgil, *Aen.* i. 651, ii. 592. So far as we know, the poet Stesichorus in the sixth century before our era was the first to broach the theory that Helen at Troy, for whom the Greeks and Trojans fought and died, was a mere wraith, while her true self was far away, whether at home in Sparta or with Proteus in Egypt; for there is nothing to show whether Stesichorus shared the opinion that Paris had spirited her away to the East before he returned, with or without her, to Troy. This view the

S 6 | Μενέλαος δὲ αἰσθόμενος τὴν ἁρπαγὴν ἧκεν εἰς
Μυκήνας πρὸς Ἀγαμέμνονα, καὶ δεῖται στρα-
τείαν ἐπὶ Τροίαν ἀθροίζειν καὶ στρατολογεῖν τὴν
Ἑλλάδα. ὁ δὲ πέμπων κήρυκα πρὸς ἕκαστον τῶν
βασιλέων τῶν ὅρκων ὑπεμίμνησκεν ὧν ὤμοσαν,
καὶ περὶ τῆς ἰδίας γυναικὸς ἕκαστον ἀσφαλίζεσθαι
παρῄνει, ἴσην λέγων γεγενῆσθαι τὴν τῆς Ἑλλάδος καταφρόνησιν καὶ κοινήν. ὄντων δὲ πολλῶν
προθύμων στρατεύεσθαι, παραγίνονται καὶ πρὸς
ES 7 Ὀδυσσέα εἰς Ἰθάκην. | ὁ δὲ οὐ βουλόμενος¹ στρα-
τεύεσθαι προσποιεῖται μανίαν. Παλαμήδης δὲ ὁ
Ναυπλίου ἤλεγξε τὴν μανίαν ψευδῆ, καὶ προσ-
ποιησαμένῳ² μεμηνέναι παρηκολούθει· ἁρπάσας
δὲ Τηλέμαχον ἐκ τοῦ κόλπου τῆς Πηνελόπης³ ὡς
κτενῶν ἐξείλκει. Ὀδυσσεὺς δὲ περὶ τοῦ παιδὸς
εὐλαβηθεὶς ὡμολόγησε τὴν προσποίητον μανίαν
καὶ στρατεύεται.

¹ ὁ δὲ οὐ βουλόμενος S: ὅτι Ὀδυσσεὺς μὴ βουλόμενος E.
² προσποιησαμένῳ E: προσποιησαμένου S.
³ ἐκ τοῦ κόλπου τῆς Πηνελόπης E: ἐκ τοῦ Πηνελόπης κόλπου S.

---

poet propounded by way of an apology to Helen for the evil
he had spoken of her in a former poem; for having lost the
sight of his eyes he ascribed the loss to the vengeance of the
heroine, and sought to propitiate her by formally retracting
all the scandals he had bruited about concerning her. See
Plato, *Phaedrus*, p. 243 A B, *Republic*, ix. p. 586 c; Isocrates,
Helene, 64; Pausanias, iii. 19. 13; *Poetae Lyrici Graeci*, ed.
Th. Bergk³, iii. 980 sqq.

¹ As to these oaths, see above, iii. 10. 9.
² As to the madness which Ulysses feigned in order to
escape going to the Trojan war, see Proclus, in *Epicorum
Graecorum Fragmenta*, ed. G. Kinkel, p. 18; Lucian, *De
domo*, 30; Philostratus, *Heroica*, xi. 2; Tzetzes, *Schol. on
Lycophron*, 818; Cicero, *De officiis*, iii. 26. 97; Hyginus,

When Menelaus was aware of the rape, he came to Agamemnon at Mycenae, and begged him to muster an army against Troy and to raise levies in Greece. And he, sending a herald to each of the kings, reminded them of the oaths which they had sworn,[1] and warned them to look to the safety each of his own wife, saying that the affront had been offered equally to the whole of Greece. And while many were eager to join in the expedition, some repaired also to Ulysses in Ithaca. But he, not wishing to go to the war, feigned madness. However, Palamedes, son of Nauplius, proved his madness to be fictitious; and when Ulysses pretended to rave, Palamedes followed him, and snatching Telemachus from Penelope's bosom, drew his sword as if he would kill him. And in his fear for the child Ulysses confessed that his madness was pretended, and he went to the war.[2]

Fab. 95 ; Servius, on Virgil, *Aen.* ii. 81 ; Lactantius Placidus, on Statius, *Achill.* i. 93 ; *Scriptores rerum mythicarum Latini*, ed. G. H. Bode, vol. i. pp. 12, 140 *sq.* (First Vatican Mythographer, 35 ; Second Vatican Mythographer, 200). The usual story seems to have been that to support his pretence of insanity Ulysses yoked an ox and a horse or an ass to the plough and sowed salt. While he was busy fertilizing the fields in this fashion, the Greek envoys arrived, and Palamedes, seeing through the deception, laid the infant son of Ulysses in front of the plough, whereupon the father at once checked the plough and betrayed his sanity. However, Lucian agrees with Apollodorus in saying that Palamedes threatened the child with his sword, though at the same time, by mentioning the unlike animals yoked together, he shows that he had the scene of the ploughing in his mind. His description purports to be based on a picture, probably a famous picture of the scene which was still exhibited at Ephesus in the time of Pliny (*Nat. Hist.* xxxv. 129). Sophocles wrote a play on the subject, called *The Mad Ulysses.* See *The Fragments of Sophocles*, ed. A. C. Pearson, vol. ii. pp. 115 *sqq.*

E 8 |῞Οτι Ὀδυσσεὺς λαβὼν αἰχμάλωτον Φρύγα
ἠνάγκασε γράψαι περὶ προδοσίας ὡς παρὰ Πριάμου πρὸς Παλαμήδην· καὶ χώσας ἐν ταῖς σκηναῖς¹
αὐτοῦ χρυσὸν τὴν δέλτον ἔρριψεν ἐν τῷ στρατο-
πέδῳ. Ἀγαμέμνων δὲ ἀναγνοὺς καὶ εὑρὼν τὸι
χρυσόν, τοῖς συμμάχοις αὐτὸν ὡς προδότην παρέ-
δωκε καταλεῦσαι.

9 ῞Οτι Μενέλαος σὺν Ὀδυσσεῖ καὶ Ταλθυβίῳ
πρὸς <Κινύραν εἰς>² Κύπρον ἐλθόντες συμμαχεῖν
ἔπειθον· ὁ δὲ Ἀγαμέμνονι μὲν οὐ παρόντι θώρακας
ἐδωρήσατο, ὀμόσας δὲ πέμψειν πεντήκοντα ναῦς,
μίαν πέμψας, ἧς ἦρχεν³ ... ὁ Μυγδαλίωνος, καὶ
τὰς λοιπὰς ἐκ γῆς πλάσας μεθῆκεν εἰς τὸ πέλαγος

10 ῞Οτι θυγατέρες Ἀνίου τοῦ⁴ Ἀπόλλωνος Ἐλαῖς

¹ We should perhaps read ἐν τῇ σκηνῇ.
² πρὸς <Κινύραν εἰς> Κύπρον Wagner: πρὸς Κύπρον E.
³ The personal name of the captain of the ship seems to
have dropped out.
⁴ Ἀνίου τοῦ Wagner: Ἀνιούτου τοῦ E.

---

¹ The Machiavellian device by which the crafty Ulysses
revenged himself on Palamedes for forcing him to go to the
war is related more fully by a Scholiast on Euripides (*Orestes*,
432) and Hyginus (*Fab.* 105). According to the Scholiast, a
servant of Palamedes was bribed to secrete the forged letter
and the gold under his master's bed, where they were discovered and treated as damning evidence of treason. According to Hyginus, Ulysses had recourse to a still more elaborate
stratagem in order to bury the gold in the earth under the
tent of Palamedes. Compare Servius, on Virgil, *Aen.* ii. 81 ;
Lactantius Placidus, on Statius, *Achill.* i. 93 ; *Scriptores
rerum mythicarum Latini*, ed. G. H. Bode, vol. i. pp. 12,
140 *sq.* (First Vatican Mythographer, 35 ; Second Vatican
Mythographer, 200). An entirely different account of the
plot against Palamedes is told by Dictys Cretensis (*Bellum*

Having taken a Phrygian prisoner, Ulysses compelled him to write a letter of treasonable purport ostensibly sent by Priam to Palamedes; and having buried gold in the quarters of Palamedes, he dropped the letter in the camp. Agamemnon read the letter, found the gold, and delivered up Palamedes to the allies to be stoned as a traitor.[1]

Menelaus went with Ulysses and Talthybius to Cinyras in Cyprus and tried to persuade him to join the allies. He made a present of breastplates to the absent Agamemnon,[2] and swore he would send fifty ships, but he sent only one, commanded by the son of Mygdalion, and the rest he moulded out of earth and launched them in the sea.[3]

The daughters of Anius, the son of Apollo, to wit,

Trojanum, ii. 15). He says that Ulysses and Diomede induced him to descend into a well, and then buried him under rocks which they hurled down on the top of him.

[2] Compare Homer, *Il.* xi. 19 *sqq.*, who describes only one richly decorated breastplate.

[3] Compare Eustathius on Homer, *Il.* xi. 20, p. 827, who says that, according to some people, Cinyras "swore to Menelaus at Paphos that he would send fifty ships, but he despatched only one, and the rest he fashioned of earth and sent them with earthen men in them ; thus he cunningly evaded his oath by keeping it with an earthenware fleet." Compare the Townley Scholia on Homer, *Il.* xi. 20, ed. E. Maass (Oxford, 1887), vol. i. p. 378. Wagner may be right in supposing that this ruse of the Cyprian king was recorded in the epic *Cypria*, though it is not mentioned in the brief summary of the poem compiled by Proclus. See R. Wagner, *Epitoma Vaticana ex Apollodori Bibliotheca*, pp. 181 *sq.* A different account of the Greek embassy to Cinyras is given by Alcidamas (*Odyss.* 20 *sq.*, pp. 181 *sq.*, ed. Blass). He says that Cinyras bribed the Greek envoy Palamedes to relieve him from military service, and that, though he promised to send a hundred ships, he sent none at all.

Σπερμὼ Οἰνώ, αἱ Οἰνότροφοι¹ λεγόμεναι· αἷς
ἐχαρίσατο Διόνυσος ποιεῖν ἐκ γῆς ἔλαιον σῖτον
οἶνον.

S 11 | Συνηθροίζετο δὲ ὁ στρατὸς ἐν Αὐλίδι. οἱ δὲ
στρατεύσαντες ἐπὶ Τροίαν ἦσαν οἵδε. Βοιωτῶν

¹ Οἰνότροφοι E: Οἰνότροποι Tzetzes, *Schol. on Lycophron*,
570 (but according to the editor, Müller, the MSS. have φ
written over the π).

---

¹ As to these three women, the Wine-growers (*Oinotrophoi*
or *Oinotropoi*) see *Epicorum Graecorum Fragmenta*, ed. G.
Kinkel, pp. 29 *sq.*; Tzetzes, *Schol. on Lycophron*, 570, 581;
Scholiast on Homer, *Od.* vi. 164; Ovid, *Metamorph.* xiii.
632-674; Servius, on Virgil, *Aen.* iii. 80; Dictys Cretensis,
Bellum Trojanum, i. 23. Each of the Wine-growers received
from Dionysus the power of producing the thing from which
she derived her name; thus Elais, who took her name from
elaia, "an olive," could produce olive oil; Spermo, who took
her name from *sperma*, "seed," could produce corn; and
Oeno, who took her name from *oinos*, "wine," could produce
wine. According to Apollodorus, the women elicited these
products from the ground; but according to Ovid and Servius,
whatever they touched was turned into olive-oil, corn, or
wine, as the case might be. Possessing these valuable powers,
the daughters of Anius were naturally much sought after.
Their father, a son of Apollo, was king of Delos and at the
same time priest of his father Apollo (Virgil, *Aen.* iii. 80), and
when Aeneas visited the island on his way from Troy, the
king, with pardonable pride, dwelt on his daughters' accom-
plishments and on the income they had brought him in (Ovid,
Metam. xiii. 650 *sqq.*). It is said by Tzetzes that when the
Greeks sailed for Troy and landed in Delos, the king, who had
received the gift of prophecy from his divine sire (Diodorus
Siculus, v. 62. 2), foretold that Troy would not be taken for
ten years, and invited them to stay with him for nine years,
promising that his daughters would find them in food all the
time. This hospitable offer was apparently not accepted at
the moment; but afterwards, when the Greeks were encamped
before Troy, Agamemnon sent for the young women and

Elais, Spermo, and Oeno, are called the Wine-growers: Dionysus granted them the power of producing oil, corn, and wine from the earth.[1]

The armament mustered in Aulis. The men who went to the Trojan war were as follows[2]:—Of the

---

ordered them peremptorily to feed his army. This they did successfully, if we may believe Tzetzes; but, to judge by Ovid's account, they found the work of the commissariat too exacting, for he says that they took to flight. Being overtaken by their pursuers, they prayed to Dionysus, who turned them into white doves. And that, says Servius, is why down to this day it is deemed a sin to harm a dove in Delos. From Tzetzes we learn that the story of these prolific damsels was told by Pherecydes and by the author of the epic *Cypria*, from whom Pherecydes may have borrowed it. Stesichorus related how Menelaus and Ulysses went to Delos to fetch the daughters of Anius (Scholiast on Homer, *Od.* vi. 164). If we may judge from the place which the brief mention of these women occupies in the *Epitome* of Apollodorus, we may conjecture that in his full text he described how their services were requisitioned to victual the fleet and army assembling at Aulis. The conjecture is confirmed by the statement of Dictys Cretensis, that before the Greek army set sail from Aulis, it had received a supply of corn, wine, and other provisions from Anius and his daughters. It may have been in order to ensure these supplies that Menelaus and Ulysses repaired to Delos for the purpose of securing the persons of the women.

[2] As to list of the Greek forces which mustered at Aulis, see Homer, *Il.* ii. 494-759; Euripides, *Iphigenia in Aulis*, 253 *sqq.*; Hyginus, *Fab.* 97; Dictys Cretensis, *Bellum Trojanum*, i. 17. The numbers of the ships and leaders recorded by Apollodorus do not always tally with those of Homer. For example, he gives the Boeotians forty ships, while Homer (*v.* 509) gives them fifty; and he says that the Phocians had four leaders, whereas Homer (*v.* 517) mentions only two. The question of the catalogue of the Greek forces, and its relation to Homer and history, are fully discussed by Dr. Walter Leaf in his *Homer and History* (London, 1915). He concludes that the catalogue forms no part of the original

μὲν ἡγεμόνες δέκα· ἦγον ναῦς μ'. Ὀρχομενίων
δ'· ἦγον ναῦς λ'. Φωκέων ἡγεμόνες δ'· ἦγον ναῦς
μ'. Λοκρῶν Αἴας Ὀιλέως·[1] ἦγε ναῦς μ'. Εὐβοέων
Ἐλεφήνωρ Χαλκώδοντος καὶ Ἀλκυόνης· ἦγε ναῦς
μ'. Ἀθηναίων Μενεσθεύς· ἦγε ναῦς ν'. Σαλα-
12 μινίων[2] Αἴας ὁ Τελαμώνιος· ἦγε ναῦς ιβ'. Ἀργείων
Διομήδης Τυδέως καὶ οἱ σὺν αὐτῷ· ἦγον ναῦς π'.
Μυκηναίων Ἀγαμέμνων Ἀτρέως καὶ Ἀερόπης
ναῦς ρ'. Λακεδαιμονίων Μενέλαος Ἀτρέως καὶ
Ἀερόπης ξ'. Πυλίων[3] Νέστωρ Νηλέως καὶ Χλω-
ρίδος ναῦς μ'. Ἀρκάδων Ἀγαπήνωρ ναῦς ζ'.
Ἠλείων Ἀμφίμαχος καὶ οἱ σὺν αὐτῷ ναῦς μ'.
Δουλιχίων Μέγης Φυλέως ναῦς μ'. Κεφαλλήνων
Ὀδυσσεὺς Λαέρτου καὶ Ἀντικλείας[4] ναῦς ιβ'.
Αἰτωλῶν Θόας Ἀνδραίμονος καὶ Γόργης· ἦγε
13 ναῦς μ'. Κρητῶν Ἰδομενεὺς Δευκαλίωνος μ'.
Ῥοδίων Τληπόλεμος[5] Ἡρακλέους καὶ Ἀστυόχης
ναῦς θ'. Συμαίων Νιρεὺς Χαρόπου[6] ναῦς γ'.

[1] Ὀιλέως Kerameus : ὁ ἰλέως S.
[2] Σαλαμινίων Kerameus : Σαλμινίων S.
[3] Πυλίων Kerameus : Πηλίων S.
[4] Ἀντικλείας Kerameus : Αὐτικλείας S.
[5] Τληπόλεμος Kerameus : τλιπόλεβος S.
[6] Συμαίων Νιρεὺς Χαρόπου Kerameus : κυμαίων νηρεὺς χαρο-
ποῦ S.

Iliad, but was added to it at a later time by a patriotic
Boeotian for the purpose of glorifying his people by claiming
that they played a very important part in the Trojan war,
although this claim is inconsistent with the statement of
Thucydides (i. 12) that the Boeotians did not migrate into
the country henceforth known as Boeotia until sixty years

Bocotians, ten leaders: they brought forty ships. Of the Orchomenians, four: they brought thirty ships. Of the Phocians, four leaders: they brought forty ships. Of the Locrians, Ajax, son of Oïleus: he brought forty ships. Of the Euboeans, Elephenor, son of Chalcodon and Alcyone: he brought forty ships. Of the Athenians, Menestheus: he brought fifty ships. Of the Salaminians, Telamonian Ajax: he brought twelve ships. Of the Argives, Diomedes, son of Tydeus, and his company: they brought eighty ships. Of the Mycenaeans, Agamemnon, son of Atreus and Aerope: a hundred ships. Of the Lacedaemonians, Menelaus, son of Atreus and Aerope: sixty ships. Of the Pylians, Nestor, son of Neleus and Chloris: forty ships. Of the Arcadians, Agapenor: seven ships. Of the Eleans, Amphimachus and his company: forty ships. Of the Dulichians, Meges, son of Phyleus: forty ships. Of the Cephallenians, Ulysses, son of Laertes and Anticlia: twelve ships. Of the Aetolians, Thoas, son of Andraemon and Gorge: he brought forty ships. Of the Cretans, Idomeneus, son of Deucalion: forty ships. Of the Rhodians, Tlepolemus, son of Hercules and Astyoche: nine ships. Of the Symaeans,

after the capture of Troy. I agree with Dr. Leaf in the belief, which he energetically maintains in this book, that the Trojan war was not a myth, but a real war, "fought out in the place, and at least generally in the manner, described in Homer," and that the principal heroes and heroines recorded by Homer were not "faded gods" but men and women of flesh and blood, of whose families and fortunes the memory survived in Greek tradition, though no doubt in course of time many mythical traits and incidents gathered round them, as they have gathered round the memories of the Hebrew patriarchs, of Alexander the Great, of Virgil, and of Charlemagne.

Κώων Φείδιππος καὶ Ἄντιφος οἱ Θεσσαλοῦ λ'.
14 Μυρμιδόνων Ἀχιλλεὺς Πηλέως καὶ Θέτιδος ν'.
ἐκ Φυλάκης Πρωτεσίλαος Ἰφίκλου μ'. Φεραίων
Εὔμηλος Ἀδμήτου ια'. Ὀλιζώνων Φιλοκτήτης
Ποίαντος ζ'. Αἰνιάνων Γουνεὺς Ὠκύτου κβ'.
Τρικκαίων Ποδαλείριος[1] ... λ'. Ὁρμενίων Εὐρύπυλος[2] ... ναῦς μ'. Γυρτωνίων[3] Πολυποίτης
Πειρίθου λ'. Μαγνήτων Πρόθοος Τενθρηδόνος[4] μ'.
νῆες μὲν οὖν αἱ πᾶσαι ,αιγ', ἡγεμόνες δὲ μγ', ἡγε-
μονεῖαι δὲ λ'·

ES 15 | Ὅτι ὄντος ἐν Αὐλίδι τοῦ στρατεύματος, θυσίας
γενομένης Ἀπόλλωνι,[5] ὁρμήσας δράκων ἐκ τοῦ
βωμοῦ παρὰ τὴν πλησίον πλάτανον, οὔσης ἐν
αὐτῇ νεοττιᾶς,[6] τοὺς ἐπ᾿[7] αὐτῇ καταναλώσας στρου-
θοὺς ὀκτὼ σὺν τῇ μητρὶ ἐνάτῃ λίθος ἐγένετο.
Κάλχας δὲ εἰπὼν κατὰ Διὸς βούλησιν γεγονέναι
αὐτοῖς τὸ σημεῖον τοῦτο, τεκμηράμενος ἐκ τῶν
γεγονότων ἔφη δεκαετεῖ χρόνῳ δεῖν Τροίαν ἁλῶναι.
16 καὶ πλεῖν παρεσκευάζοντο ἐπὶ Τροίαν.[8] Ἀγαμέμνων οὖν αὐτὸς ἡγεμὼν[9] τοῦ σύμπαντος στρατοῦ

---

[1] The blank is doubtless to be supplied thus: Ποδαλείριος
<καὶ Μαχάων Ἀσκληπιοῦ>, "Podalirius <and Machaon,
sons of Aesculapius>," as Wagner observes, comparing
Homer, *Il.* ii. 731 *sq.*

[2] Εὐρύπυλος. Add <Εὐαίμονος>, "Eurypylus, <son of
Euaemon>, as Wagner observes, comparing Homer, *Il.* ii.
736.

[3] Γυρτωνίων Kerameus: γοργυτίων S.

[4] Τενθρηδόνος Kerameus: Πενθρηδόνος S.

[5] Ὅτι ὄντος ἐν Αὐλίδι τοῦ στρατεύματος, θυσίας γενομένης
Ἀπόλλωνι E: θυσίας δὲ γενομένης ἐν Αὐλίδι τῷ Ἀπόλλωνι,
ὄντος ἐκεῖ τοῦ στρατεύματος S.

Nireus, son of Charopus: three ships. Of the Coans, Phidippus and Antiphus, the sons of Thessalus: thirty ships. Of the Myrmidons, Achilles, son of Peleus and Thetis: fifty ships. From Phylace, Protesilaus, son of Iphiclus: forty ships. Of the Pheraeans, Eumelus, son of Admetus: eleven ships. Of the Olizonians, Philoctetes, son of Poeas: seven ships. Of the Aeanianians, Guneus, son of Ocytus: twenty-two ships. Of the Triccaeans, Podalirius: thirty ships. Of the Ormenians, Eurypylus: forty ships. Of the Gyrtonians, Polypoetes, son of Pirithous: thirty ships. Of the Magnesians, Prothous, son of Tenthredon: forty ships. The total of ships was one thousand and thirteen; of leaders, forty-three; of leaderships, thirty.

When the armament was in Aulis, after a sacrifice to Apollo, a serpent darted from the altar beside the neighbouring plane-tree, in which there was a nest; and having consumed the eight sparrows in the nest, together with the mother-bird, which made the ninth, it was turned to stone. Calchas said that this sign was given them by the will of Zeus, and he inferred from what had happened that Troy was destined to be taken in a period of ten years.[1] And they made ready to sail against Troy. So Agamemnon in person was in command of the whole

---

[1] Compare Homer, *Il.* ii. 299–330; Proclus, in *Epicorum Graecorum Fragmenta*, ed. G. Kinkel, p. 18; Cicero, *De divinatione*, ii. 30. 63–65; Ovid, *Metamorph.* xii. 11–23.

---

[6] νεοττιᾶς E : νεοττείας S.   [7] ἐν S : ἐφ᾽ E.
[8] καὶ πλεῖν παρεσκευάζοντο ἐπὶ Τροίαν. These words are wanting in E.
[9] Ἀγαμέμνων οὖν αὐτὸς ἡγεμὼν S : Ὅτι Ἀγαμέμνων ἡγεμὼν E.

ἦν, ἐναυάρχει¹ δ' Ἀχιλλεὺς πεντεκαιδεκαέτης
τυγχάνων.

E 17 | Ἀγνοοῦντες δὲ τὸν ἐπὶ Τροίαν πλοῦν Μυσίᾳ
προσίσχουσι καὶ ταύτην ἐπόρθουν, Τροίαν νομίζοντες εἶναι. βασιλεύων δὲ Τήλεφος Μυσῶν,
Ἡρακλέους παῖς, ἰδὼν τὴν χώραν λεηλατουμένην,
τοὺς Μυσοὺς καθοπλίσας ἐπὶ τὰς ναῦς συνεδίωκε
τοὺς Ἕλληνας καὶ πολλοὺς ἀπέκτεινεν, ἐν οἷς καὶ
Θέρσανδρον τὸν Πολυνείκους ὑποστάντα. ὁρμή-
σαντος δὲ Ἀχιλλέως ἐπ' αὐτὸν οὐ μείνας ἐδιώκετο·
καὶ διωκόμενος ἐμπλακεὶς εἰς ἀμπέλου κλῆμα²
18 τὸν μηρὸν τιτρώσκεται δόρατι. τῆς δὲ Μυσίας
ἐξελθόντες Ἕλληνες ἀνάγονται, καὶ χειμῶνος
ἐπιγενομένου σφοδροῦ διαζευχθέντες ἀλλήλων εἰς
τὰς πατρίδας καταντῶσιν. ὑποστρεψάντων οὖν
τῶν Ἑλλήνων τότε λέγεται τὸν πόλεμον εἰκοσαετῆ
γενέσθαι· μετὰ γὰρ τὴν Ἑλένης ἁρπαγὴν ἔτει

¹ ἐναυάρχει E: ἐναυάρχη S.
² ἐμπλακεὶς εἰς ἀμπέλου κλῆμα E.   Perhaps we should read
ἐμπλακεὶς ἀμπέλου κλήματι.   Compare *Epitome*, i. 19, ii. 7.
But the construction with εἰς and the accusative occurs in
Aeschylus, *Prometheus*, 1078 *sq.*

¹ No other ancient writer mentions that Achilles was high
admiral of the fleet, though as son of a sea-goddess he was
obviously fitted for the post.   Dictys Cretensis, however,
tells us (*Bellum Trojanum*, i. 16) that Achilles shared the
command of the ships with Ajax and Phoenix, while that of
the land forces was divided between Palamedes, Diomedes,
and Ulysses.
² With the following account of the landing of the Greeks
in Mysia and their encounter with Telephus, compare Proclus,
in *Epicorum Graecorum Fragmenta*, ed. G. Kinkel, pp.
18 *sq.*; Scholiast on Homer, *Il.* i. 59.   The accounts of both
these writers agree, to some extent verbally, with that of
Apollodorus and are probably drawn from the same source,
which may have been the epic *Cypria* summarized by Proclus.

army, and Achilles was admiral,[1] being fifteen years old.

But not knowing the course to steer for Troy, they put in to Mysia and ravaged it, supposing it to be Troy.[2] Now Telephus son of Hercules, was king of the Mysians, and seeing the country pillaged, he armed the Mysians, chased the Greeks in a crowd to the ships, and killed many, among them Thersander, son of Polynices, who had made a stand. But when Achilles rushed at him, Telephus did not abide the onset and was pursued, and in the pursuit he was entangled in a vine-branch and wounded with a spear in the thigh. Departing from Mysia, the Greeks put to sea, and a violent storm coming on, they were separated from each other and landed in their own countries.[3] So the Greeks returned at that time, and it is said that the war lasted twenty years.[4] For it was in the second year after the rape of Helen that the Greeks,

The Scholiast tells us that it was Dionysus who caused Telephus to trip over a vine-branch, because Telephus had robbed the god of the honours that were his due. The incident is alluded to by Pindar ; see *Isthm.* viii. 48 (106) *sqq.* The war in Mysia is narrated in more detail by Philostratus (*Heroica*, iii. 28–36) and Dictys Cretensis (*Bellum Trojanum*, ii. 1–7). Philostratus says (§ 35) that the wounded were washed in the waters of the hot Ionian springs, which the people of Smyrna called the springs of Agamemnon.

[3] Compare Proclus, in *Epicorum Graecorum Fragmenta*, ed. G. Kinkel, p. 19, according to whom Achilles, on this return voyage, landed in Scyros and married his youthful love Deidamia, daughter of Lycomedes. See above, iii. 13. 8.

[4] Compare Homer, *Il.* xxiv. 765 *sq.*, where Helen at Troy says that it was now the twentieth year since she had quitted her native land. The words have puzzled the Scholiasts and commentators, but are explained by the present passage of Apollodorus.

δευτέρῳ τοὺς Ἕλληνας παρασκευασαμένους στρατεύεσθαι, ἀναχωρήσαντας¹ δὲ ἀπὸ Μυσίας εἰς
Ἑλλάδα μετὰ ἔτη ὀκτὼ πάλιν εἰς Ἄργος μετα-
στραφέντας² ἐλθεῖν εἰς Αὐλίδα.

19 Συνελθόντων δὲ αὐτῶν ἐν Ἄργει αὖθις μετὰ τὴν
ῥηθεῖσαν ὀκταετίαν, ἐν ἀπορίᾳ τοῦ πλοῦ πολλῇ
καθεστήκεσαν, καθηγεμόνα μὴ ἔχοντες, ὃς ἦν
20 δυνατὸς δεῖξαι τὴν εἰς Τροίαν. Τήλεφος δὲ ἐκ
τῆς Μυσίας, ἀνίατον τὸ τραῦμα ἔχων, εἰπόντος
αὐτῷ τοῦ Ἀπόλλωνος τότε τεύξεσθαι θεραπείας,
ὅταν ὁ τρώσας ἰατρὸς γένηται, τρύχεσιν ἠμφιεσ-
μένος εἰς Ἄργος ἀφίκετο, καὶ δεηθεὶς Ἀχιλλέως
καὶ ὑπεσχημένος τὸν εἰς Τροίαν πλοῦν δεῖξαι
θεραπεύεται ἀποξύσαντος Ἀχιλλέως τῆς Πηλιά-
δος μελίας τὸν ἰόν. θεραπευθεὶς οὖν ἔδειξε τὸν

---

¹ ἀναχωρήσαντας Wagner : ἀναχωρήσαντες E.
² μεταστραφέντας Wagner : μεταστραφέντες E.

---

[1] This account of how Telephus steered the Greek fleet to
Troy after being healed of his grievous wound by Achilles, is
probably derived from the epic *Cypria*; since it agrees on
these points with the brief summary of Proclus. See *Epicorum
Graecorum Fragmenta*, ed. G. Kinkel, p. 19. Compare Scholiast on Homer, *Il.* i. 59 ; Dictys Cretensis, *Bellum Trojanum*,
ii. 10. As to the cure of Telephus's wound by means of the rust
of the spear, see also Hyginus, *Fab.* 101 ; Propertius, ii. 1.
63 *sq.*; Ovid, *Ex Ponto*, ii. 2. 6. Pliny describes a painting in
which Achilles was represented scraping the rust from the
blade of his spear with a sword into the wound of Telephus
(*Nat. Hist.* xxv. 42, xxxiv. 152). The spear was the famous one
which Chiron had bestowed on Peleus, the father of Achilles ;
the shaft was cut from an ash-tree on Mount Pelion, and none
of the Greeks at Troy, except Achilles, could wield it. See
Homer, *Il.* xvi. 140–144, xix. 387–391, xxii. 133 *sq.* The
healing of Telephus's wound by Achilles is also reported,
though without mention of the spear, by Dictys Cretensis

having completed their preparations, set out on the expedition and after their retirement from Mysia to Greece eight years elapsed before they again returned to Argos and came to Aulis.

Having again assembled at Aulis after the aforesaid interval of eight years, they were in great perplexity about the voyage, because they had no leader who could show them the way to Troy. But Telephus, because his wound was unhealed, and Apollo had told him that he would be cured when the one who wounded him should turn physician, came from Mysia to Argos, clad in rags, and begged the help of Achilles, promising to show the course to steer for Troy. So Achilles healed him by scraping off the rust of his Pelian spear. Accordingly, on being healed, Telephus showed the course to steer,[1] and

(*l.c.*), a Scholiast on Homer (*Il.* i. 59) and a Scholiast on Aristophanes (*Clouds*, 919). The subject was treated by Sophocles in a play called *The Assembly of the Achaeans*, and by Euripides in a play called *Telephus*. See *The Fragments of Sophocles*, ed. A. C. Pearson, i. 94 *sqq.*; *Griechische Dichterfragmente.* ii. *Lyrische und dramatische Fragmente*, ed. W. Schubart und U. von Wilamowitz-Moellendorff (Berlin, 1907), pp. 64 *sqq.*; *Tragicorum Graecorum Fragmenta*, ed. A. Nauck², pp. 161 *sqq.*, 579 *sqq.* Aristophanes ridiculed the rags and tatters in which Telephus appeared on the stage in Euripides's play (*Acharn.* 430 *sqq.*). Apollodorus may have had the passage of Euripides or the parody of Aristophanes in mind when he describes Telephus as clad in rags.

The cure of a wound by an application to it of rust from the weapon which inflicted the hurt is not to be explained, as Pliny supposed, by any medicinal property inherent in rust as such, else the rust from any weapon would serve the purpose. It is clearly a folk-lore remedy based on the principle of sympathetic magic. Similarly Iphiclus was cured of impotence by the rust of the same knife which had caused the infirmity. See Apollodorus, i. 9. 12. The

πλοῦν, τὸ τῆς δείξεως ἀσφαλὲς πιστουμένου τοῦ
Κάλχαντος διὰ τῆς ἑαυτοῦ μαντικῆς.

21   Ἀναχθέντων δὲ αὐτῶν ἀπ᾿ Ἄργους καὶ παραγε-
ES νομένων τὸ δεύτερον εἰς Αὐλίδα,|τὸν στόλον ἄπλοια
κατεῖχε.[1] Κάλχας δὲ ἔφη οὐκ[2] ἄλλως δύνασθαι
πλεῖν αὐτούς, εἰ μὴ τῶν Ἀγαμέμνονος θυγατέρων
ἡ κρατιστεύουσα κάλλει σφάγιον Ἀρτέμιδι[3] πα-
ραστῇ, διὰ τὸ μηνίειν[4] τὴν θεὸν τῷ Ἀγαμέμνονι,
ὅτι τε βαλὼν ἔλαφον εἶπεν· οὐδὲ ἡ Ἄρτεμις, καὶ ὅτι
22 Ἀτρεὺς οὐκ ἔθυσεν αὐτῇ τὴν χρυσῆν ἄρνα. τοῦ δὲ
χρησμοῦ τούτου γενομένου, πέμψας Ἀγαμέμνων[5]
πρὸς Κλυταιμνήστραν Ὀδυσσέα καὶ Ταλθύβιον
Ἰφιγένειαν ᾔτει, λέγων[6] ὑπεσχῆσθαι δώσειν αὐτὴν
S Ἀχιλλεῖ γυναῖκα μισθὸν τῆς στρατείας.[7] | πεμψά-
σης δὲ ἐκείνης Ἀγαμέμνων τῷ βωμῷ παραστήσας
ES ἔμελλε σφάζειν, | Ἄρτεμις δὲ αὐτὴν ἁρπάσασα

---

[1] τὸν στόλον ἄπλοια κατεῖχε E: ἄπλοια οὖν κατεῖχε τὸν
στόλον S.

[2] οὐκ S: μὴ E.

[3] Ἀρτέμιδι E: Ἀρτέμιδος S.

[4] διὰ τὸ μηνίειν . . . τὴν χρυσῆν ἄρνα E: ἔλεγε γὰρ μηνῖσαι
Ἀγαμέμνονι τὴν θεόν, κατὰ μέν τινας ἐπεὶ κατὰ θήραν ἐν Ἰκαρίῳ
βαλὼν ἔλαφον εἶπεν οὐ δύνασθαι σωτηρίας αὐτὴν τυχεῖν οὐδ᾿
Ἀρτέμιδος θελούσης, κατὰ δέ τινας ὅτι τὴν χρυσῆν ἄρνα οὐκ ἔθυσεν
αὐτῇ Ἀτρεύς S.

[5] τοῦ δὲ χρησμοῦ . . . Ἀγαμέμνων S: πέμψας οὖν Ἀγαμέμνων E.

[6] Ἰφιγένειαν ᾔτει, λέγων S: ἄγει τὴν Ἰφιγένειαν, εἰπὼν E.

[7] τῆς στρατείας S: τῆς στρατείας αὐτοῦ E.

---

proverbial remedy for the bite of a dog "the hair of the dog
that bit you," is strictly analogous in principle; for it is not
the hair of any dog that will work the cure, but only the
hair of the particular dog that inflicted the bite. Thus we
read of a beggar who was bitten by a dog, at the vicarage of
Heversham, in Westmoreland, and went back to the house
to ask for some of the animal's hair to put on the wound.
See W. Henderson, *Notes on the Folk-lore of the Northern*

the accuracy of his information was confirmed by Calchas by means of his own art of divination.

But when they had put to sea from Argos and arrived for the second time at Aulis, the fleet was wind-bound, and Calchas said that they could not sail unless the fairest of Agamemnon's daughters were presented as a sacrifice to Artemis; for the goddess was angry with Agamemnon, both because, on shooting a deer, he had said, "Artemis herself could not (do it better)," [1] and because Atreus had not sacrificed to her the golden lamb. On receipt of this oracle, Agamemnon sent Ulysses and Talthybius to Clytaemnestra and asked for Iphigenia, alleging a promise of his to give her to Achilles to wife in reward for his military service. So Clytaemnestra sent her, and Agamemnon set her beside the altar, and was about to slaughter her, when Artemis carried her off to the Taurians

Counties of England (London, 1879), p. 160, note [1]. A precisely similar remedy for similar hurts appears to be popular in China; for we hear of a missionary who travelled about the province of Canton accompanied by a powerful dog, which bit children in the villages through which his master passed; and when a child was bitten, its mother used to run after the missionary and beg for a hair from the dog's tail to lay on the child's wound as a remedy. See N. B. Dennys, *The Folk-lore of China* (London and Hongkong, 1876), p. 52. For more examples of supposed cures based on the principle of sympathy between the animal who bites and the person who is bitten, see W. Henderson, *l.c.*; W. G. Black, *Folk-Medicine* (London, 1883), pp. 50 *sqq.*; W. Gregor, *Notes on the Folk-lore of the North-East of Scotland* (London, 1881), p. 127.

[1] Compare Tzetzes, *Schol. on Lycophron*, 183. The full expression is reported by the Scholiast on Homer, *Il.* i. 108, οὐδὲ ἡ "Αρτεμις οὕτως ἂν ἐτόξευσε, "Not even Artemis could have shot like that." The elliptical phrase is wrongly interpreted by the Sabbaitic scribe. See the Critical Note.

S   εἰς Ταύρους ἱέρειαν ἑαυτῆς¹ κατέστησεν, ἔλαφον
ἀντ' αὐτῆς παραστήσασα τῷ βωμῷ·² | ὡς δὲ ἔνιοι
λέγουσιν, ἀθάνατον αὐτὴν ἐποίησεν.

E 23 | Οἱ δὲ ἀναχθέντες ἐξ Αὐλίδος προσέσχον Τενέδῳ.
ταύτης ἐβασίλευε Τένης ὁ Κύκνου καὶ Προκλείας,
ὡς δέ τινες Ἀπόλλωνος· οὗτος ὑπὸ τοῦ πατρὸς
24 φυγαδευθεὶς ἐνταῦθα³ κατῴκει. Κύκνος γὰρ ἔχων
ἐκ Προκλείας τῆς Λαομέδοντος παῖδα μὲν Τένην,
θυγατέρα δὲ Ἡμιθέαν, ἐπέγημε τὴν Τραγάσου⁴
Φιλονόμην· ἥτις Τένου ἐρασθεῖσα καὶ μὴ πείθουσα καταψεύδεται πρὸς Κύκνον αὐτοῦ φθοράν,
καὶ τούτου μάρτυρα παρεῖχεν αὐλητὴν Εὔμολπον
25 ὄνομα. Κύκνος δὲ πιστεύσας, ἐνθέμενος αὐτὸν
μετὰ τῆς ἀδελφῆς εἰς λάρνακα μεθῆκεν εἰς τὸ

---

¹ Ἄρτεμις δὲ αὐτὴν ἁρπάσασα εἰς Ταύρους ἱέρειαν αὐτῆς S:
ἀλλὰ ταύτην μὲν Ἄρτεμις ἁρπάσασα ἱέρειαν ἑαυτῆς εἰς Σκυθο-
ταύρους E.

² παραστήσασα τῷ βωμῷ S: τῷ βωμῷ παραστήσασα E.

³ ἐνταῦθα Frazer : ἐνταυθοῖ E.

⁴ Τραγάσου E : Τραγάσου or Τραγανδάσου (the MSS. seem to
vary) Tzetzes, *Schol. on Lycophron*, 232: Κραγάσου Pausanias, x. 14. 2.

---

[1] This account of the attempted sacrifice of Iphigenia at
Aulis and the substitution of a doe agrees with the narrative
of the same events in the epic *Cypria* as summarized by Proclus
(*Epicorum Graecorum Fragmenta*, ed. G. Kinkel, p. 19). It
is also in harmony with the tragedy of Euripides on the
same subject. See Euripides, *Iphigenia in Aulis*, especially
vv. 87 *sqq.*, 358 *sqq.*, 1541 *sqq.* Compare Tzetzes, *Schol. on
Lycophron*, 183 ; Scholiast on Homer, *Il.* i. 108 ; Hyginus, *Fab.*
98 ; Ovid, *Metamorph.* xii. 24–38 ; Dictys Cretensis, *Bellum
Trojanum*, i. 19–22 ; *Scriptores rerum mythicarum Latini*, ed.
G. H. Bode, vol. i. pp. 6 *sq.*, 141 (First Vatican Mythographer,
20 ; Second Vatican Mythographer, 202). Some said that Iphigenia was turned by the goddess into a bear or a bull (Tzetzes,
l.c.). Dictys Cretensis dispenses with the intervention of

and appointed her to be her priestess, substituting a
deer for her at the altar; but some say that Artemis
made her immortal.[1]

After putting to sea from Aulis they touched at
Tenedos. It was ruled by Tenes, son of Cycnus and
Proclia, but according to some, he was a son of Apollo.
He dwelt there because he had been banished by
his father.[2] For Cycnus had a son Tenes and a
daughter Hemithea by Proclia, daughter of Laomedon,
but he afterwards married Philonome, daughter of
Tragasus; and she fell in love with Tenes, and, failing
to seduce him, falsely accused him to Cycnus of
attempting to debauch her, and in witness of it she
produced a fluteplayer, by name Eumolpus. Cycnus
believed her, and putting him and his sister in a chest
he set them adrift on the sea. The chest was washed

Artemis to save Iphigenia; according to him it was Achilles
who rescued the maiden from the altar and conveyed her
away to the Scythian king.

[2] The following story of Tenes, his stepmother's calumny,
his banishment, and his elevation to the throne of Tenedos,
is similarly told by Pausanias, x. 14. 2-4; Tzetzes, *Schol.
on Lycophron*, 232; Scholiast on Homer, *Il.* i. 38; Eustathius on Homer, *Il.* i. 38, p. 33. Eustathius and the Scholiast
on Homer call Tenes's sister Leucothea, and give Polyboea
as an alternative name of their stepmother. According to
Pausanias, the first wife of Cycnus was a daughter of Clytius,
not of Laomedon. As to the names, Tzetzes agrees with
Apollodorus, whom he probably copied. A rationalized
version of the story is told by Diodorus Siculus (V. 83).
According to him, Tenes was worshipped after his death as a
god by the people of Tenedos, who made a precinct for him
and offered sacrifices to him down to late times. No fluteplayer was allowed to enter the precinct, because a fluteplayer had borne false witness against Tenes; and the name
of Achilles might not be mentioned within it, because
Achilles had killed Tenes. Compare Plutarch, *Quaestiones
Graecae*, 28.

πέλαγος· προσσχούσης δὲ αὐτῆς Λευκόφρυι νήσῳ
ἐκβὰς ὁ Τένης κατῴκησε ταύτην καὶ ἀπ' αὐτοῦ
Τένεδον ἐκάλεσε. Κύκνος δὲ ὕστερον ἐπιγνοὺς
τὴν ἀλήθειαν τὸν μὲν αὐλητὴν κατέλευσε, τὴν δὲ
γυναῖκα ζῶσαν εἰς γῆν κατέχωσε.

26 Προσπλέοντας οὖν Τενέδῳ τοὺς Ἕλληνας ὁρῶν
Τένης ἀπεῖργε βάλλων πέτρους, καὶ ὑπὸ Ἀχιλλέως ξίφει πληγεὶς κατὰ τὸ στῆθος θνήσκει,
καίτοι Θέτιδος προειπούσης Ἀχιλλεῖ μὴ κτεῖναι
Τένην· τεθνήξεσθαι γὰρ ὑπὸ Ἀπόλλωνος αὐτόν,
27 ἐὰν κτείνῃ Τένην. τελούντων δὲ αὐτῶν Ἀπόλλωνι θυσίαν, ἐκ τοῦ βωμοῦ προσελθὼν ὕδρος
δάκνει Φιλοκτήτην· ἀθεραπεύτου δὲ τοῦ ἕλκους
καὶ δυσώδους γενομένου τῆς τε ὀδμῆς οὐκ ἀνεχο-
μένου τοῦ στρατοῦ, Ὀδυσσεὺς αὐτὸν εἰς Λῆμνον
μεθ' ὧν εἶχε τόξων Ἡρακλείων ἐκτίθησι κελεύ-
σαντος Ἀγαμέμνονος. ὁ δὲ ἐκεῖ τὰ πτηνὰ τοξεύων
ἐπὶ τῆς ἐρημίας τροφὴν εἶχεν.

---

[1] Compare Plutarch, *Quaestiones Graecae*, 28. Plutarch
mentions the warning given by Thetis to Achilles not to kill
Tenes, and says that the goddess specially charged one of
Achilles's servants to remind her son of the warning. But
in scouring the island Achilles fell in with the beautiful
sister of Tenes and made love to her; Tenes defended his
sister against her seducer, and in the brawl was slain by
Achilles. When the slayer discovered whom he had slain,
he killed the servant who ought to have warned him in
time, and he buried Tenes on the spot where the sanctuary
was afterwards dedicated to his worship. This version of the
story clearly differs from the one followed by Apollodorus.
[2] This story of the exposure and desertion of Philoctetes
in Lemnos appears to have been told in the epic *Cypria*, as
we may judge by the brief summary of Proclus. See *Epicorum Graecorum Fragmenta*, ed. G. Kinkel, p. 19. According to Proclus, the Greeks were feasting in Tenedos when

up on the island of Leucophrys, and Tenes landed and settled in the island, and called it Tenedos after himself. But Cycnus afterwards learning the truth, stoned the fluteplayer to death and buried his wife alive in the earth.

So when the Greeks were standing in for Tenedos, Tenes saw them and tried to keep them off by throwing stones, but was killed by Achilles with a sword-cut in the breast, though Thetis had forewarned Achilles not to kill Tenes, because he himself would die by the hand of Apollo if he slew Tenes.[1] And as they were offering a sacrifice to Apollo, a water-snake approached from the altar and bit Philoctetes; and as the sore did not heal and grew noisome, the army could not endure the stench, and Ulysses, by the orders of Agamemnon, put him ashore on the island of Lemnos, with the bow of Hercules which he had in his possession; and there, by shooting birds with the bow, he subsisted in the wilderness.[2]

Philoctetes was bitten by a water-snake. This is not necessarily inconsistent with the statement of Apollodorus that the accident happened while the Greeks were sacrificing to Apollo, for the feast mentioned by Proclus may have been sacrificial. According to another version of the story, which Sophocles followed in his *Philoctetes*, the accident to Philoctetes happened, not in Tenedos, but in the small island of Chryse, where a goddess of that name was worshipped, and the serpent which bit Philoctetes was the guardian of her shrine. See Sophocles, *Philoctetes*, 263-270, 1326-1328. Later writers identified Chryse with Athena, and said that Philoctetes was stung while he was cleansing her altar or clearing it of the soil under which it was buried, as Tzetzes has it. See Scholiast on Homer, *Il.* ii. 722; Tzetzes, *Schol. on Lycophron*, 911; Eustathius on Homer, *Il.* ii. 724, p. 330. But this identification is not supported by Sophocles nor by the evidence of a vase painting, which represents the shrine of Chryse with her name attached to her image. See Jebb's

ES 28 | Ἀναχθέντες δὲ ἀπὸ τῆς Τενέδου¹ προσέπλεον
Τροία, καὶ πέμπουσιν Ὀδυσσέα καὶ Μενέλαον
τὴν Ἑλένην καὶ τὰ χρήματα ἀπαιτοῦντας.² συνα-
θροισθείσης δὲ παρὰ τοῖς Τρωσὶν ἐκκλησίας, οὐ
μόνον τὴν Ἑλένην οὐκ ἀπεδίδουν ἀλλὰ καὶ τού-
29 τους κτείνειν ἤθελον. ἀλλὰ τοὺς μὲν³ ἔσωσεν

¹ ἀπὸ τῆς Τενέδου. These words are wanting in S.
² ἀπαιτοῦντας E : αἰτοῦντες S.
³ ἀλλὰ τοὺς μὲν E : τούτους μὲν οὖν S.

edition of Sophocles, *Philoctetes*, p. xxxviii. § 21 ; A. Baumeister, *Denkmäler des klassischen Altertums*, iii. 1326, fig.
1325. The island of Chryse is no doubt the "desert island
near Lemnos" in which down to the first century B.C. were to
be seen "an altar of Philoctetes, a bronze serpent, a bow, and
a breastplate bound with fillets, the memorial of his sufferings"
(Appian, *Mithridat.* 77). The island had sunk in the sea
before the time of Pausanias in the second century of our era
(Pausanias, viii. 33. 4). According to a different account, the
unfortunate encounter of Philoctetes with the snake took
place in Lemnos itself, the island where he was abandoned
by his comrades. See Scholiast on Homer and Eustathius,
ll.cc.; Scholiast on Sophocles, *Philoctetes*, 270; Hyginus, *Fab.*
102. Philoctetes was commonly supposed to have received
the bow and arrows of Hercules from that hero as a reward
for his service in kindling the pyre on Mount Oeta. See
Sophocles, *Philoctetes*, 801–803 ; Diodorus Siculus, iv. 38. 4;
Scholiast on Homer, *Il.* ii. 724 ; Hyginus, *Fab.* 102 ; Ovid,
Metamorph. ix. 229–234. According to one account, which
Servius has preserved, it was from these arrows, envenomed
with the poison of the hydra, and not from a serpent, that
Philoctetes received his grievous hurt. It is said that Hercules on the pyre solemnly charged his friend never to reveal
the spot where his ashes should repose. Philoctetes promised
with an oath to observe the wish of his dying friend, but afterwards he betrayed the secret by stamping with his foot on the
grave. Hence on his way to the war one of the poisoned
arrows fell upon and wounded the traitor foot. See Servius,
on Virgil, *Aen.* iii. 402 ; *Scriptores rerum mythicarum
Latini*, ed. G. H. Bode, vol. i. pp. 21, 132 (First Vatican

Putting to sea from Tenedos they made sail for Troy, and sent Ulysses and Menelaus to demand the restoration of Helen and the property. But the Trojans, having summoned an assembly, not only refused to restore Helen, but threatened to kill the envoys. These were, however, saved by Antenor; [1]

Mythographer, 59; Second Vatican Mythographer, 165). Homer speaks of Philoctetes marooned by the Greeks in Lemnos and suffering agonies from the bite of the deadly water-snake (*Il.* ii. 721-725), but he does not say how or where the sufferer was bitten. Sophocles represents Lemnos as a desert island (*Philoctetes*, 1 *sq.*). The fate of the forlorn hero, the ancient Robinson Crusoe, dwelling for ten years in utter solitude on his lonely isle, was a favourite theme of tragedy. Aeschylus, Sophocles, and Euripides all composed plays on the subject under the title of *Philoctetes*. See Dio Chrysostom, *Or.* lii; Jebb's Introduction to Sophocles, *Philoctetes*, pp. xiii. *sqq.*; *Tragicorum Graecorum Fragmenta*, ed. A. Nauck[2], pp. 79 *sqq.*, 613 *sqq.*

[1] As to the embassy of Ulysses and Menelaus to Troy to demand the surrender of Helen, see Homer, *Il.* iii. 205 *sqq.*, xi. 138 *sqq.*; Proclus, in *Epicorum Graecorum Fragmenta*, ed. G. Kinkel, p. 19; Bacchylides, xiv. [xv.]; Herodotus, ii. 118; J. Tzetzes, *Antehomerica*, 154 *sqq.*; Scholiast on Homer, *Il.* iii. 206. According to the author of the epic *Cypria*, as reported by Proclus (*l.c.*), the embassy was sent before the first battle, in which Protesilaus fell (see below); according to Tzetzes, it was sent before the Greek army assembled at Aulis; according to the Scholiast on Homer (*l.c.*), it was despatched from Tenedos. Herodotus says that the envoys were sent after the landing of the army in the Troad. Sophocles wrote a play on the subject of the embassy, called *The demand for the surrender of Helen*. See *Tragicorum Graecorum Fragmenta*, ed. A. Nauck[2], pp. 171 *sq.*; *The Fragments of Sophocles*, ed. A. C. Pearson, vol. i. pp. 121 *sqq.* Libanius has bequeathed to us two imaginary speeches, which are supposed to have been delivered by the Greek ambassadors, Menelaus and Ulysses, to the Trojan assembly before the opening of hostilities, while the Greek army was encamped within sight of the walls of Troy. See Libanius, *Declamationes*, iii. and iv. (vol. v. pp. 199 *sqq.*, ed. R. Foerster).

Ἀντήνωρ, οἱ δὲ Ἕλληνες, ἀχθόμενοι ἐπὶ τῇ τῶν
βαρβάρων καταφρονήσει,[1] ἀναλαβόντες τὴν πανοπλίαν ἔπλεον ἐπ' αὐτούς. Ἀχιλλεῖ δὲ ἐπιστέλλει
Θέτις πρῶτον[2] μὴ ἀποβῆναι τῶν νεῶν· τὸν γὰρ
ἀποβάντα πρῶτον πρῶτον[3] μέλλειν τελευτήσειν.[4]

S | πυθόμενοι δὲ οἱ βάρβαροι τὸν στόλον ἐπιπλεῖν,[5]
σὺν ὅπλοις ἐπὶ τὴν θάλασσαν ὥρμησαν καὶ
ES 30 βάλλοντες πέτροις ἀποβῆναι ἐκώλυον. | τῶν δὲ
Ἑλλήνων πρῶτος[6] ἀπέβη τῆς νεώς[7] Πρωτεσίλαος, καὶ κτείνας οὐκ ὀλίγους τῶν βαρβάρων[8]
ὑφ' Ἕκτορος θνήσκει. τούτου <ἡ>[9] γυνὴ Λαοδάμεια καὶ μετὰ θάνατον ἤρα, καὶ ποιήσασα
εἴδωλον Πρωτεσιλάῳ παραπλήσιον τούτῳ προσω-
E μίλει. | Ἑρμῆς δὲ ἐλεησάντων θεῶν ἀνήγαγε
Πρωτεσίλαον ἐξ Ἅιδου. Λαοδάμεια δὲ ἰδοῦσα

[1] ἐπὶ τῇ τῶν βαρβάρων καταφρονήσει E: τῶν βαρβάρων τὴν
καταφρόνησιν S.
[2] πρῶτον E: πρώτῳ S.
[3] πρῶτον πρῶτον E: πρῶτον S.
[4] τελευτήσειν E: καὶ τελευτᾶν S.
[5] ἐπιπλεῖν Bücheler: πλεῖν S.
[6] τῶν δὲ Ἑλλήνων πρῶτος S: πρῶτος τοίνυν E.
[7] νεώς E: νηὸς S.
[8] οὐκ ὀλίγους τῶν βαρβάρων E: οὐκ ὀλίγους S.
[9] ἡ inserted by Bücheler.

---

[1] Compare Homer, *Il.* ii. 698–702; Proclus, in *Epicorum
Graecorum Fragmenta*, ed. G. Kinkel, p. 19; Tzetzes,
Schol. on Lycophron, 245; *id. Chiliades*, ii. 759 *sqq.*; *id.
Antehomerica*, 221 *sqq.*; Eustathius on Homer, *Il.* ii. 701, p.
325, and on *Od.* xi. 521, p. 1697; Pausanias, iv. 2. 5; Hyginus,
Fab. 103; Dictys Cretensis, *Bellum Trojanum*, ii. 11. The
common tradition, followed by Apollodorus, was that Protesilaus fell by the hand of Hector; but according to others, his
slayer was Aeneas, or Achates, or Euphorbus. See Eustathius,
ll.cc.; J. Tzetzes, *Antehomerica*, 230 *sq.* The Greeks had
received an oracle that the first of their number to leap from

but the Greeks, exasperated at the insolence of the barbarians, stood to arms and made sail against them. Now Thetis charged Achilles not to be the first to land from the ships, because the first to land would be the first to die. Being apprized of the hostile approach of the fleet, the barbarians marched in arms to the sea, and endeavoured by throwing stones to prevent the landing. Of the Greeks the first to land from his ship was Protesilaus, and having slain not a few of the barbarians, he fell by the hand of Hector.[1] His wife Laodamia loved him even after his death, and she made an image of him and consorted with it. The gods had pity on her, and Hermes brought up Protesilaus from Hades. On seeing him, Laodamia

the ships would be the first to perish. See Tzetzes, *Schol. on Lycophron*, 245; Hyginus, *Fab.* 113; Ovid, *Heroid.* xiii. 93 *sq.* Protesilaus was reckoned by Pausanias (i. 34. 2) among the men who after death received divine honours from the Greeks. He was buried in the Thracian Chersonese, opposite the Troad, and was there worshipped as a god (Tzetzes, *Schol. on Lycophron*, 532). His grave at Elaeus, or Eleus, in the peninsula was enclosed in a sacred precinct, and his worshippers testified their devotion by dedicating to him many vessels of gold and silver and bronze, together with raiment and other offerings; but when Xerxes invaded Greece, these treasures were carried off by the Persians, who desecrated the holy ground by sowing it with corn and turning cattle loose on it to graze (Herodotus, ix. 116). Tall elms grew within the sacred precinct and overshadowed the grave; and it is said that the leaves of the trees that looked across the narrow sea to Troy, where Protesilaus perished, burgeoned early but soon faded and fell, like the hero himself, while the trees that looked away from Troy still kept their foliage fresh and fair. See Philostratus, *Heroica*, iii 1. Others said that when the elms had shot up so high that Troy could be seen from them away across the water, the topmost boughs immediately withered. See Quintus Smyrnaeus, *Posthomerica*, vii. 408 *sqq.*; Pliny, *Nat. Hist.* xvi. 238.

καὶ νομίσασα αὐτὸν ἐκ Τροίας παρεῖναι τότε
μὲν ἐχάρη, πάλιν δὲ ἐπαναχθέντος εἰς Ἅιδου
ἑαυτὴν ἐφόνευσεν.

S 31 | Πρωτεσιλάου δὲ τελευτήσαντος, ἐκβαίνει μετὰ
Μυρμιδόνων Ἀχιλλεὺς καὶ λίθον <βα>λὼν εἰς
τὴν κεφαλὴν Κύκνου κτείνει. ὡς δὲ τοῦτον νεκρὸν
εἶδον οἱ βάρβαροι, φεύγουσιν εἰς τὴν πόλιν, οἱ
δὲ Ἕλληνες ἐκπηδήσαντες τῶν νεῶν ἐνέπλησαν
σωμάτων τὸ πεδίον. καὶ κατακλείσαντες[1] τοὺς
32 Τρῶας ἐπολιόρκουν· ἀνέλκουσι δὲ τὰς ναῦς. μὴ
θαρρούντων δὲ τῶν βαρβάρων, Ἀχιλλεὺς ἐνεδρεύσας Τρωίλον ἐν τῷ τοῦ Θυμβραίου Ἀπόλλωνος
ἱερῷ φονεύει, καὶ νυκτὸς ἐλθὼν ἐπὶ τὴν πόλιν

---

[1] κατακλείσαντες Bücheler : καταλείσαντες S.

---

[1] According to the author of the epic *Cypria* the name of
Protesilaus's wife was Polydora, daughter of Meleager (Pausanias, iv. 2. 7). Later writers, like Apollodorus, called her
Laodamia. As to her tragic tale, see Lucian, *Dial. Mort.*
xxiii. (who does not name her) ; Eustathius, on Homer, *Il.* ii.
701, p. 325 ; Scholiast on Aristides, vol. iii. pp. 671 *sq.*, ed.
Dindorf ; J. Tzetzes, *Chiliades*, ii. 763 *sqq.*; Propertius, i. 19.
7–10 ; Hyginus, *Fab.* 103, 104 ; Ovid, *Heroid.* xiii. ; Servius,
on Virgil, *Aen.* vi. 447 ; *Scriptores rerum mythicarum Latini*,
ed. G. H. Bode, vol. i. pp. 51, 147 (First Vatican Mythographer, 158 ; Second Vatican Mythographer, 215). According
to Hyginus (*Fab.* 103), Laodamia had prayed that Protesilaus
might be restored to her for only three hours ; her prayer
was granted, but she could not bear the grief of parting with
him, and died in his arms (Servius, *l.c.*). A rationalistic version
of the story ran that Laodamia had made a waxen image of
her dead husband and secretly embraced it, till her father
ordered it to be burned, when she threw herself into the fire
and perished with the image (Hyginus, *Fab.* 104). According
to Ovid, Laodamia made the waxen image of her absent lord
and fondled it even in his lifetime. Her sad story was the
theme of a tragedy of Euripides (*Tragicorum Graecorum*

thought it was himself returned from Troy, and she was glad; but when he was carried back to Hades, she stabbed herself to death.[1]

On the death of Protesilaus, Achilles landed with the Myrmidons, and throwing a stone at the head of Cycnus, killed him.[2] When the barbarians saw him dead, they fled to the city, and the Greeks, leaping from their ships, filled the plain with bodies. And having shut up the Trojans, they besieged them; and they drew up the ships. The barbarians showing no courage, Achilles waylaid Troilus and slaughtered him in the sanctuary of Thymbraean Apollo,[3] and coming

---

Fragmenta, ed. Nauck[2], pp. 563 *sqq.*), as it is of a well-known poem of Wordsworth (*Laodameia*).

[2] Compare Proclus, in *Epicorum Graecorum Fragmenta*, ed. G. Kinkel, p. 19; Pindar, *Olymp.* ii. 82 (147); Aristotle, *Rhetoric*, ii. 22, p. 1396 b 16–18, ed. Bekker; Quintus Smyrnaeus, *Posthomerica*, iv. 468 *sqq.*; J. Tzetzes, *Antehomerica*, 257 *sqq.*; Scholiast on Theocritus, xvi. 49; Ovid, *Metamorph.* xii. 70–140; Dictys Cretensis, *Bellum Trojanum*, ii. 12. Cycnus was said to be invulnerable (Aristotle, *l.c.*): hence neither the spear nor the sword of Achilles could make any impression on his body, and the hero was reduced to the necessity of throttling him with the thongs of his own helmet. So Ovid tells the tale, adding that the sea-god, his father Poseidon, changed the dead Cycnus into a swan, whose name (Cygnus, κύκνος) he had borne in life.

[3] Compare Proclus, in *Epicorum Graecorum Fragmenta*, ed. G. Kinkel, p. 20; Scholiast on Homer, *Il.* xxiv. 257 (where for ὀχευθῆναι it has been proposed to read λοχηθῆναι or λογχευθῆναι); Eustathius, on Homer, *Il.* xxiv. 251, p. 1348; Dio Chrysostom, *Or.* xi. vol. i. p. 189, ed. L. Dindorf; Tzetzes, *Schol. on Lycophron*, 307–313; Virgil, *Aen.* i. 474 *sqq.*; Servius, on Virgil, *Aen.* i. 474; *Scriptores rerum mythicarum Latini*, ed. G. H. Bode, vol. i. p. 66 (First Vatican Mythographer, 210). Troilus is represented as a youth, but the stories concerning his death are various. According to Eustathius, the lad was exercising his horses in

Λυκάονα λαμβάνει. παραλαβὼν δὲ Ἀχιλλεὺς
τινας τῶν ἀριστέων τὴν χώραν ἐπόρθει, καὶ παραγίνεται εἰς Ἴδην ἐπὶ τὰς Αἰνείου [τοῦ Πριάμου][1]
βόας. φυγόντος δὲ αὐτοῦ, τοὺς βουκόλους κτείνας
καὶ Μήστορα[2] τὸν Πριάμου τὰς βόας ἐλαύνει.
33 αἱρεῖ δὲ καὶ Λέσβον καὶ Φώκαιαν,[3] εἶτα Κολοφῶνα καὶ Σμύρναν καὶ Κλαζομενὰς καὶ Κύμην,
μεθ' ἃς Αἰγιαλὸν καὶ Τῆνον,[4] [τὰς ἑκατὸν καλου-
μένας πόλεις]· εἶτα ἑξῆς Ἀδραμύτιον καὶ Σίδην,[5]
εἶτα Ἔνδιον καὶ Λιναῖον[6] καὶ Κολώνην.[7] αἱρεῖ
δὲ καὶ Θήβας τὰς Ὑποπλακίας[8] καὶ Λυρνησσόν,
ἔτι δὲ καὶ <Ἄντ>ανδρον[9] καὶ ἄλλας πολλάς.
34 Ἐνναετοῦς δὲ χρόνου διελθόντος παραγίνονται
τοῖς Τρωσὶ σύμμαχοι· ἐκ τῶν περιοίκων πόλεων

[1] τοῦ Πριάμου S : καὶ Πριάμου Wagner.
[2] καὶ Μήστορα Kerameus : καμήστορα S.
[3] Φώκαιαν Kerameus : φωκέας S.
[4] Τῆνον S. Kerameus conjectured Τήμνον : Wagner proposed Τίειον.
[5] Σίδην S. Kerameus conjectured Ἴδην or Σιδήνην : Wagner proposed Σίγην, comparing Stephanus Byzantius, s.v.
Σίγη, πόλις Τρωάδος, ὡς Ἑκαταῖος Ἀσίᾳ.
[6] Λιναῖον S. Kerameus conjectured Κίλλαιον : Wagner
proposed Αἰνέαν, comparing Strabo, xiii. i. 45, p. 603, where,
however, Meineke reads Νέας for Αἰνέας.
[7] Κολώνην S. Kerameus conjectured Καλλικολώνην ; but
Wagner compares Diodorus Siculus, v. 83. 1, Κολώνης τῆς ἐν
τῇ Τρῳάδι, and Strabo, xiii. i. 46, p. 604, βασιλέα δὲ Κολωνῶν.
[8] Ὑποπλακίας Kerameus : ὑπὸ πλακείας S.
[9] <Ἄντ>ανδρον Kerameus : ἄνδρον S.

the Thymbraeum or sanctuary of the Thymbraean Apollo,
when Achilles killed him with his spear. Tzetzes says that
he was a son of Hecuba by Apollo, though nominally by
Priam, that he fled from his assailant to the temple of
Apollo, and was cut down by Achilles at the altar. There
was a prophecy that Troy could not be taken if Troilus should
live to the age of twenty (so the First Vatican Mythographer).

by night to the city he captured Lycaon.[1] Moreover, taking some of the chiefs with him, Achilles laid waste the country, and made his way to Ida to lift the kine of Aeneas. But Aeneas fled, and Achilles killed the neatherds and Mestor, son of Priam, and drove away the kine.[2] He also took Lesbos[3] and Phocaea, then Colophon, and Smyrna, and Clazomenae, and Cyme; and afterwards Aegialus and Tenos, the so-called Hundred Cities; then, in order, Adramytium and Side; then Endium, and Linaeum, and Colone. He took also Hypoplacian Thebes[4] and Lyrnessus,[5] and further Antandrus, and many other cities.

A period of nine years having elapsed, allies came to join the Trojans:[6] from the surrounding cities,

This may have been the motive of Achilles for slaying the lad. According to Dictys Cretensis (*Bellum Trojanum*, iv. 9), Troilus was taken prisoner and publicly slaughtered in cold blood by order of Achilles. The indefatigable Sophocles, as usual, wrote a tragedy on the subject. See *The Fragments of Sophocles*, ed. A. C. Pearson, vol. ii. pp. 253 *sqq.*

[1] Compare Homer, *Il.* xxi. 34 *sqq.*, xxiii. 746 *sq.* Lycaon was captured by Achilles when he was cutting sticks in the orchard of his father Priam. After being sold by his captor into slavery in Lemnos he was ransomed and returned to Troy, but meeting Achilles in battle a few days later, he was ruthlessly slain by him. The story seems to have been told also in the epic *Cypria*. See Proclus, in *Epicorum Graecorum Fragmenta*, ed. G. Kinkel, p. 20.

[2] Compare Homer, *Il.* xx. 90 *sqq.*, 188 *sqq.*; Proclus, in *Epicorum Graecorum Fragmenta*, ed. G. Kinkel, p. 20.

[3] Compare Homer, *Il.* ix. 129; Dictys Cretensis, *Bellum Trojanum*, ii. 16.

[4] Compare Homer, *Il.* ii. 691, vi. 397.

[5] It was at the sack of Lyrnessus that Achilles captured his concubine Briseis after slaying her husband. See Homer, *Il.* ii. 688 *sqq.*, xix. 60, 291 *sqq.*, xx. 92, 191 *sqq.* Compare Dictys Cretensis, *Bellum Trojanum*, ii. 17.

[6] With the following list of the Trojans and their allies, compare Homer, *Il.* ii. 816–877.

Αἰνείας Ἀγχίσου καὶ σὺν αὐτῷ Ἀρχέλοχος[1] καὶ
Ἀκάμας Ἀντήνορος[2] καὶ Θεανοῦς, Δαρδανίων
ἡγούμενοι, Θρᾳκῶν Ἀκάμας Εὐσώρου, Κικόνων
Εὔφημος Τροιζήνου,[3] Παιόνων Πυραίχμης,[4] Πα-
35 φλαγόνων Πυλαιμένης Βιλσάτου,[5] ἐκ Ζελίας
Πάνδαρος Λυκάονος, ἐξ Ἀδραστείας Ἄδραστος[6]
καὶ Ἄμφιος Μέροπος,[7] ἐκ δ' Ἀρίσβης Ἄσιος
Ὑρτάκου, ἐκ Λαρίσσης Ἱππόθοος Πελασγοῦ,[8] ἐκ
Μυσίας Χρόμιος καὶ Ἔννομος[9] Ἀρσινόου, Ἀλι-
ζώνων Ὀδίος[10] καὶ Ἐπίστροφος Μηκιστέως,[11]
Φρυγῶν Φόρκυς καὶ Ἀσκάνιος Ἀρετάονος, Μαιό-
νων Μέσθλης καὶ Ἄντιφος Ταλαιμένους, Καρῶν[12]
Νάστης καὶ Ἀμφίμαχος Νομίονος,[13] Λυκίων Σαρ-
πηδὼν Διὸς καὶ Γλαῦκος[14] Ἱππολόχου.

IV. Ἀχιλλεὺς δὲ μηνίων ἐπὶ τὸν πόλεμον οὐκ
ἐξῄει διὰ Βρισηίδα . . . τῆς θυγατρὸς Χρύσου τοῦ
ἱερέως. διὸ θαρσήσαντες οἱ βάρβαροι ἐκ τῆς

---

[1] Ἀρχέλοχος Wagner (comparing Homer, Il. ii. 823):
ἀρχέλαος S.

[2] Ἀντήνορος Kerameus (compare Homer, Il. ii. 822 sq):
Αὐτήνορος S.

[3] Τροιζήνου Wagner (comparing Homer, Il. ii. 847): Τροι-
ζῆνος S.

[4] Πυραίχμης Kerameus (compare Homer, Il. ii. 848):
πυραιχάγης S.

[5] Βιλσάτου S. Wagner conjectures Βισάλτου.

[6] Ἄδραστος Kerameus (compare Homer, Il. ii. 830):
ἄδρας S.

[7] Μέροπος Kerameus (compare Homer, Il. ii. 831): Μερό-
πης S.

[8] Ἱππόθοος Πελασγοῦ S. Compare Homer, Il. ii. 842 sq.:
Ἱππόθοός τε Πύλαιός τ', ὅζος Ἄρηος, ‖ υἷε δύω Λήθοιο Πελασγοῦ
Τευταμίδαο, which Apollodorus has misunderstood. See the
exegetical note.

[9] Ἔννομος Kerameus (compare Homer, Il. ii. 858): ἐννό-
μιος S.

Aeneas, son of Anchises, and with him Archelochus and Acamas, sons of Antenor, and Theano, leaders of the Dardanians; of the Thracians, Acamas, son of Eusorus; of the Cicones, Euphemus, son of Troezenus; of the Paeonians, Pyraechmes; of the Paphlagonians, Pylaemenes, son of Bilsates; from Zelia, Pandarus, son of Lycaon; from Adrastia, Adrastus and Amphius, sons of Merops; from Arisbe, Asius, son of Hyrtacus; from Larissa, Hippothous, son of Pelasgus;[1] from Mysia, Chromius[2] and Ennomus, sons of Arsinous; of the Alizones, Odius and Epistrophus, sons of Mecisteus; of the Phrygians, Phorcys and Ascanius, sons of Aretaon; of the Maeonians, Mesthles and Antiphus, sons of Talaemenes; of the Carians, Nastes and Amphimachus, sons of Nomion; of the Lycians, Sarpedon, son of Zeus, and Glaucus, son of Hippolochus.

IV. Achilles did not go forth to the war, because he was angry on account of Briseis, the daughter of Chryses the priest.[3] Therefore the barbarians

---

[1] Compare Homer, *Il.* ii. 842 *sq.*, where the poet describes Hippothous as the son of the Pelasgian Lethus. Apollodorus, misunderstanding the passage, has converted the adjective Pelasgian into a noun Pelasgus.

[2] Homer calls him Chromis (*Il.* ii. 858).

[3] Compare Homer, *Il.* i. 1 *sqq.* From this point Apollodorus follows the incidents of the Trojan war as related by Homer.

---

[10] Ἀλιζώνων Ὀδίος Kerameus (compare Homer, *Il.* ii. 856): ἀλιζόνων ὁ δῖος S.

[11] Μηκιστέως Kerameus : μηκιστεύς S.

[12] Ἄντιφος Ταλαιμένους, Καρῶν Kerameus (compare Homer, *Il.* ii. 864–867): Ἄντυφος Πυλαιμένου, σκάρων S.

[13] Ἀμφίμαχος Νομίονος Kerameus (compare Homer, *Il.* ii. 870 *sq.*): ἀμφίναχος νομίωνος S.

[14] Γλαῦκος Kerameus : γλαύχος S.

πόλεως προῆλθον. καὶ μονομαχεῖ Ἀλέξανδρος
πρὸς Μενέλαον, Ἀλέξανδρον δὲ ἡττώμενον ἁρπάζει
Ἀφροδίτη. Πάνδαρος δὲ τοξεύσας Μενέλαον τοὺς
ὅρκους ἔλυσεν.

E 2 | Ὅτι Διομήδης ἀριστεύων Ἀφροδίτην Αἰνείᾳ
βοηθοῦσαν τιτρώσκει, καὶ Γλαύκῳ συστάς, ὑπο-
μνησθεὶς πατρῴας φιλίας, ἀλάσσει τὰ ὅπλα.

ES | προκαλουμένου δὲ[1] Ἕκτορος τὸν ἄριστον εἰς μονο-
μαχίαν, πολλῶν ἐλθόντων[2] Αἴας κληρωσάμενος
ἀριστεύει·[3] νυκτὸς δὲ ἐπιγενομένης κήρυκες δια-
λύουσιν αὐτούς.

S 3 | Οἱ δὲ Ἕλληνες πρὸς τοῦ ναυστάθμου τεῖχος
ποιοῦνται καὶ τάφρον, καὶ γενομένης μάχης ἐν
τῷ πεδίῳ οἱ Τρῶες τοὺς Ἕλληνας εἰς τὸ τεῖχος
διώκουσιν· οἱ δὲ πέμπουσι πρὸς Ἀχιλλέα πρέσ-
βεις Ὀδυσσέα καὶ Φοίνικα καὶ Αἴαντα, συμμαχεῖν
ἀξιοῦντες καὶ Βρισηίδα καὶ ἄλλα δῶρα ὑπισχνού-
4 μενοι. νυκτὸς δὲ ἐπιγενομένης κατασκόπους πέμπουσιν Ὀδυσσέα καὶ Διομήδην· οἱ δὲ ἀναιροῦσι
Δόλωνα τὸν Εὐμήλου καὶ Ῥῆσον τὸν Θρᾷκα (ὃς
πρὸ μιᾶς ἡμέρας παραγενόμενος Τρωσὶ σύμμαχος
οὐ συμβαλὼν ἀπωτέρω[4] τῆς Τρωικῆς δυνάμεως
χωρὶς Ἕκτορος ἐστρατοπέδευσε) τούς τε περὶ
αὐτὸν δώδεκα κοιμωμένους κτείνουσι καὶ τοὺς

---

[1] προκαλουμένου δὲ E : προκαλουμένου S.
[2] ἐλθόντων. We should perhaps read θελόντων.
[3] ἀριστεύει Frazer (compare a few lines above Διομήδης
ἀριστεύων, and τὸν ἄριστον; below, iv. 7, Αἴας ἀριστεύσας, v. 12,
τοῦτον ἀριστεύσαντα) : πυκτεύει ES, Wagner : πρωτεύει Herwerden (Mnemosyne, N.S. xx. (1892), p. 199).
[4] ἀπωτέρω Kerameus : ἀποτέρω S.

---

[1] Compare Homer, Il. iii. 15–382.
[2] Compare Homer, Il. iv. 85 sqq.

took heart of grace and sallied out of the city. And
Alexander fought a single combat with Menelaus;
and when Alexander got the worst of it, Aphrodite
carried him off.[1] And Pandarus, by shooting an arrow
at Menelaus, broke the truce.[2]

Diomedes, doing doughty deeds, wounded Aphrodite when she came to the help of Aeneas;[3] and
encountering Glaucus, he recalled the friendship
of their fathers and exchanged arms.[4] And Hector
having challenged the bravest to single combat, many
came forward, but the lot fell on Ajax, and he did
doughty deeds; but night coming on, the heralds
parted them.[5]

The Greeks made a wall and a ditch to protect the
roadstead,[6] and a battle taking place in the plain,
the Trojans chased the Greeks within the wall.[7] But
the Greeks sent Ulysses, Phoenix, and Ajax as ambassadors to Achilles, begging him to fight for them,
and promising Briseis and other gifts.[8] And night
coming on, they sent Ulysses and Diomedes as spies;
and these killed Dolon, son of Eumelus, and Rhesus,
the Thracian (who had arrived the day before as an
ally of the Trojans, and having not yet engaged in
the battle was encamped at some distance from the
Trojan force and apart from Hector); they also slew
the twelve men that were sleeping around him, and

[3] Compare Homer, *Il.* v. 1-417.
[4] Compare Homer, *Il.* vi. 119-236.
[5] Compare Homer, *Il.* vii. 66-312.
[6] Compare Homer, *Il.* vii. 436-441.
[7] Compare Homer, *Il.* viii. 53-565.
[8] The embassy of Ulysses, Phoenix, and Ajax to Achilles
is the subject of the ninth book of the *Iliad*. Libanius composed an imaginary reply to the speech of Ulysses (*Declam.*
v., vol. v. pp. 303-360, ed. R. Foerster).

5 ἵππους ἐπὶ τὰς ναῦς ἄγουσι. μεθ᾽ ἡμέραν δὲ
ἰσχυρᾶς μάχης γενομένης, τρωθέντων Ἀγαμέμνονος καὶ Διομήδους Ὀδυσσέως Εὐρυπύλου Μαχά-
ονος καὶ τροπῆς τῶν Ἑλλήνων γενομένης, Ἕκτωρ
ῥήξας τὸ τεῖχος εἰσέρχεται καὶ ἀναχωρήσαντος
Αἴαντος πῦρ ἐμβάλλει ταῖς ναυσίν.

6 Ὡς δὲ εἶδεν Ἀχιλλεὺς τὴν Πρωτεσιλάου ναῦν
καιομένην, ἐκπέμπει Πάτροκλον καθοπλίσας τοῖς
ἰδίοις ὅπλοις μετὰ τῶν Μυρμιδόνων, δοὺς αὐτῷ
τοὺς ἵππους. ἰδόντες δὲ αὐτὸν οἱ Τρῶες καὶ
νομίσαντες Ἀχιλλέα εἶναι εἰς φυγὴν τρέπονται.
καταδιώξας δὲ αὐτοὺς εἰς τὸ τεῖχος πολλοὺς
ἀναιρεῖ, ἐν οἷς καὶ Σαρπηδόνα τὸν Διός, καὶ ὑφ᾽
Ἕκτορος ἀναιρεῖται, τρωθεὶς πρότερον ὑπὸ Εὐφόρ-
7 βου. μάχης δὲ ἰσχυρᾶς γενομένης περὶ τοῦ νεκροῦ,
μόλις Αἴας ἀριστεύσας σῴζει τὸ σῶμα. Ἀχιλλεὺς δὲ τὴν ὀργὴν ἀποθέμενος καὶ τὴν Βρισηΐδα
κομίζεται. καὶ πανοπλίας αὐτῷ κομισθείσης παρὰ
Ἡφαίστου, καθοπλισάμενος ἐπὶ τὸν πόλεμον ἐξ-
έρχεται, καὶ συνδιώκει τοὺς Τρῶας ἐπὶ τὸν Σκά-
μανδρον, κἀκεῖ πολλοὺς μὲν ἄλλους ἀναιρεῖ, κτείνει
δὲ καὶ Ἀστεροπαῖον τὸν Πηλεγόνος[1] τοῦ Ἀξιοῦ
ποταμοῦ· καὶ αὐτῷ λάβρος ὁ ποταμὸς ἐφορμᾷ.
καὶ τούτου μὲν ὁ Ἥφαιστος τὰ ῥεῖθρα ἀναξηραίνει
πολλῇ φλογὶ διώξας, ὁ δ᾽ Ἀχιλλεὺς Ἕκτορα ἐκ

---

[1] Πηλεγόνος Kerameus : τηλεγόνου S.

---

[1] These events are narrated in the tenth book of the *Iliad*.
They form the subject of Euripides's tragedy *Rhesus*, the only
extant Greek drama of which the plot is derived from the
action of the *Iliad*.

[2] These events are told in the eleventh book of the *Iliad*

[3] Compare Homer, *Il.* xii. 436 *sqq.*

drove the horses to the ships.[1] But by day a fierce
fight took place; Agamemnon and Diomedes, Ulysses,
Eurypylus, and Machaon were wounded, the Greeks
were put to flight,[2] Hector made a breach in the
wall and entered[3] and, Ajax having retreated, he
set fire to the ships.[4]

But when Achilles saw the ship of Protesilaus burning, he sent out Patroclus with the Myrmidons, after
arming him with his own arms and giving him the
horses. Seeing him the Trojans thought that he was
Achilles and turned to flee. And having chased them
within the wall, he killed many, amongst them
Sarpedon, son of Zeus, and was himself killed by
Hector, after being first wounded by Euphorbus.[5]
And a fierce fight taking place for the corpse, Ajax
with difficulty, by performing feats of valour, rescued
the body.[6] And Achilles laid aside his anger and
recovered Briseis. And a suit of armour having been
brought him from Hephaestus, he donned the armour[7]
and went forth to the war, and chased the Trojans in a
crowd to the Scamander, and there killed many, and
amongst them Asteropaeus, son of Pelegon, son of
the river Axius; and the river rushed at him in fury.
But Hephaestus dried up the streams of the river,
after chasing them with a mighty flame.[8] And Achilles

[4] Compare Homer, *Il.* xv. 716 *sqq.*

[5] These events are narrated in the sixteenth book of the
Iliad.

[6] These events are the subject of the seventeenth book of
the *Iliad.*

[7] These events are narrated in the eighteenth and nineteenth books of the *Iliad.*

[8] These events are related in the twentieth and twenty-first
books of the *Iliad.* As to the slaying of Asteropaeus by
Achilles, see *Il.* xxi. 139-204. As to the combat of Achilles
with the river Scamander, and the drying up of the streams

μονομαχίας ἀναιρεῖ καὶ ἐξάψας αὐτοῦ τὰ σφυρὰ
ἐκ τοῦ ἅρματος σύρων ἐπὶ τὰς ναῦς παραγίνεται.
καὶ θάψας Πάτροκλον ἐπ᾽ αὐτῷ ἀγῶνα τίθησιν,
ἐν ᾧ νικᾷ ἵπποις Διομήδης, Ἐπειὸς πυγμῇ, Αἴας
καὶ Ὀδυσσεὺς πάλῃ. μετὰ δὲ τὸν ἀγῶνα παραγενόμενος Πρίαμος πρὸς Ἀχιλλέα λυτροῦται τὸ
Ἕκτορος σῶμα καὶ θάπτει.

E   V. | Ὅτι Πενθεσίλεια, Ὀτρηρῆς καὶ Ἄρεος,
ἀκουσίως Ἱππολύτην κτείνασα καὶ ὑπὸ Πριάμου
καθαρθεῖσα, μάχης γενομένης πολλοὺς κτείνει,
ἐν οἷς καὶ Μαχάονα· εἶθ᾽ ὕστερον θνήσκει ὑπὸ
Ἀχιλλέως,[1] ὅστις μετὰ θάνατον ἐρασθεὶς τῆς
Ἀμαζόνος κτείνει Θερσίτην λοιδοροῦντα αὐτόν.

---

[1] This and the following paragraph are from E. The
death of Penthesilia seems also to have been told in S, but
the passage is incomplete. It runs thus: καὶ μάχης γενομένης πολλοὺς κτείνει, θνήσκει δ᾽ ὁ τρι‖ὴς ὑπὸ Ἀχιλλέως, where
for the corrupt δ᾽ ὁ τρι‖ὴς we should perhaps, following E,
read δὲ ὕστερον. Bücheler thought that in ὁ τρι‖ὴς there
lurks Ὀτρήρη, the name of Penthesilia's mother. Perhaps
the whole passage in S originally ran thus: καὶ μάχης γενομένης <Πενθεσίλεια, Ὀτρηρῆς καὶ Ἄρεος,> πολλοὺς κτείνει,
θνήσκει δ᾽ ὕστερον ὑπὸ Ἀχιλλέως, "and a battle taking place,
Penthesilia, daughter of Otrere and Ares, slays many and is
afterwards slain by Achilles." Wagner prints in the text
θνήσκει δ᾽ Ὀτρηρῆς ὑπὸ Ἀχιλλέως, apparently taking Ὀτρηρῆς
for the name of a man.

---

of the river by the fire-god Hephaestus, see *Il.* xxi. 211–382.
The whole passage affords a striking example of the way in
which the Greeks conceived rivers as personal beings, endowed with human shape, human voice, and human passions.
Incidentally (*vv.* 130–132) we hear of sacrifices of bulls and
horses to a river, the horses being thrown alive into the
stream.

[1] The combat of Achilles with Hector, and the death of
Hector, form the subject of the twenty-second book of the
Iliad.

slew Hector in single combat, and fastening his ankles to his chariot dragged him to the ships.[1] And having buried Patroclus, he celebrated games in his honour, at which Diomedes was victorious in the chariot race, Epeus in boxing, and Ajax and Ulysses in wrestling.[2] And after the games Priam came to Achilles and ransomed the body of Hector, and buried it.[3]

V. Penthesilia, daughter of Otrere and Ares, accidentally killed Hippolyte and was purified by Priam. In battle she slew many, and amongst them Machaon, and was afterwards herself killed by Achilles, who fell in love with the Amazon after her death and slew Thersites for jeering at him.[4]

[2] The burial of Patroclus and the funeral games celebrated in his honour, are described in the twenty-third book of the *Iliad*.

[3] These events are narrated in the twenty-fourth book of the *Iliad*.

[4] These events were narrated in the *Aethiopis* of Arctinus, as we learn from the summary of that poem drawn up by Proclus. See *Epicorum Graecorum Fragmenta*, ed. G. Kinkel, p. 33. Compare Diodorus Siculus, ii. 46. 5; Quintus Smyrnaeus, *Posthomerica*, i. 18 *sqq.*, 227 *sqq.*, 538 *sqq* ; J. Tzetzes, *Posthomerica*, 6 *sqq.*, 100 *sqq.*, 136 *sqq.* ; *id. Schol. on Lycophron*, 999 ; Dictys Cretensis, *Bellum Trojanum*, iv. 2 *sq.* Quintus Smyrnaeus explains more fully than Apollodorus the reason why Penthesilia came to Troy (*Posthomerica*, i. 18 *sqq.*). Aiming at a deer in the chase, she had accidentally killed her sister Hippolyte with her spear, and, haunted by the Furies of the slain woman, she came to Troy to be purified from her guilt. The same story is told more briefly by Diodorus Siculus. According to Tzetzes (*Schol. on Lycophron*, 999), Thersites excited the wrath of Achilles, not only by his foul accusations, but by gouging out the eyes of the beautiful Amazon. In the *Aethiopis* it was related how, after killing the base churl, Achilles sailed to Lesbos and was there purified from the guilt of murder by Ulysses, but not until he had offered sacrifice to Apollo, Artemis, and Latona. See Proclus, in *Epicorum Graecorum Fragmenta*,

2   Ην δὲ Ἱππολύτη ἡ τοῦ Ἱππολύτου μήτηρ, ἡ
καὶ Γλαύκη καὶ Μελανίππη. αὕτη γάρ,[1] ἐπιτε-
λουμένων τῶν γάμων Φαίδρας, ἐπιστᾶσα σὺν
ὅπλοις ἅμα ταῖς μεθ' ἑαυτῆς Ἀμαζόσιν ἔλεγε
κτείνειν τοὺς συνανακειμένους Θησεῖ. μάχης οὖν
γενομένης ἀπέθανεν, εἴτε ὑπὸ τῆς συμμάχου Πεν-
θεσιλείας ἀκούσης, εἴτε ὑπὸ Θησέως, εἴτε ὅτι οἱ
περὶ Θησέα, τὴν τῶν Ἀμαζόνων ἑωρακότες ἐπι-
στασίαν, κλείσαντες διὰ τάχους τὰς θύρας καὶ
ταύτην ἀπολαβόντες ἐντὸς ἀπέκτειναν.

ES 3 | Ὅτι Μέμνονα[2] τὸν Τιθωνοῦ καὶ Ἠοῦς μετὰ
πολλῆς Αἰθιόπων δυνάμεως παραγενόμενον ἐν
Τροίᾳ καθ' Ἑλλήνων καὶ πολλοὺς τῶν Ἑλλήνων
κτείναντα καὶ Ἀντίλοχον κτείνει ὁ Ἀχιλλεύς.
διώξας δὲ καὶ τοὺς[2] Τρῶας πρὸς ταῖς Σκαιαῖς

---

[1] With what follows compare Epitome, i. 17, which is
from S, while the present passage is from E.

[2] Ὅτι Μέμνονα . . . κτείνει ὁ Ἀχιλλεύς E : Μέμνων δὲ ὁ
Τιθωνοῦ καὶ Ἠοῦς πολλὴν Αἰθιόπων δύναμιν ἀθροίσας παραγίνεται
καὶ τῶν Ἑλλήνων οὐκ ὀλίγους ἀναιρεῖ, κτείνει καὶ Ἀντίλοχον καὶ
αὐτὸς θνήσκει ὑπὸ Ἀχιλλέως S.   [3] δὲ καὶ τοὺς E : δὲ τοὺς S.

---

p. 33. The mother of Penthesilia is named Otrere (Otrera)
by Tzetzes (Schol. on Lycophron, 997) and Hyginus (Fab.
112), in agreement with Apollodorus. Machaon is usually
said to have been killed by Eurypylus, and not, as Apollodorus says, by Penthesilia. See Pausanias, iii. 26. 9 ; Quintus
Smyrnaeus, Posthomerica, vi. 390 sqq. ; J. Tzetzes, Posthomerica, 520 sqq. ; Hyginus, Fab. 113. From Pausanias (l.c.)
we learn that Eurypylus, not Penthesilia, was represented
as the slayer in the Little Iliad of Lesches.

[1] See above, Epitome, i. 17. The two passages are prac-
tically duplicates of each other. The former occurs in the
Sabbaitic, the latter in the Vatican Epitome of Apollodorus.
The author of the one compendium preferred to relate the
incident in the history of Theseus, the other in the history
of Troy.

Hippolyte was the mother of Hippolytus; she also goes by the names of Glauce and Melanippe. For when the marriage of Phaedra was being celebrated, Hippolyte appeared in arms with her Amazons, and said that she would slay the guests of Theseus. So a battle took place, and she was killed, whether involuntarily by her ally Penthesilia, or by Theseus, or because his men, seeing the threatening attitude of the Amazons, hastily closed the doors and so intercepted and slew her.[1]

Memnon, the son of Tithonus and the Dawn, came with a great force of Ethiopians to Troy against the Greeks, and having slain many of the Greeks, including Antilochus, he was himself slain by Achilles.[2] Having chased the Trojans also, Achilles

[2] These events were narrated in the *Aethiopis* of Arctinus, as we learn from the summary of Proclus. See *Epicorum Graecorum Fragmenta*, ed. G. Kinkel, p. 33. Compare Quintus Smyrnaeus, *Posthomerica*, ii. 100 *sqq.*, 235 *sqq.*, 452 *sqq.* ; J. Tzetzes, *Posthomerica*, 234 *sqq.* ; Dictys Cretensis, *Bellum Trojanum*, iv. 6. The fight between Memnon and Achilles was represented on the throne of Apollo at Amyclae, and on the chest of Cypselus at Olympia (Pausanias, iii. 18. 12, v. 19. 1). It was also the subject of a group of statuary, which was set up beside the Hippodamium at Olympia (Pausanias, v. 22. 2). Some fragments of the pedestal which supported the group have been discovered : one of them bears the name MEMNON inscribed in archaic letters. See *Die Inschriften von Olympia*, No. 662 ; and my commentary on Pausanias, vol. iii. pp. 629 *sq.* Aeschylus wrote a tragedy on the subject called *Psychostasia*, in which he described Zeus weighing the souls of the rival heroes in scales. See Plutarch, *De audiendis poetis*, 2 ; Scholiast on Homer, *Il.* viii. 70 ; *Tragicorum Graecorum Fragmenta*, ed. A. Nauck², pp. 88 *sq.* A play of Sophocles, called *The Ethiopians*, probably dealt with the same theme. See *The Fragments of Sophocles*, ed. A. C. Pearson, vol. i. pp. 22 *sqq.* The slaying of Antilochus by Memnon is mentioned by Homer (*Od.* iv. 187 *sq.*).

πύλαις τοξεύεται[1] ὑπὸ ᾿Αλεξάνδρου καὶ ᾿Απόλ-
4 λωνος εἰς τὸ σφυρόν. γενομένης δὲ μάχης περὶ
τοῦ νεκροῦ,[2] Αἴας Γλαῦκον ἀναιρεῖ, καὶ τὰ ὅπλα
δίδωσιν ἐπὶ τὰς ναῦς κομίζειν, τὸ δὲ σῶμα βαστάσας Αἴας βαλλόμενος βέλεσι μέσον τῶν πολεμίων
διήνεγκεν, ᾿Οδυσσέως πρὸς τοὺς ἐπιφερομένους
S 5 μαχομένου. | ᾿Αχιλλέως δὲ ἀποθανόντος συμφορᾶς

---

[1] τοξεύεται E : ἐτοξεύθη S.
[2] μάχης περὶ τοῦ νεκροῦ E : περὶ τοῦ νεκροῦ μάχης S.

---

[1] The death of Achilles was similarly related in the *Aethiopis* of Arctinus. See Proclus, in *Epicorum Graecorum
Fragmenta*, ed. G. Kinkel, pp. 33 *sq.* Compare Quintus
Smyrnaeus, *Posthomerica*, iii. 26–387; Hyginus, *Fab.* 107.
All these writers agree with Apollodorus in saying that the
fatal wound was inflicted on the heel of Achilles. The story
ran that at his birth his mother Thetis made Achilles invulnerable by dipping him in the water of Styx ; but his
heel, by which she held him, was not wetted by the water
and so remained vulnerable. See Servius, on Virgil, *Aen.*
vi. 57 ; Lactantius Placidus, on Statius, *Achill.* i. 134 ; *id.
Narrat. fabul.* xii. 6 ; Fulgentius, *Mytholog.* iii. 7. Tradition
varied as to the agent of Achilles's death. Some writers, like
Arctinus and Apollodorus, say that the hero was killed by
Apollo and Paris jointly. Thus in Homer (*Il.* xxii. 359 *sq.*)
the dying Hector prophesies that Achilles will be slain by
Paris and Apollo at the Scaean gate ; and the same prophecy
is put by Homer more darkly into the mouth of the talking
horse Xanthus, who, like Balaam's ass, warns his master of
the danger that besets his path (*Il.* xix. 404 *sqq.*). According
to Virgil and Ovid, it was the hand of Paris that discharged
the fatal arrow, but the hand of Apollo that directed it to
the mark. See Virgil, *Aen.* vi. 56–58 ; Ovid, *Metamorph.*
xii. 597–609. According to Hyginus, it was Apollo in the
guise of Paris who transfixed the mortal heel of Achilles with
an arrow (*Fab.* 107). But in one passage (*Il.* xxi. 277 *sq.*)
Homer speaks of the death of Achilles as wrought by the
shafts of Apollo alone ; and this version was followed by

was shot with an arrow in the ankle by Alexander and Apollo at the Scaean gate. A fight taking place for the corpse, Ajax killed Glaucus, and gave the arms to be conveyed to the ships, but the body he carried, in a shower of darts, through the midst of the enemy, while Ulysses fought his assailants.[1] The death

Quintus Smyrnaeus (iii. 60 *sqq.*) and apparently by Aeschylus, Sophocles and Horace. See Plato, *Republic*, ii. 21, p. 383 A B ; Sophocles, *Philoctetes*, 334 *sq.*; Horace, *Odes*, iv. 6. 1 *sqq.* Other writers, on the contrary, speak of Paris alone as the slayer of Achilles. See Euripides, *Andromache*, 655 ; *id. Hecuba*, 387 *sq.*; Plutarch, *Quaest. Conviv.* ix. 13. 2 ; *id. Comparison of Lysander and Sulla*, 4. A very different version of the story connected the death of Achilles with a romantic passion he had conceived for Polyxena, daughter of Priam. It is said that Priam offered her hand in marriage to Achilles on condition that the siege of Troy was raised. In the negotiations which were carried on for this purpose Achilles went alone and unarmed to the temple of Thymbraean Apollo and was there treacherously assassinated, Deiphobus clasping him to his breast in a pretended embrace of friendship while Paris stabbed him with a sword. See J. Tzetzes, *Posthomerica*, 385–423 ; Philostratus, *Heroica*, xx. 16 *sq.*; Hyginus, *Fab.* 110 ; Dictys Cretensis, *Bellum Trojanum*, iv. 10 *sq.* ; Servius, on Virgil, *Aen.* vi 57 ; Lactantius Placidus, on Statius, *Achill.* i. 134 ; Dares Phrygius, *De excidio Trojae*, 34 ; *Scriptores rerum mythicarum Latini*, ed. G. H. Bode, vol. i. pp. 13, 143 (First Vatican Mythographer, 36 ; Second Vatican Mythographer, 205). Of these writers, the Second Vatican Mythographer tells us that Achilles first saw Polyxena, Hector's sister, when she stood on a tower in the act of throwing down bracelets and earrings with which to ransom Hector's body, and that when Achilles came to the temple of the Thymbraean Apollo to ratify the treaty of marriage and peace, Paris lurked behind the image of the god and shot the confiding hero with an arrow. This seems to be the account of the death which Servius and Lactantius Placidus (*ll.cc.*) followed in their briefer narrative. Compare Nonnus, in Westermann's *Mythographi Graeci, Appendix Narrationum*, p. 382, No. 62.

ES ἐπληρώθη τὸ στράτευμα. | θάπτουσι δὲ αὐτὸν[1]
[ἐν Λευκῇ νήσῳ][2] μετὰ Πατρόκλου, τὰ ἑκατέρων
ὀστᾶ συμμίξαντες. λέγεται δὲ[3] μετὰ θάνατον
Ἀχιλλεὺς ἐν Μακάρων νήσοις Μηδείᾳ συνοικεῖν.[4]

S | τιθέασι δὲ ἐπ' αὐτῷ ἀγῶνα, ἐν ᾧ νικᾷ Εὔμηλος
ἵπποις, Διομήδης σταδίῳ, Αἴας δίσκῳ, Τεῦκρος

ES 6 τόξῳ. | ἡ δὲ πανοπλία αὐτοῦ τῷ ἀρίστῳ νικητή-

---

[1] θάπτουσι δὲ αὐτὸν S: Ὅτι θάπτουσι τὸν Ἀχιλλέα E.
[2] ἐν Λευκῇ νήσῳ . . . συμμίξαντες E: τοῖς Πατρόκλου μίξαντες
ὀστοῖς ἐν Λευκῇ νήσῳ S.   [3] λέγεται δὲ E: καὶ λέγεται S.
[4] Ἀχιλλεὺς ἐν Μακάρων νήσοις Μηδείᾳ συνοικεῖν E: ἐν
Μακάρων νήσοις αὐτῷ Μήδειαν συνοικεῖν S.

---

[1] According to Arctinus in the *Aethiopis*, when the body
of Achilles was lying in state, his mother Thetis came with
the Muses and her sisters and mourned over her dead son;
then she snatched it away from the pyre and conveyed it to
the White Isle; but the Greeks raised a sepulchral mound
and held games in honour of the departed hero. See Proclus,
in *Epicorum Graecorum Fragmenta*, ed. G. Kinkel, p. 34.
Compare Homer, *Od.* xxiv. 43–92; Quintus Smyrnaeus,
Posthomerica, iii. 525–787 (the laying-out of the body, the
lamentation of Thetis, the Nereids, and the Muses, and the
burning of the corpse); J. Tzetzes, *Posthomerica*, 431–467;
Dictys Cretensis, *Bellum Trojanum*, iv. 13 and 15. Homer
tells how the bones of Achilles, after his body had been
burnt on the pyre, were laid with the bones of his friend
Patroclus in a golden urn, made by Hephaestus, which
Thetis had received from Dionysus. The urn was buried
at the headland of Sigeum, according to Tzetzes and Dictys
Cretensis. In Quintus Smyrnaeus (iii. 766–780) we read
how Poseidon comforted Thetis by assuring her that Achilles,
her sorrow, was not dead, for he himself would bestow on
the departed hero an island in the Euxine Sea where he
should be a god for evermore, worshipped with sacrifices
by the neighbouring tribes. The promised land was the
White Isle mentioned by Apollodorus. It is described as a
wooded island off the mouth of the Danube. In it there was
a temple of Achilles with an image of him; and there the
hero was said to dwell immortal with Helen for his wife and

of Achilles filled the army with dismay, and they buried him with Patroclus in the White Isle, mixing the bones of the two together.[1] It is said that after death Achilles consorts with Medea in the Isles of the Blest.[2] And they held games in his honour, at which Eumelus won the chariot-race, Diomedes the foot-race, Ajax the quoit-match, and Teucer the competition in archery.[3] Also his arms were offered

his friends Patroclus and Antilochus for his companions. There he chanted the verses of Homer, and mariners who sailed near the island could hear the song wafted clearly across the water ; while such as put in to the shore or anchored off the coast, heard the trampling of horses, the shouts of warriors, and the clash of arms. See Pausanias, iii. 19. 11–13 ; Philostratus, *Heroica*, xx. 32–40. As the mortal remains of Achilles were buried in the Troad, and only his immortal spirit was said to dwell in the White Isle, the statement of Apollodorus that the Greeks interred him in the White Isle must be regarded as erroneous, whether the error is due to Apollodorus himself, or, as is more probable, either to his abbreviator or to a copyist. Perhaps in the original form of his work Apollodorus followed Arctinus in describing how Thetis snatched the body of Achilles from the pyre and transported it to the White Isle.

[2] Compare Apollonius Rhodius, *Argon.* iv. 810 *sqq.*; Tzetzes, *Schol. on Lycophron*, 174. According to the Scholiast on Apollonius Rhodius (*Argon.* iv. 815), the first to affirm that Achilles married Medea in the Elysian Fields was the poet Ibycus, and the tale was afterwards repeated by Simonides. The story is unknown to Homer, who describes the shade of Achilles repining at his lot and striding alone in the Asphodel Meadow (*Od.* xi. 471–540).

[3] The funeral games in honour of Achilles are described at full length, in the orthodox manner, by Quintus Smyrnaeus, *Posthomerica*, iv. 88–595. He agrees with Apollodorus in representing Teucer and Ajax as victorious in the contests of archery and quoit-throwing respectively (*Posthomerica*, iv. 405 *sqq.*, 436 *sqq.*) ; and he seems to have described Eumelus as the winner of the chariot-race (iv. 500 *sqq.*), but the conclusion of the race is lost through a gap in the text.

S   ριον τίθεται,[1] καὶ καταβαίνουσιν εἰς ἅμιλλαι
Αἴας καὶ Ὀδυσσεύς. | καὶ κρινάντων τῶν Τρώων,
ES ὡς δέ τινες τῶν συμμάχων, | Ὀδυσσεὺς προκρί-
νεται.[2] Αἴας δὲ ὑπὸ λύπης ταραχθεὶς ἐπιβου-
λεύεται νύκτωρ τῷ στρατεύματι, καὶ αὐτῷ μανίαν
ἐμβαλοῦσα Ἀθηνᾶ εἰς τὰ βοσκήματα ἐκτρέπει
ξιφήρη· ὁ δὲ ἐκμανεὶς σὺν τοῖς νέμουσι τὰ βοσκή-
7 ματα ὡς Ἀχαιοὺς φονεύει. ὕστερον δὲ σωφρονήσας
κτείνει καὶ ἑαυτόν.[3] Ἀγαμέμνων δὲ κωλύει τὸ
σῶμα αὐτοῦ καῆναι, καὶ μόνος οὗτος τῶν ἐν Ἰλίῳ
ἀποθανόντων ἐν σορῷ κεῖται· ὁ δὲ τάφος ἐστὶν
ἐν Ῥοιτείῳ.

[1] ἡ δὲ πανοπλία αὐτοῦ τῷ ἀρίστῳ νικητήριον τίθεται Ε: τὴν δὲ
Ἀχιλλέως πανοπλίαν τίθεισι (sic) τῷ ἀρίστῳ νικητήριον S.

[2] Ὀδυσσεὺς προκρίνεται . . . ὡς Ἀχαιοὺς φονεύει S: προκριθέντος δὲ Ὀδυσσέως Αἴας ὑπὸ λύπης ταράττεται καὶ νύκτωρ ἐπι-
βουλεύεται τῷ στρατεύματι· καὶ ὑπὸ Ἀθηνᾶς μανεὶς εἰς τὰ βοσκήματα ξιφήρης ἐκτρέπεται καὶ ταῦτα κτείνει σὺν τοῖς νέμουσιν ὡς
Ἀχαίους Ε.

[3] ὕστερον δὲ σωφρονήσας κτείνει καὶ ἑαυτόν Ε: καὶ σωφρονήσας ὕστερον ἑαυτὸν κτείνει S.

---

[1] These events were narrated in the *Little Iliad* of Lesches.
See Proclus, in *Epicorum Graecorum Fragmenta*, ed. G.
Kinkel, p. 36; compare Aristotle, *Poetics*, 23, p. 1459 b 4 *sq.*
The contest between Ajax and Ulysses for the arms of
Achilles was also related in the *Aethiopis* of Arctinus. See
Epicorum Graecorum Fragmenta, ed. G. Kinkel, p. 34. It
was known to Homer (*Od.* xi. 542 *sqq.*), who tells us that the
Trojans and Pallas Athena acted as judges and awarded the
arms to Ulysses. A Scholiast on this passage of Homer (*v.*
547) informs us that Agamemnon, unwilling to undertake the
invidious duty of deciding between the two competitors,
referred the dispute to the decision of the Trojan prisoners,
inquiring of them which of the two heroes had done most harm
to the Trojans. The prisoners decided that Ulysses was the
man, and the arms were therefore awarded to him. According
to another account, which was adopted by the author of the

as a prize to the bravest, and Ajax and Ulysses came forward as competitors. The judges were the Trojans or, according to some, the allies, and Ulysses was preferred. Disordered by chagrin, Ajax planned a nocturnal attack on the army. And Athena drove him mad, and turned him, sword in hand, among the cattle, and in his frenzy he slaughtered the cattle with the herdsmen, taking them for the Achaeans. But afterwards he came to his senses and slew also himself.[1] And Agamemnon forbade his body to be burnt; and he alone of all who fell at Ilium is buried in a coffin.[2] His grave is at Rhoeteum.

[1] *Little Iliad*, the Greeks on the advice of Nestor sent spies to the walls of Troy to overhear the Trojans discussing the respective merits of the two champions. They heard two girls debating the question, and thinking that she who gave the preference to Ulysses reasoned the better, they decided accordingly. See Scholiast on Aristophanes, *Knights*, 1056. According to Pindar (*Nem.* viii. 26 (45) *sq.*), it was the Greeks who by secret votes decided in favour of Ulysses. The subject was treated by Aeschylus in a lost play called *The Decision of the Arms.* See *Tragicorum Graecorum Fragmenta*, ed. A. Nauck[2], pp. 57 *sq.* The madness and suicide of Ajax, consequent on his disappointment at not being awarded the arms, are the theme of Sophocles's extant tragedy *Ajax.* As to the contest for the arms, see further Quintus Smyrnaeus, *Posthomerica*, v. 121 *sqq.*; J. Tzetzes, *Posthomerica*, 481 *sqq.*; Zenobius, *Cent.* i. 43; Hyginus, *Fab.* 107; Ovid, *Metamorph.* xii. 620-628, xiii. 1–398. Quintus Smyrnaeus and Tzetzes agree in representing the Trojan captives as the judges in the dispute, while Ovid speaks of the Greek chiefs sitting in judgment and deciding in favour of Ulysses. According to Zenobius (*l.c.*), Ajax in his frenzy scourged two rams, believing that he was scourging Agamemnon and Menelaus. This account is based on the description of the frenzy of Ajax in Sophocles (*Ajax*, 97–110, 237–244).

[2] Similarly the author of the *Little Iliad* said that the body of Ajax was not burned, but placed in a coffin "on account of

E 8
ES

|"Ηδη δὲ ὄντος τοῦ πολέμου δεκαετοῦς ἀθυμοῦσι
τοῖς "Ελλησι | Κάλχας θεσπίζει, οὐκ¹ ἄλλως ἀλῶ-
ναι δύνασθαι Τροίαν, ἂν μὴ² τὰ Ἡρακλέους ἔχωσι³

¹ οὐκ S : μὴ E. ² ἂν μὴ S : ἢ E.
³ ἔχωσι S : ἔχουσι E.

the wrath of the king." See Eustathius on Homer, *Il.* ii. 557,
p. 285. Philostratus tells us that the body was laid in the
earth by direction of the seer Calchas, "because suicides may
not lawfully receive the burial by fire" (*Heroica*, xiii. 7).
This was probably the true reason for the tradition that the
corpse was not cremated in the usual way. For the ghosts of
suicides appear to be commonly dreaded; hence unusual
modes of disposing of their bodies are adopted in order to
render their spirits powerless for mischief. For example, the
Baganda of Central Africa, who commonly bury their dead in
the earth, burn the bodies of suicides on waste land or at
cross-roads in order to destroy the ghosts; for they believe
that if the ghost of a suicide is not thus destroyed, it will
tempt other people to imitate its example. As an additional
precaution everyone who passed the place where the body of
a suicide had been burnt threw some grass or a few sticks on
the spot, "so as to prevent the ghost from catching him, in
case it had not been destroyed." For the same reason, if a
man took his life by hanging himself on a tree, the tree was
torn up by the roots and burned with the body; if he had
killed himself in a house, the house was pulled down and
the materials consumed with fire; for "people feared to live
in a house in which a suicide had taken place, lest they
too should be tempted to commit the same crime." See
J. Roscoe, *The Baganda* (London, 1911), pp. 20 *sq.*, 289.
Similar customs prevailed among the Banyoro, a neighbouring nation of Central Africa. "It was said to be necessary
to destroy a tree upon which a person had hanged himself
and to burn down a house in which a person had committed
suicide, otherwise they would be a danger to people in
general and would influence them to commit suicide." See J.
Roscoe, *The Northern Bantu* (Cambridge, 1915), pp. 24 *sq.*
(where, however, the burning of the body is not expressly mentioned). In like manner the Hos of Togoland, in West Africa,

When the war had already lasted ten years, and the Greeks were despondent, Calchas prophesied to them that Troy could not be taken unless they had the bow

are much afraid of the ghost of a suicide. They believe that the ghost of a man who has hanged himself will torment the first person who sees the body. Hence when the relations of such a man approach the corpse they protect themselves against the ghost by wearing magical cords and smearing their faces with a magical powder. The tree on which a man hanged himself is cut down, and the branch on which he tied the fatal noose is lopped off. To this branch the corpse is then tied and dragged ruthlessly through the woods, over stones and through thorny bushes, to the place where "men of blood," that is, all who die a violent death, are buried. There they dig a shallow grave in great haste and throw the body in. Having done so they run home; for they say that the ghosts of "men of blood" fling stones at such as do not retreat fast enough, and that he who is struck by one of these stones must die. The houses of such men are broken down and burnt. A suicide is believed to defile the land and to prevent rain from falling. Hence the district where a man has killed himself must be purified by a sacrifice offered to the Earth-god. See J. Spieth, *Die Ewe-Stämme* (Berlin, 1906), pp. 272, 274, 276 *sq.* 756, 758. As to the special treatment of the bodies of suicides, see R. Lasch, "Die Behandlung der Leiche des Selbstmörders," *Globus,* lxxvi. (Brunswick, 1899, pp. 63–66.) In the *Ajax* of Sophocles the rites of burial are at first refused, but afterwards conceded, to the dead body of Ajax; and though these ceremonies are not described, we may assume that they included the burning of the corpse on a pyre. This variation from what appears to be the usual tradition may have been introduced by Sophocles out of deference to the religious feelings of the Athenians, who worshipped Ajax as a hero, and who would have been shocked to think of his remains being denied the ordinary funeral honours. See Jebb's Introduction to his edition of the *Ajax* (Cambridge, 1896), pp. xxix. *sqq.* As to the worship of Ajax at Athens, see Pausanias, i. 35. 3; *Corpus Inscriptionum Atticarum*, ii. Nos. 467–471; Dittenberger, *Sylloge Inscriptionum Graecarum*[3], No. 717, vol. ii. p. 370. From these inscriptions we learn that the Athenian youths used to sail across every year to Salamis and there sacrifice to Ajax.

τόξα συμμαχοῦντα.¹ τοῦτο ² ἀκούσας Ὀδυσσεὺς
μετὰ Διομήδους εἰς Λῆμνον ἀφικνεῖται πρὸς Φιλο-
κτήτην, καὶ δόλῳ ἐγκρατὴς γενόμενος τῶν τόξων
πείθει πλεῖν αὐτὸν ἐπὶ Τροίαν. ὁ δὲ παραγενόμενος καὶ θεραπευθεὶς ὑπὸ Ποδαλειρίου Ἀλέξ-
9 ανδρον τοξεύει. τούτου δὲ ἀποθανόντος εἰς ἔριν
ἔρχονται Ἕλενος καὶ Δηίφοβος ὑπὲρ τῶν Ἑλένης
γάμων· προκριθέντος δὲ τοῦ Δηιφόβου Ἕλενος
ἀπολιπὼν Τροίαν ἐν Ἴδῃ διετέλει. εἰπόντος δὲ
Κάλχαντος Ἕλενον εἰδέναι τοὺς ῥυομένους τὴν
πόλιν χρησμούς, ἐνεδρεύσας αὐτὸν Ὀδυσσεὺς καὶ
10 χειρωσάμενος ἐπὶ τὸ στρατόπεδον ἤγαγε· καὶ
ἀναγκαζόμενος ὁ Ἕλενος λέγει πῶς ἂν αἱρεθείη ἡ

¹ τόξα συμμαχοῦντα E : συμμαχοῦντα τόξα S.
² τοῦτο E : ταῦτα S.

---

[1] These events are related in precisely the same way,
though with many poetic embellishments, by Quintus Smyrnaeus, *Posthomerica*, ix. 325-479 (the fetching of Philoctetes
from Lemnos and the bealing of him by Podalirius), x. 206 *sqq.*
(Paris wounded to death by the arrows of Philoctetes). The
story was told somewhat differently by Lesches in the *Little
Iliad*. According to him, the prophecy that Troy could not
be taken without the help of Philoctetes was uttered, not by
Calchas, but by the Trojan seer Helenus, whom Ulysses had
captured; Philoctetes was brought from Lemnos by Diomedes
alone, and he was healed, not by Podalirius, but by Machaon.
The account of Tzetzes (*Posthomerica*, 571-595) agrees with
that of Lesches in respect of the prophecy of Helenus and the
cure by Machaon. Sophocles also followed the *Little Iliad* in
putting the prophecy in the mouth of the captured Trojan
seer Helenus (*Philoctetes*, 604-613). Compare Tzetzes, *Schol.
on Lycophron*, 911. In their plays on the subject (see
above, note on *Epitome*, iii. 27) Euripides and Sophocles
differed as to the envoys whom the Greeks sent to bring the
wounded Philoctetes from Lemnos to Troy. According to
Euripides, with whom Apollodorus, Quintus Smyrnaeus, and

and arrows of Hercules fighting on their side. On hearing that, Ulysses went with Diomedes to Philoctetes in Lemnos, and having by craft got possession of the bow and arrows he persuaded him to sail to Troy. So he went, and after being cured by Podalirius, he shot Alexander.[1] After the death of Alexander, Helenus and Deiphobus quarrelled as to which of them should marry Helen; and as Deiphobus was preferred, Helenus left Troy and abode in Ida.[2] But as Chalcas said that Helenus knew the oracles that protected the city, Ulysses waylaid and captured him and brought him to the camp; and Helenus was forced to tell how Ilium could be

---

Hyginus (*Fab.* 103) agree, the envoys were Ulysses and Diomedes; according to Sophocles, they were Ulysses and Neoptolemus, son of Achilles. See Dio Chrysostom, *Or.* lii. vol. ii. p. 161, ed. L. Dindorf; Jebb's Introduction to his edition of Sophocles, *Philoctetes* (Cambridge, 1898), pp. xv. *sqq.*; *Tragicorum Graecorum Fragmenta*, ed. A. Nauck², pp. 613 *sqq.* However, while Sophocles diverges from what seems to have been the usual story by representing Neoptolemus instead of Diomedes as the companion of Ulysses on this errand, he implicitly recognizes the other version by putting it in the mouth of the merchant (*Philoctetes*, 570–597). A painting at the entrance to the acropolis of Athens represented Ulysses or Diomedes (it is uncertain which) in the act of carrying off the bow of Philoctetes. See Pausanias, i. 22. 6, with my commentary (vol. ii. pp. 263 *sq.*). The combat between Philoctetes and Paris is described by John Malalas, *Chronogr.* v. pp. 110 *sq.*, ed. L. Dindorf.

[2] Compare Conon, *Narrat.* 34; Servius, on Virgil, *Aen.* ii. 166. The marriage of Deiphobus to Helen after the death of Paris was related in the *Little Iliad*. See Proclus, in *Epicorum Graecorum Fragmenta*, ed. G. Kinkel, p. 36. Compare J. Tzetzes, *Posthomerica*, 600 *sq.*; *id. Schol. on Lycophron*, 143, 168; Euripides, *Troades*, 959 *sq.*; Scholiast on Homer, *Il.* xxiv. 251, and on *Od.* iv. 276; Dictys Cretensis, *Bellum Trojanum*, iv. 22. The marriage was seemingly known to Homer (*Od.* iv. 276).

Ἴλιος,[1] πρῶτον[2] μὲν εἰ τὰ Πέλοπος ὀστᾶ κομι-
σθείη παρ' αὐτούς,[3] ἔπειτα εἰ Νεοπτόλεμος συμμα-
χοίη, τρίτον εἰ τὸ διιπετὲς παλλάδιον ἐκκλαπείη·
τούτου γὰρ ἔνδον ὄντος οὐ δύνασθαι τὴν πόλιν
ἁλῶναι.

11   Ταῦτα[4] ἀκούσαντες Ἕλληνες[5] τὰ μὲν Πέλοπος
ὀστᾶ μετακομίζουσιν, Ὀδυσσέα δὲ καὶ Φοίνικα
πρὸς Λυκομήδην πέμπουσιν εἰς Σκῦρον, οἱ δὲ πείθουσι <αὐ>τὸν Νεοπτόλεμον[6] προέσθαι. παραγενόμενος δὲ οὗτος εἰς τὸ στρατόπεδον καὶ λαβὼν
παρ' ἑκόντος Ὀδυσσέως τὴν τοῦ πατρὸς πανο-

---

[1] ἡ Ἴλιος E : τὸ Ἴλιον S.   [2] πρῶτον S : καὶ πρῶτον E.
[3] αὐτούς Bücheler : αὐτοῖς E : αὐταῖς S.
[4] ταῦτα S : τούτων E.   [5] Ἕλληνες wanting in S.
[6] πείθουσι <αὐ>τὸν Νεοπτόλεμον Wagner (conjecture):
πείθουσι τὸν Νεοπτόλεμον S : πείθουσι Νεοπτόλεμον E.

---

[1] As to the capture of Helenus and his prophecy, see
Sophocles, *Philoctetes*, 604 *sqq*., 1337 *sqq.*; Conon, *Narrat.*
34; J. Tzetzes, *Posthomerica*, 571–579; *id. Chiliades*, vi.
508–515; Servius, on Virgil, *Aen.* ii. 166; Dictys Cretensis,
Bellum Trojanum, ii. 18. The mode of his capture and the
substance of his prophecies were variously related. The need
of fetching the bones of Pelops is mentioned by Tzetzes among
the predictions of Helenus; and the necessity of obtaining
the Palladium is recorded by Conon and Servius. According
to Pausanias (v. 13. 4), it was a shoulder-blade of Pelops
that was brought from Pisa to Troy; on the return from
Troy the bone was lost in a shipwreck, but afterwards
recovered by a fisherman.

[2] As to the Palladium, see above, iii. 12. 3.

[3] As to the fetching of Neoptolemus from Scyros, see
Homer, *Od.* xi. 506 *sqq.*; the *Little Iliad* of Lesches, summarized by Proclus, in *Epicorum Graecorum Fragmenta*, ed.
G. Kinkel, pp. 36 *sq.*; Pindar,*Paean*, vi. 98 *sqq.*, ed Sandys;
Sophocles, *Philoctetes*, 343–356; Philostratus Junior, *Imag.*
2; Quintus Smyrnaeus, *Posthomerica*, vi. 57–113, vii. 169–
430; J. Tzetzes,*Posthomerica*, 523–534. Apollodorus agrees
with Sophocles in saying that the Greek envoys who fetched

taken,[1] to wit, first, if the bones of Pelops were brought to them; next, if Neoptolemus fought for them; and third, if the Palladium,[2] which had fallen from heaven, were stolen from Troy, for while it was within the walls the city could not be taken.

On hearing these things the Greeks caused the bones of Pelops to be fetched, and they sent Ulysses and Phoenix to Lycomedes at Scyros, and these two persuaded him to let Neoptolemus go.[3] On coming to the camp and receiving his father's arms from Ulysses, who willingly resigned them, Neoptolemus slew many

---

Neoptolemus from Scyros were Ulysses and Phoenix. According to Quintus Smyrnaeus, they were Ulysses and Diomedes. Ulysses is the only envoy mentioned by Homer, Lesches, and Tzetzes; and Phoenix is the only envoy mentioned by Philostratus. Pindar speaks vaguely of "messengers." In this passage I have adopted Wagner's conjecture πείθουσι <αὐ>τὸν Νεοπτόλεμον προέσθαι, "persuaded him to let Neoptolemus go." If this conjecture is not accepted, we seem forced to translate the passage "persuaded Neoptolemus to venture." But I cannot cite any exact parallel to such a use of the middle of προΐημι. When employed absolutely, the verb seems often to convey a bad meaning. Thus Demosthenes uses it in the sense of "throwing away a chance," "neglecting an opportunity" (Or. xix. De falsa legatione, p. 388, §§ 150, 152, μὴ πρόεσθαι, οὐ προΐησεσθαι). Iphicrates employed it with the same significance (quoted by Aristotle, Rhetoric, ii. 23. 6 διότι προεῖτο). Aristotle applied the verb to a man who had "thrown away" his health (Nicom. Ethics, iii. 5. 14, τότε μὲν οὖν ἐξῆν αὐτῷ μὴ νοσεῖν, προεμένῳ δ' οὐκέτι, ὥσπερ οὐδ' ἀφέντι λίθον ἔτ' αὐτὸν δυνατὸν ἀναλαβεῖν). However, elsewhere Aristotle uses the word to describe the lavish liberality of generous men (Rhetoric, i. 9. 6, εἶτα ἡ ἐλευθεριότης· προΐενται γὰρ καὶ οὐκ ἀνταγωνίζονται περὶ τῶν χρημάτων, ὧν μάλιστα ἐφίενται ἄλλοι). In the present passage of Apollodorus, if Wagner's emendation is not accepted, we might perhaps read <μὴ>πρόεσθαι and translate, "persuaded Neoptolemus not to throw away the chance." But it is better to acquiesce in Wagner's simple and probable correction.

12 πλίαν πολλοὺς τῶν Τρώων ἀναιρεῖ. ἀφικνεῖται δὲ
ὕστερον Τρωσὶ σύμμαχος Εὐρύπυλος ὁ Τηλέφου
πολλὴν Μυσῶν δύναμιν ἄγων· τοῦτον ἀριστεύ-
13 σαντα Νεοπτόλεμος ἀπέκτεινεν. Ὀδυσσεὺς δὲ
μετὰ Διομήδους παραγενόμενος νύκτωρ εἰς τὴν
πόλιν Διομήδην μὲν αὐτοῦ μένειν εἴα, αὐτὸς δὲ
ἑαυτὸν¹ αἰκισάμενος καὶ πενιχρὰν στολὴν ἐνδυ-
σάμενος² ἀγνώστως εἰς τὴν πόλιν εἰσέρχεται ὡς
ἐπαίτης· γνωρισθεὶς δὲ ὑπὸ Ἑλένης δι' ἐκείνης τὸ
παλλάδιον ἔκλεψε³ καὶ πολλοὺς κτείνας τῶν
φυλασσόντων ἐπὶ τὰς ναῦς μετὰ Διομήδους
κομίζει.

¹ ἑαυτὸν E: αὑτὸν S.
² ἐνδυσάμενος ἀγνώστως εἰς τὴν πόλιν E: ἐνδὺς εἰς τὴν πόλιν
ἀγνώστως S. Perhaps for ἀγνώστως we should read ἄγνωστος.
³ ἔκλεψε S: ἐκκλέψας E.

---

¹ As to the single combat of Eurypylus and Neoptolemus,
and the death of Eurypylus, see Homer, *Od.* xi. 516–521 ; the
Little Iliad of Lesches, summarized by Proclus, in *Epicorum
Graecorum Fragmenta*, ed. G. Kinkel, p. 37 ; Quintus Smyrnaeus, *Posthomerica*, viii. 128–220 ; J. Tzetzes, *Posthomerica*,
560–565 ; Dictys Cretensis, *Bellum Trojanum*, iv. 17. Eury-
pulus was king of Mysia. At first his mother Astyoche
refused to let him go to the Trojan war, but Priam overcame
her scruples by the present of a golden vine. See Scholiast
on Homer, *Od.* xi. 520. The brief account which Apollodorus
gives of the death of Eurypylus agrees closely with the equally
summary narrative of Proclus. Sophocles composed a tragedy
on the subject, of which some very mutilated fragments have
been discovered in Egypt. See *The Fragments of Sophocles*,
ed. A. C. Pearson, vol. i. pp. 146 *sqq.* ; A. S. Hunt, *Tragicorum Graecorum Fragmenta Papyracea nuper reperta* (Oxford, the Clarendon Press ; no date, no pagination).
² These events were narrated in the *Little Iliad* of Lesches,
as we learn from the summary of Proclus (*Epicorum Graecorum Fragmenta*, ed. G. Kinkel, p. 37), which runs thus :
" And Ulysses, having disfigured himself, comes as a spy to

of the Trojans. Afterwards, Eurypylus, son of Telephus, arrived to fight for the Trojans, bringing a great
force of Mysians. He performed doughty deeds, but
was slain by Neoptolemus.[1] And Ulysses went with
Diomedes by night to the city, and there he let Diomedes wait, and after disfiguring himself and putting
on mean attire he entered unknown into the city as
a beggar. And being recognized by Helen, he with
her help stole away the Palladium, and after killing
many of the guards, brought it to the ships with the
aid of Diomedes.[2]

Troy, and being recognized by Helen he makes a compact
with her concerning the capture of the city; and having
slain some of the Trojans he arrives at the ships. And after
these things he with Diomedes conveys the Palladium out of
Ilium." From this it appears that Ulysses made two different
expeditions to Troy: in one of them he went by himself as a
spy in mean attire, and being recognized by Helen concerted
with her measures for betraying Troy to the Greeks; in the
other he went with Diomedes, and together the two stole the
Palladium. The former of these expeditions is described by
Homer in the *Odyssey* (iv. 242 *sqq.*), where Helen tells how
Ulysses disfigured himself with wounds, and disguising himself in mean attire came as a beggar to Troy; how she alone
detected him, wormed the secrets of the Greeks out of him,
and having sworn not to betray him till he had returned in
safety to the ships, let him go free, whereupon on his way
back he killed many Trojans. Euripides also relates this
visit of Ulysses to Troy, adding that Helen revealed his
presence to Hecuba, who spared his life and sent him out of
the country (*Hecuba*, 239–250). These two quite distinct
expeditions of Ulysses have been confused and blended into
one by Apollodorus. As to the joint expedition of Ulysses
and Diomedes to Troy, and the stealing of the Palladium, see
further Conon, *Narrat.* 34 ; Quintus Smyrnaeus, *Posthomerica*, x. 350–360 ; Scholiast on Homer, *Il.* vi. 311 ; J.
Malalas, *Chronogr.* v. pp. 109, 111 *sq.*, ed. L. Dindorf ; Zenobius, *Cent.* iii. 8 ; Apostolius, *Cent.* vi. 15 ; Suidas, *s.vv.*
Διομήδειος ἀνάγκη and Παλλάδιον ; Hesychius, *s.v.* Διομήδειος

14 Ὕστερον δὲ ἐπινοεῖ δουρείου ἵππου κατασκευὴν καὶ ὑποτίθεται Ἐπειῷ, ὃς ἦν ἀρχιτέκτων· οὗτος

ἀνάγκη; Eustathius, on Homer, *Il.* x. 531, p. 822 ; Scholiast on Plato, *Republic*, vi. 493 B ; Virgil, *Aen.* ii. 162-170 ; Servius, on Virgil, *Aen.* ii. 166 ; Dictys Cretensis, *Bellum Trojanum*, v. 5 and 8 *sq.* The narrative of Apollodorus suggests that Ulysses had the principal share in the exploit. But according to another and seemingly more prevalent tradition it was Diomedes who really bore off the image. This emerges particularly from Conon's account. Diomedes, he tells us, mounted on the shoulders of Ulysses, and having thus scaled the wall, he refused to draw his comrade up after him, and went in search of the Palladium. Having secured it, he returned with it to Ulysses, and together they retraced their steps to the Greek camp. But by the way the crafty Ulysses conceived the idea of murdering his companion and making himself master of the fateful image. So he dropped behind Diomedes and drew his sword. But the moon shone full ; and as he raised his arm to strike, the flash of the blade in the moonlight caught the eye of the wary Diomedes. He faced round, drew his sword, and, upbraiding the other with his cowardice, drove him before him, while he beat the back of the recreant with the flat of his sword. This incident gave rise to the proverb, "Diomedes's compulsion," applied to such as did what they were forced to do by dire necessity. The proverb is similarly explained by the other Greek proverb-writers and lexicographers cited above, except that, instead of the flash of the sword in the moonlight, they say it was the shadow of the sword raised to strike him which attracted the attention of Diomedes. The picturesque story appears to have been told in the *Little Iliad* (Hesychius, *s.v.* Διομήδειος ἀνάγκη). According to one account, Diomedes and Ulysses made their way into the Trojan citadel through a sewer (Servius, on Virgil, *Aen.* ii. 166), indeed a narrow and muddy sewer, as Sophocles called it in the play which he composed on the subject. See Julius Pollux, ix. 49 ; *The Fragments of Sophocles*, ed. A. C. Pearson, vol. ii. p. 36, frag. 367. Some affirmed that the Palladium was treacherously surrendered to the Greek heroes by Theano, the priestess of the goddess (Scholiast on Homer, *Il.* vi. 311 ; Suidas, *s.v.* Παλλά-

But afterwards he invented the construction of the Wooden Horse and suggested it to Epeus, who was an architect.[1] Epeus felled timber on Ida,

δίον); to this step she was said to have been instigated by her husband Antenor (J. Malalas, *Chronogr.* v. p. 109, ed. L. Dindorf; Dictys Cretensis, *Bellum Trojanum*, v. 5 and 8). As to Theano in her capacity of priestess, see Homer, *Il.* vi. 297 *sqq.*

The theft of the Palladium furnished a not infrequent subject to Greek artists; but the artistic, like the literary, tradition was not agreed on the question whether the actual thief was Diomedes or Ulysses. See my note on Pausanias, i. 22. 6 (vol. ii. pp. 264 *sq.*).

[1] As to the stratagem of the Wooden Horse, by which Troy is said to have been captured, see Homer, *Od.* iv. 271–289, viii. 492–515, xi. 523–532; the *Little Iliad* of Lesches, summarized by Proclus, in *Epicorum Graecorum Fragmenta*, ed. G. Kinkel, p. 37; the *Ilii Persis* ("Sack of Troy") by Arctinus, summarized by Proclus, in *Epicorum Graecorum Fragmenta*, ed. G. Kinkel, p. 49; Quintus Smyrnaeus, *Posthomerica*, xii. 23–83, 104–156, 218–443, 539–585, xiii. 21–59; Tryphiodorus, *Excidium Ilii*, 57–541; J. Tzetzes, *Posthomerica*, 629–723; *id. Schol. on Lycophron*, 930; Virgil, *Aen.* ii. 13–267; Hyginus, *Fab.* 108; Dictys Cretensis, *Bellum Trojanum*, v. 9 and 11 *sq.* The story is only alluded to by Homer, but was no doubt fully told by Lesches and Arctinus, though of their narratives we possess only the brief abstracts of Proclus. The accounts of later writers, such as Virgil, Quintus Smyrnaeus, Tryphiodorus, Tzetzes, and Apollodorus himself, are probably based on the works of these early cyclic poets. The poem of Arctinus, if we may judge by Proclus's abstract, opened with the deliberations of the Trojans about the Wooden Horse, and from the similarity of the abstract to the text of Apollodorus we may infer that our author followed Arctinus generally, though not in all details; for instance, he differed from Arctinus in regard to the affair of Laocoon and his sons. See below.

With the stratagem of the Wooden Horse we may compare the stratagem by which, in the war of Independence waged by the United Provinces against Spain, Prince Maurice contrived to make himself master of Breda. The city was then held by

ἀπὸ τῆς Ἴδης [1] ξύλα τεμὼν ἵππον κατασκευάζει
κοῖλον ἔνδοθεν εἰς τὰς πλευρὰς ἀνεῳγμένον. εἰς
τοῦτον Ὀδυσσεὺς εἰσελθεῖν πείθει πεντήκοντα
τοὺς ἀρίστους, ὡς δὲ ὁ τὴν μικρὰν γράψας Ἰλιάδα
φησί, τρισχιλίους, τοὺς δὲ λοιποὺς γενομένης
νυκτὸς ἐμπρήσαντας τὰς σκηνάς, ἀναχθέντας
περὶ [2] τὴν Τένεδον ναυλοχεῖν καὶ μετὰ τὴν
15 ἐπιοῦσαν νύκτα καταπλεῖν. οἱ δὲ πείθονται καὶ
τοὺς μὲν ἀρίστους ἐμβιβάζουσιν εἰς τὸν ἵππον,
ἡγεμόνα καταστήσαντες αὐτῶν Ὀδυσσέα, γράμ-

---

[1] ἀπὸ τῆς Ἴδης E : ἐπὶ τῶν Ἴδης S.
[2] περὶ S : ἐπὶ E.

---

a Spanish garrison, which received its supply of fuel by boats.
The master of one of these boats, Adrian Vandenberg by name,
noticed that in the absence of the governor there was great
negligence in conducting the examination to which all boats
were subjected before they were allowed to enter the town.
This suggested to Vandenberg a plan for taking the citadel by
surprise. He communicated his plan to Prince Maurice, who
readily embraced it. Accordingly the boat was loaded in
appearance with turf as usual ; but the turf was supported by
a floor of planks fixed at the distance of several feet from the
bottom ; and beneath this floor seventy picked soldiers were
placed under the command of an able officer named Harauguer.
The boat had but a few miles to sail, yet through unexpected
accidents several days passed before they could reach Breda.
The wind veered against them, the melting ice (for it was the
month of February) retarded their course, and the boat, having
struck upon a bank, was so much damaged that the soldiers
were for some time up to their knees in water. Their provisions were almost spent, and to add to their anxieties one of
their number was seized with a violent cough, which, if it had
continued, would inevitably have betrayed them to the enemy.
The man generously entreated his comrades to kill him,
offering them his own sword for the purpose ; but they as
generously refused, and happily the soldier's cough left him
before they approached the walls. Even the leak in the boat

and constructed the horse with a hollow interior and
an opening in the sides.   Into this horse Ulysses
persuaded fifty (or, according to the author of the
Little Iliad, three thousand) of the doughtiest to
enter,[1] while the rest, when night had fallen, were
to burn their tents, and, putting to sea, to lie to off
Tenedos, but to sail back to land after the ensuing
night.   They followed the advice of Ulysses and
introduced the doughtiest into the horse, after
appointing Ulysses their leader and engraving on

was stopped by some accident. On reaching the fortifications
the boat was searched, but only in the most superficial manner.
Still the danger was great, for the turf was immediately
purchased and the soldiers of the garrison set to work to
unload it. They would soon have uncovered the planks and
detected the ambush, if the ready-witted master of the boat
had not first amused them with his discourse and then invited
them to drink wine with him. The offer was readily accepted.
The day wore on, darkness fell, and the Spanish soldiers were
all drunk or asleep. At dead of night Harauguer and his men
issued from the boat, and dividing into two bodies they
attacked the guards and soon made themselves masters of two
gates.   Seized with a panic, the garrison fled the town.
Prince Maurice marched in and took possession of the citadel.
These events happened in the year 1590. See Robert Watson,
History of the Reign of Philip the Second, Fourth Edition
(London, 1785), bk. xxi. vol. iii. pp. 157-161.

[1] According to Tzetzes the number of men who entered
into the Wooden Horse was twenty-three, and he gives the
names of them all (*Posthomerica*, 641-650).   Quintus Smyrnaeus gives the names of thirty, and he says that there were
more of them (*Posthomerica*, xii. 314-335).   He informs us
that the maker of the horse, Epeus, entered last and drew
up the ladder after him ; and knowing how to open and shut
the trapdoor, he sat by the bolt.   To judge by Homer's
description of the heroes in the Horse (*Od.* xi. 526 *sqq.*), the
hearts of most of them failed them, for they blubbered and
their knees knocked together ; but Neoptolemus never
blenched and kept fumbling with the hilt of his sword.

ματα ἐγχαράξαντες τὰ δηλοῦντα· τῆς εἰς οἶκον
ἀνακομιδῆς [1] Ἕλληνες Ἀθηνᾷ χαριστήριον.
αὐτοὶ [2] δὲ ἐμπρήσαντες τὰς σκηνὰς καὶ καταλι-
πόντες Σίνωνα, ὃς ἔμελλεν αὐτοῖς πυρσὸν ἀνάπτειν,
τῆς νυκτὸς ἀνάγονται καὶ περὶ Τένεδον ναυλο-
χοῦσιν.

16 Ἡμέρας δὲ γενομένης ἔρημον οἱ Τρῶες τὸ τῶν
Ἑλλήνων στρατόπεδον θεασάμενοι [3] καὶ νομίσαντες αὐτοὺς πεφευγέναι, περιχαρέντες εἷλκον
τὸν ἵππον καὶ παρὰ τοῖς Πριάμου βασιλείοις
17 στήσαντες ἐβουλεύοντο τί χρὴ ποιεῖν. Κασάνδρας
δὲ λεγούσης ἔνοπλον ἐν αὐτῷ δύναμιν εἶναι καὶ
προσέτι Λαοκόωντος τοῦ μάντεως, τοῖς μὲν ἐδόκει
κατακαίειν, τοῖς δὲ κατὰ βαράθρων ἀφιέναι· δόξαν
δὲ τοῖς πολλοῖς ἵνα αὐτὸν ἐάσωσι θεῖον ἀνάθημα,
18 τραπέντες ἐπὶ θυσίαν εὐωχοῦντο. Ἀπόλλων δὲ
αὐτοῖς σημεῖον ἐπιπέμπει· δύο γὰρ δράκοντες
διανηξάμενοι διὰ τῆς θαλάσσης ἐκ τῶν πλησίον [4]
19 νήσων τοὺς Λαοκόωντος υἱοὺς κατεσθίουσιν. ὡς
δὲ ἐγένετο νὺξ καὶ πάντας ὕπνος κατεῖχεν, οἱ ἀπὸ

----

[1] τῆς εἰς οἶκον ἀνακομιδῆς S : τὴν εἰς οἶκον κομιδὴν E.
[2] αὐτοὶ δὲ E : οἱ δὲ S.
[3] στρατόπεδον θεασάμενοι E : θεασάμενοι στράτευμα S.
[4] πλησίον E : πλησίων S.

----

[1] As to these deliberations of the Trojans, compare Homer,
Od. viii. 505 *sqq.*; Arctinus, *Ilii Persis*, summarized by
Proclus, in *Epicorum Graecorum Fragmenta*, ed. G. Kinkel,
p. 49; Tryphiodorus, *Excidium Ilii*, 250 *sqq.*
[2] Compare the *Ilii Persis* of Arctinus, summarized by
Proclus, in *Epicorum Graecorum Fragmenta*, ed. G. Kinkel,
p. 49; Dionysius Halicarnasensis, *Antiquit. Roman.* i. 48. 2;
Quintus Smyrnaeus, *Posthomerica*, xii. 444–497; Tzetzes,
Schol. on Lycophron, 347; Virgil, *Aen.* ii. 199–227; Hyginus,
Fab. 135; Servius, on Virgil, *Aen.* ii. 201; *Scriptores rerum*

the horse an inscription which signified, "For their return home, the Greeks dedicate this thankoffering to Athena." But they themselves burned their tents, and leaving Sinon, who was to light a beacon as a signal to them, they put to sea by night, and lay to off Tenedos.

And at break of day, when the Trojans beheld the camp of the Greeks deserted and believed that they had fled, they with great joy dragged the horse, and stationing it beside the palace of Priam deliberated what they should do. As Cassandra said that there was an armed force in it, and she was further confirmed by Laocoon, the seer, some were for burning it, and others for throwing it down a precipice; but as most were in favour of sparing it as a votive offering sacred to a divinity,[1] they betook them to sacrifice and feasting. However, Apollo sent them a sign; for two serpents swam through the sea from the neighbouring islands and devoured the sons of Laocoon.[2] And when night fell, and all were

mythicarum Latini, ed. G. H. Bode, vol. i. pp. 144 sq. (Second Vatican Mythographer, 207). According to Arctinus, our oldest authority for the tragedy of Laocoon, the two serpents killed Laocoon himself and one of his sons. According to Virgil, Hyginus, and Servius, they killed Laocoon and both his sons. According to Quintus Smyrnaeus, the serpents killed the two sons but spared the father, who lived to lament their fate. This last seems to have been the version followed by Apollodorus. The reason of the calamity which befel Laocoon is explained by Servius on the authority of Euphorion. He tells us that when the Greek army landed in the Troad, the Trojans stoned the priest of Poseidon to death, because he had not, by offering sacrifices to the sea god, prevented the invasion. Accordingly, when the Greeks seemed to be departing, it was deemed advisable to sacrifice to Poseidon, no doubt in order to induce him to give the Greeks a stormy passage. But the priesthood was vacant, and it was necessary

Τενέδου προσέπλεον, καὶ Σίνων αὐτοῖς ἀπὸ τοῦ
Ἀχιλλέως τάφου πυρσὸν ἧπτεν. Ἑλένη δὲ ἐλθοῦ-
σα περὶ τὸν ἵππον, μιμουμένη τὰς φωνὰς ἑκάστης
τῶν γυναικῶν, τοὺς ἀριστέας ἐκάλει. ὑπακοῦσαι
δὲ Ἀντίκλου θέλοντος Ὀδυσσεὺς τὸ στόμα κατέ-
20 σχεν. ὡς δ' ἐνόμισαν κοιμᾶσθαι τοὺς πολεμίους,
ἀνοίξαντες σὺν τοῖς ὅπλοις ἐξῇεσαν· καὶ πρῶτος
μὲν Ἐχίων Πορθέως ἀφαλλόμενος¹ ἀπέθανεν, οἱ
δὲ λοιποὶ σειρᾷ ἐξάψαντες ἑαυτοὺς² ἐπὶ τὰ τείχη
παρεγένοντο καὶ τὰς πύλας ἀνοίξαντες ὑπεδέ-
21 ξαντο τοὺς ἀπὸ Τενέδου καταπλεύσαντας. χωρή-
σαντες δὲ μεθ' ὅπλων εἰς τὴν πόλιν, εἰς τὰς οἰκίας

¹ ἀφαλλόμενος E : ἐφαλλόμενος S.
² ἑαυτοὺς E : αὐτοὺς S.

to choose a priest by lot. The lot fell on Laocoon, priest of the Thymbraean Apollo, but he had incurred the wrath of Apollo by sleeping with his wife in front of the divine image, and for this sacrilege he perished with his two sons. This narrative helps us to understand the statement of Apollodorus that the two serpents were sent by Apollo for a sign. According to Tzetzes, the death of Laocoon's son took place in the temple of the Thymbraean Apollo, the scene of the crime thus becoming the scene of the punishment. Sophocles wrote a tragedy on the subject of Laocoon, but though a few fragments of the play have survived, its contents are unknown. See *Tragicorum Graecorum Fragmenta*, ed. A. Nauck², pp. 211 *sqq.*; *The Fragments of Sophocles*, ed. A. C Pearson, vol. ii. pp. 38 *sqq.* In modern times the story of Laocoon is probably even better known from the wonderful group of statuary in the Vatican than from the verses of Virgil. That group, the work of three Rhodian sculptors, graced the palace of the emperor Titus in the time of Pliny, who declared that it was to be preferred to any other work either of sculpture or painting (*Nat. Hist.* xxxvi. 37). Lessing took the group for the text of his famous essay on the comparative limitations of poetry and art.

¹ The beacon-light kindled by the deserter and traitor

plunged in sleep, the Greeks drew near by sea from
Tenedos, and Sinon kindled the beacon on the grave
of Achilles to guide them.[1] And Helen, going round
the horse, called the chiefs, imitating the voices of
each of their wives. But when Anticlus would
have answered, Ulysses held fast his mouth.[2] And
when they thought that their foes were asleep, they
opened the horse and came forth with their arms.
The first, Echion, son of Portheus, was killed by leaping from it; but the rest let themselves down by a
rope, and lighted on the walls, and having opened the
gates they admitted their comrades who had landed
from Tenedos. And marching, arms in hand, into

[1] Sinon to guide the Greeks across the water to the doomed
city is a regular feature in the narratives of the taking of
Troy; but the only other writer who mentions that it shone
from the grave of Achilles is Tryphiodorus, who adds that all
night long there blazed a light like the full moon above Helen's
chamber, for she too was awake and signalling to the enemy,
while all the town was plunged in darkness and silence; the
sounds of revelry and music had died away, and not even the
barking of a dog broke the stillness of the summer night.
See Tryphiodorus, *Excidium Ilii*, 487-521. That the poet
conceived the fall of Troy to have happened in the summer
time is shown by his describing how the Trojans wreathed
the mane of the Wooden Horse with flowers culled on river
banks, and how the women spread carpets of roses under
its feet (verses 316 *sq.*, 340-344). For these flowers of fancy
Tryphiodorus is severely taken to task by the pedantic
Tzetzes on the ground that Troy fell at midwinter; and he
clinches the lesson administered to his predecessor by observing that he had learned from Orpheus, "who had it from
another man," never to tell a lie. Such was the state of the
Higher Criticism at Byzantium in the twelfth century of our
era. See J. Tzetzes, *Posthomerica*, 700-707.

[2] This incident is derived from Homer, *Od.* iv. 274-289.
It is copied and told with fuller details by Tryphiodorus, who
says that Anticlus expired under the iron grip of Ulysses
(*Excidium Ilii*, 463-490).

APOLLODORUS

ἐπερχόμενοι κοιμωμένους ἀνῄρουν. καὶ Νεοπτόλεμος μὲν ἐπὶ τοῦ ἑρκείου Διὸς βωμοῦ κατα-
E φεύγοντα Πρίαμον ἀνεῖλεν· | Ὀδυσσεὺς δὲ καὶ
Μενέλαος Γλαῦκον τὸν Ἀντήνορος¹ εἰς τὴν οἰκίαν
φεύγοντα γνωρίσαντες μεθ᾽ ὅπλων ἐλθόντες² ἔσω-
σαν. Αἰνείας δὲ Ἀγχίσην τὸν πατέρα βαστάσας
ἔφυγεν, οἱ δὲ Ἕλληνες αὐτὸν διὰ τὴν εὐσέβειαν
ES 22 εἴασαν. | Μενέλαος δὲ Δηίφοβον κτείνας Ἑλένην
E ἐπὶ τὰς ναῦς ἄγει· ἀπάγουσι δὲ καὶ τὴν Θησέως
μητέρα Αἴθραν οἱ Θησέως παῖδες | Δημοφῶν καὶ
Ἀκάμας· καὶ γὰρ τούτους λέγουσιν εἰς Τροίαν

---

¹ Ἀντήνορος Wagner: ἀγήνορος E.
² ἐλθόντες Frazer: θέλοντες E, Wagner.

---

¹ As to the death of Priam at the altar, compare Arctinus,
Ilii Persis, summarized by Proclus, in *Epicorum Graecorum
Fragmenta*, ed. G. Kinkel, p. 49 ; Euripides, *Troades*, 16 *sq.*,
481–483 ; *id. Hecuba*, 22–24 ; Pausanias, iv. 17. 4 ; Quintus
Smyrnaeus, *Posthomerica*, xiii. 220–250 ; Tryphiodorus, *Exci-
dium Ilii*, 634–639 ; J. Tzetzes, *Posthomerica*, 732 *sq.* ; Virgil,
Aen. ii. 533–558 ; Dictys Cretensis, *Bellum Trojanum*, v. 12.
According to Lesches, the ruthless Neoptolemus dragged
Priam from the altar and despatched him at his own door.
See Pausanias, x. 27. 2, with my note (vol. v. p. 371). The
summary account of Proclus agrees almost verbally with the
equally summary account of Apollodorus.
² Ulysses and Menelaus were bound by ties of hospitality
to Antenor ; for when they went as ambassadors to Troy to
treat of the surrender of Helen, he entertained them hospitably in his house. See Homer, *Il.* iii. 203–207. Moreover,
Antenor had advocated the surrender of Helen and her
property to the Greeks. See Homer, *Il.* iii. 347–353.
According to Lesches, one of Antenor's sons, Lycaon, was
wounded in the sack of Troy, but Ulysses recognized him
and carried him safe out of the fray. See Pausanias, x. 26. 8.
Sophocles composed a tragedy on the subject of Antenor and
his sons, in which he said that at the storming of Troy the
Greeks hung a leopard's skin in front of Antenor's house in

the city, they entered the houses and slew the
sleepers. Neoptolemus slew Priam, who had taken
refuge at the altar of Zeus of the Courtyard.[1] But
when Glaucus, son of Antenor, fled to his house,
Ulysses and Menelaus recognized and rescued him
by their armed intervention.[2] Aeneas took up his
father Anchises and fled, and the Greeks let him
alone on account of his piety.[3] But Menelaus slew
Deiphobus and led away Helen to the ships[4]; and
Aethra, mother of Theseus, was also led away by
Demophon and Acamas, the sons of Theseus; for
they say that they afterwards went to Troy.[5] And

token that it was to be respected by the soldiery. See Strabo,
xiii. 1. 53, p. 608. In Polygnotus's great picture of the sack
of Troy, which was one of the sights of Delphi, the painter
depicted the house of Antenor with the leopard's skin hung
on the wall; in front of it were to be seen Antenor and his
wife, with their children, including Glaucus, while beside
them servants were lading an ass, to indicate the long journey
which the exiles were about to undertake. See Pausanias, x.
27. 3 *sq.* According to Roman tradition, Antenor led a colony
of Enetians to the head of the Adriatic, where the people
were thenceforth called Venetians (Livy i. 1). As to Sophocles's
play, *The Antenorids,* see *Tragicorum Graecorum Fragmenta,*
ed. A. Nauck², p. 160; *The Fragments of Sophocles,* ed. A.
C. Pearson, vol. i. pp. 86 *sqq.*

[3] Compare Xenophon, *Cyneg.* i. 15; Quintus Smyrnaeus,
Posthomerica, xiii. 315–327; Virgil, *Aen.* ii. 699 *sqq.*

[4] Compare Arctinus, *Ilii Persis,* summarized by Proclus,
in *Epicorum Graecorum Fragmenta,* ed. G. Kinkel, p. 49:
Quintus Smyrnaeus, *Posthomerica,* xiii. 354 *sqq.*; Tryphiodorus, *Excidium Ilii,* 627–633; J. Tzetzes, *Posthomerica,*
729–731; Dictys Cretensis, *Bellum Trojanum,* v. 12. Deiphobus had married Helen after the death of Paris. See
above, *Epitome,* v. 8. 9.

[5] Compare Arctinus, *Ilii Persis,* summarized by Proclus,
in *Epicorum Graecorum Fragmenta,* ed. G. Kinkel, p. 50;
Pausanias, x. 25. 8; Quintus Smyrnaeus, *Posthomerica,*
xiii. 496–543; Scholia on Euripides, *Hecuba,* 123, and

ἐλθεῖν ὕστερον. Αἴας δὲ ὁ Λοκρὸς Κασάνδραν
ὁρῶν περιπεπλεγμένην τῷ ξοάνῳ τῆς Ἀθηνᾶς
βιάζεται· διὰ <τοῦ>το τὸ¹ ξόανον εἰς οὐρανὸν
βλέπειν.²

ES 23 | Κτείναντες δὲ τοὺς Τρῶας τὴν πόλιν ἐνέπρησαν
καὶ τὰ λάφυρα ἐμερίσαντο. καὶ θύσαντες πᾶσι
τοῖς θεοῖς Ἀστυάνακτα ἀπὸ τῶν πύργων ἔρριψαν,
Πολυξένην δὲ ἐπὶ τῷ Ἀχιλλέως τάφῳ κατέ-

¹ διὰ <τοῦ>το τὸ Wagner : διὰ τὸ τὸ E.
² For βλέπειν we should perhaps read βλέπει.

on *Troades*, 31 ; Dictys Cretensis, *Bellum Trojanum*,
v. 13. Homer mentions Aethra as one of the handmaids of
Helen at Troy (*Il.* iii. 53). Quintus Smyrnaeus (*l.c.*) has
described at length the recognition of the grandmother by
the grandsons, who, according to Hellanicus, went to Troy
for the purpose of rescuing or ransoming her (Scholiast on
Euripides, *Hecuba*, 123). The recognition was related also
by Lesches (Pausanias, *l.c.*). Aethra had been taken prisoner
at Athens by Castor and Pollux when they rescued their
sister Helen. See above, iii. 7. 4, *Epitome*, i. 23. On the
chest of Cypselus at Olympia the artist portrayed Helen
setting her foot on Aethra's head and tugging at her hand-
maid's hair. See Pausanias, v. 19. 3 ; Dio Chrysostom, *Or.*
xi. vol. i. p. 179, ed. L. Dindorf.
¹ As to the violence offered to Cassandra by Ajax, compare Arctinus, *Ilii Persis*, summarized by Proclus, in *Epicorum Graecorum Fragmenta*, ed. G. Kinkel, pp. 49 *sq.* ;
Scholiast on Homer, *Il.* xiii. 66, referring to Callimachus ;
Pausanias, i. 15. 2, v. 11. 6, v. 19. 5, x. 26. 3, x. 31. 2 ;
Quintus Smyrnaeus, *Posthomerica*, xiii. 420–429 ; Tryphiodorus, *Excidium Ilii*, 647–650 ; Virgil, *Aen.* ii. 403–406 ;
Dictys Cretensis, *Bellum Trojanum*, v. 12 ; *Scriptores rerum
mythicarum Latini*, ed. G. H. Bode, vol. i. p. 55 (First
Vatican Mythographer, 181). Arctinus described how, in
dragging Cassandra from the image of Athena, at which she
had taken refuge, Ajax drew down the image itself. This
incident was carved on the chest of Cypselus at Olympia
(Pausanias, v. 19. 5), and painted by Polygnotus in his great

the Locrian Ajax, seeing Cassandra clinging to the wooden image of Athena, violated her; therefore they say that the image looks to heaven.[1]

And having slain the Trojans, they set fire to the city and divided the spoil among them. And having sacrificed to all the gods, they threw Astyanax from the battlements [2] and slaughtered Polyxena on the

picture of the sack of Troy at Delphi (Pausanias, x. 26. 3). The Scholiast on Homer (*l.c.*) and Quintus Smyrnaeus describe how the image of Athena turned up its eyes to the roof in horror at the violence offered to the suppliant.

[2] Compare Arctinus, *Ilii Persis*, summarized by Proclus, in *Epicorum Graecorum Fragmenta*, ed. G. Kinkel, p. 50; Euripides, *Troades*, 719–739, 1133–1135; *id. Andromache*, 8–11; Pausanias, x. 26. 9; Quintus Smyrnaeus, *Posthomerica*, xiii. 251–257; Tryphiodorus, *Excidium Ilii*, 644–646; Tzetzes, *Schol. on Lycophron*, 1263; Scholiast on Euripides, *Andromache*, 10; Ovid, *Metamorph.* xiii. 415–417; Hyginus, *Fab.* 109; Seneca, *Troades*, 524 *sqq.*, 1063 *sqq.* While ancient writers generally agree that Astyanax was killed by being thrown from a tower at or after the sack of Troy, they differ as to the agent of his death. Arctinus, as reported by Proclus, says merely that he was killed by Ulysses. Tryphiodorus reports that he was hurled by Ulysses from a high tower. On the other hand, Lesches in the *Little Iliad* said that it was Neoptolemus who snatched Astyanax from his mother's lap and cast him down from the battlements (J. Tzetzes and Pausanias, *ll.cc.*). According to Euripides and Seneca, the murder of the child was not perpetrated in hot blood during the sack of Troy, but was deliberately executed after the capture of the city in pursuance of a decree passed by the Greeks in a regular assembly. This seems to have been the version followed by Apollodorus, who apparently regarded the death of Astyanax as a sacrifice, like the slaughter of Polyxena on the grave of Achilles. But the killing of Astyanax was not thus viewed by our other ancient authorities, unless we except Seneca, who describes how Astyanax leaped voluntarily from the wall, while Ulysses was reciting the words of the soothsayer Calchas and invoking the cruel gods to attend the rite.

σφαξαν. λαμβάνει δὲ Ἀγαμέμνων μὲν κατ᾽ ἐξαί-
ρετον Κασάνδραν, Νεοπτόλεμος δὲ Ἀνδρομάχην,
Ὀδυσσεὺς δὲ Ἑκάβην. ὡς δὲ ἔνιοι λέγουσιν,
Ἕλενος αὐτὴν λαμβάνει, καὶ διακομισθεὶς εἰς
Χερρόνησον σὺν αὐτῇ κύνα γενομένην θάπτει,
ἔνθα νῦν λέγεται Κυνὸς σῆμα. Λαοδίκην μὲν γὰρ
κάλλει τῶν Πριάμου θυγατέρων διαφέρουσαν βλε-
S   πόντων πάντων γῇ χάσματι ἀπέκρυψεν. | ὡς δὲ

---

¹ As to the sacrifice of Polyxena on the grave of Achilles,
see Arctinus, *Ilii Persis,* summarized by Proclus, in *Epicorum
Graecorum Fragmenta,* ed. G. Kinkel, p. 50; Euripides,
Hecuba, 107 *sqq.,* 218 *sqq.,* 391–393, 521–582; Quintus Smyrnaeus, *Posthomerica,* xiv. 210-328; Tryphiodorus, *Excidium
Ilii,* 686 *sq.*; Tzetzes, *Schol. on Lycophron,* 323; Hyginus,
Fab. 110; Ovid, *Metamorph.* xiii. 439–480; Seneca, *Troades,*
168 *sqq.,* 938–944, 1118-1164; Dictys Cretensis, *Bellum Trojanum,* v. 13; Servius, on Virgil, *Aen.* iii. 322. According to
Euripides and Seneca, the ghost of Achilles appeared above
his grave and demanded the sacrifice of the maiden. Others
said that the spirit of the dead showed himself in a dream to
Neoptolemus (so Quintus Smyrnaeus) or to Agamemnon (so
Ovid). In Quintus Smyrnaeus the ghost threatens to keep
the Greeks windbound at Troy until they have complied with
his demand, and accordingly the offering of the sacrifice is
followed by a great calm. Euripides seems to have contemplated the sacrifice, in primitive fashion, as a means of
furnishing the ghost with the blood needed to quench his
thirst (*Hecuba,* 391–393, 536 *sq.*); but Seneca represents the
ghost as desiring to have Polyxena as his wife in the Elysian
Fields (*Troades,* 938–944). A more romantic turn is given
to the tradition by Philostratus, who says that after the
death of Achilles, and before the fall of Troy, the amorous
Polyxena stole out from the city and stabbed herself to death
on the grave of Achilles, that she might be his bride in the
other world. See Philostratus, *Heroica,* xx. 18; *id. Vit.
Apollon.* iv. 16. 4. According to the usual tradition, it was
Neoptolemus who slew the maiden on his father's tomb.
Pictures of the sacrifice were to be seen at Athens and Per-

grave of Achilles.[1] And as special awards Agamemnon got Cassandra, Neoptolemus got Andromache,
and Ulysses got Hecuba.[2] But some say that
Helenus got her, and crossed over with her to the
Chersonese[3]; and that there she turned into a
bitch, and he buried her at the place now called
the Bitch's Tomb.[4] As for Laodice, the fairest of the
daughters of Priam, she was swallowed up by a
chasm in the earth in the sight of all.[5] When they

gamus (Pausanias, i. 22. 6, x. 25. 10). Sophocles wrote a
tragedy on the theme. See *The Fragments of Sophocles*, ed
A. C. Pearson, vol. ii. pp. 161 *sqq.*

[2] Compare Quintus Smyrnaeus, *Posthomerica*, xiv. 20–23,
who agrees with Apollodorus as to the partition of these
captive women among the Greek leaders.

[3] This is the version of the story adopted by Dares
Phrygius, who says that Helenus went to the Chersonese
along with Hecuba, Andromache, and Cassandra (*De Excidio
Trojae*, 43).

[4] As to the transformation of Hecuba into a bitch, compare Euripides, *Hecuba*, 1259–1273 ; Quintus Smyrnaeus,
Posthomerica, xiv. 347–351 ; Dio Chrysostom, *Or.* xxxii.
vol. ii. p. 20, ed. L. Dindorf ; Agatharchides, *De Erythraeo
Mari*, in Photius, *Bibliotheca*, p. 442a 23 *sq.*, ed. Bekker ;
Julius Pollux, v. 45 ; Tzetzes, *Schol. on Lycophron*, 315,
1176 ; Cicero, *Tuscul. Disput.* iii. 26. 63 ; Ovid, *Metamorph.*
xiii. 565–571 ; Hyginus, *Fab.* 111 ; Servius, on Virgil, *Aen*
iii. 6 ; *Scriptores rerum mythicarum Latini*, ed. G. H. Bode,
vol. i. p. 145 (Second Vatican Mythographer, 209). A rationalistic version of the story is told by Dictys Cretensis (*Bellum
Trojanum*, v. 16). We may conjecture that the fable of the
transformation originated in the resemblance of the name
Hecuba to the name Hecate ; for Hecate was supposed to be
attended by dogs, and Hecuba is called an attendant of Hecate
(Tzetzes, *Schol. on Lycophron*, 1176).

[5] Compare Quintus Smyrnaeus, *Posthomerica*, xiii. 544–551;
Tryphiodorus, *Excidium Ilii*, 660–663 ; J. Tzetzes, *Posthomerica*, 736 ; *id. Schol on Lycophron*, 314.

ἔμελλον ἀποπλεῖν πορθήσαντες Τροίαν, ὑπὸ Κάλχαντος κατείχοντο, μηνίειν Ἀθηνᾶν αὐτοῖς λέγον-
ES τος διὰ τὴν Αἴαντος ἀσέβειαν. | καὶ τὸν μὲν
Αἴαντα[1] κτείνειν ἔμελλον, φεύγοντα[2] δὲ ἐπὶ
βωμὸν εἴασαν.

S VI. | Καὶ μετὰ ταῦτα συνελθόντων εἰς ἐκκλησίαν,
Ἀγαμέμνων καὶ Μενέλαος ἐφιλονείκουν, Μενελάου λέγοντος ἀποπλεῖν, Ἀγαμέμνονος δὲ ἐπιμέ-
ES νειν κελεύοντος καὶ θύειν Ἀθηνᾷ. | ἀναχθέντες[3]
δὲ Διομήδης <καὶ>[4] Νέστωρ καὶ Μενέλαος ἅμα,
οἱ μὲν εὐπλοοῦσιν, ὁ δὲ Μενέλαος χειμῶνι περι-
πεσών, τῶν λοιπῶν ἀπολομένων σκαφῶν, πέντε
ναυσὶν ἐπ' Αἴγυπτον ἀφικνεῖται.

2 Ἀμφίλοχος δὲ καὶ Κάλχας καὶ Λεοντεὺς καὶ
Ποδαλείριος καὶ Πολυποίτης[5] ἐν Ἰλίῳ τὰς ναῦς
ἀπολιπόντες ἐπὶ Κολοφῶνα πεζῇ πορεύονται,
κἀκεῖ θάπτουσι Κάλχαντα τὸν μάντιν· ἦν γὰρ
αὐτῷ λόγιον τελευτήσειν, ἐὰν ἑαυτοῦ[6] σοφωτέρῳ
3 περιτύχῃ μάντει. ὑποδεχθέντων οὖν ὑπὸ Μόψου
μάντεως, ὃς Ἀπόλλωνος καὶ Μαντοῦς παῖς ὑπῆρ-
χεν, οὗτος ὁ Μόψος περὶ μαντικῆς ἤρισε Κάλχαντι. καὶ Κάλχαντος ἀνακρίναντος ἐρινεοῦ

---

[1] καὶ τὸν μὲν Αἴαντα κτείνειν S : τὸν μέντοι Αἴαντα διὰ τὴν
ἀσεβείαν κτείνειν E.

[2] φεύγοντα ES : we should perhaps read φυγόντα.

[3] ἀναχθέντες δὲ Διομήδης Νέστωρ καὶ Μενέλαος ἅμα, οἱ μὲν
ἀποπλοοῦσιν, ὁ δὲ Μενέλαος χειμῶνι περιπεσὼν E : Διομήδης μὲν
οὖν καὶ Νέστωρ εὐπλοοῦσι, Μενέλαος δὲ μετὰ τούτων ἀναχθεὶς
χειμῶνι περιπεσὼν S. In the text I have corrected the ἀποπλοοῦσιν of E by the εὐπλοοῦσιν of S.

[4] καὶ inserted by Frazer.

[5] καὶ Ποδαλείριος καὶ Πολυποίτης E, wanting in S.

[6] ἑαυτοῦ S : αὐτοῦ E.

242

had laid Troy waste and were about to sail away, they were detained by Calchas, who said that Athena was angry with them on account of the impiety of Ajax. And they would have killed Ajax, but he fled to the altar and they let him alone.[1]

VI. After these things they met in assembly, and Agamemnon and Menelaus quarrelled, Menelaus advising that they should sail away, and Agamemnon insisting that they should stay and sacrifice to Athena. When they put to sea, Diomedes, Nestor, and Menelaus in company, the two former had a prosperous voyage, but Menelaus was overtaken by a storm, and after losing the rest of his vessels, arrived with five ships in Egypt.[2]

But Amphilochus, and Calchas, and Leonteus, and Podalirius, and Polypoetes left their ships in Ilium and journeyed by land to Colophon, and there buried Calchas the diviner[3]; for it was foretold him that he would die if he met with a wiser diviner than himself. Well, they were lodged by the diviner Mopsus, who was a son of Apollo and Manto, and he wrangled with Calchas about the art of divination. A wild fig-tree grew on the spot,

[1] Compare Arctinus, *Ilii Persis*, summarized by Proclus, in *Epicorum Graecorum Fragmenta*, ed. G. Kinkel, pp. 49 *sq.* Ulysses advised the Greeks to stone Ajax to death for his crime against Cassandra (Pausanias, x. 31. 2).

[2] Compare Homer, *Od.* iii. 130 *sqq.*, 276 *sqq* ; Hagias, *Returns* (*Nostoi*), summarized by Proclus, in *Epicorum Graecorum Fragmenta*, ed. G. Kinkel, p. 53.

[3] Compare Hagias, *Returns*, summarized by Proclus, in *Epicorum Graecorum Fragmenta*, ed. G. Kinkel, p. 53 ; Strabo, xiv. 1. 27, p. 642 ; Tzetzes, *Schol. on Lycophron*, 427–430, 980.

APOLLODORUS

ἑστώσης "Πόσους¹ ὀλύνθους φέρει;" ὁ Μόψος·
"Μυρίους" ἔφη "καὶ μέδιμνον καὶ ἕνα ὄλυνθον
4 περισσόν" καὶ εὑρέθησαν οὕτω. Μόψος δὲ συὸς
οὔσης ἐπιτόκου ἠρώτα Κάλχαντα,² πόσους χοί-
S   ρους³ κατὰ γαστρὸς ἔχει καὶ πότε τέκοι·⁴ | τοῦ δὲ
εἰπόντος·⁵ "Ὀκτώ," μειδιάσας ὁ Μόψος ἔφη·
"Κάλχας τῆς ἀκριβοῦς μαντείας ἀπεναντίως⁶
διακεῖται, ἐγὼ δ' Ἀπόλλωνος καὶ Μαντοῦς παῖς
ὑπάρχων τῆς ἀκριβοῦς μαντείας τὴν ὀξυδορκίαν
πάντως πλουτῶ, καὶ οὐχ ὡς ὁ Κάλχας ὀκτώ, ἀλλ'
ἐννέα κατὰ γαστρός, καὶ τούτους ἄρρενας ὅλους
ἔχειν μαντεύομαι, καὶ αὔριον ἀνυπερθέτως ἐν ἕκτῃ
ES   ὥρᾳ τεχθήσεσθαι." | ὧν⁷ γενομένων Κάλχας ἀθυ-
S   μήσας ἀπέθανε⁸ | καὶ ἐτάφη ἐν Νοτίῳ.

¹ "πόσους ὀλύνθους . . . καὶ εὑρέθησαν οὕτω E: "πόσα ἔχει;"
τοῦ δὲ εἰπόντος μύρια καὶ μέτρῳ μέδιμνον καὶ ἐν περισσόν," καταστήσας Κάλχας μυριάδα εὖρε καὶ μέδιμνον καὶ ἐν πλεονάζον κατὰ
τὴν τοῦ Μόψου πρόρρησιν S. Here καταστήσας is clearly
wrong. Herwerden conjectured καταστείσας (*Mnemosyne*,
N.S. xx. (1892), p. 200): Wagner suggested καταπλήσας (viz.
τὸ μέτρον). Perhaps we should read καταμετρήσας (comparing
Tzetzes, *Schol. on Lycophron*, 427, καὶ μετρήσαντες εὗρον οὕτω).
² ἠρώτα Κάλχαντι (sic) S: ἠρώτησε Κάλχαντα Tzetzes, *Schol.
on Lycophron*, 427: ἠρώτα E.
³ πόσους χοίρους S (compare Tzetzes, *Schol. on Lycophron*,
980, Πόσους χοίρους ἔχει κατὰ γαστρός): πόσους E.
⁴ καὶ πότε τέκοι E, wanting in S.
⁵ τοῦ δὲ εἰπόντος . . . ἐν ἕκτῃ ὥρᾳ τεχθήσεσθαι S: τοῦ δὲ
μηδὲν εἰπόντος αὐτὸς ἔφη δέκα χοίρους ἔχειν καὶ τὸν ἕνα τούτων
ἄρρενα, τέξεσθαι δὲ αὔριον E, "and when he (Calchas) said
nothing, he himself (Mopsus) said that the sow had ten pigs,
and that one of them was a male, and that she would farrow
on the morrow." Thus the versions of S and E differ on some
points. The version of Tzetzes (*Schol. on Lycophron*, 980)
agrees substantially, though not verbally, with that of E.
It runs thus: Μόψος δὲ συὸς ἐπὶ τόκου ἑστώσης, ἤρετο, Πόσους
χοίρους ἔχει κατὰ γαστρός, καὶ πότε τέξεται; Κάλχαντος δὲ μὴ
ἀποκριναμένου, αὐτὸς ὁ Μόψος πάλιν εἶπε, Δέκα χοίρους ἔχει, ὧν

244

and when Calchas asked, "How many figs does it bear?" Mopsus answered, "Ten thousand, and a bushel, and one fig over," and they were found to be so. And when Mopsus asked Calchas concerning a pregnant sow, "How many pigs has she in her womb, and when will she farrow?" Calchas answered, "Eight." But Mopsus smiled and said, "The divination of Calchas is the reverse of exact; but I, as a son of Apollo and Manto, am extremely rich in the sharp sight which comes of exact divination, and I divine that the number of pigs in the womb is not eight, as Calchas says, but nine, and that they are all male and will be farrowed without fail to-morrow at the sixth hour." So when these things turned out so, Calchas died of a broken heart and was buried at Notium.[1]

[1] Compare Strabo, xiv. 1. 27, pp. 642 sq.; Tzetzes, Schol. on Lycophron, 427–430, 980. From Strabo we learn that the riddle of Calchas concerning the wild fig-tree was recorded by Hesiod, and that the riddle of Mopsus concerning the sow was recorded by Pherecydes. Our authorities vary somewhat in regard to the latter riddle. According to Pherecydes, the true answer was, "Three little pigs, and one of them a female." According to Tzetzes, Calchas could not solve the riddle, so Mopsus solved it by saying that the sow would farrow ten little pigs, of which one would be a male. Strabo also tells us that the oracle which doomed Calchas to death whenever he should meet a diviner more skilful than himself, was mentioned by Sophocles in his play *The Demand for Helen*. As to that play, see *The Fragments of Sophocles*, ed. A. C. Pearson, vol. i. pp. 121 sqq. A different story of the rivalry of the two seers is told by Conon (*Narrat.* 6).

ὁ εἷς ἄρρην· τέξεται δὲ κατὰ τὴν αὔριον. οὗ γενομένου Κάλχας ἀθυμήσας τελευτᾷ. The same version is repeated by Tzetzes elsewhere (*Schol. on Lycophron*, 427) with a few verbal variations. [6] ἀπεναντίως Frazer : ἀπεναντίας S.

[7] ὧν E : τούτων γοῦν S.

[8] ἀπέθανε S : τελευτᾷ E, Tzetzes, *Schol. on Lycophron*, 427 and 980.

5   Ἀγαμέμνων δὲ θύσας ἀνάγεται καὶ Τενέδῳ προσίσχει, Νεοπτόλεμον δὲ πείθει Θέτις ἀφικομένη
ἐπιμεῖναι δύο ἡμέρας καὶ θυσιάσαι, καὶ ἐπιμένει.
οἱ δὲ ἀνάγονται καὶ περὶ Τῆνον χειμάζονται.
Ἀθηνᾶ γὰρ ἐδεήθη Διὸς τοῖς Ἕλλησι χειμῶνα
ἐπιπέμψαι. καὶ πολλαὶ νῆες βυθίζονται.

ES 6 | Ἀθηνᾶ δὲ[1] ἐπὶ τὴν Αἴαντος ναῦν κεραυνὸν
βάλλει, ὁ δὲ τῆς νεὼς διαλυθείσης ἐπί τινα πέτραν
διασωθεὶς παρὰ τὴν θεοῦ ἔφη πρόνοιαν σεσῶσθαι.
Ποσειδῶν δὲ πλήξας τῇ τριαίνῃ[2] τὴν πέτραν
ἔσχισεν, ὁ δὲ πεσὼν εἰς τὴν θάλασσαν τελευτᾷ,
καὶ ἐκβρασθέντα θάπτει Θέτις ἐν Μυκόνῳ.

7   Τῶν δὲ ἄλλων Εὐβοίᾳ προσφερομένων νυκτὸς
Ναύπλιος ἐπὶ τοῦ Καφηρέως ὄρους[3] πυρσὸν
ἀνάπτει· οἱ δὲ νομίσαντες εἶναί τινας τῶν
σεσωσμένων προσπλέουσι, καὶ περὶ τὰς Καφη-
ρίδας πέτρας θραύεται τὰ σκάφη καὶ πολλοὶ

---

[1] Ἀθηνᾶ δὲ S : Ὅτι Ἀθηνᾶ Ε.
[2] πλήξας τῇ τριαίνῃ S : τριαίνῃ πλήξας Ε.
[3] ὄρους Ε : ὄρους τῆς Εὐβοίας S.

---

[1] As to the shipwreck and death of the Locrian Ajax, compare Homer, *Od.* iv. 499-511 ; Hagias, *Returns,* summarized
by Proclus, in *Epicorum Graecorum Fragmenta,* ed. G.
Kinkel, p. 53 ; Scholiast on Homer, *Il.* xiii. 66 ; Quintus
Smyrnaeus, *Posthomerica,* xiv. 530-589 ; Tzetzes, *Schol.
on Lycophron,* 365, 387, 389, 402 ; Virgil, *Aen.* i. 39-45 ;
Hyginus, *Fab.* 116 ; Seneca, *Agamemnon,* 532-556 ; Dictys
Cretensis, *Bellum Trojanum,* vi. 1. In his great picture of
the underworld, which Polygnotus painted at Delphi, the
artist depicted Ajax as a castaway, the brine forming a scurf
on his skin (Pausanias, x. 31. 1). According to the Scholiast
on Homer (*l.c.*) Ajax was cast up on the shore of Delos, where
Thetis found and buried him. But as it was unlawful to be
buried or even to die in Delos (Thucydides, iii. 104), the

After sacrificing, Agamemnon put to sea and touched at Tenedos. But Thetis came and persuaded Neoptolemus to wait two days and to offer sacrifice; and he waited. But the others put to sea and encountered a storm at Tenos; for Athena entreated Zeus to send a tempest against the Greeks; and many ships foundered.

And Athena threw a thunderbolt at the ship of Ajax; and when the ship went to pieces he made his way safe to a rock, and declared that he was saved in spite of the intention of Athena. But Poseidon smote the rock with his trident and split it, and Ajax fell into the sea and perished; and his body, being washed up, was buried by Thetis in Myconos.[1]

The others being driven to Euboea by night, Nauplius kindled a beacon on Mount Caphereus; and they, thinking it was some of those who were saved, stood in for the shore, and the vessels were wrecked on the Capherian rocks, and many men perished.[2]

---

statement of Apollodorus that Ajax was buried in Myconus, a small island to the east of Delos, is more probable. It is said that on hearing of his death the Locrians mourned for him and wore black for a year, and every year they laded a vessel with splendid offerings, hoisted a black sail on it, and, setting the ship on fire, let it drift out to sea, there to burn down to the water's edge as a sacrifice to the drowned hero. See Tzetzes, *Schol. on Lycophron*, 365. Sophocles wrote a tragedy, *The Locrian Ajax*, on the crime and punishment of the hero. See *The Fragments of Sophocles*, ed. A. C. Pearson, vol. i. pp. 8 *sqq*.

[2] As to the false lights kindled by Nauplius to lure the Greek ships on to the breakers, see above, ii. 1. 5; Euripides, *Helen*, 766 *sq*., 1126 *sqq*.; Scholiast on Euripides, *Orestes*, 432; Quintus Smyrnaeus, *Posthomerica*, xiv. 611-628; Tzetzes, *Schol. on Lycophron*, 384; Propertius, v. 1. 115 *sq*.; Hyginus, *Fab.* 116; Seneca, *Agamemnon*, 557-575; Dictys Cretensis, *Bellum Trojanum*, vi. 1; Servius on Virgil, *Aen.*

Ε 8 τελευτῶσιν. | ὁ γὰρ τοῦ Ναυπλίου[1] καὶ Κλυμένης
τῆς Κατρέως υἱὸς Παλαμήδης ἐπιβουλαῖς Ὀδυσσέως λιθοβοληθεὶς ἀναιρεῖται. τοῦτο μαθὼν Ναύπλιος ἔπλευσε πρὸς τοὺς Ἕλληνας καὶ τὴν τοῦ
9 παιδὸς ἀπῄτει ποινήν· ἄπρακτος δὲ ὑποστρέψας,
ὡς πάντων χαριζομένων τῷ βασιλεῖ Ἀγαμέμνονι,
μεθ' οὗ τὸν Παλαμήδην ἀνεῖλεν Ὀδυσσεύς, παρα-
πλέων τὰς χώρας τὰς Ἑλληνίδας παρεσκεύασε
τὰς τῶν Ἑλλήνων γυναῖκας μοιχευθῆναι, Κλυταιμνήστραν Αἰγίσθῳ, Αἰγιάλειαν τῷ Σθενέλου
10 Κομήτῃ, τὴν Ἰδομενέως Μήδαν ὑπὸ Λεύκου· ἣν
καὶ ἀνεῖλε Λεῦκος ἅμα Κλεισιθύρᾳ[2] τῇ θυγατρὶ
ταύτης ἐν τῷ ναῷ[3] προσφυγούσῃ, καὶ δέκα πόλεις
ἀποσπάσας[4] τῆς Κρήτης ἐτυράννησε· καὶ μετὰ
τὸν Τρωικὸν πόλεμον καὶ τὸν Ἰδομενέα κατάραντα
11 τῇ Κρήτῃ ἐξήλασε. ταῦτα πρότερον κατασκευάσας ὁ Ναύπλιος, ὕστερον μαθὼν τὴν εἰς τὰς
πατρίδας τῶν Ἑλλήνων ἐπάνοδον, τὸν εἰς τὸν
Καφηρέα, νῦν δὲ Ξυλοφάγον λεγόμενον, ἀνῆψε
φρυκτόν· ἔνθα προσπελάσαντες Ἕλληνες ἐν τῷ
δοκεῖν λιμένα εἶναι διεφθάρησαν.

---

[1] τοῦ Ναυπλίου Frazer : αὐτοῦ τοῦ Ναυπλίου E, Wagner.
[2] Κλεισιθύρᾳ E : Κλεισιθήρα Lycophron, *Alexandra*, 1222,
Tzetzes, *Schol. on Lycophron*, 384, *id. Chiliades*, iii. 294.
[3] The name of the deity of the temple seems wanting,
perhaps τῆς Ἀθηνᾶς.
[4] ἀποσπάσας E, Tzetzes, *Schol. on Lycophron*, 384. We
should perhaps read ἀποστήσας, "having caused to revolt."

---

xi. 260 ; Lactantius Placidus on Statius, *Achil.* i. 93 ; *Scriptores rerum mythicarum Latini*, ed. G. H Bode, vol. i. pp.
46, 141 (First Vatican Mythographer, 144 ; Second Vatican
Mythographer, 201). The story was probably told by Hagias
in his epic *The Returns* (*Nostoi*), though in the abstract of

For Palamedes, the son of Nauplius and Clymene daughter of Catreus, had been stoned to death through the machinations of Ulysses.[1] And when Nauplius learned of it,[2] he sailed to the Greeks and claimed satisfaction for the death of his son; but when he returned unsuccessful (for they all favoured King Agamemnon, who had been the accomplice of Ulysses in the murder of Palamedes), he coasted along the Grecian lands and contrived that the wives of the Greeks should play their husbands false, Clytaemnestra with Aegisthus, Aegialia with Cometes, son of Sthenelus, and Meda, wife of Idomeneus, with Leucus. But Leucus killed her, together with her daughter Clisithyra, who had taken refuge in the temple; and having detached ten cities from Crete he made himself tyrant of them; and when after the Trojan war Idomeneus landed in Crete, Leucus drove him out.[3] These were the earlier contrivances of Nauplius; but afterwards, when he learned that the Greeks were on their way home to their native countries, he kindled the beacon fire on Mount Caphereus, which is now called Xylophagus; and there the Greeks, standing in shore in the belief that it was a harbour, were cast away.

that poem there occurs merely a mention of "the storm at the Capherian Rocks." See *Epicorum Graecorum Fragmenta*, ed. G. Kinkel, p. 53. The wrecker Nauplius was the subject of a tragedy by Sophocles. See *The Fragments of Sophocles*, ed. A. C. Pearson, vol. ii. pp. 80 *sqq.*

[1] As to the death of Palamedes, see above, *Epitome*, iii. 8.

[2] This passage, down to the end of § 12, is quoted with some slight verbal changes, but without citing his authority, by Tzetzes, *Schol. on Lycophron*, 384–386; compare *id.* on *v.* 1093.

[3] See Appendix, "The vow of Idomeneus."

APOLLODORUS

12 Νεοπτόλεμος δὲ μείνας ἐν Τενέδῳ δύο ἡμέρας
ὑποθήκαις τῆς Θέτιδος εἰς Μολοσσοὺς πεζῇ ἀπῄει
μετὰ Ἑλένου, καὶ παρὰ τὴν ὁδὸν ἀποθανόντα
Φοίνικα θάπτει, καὶ νικήσας μάχῃ Μολοσσοὺς
βασιλεύει, καὶ ἐξ Ἀνδρομάχης γεννᾷ Μολοσσόν.

13 Ἕλενος δὲ κτίσας ἐν τῇ Μολοσσίᾳ πόλιν κατοικεῖ,
καὶ δίδωσιν αὐτῷ Νεοπτόλεμος εἰς γυναῖκα τὴν
μητέρα Δηιδάμειαν. Πηλέως δὲ ἐκ Φθίας ἐκβλη-
θέντος ὑπὸ τῶν Ἀκάστου παίδων καὶ ἀποθαν-

---

[1] Compare Hagias, *Returns*, summarized by Proclus, in
Epicorum Graecorum Fragmenta, ed. G. Kinkel, p. 53;
Tzetzes, *Schol. on Lycophron*, 902, quoting "Apollodorus
and the rest." According to Servius (on Virgil, *Aen.* ii. 166),
it was the soothsayer Helenus who, foreseeing the shipwreck
of the Greek leaders, warned Neoptolemus to return home
by land; hence in gratitude for this benefit Neoptolemus at
his death bequeathed Andromache to Helenus to be his wife
(Servius, on Virgil, *Aen.* iii. 297). Neoptolemus was on
friendly terms with Helenus, because the seer had revealed
to the Greeks the means by which Troy could be taken, and
because in particular he had recommended the fetching of
Neoptolemus himself from Scyros. See above, *Epitome*, v.
10. A different tradition is recorded by Eustathius, on
Homer, *Od.* iii. 189, p. 1463. He says that Neoptolemus
sailed across the sea to Thessaly and there burned his ships
by the advice of Thetis; after which, being directed by the
soothsayer Helenus to settle wherever he should find a house
with foundations of iron, walls of wood, and roof of wool, he
marched inland till he came to the lake Pambotis in Epirus,
where he fell in with some people camping under blankets
supported by spears, of which the blades were stuck into the
earth. Compare Scholiast on Homer, *Od.* iii. 188, who adds
that, "having laid waste Molossia, he begot Molossus by
Andromache, and from Molossus is descended the race of the
kings of Molossia, as Eratosthenes relates." The lake Pambotis is believed to be what is now called the lake of Joannina,
near which Dodona was situated. Pausanias (i. 11. 1) mentions that Pyrrhus (Neoptolemus) settled in Epirus "in

After remaining in Tenedos two days at the advice of Thetis, Neoptolemus set out for the country of the Molossians by land with Helenus, and on the way Phoenix died, and Neoptolemus buried him;[1] and having vanquished the Molossians in battle he reigned as king and begat Molossus on Andromache. And Helenus founded a city in Molossia and inhabited it, and Neoptolemus gave him his mother Deidamia to wife.[2] And when Peleus was expelled from Phthia by the sons of Acastus[3] and died, Neoptolemus

compliance with the oracles of Helenus," and that he had Molossus, Pielus, and Pergamus by Andromache.

[2] As to Deidamia, mother of Neoptolemus, see above, iii. 13. 8. The marriage of Helenus to Deidamia appears not to be mentioned by any other ancient writer.

[3] According to Euripides (*Troades*, 1126-1130), while Neoptolemus was still at Troy, he heard that his grandfather Peleus had been expelled by Acastus ; hence he departed for home in haste, taking Andromache with him. The Scholiast on this passage of Euripides (*v.* 1128) says that Peleus was expelled by Acastus's two sons, Archander and Architeles, and that the exiled king, going to meet his grandson Neoptolemus, was driven by a storm to the island of Cos, where he was entertained by a certain Molon and died. As to an early connexion between Thessaly and Cos, see W. R. Paton and E. L. Hicks, *The Inscriptions of Cos*, pp. 344 *sqq*. A different and much more detailed account of the exile of Peleus is furnished by Dictys Cretensis, *Bellum Trojanum*, vi. 7-9. According to it, when Neoptolemus was refitting his shattered ships in Molossia, he heard that Peleus had been deposed and expelled by Acastus. Hastening to the aid of his aged grandfather, he found him hiding in a dark cave on the shore of one of the Sepiades Islands, where he eagerly scanned every passing sail in hopes that one of them would bring his grandson to his rescue. By disguising himself Neoptolemus contrived to attack and kill Acastus's two sons, Menalippus and Plisthenes, when they were out hunting. Afterwards, disguising himself as a Trojan captive, he lured Acastus himself to the cave and would have slain him there,

ὄντος, Νεοπτόλεμος τὴν βασιλείαν τοῦ πατρὸς
14 παρέλαβε. καὶ μανέντος Ὀρέστου ἁρπάζει τὴν
ἐκείνου γυναῖκα Ἑρμιόνην κατηγγυημένην αὐτῷ
πρότερον ἐν Τροίᾳ, καὶ διὰ τοῦτο ἐν Δελφοῖς ὑπὸ

---

if it had not been for the intercession of Thetis, who had opportunely arrived from the sea to visit her old husband Peleus. Happy at his escape, Acastus resigned the kingdom on the spot to Neoptolemus, and that hero at once took possession of the realm in company with his grandfather, his divine grandmother Thetis, and the companions of his voyage. This romantic narrative may be based on a lost Greek tragedy, perhaps on the *Peleus* of Sophocles, a play in which the dramatist appears to have dealt with the fortunes of Peleus in his old age. See *The Fragments of Sophocles*, ed. A. C. Pearson, vol. ii. pp. 140 *sqq.* The statement of Dictys Cretensis that Peleus took refuge in one of the Sepiades Islands suggests that in the scholium on Euripides (*l.c.*) the name Icos should be read instead of Cos, as has been argued by several scholars (A. C. Pearson, *op. cit.* ii. 141); for Icos was a small island near Euboea (Stephanus Byzantius, *s.v.* Ἴκός), and would be a much more natural place of refuge for Peleus than the far more distant island of Cos. Moreover, we have the positive affirmation of the poet Antipater of Sidon that Peleus was buried in Icos (*Anthologia Palatina*, vii. 2. 9 *sq.*). The connexion of Peleus with the Sepiades Islands is further supported by Euripides; for in his play *Andromache* (*vv.* 1253–1269) he tells how Thetis bids her old husband Peleus tarry in a cave of these islands, till she should come with a band of Nereids to fetch him away, that he might dwell with her as a god for ever in the depths of the sea. In the same play (*vv.* 22 *sq.*) Euripides says that Neoptolemus refused to accept the sceptre of Pharsalia in the lifetime of his grandfather Peleus.

[1] In this passage Apollodorus appears to follow the account given by Euripides in his *Andromache*, 967–981. According to that account, Menelaus gave his daughter Hermione in marriage to her cousin Orestes, the son of Agamemnon and Clytaemnestra. But in the Trojan war he afterwards promised the hand of Hermione to Neoptolemus, if Neoptolemus should succeed in capturing Troy. Accordingly on his return

succeeded to his father's kingdom. And when
Orestes went mad, Neoptolemus carried off his wife
Hermione, who had previously been betrothed to him
in Troy[1]; and for that reason he was slain by Orestes

from the war Neoptolemus claimed his bride from her husband
Orestes, who was then haunted and maddened by the Furies
of his murdered mother Clytaemnestra. Orestes protested,
but in vain; Neoptolemus insolently reproached him with his
crime of matricide and with the unseen avengers of blood by
whom he was pursued. So Orestes was obliged to yield up
his wife to his rival, but he afterwards took his revenge by
murdering Neoptolemus at Delphi. This version of the legend
is followed also by Hyginus (*Fab.* 123). An obvious difficulty
is presented by the narrative; for if Menelaus had given his
daughter in marriage to Orestes, how could he afterwards
have promised her to Neoptolemus in the lifetime of her first
husband? This difficulty was met by another version of the
story, which alleged that Hermione was betrothed or married
to Orestes by her grandfather Tyndareus in the absence of
her father Menelaus, who was then away at the Trojan war;
that meantime, in ignorance of this disposal of his daughter,
Menelaus had promised her hand to Neoptolemus before Troy,
and that on his return from the war Neoptolemus took her
by force from Orestes. See Eustathius, on Homer, *Od.* iv. 3,
p. 1479; Scholiast on Homer, *Od.* iv. 4; Ovid, *Heroides*, viii.
31 *sqq.*; Servius, on Virgil, *Aen.* iii. 330, compare *id.* on *v.*
297. According to the tragic poet Philocles, not only had
Hermione been given in marriage by Tyndareus to Orestes,
but she was actually with child by Orestes when her father
afterwards married her to Neoptolemus. See Scholiast on
Euripides, *Andromache*, 32. This former marriage of Hermione to Orestes, before she became the wife of Neoptolemus,
is recognized by Virgil (*Aen.* iii. 330), and Ovid (*Heroides*,
viii. *passim*), but it is unknown to Homer. On the other
hand, Homer records that Menelaus betrothed Hermione to
Neoptolemus at Troy, and celebrated the marriage after his
return to Sparta (*Od.* iv. 1–9). Sophocles wrote a tragedy
Hermione, the plot of which seems to have resembled that of
the *Andromache* of Euripides. See *The Fragments of Sophocles*, ed. A. C. Pearson, vol. ii. pp. 141 *sqq.* Euripides
does not appear to have been consistent in his view that

APOLLODORUS

Ὀρέστου κτείνεται. ἔνιοι δὲ αὐτόν φασι παραγενόμενον εἰς Δελφοὺς ἀπαιτεῖν ὑπὲρ τοῦ πατρὸς
τὸν Ἀπόλλωνα δίκας καὶ συλᾶν τὰ ἀναθήματα
καὶ τὸν νεὼν ἐμπιμπράναι, καὶ διὰ τοῦτο ὑπὸ
Μαχαιρέως [1] τοῦ Φωκέως ἀναιρεθῆναι.

---

[1] Μαχαιρέως Wagner : βαχαιρέως E.

Neoptolemus forcibly deprived Orestes of Hermione and
married her himself; for in his play *Orestes* (vv. 1653–1657)
he makes Apollo prophesy to Orestes that he shall wed Hermione, but that Neoptolemus shall never do so.

[1] The murder of Neoptolemus at Delphi, as Apollodorus
observes, was variously related. According to Euripides,
Neoptolemus paid two visits to Delphi. On the first occasion he went to claim redress from Apollo, who had shot his
father Achilles at Troy (see above, *Epitome*, v. 3). On the
second occasion he went to excuse himself to the god for the
rashness and impiety of which he had been guilty in calling
the deity to account for the murder ; and it was then that
Orestes, enraged at having been robbed of his wife Hermione
by Neoptolemus, waylaid and murdered his rival in the
temple of Apollo, the fatal blow being struck, however, not
by Orestes but by "a Delphian man." See Euripides,
Andromache, 49–55, 1086–1165 ; compare *id. Orestes*, 1656
sq. This is the version of the story which Apollodorus
appears to prefer. It is accepted also by Hyginus (*Fab.*
123), Velleius Paterculus (i. 1. 3), Servius (on Virgil, *Aen.*
iii. 297 and 330), and somewhat ambiguously by Dictys
Cretensis (*Bellum Trojanum*, vi. 12 *sq.*). The murder of
Neoptolemus by Orestes is mentioned, but without any
motive assigned, by Heliodorus (ii. 34) and Justin (xvii. 3. 7).
A different account is given by Pindar. He says that Neoptolemus went to consult the god at Delphi, taking with him
first-fruit offerings of the Trojan spoil ; that there he was
stabbed to death by a man in a brawl concerning the flesh of
the victim, and that after death he was supposed to dwell
within the sacred precinct and to preside over the processions
and sacrifices in honour of heroes. See Pindar, *Nem.* vii. 34
(50)–47 (70) ; compare *id. Paean*, vi. 117 *sqq.*, ed. Sandys.
The Scholiast on the former of these passages of Pindar, verse

at Delphi. But some say that he went to Delphi to demand satisfaction from Apollo for the death of his father, and that he rifled the votive offerings and set fire to the temple, and was on that account slain by Machaereus the Phocian.[1]

---

42 (62), explains the brawl by saying that it was the custom of the Delphians to appropriate (ἁρπάζειν) the sacrifices; that Neoptolemus attempted to prevent them from taking possession of his offerings, and that in the squabble the Delphians despatched him with their swords. This explanation seems to be due to Pherecydes, for a Scholiast on Euripides (*Orestes*, 1655) quotes the following passage from that early historian: "When Neoptolemus married Hermione, daughter of Menelaus, he went to Delphi to inquire about offspring; for he had no children by Hermione. And when at the oracle he saw the Delphians scrambling for (διαρπάζοντας) the flesh, he attempted to take it from them. But their priest Machaereus killed him and buried him under the threshold of the temple." This seems to have been the version of the story followed by Pausanias, for he mentions the hearth at Delphi on which the priest of Apollo slew Neoptolemus (x. 24. 4), and elsewhere he says that "the Pythian priestess ordered the Delphians to kill Pyrrhus (Neoptolemus), son of Achilles" (i. 13. 9; compare iv. 17. 4). That the slayer of Neoptolemus was called Machaereus is mentioned also by a Scholiast on Euripides (*Andromache*, 53) and by Strabo (ix. 3. 9, p. 421), who says that Neoptolemus was killed "because he demanded satisfaction from the god for the murder of his father, or, more probably, because he had made an attack on the sanctuary." Indeed, Asclepiades, in his work *Tragodoumena*, wrote as follows: "About his death almost all the poets agree that he was killed by Machaereus and buried at first under the threshold of the temple, but that afterwards Menelaus came and took up his body, and made his grave in the precinct. He says that Machaereus was a son of Daetas." See Scholiast on Pindar, *Nem.* vii. 42 (62). The story that Neoptolemus came to Delphi to plunder the sanctuary, which is noticed by Apollodorus and preferred by Strabo, is mentioned by Pausanias (x. 7. 1) and a Scholiast on Pindar (*Nem.* vii. 58, Boeckh). It is probably

E 15 |"Οτι πλανηθέντες[1] "Ελληνες ἄλλοι ἀλλαχοῦ
κατάραντες κατοικοῦσιν, οἱ μὲν εἰς Λιβύην, οἱ
δὲ εἰς Ἰταλίαν, εἰς Σικελίαν ἕτεροι, τινὲς δὲ
πρὸς τὰς πλησίον Ἰβηρίας νήσους, ἄλλοι παρὰ
τὸν Σαγγάριον ποταμόν· εἰσὶ δὲ οἳ καὶ Κύπρον

S   ᾤκησαν. | τῶν δὲ ναυαγησάντων περὶ τὸν Καφη-
ρέα[2] ἄλλος ἀλλαχῆ φέρεται, Γουνεὺς μὲν εἰς
Λιβύην, Ἄντιφος δὲ ὁ Θεσσαλοῦ εἰς Πελασγοὺς
καὶ <τὴν> χώραν[3] κατασχὼν Θεσσαλίαν ἐκάλεσεν, ὁ δὲ Φιλοκτήτης πρὸς Ἰταλίαν εἰς Καμπανούς,

---

[1] "Οτι πλανηθέντες . . . Κύπρον ᾤκησαν. This passage is
from E : the passage immediately following (τῶν δὲ ναυαγη-
σάντων . . . καὶ ἄλλος ἀλλαχοῦ) is from S. The two passages
are perhaps duplicate versions of the same passage in the
original unabridged work of Apollodorus; but as they
supplement each other, each giving details which are omitted
by the other, I have printed them consecutively in the text.
Wagner prints them in parallel columns to indicate that
they are duplicates.

[2] Καφηρέα Kerameus : κηφέα S.

[3] <τὴν> χώραν Wagner (comparing Tzetzes, Schol. on
Lycophron, 911, καὶ τὴν χώραν κατασχών).

---

not inconsistent with the story that he went to demand
satisfaction from, or to inflict punishment on, the god for the
death of his father ; for the satisfaction or punishment would
naturally take the shape of a distress levied on the goods and
chattels of the defaulting deity. The tradition that the slain
Neoptolemus was buried under the threshold of Apollo's
temple is remarkable and, so far as I remember, unique in
Greek legend. The statement that the body was afterwards
taken up and buried within the precinct agrees with the
observation of Pausanias (x. 24. 6) that "quitting the temple
and turning to the left you come to an enclosure, inside of
which is the grave of Neoptolemus, son of Achilles. The
Delphians offer sacrifice to him annually as to a hero."
From Pindar (Nem. vii. 44 (65) sqq.) we learn that Neoptolemus even enjoyed a pre-eminence over other heroes at

After their wanderings the Greeks landed and settled in various countries, some in Libya, some in Italy, others in Sicily, and some in the islands near Iberia, others on the banks of the Sangarius river; and some settled also in Cyprus. And of those that were shipwrecked at Caphereus, some drifted one way and some another.[1] Guneus went to Libya; Antiphus, son of Thessalus, went to the Pelasgians, and, having taken possession of the country, called it Thessaly. Philoctetes went to the Cam-

Delphi, being called on to preside over the processions and sacrifices in their honour. The Aenianes of Thessaly used to send a grand procession and costly sacrifices to Delphi every fourth year in honour of Neoptolemus. The ceremony fell at the same time as the Pythian games. See Heliodorus, *Aethiop.* ii. 34–iii. 6. It is a little difficult to understand how a man commonly accused of flagrant impiety and sacrilege should have been raised to such a pitch of glory at the very shrine which he was said to have attacked and robbed. The apparent contradiction might be more intelligible if we could suppose that, as has been suggested, Neoptolemus was publicly sacrificed as a scapegoat, perhaps by being stoned to death, as seems to have been the fate of the human victims at the Thargelia, whose sacrifice was justified by a legend that the first of their number had stolen some sacred cups of Apollo. See Harpocration, *s.v.* φάρμακος ; and as to the suggestion that Neoptolemus may have been sacrificed as a scapegoat, see J. Toepffer, "Thargelienbräuche," *Beiträge zur griechischen Altertumswissenschaft* (Berlin, 1897), pp. 132 *sq.*, who points out that according to Euripides (*Andromache*, 1127 *sqq.*) Neoptolemus was stoned as well as stabbed at the altar of Apollo. As to the custom of burying the dead under a threshold, see *Folk-lore in the Old Testament*, iii. 13 *sq.*

[1] The wanderings described in the remainder of this paragraph, except those of Agapenor, are resumed and told somewhat more fully in the following three paragraphs (15a, 15b, 15c), which do not occur in our text of the *Epitome*, but are conjecturally restored to it from the scholia on Lycophron of Tzetzes, who probably had before him the full text of Apollodorus, and not merely the *Epitome*.

APOLLODORUS

Φείδιππος μετὰ τῶν Κῴων ἐν Ἄνδρῳ κατῴκησεν,
Ἀγαπήνωρ ἐν Κύπρῳ, καὶ ἄλλος ἀλλαχοῦ.

ΤΖ 15a <902 : Ἀπολλόδωρος δὲ[1] καὶ οἱ λοιποὶ οὕτω
φασί· Γουνεὺς εἰς Λιβύην λιπὼν τὰς ἑαυτοῦ ναῦς
ἐλθὼν ἐπὶ Κίνυφα[2] ποταμὸν κατοικεῖ. Μέγης[3] δὲ
καὶ Πρόθοος ἐν Εὐβοίᾳ περὶ τὸν Καφηρέα σὺν
πολλοῖς ἑτέροις διαφθείρεται . . . τοῦ δὲ Προθόου
περὶ τὸν Καφηρέα ναυαγήσαντος, οἱ σὺν αὐτῷ
Μάγνητες εἰς Κρήτην ῥιφέντες ᾤκησαν.>

15b <911 : Μετὰ δὲ τὴν Ἰλίου πόρθησιν Μενεσθεὺς
Φείδιππός τε καὶ Ἄντιφος καὶ οἱ Ἐλεφήνορος[4] καὶ
Φιλοκτήτης μέχρι Μίμαντος κοινῇ ἔπλευσαν. εἶτα
Μενεσθεὺς μὲν εἰς Μῆλον ἐλθὼν βασιλεύει, τοῦ
ἐκεῖ βασιλέως Πολυάνακτος τελευτήσαντος. Ἄντιφος δὲ ὁ Θεσσαλοῦ εἰς Πελασγοὺς ἐλθὼν καὶ
τὴν χώραν κατασχὼν Θεσσαλίαν ἐκάλεσε. Φείδιππος δὲ μετὰ Κῴων ἐξωσθεὶς περὶ τὴν Ἄνδρον,[5]
εἶτα περὶ Κύπρον ἐκεῖ κατῴκησεν. Ἐλεφήνωρ
δὲ ἀποθανόντος ἐν Τροίᾳ, οἱ σὺν αὐτῷ ἐκριφέντες
περὶ τὸν Ἰόνιον κόλπον Ἀπολλωνίαν ᾤκησαν τὴν
ἐν Ἠπείρῳ. καὶ οἱ τοῦ Τληπολέμου προσίσχουσι

---

[1] The following three paragraphs are extracted from the
Scholia on Lycophron of Tzetzes, who seems to have borrowed
them from Apollodorus.

[2] Κίνυφα Tzetzes : Κίνυπα Wagner. Either form is legitimate. See Pape, *Wörterbuch der griech. Eigennamen, s.v.*
Κίνυψ, p. 663.

[3] Μέγης Stiehle, Wagner. The MSS. of Tzetzes read
Μέγας or Μάγνητες.

[4] οἱ Ἐλεφήνορος. Some MSS. of Tzetzes read Ἐλεφήνωρ.

[5] τὴν Ἄνδρον Wagner : τὸν ἀδρίαν Tzetzes.

---

[1] Compare Pausanias, viii. 5. 2, who says that, driven by
the storm to Cyprus, Agapenor founded Paphos and built the
sanctuary of Aphrodite at Old Paphos. Compare Aristotle,
Peplos, 30 (16), in Bergk's *Poetae Lyrici Graeci*[3], ii. 654.

panians in Italy ; Phidippus with the Coans settled in
Andros, Agapenor in Cyprus,[1] and others elsewhere.

Apollodorus and the rest[2] say as follows. Guneus
left his own ships, and having come to the Cinyps
river in Libya he dwelt there.[3] But Meges and
Prothous, with many others, were cast away at
Caphereus in Euboea[4] . . . and when Prothous was
shipwrecked at Caphereus, the Magnesians with him
drifted to Crete and settled there.

After the sack of Ilium,[5] Menestheus, Phidippus
and Antiphus, and the people of Elephenor, and
Philoctetes sailed together as far as Mimas. Then
Menestheus went to Melos and reigned as king, because the king there, Polyanax, had died. And
Antiphus the son of Thessalus went to the Pelasgians,
and having taken possession of the country he called
it Thessaly.[6] Phidippus with the Coans was driven
first to Andros, and then to Cyprus, where he settled.
Elephenor died in Troy,[7] but his people were cast
away in the Ionian gulf and inhabited Apollonia in
Epirus. And the people of Tlepolemus touched

[2] This paragraph is quoted from Tzetzes, *Schol. on Lycophron*, 902.

[3] According to another account, Guneus was drowned at
sea. See Aristotle, *Peplos*, 32 (37), in Bergk's *Poetae Lyrici
Graeci*[3], ii. 654.

[4] Epitaphs on these two drowned men are ascribed to
Aristotle, *Peplos*, 25 (19) and 28 (38). See Bergk's *Poetae
Lyrici Graeci*[3], ii. 653, 654. Meges was leader of the
Dulichians, and Prothous was leader of the Magnesians. See
Epitome, iii. 12 and 14.

[5] This paragraph is quoted from Tzetzes, *Schol. on Lycophron*, 911.

[6] Compare Strabo, ix. 5. 23, p. 444.

[7] Elephenor was killed in battle by Agenor. See Homer,
Il. iv. 463–472. Compare Aristotle, *Peplos*, 33 (4), in Bergk's
Poetae Lyrici Graeci[3], ii. 654.

Κρήτῃ, εἶτα ὑπ' ἀνέμων ἐξωσθέντες περὶ τὰς
Ἰβηρικὰς νήσους ᾤκησαν. . . . οἱ τοῦ Πρωτεσιλάου εἰς Πελλήνην[1] ἀπερρίφησαν πλησίον πεδίου
Κανάστρου. Φιλοκτήτης δὲ ἐξώσθη εἰς Ἰταλίαν
πρὸς Καμπανοὺς καὶ πολεμήσας Λευκανοὺς πλησίον Κρότωνος καὶ Θουρίου Κρίμισσαν κατοικεῖ·
καὶ παυθεὶς τῆς ἄλης Ἀλαίου Ἀπόλλωνος ἱερὸν
κτίζει, ᾧ καὶ τὸ τόξον αὐτοῦ ἀνέθηκεν, ὥς φησιν
Εὐφορίων.>

15c   <921: Ναναίθος] ποταμός ἐστιν Ἰταλίας·
ἐκλήθη δὲ οὕτω κατὰ μὲν Ἀπολλόδωρον καὶ τοὺς
λοιπούς, ὅτι μετὰ τὴν Ἰλίου ἅλωσιν αἱ Λαομέ-

---

[1] εἰς Πελλήνην omitted by Wagner in his edition of
Apollodorus, probably by mistake. For Πελλήνην we should
perhaps read Παλλήνην. See exegetical note.

---

[1] Canastrum, or Canastra, is the extreme southern cape of
the peninsula of Pallene (Pellene) in Macedonia. See Herodotus, vii. 123; Apollonius Rhodius, *Argon.* i. 599, with the
Scholiast; Strabo, vii. frag. 25, p. 330 (vol. ii. p 462, ed.
Meineke); Apostolius, *Cent.* ii. 20; Tzetzes, *Schol. on Lycophron*, 526; Livy, xxx. 45. 15, xliv. 11. 3.

[2] It is said that in a sedition Philoctetes was driven from
his city of Meliboea in Thessaly (Homer, *Il.* ii. 717 *sq.*), and
fled to southern Italy, where he founded the cities of Petilia,
Old Crimissa, and Chone, between Croton and Thurii. See
Strabo, vi. 1. 3, p. 254, who, after recording the foundation
of Petilia and Old Crimissa by Philoctetes, proceeds as follows:
"And Apollodorus, after mentioning Philoctetes in his *Book
of the Ships*, says that some people relate how, on arriving
in the country of Croton, he founded Crimissa on the headland
and above it the city of Chone, from which the Chonians
hereabout took their name, and how men sent by him to
Sicily fortified Segesta near Eryx with the help of Aegestes
the Trojan." The book from which Strabo makes this
quotation is not the *Library* of our author, but the *Catalogue*

at Crete; then they were driven out of their course by winds and settled in the Iberian islands. . . . The people of Protesilaus were cast away on Pellene near the plain of Canastrum.[1] And Philoctetes was driven to Campania in Italy, and after making war on the Lucanians, he settled in Crimissa, near Croton and Thurium[2]; and, his wanderings over, he founded a sanctuary of Apollo the Wanderer (*Alaios*), to whom also he dedicated his bow, as Euphorion says.[3]

Navaethus is a river of Italy.[4] It was called so, according to Apollodorus and the rest, because after the capture of Ilium the daughters of Laomedon, the

of the Ships, a work on the Homeric Catalogue by the Athenan grammarian Apollodorus. According to Strabo (viii. 3. 6, p. 339), Apollodorus borrowed most of his materials for this work from Demetrius of Scepsis. For the fragments of the work see Heyne's *Apollodorus* (Second Edition, 1803), vol. i. pp. 417 *sqq.* ; *Fragmenta Historicorum Graecorum*, ed. C. Müller, i. 453 *sqq.*

[3] Compare Aristotle, *Mirab. Auscult.* 107 (115): "It is said that Philoctetes is worshipped by the Sybarites; for on his return from Troy he settled in the territory of Croton at the place called Macalla, which they say is distant a hundred and twenty furlongs, and they relate that he dedicated the bow of Hercules in the sanctuary of the Halian Apollo. But they say that in the time of their sovereignty the people of Croton fetched the bow from there and dedicated it in the sanctuary of Apollo in their country. It is said, too, that when he died he was buried beside the river Sybaris; for he had gone to the help of the Rhodians under Tlepolemus, who had been carried out of their course to these regions and had engaged in battle with the barbarous inhabitants of that country." This war with the barbarians is no doubt the "war on the Lucanians," in which Apollodorus, or at all events, Tzetzes here tells us that Philoctetes engaged after his arrival in Italy.

[4] This paragraph is quoted from Tzetzes, *Schol. on Lycophron*, 921.

δοντος θυγατέρες, Πριάμου δὲ ἀδελφαί,[1] Αἴθυλλα
Ἀστυόχη Μηδεσικάστη μετὰ τῶν λοιπῶν αἰχμα-
λωτίδων ἐκεῖσε γεγονυῖαι τῆς Ἰταλίας, εὐλαβού-
μεναι τὴν ἐν τῇ Ἑλλάδι δουλείαν τὰ σκάφη
ἐνέπρησαν, ὅθεν ὁ ποταμὸς Ναύαιθος ἐκλήθη καὶ
αἱ γυναῖκες Ναυπρήστιδες· οἱ δὲ σὺν αὐταῖς
Ἕλληνες ἀπολέσαντες τὰ σκάφη ἐκεῖ κατῴκησαν.>

E 16 | Δημοφῶν δὲ[2] Θρᾳξὶ Βισάλταις μετ' ὀλίγων
νεῶν προσίσχει, καὶ αὐτοῦ ἐρασθεῖσα Φυλλὶς ἡ
θυγάτηρ τοῦ βασιλέως ἐπὶ προικὶ τῇ βασιλείᾳ
συνευνάζεται ὑπὸ τοῦ πατρός. ὁ δὲ βουλόμενος
εἰς τὴν πατρίδα ἀπιέναι, πολλὰ δεηθεὶς ὀμόσας
ἀναστρέψειν ἀπέρχεται· καὶ Φυλλὶς αὐτὸν ἄχρι
τῶν Ἐννέα ὁδῶν[3] λεγομένων προπέμπει καὶ
δίδωσιν αὐτῷ κίστην, εἰποῦσα ἱερὸν <τῆς> μητρὸς[4]
Ῥέας ἐνεῖναι, καὶ ταύτην μὴ ἀνοίγειν, εἰ μὴ ὅταν

---

[1] Πριάμου δὲ ἀδελφαί. These words were omitted, doubtless
by accident, in Wagner's edition of Apollodorus.

[2] The following story of the loves of Demophon and
Phyllis is repeated by Tzetzes (*Schol. on Lycophron*, 495) in
a passage which to a great extent agrees verbally with the
present passage of Apollodorus.

[3] Ἐννέα ὁδῶν Wagner (comparing Tzetzes, *Schol. on Lycophron*, 495): ἐννεάδων E.

[4] <τῆς> μητρὸς Wagner (comparing Tzetzes, *Schol. on
Lycophron*, 495): μητρὸς E.

---

[1] The same story is told by Strabo, who calls the river
Neaethus (vi. 1. 12, p. 262). Stephanus Byzantius agrees
with Apollodorus in giving Navaethus (Ναύαιθος) as the form
of the name. Apollodorus derives the name from ναῦς, "a
ship," and αἴθω, "to burn." Virgil tells a similar tale of the
founding of Segesta or, as he calls it, Acesta in Sicily. See
Virgil, *Aen.* v. 604–771.

[2] Demophon and his brother Acamas, the sons of Theseus,
had gone to Troy to rescue their grandmother Aethra from

sisters of Priam, to wit, Aethylla, Astyoche, and Medesicaste, with the other female captives, finding themselves in that part of Italy, and dreading slavery in Greece, set fire to the vessels ; whence the river was called Navaethus and the women were called Nauprestides ; and the Greeks who were with the women, having lost the vessels, settled there.[1]

Demophon with a few ships put in to the land of the Thracian Bisaltians,[2] and there Phyllis, the king's daughter, falling in love with him, was given him in marriage by her father with the kingdom for her dower. But he wished to depart to his own country, and after many entreaties and swearing to return, he did depart. And Phyllis accompanied him as far as what are called the Nine Roads, and she gave him a casket, telling him that it contained a sacrament of Mother Rhea, and that he was not to open it until he

captivity. See above, *Epitome*, v. 22. The following story of the loves and sad fate of Demophon and Phyllis is told in almost the same words by Tzetzes, *Schol. on Lycophron*, 495, except that for the name of Demophon he substitutes the name of his brother Acamas. Lucian also couples the names of Acamas and Phyllis (*De saltatione*, 40). A pretty story is told of the sad lovers by Servius. He says that Phyllis, despairing of the return of Demophon, hanged herself and was turned into a leafless almond tree ; but that when Demophon came and embraced the trunk of the tree, it responded to his endearments by bursting into leaf ; hence leaves, which had been called *petala* before, were ever after called *phylla* in Greek. See Servius, on Virgil, *Ecl.* v. 10. Compare *Scriptores rerum mythicarum Latini*, ed. G. H. Bode, vol. i. pp. 51 and 146 *sq.* (First Vatican Mythographer, 159 ; Second Vatican Mythographer, 214). The story is told in a less romantic form by Hyginus (*Fab.* 59, compare 243). He says that when Phyllis died for love, trees grew on her grave and mourned her death at the season when their leaves withered and fell.

17 ἀπελπίσῃ τῆς πρὸς αὐτὴν ἀνόδου.[1] Δημοφῶν δὲ
ἐλθὼν εἰς Κύπρον ἐκεῖ κατῴκει. καὶ τοῦ τακτοῦ
χρόνου διελθόντος Φυλλὶς ἀρὰς θεμένη κατὰ Δημο-
φῶντος ἑαυτὴν ἀναιρεῖ· Δημοφῶν δὲ τὴν κίστην
ἀνοίξας φόβῳ κατασχεθεὶς[2] ἄνεισιν ἐπὶ τὸν ἵππον
καὶ τοῦτον ἐλαύνων ἀτάκτως ἀπόλλυται· τοῦ γὰρ
ἵππου σφαλέντος κατενεχθεὶς ἐπὶ τὸ ξίφος ἔπεσεν.
οἱ δὲ σὺν αὐτῷ κατῴκησαν ἐν Κύπρῳ.

18 Ποδαλείριος δὲ ἀφικόμενος εἰς Δελφοὺς ἐχρᾶτο
ποῦ κατοικήσει· χρησμοῦ δὲ δοθέντος, εἰς ἣν
πόλιν τοῦ περιέχοντος οὐρανοῦ πεσόντος οὐδὲν
πείσεται,[3] τῆς Καρικῆς Χερρονήσου τὸν πέριξ
οὐρανοῦ κυκλούμενον ὄρεσι τόπον κατῴκησεν.

19 Ἀμφίλοχος δὲ ὁ Ἀλκμαίωνος, κατά τινας
ὕστερον παραγενόμενος εἰς Τροίαν, κατὰ [τὸν][4]
χειμῶνα ἀπερρίφη πρὸς Μόψον, καί, ὥς τινες
λέγουσιν, ὑπὲρ τῆς βασιλείας μονομαχοῦντες
ἔκτειναν ἀλλήλους.

---

[1] τῆς πρὸς αὐτὴν ἀνόδου E : τὴν πρὸς αὐτὴν ἄνοδον Tzetzes,
Schol. on Lycophron, 495.

[2] φόβῳ κατασχεθεὶς E : φάσματι κρατηθεὶς Tzetzes, *Schol. on
Lycophron,* 495.

[3] οὐδὲν πείσεται E. Wagner conjectures οὐδὲν <δεινὸν>
πείσεται, comparing Tzetzes, *Schol. on Lycophron,* 1047, οὐδὲν δεινὸν πείσεται.

[4] κατὰ [τὸν] χειμῶνα. As Wagner observes, the article
should perhaps be omitted, as in the quotation of the passage
by Tzetzes, *Schol. on Lycophron,* 440, κατὰ χειμῶνα ἀπερρίφη
πρὸς Μόψον, who cites Apollodorus by name. Yet perhaps
our author was thinking of the famous storm that overtook
the Greeks on their return from Troy and wrecked so many
gallant ships.

---

[1] The same story is told, nearly in the same words, by
Tzetzes (*Schol. on Lycophron,* 1047), who probably copied
Apollodorus. As to the settlement of Podalirius in Caria,

264

should have abandoned all hope of returning to her.
And Demophon went to Cyprus and dwelt there.
And when the appointed time was past, Phyllis
called down curses on Demophon and killed herself;
and Demophon opened the casket, and, being struck
with fear, he mounted his horse and galloping wildly
met his end; for, the horse stumbling, he was thrown
and fell on his sword. But his people settled in
Cyprus.

Podalirius went to Delphi and inquired of the
oracle where he should settle; and on receiving an
oracle that he should settle in the city where, if the
encompassing heaven were to fall, he would suffer no
harm, he settled in that place of the Carian Chersonese which is encircled by mountains all round the
horizon.[1]

Amphilochus son of Alcmaeon, who, according to
some, arrived later at Troy, was driven in the storm
to the home of Mopsus; and, as some say, they fought
a single combat for the kingdom, and slew each
other.[2]

---

[1] compare Pausanias, iii. 26. 10; Stephanus Byzantius, *s.v.*
Σύρνα. Podalirius was worshipped as a hero in Italy. He had
a shrine at the foot of Mount Drium in Daunia, and the seer
Calchas was worshipped in a shrine on the top of the same
mountain, where his worshippers sacrificed black rams and
slept in the skins of the victims for the purpose of receiving
revelations in dreams. See Strabo, vi. 3. 9, p. 284; Lycophron, *Cassandra*, 1047 *sqq.* Hence Lycophron said that
Podalirius was buried in Italy, and for so saying he was
severely taken to task by his learned but crabbed commentator Tzetzes, who roundly accused him of lying (*Schol. on
Lycophron*, 1047).

[2] This passage is quoted from Apollodorus, with the
author's name, by Tzetzes (*Schol. on Lycophron*, 440-442),
who says that according to the usual tradition Amphilochus
and Mopsus had gone together to Cilicia after the capture of

APOLLODORUS

20 Λοκροὶ δὲ μόλις τὴν ἑαυτῶν καταλαβόντες, ἐπεὶ μετὰ τρίτον ἔτος τὴν Λοκρίδα¹ κατέσχε φθορά, δέχονται χρησμὸν ἐξιλάσασθαι τὴν ἐν Ἰλίῳ Ἀθηνᾶν καὶ δύο παρθένους πέμπειν ἱκέτιδας ἐπὶ ἔτη χίλια. καὶ λαγχάνουσι πρῶται Περίβοια καὶ
21 Κλεοπάτρα. αὗται δὲ εἰς Τροίαν ἀφικόμεναι, διωκόμεναι παρὰ τῶν ἐγχωρίων εἰς τὸ ἱερὸν κατέρχονται· καὶ τῇ μὲν θεᾷ οὐ προσήρχοντο, τὸ δὲ ἱερὸν ἔσαιρόν² τε καὶ ἔρραινον· ἐκτὸς δὲ τοῦ νεὼ οὐκ ἐξῄεσαν, κεκαρμέναι δὲ ἦσαν καὶ μονοχίτωνες

¹ Λοκρίδα Wagner (comparing Tzetzes, *Schol. on Lycophron*, 1141): Λοκρίαν Ε.
² ἔσαιρον Wagner (comparing Tzetzes, *Schol. on Lycophron*, 1141): ἔσηρον Ε.

Troy. This statement is confirmed by the testimony of Strabo (xiv. 5. 16, pp. 675 *sq.*), who tells us that Amphilochus and Mopsus came from Troy and founded Mallus in Cilicia. The dispute between Amphilochus and Mopsus is related more fully both by Tzetzes and Strabo (*ll.cc.*). According to them, Amphilochus wished to go for a time to Argos (probably Amphilochian Argos; see above, iii. 7. 7). So he departed after entrusting the kingdom or priesthood to Mopsus in his absence. Dissatisfied with the state of affairs at Argos, he returned in a year and reclaimed the kingdom or priesthood from Mopsus. But, acting on the principle *Beati possidentes*, the viceroy refused to cede the crown or the mitre to its proper owner; accordingly they had recourse to the ordeal of battle, in which both combatants perished. Their bodies were buried in graves which could not be seen from each other; for the people built a tower between them, in order that the rivals, who had fought each other in life, might not scowl at each other in death. However, their rivalry did not prevent them working an oracle in partnership after their decease. In the second century of our era the oracle enjoyed the highest reputation for infallibility (Pausanias, i. 34. 3). The leading partner of the firm was apparently Amphilochus, for he is usually men-

The Locrians regained their own country with difficulty, and three years afterwards, when Locris was visited by a plague, they received an oracle bidding them to propitiate Athena at Ilium and to send two maidens as suppliants for a thousand years. The lot first fell on Periboea and Cleopatra. And when they came to Troy they were chased by the natives and took refuge in the sanctuary. And they did not approach the goddess, but swept and sprinkled the sanctuary; and they did not go out of the temple, and their hair was cropped, and they wore single garments

---

tioned alone in connexion with the oracle; Plutarch (*De defectu oraculorum*, 45) is the only ancient writer from whom we learn that Mopsus took an active share in the business, though Cicero mentions the partners together (*De divinatione*, i. 40. 88). According to Plutarch and Dio Cassius (lxxii. 7), the oracles were communicated in dreams; but Lucian says (*Philopseudes*, 38) that the inquirer wrote down his question on a tablet, which he handed to the prophet. The charge for one of these infallible communications was only two obols, or about twopence halfpenny. See Lucian, *Alexander*, 19; *id. Deorum concilium*, 12. The ancients seem to have been divided in opinion on the important question whether the oracular Amphilochus at Mallus was the son or the grandson of Amphiaraus. Apollodorus calls him the son of Alcmaeon, which would make him the grandson of Amphiaraus, for Alcmaeon was a son of Amphiaraus. But Tzetzes, in reporting what he describes as the usual version of the story, calls Amphilochus the son, not the grandson of Amphiaraus (*Schol. on Lycophron*, 440–442). Compare Strabo, xiv. 1. 27, p. 642; Quintus Smyrnaeus, *Posthomerica*, xiv. 365–369. Lucian is inconsistent on the point; for while in one passage he calls Amphilochus the son of Amphiaraus (*Alexander*, 19), in another passage he speaks of him sarcastically as the noble son of an accurst matricide, by whom he means Alcmaeon (*Deorum concilium*, 12). Elsewhere Apollodorus mentions both Amphilochus, the son of Amphiaraus, and Amphilochus, the son of Alcmaeon. See above, iii. 7. 2 and 7.

267

22 καὶ ἀνυπόδετοι. τῶν δὲ πρώτων ἀποθανουσῶν
ἄλλας ἔπεμπον· εἰσῄεσαν δὲ εἰς τὴν πόλιν νύκτωρ,
ἵνα μὴ φανεῖσαι τοῦ τεμένους ἔξω φονευθῶσι·
μετέπειτα δὲ βρέφη μετὰ τροφῶν ἔπεμπον. χιλίων
δὲ ἐτῶν παρελθόντων μετὰ τὸν Φωκικὸν πόλεμον
ἱκέτιδας ἐπαύσαντο πέμποντες.

ES 23 | Ἀγαμέμνων δὲ καταντήσας εἰς Μυκήνας μετὰ
Κασάνδρας ἀναιρεῖται ὑπὸ Αἰγίσθου καὶ Κλυται-
μνήστρας· δίδωσι γὰρ αὐτῷ χιτῶνα ἄχειρα καὶ
ἀτράχηλον, καὶ τοῦτον ἐνδυόμενος φονεύεται, καὶ
βασιλεύει Μυκηνῶν Αἴγισθος· κτείνουσι δὲ καὶ

---

¹ The story of the custom of propitiating Athena at Troy
by sending two Locrian virgins to her every year is similarly
told by Tzetzes, who adds some interesting particulars
omitted by Apollodorus. From him we learn that when the
maidens arrived, the Trojans met them and tried to catch
them. If they caught the maidens, they killed them and
burned their bones with the wood of wild trees which bore
no fruit. Having done so, they threw the ashes from Mount
Traron into the sea But if the maidens escaped from their
pursuers, they ascended secretly to the sanctuary of Athena
and became her priestesses, sweeping and sprinkling the
sacred precinct; but they might not approach the goddess,
nor quit the sanctuary except by night. Tzetzes agrees with
Apollodorus in describing the maidens during their term of
service as barefoot, with cropped hair, and clad each in a
single tunic. He refers to the Sicilian historian Timaeus as
his authority for the statement that the custom was observed
for a thousand years, and that it came to an end after the
Phocian war (357–346 B.C.). See Tzetzes, Schol. on Lycophron,
1141. The maidens were chosen by lot from the hundred
noblest families in Locris (Polybius, xii. 5); and when they
escaped death on landing, they served the goddess in the
sanctuary for the term of their lives (Plutarch, De sera
numinis vindicta, 12), or, at all events, till their successors
arrived (Suidas, s.v. κατεγήρασαν). For other references to
this very remarkable custom, which appears to be well

and no shoes. And when the first maidens died, they sent others; and they entered into the city by night, lest, being seen outside the precinct, they should be put to the sword; but afterwards they sent babes with their nurses. And when the thousand years were passed, after the Phocian war they ceased to send suppliants.[1]

After Agamemnon had returned to Mycenae with Cassandra, he was murdered by Aegisthus and Clytaemnestra; for she gave him a shirt without sleeves and without a neck, and while he was putting it on he was cut down, and Aegisthus reigned over Mycenae.[2] And they killed Cassandra

authenticated, see Strabo, xiii. 1. 40, pp. 600 *sq.*; Scholiast on Homer, *Il.* xiii. 66; Iamblichus, *De Pythagorica vita*, viii. 42; Suidas, *s.v.* ποινή (quoting Aelian); Servius, on Virgil, *Aen.* i. 41. Servius, in contradiction to our other authorities, says that only one maiden was sent annually. Strabo appears to affirm that the custom originated as late as the Persian period (τὰς δὲ Λοκρίδας πεμφθῆναι Περσῶν ἤδη κρατούντων συνέβη). This view is accepted by Clinton, who accordingly holds that the custom lasted from 559 B.C. to 346 B.C. (*Fasti Hellenici*, i. 134 *sq.*).

[2] As to the murder of Agamemnon, see Homer, *Od.* iii. 193 *sq.*, 303–305, iv. 529–537, xi. 404–434; Hagias, *Returns*, summarized by Proclus, in *Epicorum Graecorum Fragmenta*, ed. G. Kinkel, p. 53; Aeschylus, *Agamemnon*, 1379 *sqq.*; *id. Eumenides*, 631–635; Sophocles, *Electra*, 95–99; Euripides, *Electra*, 8–10; *id. Orestes*, 25 *sq.*; Pausanias, ii. 16. 6; Tzetzes, *Schol. on Lycophron*, 1108 and 1375; Hyginus, *Fab.* 117; Seneca, *Agamemnon*, 875–909; Servius, on Virgil, *Aen.* xi. 268; *Scriptores rerum mythicarum Latini*, ed. G. H. Bode, vol. i. pp. 47, 126, 141 *sq.* (First Vatican Mythographer, 147; Second Vatican Mythographer, 147 and 202); Dictys Cretensis, *Bellum Trojanum*, vi. 2. According to Homer and the author of the *Returns*, with whom Pausanias agrees, it was Aegisthus who killed Agamemnon; according to Aeschylus, it was Clytaemnestra. Sophocles and Euripides speak of the murder being perpetrated by the

24 Κασάνδραν. 'Ηλέκτρα δὲ μία τῶν 'Αγαμέμνονος θυγατέρων 'Ορέστην τὸν ἀδελφὸν ἐκκλέπτει καὶ δίδωσι Στροφίῳ Φωκεῖ[1] τρέφειν, ὁ δὲ αὐτὸν ἐκτρέφει μετὰ Πυλάδου παιδὸς ἰδίου. τελειωθεὶς δὲ 'Ορέστης εἰς Δελφοὺς παραγίνεται καὶ τὸν θεὸν ἐρωτᾷ,[2] εἰ τοὺς αὐτόχειρας τοῦ πατρὸς μετέλθοι.

25 τοῦτο δὲ τοῦ θεοῦ ἐπιτρέποντος[3] ἀπέρχεται εἰς Μυκήνας[4] μετὰ Πυλάδου λαθραίως καὶ κτείνει[5] τήν τε μητέρα καὶ τὸν Αἴγισθον, καὶ μετ' οὐ πολὺ μανίᾳ κατασχεθεὶς ὑπὸ 'Ερινύων[6] διωκόμενος εἰς 'Αθήνας παραγίνεται καὶ κρίνεται[7] ἐν 'Αρείῳ πάγῳ,[8] | ὡς μὲν λέγουσί τινες ὑπὸ 'Ερινύων, ὡς δέ τινες ὑπὸ Τυνδάρεω, ὡς δέ τινες ὑπὸ 'Ηριγόνης τῆς Αἰγίσθου καὶ Κλυταιμνήστρας, καὶ κριθεὶς ἴσων γενομένων τῶν ψήφων ἀπολύεται.

[1] Στροφίῳ Φωκεῖ E: Φωκεῖ Στροφίῳ S.
[2] καὶ τὸν θεὸν ἐρωτᾷ S: κἀκεῖ ἐρωτᾷ E.
[3] τοῦ θεοῦ ἐπιτρέποντος S: τοῦτο δ' ἐπιτραπεὶς E.
[4] ἀπέρχεται Μυκήνας E: ἀπερχόμενος εἰς Μυκήνας S.
[5] καὶ κτείνει τήν τε μητέρα καὶ τὸν Αἴγισθον E: τόν τε Αἴγισθον καὶ τὴν μητέρα κτείνει S.
[6] 'Ερινύων S: 'Ερινύων E.
[7] καὶ κρίνεται E: κρίνεται δὲ 'Ορέστης S.
[8] ἐν 'Αρείῳ πάγῳ S: ἐν 'Αρείῳ πάγῳ καὶ ἀπολύεται E.

---

two jointly. The sleeveless and neckless garment in which Clytaemnestra entangled her husband, while she cut him down, is described with tragic grandiloquence and vagueness by Aeschylus, but more explicitly by later writers (Tzetzes, Seneca, Servius, and the Vatican Mythographers).

[1] As to the murder of Cassandra, see Homer, *Od.* xi. 421–423; Pindar, *Pyth.* xi. 19 (29) *sqq.*; Philostratus, *Imagines,* ii. 10; Athenaeus, xiii. 3, p. 556 c; Hyginus, *Fab.* 117. According to Hyginus, both Clytaemnestra and Aegisthus had a hand in the murder of Cassandra; according to the other writers, she was despatched by Clytaemnestra alone.

[2] Compare Pindar, *Pyth.* xi. 34 (52) *sqq.*; Sophocles, *Electra,* 11 *sqq.*; Euripides, *Electra,* 14 *sqq.*; Hyginus, *Fab.*

also.[1] But Electra, one of Agamemnon's daughters, smuggled away her brother Orestes and gave him to Strophius, the Phocian, to bring up; and he brought him up with Pylades, his own son.[2] And when Orestes was grown up, he repaired to Delphi and asked the god whether he should take vengeance on his father's murderers. The god gave him leave, so he departed secretly to Mycenae in company with Pylades, and killed both his mother and Aegisthus.[3] And not long afterwards, being afflicted with madness and pursued by the Furies, he repaired to Athens and was tried in the Areopagus. He is variously said to have been brought to trial by the Furies, or by Tyndareus, or by Erigone, daughter of Aegisthus and Clytaemnestra; and the votes at his trial being equal he was acquitted.[4]

117. Pindar tells how, after the murder of his father Agamemnon, the youthful Orestes was conveyed to the aged Strophius at the foot of Parnassus; but he does not say who rescued the child and conveyed him thither. According to Sophocles and Euripides, it was an old retainer of the family who thus saved Orestes, but Sophocles says that the old man had received the child from the hands of Electra. Hyginus, in agreement with Apollodorus, relates how, after the murder of Agamemnon, Electra took charge of (*sustulit*) her infant brother Orestes and committed him to the care of Strophius in Phocis.

[3] This vengeance for the murder of Agamemnon is the theme of three extant Greek tragedies, the *Choephori* of Aeschylus, the *Electra* of Sophocles, and the *Electra* of Euripides. It was related by Hagias in his epic, the *Returns*, as we learn from the brief summary of Proclus (*Epicorum Graecorum Fragmenta*, ed. G. Kinkel, p. 53). Compare Pindar, *Pyth.* xi. 36 (55) *sq.*; Hyginus, *Fab.* 119. Homer briefly mentions the murder of Aegisthus by Orestes (*Od* i. 29 *sq.*, 298–300, iii. 306 *sqq.*); he does not expressly mention, but darkly hints at, the murder of Clytaemnestra by her son (*Od.* iii 309 *sq.*).

[4] The trial and acquittal of Orestes in the court of the Areopagus at Athens is the subject of Aeschylus's tragedy,

ES 26 | Ἐρομένῳ¹ δὲ αὐτῷ, πῶς ἂν ἀπαλλαγείη τῆς
νόσου, ὁ θεὸς εἶπεν, εἰ τὸ ἐν Ταύροις ξόανον μετα-
S κομίσειεν.² | οἱ δὲ Ταῦροι μοῖρά ἐστι Σκυθῶν, οἳ
τοὺς ξένους φονεύουσι καὶ εἰς τὸ ἱερὸν <πῦρ>³
ῥίπτουσι. τοῦτο ἦν ἐν τῷ τεμένει διά τινος πέτρας
ES 27 ἀναφερόμενον ἐξ Ἅιδου. | παραγενόμενος οὖν εἰς

---

¹ For ἐρομένῳ we should perhaps read χρωμένῳ.

² ἐρομένῳ δὲ . . . ξόανον μετακομίσειεν S : καὶ λαμβάνει χρησμὸν ἀπαλλαγῆναι τῆς νόσου, εἰ τὸ ἐν Ταύροις μετακομίσοι βρέ-
τας E.

³ εἰς τὸ ἱερὸν <πῦρ> ῥίπτουσι Herwerden (*Mnemosyne*,
xx. (1892), p. 200) (compare Euripides, *Iphigenia in Tauris*,
626, πῦρ ἱερόν): εἰς τὸ ἱερὸν ῥίπτουσι S, Wagner.

---

the *Eumenides*, where the poet similarly represents the matricide as acquitted because the votes were equal (verses 752 *sq.*).
The *Parian Chronicle* also records the acquittal on the same
ground, and dates it in the reign of Demophon, king of Athens.
See *Marmor Parium*, 40 *sq.* (*Fragmenta Historicorum Graecorum*, ed. C. Müller, i. 546). Compare Euripides, *Iphigenia
in Tauris*, 940–967, 1469–1472; *id. Orestes*, 1648–1652;
Tzetzes, *Schol. on Lycophron*, 1374; Pausanias, i. 28. 5,
viii. 34. 4; Dictys Cretensis, *Bellum Trojanum*, vi. 4. In the
Eumenides the accusers of Orestes are the Furies. According
to the Parian Chronicler, it was Erigone, the daughter of
Aegisthus and Clytaemnestra, who instituted the prosecution
for the murder of her father; the chronicler does not mention
the murder of Clytaemnestra as an article in the indictment
of Orestes. According to the author of the *Etymologicum
Magnum* (p. 42, *s.v.* Αἰώρα), the prosecution was conducted
at Athens jointly by Erigone and her grandfather Tyndareus,
and when it failed, Erigone hanged herself. Peloponnesian
antiquaries, reported by Pausanias (viii. 34. 4), alleged that
the accuser was not Tyndareus, who was dead, but Perilaus,
a cousin of Clytaemnestra. According to Hyginus (*Fab.* 119),
Orestes was accused by Tyndareus before the people of Mycenae, but was suffered to retire into banishment for the sake
of his father. As to the madness of Orestes, caused by the
Furies of his murdered mother, see Euripides, *Orestes*, 931 *sqq.*;
Pausanias, iii. 22. 1, viii. 34. 1–4. The incipient symptoms of

When he inquired how he should be rid of his disorder, the god answered that he would be rid of it if he should fetch the wooden image that was in the land of the Taurians.[1] Now the Taurians are a part of the Scythians, who murder strangers[2] and throw them into the sacred fire, which was in the precinct, being wafted up from Hades through a certain rock.[3] So when Orestes was come with

madness, showing themselves immediately after the commission of the crime, are finely described by Aeschylus (*Choephori*, 1021 *sqq.*).

[1] As to the oracle, compare Euripides, *Iphigenia in Tauris*, 77–92, 970–978; Tzetzes, *Schol. on Lycophron*, 1374; Hyginus, *Fab.* 120.

[2] The Taurians inhabited the Crimea. As to their custom of sacrificing castaways and strangers, see Herodotus, iv. 103; Euripides, *Iphigenia in Tauris*, 34–41; Diodorus Siculus, iv. 44. 7; Pausanias, i. 43. 1; *Orphica, Argon.* 1075 *sq.*, ed. Abel; Ovid, *Ex Ponto*, iii. 2. 45–58; Mela, ii. 11; Ammianus Marcellinus, xxii. 8. 34. According to Herodotus, these Taurians sacrificed human beings to a Virgin Goddess, whom they identified with Iphigenia, daughter of Agamemnon. The victims were shipwrecked persons and any Greeks on whom they could lay hands. They were slaughtered by being knocked on the head with a club, after which their heads were set up on stakes and their bodies thrown down a precipice into the sea or buried in the ground; for reports differed in regard to the disposal of the corpses, though all agreed as to the setting of the heads on stakes. Ammianus Marcellinus says that the native name of the goddess was Orsiloche.

[3] This account of the disposal of the bodies of the victims is based on Euripides, *Iphigenia in Tauris*, 625 *sq.* :—

OP. τάφος δὲ ποῖός δέξεταί μ', ὅταν θάνω;

ΙΦ. πῦρ ἱερὸν ἔνδον χάσμα τ' εὐρωπὸν πέτρας.

Compare *id.* 1154 *sq.* :—

ἤδη τῶν ξένων κατήρξατο,

ἀδύτοις τ' ἐν ἁγνοῖς σῶμα λάμπονται πυρί;

Thus Apollodorus differs from the account which Herodotus gives of the disposal of the bodies. See the preceding note.

APOLLODORUS

Ταύρους Ὀρέστης[1] μετὰ Πυλάδου φωραθεὶς ἑάλω
καὶ ἄγεται πρὸς Θόαντα τὸν βασιλέα δέσμιος,
ὁ δὲ ἀμφοτέρους πρὸς τὴν ἱέρειαν ἀποστέλλει.
ἐπιγνωσθεὶς δὲ ὑπὸ τῆς ἀδελφῆς ἱερὰ ποιούσης
ἐν Ταύροις,[2] ἄρας τὸ ξόανον σὺν αὐτῇ φεύγει.

S | κομισθὲν δὲ εἰς Ἀθήνας νῦν λέγεται τὸ τῆς Ταυ-
ροπόλου· ἔνιοι δὲ αὐτὸν κατὰ χειμῶνα προσενε-

---

[1] παραγενόμενος οὖν εἰς Ταύρους Ὀρέστης S : καὶ δὴ παραγενό
μενος ἐν Ταύροις Ε.

[2] τῆς ἀδελφῆς ἱερὰ ποιούσης ἐν Ταύροις S : τῆς ἀδελφῆς Ε.

---

[1] This account of the expedition of Orestes and Pylades to
the land of the Taurians, and their escape with the image of
Artemis, is the subject of Euripides's play *Iphigenia in Tauris*,
which Apollodorus seems to have followed closely.   The gist
of the play is told in verse by Ovid (*Ex Ponto*, iii. 2. 43–96)
and in prose by Hyginus (*Fab.* 120).   Compare Tzetzes,
Schol. on Lycophron, 1374 ; *Scriptores rerum mythicarum
Latini*, ed. G. H. Bode, vol. i. pp. 7, 141 *sq.* (First Vatican
Mythographer, 20 ; Second Vatican Mythographer, 202)

[2] In saying that the image of the Tauric Artemis was
taken to Athens our author follows Euripides.   See *Iphigenia in Tauris*, 89–91, 1212–1214.   But according to Euripides the image was not to remain in Athens but to be
carried to a sacred place in Attica called Halae, where it was
to be set up in a temple specially built for it and to be called
the image of Artemis Tauropolus or Brauronian Artemis
(*Iphigenia in Tauris*, 1446–1467).   An old wooden image of
Artemis, which purported to be the one brought from the
land of the Taurians, was shown at Brauron in Attica as late
as the second century of our era ; Iphigenia is said to have
landed with the image at Brauron and left it there, while she
herself went on by land to Athens and afterwards to Argos.
See Pausanias, i. 23. 7, i. 33. 1.   But according to some the
original image was carried off by Xerxes to Susa, and was
afterwards presented by Seleucus to Laodicea in Syria, where
it was said to remain down to the time of Pausanias in the
second century of our era (Pausanias, iii. 16. 8, viii. 46. 3).

Pylades to the land of the Taurians, he was detected, caught, and carried in bonds before Thoas the king, who sent them both to the priestess. But being recognized by his sister, who acted as priestess among the Taurians, he fled with her, carrying off the wooden image.[1] It was conveyed to Athens and is now called the image of Tauropolus.[2] But some say

Euripides has recorded, in the form of prophecy, two interesting features in the ritual of Artemis at Halae or Brauron. In sacrificing to the goddess the priest drew blood with a sword from the throat of a man, and this was regarded as a substitute for the sacrifice of Orestes, of which the goddess had been defrauded by his escape. Such a custom is explained most naturally as a mitigation of an older practice of actually sacrificing human beings to the goddess; and the tradition of such sacrifices at Brauron would suffice to give rise to the story that the image of the cruel goddess had been brought from the land of ferocious barbarians on the Black Sea. For similar mitigations of an old custom of human sacrifice, see *The Dying God*, pp. 214 *sqq.* The other feature in the ritual at Brauron which Euripides notices was that the garments of women dying in childbed used to be dedicated to Iphigenia, who was believed to be buried at Brauron. See Euripides, *Iphigenia in Tauris*, 1458–1467. As to Brauron and Halae, see my note on Pausanias, i. 33. 1 (vol. ii. pp. 445 *sqq.*). But other places besides Brauron claimed to possess the ancient idol of the Tauric Artemis The wooden image of Artemis Orthia at Sparta, at whose altar the Spartan youths were scourged to the effusion of blood, was supposed by the Lacedaemonians to be the true original image brought by Iphigenia herself to Sparta; and their claim was preferred by Pausanias to that of the Athenians (Pausanias, iii. 16. 7–10). Others said that Orestes and Iphigenia carried the image, hidden in a bundle of faggots, to Aricia in Italy. See Servius, on Virgil, ii. 116, vi. 136; *Scriptores rerum mythicarum Latini*, ed. G. H. Bode, vol. i. pp. 7, 142 (First Vatican Mythographer, 20; Second Vatican Mythographer, 202); compare Strabo, v. 3. 12, p. 239. Indeed, it was affirmed by some people that on his wanderings Orestes had deposited, not one, but many

χθῆναι τῇ νήσῳ Ῥόδῳ λέγουσιν . . . αὐτὸν καὶ
ES 28 κατὰ χρησμὸν ἐν τείχει καθοσιωθῆναι.[1] | καὶ δὴ
ἐλθὼν εἰς Μυκήνας Πυλάδῃ μὲν τὴν ἀδελφὴν
Ἠλέκτραν συζεύγνυσιν,[2] αὐτὸς δὲ γήμας Ἑρμιόνην,
E ἢ κατά τινας Ἠριγόνην,[3] τεκνοῖ Τισαμενόν,[4] | καὶ
δηχθεὶς ὑπὸ ὄφεως ἐν Ὀρεστείῳ τῆς Ἀρκαδίας
θνήσκει.

[1] λέγουσιν αὐτὸν καὶ κατὰ χρησμὸν ἐν τείχει καθοσιωθῆναι S.
There seems to be a lacuna after λέγουσιν. Bücheler proposed to correct the passage and supply the lacuna as follows:
λέγουσι <καὶ τὸ ξόανον μεῖναι> αὐτοῦ καὶ κατὰ χρησμὸν ἐν
τείχει καθοσιωθῆναι, "They say that the image remained
there and in accordance with an oracle was dedicated in a
fortification wall." This may give the sense. Kerameus
proposed to change αὐτὸν into ναυαγὸν, but this would still
leave the verb καθοσιωθῆναι without a proper subject.

[2] καὶ δὴ ἐλθὼν εἰς Μυκήνας Πυλάδῃ μὲν τὴν ἀδελφὴν Ἠλέκτραν
συζεύγνυσιν E: Ὀρέστης δὲ τὴν ἀδελφὴν Ἠλέκτραν Πυλάδῃ
συνῴκισεν S.

[3] ἢ κατά τινας Ἠριγόνην E, wanting in S.

[4] ἐγέννησε Τισαμενόν S: τεκνοῖ (without an accusative)
E. The original text of Apollodorus in this passage is probably
reproduced more fully by Tzetzes (Schol. on Lycophron, 1374)
as follows: Ὕστερον δὲ ἦλθεν εἰς Ἀθήνας, καὶ Πυλάδῃ μὲν
Ἠλέκτραν ζευγνύει, αὐτὸς δὲ μετὰ τῶν ἀδελφῶν ἀνελὼν Νεοπτόλεμον τὸν Ἀχιλλέως ἔγημεν Ἑρμιόνην, ἐξ ἧς γεννᾷ Τισαμενόν, ἢ
κατά τινας Ἠριγόνην γήμας, τὴν Αἰγίσθου, Πένθιλον γεννᾷ, οἰκῶν
ἐν Ὀρεστίᾳ τῆς Ἀρκαδίας, ὅπου ὑπὸ ὄφεως δηχθεὶς ἀναιρεῖται.
"Afterwards he came to Athens and united Electra in
marriage to Pylades, but he himself, with the help of his
brothers, killed Neoptolemus, son of Achilles, and married
Hermione, by whom he begat Tisamenus; or, according to
some, he married Erigone, daughter of Aegisthus, and begat
Penthilus, dwelling in Orestia, a district of Arcadia, where
he was killed by the bite of a snake."

images of Artemis in many places (Aelius Lampridius, Helio-
gabalus, 7). Such stories have clearly no historical value.
In every case they were probably devised to explain or excuse
a cruel and bloody ritual by deriving it from a barbarous
country.

that Orestes was driven in a storm to the island of Rhodes, and in accordance with an oracle the image was dedicated in a fortification wall.[1] And having come to Mycenae, he united his sister Electra in marriage to Pylades,[2] and having himself married Hermione, or, according to some, Erigone, he begat Tisamenus,[3] and was killed by the bite of a snake at Oresteum in Arcadia.[4]

[1] This drifting of Orestes to Rhodes seems to be mentioned by no other ancient writer. The verb ($καθοσιωθῆναι$), which I have taken to refer to the image and have translated by "dedicated," may perhaps refer to Orestes; if so, it would mean "purified" from the guilt of matricide. According to Hyginus (*Fab.* 120), Orestes sailed with Iphigenia and Pylades to the island of Sminthe, which is otherwise unknown. Another place to which Orestes and Iphigenia were supposed to have come on their way from the Crimea was Comana in Cappadocia; there he was said to have introduced the worship of Artemis Tauropolus and to have shorn his hair in token of mourning. Hence the city was said to derive its name ($Κόμανα$ from $κόμη$). See Strabo, xii. 2. 3, p. 535. According to Tzetzes (*Schol. on Lycophron*, 1374), Orestes was driven by storms to that part of Syria where Seleucia and Antioch afterwards stood; and Mount Amanus, on the borders of Syria and Cilicia, was so named because there the matricide was relieved of his madness ('$Αμανός$, from $μανία$ "madness" and $ἀ$ privative). Such is a sample of Byzantine etymology.

[2] As to the marriage of Electra to Pylades, see Euripides, *Electra*, 1249; *id. Orestes*, 1658 *sq.*; Hyginus, *Fab.* 122.

[3] As to the marriage of Orestes and Hermione, see above, *Epitome*, v. 14, with the note. According to Pausanias (ii. 18. 6), Orestes had by Hermione a son Tisamenus, who succeeded his father on the throne of Sparta. But Pausanias also mentions a tradition that Orestes had a bastard son Penthilus by Erigone, daughter of Aegisthus, and for this tradition he cites as his authority the old epic poet Cinaethon. Compare Tzetzes, *Schol. on Lycophron*, 1474.

[4] Compare Scholiast on Euripides, *Orestes*, 1645, quoting Asclepiades as his authority; Tzetzes, *Schol. on Lycophron*, 1374. In the passage of Euripides on which the

ES 29 | Μενέλαος δὲ πέντε ναῦς τὰς πάσας [1] ἔχων μεθ'
ἑαυτοῦ προσσχὼν [2] Σουνίῳ τῆς Ἀττικῆς ἀκρω-
τηρίῳ κἀκεῖθεν εἰς Κρήτην ἀπορριφεὶς πάλιν ὑπὸ
ἀνέμων μακρὰν ἀπωθεῖται, καὶ πλανώμενος ἀνά
τε Λιβύην καὶ Φοινίκην καὶ Κύπρον καὶ Αἴγυπτον
πολλὰ συναθροίζει χρήματα. καὶ κατά τινας
εὑρίσκεται παρὰ Πρωτεῖ τῷ τῶν Αἰγυπτίων βασιλεῖ Ἑλένη, μέχρι τότε εἴδωλον ἐκ νεφῶν ἐσχη-
κότος τοῦ Μενελάου. ὀκτὼ δὲ πλανηθεὶς ἔτη
κατέπλευσεν εἰς Μυκήνας, κἀκεῖ κατέλαβεν Ὀρέ-
στην μετεληλυθότα τὸν τοῦ πατρὸς φόνον. ἐλθὼν
δὲ εἰς Σπάρτην τὴν ἰδίαν [3] ἐκτήσατο βασιλείαν.

S   καὶ [4] | ἀποθανατισθεὶς ὑπὸ Ἥρας εἰς τὸ Ἠλύσιον
ἦλθε πεδίον μεθ' Ἑλένης.

VII. Ὁ δὲ Ὀδυσσεύς, ὡς μὲν ἔνιοι λέγουσιν,
ἐπλανᾶτο κατὰ Λιβύην, ὡς δὲ ἔνιοι κατὰ Σικελίαν,

---

[1] τὰς πάσας S: τὰς ὅλας E.
[2] προσσχὼν Σουνίῳ . . . Κύπρον καὶ Αἴγυπτον S: πολλὰς
χώρας παραμείψας E.   [3] τὴν ἰδίαν E: ἰδίαν S.
[4] Here the Vatican Epitome ends. What follows is found
in the Sabbaitic fragments alone.

Scholiast comments (*Orestes*, 1643–1647), Orestes is bidden
by Apollo to retire to Parrhasia, a district of Arcadia, for
the space of a year, after which he is to go and stand his
trial for the murder of his mother at Athens. This year to
be spent in Arcadia is no doubt the year of banishment to
which homicides had to submit before they were allowed to
resume social intercourse with their fellows. See above note
on ii. 5. 11 (vol. i. pp. 218 *sq.*). The period is so interpreted by
a Scholiast on Euripides (*Orestes*, 1645). As to Oresteum in
Arcadia, see Pausanias, viii. 3. 1 *sq.*, who says that it was
formerly called Oresthasium. A curious story of the madness
of Orestes in Arcadia is told by Pausanias (viii. 34. 1–4). He
says that, when the Furies were about to drive him mad, they
appeared to him black, but that he bit off one of his own

278

Menelaus, with five ships in all under his command, put in at Sunium, a headland of Attica; and being again driven thence by winds to Crete he drifted far away, and wandering up and down Libya, and Phoenicia, and Cyprus, and Egypt, he collected much treasure.[1] And according to some, he discovered Helen at the court of Proteus, king of Egypt; for till then Menelaus had only a phantom of her made of clouds.[2] And after wandering for eight years he came to port at Mycenae, and there found Orestes, who had avenged his father's murder. And having come to Sparta he regained his own kingdom,[3] and being made immortal by Hera he went to the Elysian Fields with Helen.[4]

VII. Ulysses, as some say, wandered about Libya, or, as some say, about Sicily, or, as others

fingers, whereupon they appeared to him white, and he immediately recovered his wits. The grave of Orestes was near Tegea in Arcadia; from there his bones were stolen by a Spartan and carried to Sparta in compliance with an oracle, which assured the Spartans of victory over their stubborn foes the Tegeans, if only they could get possession of these valuable relics. See Herodotus, i. 67 *sq.*; Pausanias, iii. 3. 5 *sq.*, iii. 11. 10, viii. 54. 3.

[1] For the wanderings of Menelaus on the voyage from Troy, see Homer, *Od.* iii. 276–302; compare Pausanias, x. 25. 2.

[2] As to the real and the phantom Helen, see above, *Epitome*, iii. 5, with the note.

[3] The return of Menelaus to his home was related by Hagias in the *Returns*, as we learn from the brief abstract of that poem by Proclus (*Epicorum Graecorum Fragmenta*, ed. G. Kinkel, p. 53).

[4] Homer in the *Odyssey* (iv. 561–569) represents Proteus prophesying to Menelaus that he was fated not to die but to be transported by the gods to the Elysian Fields, there to dwell at ease where there was neither snow, nor storm, or rain, because he had married Helen and was thereby a son-in-law of Zeus. Compare Euripides, *Helen*, 1676–1679.

APOLLODORUS

ὡς δὲ ἄλλοι κατὰ τὸν Ὠκεανὸν ἢ κατὰ τὸ Τυρρη-
νικὸν πέλαγος.

2 Ἀναχθεὶς δὲ ἀπὸ Ἰλίου προσίσχει πόλει Κικόνων Ἰσμάρῳ καὶ ταύτην αἱρεῖ πολεμῶν καὶ λαφυ-
ραγωγεῖ, μόνου φεισάμενος Μάρωνος, ὃς ἦν ἱερεὺς
Ἀπόλλωνος. αἰσθόμενοι δὲ οἱ τὴν ἤπειρον οἰ-
κοῦντες Κίκονες σὺν ὅπλοις ἐπ' αὐτὸν παραγίνονται·
ἀφ' ἑκάστης δὲ νεὼς ἐξ ἀποβαλὼν ἄνδρας ἀνα-
3 χθεὶς ἔφευγε. καὶ καταντᾷ εἰς τὴν Λωτοφάγων
χώραν καὶ πέμπει τινὰς [1] μαθησομένους τοὺς
κατοικοῦντας· οἱ δὲ γευσάμενοι τοῦ λωτοῦ κατέ-
μειναν· ἐφύετο γὰρ ἐν τῇ χώρᾳ καρπὸς ἡδὺς
λεγόμενος λωτός, ὃς τῷ γευσαμένῳ πάντων ἐποίει
λήθην. Ὀδυσσεὺς δὲ αἰσθόμενος, τοὺς λοιποὺς
κατασχών, τοὺς γευσαμένους μετὰ βίας ἐπὶ τὰς
ναῦς ἄγει, καὶ προσπλεύσας [2] τῇ Κυκλώπων γῇ
προσπελάζει.

4 Καταλιπὼν δὲ τὰς λοιπὰς ναῦς ἐν τῇ πλησίον
νήσῳ, μίαν ἔχων τῇ Κυκλώπων γῇ προσπελάζει,
μετὰ δώδεκα ἑταίρων ἀποβὰς τῆς νεώς. ἔστι δὲ
τῆς θαλάσσης πλησίον ἄντρον, εἰς ὃ ἔρχεται ἔχων

---

[1] τινὰς Wagner: τοὺς S.
[2] προσπλεύσας S. Wagner conjectures ἀποπλεύσας, which
would be better.

---

[1] As to the adventures of Ulysses with the Cicones, see
Homer, *Od.* ix. 39–66. The Cicones were a Thracian tribe ;
Xerxes and his army marched through their country (Herodotus, vii. 110). As to Maro, the priest of Apollo at Ismarus,
see Homer, *Od.* ix. 196–211. He dwelt in a wooded grove
of Apollo, and bestowed splendid presents and twelve jars of
red honey-sweet wine, in return for the protection which he
and his wife received at the hands of Ulysses.

[2] As to the adventures of Ulysses with the Lotus-eaters,
see Homer, *Od.* ix. 82–104 ; Hyginus, *Fab.* 125. The Lotus-

say, about the ocean or about the Tyrrhenian Sea.

And putting to sea from Ilium, he touched at Ismarus, a city of the Cicones, and captured it in war, and pillaged it, sparing Maro alone, who was priest of Apollo.[1] And when the Cicones who inhabited the mainland heard of it, they came in arms to withstand him, and having lost six men from each ship he put to sea and fled. And he landed in the country of the Lotus-eaters,[2] and sent some to learn who inhabited it, but they tasted of the lotus and remained there; for there grew in the country a sweet fruit called lotus, which caused him who tasted it to forget everything. When Ulysses was informed of this, he restrained the rest of his men, and dragged those who had tasted the lotus by force to the ships. And having sailed to the land of the Cyclopes, he stood in for the shore.

And having left the rest of the ships in the neighbouring island, he stood in for the land of the Cyclopes with a single ship, and landed with twelve companions.[3] And near the sea was a cave which he entered,

eaters were a tribe of northern Africa, inhabiting the coast of Tripolis (Scylax, *Periplus*, 110; Pliny, *Nat. Hist.* v. 28). As to the lotus, see Herodotus, iv. 177; Polybius, xii. 2. 1, quoted by Athenaeus, xiv. 65, p. 651 D–F; Theophrastus, *Hist. Plant.* iv. 3. 1 *sq.* The tree is the *Zizyphus Lotus* of the botanists. Theophrastus says that the tree was common in Libya, that is, in northern Africa, and that an army marching on Carthage subsisted on its fruit alone for several days. The modern name of the tree is *ssodr* or *ssidr*. A whole district in Tripolis is named *Ssodria* after it. See A. Wiedemann, *Herodots zweites Buch*, p. 385, note on Herodotus, ii. 96.

[3] As to the adventures of Ulysses and his companions among the Cyclopes, see Homer, *Od.* ix. 105–542; Hyginus, *Fab.* 125. The story is a folk-tale found in many lands. See Appendix, "Ulysses and Polyphemus."

ἀσκὸν οἴνου τὸν ὑπὸ Μάρωνος αὐτῷ δοθέντα.[1] ἦν
δὲ Πολυφήμου τὸ ἄντρον, ὃς ἦν Ποσειδῶνος καὶ
Θοώσης νύμφης, ἀνὴρ ὑπερμεγέθης ἄγριος ἀνδρο-
φάγος, ἔχων ἕνα ὀφθαλμὸν ἐπὶ τοῦ μετώπου.
5 ἀνακαύσαντες δὲ πῦρ καὶ τῶν ἐρίφων θύσαντες
εὐωχοῦντο. ἐλθὼν δὲ ὁ Κύκλωψ καὶ εἰσελάσας
τὰ ποίμνια τῇ μὲν θύρᾳ προσέθηκε πέτρον ὑπερ-
μεγέθη καὶ θεασάμενος αὐτοὺς ἐνίους κατήσθιεν.
6 Ὀδυσσεὺς δὲ αὐτῷ δίδωσιν ἐκ τοῦ Μάρωνος οἴνου
πιεῖν· ὁ δὲ πιὼν πάλιν ᾔτησε, καὶ πιὼν τὸ δεύτερον ἐπηρώτα τὸ ὄνομα. τοῦ δὲ εἰπόντος <ὅτι>[2]
Οὖτις καλεῖται, Οὖτιν ἠπείλει ὕστερον ἀναλῶσαι,
τοὺς δὲ ἄλλους ἔμπροσθεν, καὶ τοῦτο αὐτῷ ξένιον
ἀποδώσειν ὑπέσχετο. κατασχεθεὶς δὲ ὑπὸ μέθης
7 ἐκοιμήθη. Ὀδυσσεὺς δὲ εὑρὼν ῥόπαλον κείμενον
σὺν τέσσαρσιν ἑταίροις ἀπώξυνε[3] καὶ πυρώσας
ἐξετύφλωσεν αὐτόν. ἐπιβοωμένου δὲ Πολυφήμου
τοὺς πέριξ Κύκλωπας, παραγενόμενοι ἐπηρώτων
τίς αὐτὸν ἀδικεῖ. τοῦ δὲ εἰπόντος "Οὖτις," νομίσαντες αὐτὸν λέγειν "ὑπὸ μηδενὸς" ἀνεχώρησαν.
8 ἐπιζητούντων δὲ τῶν ποιμνίων τὴν συνήθη νομήν,
ἀνοίξας καὶ ἐπὶ τοῦ προθύρου στὰς τὰς χεῖρας
ἐκπετάσας ἐψηλάφα τὰ ποίμνια. Ὀδυσσεὺς δὲ
τρεῖς κριοὺς ὁμοῦ συνδέων . . . καὶ αὐτὸς τῷ μεί-
ζονι ὑποδύς, ὑπὸ τὴν γαστέρα κρυβείς, σὺν τοῖς
ποιμνίοις ἐξῆλθε, καὶ λύσας τοὺς ἑταίρους τῶν
ποιμνίων, ἐπὶ τὰς ναῦς ἐλάσας ἀποπλέων ἀνε-
βόησε Κύκλωπι ὡς Ὀδυσσεὺς εἴη καὶ ἐκπεφεύγοι[4]

---

[1] For τὸν . . . δοθέντα we should perhaps read τοῦ . . . δοθέντος, as Wagner suggests, since it was not the wine-skin
(ἄσκος), but the wine, which Maron gave to Ulysses. See
Homer, *Od.* ix. 196 *sq.*, 203–205.

taking with him the skin of wine that had been given him by Maro. Now the cave belonged to Polyphemus, who was a son of Poseidon and the nymph Thoösa, a huge, wild, cannibal man, with one eye on his forehead. And having lit a fire and sacrificed some of the kids, they feasted. But the Cyclops came, and when he had driven in his flocks, he put a huge stone to the door, and perceiving the men he ate some of them. But Ulysses gave him of Maro's wine to drink, and when he had drunk, he asked for another draught, and when he had drunk the second, he inquired his name; and when Ulysses said that he was called Nobody, he threatened to devour Nobody last and the others first, and that was the token of friendship which he promised to give him in return. And being overcome by wine, he fell asleep. But Ulysses found a club lying there, and with the help of four comrades he sharpened it, and, having heated it in the fire, he blinded him. And when Polyphemus cried to the Cyclopes round about for help, they came and asked who was hurting him, and when he said, "Nobody," they thought he meant that he was being hurt by nobody, and so they retired. And when the flocks sought their usual pasture, he opened the cave, and standing at the doorway spread out his hands and felt the sheep. But Ulysses tied three rams together, and himself getting under the bigger, and hiding under its belly, he passed out with the sheep. And having released his comrades from the sheep, he drove the animals to the ships, and sailing away shouted to the Cyclops that he was Ulysses and that he had escaped

---

2 ὅτι wanting in S, inserted by Bücheler.
3 ἀπώξυνε Kerameus: ἀπώξενε S.
4 ἐκπεφεύγοι Bücheler: ἐπιφεύγει S.

9 τὰς ἐκείνου χεῖρας. ἦν δὲ λόγιον Κύκλωπι εἰρη-
μένον ὑπὸ μάντεως τυφλωθῆναι ὑπὸ Ὀδυσσέως.
καὶ μαθὼν τὸ ὄνομα πέτρας ἀποσπῶν ἠκόντιζεν
εἰς τὴν θάλασσαν, μόλις δὲ ἡ ναῦς σῴζεται
πρὸς τὰς πέτρας. ἐκ τούτου δὲ μηνίει Ποσειδῶν
Ὀδυσσεῖ.

10 Ἀναχθεὶς δὲ συμπάσαις <ναυσὶ>[1] παραγίνεται
εἰς Αἰολίαν νῆσον, ἧς ὁ βασιλεὺς ἦν Αἴολος.
οὗτος ἐπιμελητὴς ὑπὸ Διὸς τῶν ἀνέμων καθεσ-
τήκει καὶ παύειν καὶ προΐεσθαι. ὃς ξενίσας Ὀδυσσέα δίδωσιν αὐτῷ ἀσκὸν βόειον, ἐν ᾧ κατέδησε
τοὺς ἀνέμους, ὑποδείξας οἷς δεῖ χρῆσθαι πλέοντα,
τοῦτον[2] ἐν τῷ σκάφει καταδήσας. ὁ δὲ Ὀδυσσεὺς
ἐπιτηδείοις ἀνέμοις χρώμενος εὐπλοεῖ, καὶ πλησίον
Ἰθάκης ὑπάρχων ἤδη τὸν ἀναφερόμενον ἐκ τῆς
11 πόλεως καπνὸν ἰδὼν ἐκοιμήθη. οἱ δὲ ἑταῖροι
νομίζοντες χρυσὸν ἐν τῷ ἀσκῷ κομίζειν αὐτόν,
λύσαντες τοὺς ἀνέμους ἐξαφῆκαν, καὶ πάλιν εἰς
τοὐπίσω παρεγένοντο ὑπὸ τῶν πνευμάτων ἁρπα-
σθέντες. Ὀδυσσεὺς δὲ ἀφικόμενος πρὸς Αἴολον
ἠξίου πομπῆς τυχεῖν, ὁ δὲ αὐτὸν ἐκβάλλει τῆς
νήσου λέγων ἀντιπρασσόντων τῶν θεῶν μὴ δύνασθαι σῴζειν.

12 Πλέων οὖν κατῆρε πρὸς Λαιστρυγόνας, καὶ . . .
τὴν ἑαυτοῦ ναῦν καθώρμισεν ἐσχάτως. Λαιστρυ-
γόνες δ᾽ ἦσαν ἀνδροφάγοι, καὶ αὐτῶν ἐβασίλευεν
Ἀντιφάτης. μαθεῖν οὖν Ὀδυσσεὺς βουλόμενος

---

[1] ναυσὶ conjectured by Kerameus, wanting in S.
[2] Perhaps we should read καὶ τοῦτον.

---

[1] As to the adventures of Ulysses with Aeolus, the Keeper
of the Winds, see Homer, *Od.* x. 1–76 ; Hyginus, *Fab.* 125 ;
Ovid, *Metamorph.* xiv. 223–232.

out of his hands. Now the Cyclops had been fore-warned by a soothsayer that he should be blinded by Ulysses; and when he learned the name, he tore away rocks and hurled them into the sea, and hardly did the ship evade the rocks. From that time Poseidon was wroth with Ulysses.

Having put to sea with all his ships, he came to the island of Aeolia, of which the king was Aeolus.[1] He was appointed by Zeus keeper of the winds, both to calm them and to send them forth. Having entertained Ulysses, he gave him an ox-hide bag in which he had bound fast the winds, after showing what winds to use on the voyage and binding fast the bag in the vessel. And by using suitable winds Ulysses had a prosperous voyage; and when he was near Ithaca and already saw the smoke rising from the town,[2] he fell asleep. But his comrades, thinking he carried gold in the bag, loosed it and let the winds go free, and being swept away by the blasts they were driven back again. And having come to Aeolus, Ulysses begged that he might be granted a fair wind; but Aeolus drove him from the island, saying that he could not save him when the gods opposed.

So sailing on he came to the land of the Laestry-gones,[3] and his own ship he moored last. Now the Laestrygones were cannibals, and their king was Antiphates. Wishing, therefore, to learn about the

[2] Homer says (*Od.* x. 30) they were so near land that they could already see the men tending the fires (πυρπολέοντας); but whether the fires were signals to guide the ship to port, or watch-fires of shepherds tending their flocks on the hills, does not appear.

[3] As to the adventures of Ulysses and his comrades among the Laestrygones, see Homer, *Od.* x. 80–132; Hyginus, *Fab.* 125; Ovid, *Metamorph.* xiv. 233–244.

τοὺς κατοικοῦντας ἔπεμψέ τινας πευσομένους.
τούτοις δὲ ἡ τοῦ βασιλέως θυγάτηρ συντυγχάνει
13 καὶ αὐτοὺς ἄγει πρὸς τὸν πατέρα. ὁ δὲ ἕνα μὲν
αὐτῶν ἁρπάσας ἀναλίσκει, τοὺς δὲ λοιποὺς ἐδίωκε
φεύγοντας κεκραγὼς καὶ συγκαλῶν τοὺς ἄλλους
Λαιστρυγόνας. οἱ δὲ ἦλθον ἐπὶ τὴν θάλασσαν
καὶ βάλλοντες πέτροις τὰ μὲν σκάφη κατέαξαν,
αὐτοὺς δὲ ἐβίβρωσκον. Ὀδυσσεὺς δὲ κόψας τὸ
πεῖσμα τῆς νεὼς ἀνήχθη, αἱ δὲ λοιπαὶ σὺν τοῖς
πλέουσιν ἀπώλοντο.
14 Μίαν δὲ ἔχων ναῦν Αἰαίῃ νήσῳ προσίσχει.
ταύτην κατῴκει Κίρκη, θυγάτηρ Ἡλίου καὶ Πέρ-
σης, Αἰήτου δὲ ἀδελφή, πάντων ἔμπειρος οὖσα
φαρμάκων. διελὼν[1] τοὺς ἑταίρους αὐτὸς μὲν
κλήρῳ μένει παρὰ τῇ νηί, Εὐρύλοχος δὲ πορεύεται
μεθ᾽ ἑταίρων[2] εἰκοσιδύο τὸν ἀριθμὸν πρὸς Κίρκην.
15 καλούσης δὲ αὐτῆς χωρὶς Εὐρυλόχου πάντες
εἰσίασιν. ἡ δ᾽ ἑκάστῳ κυκεῶνα πλήσασα τυροῦ
καὶ μέλιτος καὶ ἀλφίτων καὶ οἴνου δίδωσι, μίξασα
φαρμάκῳ. πιόντων δὲ αὐτῶν, ἐφαπτομένη ῥάβδῳ
τὰς μορφὰς ἠλλοίου, καὶ τοὺς μὲν ἐποίει λύκους,
τοὺς δὲ σῦς, τοὺς δὲ ὄνους, τοὺς δὲ λέοντας.
16 Εὐρύλοχος δὲ ἰδὼν ταῦτα Ὀδυσσεῖ ἀπαγγέλλει.

---

[1] Wagner conjectures διελὼν <δὲ>, which would be better.
[2] ἑταίρων Kerameus : ἑτέρων S.

---

[1] As to the adventures of Ulysses and his comrades with
the enchantress Circe, see Homer, *Od.* x. 133–574 ; Hyginus,
Fab. 125 ; Ovid, *Metamorph.* xiv. 246–440. The word (φάρμακα) here translated "enchantments" means primarily
drugs ; but in the early stages of medicine drugs were supposed to be endowed with magical potency, partly in virtue
of the spells, that is, the form of words, with which the

inhabitants, Ulysses sent some men to inquire. But the king's daughter met them and led them to her father. And he snatched up one of them and devoured him; but the rest fled, and he pursued them, shouting and calling together the rest of the Laestrygones. They came to the sea, and by throwing stones they broke the vessels and ate the men. Ulysses cut the cable of his ship and put to sea; but the rest of the ships perished with their crews.

With one ship he put in to the Aeaean isle. It was inhabited by Circe, a daughter of the Sun and of Perse, and a sister of Aeetes; skilled in all enchantments was she.[1] Having divided his comrades, Ulysses himself abode by the ship, in accordance with the lot, but Eurylochus with two and twenty comrades repaired to Circe. At her call they all entered except Eurylochus; and to each she gave a tankard she had filled with cheese and honey and barley meal and wine, and mixed with an enchantment. And when they had drunk, she touched them with a wand and changed their shapes, and some she made wolves, and some swine, and some asses, and some lions.[2] But Eurylochus saw these things and

medical practitioner administered them to the patient. Hence druggist and enchanter were nearly synonymous terms. As Circe used her knowledge of drugs purely for magical purposes, without any regard to the medical side of the profession, it seems better to translate her φάρμακα by "enchantments" or "charms" rather than "drugs," and to call her an enchantress instead of a druggist.

[2] In Homer (*Od.* x. 237 *sqq.*) the companions of Ulysses are turned into swine only; nothing is said about a transformation of them into wolves, lions, and asses, though round about the house of the enchantress they saw wolves and lions, which stood on their hind legs, wagged their tails, and fawned upon them, because they were men enchanted (*Od.* x. 210–219).

APOLLODORUS

ὁ δὲ λαβὼν μῶλυ παρὰ Ἑρμοῦ πρὸς Κίρκην
ἔρχεται, καὶ βαλὼν εἰς τὰ φάρμακα τὸ μῶλυ
μόνος πιὼν οὐ φαρμάσσεται· σπασάμενος δὲ τὸ
ξίφος ἤθελε[1] Κίρκην ἀποκτεῖναι. ἡ δὲ τὴν ὀργὴν
παύσασα τοὺς ἑταίρους ἀποκαθίστησι. καὶ λαβὼν
ὅρκους Ὀδυσσεὺς παρ' αὐτῆς μηδὲν ἀδικηθῆναι
συνευνάζεται, καὶ γίνεται αὐτῷ παῖς Τηλέγονος.

17 ἐνιαυτὸν δὲ μείνας ἐκεῖ, πλεύσας[2] τὸν Ὠκεανόν,
σφάγια[3] ταῖς ψυχαῖς ποιησάμενος μαντεύεται
παρὰ Τειρεσίου, Κίρκης ὑποθεμένης, καὶ θεωρεῖ
τάς τε τῶν ἡρώων ψυχὰς καὶ[4] τῶν ἡρωίδων.
βλέπει δὲ καὶ τὴν μητέρα Ἀντίκλειαν καὶ Ἐλπή-
νορα, ὃς ἐν τοῖς Κίρκης πεσὼν ἐτελεύτησε.

18 Παραγενόμενος δὲ πρὸς Κίρκην ὑπ' ἐκείνης
προπεμφθεὶς ἀνήχθη, καὶ τὴν νῆσον παρέπλει[5]

    [1] ἤθελε Bücheler : ἦλθε S.
    [2] Perhaps we should read πλεύσας <εἰς> τὸν Ὠκεανόν.
    [3] Wagner conjectured <καὶ> σφάγια.
    [4] Perhaps we should read καὶ τὰς.
    [5] παρέπλει Wagner : παραπλέει S.

---

[1] As to moly, see Homer, *Od.* x. 302–306. Homer says
that it was a plant dug up from the earth, with a black root
and a white flower. According to Theophrastus (*Hist. Plant.*
ix. 15. 7), moly resembled *Allium nigrum*, which was found
in the valley of Pheneus and on Mount Cyllene in northern
Arcadia ; he says it had a round root, like an onion, and a
leaf like a squill, and that it was used as an antidote to spells
and enchantments. But probably the moly of Homer grew
on no earthly hill or valley, but only in "fairyland forlorn."

[2] Telegonus is unknown to Homer, who mentions no offspring of Ulysses by the enchantress Circe. He is named
as a son of Ulysses and Circe by Hesiod in a line which is
suspected, however, of being spurious (*Theogony*, 1014). He
was recognized by Hagias in his epic, *The Returns*, and by
another Cyclic poet Eugammon of Cyrene ; indeed Eugammon
composed an epic called the *Telegony* on the adventures of
Telegonus, but according to him Telegonus was a son of

reported them to Ulysses. And Ulysses went to Circe
with moly,[1] which he had received from Hermes,
and throwing the moly among her enchantments, he
drank and alone was not enchanted. Then drawing
his sword, he would have killed her, but she appeased
his wrath and restored his comrades. And when he
had taken an oath of her that he should suffer no harm,
Ulysses shared her bed, and a son, Telegonus, was
born to him.[2] Having tarried a year there, he sailed
the ocean, and offered sacrifices to the souls,[3] and by
Circe's advice consulted the soothsayer Tiresias,[4] and
beheld the souls both of heroes and of heroines. He
also looked on his mother Anticlia[5] and Elpenor,
who had died of a fall in the house of Circe.[6]

And having come to Circe he was sent on his way
by her, and put to sea, and sailed past the isle of the

Ulysses by Calypso, not by Circe. See *Epicorum Graecorum
Fragmenta*, ed. G. Kinkel, pp. 56, 57 *sq.*; Eustathius on
Homer, *Od.* xvi. 118, p. 1796. According to Hyginus (*Fab.*
125), Ulysses had two sons, Nausithous and Telegonus, by
Circe. As to Telegonus, see also below, *Epitome*, vii. 36 *sq.*

[3] The visit of Ulysses to the land of the dead is the theme
of the eleventh book of the *Odyssey*. Compare Hyginus,
Fab. 125. The visit was the subject of one of the two great
pictures by Polygnotus at Delphi. See Pausanias, x. 28–31.

[4] As to the consultation with Tiresias, see Homer, *Od.* xi.
90–151.

[5] As to the interview of Ulysses with his mother, see
Homer, *Od.* xi. 153–224.

[6] In the hot air of Circe's enchanted isle Elpenor had
slept for coolness on the roof of the palace; then, suddenly wakened by the noise and bustle of his comrades
making ready to depart, he started up and, forgetting to
descend by the ladder, tumbled from the roof and broke his
neck. In his hurry to be off, Ulysses had not stayed to bury
his dead comrade; so the soul of Elpenor, unwept and unburied, was the first to meet his captain on the threshold of
the spirit land See Homer, *Od.* x. 552–560, xi. 51–83.

L 289

τῶν Σειρήνων. αἱ δὲ Σειρῆνες ἦσαν Ἀχελῴου
καὶ Μελπομένης μιᾶς τῶν Μουσῶν θυγατέρες,
Πεισινόη Ἀγλαόπη Θελξιέπεια. τούτων ἡ μὲν
ἐκιθάριζεν, ἡ δὲ ᾖδεν, ἡ δὲ ηὔλει, καὶ διὰ τούτων
19 ἔπειθον καταμένειν τοὺς παραπλέοντας. εἶχον δὲ
ἀπὸ τῶν μηρῶν ὀρνίθων μορφάς. ταύτας παρα-
πλέων Ὀδυσσεύς, τῆς ᾠδῆς βουλόμενος ὑπακοῦσαι,
Κίρκης ὑποθεμένης τῶν μὲν ἑταίρων τὰ ὦτα ἔβυσε
κηρῷ, ἑαυτὸν δὲ ἐκέλευσε προσδεθῆναι τῷ ἱστῷ.
πειθόμενος δὲ ὑπὸ τῶν Σειρήνων καταμένειν ἠξίου
λυθῆναι, οἱ δὲ μᾶλλον αὐτὸν ἐδέσμευον, καὶ οὕτω

---

[1] As to the return of Ulysses to the isle of Circe, and his sailing past the Sirens, see Homer, *Od.* xii. 1–200 ; Hyginus, *Fab.*
125. Homer does not name the Sirens individually nor mention their parentage, but by using the dual in reference to them
(verses 52, 167) he indicates that they were two in number.
Sophocles, in his play *Ulysses*, called the Sirens daughters of
Phorcus, and agreed with Homer in recognizing only two of
them. See Plutarch, *Quaest. Conviv.* ix. 14. 6 ; *The Fragments of Sophocles*, ed. A. C. Pearson, vol. iii. p. 66, frag.
861. Apollonius Rhodius says that the Muse Terpsichore
bore the Sirens to Achelous (*Argonaut.* iv. 895 *sq.*). Hyginus
names four of them, Teles, Raidne, Molpe, and Thelxiope
(*Fabulae, praefat.* p. 30, ed. Bunte), and, in agreement with
Apollodorus, says that they were the offspring of Achelous
by the Muse Melpomene. Tzetzes calls them Parthenope,
Leucosia, and Ligia, but adds that other people named them
Pisinoe, Aglaope, and Thelxiepia, and that they were the
children of Achelous and Terpsichore. With regard to the
parts which they took in the bewitching concert, he agrees
with Apollodorus. See Tzetzes, *Schol. on Lycophron*, 712.
According to a Scholiast on Apollonius Rhodius (*Argonaut.*
iv. 892), their names were Thelxiope, or Thelxione, Molpe,
and Aglaophonus. As to their names and parents see also
Eustathius on Homer, *Od.* xii. p. 1709, Scholiast on Homer,
Od. xii. 39, who mention the view that the father of the
Sirens was Achelous, and that their mother was either the
Muse Terpsichore, or Sterope, daughter of Porthaon.

Sirens.[1] Now the Sirens were Pisinoe, Aglaope, and Thelxiepia, daughters of Achelous and Melpomene, one of the Muses. One of them played the lyre, another sang, and another played the flute, and by these means they were fain to persuade passing mariners to linger; and from the thighs they had the forms of birds.[2] Sailing by them, Ulysses wished to hear their song, so by Circe's advice he stopped the ears of his comrades with wax, and ordered that he should himself be bound to the mast. And being persuaded by the Sirens to linger, he begged to be released, but they bound him the more, and so he

[2] Similarly Apollonius Rhodius (*Argon.* iv. 898 *sq.*) describes the Sirens as partly virgins and partly birds. Aelian tells us (*De natura animalium*, xvii. 23) that poets and painters represented them as winged maidens with the feet of birds. Ovid says that the Sirens had the feet and feathers of birds, but the faces of virgins; and he asks why these daughters of Achelous, as he calls them, had this hybrid form. Perhaps, he thinks, it was because they had been playing with Persephone when gloomy Dis carried her off, and they had begged the gods to grant them wings, that they might search for their lost playmate over seas as well as land. See Ovid, *Metamorph.* v. 552-562. In like manner Hyginus describes the Sirens as women above and fowls below, but he says that their wings and feathers were a punishment inflicted on them by Demeter for not rescuing Persephone from the clutches of Pluto. See Hyginus, *Fab.* 125, 141. Another story was that they were maidens whom Aphrodite turned into birds because they chose to remain unmarried. See Eustathius, on Homer, *Od.* xii. 47, p. 1709. It is said that they once vied with the Muses in singing, and that the Muses, being victorious, plucked off the Siren's feathers and made crowns out of them for themselves (Pausanias, ix. 34. 3). In ancient art, as in literature, the Sirens are commonly represented as women above and birds below. See Miss J. E. Harrison, *Myths of the Odyssey* (London, 1882), pp. 146 *sqq.* Homer says nothing as to the semi-bird shape of the Sirens, thus leaving us to infer that they were purely human.

παρέπλει. ἦν δὲ αὐταῖς¹ Σειρῆσι λόγιον τελευτῆσαι νεὼς² παρελθούσης. αἱ μὲν οὖν ἐτελεύτων.
20 Μετὰ δὲ τοῦτο παραγίνεται ἐπὶ δισσὰς ὁδούς.
ἔνθεν μὲν ἦσαν αἱ Πλαγκταὶ πέτραι, ἔνθεν δὲ
ὑπερμεγέθεις σκόπελοι δύο. ἦν δὲ ἐν μὲν θατέρῳ
Σκύλλα, Κραταιίδος θυγάτηρ καὶ † Τριήνου³ ἢ
Φόρκου, πρόσωπον ἔχουσα καὶ στέρνα γυναικός,
ἐκ λαγόνων δὲ κεφαλὰς ἓξ καὶ δώδεκα πόδας
21 κυνῶν. ἐν δὲ θατέρῳ [τῷ σκοπέλῳ] ἦν Χάρυβδις,
ἣ τῆς ἡμέρας τρὶς ἀνασπῶσα⁴ τὸ ὕδωρ πάλιν
ἀνίει. ὑποθεμένης δὲ Κίρκης, τὸν μὲν παρὰ τὰς
Πλαγκτὰς πλοῦν ἐφυλάξατο, παρὰ δὲ τὸν τῆς
Σκύλλης σκόπελον <πλέων>⁵ ἐπὶ τῆς πρύμνης
ἔστη καθωπλισμένος. ἐπιφανεῖσα δὲ ἡ Σκύλλα

---

¹ αὐταῖς S. Wagner conjectures αὖ ταῖς.

² νεὼς Wagner : νηὸς S.

³ Τριήνου S: Τυρρήνου Scholiast on Plato, *Republic*, ix.
p. 588 c. Bücheler conjectured Τριαίου or Τυφῶνος (compare
Hyginus, *Fab.*, p. 31, ed. Bunte): Wagner proposed Τρί-
τωνος, comparing Eustathius on Homer, *Od.* xii. 85, p. 1714.

⁴ τρὶς ἀνασπῶσα Wagner: τρίτον σπῶσα S: τρὶς σπῶσα
Kerameus.

⁵ σκόπελον <πλέων> ἐπὶ Wagner (conjecture): σκόπελον
ἐπὶ S.

---

¹ This is not mentioned by Homer, but is affirmed by
Hyginus (*Fab.* 125, 141). Others said that the Sirens cast
themselves into the sea and were drowned from sheer vexation at the escape of Ulysses. See Scholiast on Homer, *Od.*
xii. 39; Eustathius on Homer, *Od.* xii. 167, p. 1709; Tzetzes,
Schol. on Lycophron, 712; compare Strabo, vi. 1. 1, p. 252.

² As to Ulysses and the Wandering Rocks, see Homer,
Od. xii. 52–72, 201–221. The poet mentions (verses 70–72)
the former passage of the Argo between the Wandering or
Clashing Rocks, as to which see above i. 9. 22, with the
note. It has been suggested that in the story of the
Wandering Rocks we have a confused reminiscence of some

sailed past. Now it was predicted of the Sirens that they should themselves die when a ship should pass them; so die they did.[1]

And after that he came to two ways. On the one side were the Wandering Rocks,[2] and on the other side two huge cliffs, and in one of them was Scylla,[3] a daughter of Crataeis and Trienus or Phorcus,[4] with the face and breast of a woman, but from the flanks she had six heads and twelve feet of dogs. And in the other cliff was Charybdis, who thrice a day drew up the water and spouted it again. By the advice of Circe he shunned the passage by the Wandering Rocks, and in sailing past the cliff of Scylla he stood fully armed on the poop. But Scylla appeared, snatched

sailor's story of floating icebergs. See Merry, on Homer, *Od.* xii. 61.

[3] As to the passage of Ulysses between Scylla and Charybdis, see Homer, *Od.* xii. 73-126, 222-259; Hyginus, *Fab.* 125, 199.

[4] Homer mentions Crataeis as the mother of Scylla, but says nothing as to her father (*Od.* xii. 124 *sq.*). According to Stesichorus, the mother of Scylla was Lamia. See Scholiast on Homer, *Od.* xii. 124; Eustathius, on Homer, *Od.* xii. 85, p. 1714. Apollonius Rhodius represents Scylla as a daughter of Phorcus by the night-wandering hag Hecate (*Argonaut.* iv. 828 *sq.*), and this parentage had the support of Acusilaus, except that he named her father Phorcys instead of Phorcus (Scholiast on Apollonius Rhodius, *Argon.* iv. 828; compare Eustathius, *l.c.*). Hyginus calls her a daughter of Typhon and Echidna (*Fab.* 125, 151, and *praefat.* p. 31, ed. Bunte). A Scholiast on Plato (*Repub.* ix. p. 588 c), who may have copied the present passage of Apollodorus, calls Scylla a daughter of Crataeis and Tyrrhenus or Phorcus, adding that she had the face and breasts of a woman, but from the flanks six heads of dogs and twelve feet. Some said that the father of Scylla was Triton (Eustathius, *l.c.*); and perhaps the name Triton should be read instead of Trienus in the present passage of Apollodorus. See the Critical Note.

ἐξ ἑταίρους ἁρπάσασα τούτους κατεβίβρωσκεν.
22 ἐκεῖθεν δὲ ἐλθὼν εἰς Θρινακίαν νῆσον οὖσαν
Ἡλίου, ἔνθα βόες ἐβόσκοντο, καὶ ἀπλοίᾳ κατασχεθεὶς ἔμεινεν αὐτοῦ. τῶν δὲ ἑταίρων σφαξάν-
των ἐκ τῶν βοῶν καὶ θοινησαμένων, λειφθέντων[1]
τροφῆς, Ἥλιος ἐμήνυσε[2] Διί. καὶ ἀναχθέντα
23 κεραυνῷ ἔβαλε. λυθείσης δὲ τῆς νεὼς Ὀδυσσεὺς
τὸν ἱστὸν κατασχὼν παραγίνεται εἰς τὴν Χάρυβ-
διν. τῆς δὲ Χαρύβδεως καταπινούσης τὸν ἱστόν,
ἐπιλαβόμενος ὑπερπεφυκότος[3] ἐρινεοῦ περιέμεινε.
καὶ πάλιν ἀνεθέντα τὸν ἱστὸν θεωρήσας, ἐπὶ τοῦτον ῥίψας εἰς Ὠγυγίαν νῆσον διεκομίσθη.
24   Ἐκεῖ δὲ ἀποδέχεται Καλυψὼ θυγάτηρ Ἄτλαντος, καὶ συνευνασθεῖσα γεννᾷ παῖδα Λατῖνον.
μένει δὲ παρ' αὐτῇ πενταετίαν, καὶ σχεδίαν
ποιήσας ἀποπλεῖ. ταύτης δὲ ἐν τῷ πελάγει διαλυθείσης ὀργῇ Ποσειδῶνος, γυμνὸς πρὸς Φαίακας
25 ἐκβράσσεται. Ναυσικάα δέ, ἡ τοῦ βασιλέως
θυγάτηρ Ἀλκινόου, πλύνουσα τὴν ἐσθῆτα ἱκετεύ-
σαντα αὐτὸν ἄγει πρὸς Ἀλκίνοον, ὃς αὐτὸν ξενίζει

---

[1] λειφθέντων Kerameus : ληφθέντων S.
[2] ἐμήνυσε Kerameus : ἐμήνισε S.
[3] ὑπερπεφυκότος Kerameus : ὑπερφυκότος S.

---

[1] As to the adventures of Ulysses in Thrinacia, the island of the Sun, see Homer, Od. xii. 127–141, 260–402.
[2] See Homer, Od. xii. 403–425.
[3] See Homer, Od. xii. 426–450, compare v. 128–135.
[4] As to the stay of Ulysses with Calypso in the island of Ogygia, and his departure in a boat of his own building, see Homer, Od. v. 13–281, vii. 243–266; Hyginus, Fab. 125. According to Homer (Od. vii. 259), Ulysses stayed seven years with Calypso, not five years, as Apollodorus says. Hyginus limits the stay to one year. Homer does not mention that

six of his comrades, and gobbled them up. And
thence he came to Thrinacia, an island of the Sun,
where kine were grazing, and being windbound, he
tarried there.[1] But when his comrades slaughtered
some of the kine and banqueted on them, for lack
of food, the Sun reported it to Zeus, and when
Ulysses put out to sea, Zeus struck him with a
thunderbolt.[2] And when the ship broke up, Ulysses
clung to the mast and drifted to Charybdis. And
when Charybdis sucked down the mast, he clutched
an overhanging wild fig-tree and waited, and when
he saw the mast shot up again, he cast himself on it,
and was carried across to the island of Ogygia.[3]

There Calypso, daughter of Atlas, received him,
and bedding with him bore a son Latinus. He stayed
with her five years, and then made a raft and sailed
away.[4] But on the high sea the raft was broken in
pieces by the wrath of Poseidon, and Ulysses was
washed up naked on the shore of the Phaeacians.[5]
Now Nausicaa, the daughter of king Alcinous, was
washing the clothes, and when Ulysses implored
her protection, she brought him to Alcinous, who
entertained him, and after bestowing gifts on him

Calypso bore a son to Ulysses. In the *Theogony* of Hesiod
(verses 1111 *sqq.*) it is said that Circe (not Calypso), bore two
sons, Agrius and Latinus, to Ulysses; the verses, however,
are probably not by Hesiod but have been interpolated by a
later poet of the Roman era in order to provide the Latins
with a distinguished Greek ancestry. The verses are quoted
by the Scholiast on Apollonius Rhodius, *Argonaut.* iii. 200.
Compare Joannes Lydus, *De mensibus*, i. 13, p. 7, ed. Bekker.
Eustathius says (on Homer, *Od.* xvi. 118, p. 1796) that,
according to Hesiod, Ulysses had two sons, Agrius and
Latinus, by Circe, and two sons, Nausithous and Nausinous,
by Calypso.

[5] See Homer, *Od.* v. 282-493; Hyginus *Fab.* 125.

καὶ δῶρα δοὺς μετὰ πομπῆς αὐτὸν εἰς τὴν πατρίδα
ἐξέπεμψε. Ποσειδῶν δὲ Φαίαξι μηνίσας τὴν μὲν
ναῦν ἀπελίθωσε, τὴν δὲ πόλιν ὄρει περικαλύπτει.

26 Ὀδυσσεὺς δὲ παραγενόμενος εἰς τὴν πατρίδα
εὑρίσκει τὸν οἶκον διεφθαρμένον· νομίσαντες γὰρ
αὐτὸν τεθνάναι Πηνελόπην ἐμνῶντο ἐκ Δουλιχίου
27 μὲν νζ΄· Ἀμφίνομος Θόας Δημοπτόλεμος Ἀμφίμαχος Εὐρύαλος, Πάραλος Εὐηνορίδης Κλυτίος
Ἀγήνωρ Εὐρύπυλος, Πυλαιμένης [1] Ἀκάμας Θερ-
σίλοχος Ἅγιος Κλύμενος, Φιλόδημος Μενε-
πτόλεμος Δαμάστωρ Βίας Τέλμιος, Πολύϊδος
Ἀστύλοχος Σχεδίος Ἀντίγονος [2] Μάρψιος, Ἰφι-
δάμας Ἀργεῖος Γλαῦκος Καλυδωνεὺς Ἐχίων,
Λάμας Ἀνδραίμων Ἀγέρωχος Μέδων Ἄγριος,
Πρόμος Κτήσιος Ἀκαρνὰν Κύκνος Ψηρᾶς, Ἑλλά-
νικος Περίφρων Μεγασθένης Θρασυμήδης Ὀρμέ-
νιος, Διοπίθης Μηκιστεὺς Ἀντίμαχος Πτολεμαῖος
28 Λεστορίδης,[3] Νικόμαχος Πολυποίτης Κεραός. ἐκ
δὲ Σάμης κγ΄· Ἀγέλαος Πείσανδρος Ἔλατος
Κτήσιππος Ἱππόδοχος, Εὐρύστρατος Ἀρχέμολος [4]
Ἴθακος Πεισήνωρ Ὑπερήνωρ, Φεροίτης [5] Ἀντι-
σθένης Κέρβερος Περιμήδης Κύννος, Θρίασος
Ἐτεωνεὺς Κλυτίος Πρόθοος Λύκαιθος,[6] Εὔμηλος
29 Ἴτανος[7] Λύαμμος. ἐκ δὲ Ζακύνθου μδ΄· Εὐρύ-

---

[1] Πυλαιμένης Kerameus : Παλαιμένης S.
[2] Ἀντίγονος Kerameus : Ἀνήγονος S.
[3] Kerameus conjectured Νεστορίδης : Wagner Θεστορίδης.
[4] Kerameus conjectured Ἀρχέμορος or Ἀρχέμαχος.
[5] Kerameus conjectured Φιλοίτιος.
[6] Λύκαιθος Kerameus : Λυκάεθος S.
[7] Bücheler conjectured Ἴταμος.

---

[1] See Homer, *Od.* vi., vii., viii., xii. 1–124 ; Hyginus,
Fab. 125.
[2] See Homer, *Od.* xii. 125–187. "Poseidon does not pro-

sent him away with a convoy to his native land.[1]
But Poseidon was wroth with the Phaeacians, and
he turned the ship to stone and enveloped the city
with a mountain.[2]

And on arriving in his native land Ulysses found
his substance wasted; for, believing that he was dead,
suitors were wooing Penelope.[3] From Dulichium
came fifty-seven:—Amphinomus, Thoas, Demopto-
lemus, Amphimachus, Euryalus, Paralus, Evenorides,
Clytius, Agenor, Eurypylus, Pylaemenes, Acamas,
Thersilochus, Hagius, Clymenus, Philodemus, Me-
neptolemus, Damastor, Bias, Telmius, Polyidus, Astylochus, Schedius, Antigonus, Marpsius, Iphidamas,
Argius, Glaucus, Calydoneus, Echion, Lamas, An-
draemon, Agerochus, Medon, Agrius, Promus, Ctesius,
Acarnan, Cycnus, Pseras, Hellanicus, Periphron,
Megasthenes, Thrasymedes, Ormenius, Diopithes,
Mecisteus, Antimachus, Ptolemaeus, Lestorides, Ni-
comachus, Polypoetes, and Ceraus. And from Same
there came twenty-three:—Agelaus, Pisander, Elatus,
Ctesippus, Hippodochus, Eurystratus, Archemolus,
Ithacus, Pisenor, Hyperenor, Pheroetes, Antisthenes,
Cerberus, Perimedes, Cynnus, Thriasus, Eteoneus,
Clytius, Prothous, Lycaethus, Eumelus, Itanus,
Lyammus. And from Zacynthos came forty-four:—

pose to bury the city, but to shut it off from the use of its
two harbours (cp. *Od.* vi. 263) by some great mountain mass"
(Merry, on verse 152).

[3] The number of the suitors, according to Homer, was one
hundred and eight, namely, fifty-two from Dulichium, twenty-
four from Same, twenty from Zacynthus, and twelve from
Ithaca. See Homer, *Od.* xvi. 245–253. Apollodorus gives
the numbers from these islands as fifty-seven, twenty-three,
forty-four, and twelve respectively, or a hundred and thirty-
six in all. Homer does not give a regular list of the names,
but mentions some of them incidentally.

λοχος Λαομήδης Μόλεβος[1] Φρένιος Ἴνδιος, Μίνις[2]
Λειώκριτος[3] Πρόνομος Νίσας Δαήμων, Ἀρχέστρατος[4] Ἱππό[μαχος Εὐρύαλος Περίαλλος
Εὐηνορίδης, Κλυτίος Ἀγήνωρ] Πόλυβος Πολύ-
δωρος Θαδύτιος,[5] Στράτιος [Φρένιος Ἴνδιος]
Δαισήνωρ Λαομέδων, Λαόδικος Ἅλιος Μάγνης
Ὀλοίτροχος[6] Βάρθας, Θεόφρων Νισσαῖος Ἀλκά-
ροψ Περικλύμενος Ἀντήνωρ, Πέλλας Κέλτος
30 Περίφας Ὄρμενος Πόλυβος, Ἀνδρομήδης. ἐκ δὲ
αὐτῆς Ἰθάκης ἦσαν οἱ μνηστευόμενοι ιβʹ οἵδε·
Ἀντίνοος Πρόνοος Λειώδης Εὐρύνομος Ἀμφίμαχος, Ἀμφίαλος Πρόμαχος Ἀμφιμέδων Ἀρί-
στρατος Ἕλενος, Δουλιχιεὺς Κτήσιππος.

31 Οὗτοι πορευόμενοι εἰς τὰ βασίλεια δαπανῶντες
τὰς Ὀδυσσέως ἀγέλας εὐωχοῦντο. Πηνελόπη δὲ
ἀναγκαζομένη τὸν γάμον ὑπέσχετο ὅτε τὸ ἐντάφιον
Λαέρτῃ πέρας ἕξει, καὶ τοῦτο ὕφηνεν ἐπὶ ἔτη τρία,
μεθ᾽ ἡμέραν μὲν ὑφαίνουσα, νύκτωρ δὲ ἀναλύουσα.
τοῦτον τὸν τρόπον ἐξηπατῶντο οἱ μνηστῆρες ὑπὸ
32 τῆς Πηνελόπης, μέχρις ὅτε ἐφωράθη. Ὀδυσσεὺς
δὲ μαθὼν τὰ κατὰ τὴν οἰκίαν, ὡς ἐπαίτης πρὸς
Εὔμαιον οἰκέτην ἀφικνεῖται, καὶ Τηλεμάχῳ ἀναγνωρίζεται, καὶ παραγίνεται εἰς τὴν πόλιν. Με-
λάνθιος δὲ αὐτοῖς συντυχὼν ὁ αἰπόλος οἰκέτης
ὑπάρχων ἀτιμάζει. παραγενόμενος δὲ εἰς τὰ
βασίλεια τοὺς μνηστῆρας μετῄτει τροφήν, καὶ

---

[1] Bücheler conjectured Μούλιος.
[2] Kerameus conjectured Μύνης.
[3] Λειώκριτος Wagner (comparing Homer, Od. ii. 242):
Λαόκριτος S.
[4] Ἀρχέστρατος Kerameus : Ἀρχέστατος S.
[5] Bücheler conjectured Θαλύτιος.
[6] Ὀλοίτροχος Bücheler : Ὀλοίροχος S.

Eurylochus, Laomedes, Molebus, Phrenius, Indius, Minis, Liocritus, Pronomus, Nisas, Daëmon, Archestratus, Hippomachus, Euryalus, Periallus, Evenorides, Clytius, Agenor, Polybus, Polydorus, Thadytius, Stratius, Phrenius, Indius, Daesenor, Laomedon, Laodicus, Halius, Magnes, Oloetrochus, Barthas, Theophron, Nissaeus, Alcarops, Periclymenus, Antenor, Pellas, Celtus, Periphas, Ormenus, Polybus and Andromedes. And from Ithaca itself the suitors were twelve, to wit:—Antinous, Pronous, Liodes, Eurynomus, Amphimachus, Amphialus, Promachus, Amphimedon, Aristratus, Helenus, Dulicheus, and Ctesippus.

These, journeying to the palace, consumed the herds of Ulysses at their feasts.[1] And Penelope was compelled to promise that she would wed when the shroud of Laertes was finished, and she wove it for three years, weaving it by day and undoing it by night. In this way the suitors were deceived by Penelope, till she was detected.[2] And Ulysses, being apprized of the state of things at home, came to his servant Eumaeus in the guise of a beggar,[3] and made himself known to Telemachus,[4] and arrived in the city. And Melanthius, the goatherd, a servant man, met them, and scorned them.[5] On coming to the palace Ulysses begged food of the suitors,[6] and

---

[1] As to the reckless waste of the suitors, see Homer, *Od.* xiv. 80–109.

[2] As to Penelope's web, see Homer, *Od.* xix. 136–158; Hyginus, *Fab.* 126.

[3] As to the meeting of Ulysses and Eumaeus, see Homer, *Od.* xiv. 1–492; Hyginus, *Fab.* 126.

[4] As to the meeting and recognition of Ulysses and Telemachus, see Homer, *Od.* xvi. 1–234.

[5] See Homer, *Od.* xvii. 184–253.

[6] See Homer, *Od.* xvii. 360–457.

εὑρὼν μεταίτην Ἶρον καλούμενον διαπαλαίει αὐτῷ.
Εὐμαίῳ δὲ μηνύσας ἑαυτὸν καὶ Φιλοιτίῳ,¹ μετὰ
τούτων ² καὶ Τηλεμάχου τοῖς μνηστῆρσιν ἐπιβου-
33 λεύει. Πηνελόπη δὲ τοῖς μνηστῆρσι τίθησιν
Ὀδυσσέως τόξον, ὃ παρὰ Ἰφίτου ποτὲ ἔλαβε, καὶ
τῷ τοῦτο τείναντί φησι συνοικήσειν. μηδενὸς δὲ
τεῖναι δυναμένου, δεξάμενος Ὀδυσσεὺς τοὺς μνηστῆρας κατετόξευσε σὺν Εὐμαίῳ καὶ Φιλοιτίῳ
καὶ Τηλεμάχῳ. ἀνεῖλε δὲ καὶ Μελάνθιον καὶ τὰς
συνευναζομένας τοῖς μνηστῆρσι θεραπαίνας, καὶ
τῇ γυναικὶ καὶ τῷ πατρὶ ἀναγνωρίζεται.
34 Θύσας δὲ Ἅιδῃ καὶ Περσεφόνῃ καὶ Τειρεσίᾳ,
πεζῇ διὰ τῆς Ἠπείρου βαδίζων εἰς Θεσπρωτοὺς
παραγίνεται καὶ κατὰ τὰς Τειρεσίου μαντείας
θυσιάσας ἐξιλάσκεται Ποσειδῶνα. ἡ δὲ βασιλεύ-

¹ καὶ Φιλοιτίῳ Kerameus : καὶ τῷ παιδὶ Φιλοιτίου S.
² τούτων Frazer : τούτου S. Eumaeus as well as Philoetius
was privy to the plot, as we know from Homer (Od. xxi.
188–244) and as Apollodorus himself recognizes a few lines
below.

¹ See Homer, Od. xviii. 1–107; Hyginus, Fab. 126. In
Homer it is in a boxing-match, not in a wrestling-bout, that
Ulysses vanquishes the braggart beggar Irus. Hyginus, like
Apollodorus, substitutes wrestling for boxing.
² See Homer, Od. xxi. 188–244.
³ See Homer, Od. xxi. 1–82; Hyginus, Fab. 126.
⁴ See Homer, Od. xxi. 140–434, xxii. 1–389; Hyginus,
Fab. 126.
⁵ See Homer, Od. xxii. 417–477.
⁶ See Homer, Od. xxiii. 153–297, xxiv. 205–348.
⁷ Tiresias had warned Ulysses that, after slaying the
suitors, he must journey inland till he came to a country
where men knew not the sea, and where a wayfarer would
mistake for a winnowing-fan the oar which Ulysses was
carrying on his shoulder. There Ulysses was to sacrifice a
ram, a bull, and a boar to Poseidon, the god whom he had

finding a beggar called Irus he wrestled with him.[1]
But he revealed himself to Eumaeus and Philoetius,
and along with them and Telemachus he laid a plot
for the suitors.[2] Now Penelope delivered to the
suitors the bow of Ulysses, which he had once received
from Iphitus; and she said that she would marry him
who bent the bow.[3] When none of them could bend
it, Ulysses took it and shot down the suitors, with
the help of Eumaeus, Philoetius, and Telemachus.[4]
He killed also Melanthius, and the handmaids that
bedded with the suitors,[5] and he made himself known
to his wife and his father.[6]

And after sacrificing to Hades, and Persephone,
and Tiresias, he journeyed on foot through Epirus,
and came to the Thesprotians, and having offered
sacrifice according to the directions of the soothsayer
Tiresias, he propitiated Poseidon.[7]   But Callidice,

offended. See Homer, *Od.* xi. 119–131. But the journey
itself and the sacrifice are not recorded by Homer. In a
little island off Cos a Greek skipper told Dr. W. H. D. Rouse
a similar story about the journey inland of the prophet Elias.
The prophet, according to this account, was a fisherman who,
long buffeted by storms, conceived a horror of the sea, and,
putting an oar on his shoulder, took to the hills and walked
till he met a man who did not know what an oar was. There
the prophet planted his oar in the ground, and there he
resolved to abide. That is why all the prophet's chapels are
on the tops of hills. This legend was published by Dr. Rouse
in *The Cambridge Review* under the heading of "A Greek
skipper."

    This and the remaining part of Apollodorus are probably
drawn from the epic poem *Telegony*, a work by Eugammon of
Cyrene, of which a short abstract by Proclus has been preserved. See *Epicorum Graecorum Fragmenta*, ed. G. Kinkel,
pp. 57 *sq.* The author of the abstract informs us that after
the death and burial of the suitors "Ulysses sacrificed to
the nymphs and sailed to Elis to inspect the herds. And
he was entertained by Polyxenus and received a present of a

ουσα τότε Θεσπρωτῶν Καλλιδίκη καταμένειν
35 αὐτὸν ἠξίου τὴν βασιλείαν αὐτῷ δοῦσα.[1] καὶ
συνελθοῦσα αὐτῷ γεννᾷ Πολυποίτην. γήμας δὲ
Καλλιδίκην Θεσπρωτῶν ἐβασίλευσε καὶ μάχῃ τῶν
περιοίκων νικᾷ τοὺς ἐπιστρατεύσαντας. Καλλι-
δίκης δὲ ἀποθανούσης, τῷ παιδὶ τὴν βασιλείαν
ἀποδιδοὺς εἰς Ἰθάκην παραγίνεται, καὶ εὑρίσκει
ἐκ Πηνελόπης Πολιπόρθην αὐτῷ γεγεννημένον.[2]
36 Τηλέγονος δὲ παρὰ Κίρκης μαθὼν ὅτι παῖς Ὀδυσσέως ἐστίν, ἐπὶ τὴν τούτου ζήτησιν ἐκπλεῖ. παραγενόμενος δὲ εἰς Ἰθάκην τὴν νῆσον ἀπελαύνει[3]
τινὰ τῶν βοσκημάτων, καὶ Ὀδυσσέα βοηθοῦντα
τῷ μετὰ χεῖρας δόρατι Τηλέγονος <τρυγόνος>[4]
κέντρον τὴν αἰχμὴν ἔχοντι τιτρώσκει, καὶ Ὀδυσ-
37 σεὺς θνήσκει. ἀναγνωρισάμενος δὲ αὐτὸν καὶ

---

[1] Bücheler conjectured διδοῦσα.
[2] γεγεννημένον Wagner (comparing Pausanias, viii. 12. 6): γεγεννημένην S: γεγεννημένην Kerameus.
[3] ἀπελαύνει Bücheler: ἀπέλαυε S.
[4] <τρυγόνος> inserted by Bücheler.

---

bowl. And after that followed the episodes of Trophonius, and Agamedes, and Augeas. Then he sailed home to Ithaca and offered the sacrifices prescribed by Tiresias. And after these things he went to the Thesprotians and married Callidice, queen of the Thesprotians. Then the Thesprotians made war on the Brygians, under the leadership of Ulysses. There Ares put Ulysses and his people to flight, and Athena engaged him in battle; but Apollo reconciled them. And after Callidice's death, Polypoetes, son of Ulysses, succeeded to the kingdom, and Ulysses himself went to Ithaca. Meanwhile Telegonus, sailing in search of his father, landed in Ithaca and ravaged the island; and marching out to repel him Ulysses was killed by his son in ignorance. Recognizing his error, Telegonus transported his father's body, and Telemachus, and Penelope to his mother, and she made them

who was then queen of the Thesprotians, urged him to stay and offered him the kingdom; and she had by him a son Polypoetes. And having married Callidice, he reigned over the Thesprotians, and defeated in battle the neighbouring peoples who attacked him. But when Callidice died he handed over the kingdom to his son and repaired to Ithaca, and there he found Poliporthes, whom Penelope had borne to him.[1] When Telegonus learned from Circe that he was a son of Ulysses, he sailed in search of him. And having come to the island of Ithaca, he drove away some of the cattle, and when Ulysses defended them, Telegonus wounded him with the spear he had in his hands, which was barbed with the spine of a stingray, and Ulysses died of the wound.[2] But when

immortal. And Telegonus married Penelope, and Telemachus married Circe." The tradition, mentioned also by Hyginus (*Fab.* 127), that one son of Ulysses (Telegonus) married his father's widow (Penelope), and that another son (Telemachus) married his father's concubine (Circe), is very remarkable, and may possibly point to an old custom according to which a son inherited his father's wives and concubines, with the exception of his own mother. Compare Apollodorus, ii. 7. 7, with the note (vol. i. p. 269). Apollodorus mentions the marriage of Telegonus to Penelope (see below), but not the marriage of Telemachus to Circe.

[1] Compare Pausanias, viii. 12. 6, from whom we learn that the birth of this son Poliporthes or Ptoliporthes, as Pausanias calls him, was mentioned in the epic poem *Thesprotis*.

[2] Compare Oppian, *Halieut.* ii. 497–500: *Scholia Graeca in Homeri Odysseam*, ed. G. Dindorf, vol. i. p. 6; Scholiast on Homer, *Od.* xi. 134; Eustathius on Homer, *Od.* xi. 133, p. 1676; Philostratus, *Vit. Apollon.* vi. 32; *id. Heroica*, iii. 42; Parthenius, *Narrat. Amat.* 3; Tzetzes, *Schol. on Lycophron*, 794; Scholiast on Aristophanes, *Plutus*, 303; Cicero, *Tusculan. Disput.* ii. 21. 48 *sq.*; Horace, *Odes*, iii. 29. 8; Hyginus, *Fab.* 127; Ovid, *Ibis*, 567 *sq.*; Dictys Cretensis, *Bellum Trojanum*, vi. 14 *sq.*; Servius, on Virgil, *Aen.*

πολλὰ κατοδυράμενος, τὸν νεκρὸν <καὶ>[1] τὴν
Πηνελόπην πρὸς Κίρκην ἄγει, κἀκεῖ τὴν Πηνελόπην γαμεῖ. Κίρκη δὲ ἑκατέρους αὐτοὺς εἰς Μακάρων νήσους ἀποστέλλει.

38 Τινὲς δὲ Πηνελόπην ὑπὸ Ἀντινόου φθαρεῖσαν
λέγουσιν ὑπὸ Ὀδυσσέως πρὸς τὸν πατέρα Ἰκάριον
ἀποσταλῆναι, γενομένην[2] δὲ τῆς Ἀρκαδίας κατὰ
39 Μαντίνειαν ἐξ Ἑρμοῦ τεκεῖν Πᾶνα· ἄλλοι δὲ δι'
Ἀμφίνομον ὑπὸ Ὀδυσσέως αὐτοῦ[3] τελευτῆσαι·
διαφθαρῆναι γὰρ αὐτὴν ὑπὸ τούτου λέγουσιν.
40 εἰσὶ δὲ οἱ λέγοντες ἐγκαλούμενον Ὀδυσσέα ὑπὸ
τῶν οἰκείων ὑπὲρ τῶν ἀπολωλότων δικαστὴν

---

[1] <καὶ> inserted by Wagner (comparing the *Telegonia*;
see *Epicorum Graecorum Fragmenta*, ed. G. Kinkel, p. 58).
[2] γενομένην Bücheler : γενομένης S.
[3] αὐτοῦ Bücheler : αὐτὸν S.

---

ii. 44. The fish (τρυγών), whose spine is said to have barbed the
fatal spear, is the common sting-ray (*Trygon pastinaca*), as I
learn from Professor D'Arcy Wentworth Thompson, who informs me that the fish is abundant in the Mediterranean and
not uncommon on our southern coasts. For ancient descrip-
tions of the fish he refers me to Oppian, *Halieut.* ii. 470 *sqq.*
(the *locus classicus*) ; Aelian, *Nat. Anim.* i. 56 ; Nicander,
Ther. 828 *sqq.* According to Aelian, the wound inflicted by the
sting-ray is incurable. Hercules is said to have lost one of his
fingers by the bite of a sting-ray (Ptolemy Hephaest., *Nov.Hist.*
ii. in Westermann's *Mythographi Graeci*, p. 184). Classical
scholars, following Liddell and Scott, sometimes erroneously
identify the fish with the roach. The death of Ulysses through
the wound of a sting-ray is foreshadowed in the prophecy of
Tiresias that his death would come from the sea (Homer,
Od. xi. 134 *sq.*). According to a Scholiast on Homer (*Scholia
Graeca in Homeri Odysseam*, ed. G. Dindorf, vol. i. p. 6),
Hyginus, and Dictys Cretensis, Ulysses had been warned by
an oracle or a dream to beware of his son, who would kill
him ; accordingly, fearing to be slain by Telemachus, he
banished him to Cephallenia (Dictys Cretensis, vi. 14). But

Telegonus recognized him, he bitterly lamented, and conveyed the corpse and Penelope to Circe, and there he married Penelope. And Circe sent them both away to the Islands of the Blest.

But some say that Penelope was seduced by Antinous and sent away by Ulysses to her father Icarius, and that when she came to Mantinea in Arcadia she bore Pan to Hermes.[1] However others say that she met her end at the hands of Ulysses himself on account of Amphinomus,[2] for they allege that she was seduced by him. And there are some who say that Ulysses, being accused by the kinsfolk of the slain, submitted the case to the judgment of

he forgot his son Telegonus, whom he had left behind with his mother Circe in her enchanted island. The death of Ulysses at the hands of his son Telegonus was the subject of a tragedy by Sophocles. See *The Fragments of Sophocles*, ed. A. C. Pearson, vol. ii. pp. 105 *sqq.*

[1] A high mound of earth was shown as the grave of Penelope at Mantinea in Arcadia. According to the Mantinean story, Ulysses had found her unfaithful and banished her the house; so she went first to her native Sparta, and afterwards to Mantinea, where she died and was buried. See Pausanias, viii. 12. 5 *sq.* The tradition that Penelope was the mother of Pan by Hermes (Mercury) is mentioned by Cicero (*De natura deorum*, iii. 22. 56). According to Duris, the Samian, Penelope was the mother of Pan by all the suitors (Tzetzes, *Schol. on Lycophron*, 772). The same story is mentioned also by Servius (on Virgil, *Aen.* ii. 44), who says that Penelope was supposed to have given birth to Pan during her husband's absence, and that when Ulysses came home and found the monstrous infant in the house, he fled and set out afresh on his wanderings.

[2] Amphinomus was one of the suitors of Penelope; his words pleased her more than those of the other suitors, because he had a good understanding. See Homer, *Od.* xvi. 394–398. He was afterwards killed by Telemachus (Homer, *Od.* xxii. 89 *sqq.*). The suspicion that Penelope was unfaithful to her husband has no support in Homer.

APOLLODORUS

Νεοπτόλεμον λαβεῖν τὸν βασιλεύοντα τῶν κατὰ
τὴν Ἤπειρον νήσων, τοῦτον δέ, νομίσαντα ἐκπο-
δὼν Ὀδυσσέως γενομένου Κεφαλληνίαν καθέξειν,
κατακρῖναι φυγὴν αὐτοῦ, Ὀδυσσέα δὲ εἰς Αἰτωλίαν
πρὸς Θόαντα[1] τὸν Ἀνδραίμονος παραγενόμενον
τὴν τούτου θυγατέρα γῆμαι, καὶ καταλιπόντα
παῖδα Λεοντοφόνον ἐκ ταύτης γηραιὸν τελευτῆσαι.

[1] Θόαντα Kerameus : θόεντα S.

---

[1] Compare Plutarch, *Quaestiones Graecae*, 14. According
to Plutarch's account, the kinsmen of the slain suitors rose
in revolt against Ulysses; but Neoptolemus, being invited
by both parties to act as arbitrator, sentenced Ulysses to
banishment for bloodshed, and condemned the friends and
relatives of the suitors to pay an annual compensation to

Neoptolemus, king of the islands off Epirus; that Neoptolemus, thinking to get possession of Cephallenia if once Ulysses were put out of the way, condemned him to exile;[1] and that Ulysses went to Aetolia, to Thoas, son of Andraemon, married the daughter of Thoas, and leaving a son Leontophonus, whom he had by her,[2] died in old age.

Ulysses for the damage they had done to his property. The sentence obliged Ulysses to withdraw not only from Ithaca, but also from Cephallenia and Zacynthus; and he retired to Italy. The compensation exacted from the heirs of the suitors was paid in kind, and consisted of barley groats, wine, honey, olive oil, and animal victims of mature age. This payment Ulysses ordered to be made to his son Telemachus.

[2] These last recorded doings of Ulysses appear to be mentioned by no other ancient writer.

APPENDIX

APPENDIX

I.—PUTTING CHILDREN ON THE FIRE

(*Apollodorus* I. v. 1)

THE story that Demeter put the infant son of Celeus on the fire to make him immortal is told by other ancient writers as well as by Apollodorus,[1] and while there is a general resemblance between the various versions of the legend, there are some discrepancies in detail. Thus, with regard to the child's parents, Apollodorus and Ovid agree with the Homeric hymn-writer in calling them Celeus and Metanira. But Hyginus calls them Eleusinus and Cothonea; while Servius in one passage [2] names them Eleusinus and Cyntinia, and in another passage [3] calls the father Celeus. Lactantius Placidus names them Eleusius and Hioma; and the Second Vatican Mythographer calls them Celeus and Hiona. Then, with regard to the child who was put on the fire, Apollodorus agrees with the Homeric hymn-writer in calling him Demophon and in distinguishing him from his elder brother Triptolemus. But Ovid, Hyginus, Servius, Lactantius Placidus, and the First Vatican Mythographer call the child who was put on the fire Triptolemus, and make no mention of Demophon. The Second Vatican Mythographer wavers on this point; for, after saying [4] that Demeter received the child Triptolemus to nurse, he proceeds [5] to name the child

---

[1] See *Homeric Hymn to Demeter*, 231–274; Ovid, *Fasti*, iv. 549–562; Hyginus, *Fab.* 147; Servius, on Virgil, *Georg.* i. 19 and 163; Lactantius Placidus, on Statius, *Theb.* ii. 382; *Scriptores rerum mythicarum Latini*, ed. G. H. Bode, vol. i. pp. 3, 107 (First Vatican Mythographer, 8; Second Vatican Mythographer, 96 *sq.*).

[2] On *Georg.* i. 19.   [3] On *Georg.* i. 163.

[4] *Fab.* 96.   [5] *Fab.* 97.

who was put on the fire Eleusius. As to the fate of the child who was put on the fire, the Homeric hymn-writer merely says that Demeter, angry at being interrupted, threw him on the ground ; whether he lived or died the author does not mention. Apollodorus definitely affirms that the child was consumed in the fire ; and the Second Vatican Mythographer says that Demeter in her rage killed it. On the other hand, the writers who call the child Triptolemus naturally do not countenance the belief that he perished in the fire, for they record the glorious mission on which he was sent by Demeter to reveal to mankind her beneficent gift of corn. Lastly, the writers are not at one in regard to the well-meaning but injudicious person who interrupted Demeter at her magic rite and thereby prevented her from bestowing the boon of immortality on her nursling. Ovid, in agreement with the Homeric hymn-writer, says that the person was the child's mother Metanira ; Apollodorus calls her Praxithea, an otherwise unknown person, who may have been the child's sister or more probably his nurse ; for Praxithea is not named by the Homeric hymn-writer among the daughters of Celeus.[1] Some critics would forcibly harmonize Apollodorus with the hymn-writer by altering our author's text in the present passage.[2] On the other hand, Hyginus, Servius, Lactantius Placidus, and the Second Vatican Mythographer say that it was the child's father who by his exclamation or his fear distracted the attention of the goddess and so frustrated her benevolent purpose.

Just as Demeter attempted to make Demophon or Triptolemus immortal by placing him on the fire, so Thetis tried to make her son Achilles immortal in like manner,[3] and so Isis essayed to confer immortality on the infant son of the king of Byblus.[4] All three goddesses were baffled by the rash intervention of affectionate but ignorant mortals. These legends point to an ancient Greek custom of passing newborn infants across a fire in order to save their lives from the dangers which beset infancy, and which, to the primitive mind, assume the form of demons or other spiritual beings lying in wait to cut short the frail thread of life. The Greek

---

[1] vv. 105 sqq. [2] See Critical Note, vol. i. p. 38.
[3] Apollodorus, iii. 13. 6, with the note.
[4] Plutarch, Isis et Osiris, 16.

I.—PUTTING CHILDREN ON THE FIRE

practice of running round the hearth with a child on the fifth or seventh day after birth may have been a substitute for the older custom of passing the child over the fire.[1] Similar customs have been observed for similar reasons in many parts of the world. Thus, in the highlands of Scotland, "it has happened that, after baptism, the father has placed a basket filled with bread and cheese on the pot-hook that impended over the fire in the middle of the room, which the company sit around; and the child is thrice handed across the fire, with the design to frustrate all attempts of evil spirits or evil eyes."[2] In the Hebrides it used to be customary to carry fire round children in the morning and at night every day until they were christened, and fire was also carried about the mothers before they were churched; and this "fire-round was an effectual means to preserve both the mother and the infant from the power of evil spirits, who are ready at such times to do mischief, and sometimes carry away the infant."[3] Customs of this sort prevailed in Scotland down to the beginning of the nineteenth century. Sometimes the father leaped across the hearth with the child in his arms; "moreover, every person entering the house was required to take up a burning fire-brand from the hearth, and therewith cross himself, before he ventured to approach a new-born child or its mother. It was also customary to carry a burning peat sun-wise round an unbaptised infant and its mother, to protect them from evil spirits."[4] The custom of leaping over a hearth or carrying a child round it, implies that the fireplace is in the middle of the floor, as it used to be in cottages in the highlands of Scotland. Miss Gordon

---

[1] Suidas, *s.v.* Ἀμφιδρόμια; Scholiast on Plato, *Theaetetus*, p. 160 E.

[2] Th. Pennant, "Second Tour in Scotland," in J. Pinkerton's *General Collection of Voyages and Travels*, iii. 383.

[3] M. Martin, "Description of the Western Islands of Scotland," in J. Pinkerton's *General Collection of Voyages and Travels*, vol iii. p. 612.

[4] Miss C. F. Gordon Cumming, *In the Hebrides*, New Edition (London, 1886), p. 101. Compare John Ramsay, *Scotland and Scotsmen in the Eighteenth Century* (Edinburgh and London, 1888), ii. 423.

APPENDIX

Cumming describes from her own observation such a cottage in Iona, "with the old-fashioned fireplace hollowed in the centre of the earthen floor, and with no chimney except a hole in the middle of the roof." [1] Ancient Greek houses must similarly have had the fireplace in the middle of the floor, and probably in them also the smoke escaped through a hole in the roof.

Sometimes the motive for putting the child on the fire was different, as will appear from the following accounts. In the north-east of Scotland, particularly in the counties of Banff and Aberdeen, "if the child became cross and began to *dwine*, fears immediately arose that it might be a 'fairy changeling,' and the trial by fire was put into operation. The hearth was piled with peat, and when the fire was at its strength the suspected changeling was placed in front of it and as near as possible not to be scorched, or it was suspended in a basket over the fire. If it was a 'changeling child' it made its escape by the *lum* [chimney], throwing back words of scorn as it disappeared." [2] Similarly in Fife we hear of "the old and widespread superstitious belief that a fairy changeling, if passed through the fire, became again the person the fairies had stolen, . . . believed but not acted on by the old women in Fife in an earlier part of this [19th] century." [3] Among the miners of Fife, "if a child cries continuously after being dressed at birth, the granny or some other wise elder will say, 'If this gangs on we'll hae to pit on the girdle' (the large circular flat baking-iron on which scones and oat-cakes are 'fired'). Sometimes this is actually done, but the practice is rare now, and very few can give the true meaning of the saying. The idea is that the crying child is a change-ling, and that if held over the fire it will go up the chimney, while the girdle will save the real child's feet from being burnt as it comes down to take its own legitimate place." [4] Similarly. in the Highlands one way of getting rid of a changeling was to seat him on a gridiron, or in a creel, with

---

[1] Miss C. F. Gordon Cumming, *op. cit.* p. 100.

[2] W. Gregor, *Notes on the Folk-lore of the North-east of Scotland* (London, 1881), pp. 8 *sq.*

[3] *County Folk-lore*, vol. vii. *Fife*, by J. E. Simpkins (London, 1914), p. 32.

[4] *County Folk-lore*, vol. vii. (as above), p. 398.

a fire burning below.[1] This mode of exchanging fairy changelings for real children by putting the changelings on the fire appears to be also Scandinavian; for a story relates how, in the little island of Christiansö, to the south-east of Sweden, a mother got rid of a changeling and recovered her own child by pretending to thrust the changeling into the oven; for no sooner had she done so than the fairy mother rushed into the room, snatched up her child, which was a puny, dwining little creature, and gave the woman her own babe back again, saying, "There is your child! I have done by it better than you have by mine." And indeed the returned infant was a fine sturdy child.[2]

A similar custom has been observed by the Jews, for Maimonides writes that "we still see the midwives wrap newborn children in swaddling bands, and, after putting foul-smelling incense on the fire, move the children to and fro over the incense on the fire."[3] Similarly, of the Jakuns, a wild people of the Malay Peninsula, "it is reported that, in several tribes, the children, as soon as born, are carried to the nearest rivulet, where they are washed, then brought back to the house, where fire is kindled, incense of kamunian wood thrown upon it, and the child then passed over it several times. We know from history that the practice of passing children over fire was in all times much practised amongst heathen nations, and that it is even now practised in China and other places."[4] In Canton, in order to render a child courageous and to ward off evil, a mother will move her child several times over a fire of glowing charcoal, after which she places a lump of alum in the fire, and the alum is supposed to assume the likeness of the creature which the child fears most.[5] In the Tenimber and Timorlaut islands (East Indies),

---

[1] J. G. Campbell, *Superstitions of the Highlands and Islands of Scotland* (Glasgow, 1900), p. 39.

[2] B. Thorpe, *Northern Mythology* (London, 1851–1852), ii. 174 *sq.*

[3] Maimonides, quoted by D. Chwolsohn, *Die Ssabier und der Ssabismus* (St. Petersburg, 1856), ii. 473.

[4] The R[d]. Favre (Apostolic Missionary), *An Account of the Wild Tribes inhabiting the Malay Peninsula*, etc. (Paris, 1865), pp. 68 *sq.*

[5] F. Warrington Eastlake, "Cantonese Superstitions about Infants," *China Review*, ix. (1880–1881), p. 303.

APPENDIX

" in order to prevent sickness, or rather to frighten the evil spirits, the child is, in the first few days, laid beside or over the fire." [1] In New Britain, after a birth has taken place, they kindle a fire of leaves and fragrant herbs, and a woman takes the child and swings it to and fro through the smoke of the fire, uttering good wishes. At the same time a sorcerer pinches up a little of the ashes from the fire, and touches with it the infant's eyes, ears, temples, nose, and mouth, " whereby the child is thenceforth protected against evil spirits and evil magic." [2] In Yule Island, off British New Guinea, " the child at birth is passed across the flames. It seems probable that in this there is the idea of purification by the fire." [3] In Madagascar a child used to be twice carefully lifted over the fire before he was carried out of the house for the first time. [4]

Among the Kafirs of South Africa "the mother makes a fire with some scented wood which gives off an abundance of pungent smoke. Over this smoke the baby is held till it cries violently. It is believed that some people at death become wizards or wizard-spirits, and that these evil beings seek malevolently to injure small babies ; they cannot abide the smell of the smoke from this scented wood, which they meet as they wander round seeking for prey, and trying to take possession of babies. The wizard is therefore repelled by the odour, and goes on its journey, hunting for a baby which is not so evil-smelling. When the baby cries in the smoke the mother calls out, 'There goes the wizard.' This smoking process has to be performed daily with closed doors

---

[1] J. G. F. Riedel, *De sluik- en kroesharige rassen tusschen Selebes en Papua* (The Hague, 1886), p. 303.

[2] R. Parkinson, *Dreissig Jahre in der Südsee* (Stuttgart, 1907), pp. 70 *sq.* Compare *id. Im Bismarck-Archipel* (Leipsic, 1887), pp. 94 *sq.*; A. Kleintitschen, *Die Küstenbewohner der Gazellehalbinsel* (Hiltrup bei Münster, n.d.), p. 204 ; *Les Missions Catholiques*, xvii. (Lyons, 1885), p. 110 ; Dr. Hahl, in *Nachrichten über Kaiser Wilhelms-Land und den Bismarck-Archipel* (Berlin, 1897), p. 81.

[3] Father Navarre, in *Annales de la Propagation de la Foi*, lix. (Lyons, 1887), p. 185.

[4] W. Ellis, *History of Madagascar* (London, n.d.), i. 151 *sq.*

for several weeks, while the mother sings special chants.[1]"
So among the Ovambo, a Bantu people of South Africa, when
the midwife or an old female friend of the mother has carried
a newborn baby out of the hut for the first time, she finds on
her return a great fire of straw burning at the entrance, and
across it she must stride, while she swings the infant several
times to and fro through the thick smoke, "in order to free
the child from the evil magic that still clings to it from its
birth. According to another version, this swinging through
the smoke is meant to impart courage to the child ; but the
first explanation appears to me to tally better with the views
of the natives."[2] At a certain festival, which occurred every
fourth year, the ancient Mexicans used to whirl their
children through the flames of a fire specially prepared for
the purpose.[3] Among the Tarahumares, an Indian tribe of
Mexico, "when the baby is three days old the shaman comes
to cure it. A big fire is made of corn-cobs, the little one is
placed on a blanket, and with the father's assistance the
shaman carries it, if it is a boy, three times through the
smoke to the four cardinal points, making the ceremonial
circuit and finally raising it upward. This is done that the
child may grow well and be successful in life, that is, in
raising corn."[4]

---

[1] Dudley Kidd, *Savage Childhood, a Study of Kafir
Children* (London, 1906), pp. 18 *sq.*

[2] Hans Schinz, *Deutsch-Südwest-Afrika* (Oldenburg and
Leipsic, n.d.), p. 307.

[3] H. H. Bancroft, *The Native Races of the Pacific States*
(London, 1875–1876), iii. 376, note [27], quoting Sahagun, "*rode-
arlos por las llamas del fuego que tenian aparejado para esto,*"
which I translate as above. Bancroft translates, "passed the
children over, or near to, or about the flame of a prepared
fire." The French translators turn the words, "*conduisaient
autour d'une flamme qu'on avait préparée pour cet objet.*"
See B. de Sahagun, *Histoire Générale des choses de la
Nouvelle-Espagne,* traduite par D. Jourdanet et R. Simeon
(Paris, 1880), p. 166. Compare C. F. Clavigero, *History of
Mexico,* translated by C. Cullen, 2nd ed. (London, 1807), i.
317.

[4] C. Lumholtz, *Unknown Mexico* (London, 1903), i. 272.

APPENDIX

II.—WAR OF EARTH ON HEAVEN

(*Apollodorus* I. vi. 1)

Some Indian tribes of North-Western America tell a story which resembles in certain respects the Greek myth of the war waged by the Earth-born Giants on the gods in heaven. The details of the story vary from tribe to tribe, but its substance is the same.

As told by the Pend' d'Oreille Indians of Montana, the story runs as follows:—

The Earth people wanted to make war on the Sky people. Grizzly-Bear was their chief, and he called all the warriors together. They were told to shoot in turn at the moon (or sky). All did as they were told, but their arrows fell short. Only Wren had not shot his arrow. Coyote said, "He need not shoot. He is too small, and his bow and arrows are too weak." However, Grizzly-Bear declared that Wren must have his turn. Wren shot his arrow, and it hit the moon (or sky) and stuck fast. Then the others shot their arrows, which stuck each in the notch of the preceding one, until they made a chain of arrows that reached from the sky to the ground. Then all the people climbed up, Grizzly-Bear going last. He was very heavy; and when he was more than half way up, the chain broke by his weight. He made a spring, and caught the part of the chain above him; and this caused the arrows to pull out at the top, where the leading warriors had made a hole to enter the sky. So the whole chain fell down and left the people up aloft without the means of descending. The Earth people attacked the Sky people, and defeated them in the first battle; but the Sky people soon mustered in such force that they far out-numbered the Earth people, and in the next battle routed them, killing a great many. The defeated Earth people ran for the ladder, but many were overtaken and killed on the way. When they found the ladder broken, each prepared himself the best way he could so as not to fall too heavily, and one after another jumped down. Flying-Squirrel was wearing a small robe, which he spread out like wings when he jumped; therefore he has something like wings now. He came down without hurting himself. Whitefish looked down the hole before jumping. When he saw the great depth, he puckered up his mouth and drew back; therefore he has a small puckered mouth at the present day. Sucker jumped down without first preparing himself, and his bones were broken; therefore the sucker's bones are now found in all parts of its flesh. At that time there were a number of different animals on earth that are not here now; but they were killed in this war and transformed into stars. Had they all come back to earth, there would be many more kinds here now. Those which we have at the present time represent only the survivors of the war.[1]

In this, as in most other versions of the story, the Earth people are conceived as animals, whether beasts, birds or fish. This comes out clearly in a parallel version of the story told by the Indians of the Okanagon tribe in British Columbia. In it we are told that each animal and bird shot at the sky, and that the Fish, Snakes, and Toads also tried, but that only the Chickadee succeeded in hitting the sky with his arrow; and in the fall from heaven the fish fared worst, because they had no wings. According to this version, the Grizzly Bear and the Black Bear were the only animals that were left on earth when all the rest had climbed up the ladder to the sky; and in quarrelling as to which of them should mount the ladder first, the two bears knocked it down.[2]

Similarly the Shuswap tribe of British Columbia tell how "Black Bear and Wolverene were great chiefs, the former of the Fish people, the latter of the Bird people. They assembled the warriors of all the fishes and birds of the earth to go on a war expedition against the people of the sky. All the men shot their arrows up towards the sky, but they fell back without hitting it. Last of all Wren,[3] who was the smallest of all the birds, shot an arrow, which stuck in the sky. The next smallest bird shot an arrow, which hit the end of the first one; and thus they shot arrows; and one stuck in the end of the other, until there was a chain of arrows forming a ladder from earth to sky. On this all the warriors ascended, leaving the two chiefs to guard the bottom. Soon after all

---

[1] *Folk-tales of Salishan and Sahaptin Tribes*, edited by Franz Boas (Lancaster, Pa., and New York, 1917), p. 118 (*Memoirs of the American Folk-Lore Society*, vol. xi.).

[2] *Folk-tales of Salishan and Sahaptin Tribes*, p. 85.

[3] "Some say Humming-Bird, others Chickadee."

had reached the sky world, Wolverene and Black Bear began to laugh at each other's tails. Black Bear grew angry, chased Wolverene around the foot of the ladder, struck against it, and knocked it down.

"Meanwhile the earth people had attacked the sky people, and at first were victorious; but afterwards the latter, gathering in great force, routed the earth people, who fled in great disorder towards the top of the ladder. By its fall their retreat was cut off; and many made a stand against the sky people, while others threw themselves down. The birds were able to reach the earth safely, for they could fly down; but many of the fishes, who tried to throw themselves into a large lake, were wounded. In their fall some missed the lake and dropped on rocks. Thus the skull of the *sematsai* came to be flattened, the *kwaak* broke its jaw, the *tcoktcitcin* got a bloody mouth, and the sucker had all its bones scattered and broken, so that it died. The grandson of a man called Tcel gathered the bones, put them back into the body, and revived it. This is the reason why the sucker has now so many bones scattered through its flesh, why the *sematsai* has a flat head, the *tcoktcitcin* a red mouth, and why the mouth of the *kwaak* appears to be broken. The earth people who remained above were all slain, and transformed by the sky people into stars."[1]

Thus the story of the attack on the Sky people purports at the same time to explain certain peculiar features of the fauna with which these Indians are acquainted. Animals naturally attract the attention of savages, especially of savage hunters; and the observation of their peculiarities, by exciting the curiosity of the observer, is a fruitful source of explanatory myths.

So far no explanation is given of the reasons which led the Earth people to make war on the Sky people. But in a version of the story told by the Quinault Indians, who inhabit a district on the western coast of Washington State, the motives for the war are fully reported. Raven's two daughters, we are told, went out on the prairie to dig roots, and night overtook them before they could reach home. Camping out in the open, they looked up at the starry sky,

---

[1] James Teit, *The Shuswap* (Leyden and New York, 1909), p. 749 (*The Jesup North Pacific Expedition*, vol. ii. part 7).

II.—WAR OF EARTH ON HEAVEN

and the younger sister said, "I wish I were up there with that big bright star!" And the elder sister said, "I wish I were there with that little star!" Soon they fell asleep, and when they awoke they were up in the sky country, where the stars are; and the younger sister found that her star was a feeble old man, while the elder sister's star was a young man. Now the younger sister was afraid of the old man; so she ran away and tried to descend to earth with the help of a rope, which she borrowed from an old woman called Spider. But the rope proved too short, and there she hung just over her father's house till she died, and her bones dropped down on the ground. Bluejay picked them up and knew them to be the bones of Raven's daughter. So he called Raven, and they agreed that it was so. "And they gathered together all the fragments, and then called upon all the people, and all the animals, and all the birds and fishes, to gather and make an attack upon the Sky People to recover the other sister." The rest of the story follows substantially as in the preceding versions. Having determined to make war on the Sky People, the animals prepared to shoot at the heavenly vault with arrows. So they made a bow of the trunk of a white cedar and an arrow of a limb of a tree. Then Grizzly Bear stepped up to string the bow, but could not bend it; after him, Elk and all the large animals tried, but all failed. At last Wren, the smallest of birds, bent the bow, strung it easily, and shot an arrow, which stuck in the sky. Then with the help of Snail, who aimed the arrows, Wren shot shaft after shaft, so that each stuck in the notch of the preceding one, till the arrows formed a chain that reached from the sky to the earth. Up the chain the animals swarmed to heaven, and there, feeling very cold in the upper air, Beaver contrived to steal fire for them from a house of the Sky People, after Robin Redbreast, Dog, and Wildcat had failed in the attempt. There, too, in a corner of the house, they found Raven's elder daughter. Having procured the fire they sent all the rats and mice among the Sky People to gnaw through all the bowstrings of the men and all the girdles of the women, and all fastenings of any kind which they could find. So, when all was ready, the Earth People attacked. The Sky men tried to use their bows, but the bowstrings were cut. The Sky women tried to put on their clothes to run away, but they could not fasten them and they had to stay where they were. Then

321

APOLL. II.   M

the Earth People went from house to house and killed great numbers of the Sky People. At last the Sky People rallied and began to beat back the Earth People. So, taking Raven's daughter with them, they retreated down the chain of arrows, and they had almost all got safely down, when the chain broke. So some were left hanging in the sky, and they can be seen there now in the stars.[1]

The story is told in a somewhat similar form by the Kathlamet Indians, whose territory lay in the south-western part of Washington State to the south of the country owned by the Quinault Indians; but in the Kathlamet version there is no mention of Raven's daughters nor of the chain of arrows. On the other hand it contains the incidents of the stealing of fire by Beaver and of the cutting of the bow-strings and girdles by Mouse and Rat. According to the Kathlamets, it was Bluejay who cut the rope by which, in their version of the tale, the animals had ascended to the sky; and among the creatures who remained up aloft in the shape of stars were the Woodpecker, the Fisher, the Skate, the Elk, and the Deer.[2]

The story of the War on the Sky is told, in the same general form, also by the Kutenai Indians in the interior of British Columbia. Their version includes the incident of the chain of arrows, and describes the shifts to which the animals in heaven were put when the chain of arrows, by which they had ascended, was broken down. The Bats, we are told, flew down, spreading out their blankets as wings. The Flying Squirrel pulled out his skin and used it as wings to fly with. All the fish threw themselves down, but the Sucker was the only one who was broken to pieces. However, he was restored to life by the touch of his brother's widow.[3]

A different account of the origin of the War on the Sky is given in a version of the story recorded among the Indians of

---

[1] L. Farrand, *Traditions of the Quinault Indians* [New York] (1902), pp. 107-109 (*The Jesup North Pacific Expedition*). I have abridged the story.

[2] Franz Boas, *Kathlamet Texts* (Washington, 1901), pp. 67-71 (*Bureau of American Ethnology, Bulletin* 26).

[3] Franz Boas, *Kutenai Tales* (Washington, 1918), pp. 73-77 (*Bureau of American Ethnology, Bulletin* 59).

II.—WAR OF EARTH ON HEAVEN

the Lower Fraser River in British Columbia. They say that the Redheaded Woodpecker and the Eagle had each a son, and that the two youths in pursuit of a beautiful bird were lured on till they came to the sky. The bereaved fathers desired to go up after them, but did not know how to do it. So they called a general assembly of the animals and inquired of them how one may ascend to heaven. First, the Pelican flew up, but returned without reaching the sky. Next the Mole attempted to scale the heavenly heights by burrowing under the water and under the earth, but naturally he failed. Even the Eagle himself, the father of one of the missing youths, could not fly so high, though he tried hard. At last a man or an animal named Tamia, a grandson of Woodpecker's wife, came forward and declared that he had learned in a dream how one may ascend up to heaven. So he painted his hair red, and having adorned his face with a streak of red paint from the forehead down over the nose to the chin, he began to sing. "I am Tamia! I fear not to shoot at the sky," while his grandmother Takt beat time to the song. Having thus attuned himself to the proper pitch, he took his bow and shot arrow after arrow at the sky, until the arrows, as usual, formed a chain stretching right down to the earth. So all the people ascended the chain, vanquished the Sky People in battle, and freed the two sons of the Woodpecker and the Eagle. When they had returned home victorious, they broke down the chain of arrows, or rather the broad road into which the chain had been converted. But they did not notice that the Snail had lagged behind and was still up aloft. So when the Snail came to heaven's gate and found no ladder, he had to throw himself down, and in his fall he broke every bone in his body. That is why he now moves so slowly.[1]

Yet another motive is assigned for the War on the Sky by the Thompson Indians of British Columbia. According to them, that war was caused by the rape of a married woman. The people of the Sky, so they say, stole the wife of Swan, who, in great wrath at this outrage, called all the people of the earth to a council. They agreed to make war on the Sky People, and under the direction

---

[1] Franz Boas, *Indianische Sagen von der Nord-Pacifischen Küste Amerikas* (Berlin, 1895), pp. 30 *sq.*

of the injured husband, they all gathered together with their bows and arrows and shot at the sky, but all their arrows fell short. After they had all tried in vain, Wren shot an arrow. The people watched it rising till it passed out of sight, and though they waited some time, it never came down again. It had stuck in the sky. Then Wren shot another arrow, which likewise disappeared and did not come down again. It had stuck in the notch of the first one. After he had discharged many arrows, the people saw them sticking one in the end of the other, like a chain hung from the sky. Wren continued to shoot till at last the arrow-chain reached the earth. Then all the people ascended one behind the other over the chain of arrows and entering the upper world (some say through a hole which they tore in the sky) they attacked the Sky People, some of whom consisted of Grizzlies, Black Bears, and Elks. A great battle was fought, in which the Sky People were victorious, and the Earth People began to retreat in great haste down the chain of arrows. When about half the people had reached the ground, the chain broke in the middle, and many were killed by the fall. Others, who were on the chain above the point at which it broke, had to ascend again, and were either killed or made prisoners by the Sky People. Those who reached the earth represent the people, animals, birds, and fishes to be found on the earth at the present time. There were formerly other different animals and birds on the earth, but they either were killed in this war or remain in the sky to this day.[1]

A short version of the story, without the assignment of any motive for the war, is reported from among the Ntlakya-pamuq Indians of British Columbia. It includes the usual incident of the sky-reaching chain of arrows.[2]

A somewhat different story of the War on the Sky is told by the Çatloltq Indians of Vancouver Island. They say that long ago Turpentine was a blind man, who could not bear the sun's heat and used to go a-fishing for red shell-fish by night.

---

[1] James Teit, *Mythology of the Thompson Indians* (Leyden and New York, 1912), p. 246 (*The Jesup North Pacific Expedition*, vol. viii. part ii.). Another, but briefer, version of the story is reported in the same work (p. 334).

[2] Franz Boas, *Indianische Sagen von der Nord-Pacifischen Küste Amerikas*, p. 17.

II.—WAR OF EARTH ON HEAVEN

Every morning, when the day began to break, his wife called him back, saying, "Come home quick! The sun is rising." So he always hurried home before it grew warm. But one day his wife slept late, and when she awoke, it was broad day. Horrified by the discovery, she rushed to the beach, shrieking, "Come home quick! The sun is high in heaven." Thus adjured, old Turpentine plied his oars as for dear life, but it was too late; the Sun shone down on him so hot that he melted away before he reached the shore. Indignant at his fate, his two sons resolved to avenge his death by killing the Sun, his murderer. So they took their bows and arrows and went to the place where the Sun rises. There they shot an arrow at the sky, and a second arrow at the first, until the usual ladder of arrows was constructed leading up to heaven. When it was finished, the elder brother shook it to see whether it was strong enough to bear his weight, and finding it quite firm, the two brothers climbed up aloft by it. On reaching the sky they killed the Sun with their arrows. Then they deliberated how to replace the dead luminary and solved the problem very simply; for the elder brother became the Sun, and the younger brother became the Moon.[1]

A different motive for the War on the Sky is assigned by the Sanpoil Indians, who live on the Columbia River and belong to the Salish stock.[2] They say that once on a time it rained so heavily that all the fires on earth were extinguished. The animals held a council and decided to make war against the sky in order to bring back the fire. In spring the people began, and tried to shoot their arrows up to the sky. Coyote tried first, but did not succeed. Finally the Chickadee contrived to shoot an arrow which stuck in the sky. He continued to shoot, making a chain of arrows by

---

[1] Franz Boas, *Indianische Sagen von der Nord-Pacifischen Küste Amerikas*, pp. 64 *sq.* The use of a chain of arrows to give access to the sky is a common incident in the folk-tales told by the Indians of North-west America, even in stories in which there is no question of an attack upon the Sky People. See Franz Boas, "Tsimshian Mythology," *Thirty-first Annual Report of the Bureau of American Ethnology* (Washington, 1916), pp. 364 *sqq.*

[2] F. W. Hodge, *Handbook of American Indians* (Washington, 1907-1910), ii. 451.

means of which the animals climbed up. The last to climb was the Grizzly Bear, but so heavy was he that he broke the chain of arrows and so could not join the other animals in the sky.

When the animals reached the sky, they found themselves in a valley near a lake where the people of the sky were fishing. Coyote wished to act as scout, but was captured. Then the Muskrat dug holes along the shore of the lake, and Beaver and Eagle set out to obtain the fire. Beaver entered one of the fish-traps and pretended to be dead. They carried him to the chief's house, where the people began to skin him. At this time the Eagle alighted on a tree near the tent. When the people saw the Eagle, they ran out, and at once Beaver took a clam-shell full of glowing coals and ran away. He jumped into the lake, and people tried to catch him in nets; but the water drained away through the holes which Muskrat had made. The animals now ran back to the chain of arrows, which they found broken. Then, as the birds could fly down and the quadrupeds could not, each bird took a quadruped on its back and flew down with it. Only Coyote and the Sucker were left up above. Coyote tied a piece of buffalo robe to each paw and jumped down. He sailed down on the skin, and finally landed on a pine-tree. Next morning he showed off his wings, but could not take them off again, and was transformed into a bat. The Sucker had to jump down, and was broken to pieces. The animals fitted his bones together; and, since some were missing, they put pine-needles into his tail. Therefore the Sucker has many bones.[1]

III.—Myths of the Origin of Fire

(*Apollodorus* I. vii. 1)

According to Hesiod and Hyginus, it was from Zeus himself that Prometheus stole the fire which he bestowed on men;[2] and Hyginus clearly conceived the theft to have been perpetrated in heaven, for he speaks of Prometheus bringing

---

[1] *Folk-tales of Salishan and Sahaptin Tribes*, edited by Franz Boas, pp. 107 *sq.*

[2] Hesiod, *Works and Days*, 50 *sqq.*, *Theog.* 565 *sqq.*; Hyginus, *Astronom.* ii 15.

III.—THE ORIGIN OF FIRE

down the stolen fire to earth in a stalk of fennel;[1] and Latin poets similarly refer to the sky as the source from which our earthly fire was procured by the artful Prometheus.[2] But according to Plato it was from the workshop of Athena and Hephaestus that Prometheus abstracted the fire. The philosopher tells us that when the time appointed for man's creation or appearance out of the earth was at hand, Prometheus, the friend of the human race, was sore puzzled what to do; for no provision had been made for supplying the new creatures with fire, and, without that element, how could the mechanical arts exist? Prometheus himself might not enter the citadel of Zeus, which was guarded by dreadful warders; so he made his way secretly into the workshop where Athena and Hephaestus laboured in common, and, stealing the fire of Hephaestus and the mechanical skill of Athena, he bestowed both these precious gifts on men.[3] This version of the story was known to Lucian, for he represents Hephaestus reproaching Prometheus with having purloined the fire and left his forge cold.[4] Cicero speaks of " the Lemnian theft" of fire committed by Prometheus;[5] which implies that the fire was obtained from the forge of Hephaestus in Lemnos, the island on which Hephaestus fell when he was hurled from heaven by Zeus.[6] Perhaps the origin of fire on earth was mythically explained by this fall of Hephaestus, who may have been supposed to carry it with him in his descent from heaven, and to have used it to light the furnace of his smithy in the island.

The notion that the first fire used by man was stolen from a deity or other fairyland being meets us in many stories told by many savages in many parts of the world. Very often, curiously enough, the thief is a bird or beast; not uncommonly the theft is committed by a number of birds or beasts, which combine together for the purpose. On the other hand, a beast or bird often figures, not as the thief, but as the first owner of fire, and the story relates how the

---

[1] Hyginus, *Fab.* 144.
[2] Horace, *Odes*, i. 3. 27 *sqq.*; Juvenal, **xv.** 84 *sqq.*
[3] Plato, *Protagoras*, 11, p. 321 C-E.
[4] Lucian, *Prometheus*, 5.
[5] Cicero, *Tuscul. Disput.* ii. 10. 23.
[6] Homer, *Il.* i. 590 *sqq.*

fire was obtained from the animal or bird and conveyed to men. Tales of the origin, and in particular of the theft, of fire are too numerous to be told here at length ; elsewhere I hope to deal with them fully.[1] But it may be worth while to illustrate the nature and wide diffusion of such tales by some examples.

The aborigines of Cape Grafton, on the eastern coast of Queensland, tell of a time when there was no such thing as fire on earth ; so Bin-jir Bin-jir, a small wren with a red back (*Malurus* sp.), went up into the skies to get some. He was successful, but lest his friends on earth should have the benefit of it, he hid it away under his tail. Asked on his return how he had fared, he told his friend that his quest had been fruitless. But his friend laughed and said, "Why, you have got some fire stuck on to the end of your tail," referring to the red spot on the bird's back. Bin-jir Bin-jir was therefore obliged to admit that he did get some fire, and finally he showed his friend from what particular wood to extract it by friction.[2] Some of the aborigines of Western Victoria thought that the first fire was procured by a little bird described as a "fire-tail wren," which stole it from the crows, who till then had had sole possession of the valuable element.[3]

According to the Booandik tribe, who used to inhabit the extreme south-east corner of South Australia, the first owner of fire was the cockatoo, who kept it jealously hidden in his red crest and produced it from there by scratching his crest whenever he wished to cook his victuals. But he took care to cook his food privately, lest the other cockatoos should learn the secret. However, one little cockatoo contrived to steal some of the fire and communicated it to his fellows.[4] One of the tribes about Maryborough in Queensland related how men originally obtained fire by knocking off a piece of

---

[1] In a volume, *The Origin of Fire, and other Essays*, to be published by Messrs. Macmillan & Co., London.

[2] Walter E. Roth, "Superstition, Magic, and Medicine," *North Queensland Ethnography, Bulletin No. 5* (Brisbane, 1903), p. 11.

[3] James Dawson, *Australian Aborigines* (Melbourne, Sydney, and Adelaide, 1881), p. 54.

[4] Mrs. James Smith, *The Booandik tribe* (Adelaide, 1880), pp. 21 *sq.*

the sun when he rose in the east.[1] The natives about Lake Condah in Victoria said that once upon a time a man threw up a spear to the clouds with a string attached to it. Then he climbed up the string and brought down fire from the sun to the earth.[2]

The natives of the Eastern Islands of Torres Straits, between Australia and New Guinea, say that fire was formerly in possession of an old woman, who kept it in a sixth finger which she had between her finger and thumb. When she wished to kindle a fire, she had only to put this finger under the fuel, and the fuel at once ignited. The animals on another island often saw the smoke of her fire and were envious, for they had no fire of their own. They tried, one after the other, to swim across the channel and get the fire by hook or crook; but they all failed until the big lizard made his way across, bit off the old woman's fiery finger, and swam back with it in his mouth. All the people, or rather all the animals, were very glad to see the fire which he brought to them. They all went into the wood and everyone got a branch from the tree he liked best; they asked each tree to come and get a fire-stick. All the trees came and got fire and have kept it ever since; and men obtain their fire-sticks from the trees.[3]

The natives of Kiwai, an island off the mouth of the Fly River in New Guinea, say that fire was first produced on the mainland of New Guinea by two men. All animals tried to steal some of the fire and swim across to Kiwai with it, but they all failed. The birds also failed in the attempt, till at last the black cockatoo succeeded in bringing a burning stick in his beak. But his mouth was terribly burnt by the fire; and he has had a red spot on both sides of his mouth from that day to this. He let the fire-stick drop at Iasa; and the people secured it, and have had fire ever since.[4]

---

[1] A. W. Howitt, *The Native Tribes of South-East Australia* (London, 1904), p. 432.

[2] R. Brough Smyth, *The Aborigines of Victoria* (Melbourne and London, 1878), i. 462.

[3] *Reports of the Cambridge Anthropological Expedition to Torres Straits*, vi. (Cambridge, 1908), pp. 29 *sq.*

[4] Rev. J. Chalmers, "Note on the Natives of Kiwai Island," *Journal of the Anthropological Institute*, xxxiii. (1903) p. 188. For other versions of the same story, see

APPENDIX

The cockatoo here referred to belongs no doubt to the genus *Microglossa*, "whose wholly black plumage is relieved by their bare cheeks of bright red."[1]

Some people in Kiwai give a different account of the origin of fire. They say that the method of making fire was discovered accidentally or through the advice of a spirit by sawing wood with a bamboo rope or a bowstring: the friction first made the wood warm and then elicited smoke and flame.[2]

At Wagawaga, on Milne Bay, near the south-eastern extremity of New Guinea, they say that people used to cook their yams and taro in the sun, because they were ignorant of fire. But a certain old woman had fire in her body and used to draw it out from between her legs when she wished to cook her own food. She carefully kept the secret from other people; but a boy detected her in the act of making fire and contrived to steal a fire-brand from her. This was the beginning of the general use of fire among men.[3] A similar story is told by the natives of Dobu, an island belonging to the D'Entrecastaux group which lies to the east of New Guinea,[4] and also by the natives of the Trobriand Islands, to the north of the D'Entrecastaux Islands.[5]

In the Admiralty Islands, to the north of New Guinea, the natives say that in the beginning there was no fire on

---

Gunnar Landtman, *The Folk-tales of the Kiwai Papuans* (Helsingfors, 1917), pp. 331 *sq.* (*Acta Societatis Scientiarum Fennicae*, vol. xlvii); W. N. Beaver, *Unexplored New Guinea* (London, 1920), p. 174.

[1] Alfred Newton and Hans Gadow, *A Dictionary of Birds* (Cambridge, 1893–1896), p. 93.

[2] Gunnar Landtman, *op. cit.* pp. 83, 334 *sq.*

[3] C. G. Seligmann, *The Melanesians of British New Guinea* (Cambridge, 1910), pp. 379 *sq.*

[4] Rev. W. E. Bromilow, "Dobuan (Papuan) beliefs and folk-lore," *Report of the Thirteenth Meeting of the Australasian Association for the Advancement of Science, held at Sydney, 1911* (Sydney, 1912), pp. 425 *sq.*

[5] The story was recorded in the Trobriands by Dr. B. Malinowski, who was good enough to communicate it to me.

III.—THE ORIGIN OF FIRE

earth. A woman sent the sea-eagle and the starling to fetch fire from heaven. The two birds brought it, and since then people have cooked their food by fire; were it not for these two birds we should still have to dry our food in the sun. But on their flight down to earth, the two birds shifted the fire between them. The starling took the fire and carried it on the back of his neck, and the wind blew up the flame, so that it singed the bird. That is why the starling is now so small and the fish-eagle so big.[1]

The Maoris of New Zealand tell how fire was procured for the earth by the great primordial hero Maui. He got it from his grandmother, Mahuika, the goddess of fire, who at his request produced fire successively from all the nails of her fingers and toes, one after the other. A great conflagration followed, which was extinguished by heavy rain. What little fire escaped extinction took refuge in certain trees, from which it is still elicited by friction.[2] Substantially the same myth, with local variations, is told in many parts of Polynesia, as in the Chatham Islands,[3] Tonga,[4] Savage Island,[5] Samoa,[6] Bowditch Island,[7] the Union Islands,[8] the

---

[1] Josef Meyer, "Mythen und Sagen der Admiralitäts-insulaner," *Anthropos*, ii. (1907), pp. 659 *sq.*

[2] Sir George Grey, *Polynesian Mythology* (London, 1855), pp. 45–49. For briefer versions of the story, see R. Taylor, *Te Ika A Maui, or New Zealand and its Inhabitants*[2] (London, 1870), pp. 130 *sq.*; John White, *The Ancient History of the Maori*, ii. (London and Wellington, 1889), pp. 108–110.

[3] A. Shand, *The Moriori People of the Chatham Islands* (Washington and New Plymouth, 1911), p. 20 (*Memoirs of the Polynesian Society*, vol. ii.).

[4] Le P. Reiter, "Traditions Tonguiennes," *Anthropos*, xii.–xiii. (1917–1918), pp. 1026-1040; E. E. Collcott, "Legends from Tonga," *Folk-lore*, xxxii. (1921), pp. 45–48.

[5] G. Turner, *Samoa* (London, 1884), pp. 211 *sq*; (Sir) Basil Thomson, *Savage Island* (London, 1902), pp. 86 *sq.*

[6] G. Turner, *op. cit.* pp. 209 211; J. B. Stair, *Old Samoa* (London, 1897), pp. 238 *sq.*

[7] G. Turner, *op. cit.* p. 270.

[8] (Sir) Basil Thomson, *op. cit.* p. 87.

Hervey Islands,[1] and the Marquesas Islands.[2] Everywhere the fire-bringer is the human or superhuman hero Maui, but there is some variation in regard to the name and sex of the deity from whom he obtained the fire. Sometimes the deity appears as a female and sometimes as a male, sometimes as the grandmother and sometimes as the grandfather of the hero; and her or his name is variously given as Mahuika, Mahuike, Mauika, Mauike, Mauimotua, Mafuie, and Mafuike. In the Maori myth the realm of the fire-goddess would seem to be in the sky, for the hero speaks of fetching down fire for the world. But in almost all the other versions the home of the fire-deity is definitely subterranean, and the hero has to descend into the nether world in order to procure the fire. Sometimes the fire-god only yields the fire on compulsion after a struggle with the hero, in which the deity gets the worst of it. In the Chatham Islands version, as in the Maori version, the fire-god produces the fire from his fingers. In the Marquesas version the fire-goddess produces the fire from her toes, knees, back, and navel; but in the other versions which I have cited nothing is said about the fire being extracted from the body of the deity. While the fire-bringer Maui is clearly conceived as a hero in human form, he is sometimes said to have assumed the form of a bird in order either to obtain access to the realm of the fire deity or to escape from the conflagration which followed his interview with that potentate. Thus in the Maori version the hero Maui is said to have assumed the form of an eagle; in one of the two Hervey Islands versions he is reported to have entered temporarily into the body of a red pigeon; while in the Marquesas version he concealed himself under the form of a *patiotio* bird. A version of the story which is reported from the Hawaii or Sandwich Islands relates how Maui learned the art of fire-making from an *alae* bird, which used to carry fire about and communicate it to its fellow-birds in order that they might roast bananas or taro with it. Being

---

[1] W. W. Gill, *Myths and Songs from the South Pacific* (London, 1876), pp. 51–58, 63–69.

[2] E. Tregear, "Polynesian folk-lore; ii.: The Origin of Fire," *Transactions and Proceedings of the New Zealand Institute*, xx. (1887), pp. 385–387.

III.—THE ORIGIN OF FIRE

caught by Maui, the bird explained to him how to make fire by rubbing two sticks together, and indicated to him the various sorts of trees from which fire-sticks could be procured. As all but one of these trees proved on trial to be quite unsuitable for the purpose, Maui in a rage applied a burning brand to the bird's head, as you may still see by the red crest on its poll.[1] In one of the Hervey Islands versions the fire-god employed a bird of white plumage, the tern, to hold down the lower fire-stick, while he himself twirled the upper fire-stick in the usual way to elicit fire. But Maui snatched the burning upper stick from the fire-god's hands, and as the bird continued to clutch the lower stick, the hero applied the flaming stick in his hands to either side of the bird's eyes and scorched both places. That is why you see the black marks on either side of the tern's eyes down to this day. Thus, while the human aspect of the fire-bringer certainly prevails in the Polynesian myths of the origin of fire, there are hints that in another and perhaps older version of the tale he may have been a bird rather than a man.

The natives of Nukufetau, one of the Ellice Islands, give a very rationalistic account of the origin of fire. They say that fire was discovered by seeing smoke rise from two crossed branches which were rubbed against each other in the wind.[2]

The Toradyas of Central Celebes say that the Creator gave fire to the first man and woman, but did not teach them how to make it. So when the fire went out, people were at a loss how to boil their rice. Accordingly they resolved to send a messenger to the sky to ask for a little fire, for in those days the sky was much nearer to the earth than it is now. The messenger chosen for the purpose was a certain insect named *tambooya*. When the insect came to the sky and asked for fire, the gods said, "We will give you fire; but you must cover your eyes with your hands, that you may not see how we make it." But the gods did not know that the insect had an eye under each shoulder; so while he lifted up his arms

---

[1] A. Bastian, *Inselgruppen in Oceanien* (Berlin, 1883), pp. 278 *sq.*; *id.*, *Allerlei aus Volks- und Menschenkunde* (Berlin, 1888), i. 120 *sq.*

[2] G. Turner, *Samoa*, pp. 285 *sq.*

to hide his eyes in his head, he saw with his eyes under his arms how the gods made fire by striking a flint with a chopping-knife, and on his return to earth he communicated the secret to mankind who have made fire in that way ever since.[1]

The natives of Nias, an island to the west of Sumatra, say that in the olden time certain evil spirits called Belas used to consort with mankind in a friendly way, but only the Belas knew how to make fire, and they kept the secret to themselves, though they were willing enough to lend fire to men. One day a man, whose fire had gone out, went to borrow it from the wife of a Bela. To prevent him from seeing how she made it, she proposed to cover him up with a garment. But he said, "I can see through a garment; put a basket over me." She did so, but while she made fire, he looked through the interstices of the basket, and so learned the secret.[2]

The Andaman Islanders say that after the great flood, which extinguished all fires on earth, the ghost of a drowned man assumed the form of a kingfisher and flew up to the sky, where he discovered the Creator seated beside his fire. The bird seized a burning log in its beak, but accidentally dropped it on the Creator, who, smarting with pain, hurled the brand at the awkward bird. The missile missed the kingfisher but dropped near the survivors of the flood, who thus recovered the use of fire.[3]

[1] A. C. Kruijt, "De legenden der Poso-Alfoeren aangaande de eerste menschen," *Mededeelingen van wege het Nederlandsche Zendelinggenootschap*, xxxviii. (1894), pp. 340 *sq.*; N. Adriani en Alb. C. Kruijt, *De Bare'e-sprekende Toradjas van Midden-Celebes* (Batavia, 1912–14), ii. 186 *sq.*

[2] L. N. H. A. Chatelin, "Godsdienst en bijgeloof der Niassers," *Tijdschrift voor Indische Taal- Land- en Volkenkunde*, xxvi. (1880), p. 132; E. Modigliani, *Un Viaggio à Nias* (Milan, 1890), pp. 629 *sq.* Compare H. Sundermann, *Die Insel Nias* (Barmen, 1905), p. 70.

[3] E. H. Man, *On the Aboriginal Inhabitants of the Andaman Islands* (London, n.d.). pp. 98 *sq.* Compare *Census of India*, 1901, vol. iii. *The Andaman and Nicobar Islands*, by Sir Richard C. Temple (Calcutta, 1903), p. 63; M. V. Portman, "The Andaman fire-legend," *The Indian Antiquary*, xxvi. (1897), pp. 14–18.

III.—THE ORIGIN OF FIRE

The Thay or Tai of Siam have likewise a legend of a great flood which extinguished all fires on earth. The survivors sent three several messengers, a man, a serpent, and an owl, one after the other, to the Spirit of the Sky to procure fire, but none of them succeeded in the task. At last they applied to the gad-fly, and he willingly undertook the duty, only stipulating that if he succeeded in his mission he should be free thenceforth to batten on the thighs of buffaloes and the legs of men. His terms being accepted, the gad-fly flew up to the sky. Now the eyes of a gad-fly are not in its head but at the root of its wings; at least the Thay think so. But when Sky asked the gad-fly, "Where are your eyes?" the cunning insect replied, "They are just where other people's eyes are." "Then," pursued the Sky, "where will you shut yourself up so as to see nothing?" The artful gad-fly answered, "I see through the sides of a pitcher just as if they did not exist; but put me in a basket with interstices, and I see absolutely nothing." The simple-minded Sky accordingly put the gad-fly in a basket with interstices and set about making fire by the process of drawing a cord rapidly to and fro in the notch of a stick. Ensconced in the basket, the gad-fly saw the whole process and communicated the secret to men.[1] In this story the gad-fly's trick of peeping through the interstices of a basket resembles the trick played by the man in the corresponding story from Nias.[2]

The Ba-ila, a tribe of Northern Rhodesia, in South Africa, tell how the Mason-Wasp brought fire from God. They say that formerly there was no fire on earth, so all the birds assembled together and asked, "Whence shall we get fire?" Mason-Wasp offered to go to God to get some, and the Vulture, the Fish-Eagle, and the Crow volunteered to go with him. So they all flew off; but first the Vulture, then the Fish-Eagle, and then the Crow expired with the effort, and their bones fell to the earth. Only Mason-Wasp won his way to God and told him that he was come to ask for fire. God gave him fire and his blessing as well, saying, "You shall not have to beget children. When you desire a child, go and look into a grainstalk and you will find an insect

---

[1] A. Bourlet, "Les Thay," *Anthropos*, ii. (1907), pp. 921-24.   [2] See above, p. 334.

whose name is Ngongwa. When you have found him, take and carry him into a house. When you arrive in the house, look out for the fireplace where men cook, and build there a dwelling for your child Ngongwa. When you have finished building, put him in and let him remain there. When many days have elapsed, just go and have a look at him ; and one day you will find he has changed and become just as you are yourself." So it is to-day: Mason-Wasp builds a house, looking for the fireplace, just as he was commanded by God.[1]

This African account of the origin of fire on earth is explained as follows by the writers who have recorded it : " The Mason-Wasp, the Prometheus of the Ba-ila, with its indigo-blue wings, yellow abdomen, and black and orange legs, is a common object in Central Africa. It builds its cell of mud not only on the fireplaces, as the tale narrates, but also (and this is a great nuisance) on walls, books, and pictures in one's dwelling. In the cell it lays its eggs, together with a caterpillar or grub, and seals them up ; then it builds other cells, until quite a large unsightly lump of clay is left on the wall. As the young grubs hatch out they eat the insects which have been benumbed, but not killed, by the sting of their parent. We have here an interesting example of how the observation of natives is correct up to a certain point ; but not taking into consideration, because they have not noticed, all the facts, the conclusion they draw is wrong. They suppose Ngongwa to metamorphose into a Mason-Wasp ; and this tale is to explain why it is so, as well as to account for the domestic fire."[2]

A very different story of the origin of fire is told by the Basongo Meno, a group of tribes in the Congo basin, whose territory lies to the north of the Sankuru and Kasai rivers. They say that from the earliest times they have made their fishing-traps out of the ribs of the Raphia palm. One day a man, constructing such a trap, wished to bore a hole in the end of one of the ribs, and he used a small pointed stick for the purpose. In the process of boring fire was elicited, and this method of procuring fire has been employed ever since.

---

[1] E. W. Smith and A. M. Dale, *The Ila-speaking Peoples of Northern Rhodesia* (London, 1920), ii. 345 *sq.*
[2] E. W. Smith and A. M. Dale, *op. cit.* ii. 346 *sq.*

III.—THE ORIGIN OF FIRE

Hence large plantations of Raphia palm are maintained by the people to supply them with fire-sticks.[1]

In Loango they say that once on a time the spider spun a long, long thread, and that the wind caught one end of the thread and carried it up to the sky. Then the woodpecker climbed up the thread, and pecking at the celestial vault made those holes in it which we call stars. After the woodpecker had thus ascended, man also clambered up the thread to the sky and fetched down fire.[2]

The Ekoi of Southern Nigeria, on the borders of the Cameroons, say that in the beginning of the world, the Sky God, Obassi Osaw, made everything, but he did not give fire to the people who were on earth. A chief named Etim 'Ne sent the Lame Boy, who at that time was not lame, to the Sky God to ask for fire. The Lame Boy went and proffered the request, but the Sky God refused it angrily and sent him back to earth. Next the chief went himself to the deity and humbled himself before him ; but he fared no better and had to return home empty-handed. Thereupon the Lame Boy undertook to steal fire from the Sky God. With that view he went and took service with the Sky God, and after he had served the deity for some days, the god said to him, " Go to the house of my wives, and ask them to send me a lamp." The boy gladly did as he was bidden, for it was in the house of the god's wives that the fire was kept. He waited till the lamp was given him, and then brought it back with all speed. Once, after he had stayed many days among the servants, the Sky God Obassi sent him again for a lamp, and this time one of the wives said, " You can light the lamp at the fire." The boy took a brand and lighted the lamp, then he wrapped the brand in plantain leaves and tied it up in his cloth. He carried the lamp to his master ; but that night, when all the people were asleep, he took the fire-brand which he had wrapped in plantain leaves, and carrying it he set out homeward. When he reached the earth once more, he took the fire to his chief and showed it to him. So the first fire was made on earth. But looking down from his house in the sky the god, Obassi Osaw, saw the smoke rising,

[1] E. Torday et T. A. Joyce, *Les Bushongo* (Brussels, 1910), pp. 275 *sq.*

[2] *Die Loango-Expedition*, iii. 2, von E. Pechuël-Loesche (Stuttgart, 1907), p. 135.

and he said to his eldest son, "Go, ask the boy if it is he who has stolen the fire." His eldest son came down to earth and delivered his father's message. The lad confessed, saying, "I was the one who stole the fire. The reason why I hid it was because I feared." The god's eldest son, whose name was Akpan, replied, "I bring you a message. Up till now you have been able to walk. From to-day you will not be able to do so any more." That is the reason why the Lame Boy cannot walk. He it was who first brought fire to earth from Obassi's house in the sky.[1]

The Lengua Indians of the Paraguayan Chaco say that in early times men, being unable to produce fire, were compelled to eat their food raw. But one day an Indian found a fire which a certain bird had kindled in order to cook snails In the bird's absence he stole some of the burning sticks and communicated the fire to his friends, who that night cooked their food for the first time. When the bird, soaring up in the sky, saw the Indians sitting round the stolen fire, he was very angry, and created a great thunderstorm, accompanied by terrible lightning, which terrified the people. Hence, whenever it thunders, it is a sign that the thunder-bird is angry and is seeking to punish the Indians by fire from the sky ; for ever since the bird lost its fire it has had to eat its food raw.[2]

The Tapietes, an Indian tribe of the Gran Chaco, say that of old the black vulture obtained fire by means of lightning from heaven, while as yet the Indians had no fire. However, a frog stole two sparks from the black vulture's fire and brought them in his mouth to the Tapietes. Since then the Tapietes have had fire, and the black vulture has had none. Robbed of his fire, the black vulture sat down with his hands over his head and wept.[3]

The Tembes, an Indian tribe of north-eastern Brazil, in the province of Grao Para, say that formerly fire was in the possession of the king vulture. The Tembes, being destitute

---

[1] P. Amaury Talbot, *In the Shadow of the Bush* (London, 1912), pp. 370 *sq.*

[2] W. B. Grubb, *An Unknown People in an Unknown Land* (London, 1911), pp. 97-99.

[3] E. Nordenskiöld, *Indianerleben. El Gran Chaco* (Leipsic, 1912), pp. 313 *sq.* For other stories of the origin of fire, see *id.*, pp. 21 *sq.*, 110 *sq.*

of fire, had to dry their meat in the sun. So they resolved to steal fire from the king vulture. For this purpose they killed a tapir and let it lie for three days, after which the carcase was rotten and full of maggots. The king vulture and his clan now came down to partake of the feast. They pulled off their garments of feathers and appeared in human form. They had brought with them a fire-brand, and with it they kindled a great fire. They gathered the maggots, wrapped them in leaves, and roasted them. Then the Tembes, who had lain in ambush ran to the spot, but the vultures flew up and bore the fire to a place of safety. Thus the Indians exerted themselves in vain for three days. Then they built a hunting-shelter beside the carrion, and an old medicine-man hid in it. The vultures came again and kindled their fire close to the shelter. And when they had laid aside their feather-garments and were roasting the maggots, the old man jumped out on them. The vultures at once made for their cast-off garments, the old man snatched a fire-brand, and by means of it he put fire into all the trees from which the Indians now extract it by friction.[1]

The Arekuna Indians of northern Brazil tell of a certain man named Makunaima, who lived with his brothers long ago before the great flood. They had as yet no fire and were compelled to eat all their food raw. So they sought for fire and found the little green bird called by the natives *mutug* (*Prionites momota*) which was said to be in possession of fire. The bird was in the act of fishing, and Makunaima tied a string to its tail without its knowledge. The string was very long, and following it up the brothers came to the bird's house, from which they carried away fire with them. Afterwards there came a great flood, and a certain rodent, which the natives call *akuli* (*Dasyprocta aguti*), saved itself from drowning by creeping into a hole in a tree and bunging up the hole. There in the hole the creature made fire ; but the fire caught the animal's hinder quarters and changed into red hair. Hence the beast has had red hairs on that part of its body to this day.[2]

---

[1] Th. Koch-Grünberg, *Indianermärchen aus Südamerika* (Jena, 1920), No. 65, pp. 186 *sq.*

[2] Th. Koch-Grünberg, *Vom Roroima zum Orinoco* (Berlin, 1916–17), ii. 33–36 For another story of the origin of fire, told by the Taulipang Indians of the same region, see *id.* ii. 76.

APPENDIX

The Tarumas, an Indian tribe inhabiting the forests in the south-eastern region of British Guiana, say that in the beginning two brothers only lived on earth ; there was no woman. Afterwards the younger brother Duid fished up the first woman from a deep pool and married her. The two brothers lived in separate houses near each other. They had always eaten their food raw, having no fire to cook it with ; but they noticed that the woman ate nothing raw except fruit. At last, after many years, when she was an old woman and had borne many children, the elder brother forced her by threats of violence to reveal her secret. So she sat down, and spreading her legs wide apart produced fire from her genital canal. From that fire is descended the fire which we now use. One day as Duid was sitting on the bank of the river with his fire beside him, an alligator came and snapped up the fire in its jaws and carried it off. However, Duid's elder brother recalled the alligator and induced it to disgorge its fiery prey. The fire itself was uninjured, but it had burned out the alligator's tongue, and in consequence the alligator has been tongueless ever since. Another day, soon afterwards, a maroudi picked up Duid's fire and flew away with it. Again the elder brother came to the rescue. The bird was recalled and gave back the fire, but her neck was burned and has remained red to this day. Another day, when Duid was absent, a jaguar came along, and stepping on the fire burned his feet so badly that he has never since been able to plant them flat on the ground, but must walk on his toes. A tapir also came along and trod on the fire, and he is so slow in his movements that he was very badly burned and has had hoofs ever since.[1]

The Cora Indians of Mexico tell how in former times the iguana, a species of lizard, was in possession of fire, and how, having quarrelled with his wife and his mother-in-law, he retired to the sky, taking the fire with him. Thus there was no more fire on earth, because the iguana had carried it all away and kept it hidden up aloft. So the people assembled and consulted. They determined to send the raven up to the sky to fetch the fire down, but he failed in the attempt ; so

---

[1] W. C. Farabee, *The Central Arawaks* (Philadelphia, 1918), pp. 143–47 (*University of Pennsylvania, Anthropological Publications*, vol. ix.).

III.—THE ORIGIN OF FIRE

did the humming-bird, and all the other birds At last the opossum contrived to climb up to the sky. There he found an old man sitting by a fire. When the old man fell asleep, the opossum seized a firebrand and dragged it towards the abyss by which the way to earth went down. Being overtaken by the old man, the opossum threw down the fire. It fell on the ground and set the earth on fire But the earth goddess extinguished the conflagration with her milk. The people carried away the fire, and it remained with them.[1]

The Sia Indians of New Mexico say that Spider was the creator of men and all animals. He lived in a house underground, and there he made fire by rubbing a sharp-pointed stone on a round flat stone. But having kindled the fire, he kept it in his house, setting a snake, a cougar, and a bear to guard the first, second, and third door, that no one might enter and see the fire. So people on earth had no fire and grew weary of browsing on grass like deer. They sent the coyote to steal fire for them from the nether world. He went, passed the warders at the doors of Spider's house, because they were all asleep, and made his way into the room where Spider himself was slumbering beside the fire. Coyote hastened to the fire and lighted at it a cedar brand which was tied to his tail. Then he hurried away, and Spider awoke ; but before he could rouse the sleeping warders, coyote was far on his way with the fire to the upper world.[2]

The Navahoes of New Mexico say that when men first emerged from the earth, they found the animals already in possession of fire, though they themselves had none. But the coyote, the bat, and the squirrel, being friends of men, agreed to aid each other in procuring fire for mankind. So while the animals were busy playing the moccasin game, Coyote appeared on the scene with splinters of resinous pinewood tied to his tail. While the attention of the animals was absorbed by the game, Coyote dashed through the fire, the splinters attached to his tail took fire, and with his fiery train he fled, pursued by all the animals. When he was exhausted, he passed the fire to the bat, and when the bat in

---

[1] K. Th. Preuss, *Die Nayarit-Expedition,* i. (Leipsic, 1912), pp 177–81.

[2] Mrs. Matilda Coxe Stevenson, "The Sia," *Eleventh Annual Report of the Bureau of Ethnology* (Washington, 1894), pp. 26 *sq.*, 70, 72 *sq.*

APPENDIX

turn could run no more, he transmitted the fire to the squirrel, who contrived to carry it safe to the Navahoes.[1]

This arrangement of relays of animal runners, who pass the stolen fire from one to another, is a common feature in North American myths of the origin of fire. A typical story of this sort, for example, is told by the Uintah Utes of north-eastern Utah. They relate how Coyote and his people the Eagle, the Humming-bird, the Hawk-Moth, the Chicken-Hawk, and so on, had no fire, and how, led by Coyote, they started out in search of it, till at last they came to the village of people who had fire. There, dancing round the fire, Coyote contrived to ignite the shredded bark which he had stuck on his head in imitation of hair. Having thus secured the fire, he ran off with it, pursued by the people whose fire he had stolen. Growing tired, he passed the fire first to Eagle, who in turn transmitted it to Humming-bird, and so on. Finally, Coyote succeeded in bringing the precious fire, in a tube of old dry sagebrush, to his people, and explained to them how to make fire by boring a hole in a piece of sagebrush with a piece of greasewood.[2] In this tale, as in many others of the same sort, the actors bear the names of animals or birds but are conceived in some measure as human. The confusion is not necessarily a product of totemism; the lack of the power to discriminate clearly between animals and men is rather a cause than an effect of totemism.

The Sioux, Menomonis, Foxes, and several other Indian tribes in the valley of the Mississippi, used to relate, like many other peoples, that the few survivors of the great flood were left without fire. To remedy this inconvenience the Master of Life sent a white raven to carry fire to them. But the bird stopped by the way to batten on carrion and allowed the fire to go out. For this negligence the Great Spirit punished him by making him black instead of white. Then the Great Spirit sent a little grey bird (the *erbette*) as his messenger to carry fire to the man and woman, who alone had escaped from the flood. The bird did as he was bidden, and the

[1] Major E. Backus, " An account of the Navajoes of New Mexico," in H. R. Schoolcraft's *Indian Tribes of the United States* (Philadelphia, 1853–1856), iv. 281 *sq.*
[2] A. L. Kroeber, " Uteh Tales," *Journal of American Folk-lore*, xiv. (1901), pp. 252–260.

III.—THE ORIGIN OF FIRE

Great Spirit rewarded him by giving him two little black bars on each side of his eyes. Hence the Indians regard the bird with great respect; they never kill it themselves, and they forbid their children to shoot it. Moreover, they imitate the bird by painting two little black bars on each side of their own eyes.[1]

The Karok Indians of California say that in the early ages of the world men were without fire. For the Creator had hidden the fire and given it to two old hags to guard jealously. However, the Coyote, who was friendly to men, contrived to procure fire for them by stealing it from the two hags and passing it along a line of animal runners. Amongst the runners was the ground-squirrel, and the black spot which you see to this day just behind his fore-shoulders is the mark of the fire which burned him there when he was carrying it. Another of the runners was the frog. In those days he had a tail, but as he could not hop fast enough, one of the old hags, who came tearing after the fire-thief, caught him up and tweaked off his tail. That is why frogs have no tails down to this day.[2]

The Tolowa Indians of California say that after the great flood there was no fire left on earth. However, the Spider Indians and the Snake Indians contrived by means of a captive balloon to ascend to the moon and to steal fire from the Indians who inhabited the lunar orb.[3] The Maidu Indians of California relate how once Thunder carried off all the fire and kept it in his house, setting Woswosim (a small bird) to guard it and to prevent people from stealing it. However, with the help of two Lizards the people discovered the house of Thunder by its smoke, and they sent Mouse, Deer, Dog, and Coyote to get the fire, and they took a flute with them in which to carry the fire when they should get it. Mouse contrived to steal the fire while the watcher slept, and the stolen element was given to the

---

[1] François-Vincent Badin, in *Annales de l'Association de la Propagation de la Foi*, iv. (Lyons and Paris, 1830), pp. 537 *sq.*

[2] S. Powers, *Tribes of California* (Washington, 1877), pp. 38 *sq.* (*Contributions to North American Ethnology*, vol. iii.).

[3] S. Powers, *op. cit.* pp. 70 *sq.* For other stories of the origin of fire, see *id.*, pp. 161, 182, 273, 343 *sq.*

swiftest runner to carry in the tube. But Deer carried some of it in the hock of his leg, and that is why there is a reddish spot in his hock to this day. While they were making off with the fire, Thunder awoke, jumped up with a roar like thunder, and came tearing after the thieves. But Skunk shot him dead. So the people got home safely with the fire, and they have had it ever since.[1]

While in the more southern tribes of North America the animal which is most commonly supposed to have procured fire for men is the coyote, in the more northerly tribe the place of the coyote in the myth is taken by other animals or birds, such as the deer, the beaver, the mink, and the raven. For example, among the tribes of Vancouver Island the thief of fire is usually the deer, who steals it in much the same way as the coyote, by tying resinous shavings of pine-wood to his tail or his head and then whisking his tail or butting with his head through the fire, so that the shavings ignite and the animal makes off with its tail or head ablaze and with the usual hue and cry after it. Such stories are told, for example, by the Nootkas or Ahts,[2] the Catloltq,[3] the Tlatlasikoala,[4] and the Kwakiutl[5] Indians, all of Van-

---

[1] Rowland B. Dixon, "Maidu Myths," *Bulletin of the American Museum of Natural History*, xvii. part ii. (New York, 1902), pp. 65-67.

[2] G. M. Sproat, *Scenes and Studies of Savage Life* (London, 1868), pp. 178 *sq.* ; George Hunt, "Myths of the Nootka," in "Tsimshian Mythology," by Franz Boas, *Thirty-first Annual Report of the Bureau of American Ethnology* (Washington, 1916), pp. 894-896. Compare Franz Boas, *Indianische Sagen von der Nord-Pacifischen Küste Amerikas* (Berlin, 1895), p. 102. In this last version Deer fails in his attempt to steal fire from the Wolves, its owners ; but the theft is successfully perpetrated by Woodpecker and a creature called Kwatiath, who, in carrying the fire, inadvertently put it to his cheek and so burned a hole in his cheek, which may be seen there to this day.

[3] Franz Boas, *Indianische Sagen von der Nord-Pacifischen Küste Amerikas*, pp. 80 *sq.*

[4] Franz Boas, *Indianische Sagen von der Nord-Pacifischen Küste Amerikas*, p. 187.

[5] George M. Dawson, "Notes and Observations on the Kwakiool people of Vancouver Island," *Transactions of the*

III.—THE ORIGIN OF FIRE

couver Island. Myths of the same sort are current among the tribes on the adjacent coast of British Columbia, such as the Awikenoq [1] and the Tsimshian. [2] Among the Heiltsuk, another tribe on the coast of British Columbia, the Deer is said to have borne a title meaning the Torch-bearer, because he stole the fire by means of wood tied to his tail. [3]

In a myth told by the Thompson Indians, who inhabit the interior of British Columbia, the Coyote reappears as the first thief of fire, who stole it in the usual way by dancing round a fire with a head-dress of combustible shavings and then running away as soon as the shavings ignited. The parallel with the southern myths is completed by a chain of animals, including Fox, Wolf, and Antelope, to which Coyote passed the fire, and who ran with it till they succumbed, one after the other. [4] But in other versions of the myth told by the Thompson Indians the thief of fire is the Beaver, assisted by the Eagle or by the Eagle and the Weasel together. [5] A very similar story of the theft of fire is told by the Lillooet Indians, who are neighbours of the Thompson Indians. In

---

Royal Society of Canada, vol. v. section ii. (1887), p. 22. In another Kwakiutl version of the myth the thief is not the Deer but the Mink, who stole the first fire for men from the ghosts. See Franz Boas, *Indianische Sagen von der Nord-Pacifischen Küste Amerikas*, p. 158.

[1] Franz Boas, *Indianische Sagen von der Nord-Pacifischen Küste Amerikas*, pp 213 *sq.*

[2] Franz Boas, "Tsimshian Mythology," *Thirty-first Annual Report of the Bureau of American Ethnology* (Washington, 1916), p. 63.

[3] Franz Boas, *Indianische Sagen von der Nord-Pacifischen Küste Amerikas*, p. 241.

[4] James A. Teit, "Thompson Tales," in *Folk-tales of Salishan and Sahaptin Tribes*, edited by Franz Boas (Lancaster, Pa., and New York, 1917), p. 2 (*Memoirs of the American Folk-lore Society*, vol. xi.).

[5] James Teit, "Mythology of the Thompson Indians," *The Jesup North Pacific Expedition*, vol. viii. part ii. (Leyden and New York, 1912), pp. 229 *sq.* 338 *sq.* (*Memoirs of the American Museum of Natural History*); *id. Traditions of the Thompson River Indians of British Columbia* (Boston and New York, 1898), pp. 56 *sq.*

their version also the thief is the Beaver, and his accomplice is the Eagle, who diverts the attention of the owners of the fire, while Beaver conveys it away in a clam-shell.[1] A like tale is told by the Okanaken Indians, who form the most easterly division of the Salish stock in British Columbia. In their version the fire is stolen from the sky people by the animals who climb up to the sky along a chain of arrows constructed in the way which has been already described.[2] Having reached the upper world in this manner, Beaver and Eagle are deputed to secure the fire, and they do so as before, Eagle attracting the attention of the Sky people, while Beaver makes off with the fire, which he has stowed away for safety under his skin. On reaching the top of the ladder of arrows in order to descend to earth, the animals scuffle among themselves as to who should go down first, and in the scuffle the ladder breaks before they could all descend by it. Hence some of them had to jump down, and Catfish and Sucker broke their heads in leaping, which explains why their heads are so funny to this day.[3] An almost precisely similar story is told by the Sanpoil Indians, another tribe of the Salish stock who live in Washington State.[4]

The Chilcotin Indians, in the interior of British Columbia, tell how in the old days there was no fire in the world except in the house of one man, who would not give it to anybody. But Raven contrived to steal fire from him by the familiar device of tying pitchwood shavings in his hair, dancing round the man's fire, and then poking his head in the fire, so that the shavings ignited. Thus Raven got fire and used it to kindle conflagrations all over the country. When the woods began to burn, the animals ran for their

---

[1] James Teit, "Traditions of the Lillooet Indians of British Columbia," *Journal of American Folk-lore*, xxv. (1912), pp. 299 *sq.*

[2] See above, Appendix, "War of Earth on Heaven," pp. 318 *sqq.*

[3] C. Hill Tout, "Report on the Ethnology of the Okanaken of British Columbia," *Journal of the Royal Anthropological Institute*, xli. (1911), p. 146.

[4] See above, Appendix, "War of Earth on Heaven," pp. 325 *sq.*

lives and most of them escaped ; but the rabbit did not run fast enough, and the fire caught him up, and burned his feet. That is why rabbits have black spots on the soles of their feet to this day. And after the trees had caught fire, the fire remained in them, which is the reason why wood burns to-day, and why you can get fire by rubbing two sticks together.[1]

The Haida Indians of Queen Charlotte Islands say that long ago people had neither fire, nor daylight, nor fresh water, nor the olachen fish, all these good things being in the possession of a great chief or deity who lived where is now the Nasse River, and who kept them all to himself. But the cunning Raven contrived to steal all these boons from the selfish chief or deity and to communicate them to mankind. The way in which he stole fire was this. He did not dare to appear in his proper shape in the chief's house ; but assuming the form of a leaf of the spruce fir he floated on the water near the house. Now the chief had a daughter, and when she went down to draw water, she drew up the leaf along with it, and afterwards, taking a draught of the water, she swallowed the leaf. Shortly afterwards she conceived and bore a child, who was no other than the subtle Raven. Thus Raven gained an entry into the lodge. Watching his chance, he one day picked up a burning brand, and donning his coat of feathers (for he could don and doff his plumage at will) he flew out of the smoke-hole, carrying fire with him and spreading it wherever he went.[2]

The Tlingit Indians of Alaska also tell of the wonderful doings of Raven in the early days of the world. They say that fire did not then exist on the earth, but only on an island in the sea. Raven flew thither, and picking up a

---

[1] Livingston Farrand, "Traditions of the Chilcotin Indians." *The Jesup North Pacific Expedition*, vol. ii. part i. ([New York], 1900), p. 3 (*Memoir of the American Museum of Natural History*).

[2] G. M. Dawson, *Report on the Queen Charlotte Islands, 1878* (Montreal, 1880), pp. 149ʙ–151ʙ (*Geological Survey of Canada*). A less romantic version of the Haida story is current in the Masset dialect. See John R. Swanton, "Haida texts—Masset dialect," *The Jesup North Pacific Expedition*, vol. x. part ii. (Leyden and New York, 1908), pp. 315 *sq.*

firebrand in his bill returned. But so great was the distance that when he came to land the brand was almost consumed, and even Raven's bill was half burnt off. As soon as he reached the shore, he dropped the glowing embers on the ground, and the scattered sparks fell on stones and wood. And that, the Tlingit say, is the reason why both stones and wood still contain fire ; for you can strike sparks from stones by striking them with steel, and you can produce fire from wood by rubbing two sticks together.[1]

In another Tlingit version of the myth it is said that in the beginning men had no fire. But Raven (Yetl) knew that Snow-Owl, who lived far out in the ocean, guarded the fire. He commanded all men, who in those days still had the form of animals, to go, one after the other, to fetch fire ; but none of them succeeded in bringing it. At last the Deer, who then had a long tail, said, "I will take fir-wood and tie it to my tail. With that I will fetch fire." So he ran to the house of Snow-Owl, danced round the fire, and at last whisked his tail close to the flames. Then the wood on his tail caught fire, and he ran away. Thus it came about that his tail was burnt off, and since that time the Deer has had only a stumpy tail.[2]

In Normandy they say that long ago there was no fire on earth and it was necessary to fetch fire from heaven. The people applied to the big birds, but they refused to undertake the task. At last the little wren offered to go, and succeeded in bringing back the fire to earth. But on the return journey all the wren's feathers were burnt by the fire ; and to supply their place the other birds out of gratitude gave each a feather from his own plumage. Since that time the wren's plumage has been speckled. The only bird that would not give a feather to clothe the wren was the screech-owl. All the birds attacked him to punish him for his

[1] H. J. Holmberg, "Ueber die Völker des Russischen Amerika," *Acta Societatis Scientiarum Fennicae*, iv. (Helsingfors, 1856), p. 339 ; Alph. Pinart, "Notes sur les Koloches," *Bulletins de la Société d'Anthropologie de Paris*, IIme série, vii. (1872), pp. 798 *sq.* ; Aurel Krause, *Die Tlinkit-Indianer* (Jena, 1885), p. 263.

[2] Franz Boas, *Indianische Sagen von der Nord-Pacifischen Küste Amerikas*, p. 314.

III.—THE ORIGIN OF FIRE

hardness of heart. Hence he is forced to hide himself by day and only comes out at night.[1] Hence in Normandy the wren is much respected, and people believe that some misfortune would befall him who should kill the bird.[2] Some say that fire from heaven would strike the house of any bad boy who should kill a wren or rob its nest.[3]

In Brittany the same story is told of the wren, and there is the same unwillingness to hurt the bird. At Saint Donan they say that if little children touch a wren's young ones, they will catch St. Lawrence's fire : that is, they will suffer from pimples or pustules on the face, legs, and other parts of the body.[4] But in some parts of Brittany the same story is told of the robin redbreast. They say it was he who fetched the fire, and in doing so he burnt all his feathers, whereupon the other birds reclothed him by each one giving him a feather. Only the screech-owl refused to lend a feather ; hence, if he shows himself by day, all the little birds cry out on him.[5] In Guernsey they say that robin redbreast was the first who brought fire to the island. But while he was crossing the water, the fire singed his feathers, and hence his breast has been red ever since.[6]

At Le Charme, in the Département of Loiret, the story goes that the wren stole the fire of heaven and was descending with it to earth, but his wings caught fire and he was obliged to entrust his precious burden to robin redbreast. But robin burned his breast by hugging the fire to it ; hence he in turn had to resign the office of fire-bearer. Then the lark took up the sacred fire, and carrying it safe to earth

---

[1] Jean Fleury, *Littérature orale de la Basse Normandie* (Paris, 1883), pp. 108 *sq.* Compare Amélie Bosquet, *La Normandie Romanesque et Merveilleuse* (Paris and Rouen, 1845), pp. 220 *sq.*

[2] Alfred de Nore, *Coutumes, Mythes, et Traditions des Provinces de France* (Paris and Lyons, 1846), p. 271.

[3] Amélie Bosquet, *op. cit.* p. 221.

[4] P. Sébillot, *Traditions et Superstitions de la Haute-Bretagne* (Paris, 1882), ii. 214 *sq.*

[5] P. Sébillot, *Traditions et Superstitions de la Haute-Bretagne*, ii. 209 *sq.*

[6] Charles Swainson, *The Folk-lore and Provincial Names of British Birds* (London, 1886), p 16.

APPENDIX

delivered the treasure to mankind.[1] This **story** resembles
the American fire-myths in which the stolen fire is said to
have been passed on from one to another along a line of
animal runners.[2]

IV.—MELAMPUS AND THE KINE OF PHYLACUS

(*Apollodorus* I. ix. 12)

The **story** of Melampus and the kine of Phylacus **or of**
Iphiclus is told by the Scholiast on Homer, who cites as his
authority the seventh book of Pherecydes.[3] Since this version
of the legend contains some picturesque details, which are
omitted by Apollodorus, and probably affords a fair specimen
of the manner of the early mythographer Pherecydes, it
may be worth while to submit it to the reader in a translation. As printed by Dindorf in his edition of the Scholia on
Homer, the tale runs as follows[4]:

"Neleus, son of Poseidon, had a daughter named Pero, of
surpassing beauty, but he would give her in marriage to
none except to him who should first drive away from Iphiclus
at Phylace the cows of his (that is, of Neleus's) mother
Tyro.[5] When all hesitated, Bias, son of Talaus,[6] alone
undertook to do it, and he persuaded his brother Melampus

---

[1] E. Rolland, *Faune Populaire de la France,* ii. (Paris,
1879), p. 294 ; P. Sébillot, *Le Folk-lore de France* (Paris,
1904–1907), iii. 156.   [2] See above, pp. 341 *sqq.*

[3] Scholiast on Homer, *Od.* xi. 287.

[4] *Scholia Graeca in Homeri Odysseam,* ed. G. Dindorf
(Oxford, 1855), vol. ii. pp. 498 *sq.*

[5] The cows belonged originally to Tyro, the mother of
Neleus. But when Neleus was under age, Iphiclus stole the
kine and kept them. On growing up, Neleus demanded back
the cattle, but Iphiclus refused to return them. Hence
Neleus was driven to promise the hand of his beautiful
daughter Pero to anyone who should succeed in recovering
the stolen kine. See Eustathius, on Homer, *Od.* xi. 292,
p. 1685. Phylace was in Thessaly (Scholiast on Homer, *Od.*
xi. 290).

[6] According to Apollodorus (i. 9. 13), Talaus was not the
father but the son of Bias.

to achieve the task. And he, although as a soothsayer he knew that he should be kept a prisoner for a year, went to Othrys[1] to get the cows. The watchmen there and the herdsmen caught him in the act of stealing, and handed him over to Iphiclus. And he was kept in bonds with two servants, a man and a woman, who were put in charge of him. Now the man treated him kindly, but the woman treated him scurvily. But when the year was nearly up, Melampus heard some worms overhead saying among themselves that they had gnawed through the beam. On hearing that, he called the attendants and bade them carry him out, the woman taking hold of the bed by the foot, and the man by the head. So they took him up and carried him out. But meantime the beam broke and fell on the woman and killed her. The man reported to Phylacus what had happened, and Phylacus reported it to Iphiclus. And they came to Melampus and asked him who he was. He said he was a soothsayer. And they promised to give him the cows if he should discover some means whereby Iphiclus might beget children. On this subject they gave mutual pledges. And Melampus sacrificed an ox to Zeus and cut it into portions for all the birds, and they all came, save one vulture. And Melampus asked all the birds if any of them knew means whereby Iphiclus might have children. And being all puzzled, they brought the vulture. He at once discovered the cause of the inability to beget children. For while Iphiclus was still a child, Phylacus had pursued him with a knife because he saw him misbehaving ; then not catching him up, Phylacus stuck the knife in a certain wild pear-tree and the bark had grown round it, and on account of his fright Iphiclus had no longer the power to get children. So the vulture advised them to get the knife from the wild pear-tree, and wiping off the rust from it to give it in wine to Iphiclus to drink for ten days ; for by that means he would get children. And having done so, Iphiclus recovered his virility and got a son Podarces. And he gave the cows

---

[1] Accepting the correction Ὄθρυν, proposed by Barnes and approved by Buttmann, for the MS. reading Ὀφρήν or Ὀφρύν. For Othrys, see Theocritus, iii. 43 :

τὰν ἀγέλαν χὠ μάντις ἀπ' Ὄθρυος ἆγε Μελάμπους
ἐς Πύλον.

APPENDIX

to Melampus, who took them and brought them to Pylus and gave them to Neleus as a bridal gift for Pero; and he got her as a bride for his brother Bias. And children were born to him, namely, Perialces and Aretus and Alphesiboea. The story is to be found in the seventh book of Pherecydes."

The story is told in a nearly identical form by Eustathius, but without mentioning his authority.[1] He adds, however, one or two touches to the narrative which deserve to be noticed. Thus he says that when Melampus heard the worms conversing overhead, he pretended to be ill and availed himself of this pretence in order to have himself transported from the house which was so soon to collapse; and again he tells us that Melampus invited all the birds to the sacrifice except the vulture, and that he questioned them all as to the means by which Iphiclus could beget children, but that none of them could answer, until last of all the vulture appeared and explained the matter. After concluding his version of the story, Eustathius calls attention to a scholium on Theocritus which adds a notable feature to the tale. According to the scholium, Phylacus, the father of Iphiclus, was gelding animals at the time when he frightened his little son by threatening him with the knife; nay, in lifting up the knife to stick it in the tree he accidentally touched his son's genital organs with it.[2] This incident, though it is not mentioned in the scholium on Theocritus as that scholium now appears in our editions,[3] is recorded in a scholium on Homer,[4] and it has all the

---

[1] Commentary on Homer, *Od.* xi. 292, p. 1685.

[2] ἐκτέμνοντί ποτε τῷ Φυλάκῳ ζῷα παρειστήκει παῖς ὢν Ἴφικλος, ὃν ἐκπλῆξαι θέλων ὁ πατὴρ καὶ ἀνατείνας ἣν κατεῖχε μάχαιραν, εἶτα εἰς τὸ πλησίον δένδρον ἐμπῆξαι θελήσας, ἐπήνεγκεν αὐτοῦ τοῖς μορίοις οὕτω σύμβαν. If the last two words are not corrupt, they seem to mean "by accident."

[3] Schol. on Theocritus, iii. 43. In this scholium, as it now stands, Phylacus is said to have been engaged in cutting a tree (ἐκτέμνοντί ποτε τῷ πατρὶ Φυλάκῳ δένδρον) instead of gelding animals.

[4] Schol. on Homer, *Od.* xi. 290 ἣν [scil. μάχαιραν] ἐπήνεγκε Φύλακος τῷ Ἰφίκλῳ ἐπὶ τῶν ἀγρῶν ἐκτέμνοντι τὰ τετράποδα. Here τῶν ἀγρῶν seems to support the reading τῶν ἀγρῶν

appearance of being an original and vital part of the narrative. It was, in fact, the contact of the gelding knife with
the boy's genitals which, on the principle of sympathetic
magic, was supposed to have deprived him of his virility because it had just deprived the rams of their generative power.
The incident is reported by Apollodorus, except that he does
not mention the actual contact of the knife with the boy's
genital organs. We can hardly doubt that the incident also
formed part of the story as told by Pherecydes, though the
scholiast on Homer, who professes to reproduce the narrative of Pherecydes, has passed it over in silence, perhaps
out of delicacy. The mode of cure recommended by the
vulture, which undoubtedly was recorded by Pherecydes,
furnishes another good example of sympathetic or, in the
strict sense, homoeopathic magic. The lad recovered his
virility by swallowing the rust of the knife which had deprived him of his generative powers, exactly as the wounded
Telephus was healed by the rust of the spear which had
wounded him.[1]

On one point of the story our authorities are not agreed.
Were the cattle which Melampus went to steal in possession
of Phylacus or of his son Iphiclus? In one passage[2] Homer
plainly says that the cattle were in possession of Iphiclus,
and that it was Iphiclus who released Melampus after a
forcible detention of a year. This is the version of the story
accepted, doubtless on Homer's authority, by Pausanias, by
the scholiasts on Homer, Theocritus, and Apollonius
Rhodius, and by Propertius.[3] But in another passage
Homer affirms that Melampus was detained a prisoner in
the house, not of Iphiclus, but of Phylacus.[4] This latter
version is clearly the one accepted by Apollodorus, who
speaks of the cows as in possession of Phylacus, and
ascribes the release of Melampus to Phylacus and not to

---

against the reading τῶν αἰδοίων in the parallel passage of
Apollodorus (i. 9. 12). See the Critical Note on that
passage, vol. i. p. 88, note [5].

[1] See Apollodorus, *Epitome*, iii. 20

[2] Homer, *Od.* xi. 288 *sqq.*

[3] Pausanias, iv. 36. 3; Scholiasts on Homer, *Od.* xi. 287
and 290; Scholiast on Theocritus, iii. 43; Scholiast on Apollonius Rhodius, *Argon.* i. 118; Propertius, ii. 3. 51 *sqq.*

[4] Homer, *Od.* xv. 231 *sq.*

APPENDIX

Iphiclus. Hence his text ought not to be altered, as it has been altered by some editors,[1] in order to bring it forcibly into accord with the passages of Homer and the other writers in which the ownership, or rather the possession, of the cows is assigned to Iphiclus instead of to his father Phylacus.

Apollodorus also differs from Eustathius and the Scholiast on Homer in describing as a sacred oak the tree into which Phylacus stuck the bloody knife with which he had been gelding the rams; whereas according to these other writers the tree was a wild pear-tree.[2] It is tempting to connect the sacred oak of which Apollodorus here speaks with the oak which a little before he had described as standing in front of the house of Melampus and as harbouring the brood of serpents to which Melampus owed his prophetic powers.[3] But the two trees can hardly have been the same, if Melampus lived at Pylus and Phylacus in Thessaly. No doubt oaks were common in ancient Greece as they still are in some parts of modern Greece, especially in the secluded highlands of Northern Arcadia. But why was the oak in which Phylacus stuck the knife a sacred tree? Thereby perhaps hangs a tale, which, like so many other stories of the olden time in Greece, is lost to us.

The calling of all the birds together for a consultation, their profession of ignorance, and the subsequent information given by the bird which was the last to arrive, are common incidents of folk-tales. Thus in a Rumanian story all the storks are assembled by the King of the Storks to say where the water of life and the water of death are to be found; but none of them can say, until at last a blind old stork comes forward from the rear and supplies the desired information.[4] So in a Hungarian story a twelve-headed dragon calls all his beasts together to tell him where Whiteland is; but none of them know. At last a lame wolf limps

---

[1] See Apollodorus, i. 9. 12, with the Critical Note, vol. i. p. 88, note ¹.

[2] The Scholiast on Theocritus iii. 43 adopts an attitude of judicial impartiality by describing the tree simply as a tree.

[3] Apollodorus, i. 9. 11.

[4] M. Gaster, *Rumanian Bird and Beast Stories* (London, 1915), pp. 263 *sq.* See below, pp. 356 *sq.*

V.—THE CLASHING ROCKS

forward and acts as a guide to Whiteland.[1] In another Hungarian story the Queen of Mice summons all the mice to tell her where a certain castle is situated; but none of them can tell her. However, soon afterwards an old bald mouse appears who knows all about it.[2] So in a modern Greek story an old woman calls all the birds together to learn where the Glass City is; but none of them know. At last she consults a lame bird, whom she had at first neglected to summon, and he knows where the Glass City is situated.[3] In another modern Greek story the eagle summons all the birds to tell him where the *Ilinen Vilinen* are to be found, but none of them can tell him. Then he remembers a lame hawk whom he had not summoned to the assembly; so he sends for the lame hawk, who, as usual, gives the desired information.[4]

In a German story the King of the Golden Castle has lost his way and comes to the Queen of Birds to ask if she can direct him to the Golden Castle. The Queen has never heard of it, and summons all her birds to inquire whether they know where the castle is; but not one of them can tell. At last, after all the rest of the birds had assembled, up comes a stork. The Queen chides him for being so late, but he answers that he had come from far, being perched on the Golden Castle when he heard the Queen's whistle summoning him home. So the stork takes the King on his back and flies with him to the Golden Castle.[5]

V.—THE CLASHING ROCKS

(*Apollodorus* i. ix. 22)

In folk-tales the water of life is sometimes said to be found between two huge cliffs, which dash together and separate again, barely allowing the hero or his messenger

---

[1] G. Stier, *Ungarische Volksmärchen* (Pesth, n.d.), p. 9.

[2] G. Stier, *op. cit.* pp. 142 *sq.*

[3] J. G. von Hahn, *Griechische und Albanesische Märchen* (Leipsic, 1864), i. 138.

[4] J. G. von Hahn, *op. cit.*, i. 184 *sq.*

[5] P. Zaunert, *Deutsche Märchen seit Grimm* (Jena, 1919), pp. 32–35. For more examples, see E. Cosquin, *Contes Populaires de Lorraine*, i. 48.

time to snatch the precious liquid before they close on each other once more. Thus in a Russian story "the hero is sent in search of 'a healing and vivifying water,' preserved between two lofty mountains which cleave closely together, except during 'two or three minutes' of each day. He follows his instructions, rides to a certain spot, and there awaits the hour at which the mountains fly apart. 'Suddenly a terrible hurricane arose, a mighty thunder smote, and the two mountains were torn asunder. Prince Ivan spurred his heroic steed, flew like a dart between the mountains, dipped two flasks in the waters, and instantly turned back.' He himself escapes safe and sound, but the hind legs of his horse are caught between the closing cliffs and smashed to pieces. The magic waters, of course, soon remedy this temporary inconvenience." [1]

In a Rumanian story the hero Floria is ordered by a king to procure for him the water of life and the water of death. In this difficulty the hero applies to a stork who, grateful for a kindness that Floria had done him, was ready to assist him to the best of his power. Accordingly the stork, who happened to be the king of storks, returned to his palace, called all the storks together, and asked them whether they had seen or heard or been near the mountains that knock against one another, at the bottom of which are the fountains of the water of life and the water of death. None of the young strong storks could tell, but at last there came from the rear a stork, lame on one foot, blind in one eye, with a shrivelled body and half his feathers plucked out. This maimed bird said, "May it please your majesty, I have been there, and the proofs of it are my blinded eye and my crooked leg." Notwithstanding these painful experiences the gallant bird undertook once more to put his life to hazard and to fetch the water of life and death. After providing himself with fresh meat and two bottles, the stork flew straight to the place where the mountains were knocking against one another, thus preventing anyone from approaching the fountains of life and death. It was when the sun had risen as high as a lance that he espied in the distance those huge mountains which, when they knocked against

---

[1] W. R. S. Ralston, *Russian Folk-tales* (London, 1873), pp. 235 sq.

V.—THE CLASHING ROCKS

each other, shook the earth and made a noise that struck fear and terror into the hearts of those even who were far away. When the mountains had recoiled a little, the stork was about to swoop down between them and get the water, when suddenly a swallow flew to him from the heart of the mountain and warned him, on peril of his life, to wait till noon, when the mountains rested for half an hour. "As soon as thou seest," said the swallow, "that a short time has passed and they do not move, then rise up as high as possible into the air, and drop down straight to the bottom of the mountain. There, standing on the ledge of the stone between the two waters, dip thy bottles into the fountains and wait until they are filled. Then rise as thou hast got down, but beware lest thou touchest the walls of the mountain or even a pebble, or thou art lost." The stork did as the swallow had told him; he waited till noontide, and when he saw that the mountains had gone to sleep, he soared up into the air, then shooting down into the depth, he settled on the ledge of stone and filled his bottles. Having done so he rose with them again, but when he had almost reached the top of the mountains, he touched a pebble. Immediately the mountains closed on him with a snap, but all they caught of him was the tail, which remained fast wedged between the two peaks of the mountains. With a great wrench he tore himself away, leaving his tail behind, but glad to escape with his life and with the two bottles of precious water.[1]

Here the nipping off of the stork's tail resembles the nipping off of the dove's tail in the Argonaut story. In a modern Greek story a girl fetches the water of life from a spring in a mountain which opens for a short time every day at noon. In issuing from the cleft she barely escapes, for the mountain closes on her and catches the skirt of her dress. But she draws her sword, severs the skirt, and having thus freed herself, she carries away the water of life and by means of it restores to life her two brothers, who had been turned to stone by the glance of a certain bird.[2] In

---

[1] M. Gaster, *Rumanian Bird and Beast Stories* (London, 1915), pp. 263-265.

[2] J. G. v. Hahn, *Griechische und albanesische Märchen* (Leipsic, 1864), ii. 46 *sq.*

another modern Greek story a young man is directed to the
water of life by an old woman. She tells him that within a
certain mountain, which opens every day at noon, there are
many springs, and that he must draw only from the particular spring to which he should be guided by a bee, otherwise he would be lost.[1]

An Eskimo story, which relates the adventurous voyage of
a certain hero named Giviok, describes how " he continued
paddling until he came in sight of two icebergs, with a
narrow passage between them ; and he observed that the
passage alternately opened and closed again. He tried to
pass the icebergs by paddling round outside them, but they
always kept ahead of him ; and at length he ventured to go
right between them. With great speed and alacrity he
pushed on, and had just passed when the bergs closed together, and the stern-point of his kayak got bruised between
them." [2]

Tylor proposed to explain the passage of the Argo between the Clashing Rocks " as derived from a broken-down
fancy of solar-myth " ; [3] but the analogies on which he based
the hypothesis seem dubious, and the episode, like the whole
story of the voyage of the Argo, savours more of a simple
folk-tale than of a solar myth. In spite of the resemblance
of the incident in the Eskimo story it would be rash to
suppose that the Greek tale of the Clashing Rocks was suggested by a sailor's reminiscence of an encounter with
icebergs in some far northern sea. More probably it is a
mere creation of a story-teller's fancy.

---

[1] J. G. v. Hahn, *op. cit.*, ii. 280 *sq.* For other stories of
the water of life enclosed between two clashing mountains or
in a mountain that only opens for a short time, see J. G. v.
Hahn, *op. cit.* i. 238, ii. 195, 284 ; A. Leskien und K.
Brugman, *Litauische Volkslieder und Märchen* (Strasbourg,
1882), p. 551.

[2] H. Rink, *Tales and Traditions of the Eskimo* (Edinburgh
and London, 1875), pp. 158 *sq.*

[3] (Sir) E. B. Tylor, *Primitive Culture*[2] (London, 1873),
i. 349.

VI.—THE RENEWAL OF YOUTH

VI.—THE RENEWAL OF YOUTH

(*Apollodorus* i. ix. 27)

Stories like that of Medea and Pelias have been recorded among European peasantry in Scandinavia, Germany, Russia, and Italy. They tell how Christ, or St. Peter, or the Devil, going about on earth in disguise, restored an old person to youth or a dead person to life by boiling him in a kettle or burning him in a smith's forge, and how a bungler (generally a smith) tried to perform the same feat but failed.[1] A similar story is told of a certain mythical king of Cambodia, named **Pra T'hong Rat Koma**, who in his later years was afflicted with leprosy. "A learned Brahmin offered to cure him of his malady; but first it was necessary that he should be killed, and thrown into a cauldron of boiling medicine, from which he would emerge alive and clean. The King refused to believe in the Brahmin's power, but the Brahmin took a dog, which he killed and threw into the boiling cauldron, when it immediately jumped out and frisked about. Still the King doubted. Thereupon the Brahmin offered to slay himself, and he gave the King three drugs which were to be thrown successively into the cauldron. The first would give form to the dead body; the second, beauty; the third, life. Then the Brahmin flung himself into the boiling medicine, but the King, forgetful of his instructions, threw in all the drugs at once, and the Brahmin was changed to a stone statue."[2] The Shans of Lakon tell a similar story of one of

---

[1] (Sir) G. W. Dasent, *Popular Tales from the Norse* (Edinburgh, 1859), pp. 106 *sqq.*, "The Master-Smith"; Grimm, *Household Tales*, No. 81, "Brother Lustig," vol. i. pp. 312 *sqq.*, 440 *sq.* (English translation by M. Hunt); W. R. S. Ralston, *Russian Folk-tales* (London, 1873), pp. 57 *sqq.*, "The Smith and the Demon"; T. F. Crane, *Italian Popular Tales* (London, 1885), pp. 188 *sq.*, "The Lord, St. Peter and the Blacksmith."

[2] P. A. Thompson, *Lotus Land* (London, 1906), pp. 300 *sq.* The story is told, with some unimportant variations, by Adolf Bastian, who calls the king Krung Phala. See A. Bastian, *Die Voelker des oestlichen Asien*, I (Leipsic, 1866), pp. 444 *sqq.*

their early kings, who lived in the time of Buddha. They say that Kom-ma Rattsee, "a famous magician, demigod, and doctor, visited Lakon, and informed the princes and people that by his medicines and charms he could add beauty and restore youth and life to anyone, however he might have been dismembered and mangled. A decrepit old prince, who was verging on dotage, and longed for a renewal of his youth, begged the magician to experiment upon him. The doctor, after mincing him up, prepared a magic broth, and, throwing the fragments into it, placed it over the fire. After performing the necessary incantations, the prince, rejuvenated and a perfect beau, was handed out of the pot. He was so pleased with his new appearance, and the new spirit of youth and joy pervading him, that he entreated the magician to re-perform the operation, as he thought the first chopping up having been so successful, still greater benefits would accrue from its repetition. On the magician refusing, he clamorously persisted in his request. The demigod, annoyed at his persistence and his covetousness, accordingly minced him up and put him into the pot, where he remains to this day. The hill where the Phya, or prince, was dipped, is called Loi Phya Cheh (the hill of the dipped Phya); and a hill near it is known as Loi Rattsee (Russi), after the magician." [1]

The Papuans of Geelvink Bay, on the northern coast of Dutch New Guinea, tell of an old man who used to earn his living by selling the intoxicating juice of the sago-palm. But to his vexation he often found that the vessels, which he had set overnight to catch the dripping juice of the tapped palms, were drained dry in the morning. As the people in his village denied all knowledge of the theft, he resolved to watch, and was lucky enough to catch the thief in the very act, and who should the thief be but the Morning Star? To ransom herself from his clutches she bestowed on him a magical stick or wand, the possession of which ensured to its owner the fulfilment of every wish. In time the old man married a wife, but she was not pleased that her husband was so old and so covered with scabs. So one day he resolved to give her a joyful surprise by renewing

---

[1] Holt S. Hallett, *A Thousand Miles on an Elephant in the Shan States* (Edinburgh and London, 1890), pp. 269 *sq.*

his youth with the help of his magic wand. For this purpose he retired into the forest and kindled a great fire of iron-wood. When the flames blazed up he flung himself among the glowing embers, and immediately his shrivelled skin peeled off, and all the scabs were turned into copper trinkets, beautiful corals, and gold and silver bracelets. He himself came forth from the fire a handsome young man, decked himself with some of the ornaments and returned to his house. But there neither his wife nor her sister recognised him; and only his little son cried out, "There comes father!" However, when he explained to the women how he had been made young again, and convinced them of the truth of his story by conducting them to the place in the wood where the remains of the fire were still to be seen, with the rest of the trinkets lying about, their joy knew no bounds.[1]

We may conjecture that these stories reflect a real belief in the possibility of renewing youth and prolonging life by means of the genial influence of fire. The conjecture derives some support from a custom observed by the Wajagga of Mount Kilimandjaro in East Africa. Among them "the wizards boast of possessing the power to protect people against sickness and death. A peculiar custom may be quoted as an example. It is called *ndumo woika ndu nnini*: 'custom of boiling a nobleman.' When a great man desires to make himself a name, and also to prolong his life, he has this ceremony performed over him. He invites all his relations to come who desire to take part in it. The wizard arrives early in the morning, and first of all causes a trench to be dug large enough to allow a man to lie on one side of it with his legs drawn up; and his wife or a girl of the family lies down beside him. The wizard usually says to him, 'Step in with your favourite wife.' Only in case she refuses does he ask a girl to do him this service. When the man with his female companion has laid himself down in the

---

[1] J. B. van Hasselt, "Die Noeforezen," *Zeitschrift für Ethnologie*, viii. (1876), pp. 176–178; J. L. van Hasselt, "Die Papuastämme an der Geelvinkbai (Neuguinea)," *Mitteilungen der Geographischen Gesellschaft zu Jena*, ix. (Jena, 1891), pp. 103–105. The story is told more briefly by A. Goudswaard, *Die Papoewa's van de Geelvinksbaai* (Schiedam, 1863), pp. 84–87.

APPENDIX

trench, poles are placed over it, and on the poles banana-
bark and earth. After the trench has thus been covered in,
the man's three hearthstones are set over them at the heads
(of the pair), a fire is kindled between them, a pot is placed
on the fire, and food is boiled in it. This fire is kept up till
evening, and the boiled food is eaten by those who take part
in the ceremony, while the two who lie in the trench get
none of it. Not till evening are they liberated from their
confinement. In the heat they have been obliged to sweat
profusely. The wizard now spits on them and says moreover, 'Long life! Even in war thou shalt not be slain, even
a musket-ball will not hit thee.'"[1] Here the process of
boiling a pot on a man's own hearthstones over his own
head, while he sweats at every pore below, is perhaps the
nearest approach that can safely be made to boiling him in
person, and the beneficial effect of it is supposed to be a
prolongation of the "boiled nobleman's" life. But we have
seen that the process of roasting, applied to babies, was
believed by the ancient Greeks to be equally effectual in
prolonging the lives of the infants, or rather in render-
ing them immortal, by stripping off their mortal flesh and
leaving only the immortal element.[2] Thus the Greeks
apparently reposed a robust faith in the renovating virtue
both of roasting and boiling, but they drew a delicate
distinction between the two, for while they roasted babies,
they boiled old people, at least theoretically, like the
Wajagga of Mount Kilimandjaro. Nor are these the only
modes in which the primitive natural philosopher has attempted to repair the decaying energies of human and
animal life by a judicious application of what we may call
thermodynamics: for this purpose he has often either leaped
over fire or walked deliberately over glowing stones and has
driven his flocks and herds through the smoke and the
flames. These experiments in the art of prolonging life,
by cauterising, so to say, the germs that threaten its con-
tinuation, have been described by me elsewhere.[3]

---

[1] Bruno Gutman, *Dichten und Denken der Dschagganeger*
(Leipsic, 1906), p. 162.

[2] Above, pp. 311 *sqq.*

[3] *Balder the Beautiful*, vol. ii. pp. 1 *sqq.*, "The Fire-
walk." Compare *Adonis, Attis, Osiris*, vol. i. pp. 179 *sqq.*,
"Purification by Fire."

VII.—THE RESURRECTION OF GLAUCUS

VII.—The Resurrection of Glaucus

(*Apollodorus* III. iii. 1)

Other ancient writers relate, like Apollodorus, how the seer Polyidus restored the dead Glaucus to life by laying on him a magical herb which he had seen a serpent apply with similar effect to a dead serpent.[1] A similar story was told of the resurrection of a Lydian legendary hero named Tylon or Tylus. It is said that one day as he was walking on the banks of the Hermus a serpent stung and killed him. His distressed sister, Moire, had recourse to a giant called Damasen, who attacked and slew the serpent. But the serpent's mate culled a herb, "the flower of Zeus," in the woods, and bringing it in her mouth put it to the lips of the dead serpent, which immediately revived. In her turn Moire took the hint and restored her brother, Tylon or Tylus, to life by touching him with the same plant.[2] The story seems to have been associated with Sardes, since it is clearly alluded to on the coins of that city.[3]

The fisherman, Glaucus of Anthedon, whom the ancients distinguished from Glaucus, the son of Minos, is said to have learned in like manner the life-giving property of a certain herb or grass by observing that when a dead or dying fish or, according to another account, hare was brought into contact

---

[1] Tzetzes, *Schol. on Lycophron*, 811 (perhaps following Apollodorus); Apostolius, *Cent.* v. 48; Palaephatus, *De incredib.* 27; Hyginus, *Fab.* 136; *id. Astronom.* ii. 14. The story is told allusively by Claudian, *De bello Getico*, 442-446:

> *Cretaque, si verax narratur fabula, vidit*
> *Minoum rupto puerum prodire sepulchro :*
> *Quem senior vates avium clangore repertum*
> *Gramine restituit : mirae nam munere sortis*
> *Dulcia mella necem, vitam dedit horridus anguis.*

[2] Nonnus, *Dionys.* xxv. 451-551; Pliny, *Nat. Hist.* xxv. 14. The story, as we learn from Pliny, was told by Xanthus, an early historian of Lydia.

[3] B. V. Head, *Catalogue of the Greek coins of Lydia*, pp. cxi.-cxiii., with pl. xxvii. 12. As to Tylon and the "herb of Zeus," see further *Adonis, Attis, Osiris*[3], i. 186 *sq.*

with it, the creature at once revived or came to life again; having tasted the herb Glaucus became himself immortal and leaped into the sea, where he continued to dwell as a marine deity.[1]

The magical herb, which brings the dead to life again by simple contact, meets us elsewhere in folk-tales. Thus a modern Greek story relates how a mother, going in search of her dead son, killed a serpent by the way; how another serpent brought the dead serpent to life by laying a herb on its body; and how the mother, taking the hint, restored her dead son to life by means of the same herb.[2] In another modern Greek story a husband and wife, going in search of their dead son, see two serpents fighting and one of them killing the other. The husband says to his wife, "Cover up the dead serpent with leaves, that no man may see it." The wife does so, and immediately the dead serpent comes to life again. Thereupon the husband says to his wife, "Fill your pocket full of that herb, for it is a good medicine." Afterwards by means of the herb they restore their dead son to life.[3] Another modern Greek story tells how three ogres, as they sat talking together at a spring, saw two serpents fighting. One of the serpents struck the other such a violent blow with its tail that it cut the body of the other clean through. But the two pieces wriggled to a herb that grew near, and wrapping themselves up in it were united into one body as before. When the youngest of the three ogres saw that, he said to his brothers, "That forebodes ill to us. Let us take some of this herb and go home, to see what is doing there." So they returned to the crystal tower in which they dwelt, and found it dark and deserted; and not far off they discovered the

---

[1] Nicander, in the first book of his *Aetolian History*, cited by Athenaeus, vii. 48, pp. 296 F–297 A; Tzetzes, *Schol. on Lycophron*, 754; Scholiast on Apollonius Rhodius, *Argon.* i. 1310: Ovid, *Metamorph.* xiii. 924 *sqq.*; Ausonius, *Mosella*, 276 *sqq.*; Servius on Virgil, *Georg.* i. 437. According to Nicander, it was a hare that was revived by the herb; according to the other writers it was the fish which Glaucus had just caught.

[2] J. G. von Hahn, *Griechische und albanesische Märchen* (Leipsic, 1864), ii. 204.

[3] J. G. von Hahn, *op. cit.* ii. 260.

headless body of the young prince who had married their sister. A little search revealed the missing head, and by applying it to the body and rubbing the herb on the severed neck, they soon joined the two together. The prince started up, saying, " Ah, brothers, how deep has been my sleep and how light my awakening ! "[1]

Again, a German folk-tale relates how a young man of humble birth married a princess on condition that, if she died before him, he should be buried alive with her. She did die before him, and accordingly her young husband was conducted down into the royal vault, there to stay with the body of his dead wife till he died. While he sat there watching by the corpse and gloomily expecting death, he saw a snake creep out of a corner of the vault and crawl towards the dead body. Thinking that the creature had come to gnaw the corpse, he drew his sword and hewed the snake in three pieces. After a time a second snake crawled out of the hole, and seeing the first snake cut in pieces, it went back again, but soon returned with three green leaves in its mouth. These leaves it laid on the three severed pieces of the dead snake, and immediately the pieces joined together, and the dead snake came to life. Thereupon the two snakes retired together, but the leaves remained lying on the ground. The young man picked them up, and by applying them to the mouth and eyes of his dead wife he resuscitated her. After that they knocked on the door of the vault and called out, till they attracted the notice of the sentinels and were released from confinement by the King in person. But the provident young man kept the three snake-leaves carefully, and it was lucky for him that he did so ; for they afterwards served to restore himself to life, when he had been treacherously done to death by his ungrateful wife with the assistance of an unscrupulous skipper.[2]

Again, in a Lithuanian story a young man on his travels sees two snakes fighting with such fury that both of them were wounded and mangled, and the young man thought they would die on the spot. But after the fight the snakes crawled to a certain bush, and plucking leaves from it applied

[1] J. G. von Hahn, *op. cit.* ii. 274.

[2] Grimm, *Household Tales*, No. 16 (vol. i. pp. 70 *sq.*, Margaret Hunt's translation).

them to their wounded bodies, which were immediately made whole. Afterwards, when the young man had been foully murdered, he was brought to life again by some helpful animals, whose life he had spared, and which now repaid his kindness by fetching leaves from the snakes' bush and laying them on his body. No sooner had they done so than he revived and asked, "Why have you wakened me? I was sleeping so soundly."[1]

In a Walachian story the hero, lying asleep, is beheaded by a gipsy, whereupon three friendly animals, a bear, a wolf, and a fox, consult how they may bring him to life again. After they have laid their heads together in vain, the fox meets a serpent which is carrying a herb in its mouth. The fox asks, "What sort of herb is that which you are carrying there?" The serpent answers, "It is a magic herb; I will restore my son's head, which has been cut off." "Let me see it nearer," says the fox. The simple serpent complies with the request, and the fox seizes the herb in his mouth and makes off with it. By means of the herb he attaches the hero's severed head to his body, and the application of a jugful of water of life, borrowed, or rather stolen, by the wolf from an old woman, soon completes the hero's resurrection.[2]

In a Russian story a mother is wandering in a wood with her dead baby at her breast. She sees an old serpent creep up to a dead serpent and restore it to life by rubbing it with a leaf. The mother snatches the leaf, and by touching her dead baby with it she resuscitates the infant.[3]

In some stories the secret of the life-giving plant is learned, not from a serpent, but from some other animal. Thus in an Irish tale a woman, whose husband has been killed in single combat, sees two birds fighting and one of them killing the other. Then birds come and put leaves of a tree on the dead bird, and in half an hour the dead bird comes to life. The widow puts the leaves on her dead husband, who had assumed

---

[1] A. Schleicher, *Litauische Märchen, Sprichworte, Rätsel und Lieder* (Weimar, 1857), pp. 57–59.

[2] Arthur und Albert Schott, *Walachische Maehrchen* (Stuttgart and Tubingen, 1845), p. 142.

[3] G. Polivka, "Zu der Erzählung von der undankbaren Gattin," *Zeitschrift des Vereins für Volkskunde*, xiii. (1903), p. 408.

the form of a bird for the purpose of the single combat; and as usual the application of the magic plant effects the resurrection of the corpse.[1]

In a mediæval romance, a weasel having been killed by the blow of a stick, his mate brings a red flower and places it in the mouth of the dead weasel, which at once returns to life. The same flower thereafter, applied to a dead maiden, works on her the same miracle of resurrection.[2]

In a story told by the Baraba, a Turkish tribe of Southern Siberia, the hero has his legs cut off through the treachery of his two elder brothers. Sitting disconsolate propped up against the wall of the house, he sees the mice gather about his severed limbs and begin to nibble them. He seizes a mouse and breaks one of its legs, saying, " If I am lame, you shall be lame too." The other mice now gather about the lame mouse, and grubbing up a little white root out of the earth, give it to the lame mouse to eat. The mouse eats it, and after a time its broken leg is made whole, and the little creature runs away. The hero takes the hint, digs up the root with his nails, and eats it. After a time his two legs join on to his body again, and you could not detect so much as a scar at the joining.[3]

In a Polish story a girl kills her too importunate lover and is buried with him in a vault. There she sees two ravens fighting and one of them killed by the other; whereupon a third raven brings a herb in its bill, and by means of it brings the dead raven to life. As usual, the girl restores her dead lover to life by an application of the herb.[4]

In an Italian story a hero rescues a princess from a horrible seven-headed dragon, which was about to devour her. In the combat the hero began by cutting off one of the dragon's heads; but so soon as this happened, the dragon rubbed the headless neck on a herb that grew near, and at once the

---

[1] W. Larminie, *West Irish Folk-tales and Romances* (London, 1893), pp. 82 *sq.*

[2] P. Sébillot, *Le Folk-lore de France*, iii. 529, referring to Marie de France, *Poésies*, ed. Roquefort, i. 475.

[3] W. Radloff, *Proben der Volkslitteratur der Türkischen Stämme Süd-Sibiriens* iv. (St. Petersburg, 1872), pp. 77 *sq.*

[4] G. Polivka, "Zu der Erzählung von der undankbaren Gattin." *Zeitschrift des Vereins für Volkskunde*, xiii. (1903), pp. 408 *sq.*

367

severed head was reunited to the body. Seeing this, the hero killed the dragon by slicing off all his seven heads at one stroke, and after that he plucked a handful of the herb which had healed the dragon's dreadful wound. As usual, the magical herb thus acquired is afterwards turned to good account by the hero; for having the misfortune to decapitate his own brother, "like a pumpkin," in consequence of a painful misunderstanding, he soon mended matters by rubbing the bleeding neck with the miraculous herb, where upon the head immediately rejoined its body, and the dead brother was restored to vigorous life.[1]

In a Kabyle story a man sees two large spiders (tarantulas) fighting; one of them kills the other and then restores it to life by pressing into its nose the sap of a herb; the man takes the herb and by means of it restores to life his dead brother, who had been devoured by an ogress.[2]

A Jewish story, in the *Midrash Tanchuma*, tells of a man who, travelling from Palestine to Babylon, saw two birds fighting with each other. In the fight one of the birds killed the other, but immediately brought it to life again by fetching a herb and laying it on the beak of the dead bird. As the herb dropped from the bird's beak, the man picked it up and took it with him, intending to raise the dead by its means. When he came to the staircase leading up to Tyre, he found a dead lion by the wayside, and experimented on the animal by laying the herb on its mouth. The experiment was perfectly successful. The dead lion came to life and devoured its benefactor. The story ends with the moral, Do not good to the wicked, lest evil befal thee. The same story is told at greater length in the *Alphabet of Ben-Sirah*.[3]

We may compare, also, an episode in a Socotran story which bears a close resemblance to the ancient Egyptian story of "The Two Brothers." One of two brothers finds

---

[1] Giambattista Basile, *Der Pentamerone*, übertragen von Felix Liebrecht (Breslau, 1846), vol. i. pp. 99–109 (First Day, Seventh Story, "Der Kaufmann").

[2] J. Rivière, *Contes populaires de la Kabylie du Djurdjura* (Paris, 1882), pp. 193–197.

[3] *Südarabische Expedition*, vol. iv. 1. *Die Mehri- und Soqotri-Sprache*, von D. H. Müller (Vienna, 1902), pp. 201–203.

VII.—THE RESURRECTION OF GLAUCUS

his brother dead in the castle of the Daughter of the Sunrise. As he sits weeping with the corpse on his lap, he sees a raven take a dead raven and plunge with it into the water, from which both birds emerge alive. The brother took the hint, tied his dead brother on his back, and leaped with him into the water, which had the effect of restoring the dead man to life.[1] Here the life-giving agent is not a magical plant, but a magical water ; but the mode of its discovery by observation of animals is similar.

A belief in the actual existence of a plant endowed with such magical virtue appears to survive in some parts of Germany to this day ; at least it is said to have survived down to the middle of the nineteenth century. At Holzhausen, near Dillingen in Swabia, an informant reported as follows : " In our country there are many large snakes in the wood. If you hew a snake in three pieces with a shovel or a hoe, without smashing the head, and go away at once, the snake seeks a herb, lays it between the wounds, and is immediately whole again. I have often searched diligently after the healing herb, but have never been able to get it ; for so long as you stand by the severed snake, it is never made whole, and after sundown never at all. But if you leave the spot, the snake quickly fetches the unknown herb and heals itself. I have often seen such snakes as have been cut in pieces and made whole again ; for a scar remains right round the parts at the point where they cohered and healed."[2]

That serpents possess a knowledge of plants which confer immortality is a popular belief among the Armenians. They think that " the springs and flowers actually confer immortality, but not on men. The belief is that snakes, if they are not killed, live for ever. There are ' wells of immortality,' the springs of which are surrounded with various flowers and herbs. Old, sick, and wounded snakes are acquainted with such springs and herbs. They come to these springs, slough their skins, eat a leaf of a flower, then crawl to the spring, bathe in it, and drink three sips of the water. Then they

---

[1] *Südarabische Expedition*, vol. iv. 1. *Die Mehri- und Soqotri-Sprache*, von D. H. Müller, p. 88.

[2] Fried. Panzer, *Beitrag zur deutschen Mythologie* (Munich, 1848–1855), ii. 206, § 360.

crawl out, and are healed, and renew their youth. If anyone knows that spring and flower, drinks three handfuls of
the water, and eats the flower, he will be himself immortal."[1]

VIII.—The Legend of Oedipus

(*Apollodorus* III. v. 7)

According to the legend, Oedipus committed a twofold
crime in ignorance : he killed his father and married his
mother. The same double tragedy meets us in a Finnish
tale, which runs as follows :—

Two wizards arrived at the cottage of a peasant and were
hospitably entertained by him. During the night a she-goat
dropped a kid, and the younger of the two wizards proposed
to assist the mother-goat in her travail, but the elder of the
two would not hear of it, " Because," said he, " the kid is
fated to be swallowed by a wolf." At the same time the
peasant's wife was overtaken by the pangs of childbirth,
and the younger of the two wizards would have gone to her
help, but was dissuaded by the elder, who told him that the
boy who was about to be born would kill his father and marry
his mother. The peasant overheard this conversation and
reported it to his wife, but they could not make up their
minds to kill the child. One day, when they were making
merry in the peasant's cottage, they put the kid to roast on
a spit, and then laid the roasted meat near the window ;
but it fell out of the window and was devoured by a passing
wolf. Seeing that one of the two predictions made by the
wizards was thus fulfilled, the peasant and his wife were sore
afraid and thought how they could get rid of their child.
Not having the courage to kill him outright, they wounded
him in the breast, tied him to a table, and threw him into the
sea. The forsaken child drifted to an island, where he was
picked up and carried to the abbot of a monastery. There
he grew up and became a clever young man. But he wearied
of the monastic life, and the abbot advised him to go out into
the world and seek his fortune. So he went. One day he

---

[1] Manuk Abeghian, *Der armenische Volksglaube* (Leipsic,
1899), p. 59.

came to a peasant's cottage. The peasant was out, but his wife was at home, and the young man asked her for work. She told him, " Go and guard the fields against robbers." So he hid under the shadow of a rock, and seeing a man enter the field and gather grass, he struck and killed him. Then he returned to his mistress, who was uneasy because her husband did not come home to dinner. So they discovered that the supposed thief, whom the young man had killed, was no other than the husband of his mistress ; but as the homicide had not been committed with any evil intent, the widow, after weeping and wailing, forgave the young man and kept him in her service ; nay, in time she consoled herself by marrying him. However, one day she noticed the scar on her second husband's breast and began to have her suspicions. Inquiry elicited the fatal truth that her husband was also her son. What were they to do ? The woman sent him to seek out wise men, who might teach him how to expiate his great sin. He went and found a monk with a book in his hand. To him the conscience-stricken husband put his question ; but when the monk, on consulting his book, replied that no expiation was possible for guilt so atrocious, the sinner in a rage killed the holy man. The same thing happened to another monk who had the misfortune to receive the confession of the penitent. But a third monk proved more compliant, and answered very obligingly that there was no sin which could not be atoned for by repentance. Accordingly he advised the repentant sinner to dig a well in the rock till he struck water ; and his mother was to stand beside him holding a black sheep in her arms, until the sheep should turn white. This attracted public attention, and passers-by used to stop and ask the pair what they were doing. One day a gentleman, after putting the usual question and receiving the usual answer, was asked by the penitent, " And who are you ? " He answered, " I am he who makes straight what was crooked, and I summon you to the bar of justice." Seeing no hope of escaping from the arm of the law, the penitent took the bull by the horns and killed the gentleman. At the same moment the rock opened, the water gushed out, and the black sheep turned white. But his fourth homicide lying heavy on his soul, the murderer returned to the monk to learn how he could expiate his latest crime. But the holy man reassured him. " The gentleman whom you

killed," said he, " offended God more than you by his pro-
fessions. Your penance has been shortened ; no expiation
is required." So the repentant sinner was able to pass the
rest of his days in peace and quietness.[1]

The same story is told, with some variations of detail, in
the Ukraine :

There was a man and his wife, and they had a son. One
day they dreamed that when their son should be grown up,
he would kill his father, marry his mother, and afterwards
kill her also. They told each other their dream. " Well,"
said the father, " let us cut open his belly, put him into a
barrel, and throw the barrel into the sea." They did so,
and the barrel with the boy in it floated away on the sea.
Some sailors found it, and hearing the squalling of a child
in the barrel, they opened it, rescued the boy, sewed up his
wound, and reared him. When he was grown to manhood,
he bid the sailors good-bye and went away to earn his bread.
He came to the house of his father, but his father did not
recognize him and took him into his service. The duty laid
on the son by his father was to watch the garden ; and if
anyone entered it, he was to challenge the intruder thrice,
and if he received no answer, he was to fire on him. After
the young man had served some time, his master said, " Go
to, let us see whether he obeys my orders." So he entered
the garden. The young man challenged him thrice, and
receiving no answer, he shot him dead, and on coming up to
his victim he recognized his master. Then he went to his
mistress in her chamber, married her, and lived with her.
One Sunday morning, when he was changing his shirt, she
saw the scar on his body and asked him what it was. " When
I was small," answered he, " some sailors found me at sea
with my belly cut open, and they sewed it up." " Then I
am your mother ! " she cried. He killed her on the spot
and went away. He walked and walked till he came to a
priest and asked him to inflict some penance on him by way
of atonement for his sins. " What are your sins ? " asked
the priest. He told the priest, and the priest refused him

---

[1] L. Constans, *La légende d'Oedipe* (Paris, 1881), pp.
106–108. The story is told more briefly by Gustav Meyer, in
his preface to E. Schreck's *Finnische Märchen* (Weimar,
1887), p. xxv., referring to Erman's *Archiv*, xvii. 14 *sqq.*

absolution. So he killed the priest and came to another priest, who, proving equally recalcitrant, was disposed of by the young man in the same summary fashion. The third priest to whom he applied was kind or prudent enough to ◆xplain to him how he might expiate his sins. "Take this staff of apple-tree wood," said the priest; "plant it on yonder mountain, and morning and evening go to it on your knees with your mouth full of water, and water the staff. When it shall have sprouted and the apples on it are ripe, then shake it; as soon as the apples shall have fallen, your sins will be forgiven you." After twenty-five years, the staff budded and the apples ripened. The sinner, no longer young, shook the tree, and all the apples fell but two. So he returned and reported to the priest. "Very good," said the priest, "I will throw you into a well." He was as good as his word, and when the sinner was at the bottom of the well, the priest shut down the iron trap door, locked it, covered it up with earth, and threw the keys into the sea. Thirty years passed, and one day, the priest's fishermen caught a jack, cut it open, and found the keys in its belly. They brought the keys to the priest. "Ah!" said the priest laconically, "my man is saved." They ran at once to the well, and on opening it they found the sinner dead, but with a taper burning above his body. Thus all his sins were forgiven and he was gathered to the saints in bliss.[1]

The same double crime of parricide and incest with a mother, both committed in ignorance, occurs in a very savage story which the Javanese of the Residency of Pekalongan tell to account for the origin of the Kalangs, an indigenous tribe of Java. In it a woman, who is a daughter of a sow, marries her son unwittingly, and the son kills a dog, who is really his father, though the man is ignorant of the relation in which he stands to the animal. In one version of the story the woman has twin sons by the dog, and afterwards unwittingly marries them both; finally she recognizes one of her sons by the scar of a wound which she had formerly inflicted on his

---

[1] Eugène Hins, "Légendes chrétiennes de l'Oukraine," *Revue des Traditions Populaires*, iv. (1889), pp. 117 *sq.*, from *Traditions et Contes populaires de la petite Russie*, by Michel Dragomanof.

APPENDIX

head with a wooden spoon.[1] According to the Javanese, such incestuous unions are still not uncommon among the Kalangs : mother and son often live together as man and wife, and the Kalangs think that worldly prosperity and riches flow from these marriages.[2] However, it is to be observed that the story of the descent of the Kalangs from a dog and a pig is not told by the people themselves, but by the Javanese, who apparently look down with contempt on the Kalangs as an inferior race. Similar stories of descent from a dog and a pig are commonly told of alien races in the Indian Archipelago, and they are usually further embellished by accounts of incest practised by the ancestors of these races in days gone by. For example, the Achinese of Sumatra tell such a tale of the natives of the Nias, an island lying off the west coast of Sumatra ; and the natives of Bantam tell a similar story of the Dutch.[3] Probably, therefore, many stories of incest told of alien peoples, whether in the past or in the present, are no more than expressions of racial hatred and contempt, and it would be unsafe to rely upon them as evidence of an actual practice of incest among the peoples in question.

In the Middle Ages the story of Oedipus was told, with variations, of Judas Iscarioth. It is thus related in *The Golden Legend* :—

There lived at Jerusalem a certain Ruben Simeon. of the race of David. His wife, Cyborea, dreamed that she gave birth to a son, who would be fatal to the family. On waking, she told her dream to her husband, who endeavoured to comfort her by saying that she had been deceived by the evil spirit. But perceiving that she was with child from that very night, she began to be very uneasy, and her husband with her. When the child was born, they shrank from killing him, but put him in a little ark and committed it to the sea. The waves washed up the ark on the shore of the island of Iscarioth. The queen of the island found it, and having no

---

[1] E. Ketjen, " De Kalangers," *Tijdschrift voor Indische Taal-, Land- en Volkenkunde,* xxiv. (1877), pp. 430–435.

[2] E. Ketjen, *op. cit.* p. 427.

[3] J. C. van Eerde, " De Kalanglegende op Lombok," *Tijdschrift voor Indische Taal-, Land- en Volkenkunde,* xlv. (1902), pp. 30 *sq.*

child of her own, she adopted the little foundling. But soon afterwards she was with child and gave birth to a son. When the two boys were grown up, Judas Iscarioth behaved very ill to his supposed brother, and the queen, seeing that expostulations had no effect on him, upbraided him with being a foundling. In a rage, Judas murdered his brother and took ship for Jerusalem. There he found a congenial soul in the governor of Judea, Pontius Pilate, who appointed him to a high office in his court. One day the governor, looking down from his balcony on the garden of a neighbour, was seized with a great longing to eat some apples which he saw hanging there from the boughs. The obsequious Judas hastened to gratify his master's desire by procuring, not to say stealing, the apples. But the old man who owned the garden, and who chanced to be no other than Judas's father, resisted the attempt, and Judas knocked him on the head with a stone. As one good turn deserves another, the governor rewarded Judas by bestowing on him the property of the deceased, together with the hand of his widow, who was no other than Cyborea, the mother of Judas. Thus it came about that Judas, without knowing it, killed his father and married his mother. Still the widow, now again a wife, was not consoled, and one day Judas found her sighing heavily. When he questioned her as to the reason of her sadness, she replied, " Wretch that I am, I drowned my son, my husband is dead, and in my affliction Pilate gave me in marriage against my will." The answer set Judas thinking, and a few more questions elicited the melancholy truth. Struck with remorse and anxious to comfort his mother, Judas flung himself at the feet of Christ, confessed his sins, and became his disciple. But being entrusted with the bag, he allowed his old evil nature to get the better of him, with the tragical consequences with which we are all familiar.[1] This monkish legend may have been concocted by a mediæval writer who, having read the story of Oedipus, turned it to the purpose of edification by casting a still deeper shade of infamy on the character of the apostate and traitor.

It has been argued that traditions of incest, of which the Oedipus legend is only one instance out of many, are derived from a former custom of incestuous unions among mankind,

---

[1] L. Constans, *La légende d'Oedipe*, pp. 95–97.

such as some inquirers believe to have prevailed at an early period in the evolution of society.[1] But this interpretation, like another which would explain the legend as a solar myth,[2] appears to be somewhat far-fetched and improbable.

IX.—APOLLO AND THE KINE OF ADMETUS

(*Apollodorus* III. x. 4)

Apollodorus tells us that when Apollo herded the cattle of Admetus, he caused all the cows to bear twins. So Callimachus says that the she-goats which Apollo tended for Admetus could not lack kids, and that the ewes could not be milkless, but that all must have had their lambs; and if any had borne but a single young one before, she would then bear twins.[3]

Perhaps, as himself a twin, Apollo may have been supposed to possess a special power of promoting the birth of twins in animals. A similar faculty may possibly have been ascribed to the patriarch and herdsman, Jacob, himself a twin, who

---

[1] L. J. B. Bérenger-Feraud, *Superstitions et Survivances*, iii. (Paris, 1896), pp. 467–514.

[2] This explanation of the story of Oedipus, put forward by the French scholar Michel Bréal, has been criticized and rightly rejected by Domenico Comparetti in his essay, *Edipo e la Mitologia Comparata* (Pisa, 1867). It was not to be expected that the parricidal and incestuous Oedipus should escape the solar net in which Sir George Cox caught so many much better men. According to him, Oedipus was the sun, his father Laius was the darkness of night, and his mother Jocasta was the violet-tinted sky; while his daughter Antigone may have been, as M. Bréal thought, "the light which sometimes flushes the eastern sky as the sun sinks to sleep in the west." Thus the old tragic story of crime and sorrow is wiped out, and an agreeable picture of sunrise and sunset is painted, in roseate hues, on the empty canvas. See Sir George W. Cox, *The Mythology of the Aryan Nations* (London, 1882), pp. 312 *sqq.*

[3] Callimachus, *Hymn to Apollo*, 47–54.

is said to have resorted to peculiar devices for the multiplication of Laban's flocks, of which he was in charge.[1] We know that a fertilizing power was ascribed to the mound which covered the grave of the twins, Amphion and Zethus, near Thebes; for every year, at the time when the sun was in Taurus, the people of Tithorea in Phocis used to try to steal earth from the mound, believing that with the earth they would transfer the fertility of the Theban land to their own.[2]

Similarly some savages ascribe to twins and their parents a power of multiplying animals and plants, so as to ensure a good catch to the fisherman and a plentiful crop to the farmer.[3] Thus the Tsimshian Indians of British Columbia believe that all the wishes of twins are fulfilled. Therefore twins are feared, as they can harm the man whom they hate. They can call the salmon and olachen, hence they are called *Sewihan*, that is, "making plentiful."[4] Among the Nootkas of Vancouver Island "numerous regulations refer to the birth of twins. The parents of twins must build a small hut in the woods, far from the village. There they have to stay two years. The father must continue to clean himself by bathing in ponds for a whole year, and must keep his face painted red. While bathing he sings certain songs that are only used on this occasion. Both parents must keep away from the people. They must not eat, or even touch, fresh food, particularly

---

[1] Genesis, xxx. 37–43.   [2] Pausanias, ix. 17. 4 *sq.*

[3] The customs and superstitions relating to twins are discussed with great learning and ingenuity by my friend Dr. Rendel Harris in his book *Boanerges* (Cambridge, 1913); see particularly pp. 73, 122, 123, 124, 143 *sq.* for the belief in the fertilizing powers of twins. The same writer has dealt more briefly with other aspects of the subject in two treatises, *The Dioscuri in the Christian Legends* (London, 1903), and *The Cult of the Heavenly Twins* (Cambridge, 1906). On this curious department of folk-lore I have also collected some facts, on which I will draw in what follows.

[4] Franz Boas, in *Fifth Report of the Committee of the British Association on the North-Western Tribes of Canada*, p. 51 (separate reprint from the *Report of the British Association, Newcastle-upon-Tyne Meeting*, 1889); *id.* "Tsimshian Mythology," *Thirty-first Annual Report of the Bureau of American Ethnology* (Washington, 1916), p. 545.

377

APPENDIX

salmon. Wooden images and masks, representing birds and fish, are placed around the hut, and others, representing fish near the river, on the bank of which the hut stands. The object of these masks is to invite all birds and fish to come and see the twins and to be friendly to them. They are in constant danger of being carried away by spirits, and the masks and images—or rather the animals which they represent —will avert this danger. The twins are believed to be in some way related to salmon, although they are not considered identical with them, as is the case among the Kwakiutl. The father's song which he sings when cleaning himself is an invitation for the salmon to come, and is sung in their praise. On hearing this song, and seeing the images and masks, the salmon are believed to come in great numbers to see the twins. Therefore the birth of twins is believed to indicate a good salmon year. If the salmon should fail to come in large numbers it is considered proof that the children will soon die, Twins are forbidden to catch salmon, nor must [may] they eat or handle fresh salmon."[1]

In this custom the twins and their father rather attract than multiply the fish, but for the purpose of the fisherman the two things come to the same. The reason why the twins and their parents are forbidden to eat or even touch fresh salmon is probably a fear of thereby deterring the salmon from coming to see the twins ; for the fish would hardly come if they knew that they were to be eaten. They visit the twins for the pleasure of seeing them, but in the innocence of their hearts they have no inkling of the fate that awaits them from the wily fisherman lurking in the background.

The Kwakiutl, another Indian tribe of British Columbia, " believe that twins are salmon that have assumed the form of men, and that they are able to bring salmon."[2] A story told by one branch of the tribe illustrates the belief in the

---

[1] Franz Boas, in *Sixth Report of the Committee of the British Association on the North-Western Tribes of Canada*, p. 39 (separate reprint from *Report of the British Association, Leeds Meeting*, 1890).

[2] Franz Boas and George Hunt, *Kwakiutl Texts*, II. (1902), p. 322 note (*The Jesup North Pacific Expedition, Memoirs of the American Museum of Natural History* [New York], vol. V.).

power of twins to attract or multiply salmon. They say that a certain old woman, who died some thirty years ago, was one of twins, and when she came to die she warned the people not to cry for her after she was gone. "If you cry," said she to her sorrowing relatives, "no more salmon will come here. Hang the box into which you will put my body on to a tree near the river after having painted it. When you pass by, ask me for salmon, and I shall send them."[1]

Another Kwakiutl story brings out the same belief still more clearly. Once upon a time, we are told, a certain chief called Chief of the Ancients wished to marry a twin woman in order that the various kinds of salmon might come to him for the sake of his wife. His aunt, the Star-Woman, advised him to go to the graves and search among them for a dead twin woman to be his wife. So he went to the graves and asked, " Is there a twin here ? " But the graves answered, "There is none here." From grave to grave he went, but there was no twin in them, till at last one of the graves answered him, saying, " I am a twin." So the chief gathered the bones from the grave, and sprinkled them with the water of life, and the dead twin became a living woman. She was a very pretty woman, and Chief of the Ancients married her. But she warned him, saying, " Just take care, Chief of the Ancients ! I am Salmon-Maker. Don't do me any harm." Then Salmon-Maker made many salmon for her husband. When she put her finger in a kettle of water, a large spring-salmon would at once be there in the water, jumping about, and when she put two fingers into the kettle, there would be two large spring-salmon jumping about in the water. When she walked into the river with the water only up to the instep of her foot, the salmon at once came jumping ; and if she were to walk right into the river, it would dry up, so full would it be of salmon. Thus the salmon-traps of the people were full of salmon, and their houses were full of dried and roasted salmon. Then Chief of the Ancients grew proud and his heart was lifted up because he had much food to eat. When the backbone of the spring-salmon caught in the hair of his head, he took it and threw it into the corner of the house. He said, " You come from the ghosts, and you catch

---

[1] Franz Boas, in *Sixth Report o the Committee*, etc. (see note [1], p. 378), p. 62.

me!" His wife, Salmon-Maker, hung her head and cried, but he laughed at her and spoke angrily to her. At last she could bear his unkindness no more. She arose. She spoke, weeping, to the dried salmon, saying, "Come, my tribe, let us go back." Thus she spoke to them. Then she started and led her tribe, the dried salmon, and they all went into the water. Chief of the Ancients tried to put his arm round his wife; but her body was like smoke, and his arms went through her. Then Chief of the Ancients and his younger brothers became poor again. They had nothing to eat.[1]

Among the Baganda of Central Africa twins were believed to be sent by Mukasa, the great god whose blessing on the crops and on the people was ensured at an annual festival. The twins were thought to be under the special protection of the god, and they bore his name, the boys being called Mukasa, and the girls Namukasa. After the birth of twins the parents, with the infants, used to make a round of visits to friends and relations. They were received with dances and rejoicing, for "the people whom they visited thought that, not only they themselves would be blessed and given children, but that their herds and crops also would be multiplied." A ceremony performed by the father and mother of the twins over a flower of the plantain indicated in the plainest,

---

[1] Franz Boas and G. Hunt, *Kwakiutl Texts*, II. pp. 322–330 (*Memoirs of the American Museum of Natural History, The Jesup North Pacific Expedition*, vol. III. [New York] 1902). Compare Franz Boas, *Kwakiutl Tales* (New York and Leyden, 1910), pp. 491 *sq.* (*Columbia University Contributions to Anthropology*, vol. II.). Similar tales are told more briefly by the Tlatlasikoala and Awikyenoq Indians of the same region. See Franz Boas, *Indianische Sagen von der Nord-Pacifischen Küste Amerikas* (Berlin, 1895), pp. 174, 209 *sq.* The Awikyenoq Indians, whose territory is situated on the coast of British Columbia immediately to the north of the Kwakiutl, also believe that twins were salmon before they were born as human beings, and that they can turn into salmon again (F. Boas, *op. cit.* p. 209 note). For other versions of the story told by the Indians of this region, see Franz Boas, "Tsimshian Mythology," *Thirty-first Annual Report of the Bureau of American Ethnology* (Washington, 1916), pp. 667 *sq.*

if the grossest, manner the belief of the Baganda that parents of twins possessed a power of magically fertilizing the plantains which form the staple food of the people.[1]

Among the Bateso, a tribe of the Uganda Protectorate, " the birth of twins is a welcome event. The midwife announces the fact to the father, who immediately orders the special drum-rhythm to be beaten to make the fact known, and women soon gather at the house uttering a peculiar shrill cry of pleasure. The mother remains secluded for three months, and during this time the father pays visits to members of his own and of his wife's clans, from whom he receives presents of food and animals for a special feast to be held when the period of seclusion is ended and the twins are presented to the members of the clans. Should no hospitality be offered to the father and no present be given at a place when he is making his round of visits, he refuses to enter the house and passes on elsewhere. This is regarded by its occupants as a loss, because the blessing of increase which rests upon the father of twins is not communicated to the inhospitable family."[2]

Among the Basoga, another tribe of the Uganda Protectorate, the birth of twins is ascribed to the intervention of the god, Gasani. When such a birth has taken place, a shrine is built near the house in which the twins live, and two fowls and a basket, containing a few beans, a little sesame, a little millet, and some earth from a cross-road, are deposited in the shrine, after they have been solemnly offered to the god, Gasani. This shrine is the place to which barren women go to make offerings to the god, to ask his blessing, and to seek the gift of children.[3] Moreover, in the Central District of Busoga, the land of the Basoga, " when a woman has twins, the people to whose clan she belongs do not sow any seed until the twins have been brought to the field. A pot of cooked grain is set before the children with a cake of sesame

[1] Rev. J. Roscoe, *The Baganda* (London, 1911), pp. 64–72. As to the annual festival in honour of Mukasa, see *id.* pp. 298 *sq.* At it the priest of the god gave the blessing to the people, their wives, children, cattle, and crops.

[2] Rev. J. Roscoe, *The Northern Bantu* (Cambridge, 1915), p. 265.

[3] Rev. J. Roscoe, *The Northern Bantu*, p. 249.

and all the seed that is to be sown. The food is eaten by the people assembled and afterwards the field is sown in the presence of the twins ; the plot is then said to be the field of the twins. The mother of twins must sow her seed before any person of her clan will sow theirs."[1]

These customs seem clearly to imply that twins and their mother are endowed with a special power of quickening the seed.

But though a belief in the fertilizing virtue of twins is found among peoples so far apart as the red men of North-western America and the black men of Central Africa, it would be rash to assume that such a belief is universal or even common ; on the contrary, it appears to be rare and exceptional. Far more usually the birth of twins is viewed with horror and dismay as a portent which must be expiated by the death of the twins and sometimes by that of the mother also. To adduce the evidence at large would be out of place here ; I will only cite a few instances in which a directly contrary influence is ascribed to twins or their mother. For example, in Unyoro, a district of the Uganda Protectorate, the explorer, Speke, was told by one of his men, who was a twin, that " in Ngura, one of the sister provinces to Unyanyembé, twins are ordered to be killed and thrown into water the moment they are born, lest droughts and famines or floods should oppress the land. Should anyone attempt to conceal twins, the whole family would be murdered by the chief."[2] Among the Nandi of British East Africa " the birth of twins is looked upon as an inauspicious event, and the mother is considered unclean for the rest of her life. She is given her own cow and may not touch the milk or blood of any other animal. She may enter nobody's house until she has sprinkled a calabash full of water on the ground, and she may never cross the threshold of a cattle kraal again."[3] Indeed, if a mother of twins goes near the cattle, the Nandi believe that the animals will die.[4]

---

[1] Rev. J. Roscoe, *The Northern Bantu*, p. 235.

[2] J. H. Speke, *Journal of the Discovery of the Source of the Nile*, ch. xviii. p. 426 (*Everyman's Library*).

[3] A. C. Hollis, *The Nandi* (Oxford, 1909), p. 68.

[4] C. W. Hobley, *Eastern Uganda, an Ethnological Study* (London, 1902), p. 40.

X.—MARRIAGE OF PELEUS AND THETIS

Again, among the Bassari of Togo, in Western Africa, women who have given birth to twins are not allowed to go into the cornfields at the time of sowing and harvest, because it is believed that, if they did so, they might spoil the crop. Only after such a woman has again been brought to bed and given birth to a single child may she once more take part in field labour.[1] Among the natives of Nias, an island to the west of Sumatra, the birth of twins is regarded as a misfortune which portends failure of the crops, epidemics, sickness among the cattle, conflagrations, and other ills ; it used, therefore, to be customary to expose one or both of the infants and leave them to perish ; sometimes, it is said, the mother would strangle one of the twins with her own hand.[2] A German missionary reports a case in Nias of a woman who gave birth to twins twice in successive years ; both sets of children were exposed by the father in a tree and left to die ; but on the second occasion the spirits were supposed to demand another victim, so the father bought a slave, a poor young man, tied him up near the village beside a river, and killed him with his own hand.[3]

Thus contrary and equally baseless, though not equally mischievous, are the superstitions of savages touching the birth of twins.

X.—THE MARRIAGE OF PELEUS AND THETIS

(*Apollodorus*, III. xiii. 5)

The story how Peleus won the sea-goddess for his wife has its parallel in a modern Cretan tale. It is said that a young man, who played the lyre beautifully, was carried off by the sea nymphs (Nereids) to their cave, where they listened with delight to his music. But he fell in love with one of them,

---

[1] H. Klose, *Togo unter deutscher Flagge* (Berlin, 1899), p. 510.

[2] J. P. Kleiweg de Zwaan, *De Geneeskunde der Menang-kabau-Maleiers* (Amsterdam, 1910), p. 149 ; *id. Die Heil-kunde der Niassers* (The Hague, 1913), p. 178. Compare E. Modigliani, *Un Viaggio a Nias* (Milan, 1890), p. 555.

[3] A. Fehr, *Der Niasser im Leben und Sterben* (Barmen, 1901), pp. 14 *sq.*

and not knowing how to win her for his wife, he asked the advice of an old woman who dwelt in his village. She advised him to seize his darling by the hair when the hour of cock-crow was near, and though she should turn into diverse shapes, he was not to be frightened or to let her go, but to hold fast till the cocks crew. He took the advice, and though the wild sea-maiden turned into a dog, a serpent, a camel, and fire, he held her by the hair till the cocks crew and the other sea-maidens vanished. Then she changed back into her own beautiful shape and followed him meekly to the village. There they lived as man and wife for a year, and she bore him a son, but she never spoke a word. Her strange silence weighed on him, and in his perplexity he again betook him to the old woman, and she gave him a piece of advice, which in an unhappy hour he followed. He heated the stove and taking up their child in his arms, he threatened to throw it into the fire if his wife would not speak to him. At that she started up, crying, "Leave my child alone, you dog!" and snatching the infant from him she vanished before his eyes. But as the other Nereids would not receive her back among them because she was a mother, she took up her abode at a spring not far from the sea-nymphs' cave, and there you may see her twice or thrice a year with her baby in her arms.[1]

This modern Greek story serves to explain a feature in the ancient story which is known only through an incidental allusion of Sophocles. In his play *Troilus* the poet spoke of the marriage of Peleus and Thetis as voiceless or silent (ἀφθόγγους γάμους).[2] In the original form of the tale it is probable that the sea-bride of Peleus remained strangely and obstinately silent until Peleus detected her in the act of placing their child on the fire to make him immortal.[3] At that sight the father cried out, no doubt reproaching his sea-wife for murdering, as he supposed, their infant; and she, offended at the interruption and hurt at the unmerited reproach, spoke to him once for all, and then, vanishing before his eyes, returned to her old home in the sea. This conjecture is

---

[1] B. Schmidt, *Das Volksleben der Neugriechen* (Leipsic, 1871), pp. 115–117.

[2] Scholiast on Pindar, *Nem.* iii. 35 (60); *The Fragments of Sophocles*, ed. A. C. Pearson, vol. ii. pp. 255 *sq.*

[3] See Apollodorus, iii. 13. 6, with the note.

X.—MARRIAGE OF PELEUS AND THETIS

partially confirmed by a fragment of Sophocles, in which the poet said that Thetis deserted Peleus because she was reproached by him.[1] The silence of the bride in the folk-tale is probably to be explained as a reminiscence of a custom of imposing silence on brides for some time after marriage. For example, among the Tedas of Tibesti, a region of the Central Sudan, a bride is shut up after marriage for seven days in a special compartment of her husband's house and does not utter a word.[2] Again, among the Wabende, of Lake Tanganyika, a wife does not speak to her husband for several days after marriage; she waits till he has made her a present.[3]

The story of Peleus and Thetis seems to belong to a familiar type of popular tale known as the Swan Maiden type. A number of swans are in the habit of divesting themselves of their plumage and appearing as beautiful maidens. In that temporary state they are seen by a young man, who falls in love with one of them, and by concealing the bird's skin, which she has stripped off, he prevents the Swan Maiden from resuming her wings and flying away. Thus placed at his mercy, she consents to marry him, and for some time they live together as husband and wife, and she bears him a child. But one day she finds by accident the bird-skin which her husband had hidden; a longing for her old life in the air comes over her; she puts on the feathery coat, and leaving husband and child behind, she flies away to return no more. The story recurs with many minor variations in many lands.

---

[1] Scholiast on Apollonius Rhodius, *Argon.* iv. 816; Scholiast on Aristophanes, *Clouds*, 1068, p. 443, ed. Fr. Dübner; *The Fragments of Sophocles*, ed. A. C. Pearson, vol. i. pp. 106 *sq.*

[2] P. Noel, "Ethnographie et Anthropologie des Tedas du Tibesti," *L'Anthropologie*, xxx. (1920), p. 121.

[3] Avon, "Vie sociale des Wabende au Tanganika," *Anthropos*, x.-xi. (1915–1916), p. 101. For more instances, see *Totemism and Exogamy*, i. 63, note[5], iv. 233-237. Compare Andrew Lang, *Custom and Myth* (London, 1884), p. 74, "M. Dozon, who has collected the Bulgarian songs, says that this custom of prolonged silence on the part of the bride is very common in Bulgaria, though it is beginning to yield to a sense of the ludicrous."

APPENDIX

Often the fairy wife is not a bird but a beast, who doffs her beast skin to be a human wife for a time, till in like manner she discovers the cast skin, and resuming with it her beast shape returns to her old life in the woods or the wilderness. Sometimes she is a fish or other marine creature, and then the resemblance to the story of Peleus and Thetis is particularly close, for she comes from the sea to be married as a human maid to her human lover, and after the last unhappy parting she returns as a fish to dwell with her finny kindred in the depths of the sea. To increase the resemblance with the tale of Peleus and Thetis, the cause of the parting is often some unkindness done to the wife or to her animal kinsfolk, or simply some cruel taunt reflecting on her relationship to the fish or the birds or the beasts.

For example, "in the Farö Islands the superstition is current that the seal casts off its skin every ninth night, assumes a human form, and dances and amuses itself like a human being until it resumes its skin, and again becomes a seal. It once happened that a man, passing during one of these transformations, and seeing the skin, took possession of it, when the seal, which was a female, not finding her skin to creep into, was obliged to continue in a human form, and being a comely person, the man made her his wife, had several children by her, and they lived happily together, until, after a lapse of several years, she chanced to find her hidden skin, which she could not refrain from creeping into, and so became a seal again."[1] A similar notion prevailed among the people of Shetland regarding mermaids, about whom it is said that "they dwell among the fishes, in the depth of the ocean, in habitations of pearl and coral; that they resemble human beings, but greatly excel them in beauty. When they wish to visit the upper world, they put on the *ham* or garb of some fish, but woe to those who lose their *ham*, for then are all hopes of return annihilated, and they must stay where they are. . . . It has also happened that earthly men have married mermaids, having taken possession of their *ham*, and thus got them into their power."[2]

---

[1] B. Thorpe, *Northern Mythology* (London, 1851-1852), ii. 173.

[2] B. Thorpe, *l.c.*, referring to Hibbert's *Shetland*, quoted by Faye, pp. 60, 61.

X.—MARRIAGE OF PELEUS AND THETIS

Again, in the Pelew Islands, in the Pacific, they tell how a man used to hang bowls on palm-trees to collect the palm-wine which oozed from incisions in the trunks. Every night he examined the bowls, but every night he found that they had been emptied by somebody. So he set himself to watch, and one night he saw a fish come out of the sea, lay aside its tail, and then in human shape climb a palm-tree. The man snatched up the tail, and taking it home with him hung it up in the storeroom. Next morning when he went to the palm-tree to collect the wine, he found a woman under the tree, who called out to him that she was naked and begged him to bring her an apron. They returned to his house together, and the unknown woman became his wife. She bore him a child, who grew up to be a very beautiful maiden. But one day, in her husband's absence, she received a visit from some chiefs. For their entertainment she needed the pestle with which to mash sweet potatoes, and searching for it in the storeroom she discovered her old tail. At sight of it a great longing for her old home came over her. She told her daughter to cleave to her father if she herself were long away, and that same evening she secretly took down the tail, ran to the beach, and plunged into the sea.[1]

The stories of "Beauty and the Beast" and "Cupid and Psyche" belong to the same type of tale, though in them it is the husband and not the wife who is the fairy spouse and is liable to vanish away from his mortal wife whenever she offends him by breaking some rule, the observance of which he had enjoined on her as a condition of their wedded bliss.[2]

---

[1] J. Kubary, " Die Religion der Pelauer," in A. Bastian's *Allerlei aus Volks- und Menschenkunde* (Berlin, 1888), i. 60 *sq*. The Kwakiutl story of Chief of the Ancients and his wife Salmon-Maker is another instance of this class of tales. See above, pp. 379 *sq*.

[2] As to these stories, see Theodor Benfey, *Pantschatantra* (Leipsic, 1859), i. 254 *sqq*.; A. Lang, *Custom and Myth* (London, 1884), pp. 64 *sqq*.; S. Baring-Gould, *Curious Myths of the Middle Ages* (London, 1884), pp. 561 *sqq*.; W. A. Clouston, *Popular Tales and Fictions*, i. 182 *sqq*.; E. Cosquin, *Contes populaires de Lorraine*, ii. 215 *sqq*.; E. S. Hartland, *The Science of Fairy Tales* (London, 1891) pp. 255 *sqq*.; Miss M. R. Cox, *Introduction to Folk-lore*,

APPENDIX

The folk-lore element in the marriage of Peleus and
Thetis was fully recognized and clearly brought out by
W. Mannhardt in his admirable study of the Peleus saga.
He was probably right in holding that the modern Cretan
story[1] is not a reminiscence of the story of the marriage of
Thetis, but an independent folk-tale, of which the Peleus
and Thetis story was merely a localized version.[2]

XI.—PHAETHON AND THE CHARIOT OF THE SUN

(*Apollodorus* III. xiv. 3)

Some Indian tribes of North-western America tell a story
which bears a close resemblance to the story of Phaethon
and the chariot of the Sun, his father. The tale of Phaethon
is related most fully by Ovid. According to the poet, the
sea-nymph, Clymene, daughter of Tethys, bore a son,
Phaethon, to the Sun. When the lad grew up, he one day
boasted of his illustrious parentage to a companion, who

New Edition (London, 1904), pp. 120 *sqq.*; *Totemism and
Exogamy*, ii. 205 *sq.*, 565–571, iii. 60–64; *The Dying God*,
pp. 124–131. To the stories of this type quoted or referred to
in these passages add E. Stack and Sir Charles Lyall, *The
Mikirs* (London, 1908), pp. 55 *sqq.*; A. Playfair, *The Garos*
(London, 1909), pp. 123 *sqq.*; S. Endle, *The Kacháris* (London, 1911), pp. 119 *sqq.*; R. Neuhauss, *Deutsch Neu-Guinea*
(Berlin, 1911), iii. 564 *sqq.*; N. Adriani en A. C. Kruijt, *De
Bare'e-sprekende Toradja's van Midden-Celebes* (Batavia,
1912–1914), iii. 401; D. Macdonald, "Efate, New Hebrides,"
*Report of the Fourth Meeting of the Australasian Association
for the Advancement of Science, held at Hobart, Tasmania,
in January*, 1892, p. 731; [D.] Macdonald, "The mythology
of the Efatese," *Report of the Seventh Meeting of the Australasian Association for the Advancement of Science, held at
Sydney*, 1898, pp. 765–767; Elsdon Best, "Maori Folk-lore,"
*Report of the Tenth Meeting of the Australasian Association
for the Advancement of Science, held at Dunedin*, 1904, pp.
450 *sq.*

[1] See above, pp. 383 *sq.*

[2] See his *Antike Wald- und Feldkulte*, pp. 60 *sqq.*

ridiculed the notion and told Phaethon that he was a fool to
believe such a cock-and-bull story. In great distress Phaethon
repaired to his mother and begged her to tell him truly
whether his father was really the Sun or not. His mother
reassured him on this point. Stretching her arms towards
the Sun, she solemnly swore that the great luminary was
indeed his father; but if he had any lingering doubts on the
question, she advised him to apply to the Sun himself. "You
can easily do so," she said. "The house of the Sun, from
which he rises, is near our land. Go and question the Sun
himself." So Phaethon journeyed to the house of the Sun
and found the deity clad in purple and seated on a throne
resplendent with emeralds in the midst of a gorgeous palace.
At first the youth could not bear the fierce light that beat on
him, so he halted afar off. But the god received him kindly,
and freely acknowledged him as his truly begotten son.
More than that, he promised by the Stygian marsh to grant
him any boon he might ask. Thus encouraged, Phaethon
requested to be allowed to drive the Sun's chariot for a single
day. The Sun, foreseeing the fatal consequences of granting
the request, endeavoured to dissuade his son from the
hazardous enterprise, by pointing out its difficulties and
dangers. But all in vain; the rash youth insisted, and bound
by his oath the deity had no choice but to comply. Even as
they talked, the rosy light of dawn flushed the eastern sky,
the starry host fled away, with Lucifer bringing up the rear,
and the horned moon grew pale. There was no time to
delay. The Sun commanded the Hours to yoke the horses,
and forth from their stalls clattered the fire-breathing steeds.
As Phaethon prepared to mount the car, his Heavenly Sire
invested him with his own beamy crown, and sighing, said:
"Spare the whip, my boy, and use the reins; the horses
need to be held in rather than urged to speed. Drive not too
high, or you will kindle the celestial vault; drive not too low,
or you will set the earth on fire. The middle is the safest
course." But the father's warnings were wasted on his
imprudent son. Once started on his mad career, Phaethon
soon lost all control of the horses, which, not feeling the
master's hand, quickly ran wild, dragging the chariot out of
its course, now to the icy north, now to the torrid south, now
high, now low, now crashing into the fixed stars and colliding
with the constellations, now brushing the earth and setting

it all on flame. The forests blazed, the rivers boiled and steamed: the Ethiopians, who had been fair before, were scorched and blackened in the heat: the Nile in terror hid his head, dry was his channel, and his seven mouths were choked with dust; and southward an arid desert stretched far in the waste Sudan. Heaven and earth might have perished in one vast conflagration if the Omnipotent Father himself, the mighty Jove, had not hurled a thunderbolt from the zenith and struck dead the helpless charioteer. Down, down he crashed, his burning hair streaming behind him like the trail of light left by a falling star; so he dropped plump into the waters of the Eridanus, which laved his charred and smoking limbs. There the Naiads of the West buried his mangled remains, and over his grave they set a stone with an inscription recording his ambitious attempt and its disastrous issue.[1]

The corresponding story as told by the Bella Coola Indians of British Columbia runs as follows :

A young woman had been married against her will by a man of the name of Stump. But their connubial bliss was short, for Stump's hair was full of toads and he expected his wife to pick them out for him. This was more than she could bear, and she fled, pursued by the too faithful Stump. He gained on her, but she delayed his pursuit by throwing over her shoulder successively a bladder full of liquid, a comb, and a grindstone. The liquid turned into a lake, the comb into a thicket, and the grindstone into a great mountain, which carried her up to heaven. There she came to the house of the Sun, and peeping in through a chink she saw the Sun sitting inside in the likeness of a man. He said, "Come in"; but the doorway was blazing with fire and she hung back. The Sun told her to jump through the fire. She did so and entered the house safely. After her up came Stump, and endeavouring to pass the fiery doorway was consumed in the flames. The woman now lived in a corner of the house of the Sun, and after a while she gave birth to a boy, the son of the Sun. His name was Totqoaya. He was very ugly, and his face was covered with sores. In time his mother longed to return to her father on earth; so, instructed by the Sun, she took her boy on her back and walked down the eyelashes

---

[1] Ovid, *Metamorph.* i. 750–ii. 328.

of the Sun, which are the sunbeams, till she came in the evening to her father's house. Her parents and friends were very glad to see her.

"The next morning the boy went out of the house, and began to play with the other children, who made fun of him. Then he told them that his father was the Sun; but they merely laughed at him, until he grew very angry. Then he told his mother that he intended to return to his father in heaven. He made a great many arrows and a bow, went outside, and began to shoot his arrows upward. The first one struck the sky. The second one struck the notch of the first one. And thus he continued until a chain of arrows was formed which reached the ground. Then he climbed up; and after reaching heaven, he went into the Sun's house. There he said, 'Father, I wish to take your place to-morrow.' The Sun consented, but said, 'Take care that you do not burn the people. I use only one torch in the morning, and increase the number of torches until noon. In the afternoon I extinguish the torches one by one.' On the following morning the boy took his father's torches and went along the path of the Sun; but very soon he lighted all the torches. It became very hot on the earth. The woods began to burn, and the rocks to crack, and many people died. But his mother waved her hands, and thus kept her own house cool. The people who had entered her house were safe. When the Sun saw what the boy was doing, he caught him and threw him down to the earth, and said, 'Henceforth you shall be the mink.' "[1]

The story is told, with variations of details, by the Kwakiutl Indians of British Columbia as follows:

---

[1] Franz Boas, *The Mythology of the Bella Coola Indians* [New York] (1898), pp. 100–103 (*Memoirs of the American Museum of Natural History*, vol. ii., *The Jesup North Pacific Expedition*). For another version of the Bella Coolan story, see Franz Boas, *Indianische Sagen von der Nord-Pacifischen Küste Amerikas* (Berlin, 1895), p. 246. In this other version the Sun says to his son Totqoaya, "I am old. Henceforth carry the sun in my place. But take care. Go straight on, bend not down, else will the earth burn." The catastrophe follows as before, and the American Phaethon is finally turned, as before, into a mink.

" The future mother of Born-to-be-the-Sun was weaving wool, facing the rear of the house. Then the sun was in the sky, and the sun was shining through the holes in the house; and the rays struck her back while she sat facing the rear of the house, on her bed. Thus she became pregnant. There was no husband of this woman. She gave birth, and Born-to-be-the-Sun (Mink) became a child. Therefore it had immediately the name Born-to-be-the-Sun, because it was known that its mother became pregnant by the sun shining on her back.

" The Born-to-be-the-Sun was fighting with his friend Bluebird. Then Bluebird made fun of Born-to-be-the-Sun because he had no father. Then Born-to-be-the-Sun cried in the house to his mother, telling his mother that he was called an orphan because he had no father. Therefore his mother said to him that his father was the Sun.

" Immediately Born-to-be-the-Sun said he would go and visit his father. Then his mother made a request of the uncle of Born-to-be-the-Sun : ' Make arrows for this child, that he may go and see his father.' He made four arrows for him. Then Born-to-be-the-Sun shot one of the arrows upward. It is said it struck our sky. Then he shot another one upward. It struck the nock of the one that he had shot upward first ; then again another one, and it hit the end of his arrow. His arrows came down sticking together. Then he shot the last one, and it hit the end of the one he had shot before. They came to the ground.

" Then the mother of Born-to-be-the-Sun took the end of the arrows and shook them, and they became a rope. Then she cautioned her child, (saying,) ' Don't be foolish at the place where you are going.' Thus Born-to-be-the-Sun was told by his mother. Then Born-to-be-the-Sun climbed the rope, going upward. He went to visit his father. He arrived, and went through to the upper side of the sky. Then Born-to-be-the-Sun sat on the ground next to his father's house. Then Born-to-be-the-Sun was seen by a boy. Then he was asked by the boy, ' Why are you sitting there ? ' ' I came to see my father.' Then the boy entered, and reported to the chief, ' This boy sitting on the ground near the house comes to see his father.' ' Ah, ah, ah ! indeed ! I obtained him by shining through. Go ask him if he will come in.'

" Then the boy went out and called Born-to-be-the-Sun. Born-to-be-the-Sun entered and sat down. Immediately he

XI.—PHAETHON AND THE SUN

was taken care of by his father. ' Thank you, child, that you will change feet with me. I have tried not to be tired from walking to and fro every day. Now you shall go, child.' Thus said the chief to his son.

" Then he was cautioned by his father. ' Don't walk fast where you are walking along. Don't look right down to those below us, else you will do mischief.' Then he dressed him up with his ear-ornaments. Then he put on his mask. Then he walked on the trail that was pointed out. He walked along. ' My dear master, don't sweep too much when you are walking along. Don't show yourself [through] entirely when you are peeping through.' Then he started in the morning. He passed noon. Then in the afternoon the sun was warm. Then he desired to peep through. He swept away his aunts (the clouds). Already this world began to burn. There was noise of the cracking of mountains, and the sea began to boil. The trees of the mountains caught fire. Therefore there are no good trees on the mountains, and therefore the rocks are cracked.

" That was the reason of the fury of Born-to-be-the-Sun's father. The chief pursued his child. He reached him when the sun was not low. Then the clothing of Born-to-be-the-Sun was taken away. ' Is that what I told you ? You have come only once.' Born-to-be-the-Sun was just taken by the neck by his father, and was thrown through the hole. Born-to-be-the-Sun came down. A canoe was paddling along, and came right to Born-to-be-the-Sun. ' Is this our chief, Born-to-be-the-Sun, floating about ?' Then he raised his head on the water when they touched him with the paddle. Born-to-be-the-Sun awoke and puffed. ' Indeed, I have been asleep on the water a long time.' He went ashore and went inland."[1]

---

[1] Franz Boas *Kwakiutl Tales* (New York and Leyden, 1910), pp. 123, 125, 127 (*Columbia University Contributions to Anthropology*, vol. ii.). For a briefer Kwakiutl version of the story, see Franz Boas, *Indianische Sagen von der Nord-Pacifischen Küste Amerikas*, p. 157. In this latter version there is no mention of the mother of the son of the Sun, but the narrator describes how the Sun's ear-rings and nose-plug were made of glittering haliotis shell, and how, when his son wore these borrowed ornaments, the light flashed from them so fiercely that it caused the rocks to split and the water to boil.

APPENDIX

The story is told more briefly, but in similar form, by the Tlatlasikoala, the Awikyenoq, and the Heiltsuk Indians of British Columbia. In the first of these three versions the Sun, as in Ovid's narrative, warns his son to go neither too high nor too low, for otherwise it would be either too cold or too hot on earth.[1]

Whether the remarkable resemblances between the Greek and the Indian versions of the tale are to be explained as due to independent invention or to European influence, is a question which, so far as I know, there is no evidence to determine, and on which therefore it would be rash to pronounce an opinion. In the Indian versions the unlucky hero always appears, sooner or later, as a mink, an animal about which the Indians of this part of America tell many stories. I have spoken of the Greek version of the story because it is probable that Ovid drew the main outlines of his narrative from Greek originals, though doubtless many of the picturesque particulars with which he embellished it are due to the poet's own imagination. But the more we compare the *Metamorphoses* with the paarllel stories in extant Greek literature, the more, I think, we shall be inclined to admire the poets' learning and the fidelity with which he followed his sources, always, however, embroidering their usually plain substance with the many-coloured threads of his exuberant fancy.

XII.—THE VOW OF IDOMENEUS

(*Apollodorus, Epitome,* VI. 10)

Apollodorus tells us that while Idomeneus, king of Crete, was away with his army at the siege of Troy, his wife Meda at home was debauched by a certain Leucus, who afterwards murdered her and her daughter, and, having seduced ten cities of Crete from their allegiance, made himself lord of the island and expelled the lawful king Idomeneus when, on his return from Troy, he endeavoured to reinstate himself in the kingdom. The same story is told, almost in the same words, by Tzetzes, who doubtless here, as in so many places, drew his information

---

[1] Franz Boas, *Indianische Sagen von der Nord-Pacifischen Küste Amerikas,* pp. 173, 215 *sq.*, 234.

XII.—THE VOW OF IDOMENEUS

direct from Apollodorus.[1] The exile of Idomeneus is mentioned by Virgil, who says that the king, driven from his ancestral dominions, settled in the Sallentine land, a district of Calabria at the south-eastern extremity of Italy.[2] The poet says nothing about the cause of the king's exile; but his old commentator Servius explains it by a story which differs entirely from the account given by Apollodorus. The story is this. When Idomeneus, king of Crete, was returning home after the destruction of Troy, he was caught in a storm and vowed to sacrifice to Neptune whatever should first meet him; it chanced that the first to meet him was his own son, and Idomeneus sacrificed him or, according to others, only wished or attempted to do so; subsequently a pestilence broke out, and the people, apparently regarding it as a divine judgment on their king's cruelty, banished him the realm.[3] The same story is repeated almost in the same words by the First and Second Vatican Mythographers, who clearly here, as in many places, either copied Servius or borrowed from the same source which he followed.[4] But on one point the First Vatican Mythographer presents an interesting variation; for according to him it was not his son but his daughter whom the king first met and sacrificed, or attempted to sacrifice.

A similar story of a rash vow is told of a certain Maeander, son of Cercaphus and Anaxibia, who gave his name to the river Maeander. It is recorded of him that, being at war with the people of Pessinus in Phrygia, he vowed to the Mother of the Gods that, if he were victorious, he would sacrifice the first person who should congratulate him on his triumph. On his return the first who met and congratulated him was his son Archelaus, with his mother and sister. In fulfilment of his vow, Maeander sacrificed them at the altar, and thereafter, broken-hearted at what he had done, threw himself into the

---

[1] Tzetzes, *Schol. on Lycophron*, 384–386, compare *Schol.* on *id.* 1093.

[2] Virgil, *Aen.* iii. 121 *sq.*, 400 *sq.*; compare *id.*, xi. 264 *sq.*

[3] Servius, on Virgil, *Aen.* iii. 121 and on xi. 264. The two passages supplement each other on some points, and in the text I have combined them.

[4] *Scriptores rerum mythicarum Latini*, ed. G. H. Bode, vol. i. pp. 59, 145 *sq.* (First Vatican Mythographer, 195; Second Vatican Mythographer, 210).

APPENDIX

river, which before had been called Anabaenon, but which
henceforth was named Maeander after him. The story is
told by the Pseudo-Plutarch, who cites as his authorities
Timolaus, in the first book of his treatise on Phrygia, and
Agathocles the Samian, in his work, *The Constitution of
Pessinus.*[1]

In this last story, according to the only possible interpretation of the words,[2] Maeander clearly intended from the
outset to offer a human sacrifice, though he had not antici-
pated that the victims would be his son, his daughter, and his
wife. Similarly in the parallel Israelitish legend of Jephthah's
vow it seems that Jephthah purposed to sacrifice a human
victim, though he did not expect that the victim would be his
daughter : "And Jephthah vowed a vow unto the Lord, and
said, If thou wilt indeed deliver the children of Ammon into
mine hand, then it shall be, that whosoever cometh forth of
the doors of my house to meet me, when I return in peace
from the children of Ammon, he shall be the Lord's, and I will
offer him up for a burnt offering."[3] For so the passage runs
in the Hebrew original,[4] in the Septuagint,[5] and in the Vulgate[6]
and so it has been understood by the best modern commentators.[7] In the sequel Jephthah did to his daughter

---

[1] Pseudo-Plutarch, *De fluviis*, ix. 1.

[2] ηὔξατο τῇ Μητρὶ τῶν θεῶν, ἐὰν ἐγκρατὴς γένηται τῆς νίκης,
θύσειν τὸν πρῶτον αὐτῷ συγχαρέντα [ἐπὶ] ταῖς ἀνδραγαθίαις
τρόπαια φέροντι.   [3] Judges, xi. 30 *sq.*

[4] Judges, xi. 31, וְהָיָה הַיּוֹצֵא אֲשֶׁר יֵצֵא מִדַּלְתֵי בֵיתִי לִקְרָאתִי . . . .
וְהַעֲלִיתִהוּ עוֹלָה

[5] καὶ ἔσται ὁ ἐκπορευόμενος ὃς ἂν ἐξέλθῃ ἀπὸ τῆς θύρας τοῦ
οἴκου μου εἰς συνάντησίν μου . . . ἀνοίσω αὐτὸν ὁλοκαύτωμα.

[6] *Quicumque primus fuerit egressus de foribus domus
meae, mihique occurrerit . . . eum holocaustum offeram
Domino.*

[7] J. S. Black (*The Smaller Cambridge Bible for Schools*,
1892), G. W. Thatcher (*The Century Bible*, n.d.), G. F.
Moore (*The International Commentary*, Second Edition,
1903), G. A. Cooke (*The Cambridge Bible for Schools and
Colleges*, 1913), C. F. Burney (1918). Professor G. F. Moore
observes, "That a human victim is intended is, in fact, as
plain as words can make it ; the language is inapplicable to

according to his vow,[1] in other words he consummated the sacrifice. "Early Arabian religion before Mohammed furnishes a parallel: 'Al-Mundhir [king of al-Hīrah] had made a vow that on a certain day in each year he would sacrifice the first person he saw; 'Abīd came in sight on the unlucky day, and was accordingly killed, and the altar smeared with his blood.'"[2]

Similar vows meet us in folk-tales. Thus in a German story from Hesse we read how a man, setting out on a long journey, promised his three daughters to bring back a present for each, whatever they should desire. The youngest of them, his favourite child, asked him to bring back a singing, soaring lark. On his way through a forest, he saw a singing, soaring lark perched on the top of a tree, and he called to his servant to climb up and catch the bird. But as he approached the tree, a lion leaped from under it, saying that he would devour whoever tried to steal his singing, soaring lark. The man prayed the lion to spare his life and to take a large sum of money instead. But the animal replied, "Nothing can save thee, unless thou wilt promise to give me for my own what first meets thee on thy return home; but if thou wilt do that, I will grant thee thy life, and thou shalt have the bird for thy daughter, into the bargain." The man accepted the offer, and on his return home the first who met him was his youngest and dearest daughter, who came running up, kissed and embraced him, and when she saw that he had brought with him a singing, soaring lark, she was beside herself with joy. But her father wept and said, "My dearest child, I have bought the little bird dear. In return for it I have been obliged to promise thee to a savage lion, and when he has thee, he will tear thee in pieces and devour thee." But the brave damsel, like Jephthah's daughter, consoled her sorrowful father, saying that he must keep his word, and that she would go to the lion and try to mollify him. The story ends happily, for the lion turned out to be no real lion but an

---

an animal, and a vow to offer the first sheep or goat that he comes across—not to mention the possibility of an unclean animal—is trivial to absurdity."

[1] Judges, xi. 39.

[2] G. A. Cooke, on Judges, **xi**. **31,** quoting Lyall, *Ancient Arabian Poetry,* p. xxviii.

enchanted prince, who married the girl, and after a series of adventures the two lived happily together.[1]

A similar tale is reported from Lorraine. Its substance is as follows : Once upon a time there was a man who had three daughters. One day he told them that he was setting out on a journey and promised to bring each of them back a present, whatever they pleased. The youngest, whom he loved the best, said she would like to have the talking rose. So one day on his travels the man came to a fine castle from which issued a sound of voices speaking and singing. On entering the castle he found himself in a courtyard, in the middle of which was a rose-bush covered with roses. It was the roses which he had heard speaking and singing. " At last," thought he, " I have found the talking rose." He was just about to pluck one of the roses, when a white wolf ran at him, crying, " Who gave you leave to enter my castle and to pluck my roses? You shall be punished with death. All who intrude here must die." The poor man offered to give back the talking rose, if only the white wolf would let him go. At first the wolf would not consent, but, on hearing that the man's daughter had begged for the talking rose, he said, " Look here. I will pardon you, and more than that I will let you keep the rose, but on one condition: it is that you will bring me the first person you meet on returning home." The poor man promised and went away back to his own country. The first person he saw on entering his house was his youngest daughter. " Ah, my daughter," said he, " what a sad journey ! " " Have you not found the talking rose ? " quoth she. " I found it," quoth he, " to my sorrow. In the castle of the white wolf I found it, and I must die." When he explained to her that the white wolf had granted him his life on condition of his bringing the first person he should meet on entering his house, she bravely declared herself ready to go with him. So together they came to the castle. There the white wolf received them very civilly and assured them that he would do them no harm. " This castle," said he, " belongs to the fairies ; we who dwell in it are all fairies ; I myself am condemned to be a white wolf by day. If you keep the secret, it will go well with you." That night the white wolf appeared to the maiden in her

---

[1] Grimm's *Household Tales*, No. 88 (vol. ii. pp. 5-10 of Margaret Hunt's translation).

XII.—THE VOW OF IDOMENEUS

chamber in the form of a handsome gentleman and promised that, if only she followed his directions, he would marry her and make her his queen, and she should be mistress of the castle. All went well till one day the girl received a visit from one of her sisters, and, yielding to her importunity, revealed the wondrous secret. A frightful howl at once rang through the castle; the maiden started up affrighted, but hardly had she passed the doorway when the white wolf fell dead at her feet. She now rued her fatal compliance, but it was too late, and she was wretched for the rest of her life.[1]

So in a Lithuanian story we read of a king who had three fair daughters, but the youngest was the fairest of them all. Once on a time the king wished to go on business to Wilna, there to engage a maid who would look after his royal household, sweep the rooms, and feed the pigs. But his youngest daughter told him that she needed no maid-servant, for she would herself discharge these domestic duties, if only he brought her back from Wilna a mat woven of living flowers. So the king went to Wilna and bought presents for his two elder daughters, but though he searched the whole town and went into every shop, he could not find a mat woven of living flowers. His way home led him through a forest, and there in the wood, a few miles from his castle, what should he see but a white wolf sitting by the side of the path with a hood of living flowers on his head. The king said to the coachman, "Get down from the box, and fetch me that hood." But the white wolf opened his mouth and said, "My lord and king, you may not get the flowery hood for nothing." The king asked him, "What would you have? I will gladly load you with treasures in return for the hood." But the wolf answered, "I want not your treasures. Promise to give me whatever you shall first meet. In three days I will come to your castle to fetch it." The king thought to himself, "It is still a long way to home. I am quite sure to meet some wild beast or bird. I'll promise it." And so he did. Then he drove away with the flowery hood in the carriage, and on the whole way home he met just nothing at all. But no sooner had he entered the courtyard of his castle than his youngest daughter came forth to meet him. The king and likewise the queen wept bitter tears. Their daughter asked, "Father and

---

[1] E. Cosquin, *Contes populaires de Lorraine* (Paris, n.d.), ii. 215-217.

mother, why do you weep so?" Her father answered, "Alas, I have promised you to a white wolf; in three days he will come to the castle, and you must go with him." Sure enough the white wolf came on the third day and carried off the princess to his castle; for he was really a prince who was a wolf by day, but put off the wolf skin by night and appeared in his true form as a handsome young man. After a series of adventures, in the course of which the wolf-skin is burnt by the mother of the princess and the prince in consequence disappears for a time, the rediscovered and now transformed prince marries the princess in his fine castle.[1]

In a Tyrolese story of the same type, a merchant, setting out on his travels, asks his three daughters what he shall bring them back from the city. The youngest asks him to bring her a leaf that dances, sings, and plays. In the city, as usual, he buys the presents for his elder daughters but cannot find the leaf on which his youngest daughter had set her heart. However, on his way home he comes to a palace with a beautiful garden; and in the middle of the garden is a tree on which all the leaves are dancing and singing and playing delightfully. Thinking that one of these leaves is just the thing his daughter wants, he plucks one; but no sooner has he done so than a great serpent appears and says: "Since you have taken a leaf, I demand of you that you send me within three days the first person whom you shall meet at home. Woe to you if you do not!" With a foreboding of evil he goes home, and the first person that meets him there is his youngest daughter. "Father," she asks, "have you brought the leaf?" "I have," he answers sadly, "but it will cost you dear." He then tells her on what condition he had received the leaf from the serpent. But his daughter goes cheerfully to the serpent, who, as usual, turns out to be an enchanted nobleman. Dancing with him at the wedding of her sisters, the young lady inadvertently treads on his tail and crushes it; this suffices to break the spell: he turns into a handsome young man in her arms: the two are married, and he introduces his bride to his noble and overjoyed parents.[2]

---

[1] A. Leskien und K. Brugman, *Litauische Volkslieder und Märchen* (Strasbourg, 1882), No. 23, pp. 438–443.

[2] Chr. Schneller *Märchen und Sagen aus Wälschtirol* (Innsbruck, 1867), No. 25, pp. 63–65.

XII.—THE VOW OF IDOMENEUS

A Hanoverian story relates how once upon a time a king had three daughters, but the youngest was the apple of his eye. Setting out one day to make some purchases at the yearly fair, he asked his daughters what presents he should bring them back. The youngest asked for a tinkling lion-leaf.[1] At the fair the king easily bought the presents for his elder daughters, but do what he would, he could not find the tinkling lion-leaf. Riding dejectedly home, he had to traverse a wide, wide wood, and in the wood he came to a great birch-tree, and under the birch-tree lay a great black poodle dog. Seeing the king so sad, the poodle asked him what ailed him, and on learning the cause of his sadness the dog said, "I can help you. The tinkling lion-leaf grows on this very tree, and you shall have it if in a year and a day from now you will give me what to-day shall first come out of your house to meet you." The king thought to himself, "What should that be but my dog?" So he gave his word. Then the poodle wagged his tail, climbed up the birch-tree, broke the leaf off with his paw, and gave it to the king, who took it and rode merrily home. But when he came near the house, his youngest daughter sprang joyfully out to meet him. Struck with horror he pushed her from him. She wept and thought, "What can be the matter that my father thus repels me?" And she went and complained to her mother. The queen asked her husband why he had so treated his youngest daughter; but he would not tell her, and for a whole year he continued in the dumps and pined away. At last, when the year was all but up, he let the cat out of the bag. At first the queen was thunderstruck, but soon she pulled herself together, and concerted with her husband a device to cheat the black poodle by palming off the goose-girl instead of their daughter on him when he came to fetch away the princess. The deception succeeded at first, but when the poodle had carried off the goose-girl to the wood, he detected the fraud and brought her back. A second time a false princess was fobbed off on him, and a second time detected. At last the parents had, amid the loud lamentation of the courtiers, to give up their real daughter to the black poodle, who led her away and lodged her, all alone, in a little cottage in the depth of a great forest. There

---

[1] *Ein klinkesklankes Lowesblatt.* I am not sure of the meaning.

she learned from an old hag that the poodle was an enchanted prince, the cottage an enchanted castle, the wood an enchanted city, and the wild beasts enchanted men, and that every day at midnight the black poodle stripped off his shaggy hide and became an ordinary man. Following the directions of the hag, the princess waited till the third night, and when the enchanted prince had laid aside the black dogskin and was fast asleep, she got hold of the skin and threw it on the fire. That broke the spell. The prince now appeared before her eyes in his true, his handsome form ; the cottage turned into a palace, the wood into a city, and the wild beasts into men and women. The prince and princess were married, and at the wedding feast the bride showed great honour to the old hag, who thereupon blessed her and, vanishing away, was never seen or heard of again.[1]

Two stories of the same general type have been recorded in Schleswig-Holstein. In one of them a king has three daughters, and when he is about to set out on a journey he asks them what presents he should bring them back. The eldest daughter wished for a golden spinning-wheel, the second for a golden reel, and the youngest for a golden jingle-jangle.[2] When the king had procured the golden spinning-wheel and the golden reel, and was about to set out for home, he was very sad, for he did not know how to get a golden jingle-jangle. While he sat and wept, an old man came up to him and inquired the cause of his sorrow. On hearing it he said, "The golden jingle-jangles are on a great tall tree in the forest, and a big bear watches over them; but if you promise the bear something, he will give you one." So the king went and found the big bear under the big tree, and begged him to let him have a golden jingle-jangle. The bear answered, "You shall have a golden jingle-jangle if you will give me whatever first meets me in your castle." The king consented, and the bear promised to come next morning to the castle and bring the golden jingle-jangle. But when the bear appeared in the castle next morning, who should first meet him but the king's youngest daughter ? The bear would have carried her off at once, but the king was sore troubled and said to the bear, "Go away;

---

[1] Carl und Theodor Colshorn, *Märchen und Sagen* (Hanover, 1854), No. 20, pp. 64-69.
[2] "*Einen goldenen Klingelklangel.*"

she will soon follow you." But instead of his own daughter the king dressed up the shepherd's daughter and sent her to the bear, who detected the fraud and returned her to the king. The same thing happened to the swineherd's daughter, whom the king next attempted to palm off on the bear instead of the princess. Last of all the king was forced to send his youngest daughter, and with her the bear was now content. Afterwards the bear brought her back on a visit to her father's castle and danced with her there. In the dance she trod heavily on one of his paws, and immediately he was changed into a rich and handsome prince and took her to wife.[1]

Another story, recorded in Schleswig-Holstein, relates how a king lost his way and wandered in a great forest, till a little black man appeared and offered to guide him home if the king would promise to give him whatever should first come out of the king's house to meet him. The king accepted the offer, and on his return to the castle the first to run out to meet him was his daughter. He told her with tears of his promise ; but she answered, " Since I have been the means of saving your life, I will willingly go away thither." Accordingly she is fetched away by a white wolf, who, as usual, turns out to be an enchanted prince, and marries her as soon as the spell which bound him is broken.[2]

In a German story of the same type a nobleman loses his way in a wood and meets a poodle who promises to guide him home if the nobleman will give the poodle whatever on his return should first come forth from the nobleman's house to meet him. As usual, the nobleman's daughter is the first to come forth to meet him ; and, as usual, the seeming calamity ends in the girl's marriage with a prince.[3]

Similarly in a Swedish story we hear of a king who had three daughters, but he loved the youngest best of all. One day he lost his way in the forest, and, whichever way he turned, he always met a man in a grey cloak, who said to him, " If you would make your way out of the forest, you must give me the

---

[1] K. Müllenhoff, *Sagen Märchen und Lieder der Herzogthümer Schleswig-Holstein und Lauenburg* (Kiel, 1845), pp. 384 *sq.*

[2] K. Müllenhoff, *op. cit.* pp. 385-388.

[3] P Zaunert, *Deutsche Märchen seit Grimm* (Jena, 1919), pp. 303 *sqq.*

APPENDIX

first living thing that meets you at your home-coming." The king thought to himself, "That will be my greyhound as usual"; so he promised. But it was his youngest and dearest daughter who met him first. The king sent his two elder daughters, one after the other, into the forest; but the man in the grey cloak sent them both back with rich presents. At last the king sent his youngest daughter, and after various adventures she was happily wedded to the man in the grey cloak, who, as usual, turned out to be an enchanted prince or nobleman, the owner of a fine castle.[1]

Thus in most of the folk-tales the rash vow turns out fortunately for the victim, who, instead of being sacrificed or killed, obtains a princely husband and wedded bliss. Yet we may suspect that these happy conclusions were simply devised by the story-teller for the sake of pleasing his hearers, and that in real life the custom, of which the stories preserve a reminiscence, often ended in the sacrifice of the victim at the altar. Of such a custom a record seems to survive in the legends of Idomeneus, Maeander, al-Mundhir, and Jephthah.

XIII.—ULYSSES AND POLYPHEMUS

(*Apollodorus, Epitome*, VII. 4–9)

Stories like that of Ulysses and Polyphemus have been recorded in modern times among many widely separated peoples. So close is the resemblance between the various versions of the tale that they must all apparently be derived from a common original, whether that original was the narrative in the *Odyssey*, or, more probably, a still older folk-tale which Homer incorporated in his epic. Some of these parallel versions were collected by Wilhelm Grimm about

---

[1] J. Bolte und G. Polívka, *Anmerkungen zu den Kinder- und Hausmärchen der Brüder Grimm*, i. (Leipsic, 1913), pp. 16 *sq.* As to stories of this type, see further E. Cosquin, *Contes populaires de Lorraine*, ii. 218 *sqq.*; W. Baumgartner, "Jephtas Gelübde," *Archiv für Religionswissenschaft*, xviii. (1915), pp. 240–249.

the middle of the nineteenth century,[1] but many others have since come to light.[2]

(1) The oldest of the modern versions of the Polyphemus story occurs in a mediaeval collection of tales which was written in or soon after 1184 A.D. by a monk, John, of the Cistercian Abbey of Haute-Seille (Alta Silva) in Lorraine. The book, dedicated to Bertrand, Bishop of Metz, is composed in very fair Latin and bears the title of *Dolopathos sive de Rege et Septem Sapientibus*. It was lost for centuries, but in 1864 a manuscript copy of the work was discovered by A. Mussafia in the Royal Library at Vienna. Subsequent research brought to light several other manuscripts at Vienna, Innsbruck, and Luxemburg, and in 1873 a complete edition of the book was published by H. Oesterley at Strasbourg.[3] Meantime the work had long been known to scholars

---

[1] Wilhelm Grimm, *Die Sage von Polyphem* (Berlin, 1857) (reprinted from the *Abhandlungen der königl. Akademie der Wissenschaften zu Berlin*, 1857). The versions recorded by Grimm are summarized by W. W. Merry in his edition of Homer, *The Odyssey, Books I–XII* (Oxford, 1876), pp. 546–550.

[2] See A. van Gennep, "La Légende de Polyphème," *Religions, Mœurs, et Légendes* (Paris, 1908), pp. 155–164. In this essay the learned author reviews a work by O. Hackman, *Die Polyphemsage in der Volksüberlieferung* (Helsingfors, 1904), which I have not seen. From M. van Gennep's notice of it, I gather that Mr. Hackman has collected, analysed, and classified no less than two hundred and twenty-one popular variations of the tale. Very many versions are referred to by Messrs. J. Bolte and G. Polívka in their erudite *Anmerkungen zu den Kinder- und Hausmärchen der Brüder Grimm* iii. (Leipzig, 1918), pp. 374–378. Thus the versions quoted by me in the following pages form apparently only a small part of those which are on record. But they may suffice to illustrate the wide diffusion of the tale and the general similarity of the versions.

[3] Joannes de Alta Silva, *Dolopathos sive de Rege et Septem Sapientibus*, herausgegeben von Hermann Oesterley (Strassburg, Karl J. Trübner, 1873). A more recent edition is that of A. Hilka (Heidelberg, 1913). Of the manuscripts the one now in the Athenæum at Luxemburg is the oldest and most complete; it was written in the thirteenth century and

through a metrical French translation which was written somewhere between the years 1222 and 1226 A.D. by a certain trouvère named Herbers. Considerable extracts from the poem, amounting to about a third of the whole, were published, with a prose analysis, by Le Roux de Lincy in 1838 ;[1] but the complete poem was first edited, from two manuscripts in the Imperial (now the National) Library in Paris, by Charles Brunet and Anatole de Montaiglon in 1856.[2]

This mediaeval collection of stories, called *Dolopathos*, whether in its original Latin form or in the metrical French translation, is clearly based, directly or indirectly, on an older mediaeval collection of tales called *The Book of Sindibad* or *The Seven Sages*, of which versions exist in many languages, both Oriental and European ;[3] for not only is the general

---

alone contains the author's dedication and preface. It formerly belonged to the Abbey of Orval (Aurea Vallis) in the diocese of Trèves and was removed, with the rest of the library, for safety to Luxemburg at the time when the Abbey was sacked by the French in 1793. As to the date of *Dolopathos*, see Oesterley's preface, p. xi. The monkish author's orthography is not equal to his diction and style. He uses such forms as *michi* for *mihi*, *nichil* for *nihil*, *herbe* for *herbae*, *nephas* for *nefas*, *etas* for *aetas*, *que* for *quae*, &c.

[1] Le Roux de Lincy, *Roman de Sept Sages de Rome*, printed as an appendix or introduction to A. Loiseleur Deslongchamps's *Essai sur les Fables Indiennes et sur leur Introduction en Europe* (Paris, 1838), but paged separately. The analysis and the extracts include the tale of Polyphemus (pp. 133–135, 239–251), who, however, is not mentioned by name, being simply referred to as " the giant."

[2] *Li Romans de Dolopathos, publié pour la première fois par Charles Brunet et Anatole de Montaiglon* (Paris, 1856). For the story of Polyphemus (who is not mentioned by name), see pp. 284–295. As to the date of this metrical translation see the editors' preface, pp. xvii–xix.

[3] As to *The Book of Sindibad* or *The Seven Sages*, see A. Loiseleur Deslongchamps, *Essai sur les Fables Indiennes et sur leur Introduction en Europe*, pp. 80 *sqq.* ; J. Dunlop, *Geschichte der Prosadichtungen*, übertragen von Felix Liebrecht (Berlin, 1851), pp. 196 *sqq.* ; D. Comparetti, *Researches concerning the Book of Sindibâd* (London. 1882), pp. 1 *sqq.*

framework or plan of *Dolopathos* the same with that of
Sindibad or *The Seven Sages*, but out of the eight stories
which it contains, three are identical with those included
in the earlier work.[1] Among the tales which the two collec-
tions have in common the story of Polyphemus is not one,
for it appears only in *Dolopathos*.

As told by the author of *Dolopathos* the story of Polyphemus
diverges in certain remarkable features from the Homeric
account, and since some of these divergences occur in popular
versions of the story recorded among various peoples, we may
reasonably infer that John de Haute-Seille herein followed
oral tradition rather than the Homeric version of the tale.[2]
At the same time he certainly appears to have been acquainted
with the *Odyssey ;* for he not only mentions Polyphemus

The fullest of the versions is the mediaeval Greek version
known as *Syntipas*, of which a critical edition was published
by A. Eberhard at Leipsic in 1872 (*Fabulae Romanenses
Graece conscriptae*, volumen prius, Leipsic, Teubner, 1872).
This version purports to be translated from the Syriac, and a
Syriac version was published with a German translation
by Fr. Baethgen in 1879 (*Sindban oder Die Sieben Weisen
Meister, syrisch und deutsch*, von Friederich Baethgen, Leipsic,
1879) ; but this version can hardly be the one which Andreo-
pulos translated into Greek, since it is somewhat shorter.
Compare D. Comparetti, *op. cit.* p. 63 note, who has made it
probable (pp. 53 *sqq.*) that the Greek version (*Syntipas*)
was made towards the end of the eleventh century by order
of Gabriel, Duke of Melitene. A French translation of the
Syriac version was published by F. Macler in 1903 (*Contes
Syriaques, Histoire de Sindban, mise en français* par Frédéric
Macler, Paris, 1903). The same scholar has since published
a French translation of an Armenian version, which seems to
have been made from the Latin. See *La version Arménienne
de l'Histoire des Sept Sages de Rome, mise en français* par
Frédéric Macler (Paris, 1919).

[1] H. Oesterley, preface to his edition of *Dolopathos*, pp.
xiii *sqq.*

[2] It is the opinion of Oesterley, his editor, that in general
John drew the materials for his work rather from oral tradition
than from literary sources. See H. Oesterley's preface, pp.
xii *sqq.*

by name but speaks of Circe, daughter of the Sun, and how she transformed the companions of Ulysses into diverse beasts.[1]

The story of Polyphemus, as recorded in *Dolopathos*, runs as follows :—

A famous robber, who had lived to old age and accumulated vast riches in the exercise of his profession, resolved to devote the remainder of his days to the practice of virtue, and in pursuance of that laudable resolution he excited by his exemplary conduct the wonder and admiration of all who remembered the crimes and atrocities of his earlier life. Being invited by the queen to recount the greatest perils and adventures which he had met with in his career of brigandage, he spoke thus : " Once on a time we heard that a giant, who owned great sums of gold and silver, dwelt in a solitary place about twenty miles distant from the abodes of men. Lured by the thirst for gold, a hundred of us robbers assembled together and proceeded with much ado to his dwelling. Arrived there, we had the pleasure of finding him not at home, so we carried off all the gold and silver on which we could lay hands. We were returning home, easy in our minds, when all of a sudden the giant with nine others comes upon us and takes us prisoners, the more shame to us that a hundred men should be captured by ten. They divided us among them, and, as ill luck would have it, I and nine others fell to the share of the one whose riches we had just been lifting. So he tied our hands behind our backs and drove us like so many sheep to his cave ; now his stature exceeded thirteen cubits. We offered to pay a great sum as ransom, but he mockingly replied that the only ransom he would accept was our flesh. With that he seized the fattest of our number, cut his throat, and rending him limb by limb, threw him into the pot to boil. He treated the rest of us, all but me, in the same fashion, and to crown it all he forced me to eat of every one of them. Why dwell on the painful subject ? When it came to my turn to have my throat cut, I pretended to be a doctor and promised that, if he spared my life, I would heal his eyes, which ached dreadfully. He agreed to these terms for my medical services, and told me to be quick about it. So I

---

[1] Joannes de Alta Silva, *Dolopathos sive de Rege et Septem Sapientibus*, herausgegeben von H. Oesterley, pp. 71, 99.

took a pint of oil and set it on the fire, and stirring it up with a good dose of lime, salt, sulphur, arsenic, and anything else I could think of that was most injurious and destructive to the eyes, I compounded a salve, and when it was nicely on the boil, I tipped the whole of it on the patient's head. The boiling oil, streaming over every inch of his body, peeled him like an onion ; his skin shrivelled up, his sinews stiffened, and what little sight he had left he lost completely. And there he was, like a man in a fit, rolling his huge body about on the floor, roaring like a lion and bellowing like a bull—a really horrid sight. After long rolling about and finding no ease to his pain, he grips his cudgel like a madman and goes groping and fumbling about for me, thumping the walls and the floor like a battering-ram. Meantime what was I to do ? and whither could I fly ? On every side the house was walled in by the most solid masonry, the only way out was by the door, and even that was barred with bolts of iron. So while he was tearing about after me in every corner, the only thing for me to do was to climb up a ladder to the roof and catch hold of a beam, and there I hung to it by my hands for a whole day and night. When I could bear it no longer, I had just to come down and dodge between the giant's legs and among his flock of sheep. For you must know that he had a thousand sheep and counted them every day. And while he kept a fat one he used to let the others go to grass ; and whether it was his skill or his witchery I know not, but at evening they would all come trooping back of themselves, and he got the full tale. So when he was counting them and letting them out as usual, I tried to escape by wrapping me in the shaggy fleece of a ram and fixing his horns on my head ; and in that guise I mingled with the flock that was going out. On my turn coming to be counted, he feels me all over, and finding me fat, he keeps me back, saying, 'To-day I'll fill my empty belly on you.' Seven times did I thus pass under his hands, seven times did he keep me back, yet every time I gave him the slip. At last, when I came under his hand once more, he drove me in a rage out of the door, saying, 'Go and be food for the wolves, you who have so often deceived your master.' When I was about a stone's throw off, I began to mock him because I had outwitted him so often and made my escape. But he drew a gold ring from his finger and said, 'Take that for a reward ; for it is not meet

that a guest should go without a gift from a man like me.'
I took the proffered ring and put it on my finger, and at once
I was bewitched by some devilry or other and began to shout,
'Here I am! Here I am!' Thereupon, blind though he
was, guided by the sound of my voice, he came tearing along,
bounding over the smaller bushes, sometimes stumbling and
collapsing like a landslide. When he was nearly up to me,
and I could neither stop shouting nor tear the ring from my
finger, I was forced to cut off the finger with the ring and to
fling it at him. Thus by the loss of a finger did I save my
whole body from imminent destruction."[1]

This version differs from the Homeric account in several
important respects. It represents the giant as merely
blear-eyed instead of one-eyed; it describes the blinding of
him as effected by a stratagem which the hero of the tale
practises on the giant with his own consent instead of as a
violence done to him in his sleep; and it adds an entirely
new episode in the trick of the magic ring and the consequent
sacrifice of the hero's finger. These discrepancies, which
recur, as we shall see, in other versions, confirm the view that
the source from which the monk John drew the story was
oral tradition rather than the narrative in the *Odyssey*.

(2) All the distinctive features which we have just remarked
in the version of John of Haute-Seille meet us again in a
West Highland version of the story, which was told by a
blind fiddler in the island of Islay. It runs thus: A certain
man called Conall Cra Bhuidhe undertook with the help of his
sons to steal the brown horse of the King of Lochlann; but
in the attempt they were caught by the king, who would
have hanged them, if Conall had not saved their lives by telling
the story of his adventures. One of his adventures was like

---

[1] Joannes de Alta Silva, *Dolopathos sive de Rege et Septem
Sapientibus*, herausgegeben von H. Oesterley, pp. 66–68;
id., herausgegeben von A. Hilka (Heidelberg, 1913), pp. 73–75.
There are a few minor discrepancies in the texts of these
editions. According to Oesterley's text, the hero was obliged
to cut off (*abscidere*) his finger; according to Hilka's text,
he was compelled to bite it off (*dentibus abscidere*). The word
dentibus is wanting in the Luxemburg manuscript. The
parallel versions are in favour of cutting off, as against biting
off, the finger. See below, pp. 412, 413 *sq.*, 415, 416, 418, 419,
421, 422.

that of Ulysses in the cave of Polyphemus. "I was there as a young lad," said Conall, "and I went out hunting, and my father's land was beside the sea, and it was rough with rocks and caves and chasms. When I was going on the shore, I saw a smoke curling up between two rocks, and while I was looking at it, I fell; but the place was so full of manure that neither skin nor bone was broken. Then I heard a great clattering, and what was there but a great giant and two dozen of goats with him, and a buck at their head? And when the giant had tied the goats, he came up and he said to me, 'Ho, Conall, it's long since my knife is rusting in my pouch waiting for thy tender flesh.' 'Och,' said I, 'it's not much thou wilt be bettered by me, though thou shouldst tear me asunder; I will make but one meal for thee. But I see thou art one-eyed. I am a good leech, and I will give thee the sight of the other eye.' The giant went and he drew the great cauldron on the site of the fire. I told him how to heat the water so that I should give its sight to the other eye. I got heather, and I made a rubber of it, and I set him upright in the cauldron. I began at the eye that was well, pretending to him that I would give its sight to the other one, till I left them as bad as each other; and surely it was easier to spoil the one that was well than to give sight to the other.

"When he saw that he could not see at all, and when I myself said to him that I would get out in spite of him, he gave a spring out of the water and stood at the mouth of the cave, and he said that he would have revenge for the sight of his eye. I had to stay there crouched all night, holding my breath that he might not feel where I was. When he heard the birds calling in the morning, and knew that it was day, he said, 'Art thou sleeping? Awake and let out my goats.' I killed the buck. He cried, 'I will not believe that thou art killing my buck.' 'I am not,' said I, 'but the ropes are so tight that I take long to loose them.' I let out one of the goats, and he caressed her, and he said to her, 'There thou art, thou shaggy white goat, and thou seest me, but I see thee not.' I let them out one by one, as I flayed the buck, and before the last one was out I had flayed him bag-wise. Then I put my legs in place of his legs, and my hands in place of his fore legs, and my head in place of his head, and the horns on top of my head, so that the brute might think that it was the buck. I went out. When I was going out, the giant laid his hand on me, and he said, 'There thou art, my pretty buck; thou seest me, but I see thee not.' When I myself got out, and I saw the world about me, surely, oh King! joy was on me.

"When I was out and had shaken the skin off me, I said to the brute, 'I am out now in spite of thee.' 'Aha!' said he, 'hast thou done this to me? Since thou wert so stalwart that thou hast got out, I will give thee a ring that I have here, and keep the ring, and it will do thee good.' 'I will not take the ring from thee,' said I, 'but throw it, and I will take it with me.' He threw the ring on the flat ground, I went myself and I lifted the ring, and I put it on my finger. Then he said, 'Does the ring fit thee?' I said to him, 'It does.' He said, 'Where art thou, ring?' And the ring said, 'I am here.' The brute came towards where the ring was speaking, and now I saw that I was in a harder case than ever I was. I drew a dirk. I cut off my finger, and I threw it from me as far as I could on the loch, and the place was very deep. He shouted, 'Where art thou, ring?' And the ring said, 'I am here,' though it was at the bottom of the ocean. He gave a leap after the ring, and down he went in the sea. I was pleased when I saw him drowning, and when he was drowned I went in, and I took with me all he had of gold and silver, and I went home, and surely great joy was on my people when I arrived. And as a sign for thee, look thou, the finger is off me."[1]

(3) In another Highland story, recorded in Argyllshire, a one-eyed giant carries the hero of the tale into his cave, intending to devour him; but with the help of a king's daughter, whom the giant had detained for seven years, the hero contrives to blind the monster by thrusting a red-hot bar into his single eye while he sleeps. There is no mention of sheep or goats in this story, and the episode of the talking ring is also absent.[2]

---

[1] J. F. Campbell, *Popular Tales of the West Highlands*, New Edition, I (Paisley and London, 1890), pp. 105–114 (Tale V). I have slightly abridged the story and changed a few words for the sake of the English idiom.

[2] D. MacInnes, *Folk and Hero Tales* (London, 1890), pp. 263, 265, 267 (*Waifs and Strays of Celtic Tradition, Argyllshire Series*, No. II).

(4) The incident of the ring and the severed finger occurs also in two Basque stories of the same type. One of them was told by the parish priest of Esquiule, in La Soule, as follows :

"In my infancy I often heard from my mother the story of the Tartaro. He was a Colossus, with only one eye in the middle of his forehead. He was a shepherd and a hunter, but a hunter of men. Every day he ate a sheep ; then, after a snooze, everyone who had the misfortune to fall into his hands. His dwelling was a huge barn, with thick walls, a high roof, and a very strong door, which he alone knew how to open. His mother, an old witch, lived in one corner of the garden, in a hut constructed of turf.

"One day a powerful young man was caught in the snares of the Tartaro, who carried him off to his house. This young man saw the Tartaro eat a whole sheep, and he knew that he was accustomed to take a snooze, and then after that his own turn would come. In his despair he said to himself that he must do something. Directly the Tartaro began to snore he put the spit into the fire, made it red-hot, and plunged it into the giant's one eye. Immediately he leapt up, and began to run after the man who had injured him ; but it was impossible to find him. ' You shall not escape. It is all very well to hide yourself,' said he, ' but I alone know the secret how to open this door.'

"The Tartaro opened the door half-way, and let the sheep out between his legs. The young man takes the big bell off the ram, and puts it round his neck, and throws over his body the skin of the sheep which the giant had just eaten, and walks on all fours to the door. The Tartaro examines him by feeling him, perceives the trick, and clutches hold of the skin ; but the young man slips off the skin, dives between his legs, and runs off.

"Immediately the mother of the Tartaro meets him, and says to him : ' O, you lucky young fellow ! You have escaped the cruel tyrant ; take this ring as a remembrance of your escape.' He accepts, puts the ring on his finger, and immediately the ring begins to cry out, ' *Heben nuk !* *Heben nuk !*' (' Thou hast me here ! Thou hast me here !') The Tartaro pursues, and is on the point of catching him, when the young man, maddened with fright, and not being able to pull off the ring, takes out his knife, and cuts off his own finger, and throws it away, and thus escapes the pursuit of the Tartaro."[1]

(5) Another Basque story of the same sort was told by Jean Sallaber of Aussurucq as follows:

Two soldiers of the same district, having got their furlough, were returning home on foot together. Night fell as they were traversing a great forest. But in the twilight they perceived a smoke in the distance, so they turned their steps towards it and discovered a poor hovel. They knocked at the door, and a voice from within answered, "Who is there?" "Two friends," they answered. "What do you want?" asked the voice. "A lodging for the night," they replied. The door opened, they were admitted, and then the door closed. Brave as the soldiers were, they were yet terrified at finding themselves in the presence of a Basa-Jaun. He had the figure of a man, but was all covered with hair, and had a single eye in the middle of his forehead.

The Basa-Jaun set food before them, and when they had finished their supper, he weighed them and said to the heavier, "You will do for to-night, and the other for to-morrow"; and without more ado he ran a big spit through the fatter of the two, without even stripping him of his clothes, and after setting him to roast on the spit before a great fire, he ate him up. The other was in a sad fright, not knowing what to do to save his life.

Having made a hearty meal, the Basa-Jaun fell asleep. Immediately the soldier laid hold of the spit which had served to roast his comrade, heated it red-hot in the fire, and plunging it into the eye of the Basa-Jaun, blinded him. Howling aloud, the Basa-Jaun ran about everywhere to find the stranger; but the soldier had made haste to hide in the fold, among the sheep of the Basa-Jaun; for he could not get out, because the door was shut.

Next morning the Basa-Jaun opened the door of the fold, and, wishing to catch the soldier, he made all the sheep, on their way out, pass one by one between his legs. But the soldier had conceived the idea of skinning a sheep and clothing himself in its fleece, in order that the blinded giant should not catch him. As the Basa-Jaun felt all the sheep,

---

[1] Wentworth Webster, *Basque Legends* (London, 1879), pp. 4 *sq.*

the skin of the flayed one remained in his hands, and he thought that the man had passed out under it.

The soldier did escape, and very glad he was to do so. But the Basa-Jaun ran after him as well as he could, crying, "Hold, take this ring, in order that, when you are at home, you may be able to tell what a marvel you have done!" And with that he threw him the ring. The soldier picked it up and put it on his finger; but the ring began to speak and to say, "Here I am! Here I am!" Away ran the soldier, and the blinded monster after him. At last, worn out with his flight, and fearing to be overtaken by the Basa-Jaun, the soldier would have thrown the ring into a stream, but he could not wrench it from his finger. So he cut off the finger and threw it with the ring into the stream. From the bottom of the river the ring continued to cry, "Here I am! Here I am!" and hearing the cry the Basa-Jaun rushed into the water and was drowned. Then the soldier crossed the stream on a bridge and escaped, very happy, to his home.[1]

(6) The episode of the talking ring and the severed finger occurs also in a Rumanian story of the same type. In it a man sends his three sons out with the flock of sheep and warns them not to answer if anyone should hail them by night. But they neglect his warning, and in the night, when a voice has hailed them thrice, they all answer, "Here we are." A giant now appears and calls to them to roast their fattest wether for him, because he is hungry. When the wether is roasted, the giant swallows it at a gulp, and orders the three brothers to follow him with the flock. He leads them to his home, where they are obliged to leave the sheep in the walled courtyard. When they enter the giant's house, they bid him good evening, but he answers that the eldest brother will serve him for supper that same evening, that the second brother will do the same the next evening, and that the youngest brother will be kept for the next day but one. He then made up a big fire, hung a huge kettle over it, and lay down to sleep, after telling the brothers to wake him when the water should boil. They did so accordingly, whereupon he seized the eldest brother, threw him into the kettle, boiled him till he was tender, and then ate

---

[1] J. Vinson, *Le Folk-lore du pays Basque* (Paris, 1883), pp. 42–45.

him. Thereupon he put water to boil on the fire again and lay down, with an injunction to wake him at the time appointed. But the youngest brother skimmed off the fat of his boiled brother as it floated on the water, and having got it he secreted it. The giant slept till evening, then waking from his nap he seized the second brother and devoured him. A third time he set water on the fire, ordering the surviving brother to waken him as usual. Meantime the survivor found a tripod in the kitchen, set his brother's fat on it, and roasted it over the fire. Then he flung the roasted fat and the tripod at the sleeping giant, thus putting out both his eyes. Up started the giant in a fury and tried to catch the young man, but the youth threw him off the scent by dropping nuts, which he had in his wallet, one after the other on the floor. In his blind rage the giant seized the latch and wrenched the door open. The young man darted out into the courtyard, slaughtered a ram, and crept into its skin. Not suspecting the trick, the giant now opened the gate of the courtyard and let the sheep out one by one in the hope of catching his prisoner when he should attempt to escape. But the disguised youth slipped through and called out mockingly to the giant, "Now you can do nothing to me." Then the giant, making believe to be friendly, called after him, "Take this ring from my little finger for a memorial." The young man picked it up and put it on. Then the ring began to call out, "This way, blind man, this way!" Away ran the youth and the giant after him. The fugitive reached the water first, but the giant was close on his heels ; so the young man cut off his own finger with the ring on it, and threw it into the waves. As the ring continued to call out, "This way, blind man, this way!" the giant leaped into the water and was drowned.[1]

(7) The episode of an enchanted, though not talking, ring and a severed finger, meets us in two Italian stories of this type. One of them, recorded in the Abruzzo, tells of two brothers who were going to a fair. As they were crossing a rugged mountain, night overtook them. They saw a gleam of light in a cave, and approaching they called out, "Master of the house, will you give us shelter ?" A voice

---

[1] W. Grimm, *Die Sage von Polyphem*, **pp.** 15 *sq.*, referring to Franz Obert (*Ausland*, 29, 717).

from within answered, "Wait." They waited, and out came a giant who had an eye in his forehead. He said, "Pray come in. Here there is no lack of anything." The two brothers went in, but they were all of a tremble, all the more because Eye-in-his-forehead shut the door with a bolt which not a hundred men could lift. Standing in front of the fire, Eye-in-his-forehead said to the two brothers, "I have a hundred sheep, but the year is long, and we must be as thrifty as may be. So which shall we eat first? Little Brother or Big Brother? You may cast lots for it." The two brothers cast lots, and the lot fell on Big Brother. So Big Brother was stuck on a spit and set on the hot coals. While Eye-in-his-forehead turned the spit, he said in an undertone, "Big Brother to-day, Little Brother to-morrow." Little Brother racked his brains to think how he could escape from the danger. Meantime Big Brother was roasted, and Eye-in-his-forehead began to eat him. He wished Little Brother to eat too, and Little Brother pretended to eat, but he threw the meat behind his back. Dinner over, Eye-in-his-forehead went to sleep in the straw, but Little Brother remained beside the fire. When he perceived that Eye-in-his-forehead snored, he heated the point of the spit red-hot and thrust it, fizzing, into the giant's eye. The giant started up to catch Little Brother, but Little Brother nimbly mixed with the sheep, and though the giant searched the sheep, feeling them one by one, he could not discover the fugitive. However, he said, "I'll catch him at break of day." Little Brother thought it was all up with him unless he could hit on some dodge or other. So he killed the ram, skinned it, and dressed himself in the skin. At break of day Eye-in-his-forehead removed the bolt and stood straddling in the doorway. And first of all he called for the ram with the bell on its neck. Little Brother came forward, jingling the bell and going on all fours. As he passed between the legs of Eye-in-his-forehead, the giant caressed him, and so he did to the rest of the sheep. But groping about in the cave he lighted on the carcass of the ram which Little Brother had killed and skinned. Then he perceived the trick which Little Brother had played him, and sniffing about in his direction he threw him an enchanted ring. Little Brother picked it up and put it on his finger, but having done so he found himself compelled, instead of running away, to draw near to the giant. In vain he tried to pull the ring from his finger ; the ring would not budge. So in order not to fall into the hands of Eye-in-his-forehead he cut off the finger on which was the ring, and threw it in the face of the giant who ate it and said to Little Brother, " At least I have tasted you."[1]

(8) Another Italian version of the story, recorded at Pisa, tells of a man of Florence who set out on his travels. On the way he picked up a curate and a workman, and the three agreed to try their fortunes together. Walking through a wood for a long time, they came at last to a very fine palace and knocked at the door. A giant opened the door in person and asked them where they were going. " Oh, just taking a turn," said they. " Very well," said the giant, " just turn in here. There's a vacancy in the curacy of my parish, and a vacancy in my workshop, and I'll find some job or other for him," alluding to the Florentine. All three closed with the offer, and put up in the giant's house. He gave them a room and said, " To-morrow I'll give you your jobs to do." Next day the giant came to them, took the curate, and led him away to another chamber. Instigated by the passion of curiosity, the Florentine followed on tiptoe, and applying his eye to the keyhole of the chamber in which the curate was getting his job, he saw the giant showing him some leaves, and while the clergyman was looking at them, what does the giant do but whip out a scimitar, and in less than no time he had the curate's head off and his body in a grave, which was in the chamber. " Good idea of mine to come here," thought the Florentine to himself. When they were at dinner, the giant said, " The curate has got his job. Now I'll give the workman his." So after dinner he led the workman to the same chamber. The Florentine followed as before, and again applying his eye to the keyhole, he saw the giant taking some leaves from his writing-desk and showing them to the workman, and while the workman was gazing at them, the giant performed the sword-trick once more. " My turn next," thought the Florentine to himself.

That evening at supper the giant remarked that the work-

---

[1] Antonio de Nino, *Usi e Costumi Abruzzesi* (Florence, 1879–1883), III. 305–307.

man had got his job, and that he, the giant, would soon find a job for the Florentine too. But the Florentine had no wish to do the job in question, and he cudgelled his brains as to how he could get out of it. At last he thought of a plan. It happened that one of the giant's eyes was defective ; so he said to the giant, " What a pity that with that fine figure of yours you should have such an eye ! But look here, I know a cure for it, it is a certain herb which I have seen here in the meadow." " Really ? " said the giant, " here in the meadow ? Then let's go and find it." When they were in the meadow, the Florentine picked up the first herb he saw, and bringing it back with him put it in a pot of oil, which he set on the fire. When the oil was boiling, the Florentine said to the giant, " I warn you that the pain will be great ; but you must keep steady, and it will be well that I should tie you to this marble table, for otherwise the opera-tion will turn out ill." The giant, who was bent on having his bad eye put right, told the Florentine to tie away. The Florentine did as he was desired, and then poured the boiling oil on both the giant's eyes. " You have blinded me," roared the giant ; but the other stole softly down the stair, opened the door, and cut away. The giant had now lost both his eyes, but such was his strength that he rose to his feet with the marble table on his back, and made after his foe. " Come here ! Come here ! " he cried, " fear not. At least take a keepsake." And he threw a ring to the Florentine, who picked it up and put it on his finger. But no sooner had he done so than his finger was turned to marble, and he could not budge from the spot. In vain did he tug at the ring ; he could not stir it from his finger. And now the giant was all but up with him. In despair the fugitive drew a knife, which he had in his pocket, and cut off his finger. Then he could move again, and away he tore, and the giant, encumbered by the table on his shoulders, could not catch him up. The wanderer reached Florence in a state of exhaustion, and by this time he had had enough of it. The wish to scour the world and to tell of his travels never came back on him.[1] In this version we miss the characteristic episode of the hero's escape under a ram or clad in a sheepskin.

---

[1] D. Comparetti, *Novelline popolari Italiane* (Rome, Turin, and Florence, 1875), No. 44, pp. 192-195.

APPENDIX

(9) A Serbian story of this type relates how a priest and his scholar were once walking through a great mountainous region when night overtook them. Seeing a fire burning in a cave some way off, they made for it. On reaching the cave they found nobody in it except a giant with one eye in his forehead. They asked him if he would let them enter, and he answered "Yes." But the mouth of the cave was blocked with a huge stone, which a hundred men could not have stirred. The giant arose, lifted the stone, and let them in. Then he rolled back the stone into the mouth of the cave and kindled a great fire. The travellers sat down beside it and warmed themselves. When they had done so, the giant felt their necks in order to know which was the fatter, that he might kill and roast him. Finding the parson the fatter of the two, he knocked him on the head, stuck him on a spit, and roasted him over the fire. When he was done to a turn, the giant invited the scholar to partake of the roasted flesh, and though the scholar protested that he was not hungry, the giant forced him to take a mouthful, which, however, he spat out on the sly. Having eaten his fill, the giant composed himself to slumber beside the fire. While he slept, the scholar sharpened a stick and thrusting it into the giant's eye, blinded him. "You have robbed me of my one eye," roared the giant, "because I had not the sense to put out both of yours. But no matter. Thank God, you will not escape me." He groped about in the cave, but could not find the scholar, because there were many sheep in it, and the scholar had drawn a ram's skin over his body and in that disguise had mingled with the flock. Then the giant went to the mouth of the cave, pushed the great stone a little aside, and let the sheep pass out, one after the other, and the scholar in the ram's skin slipped out with them. Having escaped into the open, he cried to the giant, "Seek for me no more. I am out." When the giant saw that his prisoner had given him the slip, he held out a staff to him, saying, "Though you have escaped me, take this staff to shepherd the sheep with ; for without it you will not get a single sheep to budge." The simple scholar took it, and no sooner had he touched it than one of his fingers clave fast to the staff. He now gave himself up for lost and began to run round and round the giant, till he remembered that he had his clasp-knife on him

Whipping it out, he cut off the finger that clave to the staff, and so he escaped. Afterwards, driving the flock before him, he mocked and jeered at the blinded giant, who pursued him till he came to the edge of the water, into which he fell and was drowned.[1]

(10) A Russian story, which belongs to the same class, tells how once upon a time there was a smith. "Well now," says he, "I've never set eyes on any harm. They say there's evil (*likho*) in the world. I'll go and seek out evil." So he went and started in search of evil, and on the way he met a tailor, who agreed to join him in the search. Well, they walked and walked till they came to a dark, dense forest, and in the forest they found a narrow path, and along the path they walked till they saw a large cottage standing before them. It was night, and there was nowhere else to go to. So they went in. There was nobody there. All looked bare and squalid. They sat down, and remained sitting there some time. Presently in came a tall woman, lank, crooked, with only one eye. "Ah!" says she, "I've visitors. Good day to you." "Good day, grandmother. We've come to pass the night under your roof." "Very good: I shall have something to sup on."

Thereupon they were greatly terrified. As for her, she went and fetched a great heap of firewood. She flung it into the stove, and set it alight. Then she took the tailor, cut his throat, trussed him, and put him in the oven. When she had finished her supper, the smith looked at the oven and said, "Granny, I'm a smith." "What can you forge?" "Anything." "Make me an eye." "Good," says he; "but have you got any cord? I must tie you up, or you won't keep still. I shall have to hammer your eye in."

She went and fetched two cords, one rather thin, the other thicker. Well, he bound her with the thinner, but she broke it. So he took the thick cord, and tied her up with it famously. She wriggled and writhed, but break it she could not. Then he took an awl, heated it red-hot, and applied the point of it to her sound eye, while he hammered away at the other end with a hatchet. She struggled like anything and broke the

---

[1] W. S. Karadschitsch, *Volksmärchen der Serben* (Berlin, 1854), No. 38, pp. 222–225; F. S. Krauss, *Sagen und Märchen der Südslaven* (Leipsic, 1883), No. 5, Vol. I, pp. 170–173.

cord; then she went and sat down at the threshold. "Ah, villain!" she cried, "you shan't get away from me now."

By and by the sheep came home from afield, and she drove them into her cottage for the night. Well, the smith spent the night there, too. In the morning she got up to let the sheep out. He took his sheep-skin pelisse and turned it inside out, so that the wool was outside, passed his arms through its sleeves, and pulled it well over him, and then crept up to her as if he had been a sheep. She let the flock go out one at a time, catching hold of each by the wool on its back, and shoving it out. Well, he came creeping up like the rest. She caught hold of the wool on his back and shoved him out. But as soon as she had shoved him out, he stood up and cried, "Farewell, Likho! I have suffered much evil (likho) at your hands. No, you can do nothing to me." "Wait a bit!" she replied, "you shall endure still more."

The smith went back through the forest along the narrow path. Presently he saw a golden-handled hatchet sticking in a tree, and he felt a strong desire to seize it. Well, he did seize that hatchet, and his hand stuck fast to it. What was to be done? There was no freeing it anyhow. He gave a look behind him. There was Likho coming after him and crying, "There you are, villain! you've not got off yet." The smith pulled out a knife and began hacking away at his hand; he cut it clean off and ran away. When he reached his village, he showed the stump of his arm as a proof that he had seen Likho at last.[1]

(11) A story which resembles this Russian tale in some points is told by the Esthonians. They call the farm-servant who has the superintendence of barns and corn the Barn-carl (*Riegenkerl*).[2] One day when a Barn-carl sat casting knobs in a mould, up comes to him the devil, bids him good-day, and asks him what he is doing. "I am casting eyes," says the Barn-carl. "Eyes?" quoth the devil. "Can you cast new eyes for me?" "Yes," says the Barn-carl, "but just at the moment I have no more in stock."

---

[1] W. R. S. Ralston, *Russian Folk-tales* (London, 1873), pp. 178–181; W. W. Strickland, *Russian and Bulgarian Folk-lore Stories* (London, 1907), pp. 38 *sqq.*

[2] *Riege* is "a building for drying corn spread out" (Lucas)

XIII.—ULYSSES AND POLYPHEMUS

" But perhaps you could do it some other time ? " asks the
devil. "That I could," says the Barn-carl. "When shall
I come then ? " asks the devil. "When you please," says
the Barn-carl. Next day the devil came to get his new pair
of eyes. "Do you want big eyes or small ones ? " asks the
Barn-carl. "Right big ones," says the devil. The man
set a lump of lead to melt on the fire and said, " I can't
mould your eyes when you are like that. You must let
yourself be tied up fast." With that he made the devil lie
down on his back on a bench, took a strong cord, and bound
him tight. When the devil was bound tight, he asked the
Barn-carl, "What is your name ? " "My name," he said,
" is Myself " (*Issi*). "That's a good name," quoth the
devil, " I never heard a better." By this time the lead was
molten, and the devil opened his eyes wide, expecting to get
new ones. "Here goes," quoth the Barn-carl, and with
that he pours the molten lead on the devil's eyes. Up jumps
the devil with the bench tied to his back and makes off at a
run. Some people were ploughing in a field, and as the poor
devil tore past them, they asked him, "Who did that to
you ? " "Myself did it," says he. They laughed. But
the devil died of his new eyes, and has never been seen since.[1]

Here the trick of " Myself " played by the Barn-carl on
the devil resembles the trick of " Nobody " played by Ulysses
on Polyphemus.

(12) A similar trick is played on a blinded giant in a Lapp
tale, which in other respects resembles the Homeric story
still more closely. Many hundred years ago, we are told,
when there were still giants and trolls among the mountains
and hills, a man might easily stumble on a troll against his
will when he passed the boundary of his home-land. Well, it
chanced once on a time that four Lapps, who had gone out
to seek their reindeer, lost their way on the mountains.
Three whole days and as many nights did they wander about
without coming to a human habitation, and they were near
dead with hunger and weariness when at last they spied a
light that seemed to shine at the foot of a mountain, whose
top reached the clouds. Joyfully they hastened to it,
expecting to find a human dwelling. But when they reached

---

[1] W. Grimm, *Die Sage von Polyphem*, pp. 16 *sq.* ; J. Grimm,
Deutsche Mythologie, II. 858 *sq.*

the foot of the mountain, they found that the light glimmered from a cave under the crag. After a moment's deliberation they resolved to enter the cave. When they had penetrated it might be a couple of musket shots into the bowels of the mountain, they found themselves in a great hall, of which the roof and the walls were of purest silver and so bright that you could see yourself in them as in a looking-glass. Not a human being was to be seen, but there were more than a hundred gigantic goats, both billy-goats and nanny-goats. In one corner of the hall there was a great hearth with a fire blazing merrily on it, and over the fire hung a prodigious big kettle with the flesh of a whole ox boiling in it. As the Lapps were very sharp set, they gathered round the kettle and began to eat the beef.

When they had satisfied their hunger, they put out the fire by pouring the hot water from the kettle on it, and having done so they filled the kettle with cold water. What was left of the beef in the kettle they hid. Then, poking about in the cave, they discovered great store of gold and silver and other precious things, but they did not dare to lay hands on them as not knowing to whom all these riches might belong. Suspecting that the owner might be no mere man, they made up their minds to quit the cave after they had rested a little from their weary wanderings. So they hid in a dark corner of the cave and fell asleep. Hardly had they done so when they were awakened by a noise so loud that they thought their last hour was come. Next moment they saw a man stride into the cave, and he was so big that they were all amazed, for they knew at once that he was a giant. To escape was impossible, and they made up their minds to keep quite still.

The giant stopped short in the middle of the cave and began to crinkle his nose and to sniff and snuff on all sides. "Very odd," he muttered at last, "it can't be that there should have been somebody here." Then he went up to the hearth, and, lifting the lid from the kettle, he looked in and was not a little surprised to find nothing in it but water. In a rage he flung the lid at the silver roof, where it stuck ; then he began to rummage every corner and crevice of the cave. It was not long before he lit upon the terrified Lapps, dragged the biggest of them out, and threw him into the kettle to boil, forgetting that the kettle could not boil without fire. The rest of the Lapps he chained up to the wall of the cave, then lay down to sleep till the Lapp in the kettle should be boiled.

Not many minutes passed before he snored so loud that the mountain shook and the cinders danced on the hearth. Then the Lapp stepped out of the kettle, freed his comrades from their chains, and with them hastened to the mouth of the cave. But to their dismay they found that the giant had barred it with a stone so huge that all four of them could not stir it.

After laying their heads together for an hour they turned back into the cave, resolved by hook or crook to play the giant a trick. The beef which they had hidden they put into the kettle again, and the three Lapps went back to the places where the giant had chained them up; but the fourth Lapp hid behind a great coop near the door.

The giant now woke up and hurried to the kettle to see whether the Lapp were boiled, but not finding him in it he went to the other prisoners and threatened to knock them on the head out of hand if they did not tell him where their friend had gone. One of the Lapps swore that sure his friend must be in the kettle, and that the giant's eyes must be blear not to see him. "That would be odd," said the giant, who was a little ashamed of his hastiness, "but now that I think of it, I do believe that of late my sight has been a bit dim." "Well," said the Lapp, "a good eye-salve will soon set that right." "Can you make up such a salve?" asked the giant. "To be sure," says the Lapp; "as soon as you get my salve in your eyes you will see fifty miles just as well as fifty yards. But you must know that it smarts horribly." "No matter," says the giant, "just you make up the salve and let me have it as quick as may be." "With all my heart," says the Lapp, "if you will pay me well for it." "You shall live with me fourteen whole days," says the giant, "till I have eaten up your friends. But you must tell me your name, lest I should eat you up instead." The Lapp said that his name was Nobody, and the giant repeated it ten times to make quite sure that he should not forget it. A fire was now made on the hearth, the Lapp heated five pounds of lead on it, and when it was molten he poured it on the giant's eyes, which of course were quite put out by it.

The giant soon perceived that Nobody had tricked him, so he began to call his neighbour to help him to serve out the

Lapp. His neighbour came running and asked who had hurt him, that he howled so dolefully. "Nobody has done it," answered the giant. On that the neighbour, thinking that he was joking, flew into a rage and said, "Then you can help yourself. Don't call me another time, or it will be the worse for you." And with that he went away.

As he got no help from his neighbour, the giant now made shift to search the cave and catch his foes; but they hid behind the goats, so that he could not find them. After groping about in this way for a long time he came to see that the beasts were in the way of his search. So he went to the doorway, took away the big stone which served as a door, and let out the goats one by one, after making sure that none of the Lapps slipped out with them.

When the Lapps saw what he was up to, they killed four billy-goats with all speed, skinned them, and wrapped themselves up in the skins, after which they crawled out of the cave on hands and feet, taking as much gold and silver with them as they could carry. When the last Lapp was about to leave the cave, the giant detained him, caressed him, and stroked his back, saying, "My poor big billy-goat, you will now be without a master." After caressing the supposed billy-goat, he let him go; then he shut up the mouth of the cave with the big stone, and with a grin cried out, "Now I've got you in the trap! Now we shall see which of us can chouse the other best, my dear Mr. Nobody!"

Nobody knows what afterwards befel the silly giant. As like as not, he went round and round the cave looking for the Lapps, till he died of hunger.[1]

(13) A Lapp variant of the preceding story runs as follows: Once on a time Slyboots[2] lost his way and came to the abode of a Stalo. This Stalo owned a house, a kitchen, and sheep. It was his way, whenever he got hold of a poor little oaf of a Lapp, to keep him by him for a time, so as to fatten him before he made a meal of him. He thought to do the same thing to Slyboots. But Slyboots thought of a dodge to blind

---

[1] J. C. Poestion, *Lappländische Märchen* (Vienna, 1886), No. 29, pp. 122–126.

[2] *Aschenputtel*, equivalent to the "Boots" of our fairy tales, a general name for the youngest son, who is supposed to be slyer than his elder brothers.

the Stalo. So he made believe to be very sharp-sighted and to be able to see all sorts of funny things ever so far off. The Stalo glowered for all he was worth in the same direction, but could make out just nothing at all. "Look here, young man," says he, "however do you come to be so sharp-sighted?" "Oh," says Slyboots, "it's in this way. I let them drip a drop of lead in my eyes. That's why I am so sharp-sighted." "Oh, that's it, is it?" says the Stalo. "Come on, my dear chap, and pour a little molten lead in my eyes. I should so like to be as sharp-sighted as you." "I'll do it with all my heart," says Slyboots, "but you could not stand it, for it hurts rather." "Not stand it?" says the Stalo. "I'll stand anything to be as sharp-sighted as you."

So Slyboots must needs, as if against his will, pour lead into the Stalo's eyes. He made him lie on his back and poured the lead first into one eye. The Stalo whimpered, but said, "Look sharp, my dear fellow, and pour the lead into the other eye also." The young man did so. "Now," said he, "you will be blind for a while, till your eyes have grown accustomed to the change; but afterwards you will see like anything."

It was now arranged that so long as the Stalo was blind, the young man should take charge of the household. So he picked out a fat ram from the Stalo's sheep and slaughtered it, and next he took the Stalo's old dog and slaughtered him too. In the evening he boiled the fat mutton for himself in one pot, and in another pot he cooked the dog's flesh for the Stalo, and when all was ready he served up the dog's flesh to the Stalo in a trough, while he devoted his own attention to the mutton. The Stalo heard him pegging away and smacking his lips, while he himself could hardly get his teeth into the tough old dog's flesh. "Look here, young man," says he, "what's all that smacking and licking of the lips that I hear, while my jaws only creak and clatter?" But the Slyboots fobbed him off with some answer or other.

However it was not long before the Stalo perceived that Slyboots had made a fool of him, for the sharp sight which had been promised him was still to seek. In fact he was blind and remained so. So he now racked his brains to know how he could pay Slyboots off for the trick he had played him. At last one day he told Slyboots to go into the fold and count the sheep. "That's easily done," says

APPENDIX

Slyboots, and in he goes. But blind as the Stalo was, he came on the heels of Slyboots and set himself plump in the doorway. "Aha!" thinks he to himself, "now I've got you in the trap! you shan't slip from my claws!" But Slyboots was not so easily to be cast down. "Let all my sheep out, one after the other," said the Stalo, "but my big ram last of all." "All right," said the youth, "so be it." Then he let the sheep out between the legs of the Stalo, who stood straddling in the doorway. But Slyboots slaughtered the big ram and skinned him. And when it came to his turn, he put on the ram's skin amd crawled on all fours between the Stalo's legs. "Aha!" said the Stalo, "that's my fine, fat ram!" and he clapped the supposed ram on the back. At last the Stalo said, "Now come out yourself, my fine fellow!" Then Slyboots cried to him from without, "I've been out ever so long."[1]

(14) A Finnish tale of the same general type, but lacking some characteristic features of the Homeric story, is as follows. A poor ostler, named Gylpho, sets out to free three king's daughters, who are kept prisoners spellbound in a subterranean cave. He arrives in an iron chamber, where one of the princesses is watched by the old rock-spirit Kammo, who has a great horn on his head, and a single eye in the middle of his forehead. The monster smells human flesh, but the maiden contrives to lull his suspicions. His eye had grown dim, and the eyelashes had grown into it, so that he could not see the young man. The stove was heated, and beside it stood a great iron poker with which the rock-spirit used to poke the fire. Gylpho took it quietly, heated it red-hot, and then poked it into the spirit's eye. Up got Kammo and screamed so loud that the rocks echoed with the shriek. He groped about, but could not find his foe, who seized a chance of hewing off the spirit's head.[2]

(15) The Finnish scholar Castren records, with some surprise, that in Russian Karelia, which borders on Finland, he met with a tale like that of Ulysses and Polyphemus in Homer. The hero of the Karelian story is shut up in a castle, where

---

[1] J. C. Poestion, *Lappländische Märchen*, No. 36, pp. 152–154.

[2] W. Grimm, *Die Sage von Polyphem*, p. 17, referring to Bertram, *Finnische Volksmärchen und Sprichwörter*, p. 9.

he is watched by a giant blind of one eye. In order to escape from the castle the Karelian hero resorts to the same stratagem as that to which the Greek hero had recourse in a similar plight. He pokes out the giant's eye by night, and next morning, when the giant sends out his sheep to graze, the hero hides himself under one of them, and so has the good luck to pass out of the castle gate.[1]

(16) From Lithuania is reported a tale which bears a close, if not a suspicious, resemblance to the Homeric story. It runs thus. One day a ship put in to an island. The skipper landed with his crew. To cook their victuals they built a hearth of stones, and looking about for a big flat stone to serve as a hearth-stone, they spied just such a stone as they wanted at the foot of a mountain. Having pried it up by their united efforts, they saw to their surprise that the big smooth stone had covered a wide opening with steps leading down into a cave. They descended and soon saw that they were in a giant's house. The house was so huge that you could hardly see the vaulted roof, in the middle of which was an aperture that allowed the sunlight to enter and the smoke to escape.

While they were looking about, they heard a sudden rumbling, and soon a giant, tall as a tower, came down the steps, after closing the entrance with the big stone. Next he planted a whole forest of trees about the hearth and set them on fire. By the light of the fire the mariners saw to their horror that the giant had only one eye in the middle of his forehead. They tried to flee to the barred entrance, but the giant perceived them, seized one of them, and swallowed him at a gulp. The others he drove back into the inner part of the cave. Then he stirred the fire and began to milk the ewes, and next he set a huge kettle on the fire to boil the milk. When the milk boiled, he quaffed it, lay down on his bed of moss, and fell asleep. Soon he slept so soundly that the whole mountain quaked with his snoring.

The sailors now plucked up courage, and the skipper unfolded a plan for their salvation. He had noticed a great iron spit belonging to the giant. The point of it he soon heated red-hot in the fire, and then with the help of the crew he

---

[1] M. A. Castren, *Reisen im Norden* (Leipsic, 1853), pp. 98 *sq.*

rammed it into the giant's eye. The glowing iron hissed, and the blood spouted up in a jet, falling back in drops that scalded like boiling water. Up started the giant, bellowing with pain, but though he groped and fumbled along the sides and floor of the cave, he could not catch his assailants, for they had hidden in the sheep-fold.

Thus baffled, the giant fell into a terrible fury, hurling the burning brands in all directions to set fire to his foes. But instead of igniting them he only set fire to his own mossy bed, and soon the cave was filled with such a thick smoke that the giant was obliged to quit it and sit down in front of the entrance, plotting revenge. But the skipper devised a new device to effect an escape. He tied every one of his men under a sheep, and getting himself under the old tup that led the flock, he and the rest passed out with the sheep when they trooped out of the cave. Thus they all escaped from the giant. Once safe on board, the skipper could not help mocking the giant, who replied by hurling mighty rocks in the direction of the voice. One of the rocks smashed the stern of the ship and killed some of the crew. It was with difficulty that the skipper and the rest of the crew contrived to save themselves in the damaged vessel.[1]

(17) A German version of the widespread tale has been recorded in the Harz mountains. A clever man, travelling with six companions, comes to a land ruled by a giant, twelve feet high, six feet broad, and furnished with only one eye, which is planted in the middle of his forehead and is as big as a cheese-bowl. The giant catches the seven and devours one of them a day. When only the clever man and one comrade are left, they devise a plan of escape. In the night they make an iron red-hot, thrust it into the giant's one eye, and take to their heels. The giant makes after them with huge strides, but in his blindness fails to catch them.[2]

(18) An English version of the Polyphemus story is reported from Yorkshire. At Dalton, in the parish of Sessay, near Thirsk, there is, or used to be, a mill, and in front of it

---

[1] Fr. Richter "Lithauische Märchen. Der einäugige Riese," *Zeitschrift für Volkskunde*, I. (1889), pp. 87–89. The writer says nothing as to the source of the tale.

[2] W. Grimm, *Die Sage von Polyphem*, p. 18, referring to H. Pröhle's *Kinder- und Volksmärchen*, p. 137.

there was a mound, which went by the name of "the Giant's Grave." In the mill was shown a long blade of iron, something like a scythe-blade, but not curved. This was said to have been the giant's razor, and there was also exhibited the stone porridge-pot or lather-dish which had been the property of the giant. This giant used to reside at the mill and to grind men's bones to make his bread. One day he captured a lad on Pilmoor, and instead of grinding him to flour as usual in the mill, he kept him as his servant and never let him go away. Jack served the giant many years without a holiday. At last he could bear it no longer. Topcliffe Fair was coming on, and the lad entreated that he might be allowed to go there to see the lasses and buy some spice. The giant surlily refused to give him leave, so Jack resolved to take it. The day was hot, and the giant was sleeping after dinner in the mill, with a great loaf of bone-bread beside him and a knife in his hand. Jack slipped the knife from the sleeper's grasp and jabbed it into his single eye. Up started the giant with a howl of agony and barred the door. Jack was again in difficulty, but he soon found a way out of it. The giant had a favourite dog which had also been sleeping when the giant was blinded. Jack killed the dog, skinned it, and throwing the hide over his back, ran on all-fours barking between the legs of the giant, and so escaped.[1]

(19) A Breton version of the story relates how a young man, returning with a well-filled purse from La Vendée, was traversing a forest, when he saw a hut, and going up to it knocked at the door. A rough voice answered, "Wait a moment and I will open to you." Then there was a loud noise, the door opened and he beheld a giant with a single eye in the middle of his forehead, holding in his hand the bolt of the door, and the bolt itself was as big as an ordinary man. On entering the house the young man saw human arms hanging, along with chitterlings, in the chimney, and feet of men and pieces of human flesh boiling in a pot on the fire. He made an excuse for retiring from the house, but he could not lift the bolt. "You need not go out," said the giant, "you may retire among the sheep there." Now in the inner part of the house there was a flock of eight sheep,

---

[1] S. Baring Gould, "The Giant of New Mills, Sessay," *Folk-lore*, I. (1890), p. 130.

every one of them as big as a colt. To hide his fear, the young man stepped up to the hearth and began to smoke his pipe. The giant asked him if he would eat some meat. " No," said the youth, " I am not hungry." " You shall eat all the same," answered the giant. But the young man drew a pistol from his pocket, and firing at the giant put out his eye. " Wretch," cried the giant, " I will kill and eat you." The youth took refuge among the sheep. The giant sought him, but could not find him. Then he opened the door and caused the sheep to go out one by one, feeling each of them as it passed. When only three or four were left, the youth got under the belly of one of them, holding fast to the fleece. In passing the door he knocked against the giant, who stopped the sheep ; but by this time the young man was out, and making his way through the forest with the sheep he sold them for a good price in the market.[1]

(20) In another Breton version of the story the hero goes by the name of Bihanic, and is, as usually happens with heroes, the youngest of three brothers. He is sent by a king to rob a certain giant of his treasures, which consisted of a wonderful parrot, endowed with the gift of second sight, a dromedary which could run faster than a bird could fly, and a carbuncle which radiated so brilliant a light that the darkness of night was turned to day for seven leagues round the giant's castle. The hero succeeded in procuring the dromedary and the carbuncle without much trouble, but to capture the parrot was a much harder task. When Bihanic drew near the giant's castle for this purpose, he met a young shepherd who was feeding the giant's sheep. " Go to the castle," he said to the shepherd, " and fetch me a light for my pipe. I'll give you a crown." The unsuspecting swain pocketed the money and ran to the castle. Meantime Bihanic took one of the sheep, the woolliest of the flock, killed it and skinned it. Then he put on the skin, and mixing with the flock at eventide, he entered into the castle, all unknown both to the giant and to the shepherd. Now it was the giant's custom morning and evening to consult his oracular parrot, and that night, when he inquired of the oracle as usual, the parrot informed him that his enemy

---

[1] P. Sébillot, " Contes de la Haute-Bretagne," *Revue des Traditions Populaires,* IX. (1894), pp. 105 *sqq.*

XIII.—ULYSSES AND POLYPHEMUS

Bihanic, who had already robbed him of his dromedary and his carbuncle, was again in the castle; more than that, the sagacious bird told him that the thief was lurking in the fold, disguised in the skin of a sheep which he had killed and skinned. The giant searched for him in the fold, but could not find him, though he felt the sheep with his hands, one after the other. Then he ordered the shepherd to let the sheep out, one by one, and as they passed out, the giant stood at the threshold and examined every one. When they were almost all out, the skin of one of them remained in his hands and he cried, " Aha, I've got him ! " " Alas," thought Bihanic to himself, " it's all up with me this time," as he felt the grip of the giant's fingers on his ribs. The giant carried him to the kitchen. " Here's that rascal of a Bihanic," said he, showing him to the other giants and giantesses, " he'll not play us any more tricks. What sauce shall we eat him with ? " " You must put him on the spit," they all answered. So they stripped him stark naked, trussed him like a fowl, and threw him into a corner of the kitchen till it was time to stick him on the spit. The cook, left alone, complained to Bihanic that she had not wood enough to roast him. " Just loose my bonds a bit, fair cook," said he, " and I'll go and fetch some." Flattered by being called " fair," the cook was mollified and undid the bonds. No sooner had she done so than the grateful Bihanic caught up a hatchet and brought it down on the head of the giantess with such hearty good will that he cleft her in two from top to toe. He then hurried to the parrot, stuffed it into his bag, and made off. When the giant came to the kitchen to see whether Bihanic was done to a turn, and saw his wife, the cook, dead and weltering in her gore, and the parrot gone, he howled and shrieked so that the other giants and giantesses came running, and between them all there was a terrible noise.[1]

(21) A Gascon version of the old heathen tale is enriched with some pious details for the edification of devout Christians. It runs thus : Once upon a time there lived a poor widow in a cottage with her two children, a boy and a girl. One day the boy said to his mother, " Mother, from morning to night

---

[1] F. M. Luzel, *Contes populaires de Basse-Bretagne* (Paris, 1887), II. 231 *sqq.*

I, you, and my sister work to earn a bare livelihood. I will go and seek my fortune. I will go to the land of the Ogres[1] to gather golden horns, horns of oxen, and horns of sheep." But his mother said, "No, no, my dear. I will not let you. The Ogres dwell far, far from here, towards the setting sun. They dwell in a wild black country, in a country of high mountains, where the streams fall from heights of three thousand feet. In that country there are no priests, nor churches, nor churchyards. The Ogres are giants seven fathoms tall. They have only one eye, right in the middle of the forehead. All the long day they watch their oxen and their sheep with golden horns, and at evening, at set of sun, they bring back these cattle to the caves. When they catch a Christian, they roast him alive on a gridiron and swallow him at one bite. No, no, my dear, you shall not go to seek your fortune. You shall not go seek golden horns, horns of oxen and sheep, in the land of the Ogres."

"Excuse me, mother," he said, "but this time you cannot have your way." Then the girl spoke. "Mother," she said, "you see my brother is wilful. Since he will not listen to reason, I will go with him. Count on me to guard him from all harm." So the poor mother had to give her consent. "Hold, my child," said she, "take this little silver cross, and never part with it, neither by day nor by night. It will bring you good luck. Go then, my poor children, go with the grace of God and the Holy Virgin Mary."

The brother and sister saluted their mother and set out, staff in hand, with their wallets on their backs. For seven months they walked, from morning to night, towards the setting sun, living on alms and sleeping in the stables of charitable folk. At last they came to a wild black country, a country of high mountains, where the streams fell from heights of three thousand feet. In that country there are no priests, nor churches, nor churchyards. In that country live the Ogres, giants seven fathoms tall. These giants have only one eye, right in the middle of their forehead. All the long day they watch their oxen and their sheep with golden horns, and at evening, at set of sun, they bring back these cattle to the caves. As for good cheer, there is no lack of

---

[1] *Bécuts.* In the Gascon dialect *Bécut* means " beaked " and by extension an ogre.

meat. For dinner they kill an ox, and for supper a sheep. But they take no account of their golden horns and throw them away. When they catch a Christian, they roast him alive on a gridiron and swallow him at one bite.

Every day, from sunrise to sunset, the brother and sister sought for the golden horns in the mountains, hiding themselves as well as they could under the bushes and among the rocks, lest they should be seen by the Ogres. At the end of seven days their wallets were full. Sitting down by a stream, they counted them, " One, two, three, four . . . ninety-eight, ninety-nine, a hundred golden horns. And now we are rich enough. To-morrow we will return to our mother."

At that moment the sun was sinking. An Ogre passed, driving before him his oxen and his sheep with golden horns. " The Ogre ! the Ogre ! " cried the children and fled at the top of their speed. But the Ogre had seen it all. He took them, threw them into a big bag, and repaired to his cave, which was shut by a flat stone weighing a hundred hundred-weights. With a push of his shoulder the Ogre shoved aside the stone and closed the entrance. That done, he shook out his big bag on the ground. " Little Christians," said he, " sup with me." " With pleasure, Ogre," said they. The Ogre threw a heap of logs on the hearth, lit a fire, bled a sheep, skinned it, threw the skin and the two golden horns in a corner, and spitted the flesh. " Little Christians," said he, " turn the spit." " Ogre, you shall be obeyed," said they. While they turned the spit, the Ogre laid a hundredweight of bread and seven great jars of wine on the table.

" Little Christians," said the Ogre, " sit down there. Want for nothing, and tell me all about your country." The boy knew a great many fine stories, and he talked till supper was done. " Little Christian master," said the Ogre, " I am pleased with you. Now it's your turn, little Christian miss." The girl knew many beautiful prayers, in honour of the Good God, of the Holy Virgin, and of the saints. But at the first word the Ogre turned blue with rage. " Oh, you hussy," cries he, " you are praying to God. Just wait a bit." Straightway he seized the girl, stripped her of her clothes, laid her on a gridiron, and roasted her alive on a slow fire. " Little Christian master," says he to her brother, " what do you think of this steak ? I'll give you your share of it presently." But the boy answered, " No, Ogre, Christians

435

do not eat one another." "Little Christian master, look, that is what I will do to you to-morrow, when you shall have told all your fine stories."

The boy was white with anger, but he could do nothing against the Ogre. He watched his sister broiling alive on a slow fire. The poor girl clasped in her right hand the little silver cross, which her mother had enjoined her never to part with, neither by night nor by day. "My God," cried she, "have pity on me! Holy Virgin, come to my help!" "Ah, hussy," said the Ogre, "so you pray God even when you are broiling alive, just wait a bit." The Ogre swallowed her alive in one mouthful. Then he lay down on the ground, the whole length of the hearth, "Little Christian master," said he, "tell me stories of your country." The boy talked till midnight. From time to time the Ogre interrupted him, saying, "Little Christian master, poke the fire. I am cold."

An hour after midnight the Ogre, glutted with meat and wine, was snoring like a hurricane. Then the boy thought to himself, "Now we shall see some fun." Softly, very softly, he drew near the hearth, seized a glowing brand, and thrust it with all his strength into the Ogre's eye. The Ogre was now blind. He ran about in the cave like one possessed by a devil, yelling so that he could be heard a hundred leagues off, "Oh, all ye gods! I am blind! I am blind!" The boy laughed, hidden under the litter, among the oxen and sheep with the golden horns.

At the cries of the Ogre his brothers awoke in their caves. "Ha! ha! ha!" they shouted, "what's the matter there? What's the matter there?" And the Ogres came running in the black night, with lanterns as big as barrels and with staves as tall as poplars. "Ha! ha! ha!" they shouted, "what's the matter there? What's all that there?" With a push of the shoulder they shoved aside the stone weighing a hundred hundredweights which stopped the mouth of the cave, from which the cries still proceeded, "Oh, ye gods, I am blind! I am blind!" "Brother," said they, "who has put you in that state?" "Brothers," he answered, "it was a little Christian. Seek him everywhere in the cave. Seek him, that I may swallow him alive. Oh, ye gods, I am blind! I am blind!" The Ogres searched everywhere, but found nothing, while the boy laughed, hidden under the straw, among the oxen and sheep with horns of gold. At last the Ogres were tired. "Good-bye, brother," they said, "try to sleep. We will come back to-morrow." So they shut up the cave and withdrew.

Then the boy tried to roll away the big stone that barred the entrance, but he had to cry, "Mother of God, this is too much for my strength." The Ogre listened. "I hear you, little Christian. I hear you, you cur. Blind as I am, you shall not escape me." For three days and nights the boy, the Ogre, and the cattle remained in the cave without eating or drinking. At last the oxen and the sheep with golden horns bellowed and bleated for hunger. "Wait a bit, poor beasts," said the Ogre, "I'll open the cave for you. But as for you, little Christian, that is quite a different matter. Blind as I am, you shall not escape me." While the Ogre groped about at the mouth of the cave, the boy put on the golden horns and the skin of the sheep that had been killed three days before.

At last the big stone fell. The Ogre seated himself outside, on the threshold of the cave, and the oxen and the sheep passed out, one by one, the oxen first. Their master felt their horns and their backs, and he counted them, one by one. Then came the sheep, and their master felt their horns and their woolly coats, and counted them, one by one. Among the sheep the boy waited on all fours. When his turn came, he advanced fearlessly. The Ogre was suspicious. On feeling the wool of his back he perceived that the fleece fitted ill. "Ah, little Christian," he called out, "ah, you cur! Just wait a bit!" But the boy made off as fleet as the wind.

The story ends by relating how the Ogre was sick and vomited up alive the girl whom he had swallowed, and how the brother and sister returned with great riches to their mother.[1]

(22) If the Homeric story of Ulysses and Polyphemus survives anywhere in oral tradition, it might be expected to survive in Sicily; and certainly a story of the same type has been recorded in that island from the lips of a girl eight years old. It is in substance as follows. There were once two monks who went begging for the church every year.

[1] J. F. Bladé, *Contes populaires de la Gascogne* (Paris, 1886), I. 32–42.

APPENDIX

One was large and the other small. They lost their way once and came to a large cave, and in the cave was a monster who was building a fire. However, the two monks did not believe it was a monster, but said, "Let us go and rest there." They entered, and saw the monster killing a sheep and roasting it. He had already killed and cooked twenty.

"Eat!" said the monster to them. "We don't want to eat," they replied, "we are not hungry." "Eat, I tell you!" he repeated. After they had eaten the sheep, they lay down, and the monster closed the entrance to the cave with a great stone. Then he took a sharp iron, heated it in the fire, and having stuck it in the throat of the bigger monk he roasted his body and desired the other monk to help him to eat it. "I don't want to eat," answered the monk, "I am full." "Get up!" said the monster, "if you don't, I will kill you." The wretched monk arose in fright, seated himself at the table, and pretended to eat, but threw the flesh away.

In the night the good man took the iron, heated it, and plunged it in the monster's eyes. Then in his terror he slipped into the skin of a sheep. The monster groped his way to the mouth of the cave, removed the stone, and let the sheep out one by one; and so the good man escaped and returned to Trapani, and told his story to some fishermen. The monster went fishing, and, being blind, stumbled against a rock and broke his head.[1]

(23) A similar Greek story has been recorded at Pharasa in Cappadocia. It runs thus: "In the old time there was a priest. He went to get a goat. He went to a village. There was another priest. He said, 'Where are you going?' The priest said, 'I am going to get a goat.' He said, 'Let me come also, to get a goat.' They rose up; they went to another village. There was there another priest. And the three went to another village. They found another priest. They took that priest also. They went on. They made up seven priests.

"As they were going to a village, there was a woman;

---

[1] G. Pitré, *Fiabe Novelle e Racconti popolari Siciliani*, ll. (Palermo, 1875), No. 51, pp. 1–3; T. F. Crane, *Italian Popular Tales* (London, 1885) pp. 89 *sqq.* I have followed Crane's summary of the story, as the Sicilian dialect is only partially intelligible to me.

438

the was cutting wood. There was also a Cyclops.[1] The
Cyclops ran up; he seized the seven priests. He carried
them to his house. In the evening he roasted one priest;
he ate him. He was fat. He ate him; he got drunk.

"The six priests rose up. They heated the spit. They
drove it into the Cyclops' eye. They blinded the Cyclops.
They ran away. Inside the stable the Cyclops had seven
hundred sheep. They went into the stable. They flayed
six sheep. They left their heads and their tails. They got
into the skins. In the morning the Cyclops rose up; he
drove out the sheep; he took them by the head and tail.
He drove out the seven hundred sheep. He shut the doors.
He went inside; he searched for the six priests. He could
not find them. He found the six sheep killed.

"The six priests took the seven hundred sheep; they
went to their houses. They also gave a hundred sheep to
the wife of the priest, whom the Cyclops had eaten. The
woman said, ' Where is my priest ? ' They said, ' He has
remained to gain yet more.' And the six priests took a
hundred sheep each. They went to their houses. They
ate, they drank, they attained their desires."[2]

(24) Another modern Greek version of the Polyphemus
story, recorded at Athens, runs as follows : A prince makes
his way into an Ogre's cave in the Ogre's absence, and finds
there a tub of milk and a cake almost as big as a threshing-
floor. Having refreshed himself by drinking of the milk
and eating of the cake, he looked about, and seeing a crevice
in the rock hid himself in it. Soon the tinkling of sheep bells
announced that the sheep were returning to the cave for
the night, and the Ogre with them. On entering the cave
the Ogre closed the entrance by rolling a great rock into the
opening, and then he sat down to eat, noticing that his supply
of milk and cake was short. However, after satisfying
his appetite as well as he could, he raked up the fire and lay
down to sleep. While he slept and snored the prince crept

---

[1] In Greek τεπεκόζης. This word is explained to be a
Turkish expression for a one-eyed giant, derived from *tepe*,
" head " and *göz*, " eye." See R. M. Dawkins, *Modern Greek
in Asia Minor*, p. 650.

[2] R. M. Dawkins, *Modern Greek in Asia Minor* (Cambridge,
1916), p. 551.

out from his place of concealment, and taking a long stake, sharpened it and held it in the fire. When the stake glowed in the fire, the Prince thrust it into the Ogre's eye and blinded him ; for the Ogre had only one eye, which was in his forehead. The shrieks of the Ogre roused the whole neighbourhood, and the other Ogres came to see what was the matter with their chief ; but finding the mouth of the cave barred by the great rock, they could not enter, and so went away again, supposing that the chief was drunk. Then the Ogre opened the cave by rolling away the stone, and sitting down at the entrance he began to let out his sheep, feeling them one by one. Now there was one big woolly ram, and clinging to its belly the prince contrived to escape from the cave, while the Ogre stroked the animal on the back.[1]

(25) Another modern Greek version of the ancient tale was told to the German archaeologist, Ludwig Ross, by a native of Psara, an island off the west coast of Chios. In outline it is as follows : Three brothers, by name Dimitri, Michael, and George, landed from a ship on an unknown coast, and separating from their comrades wandered about till they came to a magnificent palace. Entering it they found in the forecourt a great flock of sheep, and in the banqueting-hall a feast set out, but no human being was to be seen. They sat down and partook of the good things, and hardly had they done so when a huge, ugly, blind Ogre appeared, and in a voice which curdled the blood in their veins cried out, " I smell human flesh, I smell human flesh ! " Pale with terror, the three brothers sprang to their feet, but the Ogre, guided by the sound, stretched out his hideous claws and seized first Dimitri and then Michael, and dashed them to pieces on the floor. George, being nimble, contrived to escape into the forecourt, but there he found the gate shut and the walls so high that he could not scale them. What was he to do ? Drawing his knife, he killed the biggest ram of the flock, stripped off its skin, and throwing the carcass into a well he wrapped himself up in the skin and attempted to creep out on all fours, as if he were a ram. Meantime the Ogre had finished his horrible meal of human flesh, and came waddling down the marble staircase, shouting, " You shall

---

[1] G. Drosinis, *Land und Leute in Nord-Euböa*, Deutsche Uebersetzung von Aug. Boltz (Leipsic, 1884), pp. 170–176.

XIII.—ULYSSES AND POLYPHEMUS

not escape me ! You shall serve me for a savoury supper ! "
Then he went to the gate and opened it just wide enough to
let out one sheep at a time. He next called all the ewes by
name, and as each came he milked it and let it out. Last
of all came the rams, amongst which George, wrapt in the
ram's skin, had taken his place. He approached the Ogre
with fear and trembling, but the monster stroked his back,
praised his size and strength, and let him go through the
gateway. So George escaped.[1]

In this version the hero does not blind the monster, and
thus one of the most characteristic incidents of the story is
wanting ; but in other respects the tale conforms to the
common type.

(26) Another modern Greek version of the story, recorded
at Lasta in Gortynia, a district of the Morea, relates how a
man of old set out to wander through the world and came to
a land where the men were of great stature, but had only
one eye each. The traveller lodged in the house of one of
these one-eyed giants, and at evening the giant's wife hid
him ; for during the day the giant, who was a wicked cannibal,
was not at home. When the giant came home, he told his
wife that he smelt something, and though she tried to persuade him that it was nothing, he searched the house and
discovered the man. At first he made as if he would devour
the man, but after putting him into his mouth, he took him
out again and spared him for the sake of his wife. However,
next day he repented of his mercifulness and would have
gobbled the man up, if his wife had not made him drunk,
and secretly fetching out the man urged him to fly. But
before he fled, the man took a burning coal and thrust it into
the giant's eye, thus blinding him. So the wicked cannibal
was punished and never devoured men afterwards.[2] This
version omits the characteristic episode of the hero's escape
by the means of a sheep or a sheepskin.

(27) An Albanian version of the story, recorded in Sicily,
runs as follows : Once on a time there were two men travelling. Night fell upon them by the way, and it rained and
thundered. Poor fellows, just think what a plight they were

---

[1] Ludwig Ross, *Erinnerungen und Mittheilungen aus
Griechenland* (Berlin, 1863), pp. 287–289.

[2] K. Dieterich, " Aus neugriechische Sagen," *Zeitschrift des
Vereins fur Volkskunde*, XV. (1905), p. 381.

APPENDIX

in! They saw a light far off and said, "Let's go and see if we can pass the night where that light is." And they went and came to the cave, for a cave it was where the light shone. They went in and saw that there were sheep and rams and two Cyclopes, who had two eyes in front and two behind. The Cyclopes saw them come in and said one to the other. "Go to, here we have got something to eat." And they proposed to eat the two men. The poor fellows stayed there two days; then the Cyclopes felt the back of their necks and said, "Good! We'll eat one of them to-morrow." Meantime they made them eat to fatten them. For in the evening they would take a sheep and a ram, roast them on spits over the fire, and compel the poor wretches to devour them, entrails and all, just to fatten them. And every now and then they would feel the back of their necks, and one would say to the other, "They're getting on very well!" But the two men said to each other by words or signs, "Let us see whether we can escape." Now, as I said, two days passed, and on the second day the Cyclopes fell asleep and slumbered with all their eyes open. Nevertheless, when the two men saw the Cyclopes sleeping, they took the spits on which the sheep had been roasted, and they heated them in the fire. Then they took rams' skins and clothed themselves in them, and going down on all fours they walked about in the rams' skins. Meanwhile the spits were heated, and each of the men took two, and going softly up to the sleeping Cyclopes, they jabbed the hot spits into their eyes. After that, they went down on all fours like sheep. The Cyclopes awoke blind, and gave themselves up for lost. But they took their stand at the door, each at a doorpost, just as they were, with all the spits sticking in their eyes. They let out all the sheep that were in the cave, saying, "The sheep will go out, and the men will stay in," and they felt the fleeces of the sheep to see whether the men were going out too. But the men had the sheepskins on their backs, and they went on all fours, and when the Cyclopes felt them, they thought they were sheep. So the men escaped with their life, and when they were some way off, they put off the skins. Either the Cyclopes died or they know themselves what they did. That is the end of the story.[1]

---

[1] D. Comparetti, *Novelline popolari Italiane* (Rome, Turin, and Florence, 1875), No. 70, pp. 308-310.

442

XIII.—ULYSSES AND POLYPHEMUS

A peculiar feature of this version is the multiplication of the eyes of the Cyclopes from one to four apiece.

(28) A Hungarian story of this type tells of three travelling craftsmen, Balzer, Laurence, and John, who, after sailing the sea for seven days and seven nights, landed in a great wood. There they lighted on a sheep-walk and followed it till they came to a stall. They entered the stall and found there a huge giant who had only one eye in his forehead. He asked them what they wanted, and when they had told him, he set food before them. Evening soon fell, and then the giant drove the sheep into the stall. Now the sheep were as big as asses are with us. To shut the stall the giant had nothing but a big stone, which sixteen men like you and me could not have stirred from the spot.

When the sheep had all been let in, the giant sat down by the fire and chatted with his guests; at the same time he felt the neck of each of them to see which was the fattest. Poor Balzer was the man, as the giant perceived; so he took a knife, cut off his head, and gave him to his sheep to devour. The two surviving friends looked anxiously at each other and consulted secretly together; and when they saw that the giant was sleeping on his back by the fire, John took a firebrand and poked it into his eye, so that he could see no more.

When morning broke and the birds began to twitter, the giant took the stone from the doorway and let the sheep out; but he was so sly that he straddled his legs and let each sheep pass between them. Now John was by trade a shoemaker; so he had with him a paring-knife and an awl. He showed Laurence what to do and gave him an awl in his hand; he was to hang on to the tail of a sheep, and just when the sheep was in the doorway he was to jab the awl into its paunch; so would the animal run through the doorway like lightning. John did just the same himself, and both came safely through. When the sheep were all out, the giant shut the door and groped all about, but found nobody. Then he set up such a shriek that the two on the shore fell all their length to the ground. And at his roar twelve more giants, each as big as he, came at a run; and when they saw him in that sorry plight they seized him straight off and tore him to bits. Then they ran all twelve to the sea, but by this time the two fugitives were twelve fathoms from the shore, so that the

443

giants could not take vengeance on them. Then the giants
began to shriek and roar so terribly that the sea rose in great
waves, and the two wretches were almost drowned. But God
in his mercy saved them, and they sailed on till they came to
a wood, where they landed and walked for pleasure.[1]

(29) A modern Syrian version of the old tale runs as follows :
Once upon a time there was a prince who had two sons.
One of them set out with a book, which he owned, to go to a
monastery. He journeyed till nightfall, when he tarried
among the mountains and slept till about midnight. Then he
heard someone crying. He thought, " I will go and see what
it is." He went and found a cave in which a fire was blazing.
Entering the cave, he saw a blind giant sleeping by the fire.
The youth sat down and pricked the giant with a needle.
The giant got up and searched for him, but could not find
him. After a while the youth pricked the giant again.
The giant arose. Little by little the day broke, and the goats
began to pass out of the cave. The giant stood straddling
at the mouth of the cave and let the goats pass out one
by one. The young man crouched under the belly of the he-
goat, and so got out. In the sequel the youth professes to be
the giant's son, and after undergoing a peculiar test of sonship
he is accepted as such by the giant and allowed to lead the
goats to grass. He even recovers the giant's lost eyes from
a she-bear, which had apparently abstracted them.[2]

This story differs from all the rest in that the hero, instead
of blinding the giant, restores his lost sight. But in other
respects, particularly in the mode of the hero's escape from
the cave, the tale conforms to the ordinary type.

(30) In the " Third Voyage of Sindibad the Sailor," which
is incorporated in *The Arabian Nights*, the voyager and his
companions are landed on an island, where they find and
enter a giant's house. Presently the giant, a huge black
monster with two eyes blazing like fire, arrived, and finding
his uninvited guests, he seized them and felt them as a butcher
feels the sheep he is about to slaughter. The first whom he
thus treated was Sindibad himself, but finding him lean

---

[1] G. Stier, *Ungarische Volksmärchen* (Pesth, n.d., preface
dated June 1857), No. 14, pp. 146–150.

[2] E. Prym and A. Socin, *Syrische Sagen und Maerchen*
(Göttingen, 1881), No. 32, pp. 115 *sq.*

from the excessive fatigue which he had undergone on the
voyage, he let him go. In this way the giant picked out the
master of the ship, a fat, stout, broad-shouldered man, broke
his neck, spitted him, and roasted him on the spit before the
fire, after which he devoured him, tearing the flesh to pieces
with his nails and gnawing the bones. Then he lay down and
slept till morning. This proceeding he repeated on the two
subsequent days; but on the third night, when three of their
number had thus perished, Sindibad and his fellows took two
spits, which they thrust into the fierce fire till they were red-
hot like burning coals. These they grasped firmly and thrust
with all their might into the giant's two eyes while he lay
snoring. Thus rudely awakened from slumber, the giant started
up and searched for his assailants right and left, but could
not find them. So he groped his way to the door and went
out, followed by Sindibad and his friends, who had prudently
prepared rafts for their escape from the island. Presently
the giant returned with a giantess, taller and uglier than
himself; but by this time the fugitives were on board the
rafts, and they now shoved off with all speed. The two giants
pelted the runaways with rocks, which killed most of them;
Sindibad and two others alone escaped on their raft to
another island.[1]

(31) In "The Story of Seyf El-Mulook," which also forms
part of *The Arabian Nights*, we have another slightly different
version of the same story. A certain man Saed, brother of
Seyf El-Mulook, relates how he was shipwrecked and drifted
ashore on a plank with a party of memlooks (male white
slaves). He and two of the memlooks walked till they came
to a great wood. There they met a person of tall stature,
with a long beard, long ears, and two eyes like cressets, who
was tending many sheep. He greeted them in a friendly
way and invited them to his cave. There they found a
number of men whom the giant had blinded by giving them
cups of milk to drink. Warned by them, Saed pretended to
drink the milk offered him by the giant, and he made believe
to be blinded by it; but really he poured the milk into a hole
in the ground. His two companions drank the milk and
became blind. Thereupon the giant arose, and having closed

---

[1] *The Arabian Nights' Entertainment*, translated by E. W.
Lane, III. (London, 1839–1841), pp. 26–30.

the entrance of the cave, drew Saed towards him and felt his ribs, but found him lean with no flesh on him. Wherefore he felt another, and saw that he was fat, and he rejoiced thereat. He then slaughtered three sheep, skinned them, spitted them, and roasted them over a fire, after which he brought the roast mutton to Saed's two companions, who ate it with him. Next he brought a leathern bottle of wine, drank the wine, and lying down fell asleep and snored.

While he slept, Saed took two spits, heated them red-hot in the fire, and thrust them into the giant's two eyes. The blinded giant arose and pursued his enemy into the inner part of the cave; but, directed by the blind men, Saed found a polished sword, with which he hewed the giant through the middle, so that he died.[1]

It is to be observed that both the versions of the story in *The Arabian Nights* omit the characteristic episode of the hero's escape in a sheepskin or under the belly of a sheep.

(32) A story resembling the Homeric tale of Ulysses and Polyphemus is reported to be widely current in the mountains of Armenia. It is told orally as a popular tale in Erzerum, Kars, Bajberd, Erzinka, Keghi, and other towns; and Armenian emigrants carry it with them to their new homes in Alexandropol, Achalzich, Achalkalak, Gumush-chane, and so forth. The tale is known as the "Story of the Eye in the Forehead." There are a number of different versions of it. One of the best, closely resembling the Homeric version, is said to be the one told at Gumush-chane, to the south of Trebizond. The version told at Achalzich runs as follows:

One day a rich man, looking out of his window, saw a porter approaching with a sack of meal on his back. When he came to the wall of the house, the porter put down his load to take breath, and began to bemoan his hard fate. "What an unlucky wretch am I!" he complained, "what a hell of a life I lead! When will God deliver me from my horrible lot!" and so on in the same strain. The rich man sent his servants to call in the porter, and when the fellow said that he could not leave his sack, the other had the sack despatched to its destination by one of his servants. It happened that the gentleman had invited friends to dinner that day, and by this

---

[1] *The Arabian Nights' Entertainment*, translated by E. W. Lane, III. 353-355.

time the guests had begun to assemble. But the best place at table was reserved for the porter. When they were all seated, the host stood up and said, " Listen, gentlemen, and you, my friend," turning to the porter, " listen you too, I have something to tell you. When I have finished my story you, gentlemen, and you, my friend" (meaning the porter) "shall judge whether the present lot of our friend here, of which he has just been complaining, is harder and more unendurable than the experience I have undergone in my life.

" I was a merchant and a handicraftsman. Once I sailed in a ship on business with twenty companions. A great storm overtook us, and our ship was cast on the rocks and broken in pieces, but we were carried ashore by the wind. So far as our vision extended, there was not a living being anywhere, neither man nor devil. For long we had nothing to eat or drink, and we wandered about till we came to a wood. In the wood we saw a building. We went in and waited. About the time when the sun went down, there appeared a frightfully big man, who had an eye in the middle of his forehead. When he saw us, he began to laugh, his face beamed with joy, and he made curious grimaces. He blinked with his eyes, kindled a great fire in the oven, and put an iron spit in it. Then he came up to us, felt every one of us, and choosing the strongest and fattest stuck him on the spit, held him over the fire for a little, and ate him. We were horrified, but could do nothing, and waited to see what would befall. Next evening he came again, stuck another of us on the spit, roasted him, and ate him. We saw that this could not last, and that something must be devised to save us.

" The giant with one eye in his forehead, who devoured our companions, laid him down every evening before the door and fell asleep, after he had partaken of his supper. In the morning he went away and walked about till evening. The third evening, when he had lain down and was sleeping quietly, whereas we could not sleep for fear, one of us by my advice got up, heated the spit in the fire, and thrust it, red-hot, into the giant's eye. The blinded giant shrieked dreadfully. We ran hastily to the sea, and embarking in a boat, rowed away at once from the shore. The giant's mates heard his shrieks and observed us. They hastened to him, and threw great stones at us from a distance, so that the whole sea rose in billows. At last our boat was hit by a stone and knocked to bits. All my comrades were drowned, I alone was saved, for I tied myself to a board, and so came to shore." [1]

In this version there is no mention of sheep, and no explanation is given of the hero's escape from the abode of the giant.

(33) A version of the tale which presents the main features of the Homeric story has been recorded in Mingrelia, a district on the southern slope of the Caucasus and on the eastern shore of the Black Sea. It is as follows :

Once upon a time a traveller on the road from Redut-Kale to Anaklia (on the eastern shore of the Black Sea) was overtaken by night, a dark and rainy night. In the midst of the forest, far from every human habitation, a pack of wolves beset him, and some of them tried to tear him from his horse. But the horse stood stock still, and neither soft nor hard words could induce him to stir from the spot. What booted it that the wanderer had tied sticks to the tail of his horse to keep the wolves at bay ? They attacked him in spite of the talisman. A cold shudder ran over the poor man, his sword hung powerless in his limp hand. All he could do was to cry aloud for help. And lo ! a light appeared in the distance, the wolves vanished, and the horse galloped towards the light. It was a torch in the hand of a man who inhabited a lonely house hard by. The traveller warmed himself in the hut and told his host of his adventures. But his host had far worse experiences to relate. " Brother," quoth he, " you are unhappy because the insects in the wood have attacked you. But if you only knew what I have endured, you would deem yourself lucky that nothing worse has befallen you.

" You see we are all here in mourning. We were seven brothers, all fishermen. Often we would be months at sea with our ship, only sending a boat home once a week with our catch. One day when we had cast our lines we noticed that our ship was moving away from the shore ; something was pulling it, and we could not stop it. Thus we were drawn on, and after some weeks we saw before us a rocky shore with a stream of honey flowing into the sea. Our ship drew in towards the honey stream, and when we were near it, a huge fish, with a mouth a fathom wide, bobbed up

---

[1] Senekerim Ter-Akobian, " Das armenische Märchen vom ' Stirnauge,' " *Globus*, XCIV. (1908), p. 205.

out of the water beside our ship. It swallowed the honey so greedily that the brook almost ran dry. Our hooks had caught in its gills, and it had been towing us along all the time. While it was busy gorging itself on the honey, we cut loose our lines, and let the fish go free. We loaded the ship with honey and wax, and the evening before we were to make sail for home, we saw a flock of sheep and goats approaching the honey stream. The shepherd was a one-eyed giant. In his hand he held a staff as thick as a pillar, and he twirled it like a spindle. A dreadful fear came over us. The giant drew our ship to the shore, and drove us with his flock to a great building, which stood in the middle of a wood. The trees were so high that we could not see the tops. The very rushes were as thick and tall as oaks are with us.

"The enormous edifice was built of huge, unhewn blocks of stone and divided into various rooms for the flocks; the goats, the sheep, the lambs, and the kids had their separate compartments. The one-eyed giant shut us in and then drove his flock away. We tried to break open the door, but in vain. Like mice in a trap we ran about from morning to night. At evening the giant returned, shut up his beasts, and made a fire. He laid on whole trunks of trees. Then he took a spit, fetched a fat wether, and roasted it, without skinning it. Nay, he did not even kill it, but stuck it alive on the spit; the animal writhed in the fire till its eyes burst. Then he ate it up, lay down, and began to snore.

"Next morning he ate two more wethers, and in the evening he took the fattest of us, stuck him on the spit, and began to roast him. Our brother writhed horribly and shrieked for help, but what could we do? When our brother's eyes burst, the giant tore off one of his legs and threw it to us; but the rest of our brother he ate. We buried the leg. The next days it came to the turn of my other brothers; at last only I and our youngest brother were left. We were almost beside ourselves with fright and longed for death, but not such a terrible one.

"Well, when he had eaten our fifth brother and lay by the fire and snored, we slunk up to the spit which he had stuck at his side in the ground, and with much ado we pulled it out. Then we thrust it into the fire, and waited anxiously till it was red-hot; and we thrust the red-hot spit into his eye. Blinded, he bounced up with such force in his pain, that we

449

thought he would have broken through the roof, but he only hurt his head. With a frightful yell he ran through the whole house, trampling on sheep and goats; but he could not find us, for we dodged between his legs.

"In the morning the beasts began to bleat, being fain to go out to graze. The giant opened the door, stood in front of it, and let the sheep and goats pass out one by one between his legs, but he felt the back, head, and belly of each. So he did till noon. Then he grew tired, and contented himself with feeling the back of each beast. Luckily my brother had still a knife, and with it we skinned two sheep. Then we wrapped ourselves up in the skins and resolved to creep between his legs. Half dead with fear, I was the first to try my luck. The giant remarked nothing, and I was out. My brother followed. We sought our ship, which was still in the same place. Our hope of escape rose. Meantime the giant's flock came up. We picked out the best animals and took them with us on board. But scarcely had we cut the cable when the giant arrived and felt for the ship. When we were out of reach, we called to him our names, that he might know who had played him such a trick. In a rage he flung his club at us, with such violence that the sea foamed up, and our ship nearly went down. After long wanderings along the coast and many hardships, we at last came home."[1]

(34) A version of the tale which also resembles the Homeric story is told by the Ossetes of the Caucasus, a people who speak an Iranian tongue. Their version runs as follows: Urysmag rode with his companions a long, long way, till they could hardly stir a step for weariness and hunger. Then Urysmag suddenly remarked at the foot of a mountain a shepherd of gigantic stature with a flock of sheep. So he rode up to him, and dismounting from his horse, caught the best ram, which was as big as an ox. But he could not hold the ram; nay, the ram drew him bit by bit, till he fell into the hands of the one-eyed giant. "O Bodsol," said the giant, addressing the ram, "I thank you for procuring me a right good roast." So saying he thrust Urysmag into his shepherd's pouch. Being hungry, Urysmag at once

---

[1] A. Dirr, *Kaukasische Märchen* (Jena, 1920), No. 65, pp. 248–251. The Mingrelian language is akin to the Georgian (*id.*, p. 290).

addressed himself to the giant's provisions. "What are you up to there?" said the giant to him, "keep still, or I'll give you such a squeeze that I'll break every rib in your body." Meantime the sun went down, and the one-eyed giant drove his flock home to a cave and rolled a great rock before the entrance. The rock shut the mouth of the cave so tight that not a single ray of light could penetrate into the cavern. "Go, my son," said the giant to his offspring, "and bring me the roasting spit. I'll roast a tit-bit for you which the ram Bodsol has brought me home to-day." The son quickly brought the iron spit. The giant took the spit, stuck Urysmag on it, and set it on the fire; then he lay down to sleep. Now the spit had not pierced Urysmag, but only passed between his body and his clothes. So when the giant had lain down and began to snore, Urysmag disengaged himself from the spit, heated it red-hot, and thrust it into the giant's eye. The giant roared and raged, and threatened what he would do to his little enemy when he caught him. Meantime Urysmag killed the giant's son; and in his fury the giant bit his own fingers, but that did not mend matters. In the morning the sheep began to bleat; the day was breaking, and it was time to let them out to pasture. "Now you'll catch it! You shall not escape me," threatened the giant, and rolling the block of stone from the mouth of the cave, he sat down on it and caused every sheep to pass before him, one by one. Now in the giant's flock there was a big white ram with long horns, and it was the giant's favourite. Urysmag hastily killed this ram, drew off the skin with the horns, put the skin with the horns on himself, and thus disguised was the first to creep on all fours out of the cave. "You are Gurtshi," said the giant to the supposed ram as he felt him, "go, my clever beast, go and guard the flock till evening, and drive them home. Alas! I'm blind, but I'll punish him who has outwitted me." So saying he stroked the back of the supposed ram and let him go out. Thus Urysmag escaped, and he waited till the whole flock was out. Then he cried out, "And here I am after all, you blind donkey!" The giant died of vexation. But Urysmag drove away the sheep to his companions and killed some rams to make a feast for his friends.[1]

---

[1] Chr. H., "Ossetische Märchen und Sagen," *Globus*, XLI. (1882), pp. 333 *sq.*; A. Dirr, *Kaukasische Märchen*, pp. 252–

APPENDIX

(35) A story of the same type is reported from Daghestan, a region situated on the north-eastern slope of the Caucasus. It is as follows : Two shipwrecked mariners meet a one-eyed giant, who is tending a flock of sheep. The giant seizes them and carries them to his abode, which is built of great blocks of stone in the forest. He sends one of the two to fetch water, and in his absence he roasts and devours the other, leaving nothing but a hand and foot, which he offers to the other shipwrecked mariner on his return. The mariner replies that he is not hungry. Then the giant shuts up his abode with an enormous rock and goes to sleep. The man puts out the giant's eye with a red-hot bar of iron. Next morning the man kills a ram, wraps himself up in the skin, and so makes his way out along with the flock. The giant becomes aware of the trick and utters a shout : other Cyclopes come in haste ; but the man reaches the shore and makes good his escape on a piece of the wreck.[1]

(36) A story of the type we are considering occurs also in a Mongolian work, dating perhaps from the thirteenth or fourteenth century, which professes to narrate the history of the Oghuz, a widely spread branch of the great Turkish family, who include the Turcomans and the Uzbegs of Bokhara and are said still to constitute perhaps the majority of the population between the Indus and Constantinople.[2] The work in question includes eight narratives. It is in the eighth narrative, entitled " How Bissat killed Depé Ghoz," that the story occurs with which we are here concerned. It runs as follows.[3] An Oghuzian herdsman surprised and caught at a spring a

---

254. There are a few unimportant variations, mostly verbal, between these two versions of the tale. In the former it is said that the outwitted giant "died of vexation"; in the latter it is said that he "almost died of vexation and rage." As to the Ossete language, see A. Dirr, *op. cit.*, p. 290.

[1] A. van Gennep, *Religions, Mœurs, et Légendes* (Paris, 1908), p. 162.

[2] As to the Oghuz, see A. H. Keane, *Man, Past and Present*, revised by A. H. Quiggin and A. C. Haddon (Cambridge, 1920), pp. 311 *sqq.*

[3] W. Grimm, *Die Sage von Polyphem*, pp. 7-12, referring to Diez, *Der neuentdeckte oghuzische cyklop verglichen mit dem homerischen*, 1815.

XIII.—ULYSSES AND POLYPHEMUS

fairy of the Swan Maiden type, and had by her a semi-divine son named Depé Ghoz, who had the form of a man, except that he possessed only a single eye on the crown of his head. His birth was attended with prodigies, and as his fairy mother flew away she prophesied that he would be the bane of the Oghuz. The prediction was unhappily fulfilled. The monster began a long career of villainy by killing the nurse who gave him the breast, and he soon began to carry off and devour his own people, the Oghuz. It was in vain that they sent troops against him, for he was invulnerable ; his fairy mother had put a ring on his finger, saying, " No arrow shall pierce thee, and no sword shall wound thy body." So no man could stand before him, and he put his foes to flight with great slaughter. Therefore they were forced to send envoys to negotiate a peace. Depé Ghoz at first, pitching his pretentions in a rather high key, stipulated for a daily ration of twelve men to be consumed by him ; but the envoys pointing out to him with much force that at such a rate of consumption the population would soon be exhausted, the Ogre consented to accept the more reasonable ration of two men and five hundred sheep a day. On this basis he made shift to subsist until a distressed mother appealed to the heroic Bissat to save her second son, who was doomed to follow his elder brother into the maw of the monster. Touched by her story, and burning to avenge his own brother, who had been one of the giant's victims, the gallant Bissat declared his resolve to beard the Ogre in his den and to rid society of a public nuisance. It was in vain that the princes endeavoured to deter him from the dangerous enterprise. He listened to none of them, but stuck a handful of arrows in his belt, slung his bow over his shoulder, girt his sword on his thigh, and bidding farewell to his father and mother set out for the giant's home.

He came to the rock where Depé Ghoz devoured his human victims. The giant was sitting there with his back to the sun. Bissat drew an arrow from his belt and shot it at the giant's breast, but the shaft shivered at contact with his invulnerable body. A second arrow fared no better ; the monster only observed, " A fly has bothered me." A third shaft likewise shivered, and a piece of it fell before the giant. He started up. " The Oghuz are waylaying me again," said he to his servants. Then he walked leisurely up to Bissat, gripped him by the throat, and carried him to his abode. There he stuck

453

him in his own ox-hide boot, saying to the servants, "I'll roast him on a spit for supper." So saying he went to sleep. But Bissat had a knife, and he slit the ox-hide and stepped out of the boot. He asked the servants how he could kill the giant. "We know not," said they, "there is no flesh on his body except in his eye." Bissat went up to the sleeper's head, and lifting his eyelid saw that the eye was indeed of flesh. He ordered the servants to heat the butcher's knife in the fire. When the knife was red-hot, Bissat thrust it into the giant's eye, destroying it entirely. Depé Ghoz bellowed so that mountains and rocks rang again. But Bissat sprang away and fell into the cave among the sheep.

The giant perceived that his foe was in the cave. So he took his stand in the doorway, setting a foot on each side of it and calling out, "Come, little rams, one after the other." As each came up, he laid his hand on its head. Meantime Bissat had killed a ram and skinned it, leaving the head and tail attached to the skin. Now he put on the skin and so arrayed drew near to the giant. But the giant knew him and said, "You knew how to rob me of my sight, but I will dash you against the wall." Bissat gave him the ram's head into his hand, and when the giant gripped one of the horns and lifted it up, the skin parted from it, and Bissat leaped out between the giant's legs. Depé Ghoz cast the horn on the ground and asked, "Are you freed?" Bissat answered, "My God has set me free." Then the giant handed him a ring and said, "Put it on your finger. Then neither arrow nor sword can harm you." Bissat put the ring on his finger. The giant attacked him and would have wounded him with a knife. Bissat leaped away and noticed that the ring again lay under the giant's feet. The giant again asked, "Are you freed?" and Bissat again replied, "My God has set me free." Finally, the hero contrived to slay the monster by cutting off his head with a sword, but this conclusion of the tale does not concern us here, having no parallel in the Homeric story.

In this Mongolian or Turkish version the giant's offer of a ring to his escaped prisoner recalls the incident of the ring in some of the other versions already noticed ;[1] but here the ring does not talk and thereby betray its wearer's presence to his vengeful enemy.

---

[1] See above, p. 410, with the note.

XIII.—ULYSSES AND POLYPHEMUS

Wilhelm Grimm interpreted the eye of Polyphemus as the sun, and found the origin of the story in the physical conflict of the elements and in the moral contrast of rude violence with crafty adroitness.[1] Such interpretations may safely be dismissed as erroneous. They illustrate the common tendency of learned men to attribute their own philosophic or mystical views to simple folk who are quite incapable, not only of conceiving, but even of comprehending them. To all appearance Polyphemus and his fellows are fairyland beings, neither more nor less, the creation of a story-teller who invented them for the sheer delight of giving the reins to his imagination and of exciting the wonder and admiration of his spellbound hearers, but who never dreamed of pointing a moral or of elucidating the dark, mysterious processes of external nature. Early man was not for ever pondering the enigmas of the universe ; he, like ourselves, had doubtless often need to relax the strain and to vary the monotony of ordinary life by excursions into the realm of fancy.

---

[1] W. Grimm, *Die Sage von Polyphem*, pp. 28 *sqq.*

INDEX

The roman numbers (i., ii.) *refer to the volumes ; the arabic numbers* (1, 2, 3, &c.) *refer to the pages.*

INDEX

201 ; captures Lycaon, 203 ; lifts the cattle of Aeneas, 203 ; takes many cities, 203 ; angry on account of Briseis, does not fight, 205 ; receives an embassy of the Greeks, 207 ; sends Patroclus to fight the Trojans, 209 ; recovers Briseis and lays aside his anger, 209 ; dons the armour of Hephaestus and goes forth to war, 209 ; his conflict with the river Scamander, 209 ; slays Hector, buries Patroclus, and allows Priam to ransom the body of Hector, 211 ; kills Penthesilia and Thersites, 211 ; slays Memnon, 213 ; shot by Alexander and Apollo, 215 ; buried with Patroclus in the White Isle, 217 ; consorts with Medea in the Isles of the Blest, 217 ; games in his honour, 217 ; his arms, contended for by Ajax and Ulysses, adjudged to Ulysses, 217, 219 ; beacon light kindled on his grave, 235 ; Polyxena slain by the Greeks on the grave of, 239, 241

Acontes, son of Lycaon, i. 389

Acrisius, twin son of Abas by Aglaia, i. 145 ; expels his twin brother Proetus, 145 ; reigns over Argos, 147 ; father of Danae, 147 ; guards her in a brazen chamber, 153, 155 ; casts her and Perseus into the sea, 155 ; fears the oracle and goes to Larissa, 161, 163 ; killed accidentally by Perseus, 163 ; husband of Eurydice, ii. 11

Acropolis (of Athens), the Erechtheis and Pandrosium on the, ii. 79 ; the sisters of Pandrosus throw themselves from the, 91 ; wooden image of Athena on the, 93 ; Daedalus throws Talos from the, 121 ; Aegeus flings himself from the, 137

Actaea, a Nereid, i. 15

Actaea, daughter of Danaus, wife of Periphas, i. 141

Actaeon, son of Aristaeus and Autonoe, a hunter, woos Semele or sees Artemis bathing, i. 323 ; torn to pieces by his dogs, 323, 325

Actaeus, father of Agraulus, ii. 81

Actaeus, father of Telamon, according to Pherecydes, ii. 53

Acte, old name of Attica, ii. 77

Actor, brother of Augeas, father of Eurytus and Cteatus, i. 249

Actor, son of Deion, i. 79 ; father of Menoetius, 97

Actor, son of Hippasus, in the Argo, i. 97

Actor, son of Myrmidon, i. 57 father of Eurytion, 67, ii. 61

Acusilaus, on Pelasgus, i. 131, 389 ; on Io, 133 ; on Argus, 133 ; on the madness of the daughters of Proetus, 147 ; on the Cretan bull, 199 ; on the death of Actaeon, 323 ; as to Megapenthes, son of Menelaus, ii. 31 ; on the parents of Asopus, 51 ; on the death of Zetes and Calais, 107

Adiante, daughter of Danaus, wife of Daiphron, i. 143

Adite, daughter of Danaus, wife of Menalces, i. 143

Admete, daughter of Eurystheus, desires the belt of the Amazon, i. 203

Admetus, son of Pheres, hunts the Calydonian boar, i. 67 ; served by Apollo, 91 ; husband of Alcestis, who dies for him, 93 ; in the Argo, 97 ; Apollo serves him as a herdsman, ii. 21 ; father of Eumelus, 27, 185

Adonis loved by Aphrodite, i. 19 ; son of Cinyras, or of Phoenix, or of Thias, ii. 85, 87 ; born of a myrrh tree, 87 ; carried by Aphrodite in a chest to Persephone, 87 ; divides his time between Aphrodite and Persephone, 87, 89 ; killed by a boar in hunting, 85, 89

Adramyttium, a city taken by Achilles, ii. 203

Adrastia, a city, allied with Troy, ii. 205

Adrastia, nurse of Zeus, i. 7

Adrastus, father of Eurydice, ii. 43

Adrastus marches against Thebes, i. 73 ; father of Aegialia, 75 ; married to Amphithea, 91 ; son of Talaus, 91 ; king of Argos, 353 ; marries his daughters to the exiles

458

INDEX

Tydeus and Polynices, and promises to restore both to their native lands, 353; musters an army with seven leaders and makes war on Thebes, 355; one of the victors in the Nemean games, 359; stationed at the Homoloidan gate of Thebes, 361; alone of the Seven Champions saved by his horse Arion, 373; flies to Athens and prays the Athenians to bury the Argive dead, 373, 375; father of Aegialeus, 379

Adrastus, son of Merops, a Trojan ally, ii. 205

Aeacus, father of Peleus and Telamon, i. 67, 97, ii. 53; son of Zeus and Aegina, father of Phocus by Psamathe, 55; prays for rain, 55; banishes Peleus and Telamon from Aegina, 57; keeps the keys of Hades, 57

Aeaea, the Argonauts purified by Circe in, i. 115

Aeaean isle of Circe, Ulysses in, ii. 287, 289

Aeanianians, their muster for the Trojan war, ii. 185

Aeetes, son of the Sun by Perseis, king of Colchis, receives Phrixus, i. 77; promises the Golden Fleece to Jason, 109; orders him to yoke brazen-footed bulls and sow dragon's teeth, 109; wishes to burn the Argo, 113; pursues Medea, 113; deposed by his brother Perses, but restored by Medea, 121; brother of Circe, ii. 287

Aegaeon, son of Lycaon, i. 389

Aegeoneus, son of Priam, ii. 49

Aegeus, father of Theseus, i. 67; married to Medea, 125; son of Pandion or of Scyrius, born at Megara, ii. 113; restored to Athens by his brothers (the sons of Pandion), 113; consults the oracle as to the begetting of children, 113, 115; at Troezen he lies with Aethra, daughter of Pittheus, 115; sends Androgeus, son of Minos, against the bull of Marathon, 115; sends

Theseus against the Marathonian bull, 133; recognizes Theseus and expels Medea, 133, 135; charges Theseus to hoist a white sail in sign of success, 135; casts himself from the acropolis at sight of the black sail, 137

Aegialeus, father of Aegialia, i. 75; son of Adrastus, 91; one of the Epigoni, 379; killed by Laodamas, 381

Aegialeus, son of Inachus, i. 129

Aegialia, daughter of Adrastus or of Aegialeus, wife of Diomedes, i. 75, 91; corrupted by Cometes, ii. 249

Aegialia, a country, named after Aegialeus, i. 129

Aegialus, a city, taken by Achilles, ii. 203

Aegimius, king of the Dorians, Hercules helps him against the Lapiths, i. 263; his sons slain in battle, 289

Aegina, daughter of Asopus, carried off by Zeus, i. 79, ii. 51; conveyed to island of Oenone (Aegina), where she bears Aeacus to Zeus, 53

Aegina, the Argonauts in, i. 119; island, formerly called Oenone, ii. 53; Peleus and Telamon banished from, 57

Aegipan steals the severed sinews of Zeus, i. 49

Aegis wrapt by Athena round the Palladium, ii. 41

Aegisthus, son of Thyestes, ii. 169; murders Atreus and restores the kingdom to Thyestes, 169; paramour of Clytaemnestra, 249; with Clytaemnestra, murders Agamemnon and Cassandra, 269; murdered by Orestes, 271; father of Erigone by Clytaemnestra, 271

Aegius, son of Egyptus, i. 141

Aegle, one of the Hesperides, i. 221

Aegleis, daughter of Hyacinth, sacrificed by the Athenians, ii. 119

Aello, a Harpy, i. 15

Aellopus, a Harpy, i. 105

Aeneas, son of Anchises and Aphrodite, ii. 37; his kine on Ida raided by Achilles, 203; an

459

INDEX

Agasthenes, father of Polyxenus, ii. 27

Agathon, son of Priam, ii. 49

Agave, a Nereid, i. 15

Agave, daughter of Cadmus, wife of Echion, i. 317; kills her son Pentheus in a fit of Bacchic frenzy, 331

Agave, daughter of Danaus, wife of Lycus, i. 139

Agelaus, a servant, exposes the infant Paris, ii. 47

Agelaus, son of Hercules by Omphale, i. 275

Agelaus, son of Temenus, hires men to murder his father, i. 291

Agelaus, suitor of Penelope, ii. 297

Agenor, father of Phineus, i. 105

Agenor, son of Amphion and Niobe, i. 341

Agenor, son of Ecbasus, i. 131

Agenor, son of Egyptus, husband of Cleopatra, i. 141

Agenor, son of Phegeus, i. 385. *See* Phegeus

Agenor, son of Pleuron, husband of Epicaste, i. 61

Agenor, son of Poseidon and Libya, i. 135; reigns in Phoenicia, 135; his children, Europa, Cadmus, Phoenix, and Cilix, 297

Agenor, suitor of Penelope, from Dulichium, ii. 297

Agenor, suitor of Penelope, from Zacynthos, ii. 299

Agerochus, suitor of Penelope, ii.297

Aglaia, a Grace, i. 17

Aglaia, daughter of Mantineus, wife of Abas, i. 145

Aglaia, daughter of Thespius, mother of Antiades by Hercules, i. 273

Aglaope, one of the Sirens, ii. 291

Aglaus, son of Thyestes, murdered by Atreus, ii. 167

Agraulus, daughter of Actaeus, wife of Cecrops, ii. 81

Agraulus, daughter of Cecrops, mother of Alcippe by Ares, ii. 81

Agrius, a centaur, repelled by Hercules, i. 193

Agrius, a giant, killed by the Fates, i. 47

Agrius, son of Porthaon, i. 63;

accuses Tydeus, 73; some of his sons killed by Tydeus, 73; two of his sons kill Oeneus, 73

Agrius, suitor of Penelope, ii. 297

Ajax, son of Oileus, suitor of Helen, ii. 27; leader of the Locrians against Troy, 183; violates Cassandra, 239; Athena angry at his impiety, 243; wrecked and drowned, 247; buried by Thetis in Myconos, 247

Ajax, son of Telamon, suitor of Helen, ii. 27, 29; named after an eagle, 61; leader of the Salaminians against Troy, 183; fights Hector, 207; sent as ambassador to Achilles, 207; retreats, 209; rescues the body of Patroclus, 209; victor in wrestling, 211; kills Glaucus, 215; carries off the dead body of Achilles, 215; victor in the quoits match, 217; contends for the arms of Achilles, 219; goes mad and kills himself, 219; his dead body not allowed to be burnt, is buried in a coffin at Rhoeteum, 219

Alastor, son of Neleus, i. 85

Alcaeus, son of Androgeus, taken as hostage by Hercules, i. 205

Alcaeus, son of Perseus, i. 163; father of Amphitryon and Anaxo, 165

Alcarops, suitor of Penelope, ii. 299

Alcathous, son of Porthaon, i. 63; killed by Tydeus, 71

Alcathus, father of Automedusa, i. 181; father of Periboea, ii. 61; son of Pelops, 61

Alces, son of Egyptus, husband of Glauce, i. 141

Alcestis, daughter of Pelias, i. 85; dies for her husband Admetus and is restored to life, 93

Alcides, name given to Hercules, i. 183

Alcidice, wife of Salmoneus, mother of Tyro, i. 81

Alcimenes, brother of Bellerophon, i. 149

Alcinous, king of Corcyra (of the Phaeacians), i. 115; his reception of the Argonauts and Medea, 117; sends Ulysses away to his native land, ii. 295, 297

INDEX

Alcinus, son of Hippocoon, slain by Hercules, ii. 23

Alcippe, daughter of Ares by Agraulus, ii. 81; Halirrothius attempts to violate her, 81

Alcippe, mother of Daedalus, ii. 121

Alcmaeon goes with Diomedes (to Calydon), i. 73; son of Amphiaraus, leader of the Epigoni against Thebes, 379; kills Laodamas, 381; learning the treachery of his mother Eriphyle, he kills her, 381, 383; haunted by her Fury, 383; is purified by Phegeus at Psophis and marries Arsinoe, daughter of Phegeus, 383; his wanderings and final purification by Achelous, 383; marries Callirrhoe, daughter of Achelous, 385; murdered by the sons of Phegeus, 385

Alcmaeonid, homicide of Tydeus mentioned in the, i. 71

Alcmena, daughter of Electryon, i. 165; her delivery retarded by the Ilithyias, 167; goes to Thebes with Amphitryon, 171; visited by Zeus in the likeness of Amphitryon, 173, 175; bears Hercules and Iphicles, 175; marries Rhadamanthys and dwells at Ocaleae, 181; gouges out the eyes of Eurystheus, 279; married to Rhadamanthys, 303

Alcmenor, son of Egyptus, husband of Hippomedusa, i. 141

Alcon, son of Hippocoon, slain by Hercules, ii. 23

Alcyone, daughter of Aeolus, wife of Ceyx, i. 57; says that her husband is Zeus, 59; turned into a kingfisher, 59

Alcyone, daughter of Atlas, one of the Pleiades, ii. 3; mother of Aethusa by Poseidon, 5

Alcyone, daughter of Sthenelus, i. 167

Alcyone, wife of Chalcodon, mother of Elephenor, ii. 183

Alcyoneus, a giant, i. 43; shot by Hercules, 45

Alecto, a Fury, i. 5

Alector, father of Iphis, i. 353

Alector, father of Leitus, i. 97, ii. 27

Aletes, son of Icarius by Periboea, ii. 23

Aleus, father of Cepheus, i. 97; father of Auge, 253, 277; exposes her child (Telephus), 255; gives her to Nauplius to sell, 257; son of Aphidas, 397; father of Auge, Cepheus, and Lycurgus, 397

Alexander, son of Eurystheus, slain by the Athenians, i. 277

Alexander, surname of Paris, ii. 47; marries Oenone, 51; warned by her not to fetch Helen, 51; carries off Helen, 51, 171; shot by Philoctetes, 51; carried to Oenone and dies, 51; judges the three goddesses and gives the prize to Aphrodite, 173; sails to Sparta, 173; entertained by Menelaus, 173; carries off Helen, 173, 175; driven by a storm to Sidon, 175; comes to Troy with Helen, 175; fights Menelaus, 207; shoots Achilles, 215; shot by Philoctetes, 223. *See* Paris

Alexiares, son of Hercules by Hebe, i. 273

Alizones, Trojan allies, ii. 205

Allies of the Trojans, ii. 203, 205

Aloads, the, Otus and Ephialtes, attack the gods, i. 59; put Ares in bonds, 59; kill each other, 61

Aloeus, son of Poseidon by Canace, i. 59

Alopius, son of Hercules by Antiope, i. 273

Alphesiboea, wife of Phoenix, mother of Adonis, according to Hesiod, ii. 85

Alpheus, river, Apollo at the, i. 87; diverted by Hercules into the cattle-yard of Augeas, 195, 197

Altar of Radiant Apollo, i. 117; of Hera of the Height, 123, 125; of Zeus, strangers sacrificed on, 225; of Hercules the Glorious Victor, 245; of Pelops at Olympia, 251; of Cenaean Zeus, built by Hercules, 267; of Mercy, 277; of Atabyrian Zeus, founded by Althaemenes, 307; of Mercy at Athens, Adrastus takes refuge at, 373, 375; of Hera, ii. 171; of

462

Thasos, 209; son of Minos, 303, 307; vanquishes all comers at the Panathenian games, ii. 115; killed by the bull of Marathon, 115; or murdered on his way to Thebes, 115, 116

Andromache, daughter of Eetion, wife of Hector, ii. 51; assigned to Neoptolemus, 241; bears him a son Molossus, 251

Andromeda, daughter of Cepheus, exposed to a sea-monster, rescued by Perseus, i. 159, 161; goes with him to Argos, 161; her sons by him, 163

Andromedes, suitor of Penelope, ii. 299

Andros, Coans settle in, ii. 259

Anicetus, son of Hercules by Hebe, i. 273

Anius, son of Apollo, his daughters called the Wine-growers, ii. 179, 181

Anogon, son of Castor by Hilaira, ii. 33

Antaeus, son of Poseidon, wrestles with Hercules and is killed by him, i. 223

Antandrus, city, taken by Achilles, ii. 203

Antenor saves Ulysses and Menelaus, ii. 197; father of Archelochus and Acamas, 205; father of Glaucus, 237

Antenor, suitor of Penelope, ii. 299

Anthea, daughter of Thespius, i. 273

Antheis, daughter of Hyacinth, slain by the Athenians, ii. 119

Anthelia, daughter of Danaus by Polyxo, i. 141

Anthemus, river, battle of Hercules with Geryon at the, i. 215

Anthippe, daughter of Thespius, mother of Hippodromus by Hercules, i. 273

Antia, daughter of Iobates, wife of Proteus, i. 145

Antiades, son of Hercules by Aglaia, i. 273

Anticlia, mother of Periphetes, ii. 123

Anticlia, mother of Ulysses, ii. 183; Ulysses sees the ghost of his mother, 289

Anticlus would answer Helen from the Wooden Horse, ii. 235

Antigone, daughter of Eurytion, married to Peleus, ii. 61; hangs herself, 65

Antigone, daughter of Oedipus, i. 349; goes with him to Attica, 351; secretly buries the dead body of Polynices, 373; herself buried alive in the grave, 373

Antigonus, suitor of Penelope, ii. 297

Antileon, son of Hercules by Procris, i. 273

Antilochus, son of Nestor, i. 85; suitor of Helen, ii. 27

Antimache, daughter of Amphidamas, wife of Eurystheus, i. 399

Antimachus, son of Hercules by Nicippe, i. 275

Antimachus, suitor of Penelope, ii. 297

Antinous, suitor of Penelope, ii. 299; said by some to have seduced Penelope, 305

Antiochus, son of Hercules, father of Phylas, i. 287

Antiochus, son of Melas, killed by Tydeus, i. 71, 73

Antiochus, son of Pterelaus, i. 165

Antiope, an Amazon, carried off by Theseus, ii. 143

Antiope, daughter of Nycteus, loved by Zeus, i. 337; runs away to Epopeus at Sicyon and is married to him, 337; captured by her uncle Lycus, 337; gives birth to Amphion and Zethus 337, 339; is tormented by Lycus and Dirce, but released by her sons, 339; mother of Zethus and Amphion by Zeus, ii. 5.

Antiope, daughter of Thespius, mother of Alopius by Hercules, i. 273

Antiphates, king of the Laestrygones, ii. 285

Antiphus, son of Hercules by Laothoe, i. 273

Antiphus, son of Myrmidon, i. 57

Antiphus, son of Priam and Hecuba ii. 49

Antiphus, son of Talaemenes, a le der of the Maeonians, ii. 205

465

INDEX

Antiphus, son of Thessalus, leader of the Coans against Troy, ii. 185; occupies the land of the Pelasgians and calls it Thessaly, 257, 259

Antisthenes, suitor of Penelope, ii. 297

Ants turned into men in Aegina, ii. 53

Apemosyne, daughter of Catreus, i. 307; loved by Hermes, 309; killed by her brother, 309

Aphareus, father of Idas and Lynceus, i. 67, 97; son of Perieres, 79; father of Lynceus, Idas, and Pisus, ii. 13, 21, 33

Aphetae, in Thessaly, Hercules left by the Argonauts at, i. 101

Aphidas, son of Arcas, joint ruler of Arcadia, i. 397

Aphidnae, Helen carried off to, ii. 25; captured by Pollux and Castor, 25

Aphrodite, daughter of Zeus and Dione, i. 15, 17; loves Adonis, 19; angry with Pierus, 19; causes Dawn to be perpetually in love, 33; afflicts the Lemnian women, 99; carries away Butes, 115; mother of Harmonia, 317; gives the golden apples to Melanion, 401; loves Anchises and bears him Aeneas and Lyrus, ii. 37; in anger causes the daughters of Cinyras to cohabit with foreigners, 85; disputes with Persephone for the possession of Adonis, 87, 89; forsakes Hephaestus, 89; a competitor for the prize of beauty, preferred by Alexander, 173; rescues Alexander (Paris) from Menelaus, 207; wounded by Diomedes, 207

Apia, old name of Peloponnese, i. 129, ii. 163

Apis, son of Phoroneus, slain by Aetolus, i. 61; tyrant of Peloponnese, 129; deemed a god, identified with Sarapis, 129; his murder avenged by Argus, 139

Apollo, father of Linus, i. 17; loves Hyacinth, 19; father of the Corybantes, 21; son of Zeus and Latona, born in Delos,

25; comes to Delphi, kills the Python, and takes over the oracle, 27; kills Tityus, 27, 29; his contest with Marsyas, 29, 31; shoots Ephialtes, 45; his intrigue with Phthia, 61; woos Marpessa, fights Idas, 61; soothsaying learned from, 87; serves Admetus, 91, 93; bids Pelias appease Artemis, 93; Radiant, the Argonauts found an altar of, 117; flashes lightning to guide Argonauts, 117; gives Hercules a bow and arrows, 183; fortifies Troy, but being defrauded by Laomedon he punishes the city with a pestilence, 205, 207; fights Hercules for the tripod, 241; precinct of, 263; father of Miletus, 301; shoots down the sons of Niobe, 343; portion of Theban booty sent to, at Delphi, 381; his oracle as to foundation of Amphilochian Argos, 389; herds kine in Pieria, ii. 5, 7; recovers the stolen kine from Hermes, 9; gets the lyre from Hermes, 9; gives him the golden wand, 11; receives from him the pipe, 11; loves Hyacinth and kills him involuntarily, 11, 13; father of Aesculapius by Arsinoe, or by Coronis, 13, 15; curses the raven that brings word of Coronis's infidelity, 15; kills Coronis, but entrusts the infant Aesculapius to Chiron, 15; kills the Cyclopes, 19; serves Admetus as a herdsman, 21; causes the cows to drop twins, 21; confers the gift of prophecy on Cassandra, 49; deprives her of the power to persuade, 49; father of Troilus by Hecuba, 49; father of Anius, 179; father of Tenes, according to some, 193; altar of, 195; will kill Achilles if Achilles kills Tenes, 195; Thymbraean, the sanctuary of, 201; and Alexander shoot Achilles, 215; sends a sign to warn the Trojans, 233; father of Mopsus by Manto, 243, 245; Neoptolemus demands satisfaction of, for the

466

INDEX

death of his father, 255; the Wanderer, sanctuary of, founded by Philoctetes, 261; Maro, priest of, 281

Apollonia, in Epirus, the people of Elephenor inhabit, ii. 259

Apollonius, *Argonautica*, on the Harpies, i. 107

Apple, prize of beauty, thrown by Strife, ii. 173

Apples of the Hesperides, i. 219, 221, 231; golden, let fall by Melanion in the race, 401

Apsyrtides Islands, the Argonauts at the, i. 115; Colchians settle in the, 117

Apsyrtus, brother of Medea, murdered by her, i. 113; the Argonauts purified for the murder of, 115

Arabia, Egyptus settled in, i. 137; Hercules passes by, 229

Arabian woman, wife of Egyptus, i. 141

Arbelus, son of Egyptus, husband of Oeme, i. 143

Arcadia, Lycurgus in, i. 67; Atalanta in, 67; the hearth of Telephus in, 73; ravaged by a bull, 131; traversed by the mad daughters of Proetus, 147; Stymphalus in, 197; the Cretan bull roams over, 199; Hercules in, 253; Arcas brought up in, 397; Cyllene in, ii. 3; booty of cattle driven from, 33; Oresteum in, 277; Mantinea in, 305

Arcadian army collected by Hercules, i. 249

Arcadians robbed of their cattle by a satyr, i. 131; join Hercules in his attack on Oechalia, 265; help the Dioscuri to capture Athens, ii. 153; their muster for the Trojan war, 183

Arcas, son of Zeus by Callisto, given by Zeus to Maia to bring up, i. 395, 397

Arcena, one of Actaeon's dogs, i. 323

Archebates, son of Lycaon, i. 389

Archedicus, son of Hercules by Eurypyle, i. 273

Archelaus, son of Egyptus, husband of Anaxibia, i. 141

Archelaus, son of Electryon, i. 165

Archelochus, son of Antenor, leader of the Dardanians, ii. 205

Archemachus, son of Hercules by Patro, i. 273

Archemachus, son of Priam, ii. 49

Archemolus, suitor of Penelope, ii. 297

Archemorus. *See* Opheltes

Archery, bride offered as prize in a contest of, i. 237, 239

Archestratus, suitor of Penelope, ii. 299

Architeles, father of Eunomus, i. 259; pardons Hercules for killing his son, 261

Arcisius, father of Laertes, i. 97.

Arene, daughter of Oebalus, wife of Aphareus, ii. 13

Areopagus, Ares tried for murder in the, ii. 81; Cephalus tried for homicide in the, 105; Daedalus tried for murder in the, 123; Orestes tried and acquitted of murder in the, 271

Ares, son of Zeus and Hera, i. 15; bedded with Dawn, 33; put in bonds by the Aloads, 59; rescued by Hermes, 59, 61; father of Oxylus by Protogonia, 61; his children by Demonice, 63; father of Meleager, 65; father of Dryas, 67; grove of, in Colchis, 77, 95; father of Ascalaphus and Ialmenus, 99, ii. 27; father of Diomedes the Thracian, i. 201; the belt of, worn by Hippolyte, queen of the Amazons, 203; father of Cycnus, champions him against Hercules, 221; father of Cycnus, 265; the spring of, at Thebes, 315; dragon, offspring of, 315; Cadmus serves Ares to atone for slaughter of dragon, 317; father of Harmonia, 317; father of Phlegyas, 337; Menoeceus offers himself as a sacrifice to, 367; father of Parthenopaeus by Atalanta, according to some, 403; father of Alcippe by Agraulus, ii. 81; kills Halirrhothius and is tried for murder in the Areopagus, 81; father of Tereus, 99; gives arms

INDEX

and horses to Oenomaus, 161;
father of Penthesilia by Otrere,
211

Arestor, father of Argus, according
to Pherecydes, i. 133

Arete, wife of Alcinous, marries
Medea to Jason, i. 117

Arethusa, one of the Hesperides,
i. 221

Aretus, son of Nestor, i. 85

Aretus, son of Priam, ii. 49

Argele, daughter of Thespius,
mother of Cleolaus by Hercules,
i. 273

Arges, a Cyclops, i. 5

Argia, daughter of Adrastus, i. 91;
wife of Polynices, 353

Argia, daughter of Autesion, wife
of Aristodemus, i. 287

Argiope, a nymph, mother of
Cercyon, ii. 131

Argiope, a nymph, mother of
Thamyris, i. 19

Argius, son of Egyptus, husband
of Evippe, i. 141

Argius, son of Licymnius, buried
by Hercules, i. 267

Argius, suitor of Penelope, ii. 297

Argive land, traversed by the mad
daughters of Proetus, i. 147;
dead cast out unburied by Creon,
373

Argives flee before the Thebans,
i. 367; capture and spoil Thebes
and pull down the walls, 381;
send Manto and a portion of the
booty to Apollo at Delphi, 381;
help to save the sons of Alcmaeon
from their pursuers, 387; their
muster for the Trojan war, ii.
183

Argo, the building of the, i. 97;
speaks with human voice, 97,
101, 103, 115; Amycus goes to
the, 103; Aeetes wishes to burn
the, 113; the Colchians search
for the, 113; find it in the land
of the Phaeacians, 117; pelted
with stones by Talos, 119;
dedicated to Poseidon at the
Isthmus of Corinth, 121

Argonautica of Apollonius, i. 105

Argonauts, list of the, i. 97, 99;
in Lemnos, i. 99; among the
Doliones, 99, 101; in Mysia,

101; among the Bebryces, 103;
deliver Phineus from the Harpies,
105; learn from him the course
of their voyage, 105; among the
Mariandynians, 109; sail from
Colchis with Medea, 113; overtaken by a storm, 113; pass the
Sirens, 115; sail from Phaeacia
with Medea, 117; Pelias despairs
of the return of the, 121; sail
with Boreas, ii. 107; punish
Phineus, 107

Argos, Amphiaraus at, i. 67;
Tydeus at, 73; madness of the
women of, 91; Melampus receives part of the kingdom of,
91; Hercules returns to, 101;
river Inachus in, 129; Danaus,
king of, 137; the inhabitants of
Argos called Danai by Danaus,
137; the sons of Egyptus come
to, 139; Lynceus, king of, 145;
Acrisius, king of, 147; Amphitryon banished from, 169,
171; allotted to Temenus, 289;
toad a symbol of, 291; Polyidus departs to, 313; Dionysus
drives the women mad at, 331;
Polynices goes to, 351; Telephus comes to, to be healed
by Achilles, ii. 189; the Greeks
sail from, to Aulis, 191. *See
also* Amphilochian Argos

Argus, son of Phrixus, i. 77; builds
the Argo, 95, 97

Argus, son of Zeus and Niobe,
i. 129; gave his name to Argos,
129; his children, 129

Argus the All-seeing, son of Agenor,
i. 131; his exploits, 131; set to
guard Io in form of a cow, 131;
killed by Hermes, 131

Argyphia, wife of Egyptus, i. 139

Aria, daughter of Cleochus, mother
of Miletus by Apollo, i. 301

Ariadne, daughter of Minos, i. 303,
307; loves Theseus and gives
him the clue to the labyrinth,
ii. 135; taken by him to Naxos,
137; carried off by Dionysus to
Lemnos, 137; her sons by
Dionysus, 137

Arion, a horse, offspring of Poseidon and Demeter, saves his
master Adrastus, i. 373

469

INDEX

Asterius, name of the Minotaur, i. 305. *See* Minotaur

Asterius, prince of Crete, marries Europa, i. 301; dies childless, 303; father of Crete, according to Asclepiades, 303

Asterius, son of Cometes, in the Argo, i. 99

Asterius, son of Neleus by Chloris, i. 85

Asterodia, daughter of Deion, i. 79

Asteropaeus, son of Pelegon, slain by Achilles, ii. 209

Asterope, daughter of Cebren, wife of Aesacus, ii. 45

Astraeus, offspring of Crius and Eurybia, i. 13

Astyanax, son of Hercules by Epilais, i. 273

Astyanax thrown by the Greeks from the battlements of Troy, ii. 239

Astybies, son of Hercules, by Calametis, i. 273

Astycratia, daughter of Amphion and Niobe, i. 341

Astydamia, daughter of Amyntor, mother of Ctesippus by Hercules, i. 277

Astydamia, daughter of Pelops, wife of Alcaeus, i. 165

Astydamia, wife of Acastus, falsely accuses Peleus, ii. 63, 65; killed by Peleus, 73

Astygonus, son of Priam, ii. 49

Astylochus, suitor of Penelope, ii. 297

Astynous, son of Phaethon, father of Sandocus, ii. 83

Astyoche, daughter of Amphion and Niobe, i. 341

Astyoche, daughter of Phylas, mother of Tlepolemus, i. 259; mother of Tlepolemus by Hercules, 277, ii. 183

Astyoche, daughter of Laomedon, ii. 45, 261, 263

Astyoche, daughter of Simoeis, wife of Erichthonius, ii. 37

Astypalaea, mother of Eurypylus by Poseidon, i. 247

Atabyrium, a mountain in Rhodes, i. 307

Atalanta, daughter of Iasus and Clymene, exposed by her father, suckled by a she-bear, i. 399; a virgin huntress, 399; kills two centaurs, 399; hunts the Calydonian boar, 399; wrestles with Peleus, 399, 401, ii. 63; races with her suitors, i. 401; won by Melanion with golden apples, 401; changed into a lion, 401; mother of Parthenopaeus, 403. *See also* Atalanta, daughter of Schoeneus

Atalanta, daughter of Schoeneus, hunts the Calydonian boar, i. 67, 69; in the Argo, 97. *See also* Atalanta, daughter of Iasus

Atas, son of Priam, ii. 49

Ate, the Phrygian, the hill of, site of Ilium, ii. 39; thrown by Zeus into the Ilian country, 41, 43

Athamantia, named after Athamas, i. 77

Athamas, son of Aeolus, i. 57; rules over Boeotia, 75; attempts to sacrifice his son Phrixus, 75; shoots his son Learchus, 77; banished from Boeotia, 77; marries Themisto, 77; husband of Ino, 317; rears Dionysus as a girl, 319; driven mad by Hera, hunts and kills his son Learchus as a deer, 319

Athena, born of the head of Zeus, i. 25; throws away the pipes, 29; kills Enceladus, 45; flays giant Pallas, 45; superintends the building of the Argo, 95, 97; gives dragon's teeth to Aeetes, 109; advises Danaus to build a ship, 137; Lindian, her image set up by Danaus, 137; and Hermes purify the Danaids for the murder of their husbands, 143; helps Perseus, 155, 159; receives the Gorgon's head from Perseus and puts it in her shield, 161; gives Hercules a robe, 183; gives Hercules brazen castanets, 199; gets the apples of the Hesperides from Hercules, 233; brings Hercules to Phlegra, 247; precinct of, at Tegea, 255; Cadmus wishes to sacrifice a cow to, 315; procures for him the kingdom (of Thebes), 317; seen naked by Tiresias, blinds him but makes him understand the notes of birds, 363 ; would make Tydeus immortal, but changes her mind, 369 ; precinct of, 397 ; gives Aesculapius the Gorgon's blood, ii. 17 ; brought up by Triton, 41 ; wounds Pallas and makes an image of her (the Palladium), 41 ; strives with Poseidon for the possession of Attica, 79, 81 ; plants an olive-tree, 79, 81 ; the country adjudged to her, 81 ; calls the city Athens, 81 ; mother of Erichthonius by Hephaestus, 89, 91 ; entrusts Erichthonius in a chest to Pandrosus, 91 ; angry with the sisters of Pandrosus for opening the chest, drives them mad, 91 ; brings up Erichthonius in the precinct, 91, 93 ; wooden image of, on the Acropolis, 93 ; Erichthonius buried in the precinct of, 95 ; Butes gets priesthood of, 101 ; a competitor for the prize of beauty, 173 ; drives Ajax mad, 219 ; the Wooden Horse dedicated to, 233 ; Cassandra violated by the Locrian Ajax at the image of, 239 ; angry with the Greeks for the impiety of Ajax, 243 ; Agamemnon proposes to sacrifice to, 243 ; asks Zeus to send a storm on the Greeks, 247 ; hurls a thunderbolt at the ship of Ajax, 247 ; propitiated at Ilium by the Locrians for a thousand years, 267, 269

Athenians refuse to surrender the sons of Hercules, i. 277 ; wage war with Eurystheus, 277 ; capture Thebes and bury the Argive dead, 375 ; their war with the Eleusinians, ii. 109 ; visited with famine and pestilence, slaughter the daughters of Hyacinth, 119 ; send seven youths and seven maidens every year to be devoured by the Minotaur, 119, 123 ; their muster for the Trojan war, 183

Athens, Theseus at, i. 67 ; the road to, cleared of evildoers by Theseus, 123 ; Amphitryon at, 173 ; altar of Mercy at, 277, 373,

375 ; the sons of Hercules come for protection to, 277 ; Daedalus banished from, 305 ; Adrastus flees to, 373 ; named after Athena, ii. 81 ; Erichthonius, king of, 93 ; Procris comes to 105 ; the Metionids expelled from, 113 ; return of Aegeus to, 115 ; attacked with a fleet by Minos, 117 ; Daedalus flees from, 121 ; Medea at, 123, 125 ; Theseus comes to, 133 ; battle of Theseus with the Amazons at, 145 ; captured by the Dioscuri, 153 ; Menestheus restored to, by the Dioscuri, 153 ; Orestes tried at, 271 ; image of Tauropolus brought to, 275

Athletic contest for brides, i. 143

Atlantia, a Hamadryad nymph, consorts with Danaus, i. 141

Atlas, son of Iapetus and Asia, i. 13 ; bears the sky, 13 ; father of Merope, 79 ; family of, 81 ; among the Hyperboreans, the golden apples of the Hesperides on, 219, 221 ; gives the apples to Hercules, 231 ; holds up the sphere, 231 ; asks Hercules to relieve him of the burden, 231 ; father of the Pleiades, by Pleione, ii. 3 ; Zeus consorts with the daughters of, 5 ; father of Electra, 35 ; father of Calypso, 295

Atonement for slaughter by servitude, i. 317. See Servitude

Atreus, son of Pelops, along with his brother Thyestes is entrusted with Midea, i. 171 ; father of Menelaus, ii. 27 ; son of Pelops, 163 ; neglects to perform his vow to Artemis, 165, 191 ; puts the golden lamb in a box, 165 ; gets the sign of the sun going backward and ousts his brother Thyestes from the kingdom of Mycenae, 165 ; murders the children of Thyestes and serves them up to him at a banquet, 167 ; killed by Aegisthus, 169 ; father of Agamemnon and Menelaus by Aerope, 183

Atromus, son of Hercules by Stratonice, i. 273

INDEX

Atropus, a Fate, i. 15

Atthis, daughter of Cranaus, ii. 89; mother of Erichthonius, according to some, 89; Attica named Atthis after her, 89

Atthis, name of Attica, ii. 89

Attica, Amphictyon, king of, i. 57; Marathon in, 201; Colonus in, 351; Cecrops the first king of, ii. 77; formerly called Acte, afterwards Cecropia, 77; Poseidon the first god to come to, 79; laid under the sea by Poseidon, 81; Demeter and Dionysus come to, 95; Sunium in, 279

Atymnius, son of Zeus, loved by Sarpedon, i. 303

Auge, daughter of Aleus, i. 253, 275; debauched by Hercules, 253, 397; priestess of Athena, hides her babe in Athena's precinct, 397; delivered by her father to Nauplius to be put to death, 397; married by Teuthras, prince of Mysia, 397

Augeas, son of the Sun, in the Argo, i. 97; king of Elis, his cattle-yard cleaned out by Hercules, 195, 197; refuses to pay Hercules his reward and expels him from Elis, 197; appoints the Molionides his generals, 249; killed by Hercules, 249; father of Epicaste, 277

Aulis in Boeotia, the Greek army musters for the Trojan war at, ii. 181; portent of the serpent and the sparrows at, 185; Greeks reassemble at, after eight years, 189

Aulis in Lydia, Syleus in, i. 241

Ausonia, Circe in, i. 115

Auspices, art of taking the, i. 87

Autesion, father of Argia, i. 287

Autolycus, father of Polymede, i. 93; son of Hermes, in the Argo, 97; teaches Hercules to wrestle, 175; steals cattle of Eurytus, 239

Automate, daughter of Danaus, wife of Busiris, i. 139

Automedusa, daughter of Alcathus, wife of Iphicles, i. 181

Autonoe, a Nereid, i. 15

Autonoe, daughter of Cadmus, wife

of Aristaeus, i. 317; mother of Actaeon, 323

Autonoe, daughter of Danaus, wife of Eurylochus, i. 141

Autonoe, daughter of Pireus, mother of Palaemon by Hercules, i. 277

Axius, river, father of Pelegon, ii. 209

Bacchanals taken prisoners by Lycurgus and then released, i. 327

Balius, an immortal horse, given by Poseidon to Peleus, ii. 69

Balius, one of Actaeon's dogs, i. 325

Banishment for homicide, i. 61. See Exile

Barrenness of earth caused by presence of matricide Alcmaeon, i. 383; of land caused by seduction of Auge (priestess of Athena), 397

Barthas, suitor of Penelope, ii. 299

Batia, a Naiad nymph, wife of Oebalus, ii. 21

Batia, daughter of Teucer, wife of Dardanus, ii. 35

Baton, charioteer of Amphiaraus, swallowed up with his master in the earth, i. 371

Bear, Callisto turned into a, i. 395; the star (constellation), Callisto turned into, 397; Atalanta suckled by a, 399; Paris suckled by a, ii. 47

Bears, Achilles fed on the marrows of, ii. 71

Bearskin, severed sinews of Zeus wrapt in a, i. 49

Bebryces, the Argonauts among the, i. 103; a Mysian tribe, conquered by Hercules, 205

Beds, the two, on which Damastes (Procrustes) stretched his guests, ii. 133

Bellerophon, son of Glaucus, kills the Chimera, i. 79; kills his brother, 149; is purified by Proetus, 151; refuses the amorous proposals of Stheneboea, 151; sent by Iobates against the Chimera, 151; shoots the Chimera, 153; conquers the Solymi and the Amazons, 153; kills an ambush of Lycians, 153; marries

472

INDEX

477

INDEX

Chrysippus, son of Egyptus, husband of Chrysippe, i. 141

Chrysippus, son of Pelops, is loved and carried off by Laius, i. 339

Chrysopelia, a nymph, wife of Arcas, i. 397

Chrysothemis, daughter of Agamemnon and Clytaemnestra, ii. 171

Chthonia, daughter of Erechtheus, ii. 103 ; married to (her father's brother) Butes, 103

Chthonius, one of the Sparti, i. 317 ; father of Nycteus, 335

Chthonius, son of Egyptus, husband of Bryce, i. 141

Cicones, Trojan allies, ii. 205 ; Ulysses among the, 281

Cilicia, Typhon in, i. 47, 49 ; Corycian cave in, 49 ; named after Cilix, 301 ; Celenderis in, ii. 83

Cilix, son of Agenor, i. 297 ; settles in Cilicia, 301

Cilla, daughter of Laomedon, ii. 43

Cimmerian land traversed by Io, i. 133

Cinyps, river in Libya, ii. 259

Cinyras, father of Laodice, i. 397 ; son of Sandocus, founds Paphos in Cyprus, ii. 83, 85 ; father of Adonis, 85 ; his daughters cohabit with foreigners and die in Egypt, 85 ; in Cyprus, promises to send ships for the war against Troy, 179

Circaean root given by Procris to Minos to drink, ii. 105

Circe, sister of Aeetes, i. 77 ; purifies the Argonauts for the murder of Apsyrtus, 115 ; daughter of the Sun, sister of Aeetes, an enchantress, turns the companions of Ulysses into beasts, ii. 287 ; Ulysses escapes her enchantments and shares her bed, 289 ; she bears him a son Telegonus, 289 ; she sends Ulysses on his way, 289

Cisseus, father of Hecuba, ii. 45

Cisseus, son of Egyptus, husband of Anthelia, i. 141

Cithaeron, the lion of, killed by Hercules, i. 177, 179 ; Actaeon devoured by his dogs on 323

Theban women rave in Bacchic frenzy on, 331 ; Pentheus torn to pieces there, 331 ; the children of Niobe killed on, 343 ; the Seven against Thebes at, 359

Cius, in Mysia, founded by Polyphemus, i. 101

Clashing Rocks, the Argo passes between the, i. 107, 109

Clazomenae taken by Achilles, ii.203

Cleoboea, mother of Eurythemis, i. 63

Cleocharia, a Naiad nymph, wife of Lelex and mother of Eurotas, ii. 11

Cleochus, father of Aria, i. 301

Cleodaeus, the sons of, inquire of the oracle, i. 285

Cleodore, daughter of Danaus, wife of Lixus, i. 141

Cleodoxa, daughter of Amphion and Niobe, i. 341

Cleolaus, son of Hercules by Argele, i. 273

Cleonae, Hercules at, i. 185, 187 ; the Molionides killed by Hercules at, 249

Cleopatra, daughter of Boreas and Orithyia, ii. 105 ; wife of Phineus, 107

Cleopatra, daughter of Danaus, wife of Agenor, i. 141

Cleopatra, daughter of Idas and Marpessa, wife of Meleager, i. 67 ; hangs herself, 71

Cleopatra, daughter of Tros, ii. 37

Cleopatra, maiden sent by the Locrians to propitiate Athena at Ilium, ii. 267

Cleophyle, wife of Lycurgus, i. 399

Clio, a Muse, i. 17 ; twits Aphrodite with her love of Adonis, 19 ; mother of Hyacinth by Pierus, 19

Clisithyra, daughter of Idomeneus and Meda, murdered by Leucus, ii. 249

Clite, daughter of Danaus, wife of Clitus, i. 141

Clitonymus, son of Amphidamas, killed by Patroclus, ii. 77

Clitor, son of Lycaon, i. 389

Clitus, son of Egyptus, husband of Clite, i. 141

Clonia, a nymph, wife of Hyrieus,

478

INDEX

Corythus, Telephus bred by the neatherds of, i. 397

Cos, Polybotes at, i. 47; ravaged by Hercules, 247

Cottus, a Hundred-handed, i. 3

Cow, Io turned into a white, i. 133; of three different colours, how described, 311; as guide to the foundation of Thebes, 313, 315; as guide to the foundation of Ilium, ii. 37, 39

Cows of the Sun driven away from Erythia by Alcyoneus, i. 43. See Kine

Crab attacks Hercules, i. 189

Cranae, daughter of Cranaus, ii. 89

Cranaechme (not Menaechme), daughter of Cranaus, ii. 89

Cranaus, king of Attica, i. 57, ii. 89; said to have arbitrated between Poseidon and Athena, ii. 81; names the country Atthis, 89; expelled by Amphictyon, 89; father of Atthis, 89

Cranto, a Nereid, i. 15

Crataeis, mother of Scylla, ii. 293

Cratieus, father of Anaxibia, i. 85

Crenidian gate of Thebes, i. 361

Creon, king of Corinth, betroths his daughter Glauce to Jason, i. 123; brings up two children of Alcmaeon, 387

Creon, king of Thebes, purifies Amphitryon, i. 171; helps him in the war on the Teleboans (Taphians), 171, 173; marries his daughters to Hercules and Iphicles, 181; father of Megara, 275; son of Menoeceus, succeeds Laius as king of Thebes, 347; his son Haemon devoured by the Sphinx, 349; promises the kingdom to him who should read the riddle of the Sphinx, 349; father of Menoeceus, 367; succeeds to the kingdom of Thebes, 373; casts out the Argive dead unburied, 373; buries Antigone alive, 373

Creon, son of Hercules, i. 273

Creontiades, son of Hercules by Megara, i. 181, 275

Cresphontes, a Heraclid, gets Messene by lot, i. 289, 291; murdered by his sons, 291

Cretans, their muster for the Trojan war, ii. 183

Crete, daughter of Asterius, wife of Minos, i. 303

Crete, daughter of Deucalion, i. 311

Crete, Zeus born in, i. 7; guarded by Talos, 119; Hercules goes to, to fetch the bull, 199; Europa brought by Zeus to, 299; Minos in, 303; Althaemenes sets out from, 307; visible from Rhodes, 307; Theseus in, ii. 135; Menelaus goes to, to bury Catreus, 173; revolt of Leucus in, 249; Idomeneus lands in, 249; Magnesians under Prothous settle in, 259; the people of Tlepolemus touch at, 259, 261; Menelaus driven to, 279

Cretheus, son of Aeolus, i. 57; brings up Tyro, 81; founds Iolcus, 85; marries Tyro, 85; father of Aeson, Amythaon, and Pheres, 87, 91

Cretinia, a district of Rhodes, i. 307

Creusa, daughter of Erechtheus, mother of Achaeus and Ion, i. 57; daughter of Erechtheus, ii. 103; married to Xuthus, 103

Creusa, daughter of Priam and Hecuba, ii. 47

Criasus, son of Argus, succeeds his father in the kingdom of Argos, i. 131

Crimissa, near Croton, Philoctetes settles at, ii. 261

Crino, wife of Danaus, i. 143

Crius, a Titan, i. 5; father of Astraeus, Pallas, and Perses, 13

Croco, father of Meganira, i. 397

Croesus, family of, descended from Agelaus, son of Hercules, i. 275

Crommyon, the sow at, offspring of Echidna and Typhon, ii. 129; slain by Theseus, 129

Cronus, youngest of the Titans, mutilates his father Sky, i. 5; his sovereignty, 7; marries Rhea, swallows his offspring, 7; deceived by Rhea, 9; father of Chiron, 13

Croton, Crimissa near, ii. 261

Crown, a golden, Procris bribed by a, ii. 103, 105

INDEX

Cteatus, father of Amphimachus, ii. 27

Cteatus. *See* Eurytus

Ctesippus, two sons of Hercules, i. 275, 277

Ctesippus, suitor of Penelope, from Ithaca, ii. 299

Ctesippus, suitor of Penelope, from Same, ii. 297

Ctesius, suitor of Penelope, ii. 297

Curetes, guards of infant Zeus, i. 7, 9; at war with the Calydonians, 69; make away with Epaphus, 135; killed by Zeus, 135; tell Minos how to recover his dead son, 311

Curetian country, Aetolia, i. 61

Curses at sacrifices to Hercules (at Lindus), i. 227

Cyanippus, son of Adrastus, i. 91

Cybela, in Phrygia, Dionysus at, i. 327

Cychreus, father of Glauce, ii. 53; son of Poseidon and Salamis, delivers island of Salamis from a snake and becomes king, 59; bequeaths the kingdom to Telamon, 59

Cyclopes, offspring of Sky and Earth, i. 3; bound and cast into Tartarus by Sky, 5; released by Zeus, they forge thunderbolts for him, 11; fortify Tiryns, 147; fashion the thunderbolt for Zeus, ii. 19; slain by Apollo, 19; Ulysses in the land of the, 281, 283, 285

Cyclops, Geraestus the, his grave at Athens, ii. 119

Cycnus, father of Tenes and Hemithea, ii. 193; believing a false accusation he sets them adrift on the sea, 193; learning the truth he stones one of the accusers, 195

Cycnus, son of Ares, his combat with Hercules, i. 221; slain by Hercules, 265

Cycnus, suitor of Penelope, ii. 297

Cyllene, a nymph, wife of Pelasgus, mother of Lycaon, according to some, i. 389

Cyllene, snakes seen copulating on, i. 365; in Arcadia, the Pleiades born at, ii. 3; Hermes born in a

cave on, 5; invents the lyre on, 9

Cyme, city, taken by Achilles, ii. 203

Cymo, a Nereid, i. 15

Cymothoe, a Nereid, i. 15

Cynaethus, son of Lycaon, i. 389

Cynnus, suitor of Penelope, ii. 297

Cynortas (Cynortes), son of Amyclas, i. 81, ii. 11; father of Perieres, 13

Cyprus, Phrasius, a seer from, i. 225; Cinyras, in ii. 83, 179; Pygmalion, king of, 85; Alexander (Paris) tarries in, 175; Greeks settle in, 257; Agapenor settles in, 259; Phidippus settles in, 259; Demophon settles in, 265

Cyrene, mother of Diomedes the Thracian, by Ares, i. 201

Cytheria, the banished Thyestes dwells in, ii. 171

Cytisorus, son of Phrixus, i. 77

Cyzicus, king of the Doliones, i. 99; slain by the Argonauts, 101

Daedalus makes a statue of Hercules at Pisa, i. 243; architect, banished from Athens for murder, 305; makes an artificial cow for Pasiphae, 305; son of Eupalamus, architect and first inventor of images, ii. 121; murders his nephew Talos, 121; tried and condemned in the Areopagus, 123; flees to Minos, 123; accomplice of Pasiphae, 123; constructs the labyrinth, 121, 123; besought by Ariadne to disclose the way out of the labyrinth, 135; shut up by Minos in the labyrinth, 139; makes wings for himself and flies to Camicus in Sicily, 139, 141; pursued and detected by Minos, 141

Daëmon, suitor of Penelope, ii. 299

Daesenor, suitor of Penelope, ii. 299

Daiphron, son of Egyptus, husband of Scaea, i. 139

Daiphron, son of Egyptus, husband of Adiante, i. 143

Damasichthon, son of Amphion and Niobe, i. 341

Damasippus, son of Icarius, ii. 23

INDEX

Damasistratus, king of Plataea, buries Laius, i. 347

Damastes, or Polypemon, a malefactor, slain by Theseus, ii. 131, 133

Damastor, suitor of Penelope, ii. 297

Danae, daughter of Acrisius, i. 147 ; shut up in a brazen chamber, 153, 155 ; conceives Perseus by Zeus, 155 ; cast into sea and drifts with Perseus to Seriphus, 155 ; loved by Polydectes, 155 ; returns with Perseus to Argos, 161

Danai, old name of the Argives, i. 137

Danaus, son of Belus, i. 137 ; settled in Libya, 137 ; has fifty daughters, 137 ; the first to build a ship, 137 ; flees with his daughters to Argos and obtains the kingdom, 137 ; consents to marry his daughters to the sons of Egyptus, 139, 141, 143 ; his daughters murder their husbands, 143 ; gives his daughters to victors in an athletic contest, 143

Dance, frenzied, of the mad daughters of Proetus, i. 149

Dardania, country named after Dardanus, ii. 35

Dardanians, Trojan allies, ii. 205

Dardanus, a city built by Dardanus, i. 35

Dardanus, son of Zeus and Electra, ii. 35 ; leaves Samothrace, marries the daughter of King Teucer, and calls the country Dardania, 35 ; father of Idaea, 107

Dascylus, father of Lycus, i. 205

Daulia, in Phocis, Procne and Philomela at, ii. 101

Dawn, daughter of Hyperion and Thia, i. 13 ; mother of winds and stars, 13 ; loves Orion, 33 ; bedded with Ares, 33 ; caused by Aphrodite to be perpetually in love, 33 ; forbidden by Zeus to shine, 45 ; carries off Cephalus, 79 ; loves Tithonus and carries him to Ethiopia, ii. 43 ; bears to him Emathion and Memnon, 43 ; carries off Cephalus and bears him a son Tithonus, 83

Dead raised to life by Aesculapius

by means of the Gorgon's blood, ii. 17

Dearth, human sacrifices as a remedy for, i. 225, 227

Deer substituted for Iphigenia at the altar, ii. 193

Deianira, daughter of Oeneus, i. 65, 257 ; Hercules wrestles for her with Achelous, 65, 257 ; receives the poison from Nessus, 261 ; sends the poisoned robe to Hercules, 269 ; hangs herself, 269 ; her sons by Hercules, 275

Deicoön, son of Hercules by Megara, i. 181, 275

Deidamia, daughter of Lycomedes, intrigue of Achilles with, ii. 75 ; mother of Pyrrhus (Neoptolemus) by Achilles, 75 ; given by Neoptolemus in marriage to Helenus, 251

Deimachus, father of Enarete, i. 57

Deimachus, son of Neleus, i. 85

Deion, son of Aeolus, i. 57 ; reigns over Phocis, 79 ; marries Diomede, father of Cephalus, 79, ii. 103

Deioneus, father of Cephalus, i. 171

Deiopites, son of Priam, ii. 49

Deiphobus, son of Hippolytus, purifies Hercules for the murder of Iphitus, i. 239

Deiphobus, son of Priam and Hecuba, ii. 49 ; awarded Helen after the death of Alexander (Paris), 223 ; slain by Menelaus, 237

Deiphontes, husband of Hyrnetho, i. 291 ; promoted with his wife to the kingdom (of Argos), 291

Deipyle, daughter of Adrastus, wife of Tydeus, i. 73, 91, 353

Deliades, brother of Bellerophon, accidentally killed by him, i. 149

Delos, formerly called Asteria, i. 25 ; birth of Apollo and Artemis in, 25 ; Orion in, 31, 33

Delphi, Apollo, Themis, and the Python at, i. 27 ; Tityus at, 29 ; oracle at, 75 ; Hercules inquires of the oracle at, 183 ; Hercules at, 239, 241 ; Hyllus inquires of the oracle at, 283 ; Cadmus inquires of the oracle at, 313 ; Oedipus inquires of the oracle at, 345 ; portion of Theban booty

INDEX

Orpheus, i. 19; kills Eurytus, 45; gives the first vine-plant to Oeneus, 63, 65; father of Deianira by Althaea, 65; drives the women of Argos mad, 91; father of Phanus and Staphylus, 97; rites of, rejected by the daughters of Proetus, 147; offspring of Zeus and Semele, 319; sewn up in his father's thigh, 319; entrusted to Hermes, 319; reared as a girl by Athamas and Ino, 319; turned into a kid, 321; brought by Hermes to the nymphs at Nysa, 321; discovers the vine, 325; driven mad by Hera he roams Egypt and Syria, 325, 327; received by Proetus, king of Egypt, 327; comes to Phrygia, where he is purified by Rhea and learns the rites of initiation, 327; passes through Thrace, 327; expelled by Lycurgus, 327; takes refuge in the sea, 327; drives Lycurgus mad, 327; causes him to be put to death, 331; traverses Thrace and India and sets up pillars, 331; comes to Thebes and sets the women raving, 331; comes to Argos and drives the women mad, 331; is ferried to Naxos by pirates, whom he turns into dolphins, 331, 333; recognized as a god, brings up his mother from Hades and ascends with her to heaven, 333; comes to Attica, ii. 95; received by Icarius, 97; carries off Ariadne from Naxos to Lemnos, 137; grants the daughters of Anius the power to produce oil, corn, and wine, 179, 181

Diopithes, suitor of Penelope, ii. 297

Dioscuri, the name given to Castor and Pollux, ii. 31; carry off and marry Hilaira and Phoebe, daughters of Leucippus, 13, 31; drive away cattle from Messene, 33; translated to the gods, 35; help Peleus to lay waste Iolcus, 71, 73; capture Athens and rescue Helen, 153; restore Menestheus and give him the sovereignty of Athens, 153. See also Castor and Pollux

Dioxippe, daughter of Danaus, i. 143

Dirce, wife of Lycus, ill-treats Antiope, i. 339; is tied by Antiope's sons to a bull, 339; her body thrown into a spring, which is called Dirce after her, 339

Disease a consequence of murder, i. 239; cured by servitude and compensation for the murder, 241

Divination, art of, taught by Polyidus to Glaucus, i. 313; learned by Hermes from Apollo, ii. 11; practised by Calchas, 191; trial of skill in the art of, between Calchas and Mopsus, 243 sq. See Prophecy, Soothsaying

Dodona, the oak of, i. 97

Doe, Telephus suckled by a, i. 255, 257, 397

Dog, unapproachable, i. 89; wonderful, given by Minos to Procris, 173. ii. 205; hunts the (Teumessian) vixen and is turned to stone, i. 173

Dogs of Actaeon, i. 323, 325

Doliche, old name of the island of Icaria, i. 243

Doliones, the Argonauts among the, i. 99, 101; harassed by the Pelasgians, 101

Dolon, son of Eumelus, killed by Ulysses and Diomedes, ii. 207

Dolopians, Phoenix made king of the, by Peleus, ii. 75

Dominion, born of Pallas and Styx, i. 13

Dorians, descended from Dorus, i. 57; Hercules fights for the, against the Lapiths, 263

Doris, an Oceanid, i. 13; wife of Nereus, 15

Dorium, daughter of Danaus, wife of Cercetes, i. 141

Dorus, father of Xanthippe, i. 61

Dorus, son of Apollo, killed by Aetolus, i. 61

Dorus, son of Hellen, ancestor of the Dorians, i. 57

Dorycleus, son of Hippocoon, ii. 21

Doryclus, son of Priam, ii. 49

Dotis, mother of Phlegyas, i. 337

Doto, a Nereid, i. 15

INDEX

INDEX

Menelaus driven by a storm to, 243; Helen found by Menelaus in, 279

Egyptians identify Demeter with Isis, i. 135

Egyptus, son of Belus, conquers and reigns over Egypt, i. 137; has fifty sons, 137; his sons come to Argos, marry the daughters of Danaus, and are murdered by them, 139, 141, 143

Egyptus, son of Egyptus, husband of Dioxippe, i. 141, 143

Eight years' period, i. 317

Eione, a Nereid, i. 15

Elachia, daughter of Thespius, mother of Buleus by Hercules, i. 275

Elais, daughter of Anius, one of the Wine-growers, ii. 179, 181

Elare, daughter of Orchomenus, mother of Tityus by Zeus, i. 27

Elato, charioteer of Amphiaraus, i. 371

Elatus, a centaur, wounded by Hercules, i. 193

Elatus, father of Polyphemus, i. 99

Elatus, son of Arcas, joint ruler of Arcadia, father of Stymphalus and Pereus, i. 397

Elatus, suitor of Penelope, ii. 297

Eleans, Polyxenus, king of the, i. 169; war of Hercules with the, 249; their muster for the Trojan war, ii. 183. See also Elis

Electra, an Oceanid, i. 11, 13; mother of Iris and the Harpies by Thaumas, 15

Electra, daughter of Atlas, one of the Pleiades, ii. 3; has Iasion and Dardanus by Zeus, 35; takes refuge at the Palladium, 41

Electra, daughter of Agamemnon, ii. 171, 271; saves Orestes and entrusts him to Strophius, 271; married to Pylades, 277

Electra, daughter of Danaus wife of Peristhenes, i. 141

Electran gate of Thebes, i. 361

Electryon, son of Perseus, i. 163; father of Alcmena, 165; king of Mycenae, 167; his sons slay the sons of Pterelaus, 169; accidentally killed by Amphitryon, 169

Elephantis, wife of Danaus, i. 141

Elephenor, son of Chalcodon, suitor of Helen, ii. 27; leader of the Euboeans against Troy, 183; dies in Troy, 259; his people inhabit Apollonia in Epirus, 259

Eleusinians, their war with the Athenians, ii. 109

Eleusis, Demeter at, i. 37, 39, ii. 95; the Laughless Rock at, i. 37; Well of the Fair Dances at, 37; the centaurs, fleeing from Hercules, are received and hidden by Poseidon at, 193, 195; Hercules initiated by Eumolpus at, 233

Eleusis, father of Triptolemus, according to Panyasis, i. 39

Eleuther, son of Apollo by Aethusa, ii. 5

Eleutherae, in Boeotia, Amphion and Zethus born at, i. 337, 339

Elis, founded by Endymion, i. 61; Salmoneus founds a city in, which is destroyed by thunderbolt, 81; Augeas, king of, 195; captured by Hercules, 249; Oxylus flees to, 289; Pisa in, ii. 163. See also Eleans

Elpenor, Ulysses sees the ghost of, ii. 289

Elymi, in Sicily, Eryx king of the, i. 217

Elysian Fields, Cadmus and Harmonia sent by Zeus to the, i. 335; Menelaus and Helen go to the, ii. 279

Emathion, son of Tithonus, slain by Hercules, i. 229; son of Tithonus and Dawn, i. 43

Emulation, born of Pallas and Styx, i. 13

Enarete, daughter of Deimachus, wife of Aeolus, i. 57

Enarophorus, son of Hippocoon, ii. 21

Enceladus, a giant, overwhelmed under Sicily by Athena, i. 45

Enceladus, son of Egyptus, husband of Amymone, i. 139

Encheleans get Cadmus and Harmonia to help them against the Illyrians, i. 335

Endeis, daughter of Sciron, wife of Aeacus, ii. 53

Endium, a city, taken by Achilles, ii. 203

INDEX

Endymion, founder of Elis, beloved by the Moon, his eternal sleep, i. 61; father of Aetolus, 61

Enipeus, river, loved by Tyro, i. 81

Ennomus, son of Arsinous, a Mysian leader, ii. 205

Entelides, son of Hercules, by Menippis, i. 273

Enyo, daughter of Phorcus, i. 155

Eone, daughter of Thespius, mother of Amestrius by Hercules, i. 275

Epaphus, son of Io, i. 135; put out of the way by the Curetes, 135; discovered in Byblus by Io, 135; reigns over Egypt, 135; founds Memphis, 135; father of Lysianassa, 225

Epeus, victor in boxing, ii. 211; an architect, constructs the Wooden Horse, 229, 231

Ephemeral fruits, i. 51

Ephesus, the Cercopes at, i. 241

Ephialtes, a giant, shot by Apollo and Hercules, i. 45

Ephialtes, one of the Aloads, son of Poseidon by Iphimedia, woos Hera, i. 59. See Otus, Aloads

Ephyra (Corinth) founded by Sisyphus, i. 79

Ephyra in Thesprotia, captured by Hercules, i. 259

Epicasta, daughter of Menoeceus, i. 343. See Jocasta

Epicaste, daughter of Augeas, mother of Thestalus by Hercules, i. 277

Epicaste, daughter of Calydon, wife of Agenor, i. 61

Epicnemedian Locrians join Hercules in his attack on Oechalia, i. 265

Epidaurus, son of Argus, i. 131

Epigoni, their war on Thebes, i. 91, 377, 379, 381

Epilais, daughter of Thespius, mother of Astyanax by Hercules, i. 273

Epilaus, son of Neleus, i. 85

Epimetheus, son of Iapetus and Asia, i. 13; husband of Pandora and father of Pyrrha, 53

Epirus, the sons of Alcmaeon, journey to, i. 387; Apollonia in,

ii. 259; Ulysses journeys through, 301; Neoptolemus, king of the islands off, 307

Epistrophus, son of Iphitus, suitor of Helen, ii. 27

Epistrophus, son of Mecisteus, leader of the Alizones, ii. 205

Epochus, son of Lycurgus, i. 399

Epopeus, son of Poseidon by Canace, i. 59; king of Sicyon, marries Antiope, 337; killed by Lycus, 337

Erasippus, son of Hercules by Lysippe, i. 275

Erato, a Muse, i. 17

Erato, a Nereid, i. 15

Erato, daughter of Danaus, wife of Bromius, i. 141

Erato, daughter of Thespius, mother of Dynastes by Hercules, i. 273

Erechtheis, the (so-called) sea on the Acropolis of Athens, produced by Poseidon, ii. 79

Erechtheus, father of Creusa, i. 57; father of Procris, 79; twin son of Pandion, ii. 99; succeeds to the kingdom, 101; marries Praxithea, 103; his children, 103; in the war with the Eleusinians he slaughters his youngest daughter for victory, and the other daughters slaughter themselves, 111; kills Eumolpus, 111; he and his house destroyed by Poseidon, 111

Erginus, son of Clymenus, king of Orchomenus, exacts tribute from the Thebans and is killed by Hercules, i. 179, 181

Erginus, son of Poseidon, in the Argo, i. 97

Erichthonius, son of Dardanus, succeeds to the kingdom, ii. 37; husband of Astyoche, father of Tros, 37

Erichthonius, son of Hephaestus and Atthis or Athena, ii. 89, 91; put in a chest and entrusted by Athena to Pandrosus, 91; brought up by Athena in the precinct, 91, 93; king of Athens, 93; sets up a wooden image of Athena, 93; institutes the Panathenaea, 93; marries Praxithea, 95; father of Pandion, 95; buried in the precinct of Athena, 95

Eridanus, river, the Argonauts at

487

INDEX

carried to Ethiopia, 109; being banished, he goes to Thrace, of which he becomes king, 109; fights for the Eleusinians against the Athenians, 109, 111; killed by Erechtheus, 111; father of Ismarus, 109

Eumolpus, a flute player, falsely accuses Tenes, ii. 193; killed by Cycnus, 195

Eumon, son of Lycaon, i. 389

Euneus, son of Jason, i. 9

Eunice, a Nereid, i. 15

Eunomus, son of Architeles, killed by Hercules, i. 259

Eupalamus, father of Metiadusa, ii. 111; son of Metion, father of Daedalus, 121

Euphemus, son of Poseidon, in the Argo, i. 97

Euphemus, son of Troezenus, leader of the Cicones, ii. 205

Euphorbus wounds Patroclus, ii.209

Euphorion, on the dedication of the bow of Philoctetes to Apollo, ii. 261

Euphrosyne, a Grace, i. 17

Eupinytus, son of Amphion and Niobe, i. 341

Euripides, on the sons of Belus, i. 137; on the death of Parthenopaeus, 369; on the children of Alcmaeon, 387; as to the father and husband of Atalanta, 401, 403

Europa on the bull, i. 199; daughter of Agenor or of Phoenix, 297, 299; loved by Zeus, who carries her on a bull through the sea to Crete, 299; she bears him Minos, Sarpedon, and Rhadamanthys, 299; sought for by her brothers, her mother, and Thasus, 299, 301; married by Asterius, 301; her descendants, 313; gives necklace to Harmonia, 317

Europe, traversed by Io, i. 133; traversed by Hercules on his way to fetch the kine of Geryon, 211; and Libya, pillars of Hercules at the boundaries of, 211, 213; and Asia embroiled by the will of Zeus, ii. 171

Europe, wife of Danaus, i. 139

Eurotas, son of Lelex, father of Sparta, ii. 11

Euryale, a Gorgon, i. 157

Euryale, mother of Orion by Poseidon, i. 31

Euryalus, son of Mecisteus, i. 91; in the Argo, 97; one of the Epigoni, 379

Euryalus, son of Melas, killed by Tydeus, i. 71, 73

Euryalus, suitor of Penelope from Dulichium, ii. 297

Euryalus, suitor of Penelope from Zacynthos, ii. 299

Eurybia, daughter of Sea, mother of Astraeus, Pallas, and Perses, i. 13, 15

Eurybia, daughter of Thespius, mother of Polylaus by Hercules, i. 273

Eurybius, son of Eurystheus, slain in battle with the Athenians, i. 277

Eurybius, son of Neleus, i. 85

Eurycapys, son of Hercules by Clytippe, i. 273

Eurydamas, son of Egyptus, husband of Phartis, i. 141

Eurydice, daughter of Adrastus, wife of Ilus, ii. 43

Eurydice, daughter of Danaus, wife of Dryas, i. 141

Eurydice, daughter of Lacedaemon, wife of Acrisius, mother of Danae, i. 147, ii. 11

Eurydice, wife of Lycurgus, mother of Opheltes, i. 91, 357

Eurydice, wife of Orpheus, dies of snake-bite, i. 17; sent up from Hades by Pluto, but obliged to return, 17, 19

Eurygania, daughter of Hyperphas, wife of Oedipus, according to some, i. 349

Eurylochus, a companion of Ulysses, reports to him the enchantments of Circe, ii. 287, 289

Eurylochus, son of Danaus, husband of Autonoe, i. 141

Eurylochus, suitor of Penelope, ii. 299

Eurymede, wife of Glaucus, mother of Bellerophon, i. 79

Eurymedon, son of Minos, in Paros, i. 203, 303

Eurymenes, son of Neleus, i. 85

Eurynome, an Oceanid, i. 13;

489

INDEX

Evadne, daughter of Iphis, burns herself with the corpse of her husband Capaneus, i. 375

Evadne, daughter of Strymon, wife of Argus, i. 131

Evaemon, father of Eurypylus, ii. 27

Evaemon, son of Lycaon, i. 389

Evagoras, son of Neleus, i. 85

Evagoras, son of Priam, ii. 49

Evagore, a Nereid, i. 15

Evander, son of Priam, ii. 49

Evenorides, suitor of Penelope from Dulichium, ii. 297

Evenorides, suitor of Penelope from Zacynthos, ii. 299

Evenus, a river, i. 63; the centaur Nessus at the, 261

Evenus, son of Ares, father of Marpessa, i. 63; throws himself into a river, which is named after him, 63

Everes, father of Tiresias, i. 361

Everes, son of Hercules by Parthenope, i. 277

Everes (Eueres), son of Pterelaus, i. 165; survives the slaughter of his brothers, 169

Evippe, daughter of Danaus, wife of Argius, i. 141

Evippe, daughter of Danaus, wife of Imbrus, i. 141

Evippus, son of Thestius, i. 63

Exile the penalty for homicide, i. 61, 261, 283, 287, 289, 305, 335, 337, ii. 57, 105

Exole, daughter of Thespius, mother of Erythras by Hercules, i. 273

Extremities of human victim cut off, i. 329

Fates, the, daughters of Zeus and Themis, i. 15; slay two giants, 47; beguile Typhon, 51; predict the death of Meleager, 65; allow Admetus a substitute to die for him, 93

Fennel, fire hidden in a stalk of, i. 51

Fire, Demophon put on the, by Demeter to make him immortal, i. 37, 39; stolen by Prometheus and given to men, 51; fire-breathing bulls, 109, 111; Her-

cules throws his children into the, 183; Achilles put by Thetis on the, to make him immortal, ii. 69, 71; Broteas throws himself into the, 155, 157; sacred fire into which the Taurians throw strangers, 273

First fruits sacrificed to the gods, i. 65, 67

Flesh of infants eaten by women in Bacchic frenzy, i. 331

Flood in Deucalion's time, i. 55, ii. 89. *See* Deucalion

Fox a symbol of Messene, i. 291

Furies, born of the flowing blood of Sky, i. 5; pursue Orestes, ii. 271

Fury, Demeter in the likeness of a, i. 373; of Eriphyle pursues her murderer Alcmaeon, 383

Gadfly sent by Hera to infest Io in cow-form, i. 133; sent by Hera to torment the cows of Hercules, 217

Gadira, the kine of Geryon in, i. 211

Galatea, a Nereid, i. 15

Games celebrated in honour of father of Teutamides, i. 163; in honour of Archemorus, 359; in honour of Pelias, 399, ii. 63; held by king of Phrygia, 37; in honour of Laius at Thebes, 117; in honour of Patroclus, 211; in honour of Achilles, 217

Ganymede, son of Tros, caught up by Zeus on an eagle and made cupbearer of the gods, ii. 37; horses given by Zeus as compensation for the rape of, i. 209

Gelanor, king of Argos, surrenders the kingdom to Danaus, i. 137

Genetor, son of Lycaon, i. 389

Geraestus, Cape, Myrtilus thrown into the sea at, ii. 163

Geraestus, the Cyclops, the daughters of Hyacinth sacrificed on the grave of, ii. 119

Gerenians, Nestor brought up among the, i. 85, 251

Geryon, son of Chrysaor, i. 159; a triple-bodied giant in Erythia, 211; killed and his kine driven away by Hercules, 215

Giants, sons of Sky and Earth,

INDEX

Deucalion's time, i. 55; kings of, go to Sparta to woo Helen, ii. 27; delivered from dearth by prayer of Aeacus, 55; army raised in, for war against Troy, 177; Trojan women dread slavery in, 263

Greeks named Hellenes after Hellen, i. 57; ravage Mysia, taking it for Troy, ii. 187; repulsed by Telephus, they return home, 187; at Troy make a wall to protect the roadstead, 207; chased by the Trojans, 207, 209; many of them slain by Memnon, 213; after ten years of war the Greeks despondent, 224; fetch the bones of Pelops, 225; dedicate the Wooden Horse to Athena, 233; lighted to Troy by a beacon, 235; spare Aeneas and Anchises, 237; Zeus sends a storm on the, 247; refuse satisfaction to Nauplius for the death of Palamedes, 249; wives of the, persuaded to be unfaithful, 249; their wanderings and settlements in various countries, 257; lose their ships and settle in Italy, 263

Guneus, father of Laonome, i. 165

Guneus, son of Ocytus, leader of the Aeanianians against Troy, ii. 185; settles in Libya, 257, 259

Gyes, a Hundred-handed, i. 3

Gyrtonians, their muster for the Trojan war, ii. 185

Hades, Tartarus a place in, i. 5; Pluto, lord of, 11; Styx in, 13; descent of Orpheus to, 17; Tityus in, 29; Side in, 31; Ascalaphus in 39, 237; Sisyphus in, 79; Alcestis brought up from, 93; the mouth of, at Taenarum, 233, 235; Hercules in, 233, 235, 237; Cerberus brought up by Hercules from, 233, 237; Theseus and Pirithous in, 235, 237; Meleager and the Gorgon Medusa in, 235; Rhadamanthys and Minos judges in, 301; Dionysus brings up his mother (Semele) from, 333; Aeacus keeps the keys of, ii. 57; descent of Theseus and Pirithous

to, 153; punishment of Tantalus in, 155; Protesilaus brought up from, 199, and carried back to, 201; fire wafted up from, 273

Hades, the cap of, which rendered the wearer invisible, i. 157, 159; the kine of, i. 215, 237; wounded by Hercules at Pylus, 251. *See* Pluto

Haemo, son of Lycaon, i. 389

Haemon, son of Creon, killed by the Sphinx, i. 349

Haemus, Mount, in Thrace, i. 51; traversed by Io, 133

Hagius, suitor of Penelope, ii. 297

Hagnias, father of Tiphys, i. 97

Hair cut off in mourning, i. 101; golden hair of Pterelaus, 165, 173; of Gorgon turns enemies to flight, 253; purple hair of Nisus, ii. 173; of Locrian maidens cropped at Troy, 267

Halie, a Nereid, i. 15

Halimede, a Nereid, i. 15

Halipherus, son of Lycaon, i. 389

Halirrhothius, son of Poseidon killed by Ares, ii. 81

Halius, suitor of Penelope, ii. 299

Halocrates, son of Hercules, by Olympusa, i. 275

Hamadryad nymphs, mothers of children by Danaus, i. 141

Hanging as a mode of suicide, i. 71, 121, 269, 349, ii. 51, 65, 97, 147

Harmonia, daughter of Ares and Aphrodite, married to Cadmus, i. 317; receives a necklace made by Hephaestus, 317; goes with Cadmus to the Encheleans and is turned into a serpent, 335; sent by Zeus to the Elysian Fields, 335

Harpaleus, son of Lycaon, i. 389

Harpalycus, son of Lycaon, i. 389

Harpies, the, offspring of Thaumas and Electra, i. 15; molest Phineus, chased away by Zetes and Calais, 105, 107, ii. 105, 107

Harpys, river in Peloponnese, i. 105

Heads of murdered sons of Egyptus buried at Lerna, i. 143; of unsuccessful suitors of Hippodamia nailed to her father's house, ii. 161

Heaven attacked by Typhon, i. 49; Hercules carried up to, 271;

493

INDEX

INDEX

against Troy, 61; kills Zetes and Calais, 107; Troy not to be taken without the bow of, 221, 223

Herds of Augeas, i. 195

Hermes slays giant Hippolytus, i. 47; steals the severed sinews of Zeus, 49; sent by Zeus to Deucalion, 55; rescues Ares, 59, 61; gives ram with golden fleece to Nephele, 75; father of Auto- lycus, 97; father of Eurytus, 97; ordered by Zeus to steal Io in form of a cow, 133; kills Argus the All-seeing, 133; hence called Argiphontes, 133; and Athena purify the Danaids for the murder of their husbands, 143; guides Perseus to the Phorcides, 155; gives Perseus an adaman- tine sickle, 157; receives the winged sandals, wallet, and cap of Hades from Perseus and re- stores them to the nymphs, 161; gives Hercules a sword, 183; father of Abderus, 201; admonishes Hercules in Hades, 235; sells Hercules to Omphale, 241; loves Apemosyne, 309; conveys infant Dionysus to Ino and Athamas, 319; brings Dionysus to the nymphs at Nysa, 321; gives Amphion a lyre, 339; son of Zeus by Maia, born on Cyllene, ii. 5; goes to Pieria and steals the kine of Apollo, 5, 7, 9; makes a lyre from tortoise-shell, 9; makes a shepherd's pipe, 9; gets from Apollo a golden wand and the art of divination, 11; appointed herald of the gods, 11; father of Cephalus by Herse, 83; sent by Zeus with a message to Atreus, 165; leads the goddesses to be judged by Alexander on Ida, 173; steals Helen and carries her to Egypt, 175; brings up Protesilaus from Hades, 199; gives moly to Ulysses, 289; father of Pan by Penelope, 305

Hermion, Pluto at, i. 35

Hermione, daughter of Menelaus and Helen, ii. 29; daughter of Helen, abandoned by her mother, 175; betrothed to Neoptolemus,

253; wife of Orestes, 253, 277; carried off by Neoptolemus, 253

Hermus, son of Egyptus, husband of Cleopatra, i. 141

Herodorus, on Hercules and Om- phale, i. 101; on the children of Niobe, 343

Heroes, sacrifices to, i. 185; and heroines, Ulysses sees the souls of, ii. 289

Herse, daughter of Cecrops, ii. 81; mother of Cephalus by Hermes,83

Herse, wife of Danaus, i. 143

Hesiod, on Periboea, i. 71; on one of the Harpies, 105; on Pelasgus, 131, 389; on Io, 131, 133; on lovers' oaths, 131; on the mad- ness of the daughters of Proetus, 147; on the Chimera, 151; on the *kibisis*, 157; on the children of Niobe, 341; on the changes of sex experienced by Tiresias, 363, 365; as to Callisto, 395; on the father of Atalanta, 401; on Adonis, ii. 85

Hesione, daughter of Laomedon, exposed to a sea monster, rescued by Hercules, i. 207, 209; given by him to Telamon, 245, 247; she ransoms her brother Podarces (Priam), 247; daughter of Laomedon, ii. 43; given as a prize to Telamon, 61; mother of Teucer by Telamon, 61

Hesione, wife of Nauplius, i. 145

Hesperia, one of the Hesperides, i. 221

Hesperides, the golden apples of the, on Atlas, among the Hyper- boreans, guarded by a dragon, i. 219, 221; given by Atlas to Hercules, who brings them to Eurystheus, 231; carried back by Athena 231

Hestia, first-born of Cronus, swal- lowed by him, i. 7

Hestiaea, city built by the exiled Thebans, i. 381

Hesychia, daughter of Thespius, mother of Oestrobles by Her- cules, i. 275

Hicetaon, son of Laomedon, ii. 43

Hierax blabs on Io, i. 133

Hieromneme, daughter of Simoeis, wife of Assaracus, ii. 37

497

INDEX

Hilaira, daughter of Leucippus, carried off by the Dioscuri, ii. 13 ; bears Anogon to Castor, 33

Hind, the Cerynitian hind with the golden horns brought by Hercules to Mycenae, i. 191

Hippalcimus, father of Peneleos, ii. 27

Hippalmus, father of Peneleus, i. 97

Hippasus, father of Actor, i. 97

Hippasus, son of Ceyx, buried by Hercules, i. 267

Hippeus, son of Hercules by Procris, i. 273

Hippo, daughter of Thespius, mother of Capylus by Hercules, i. 273

Hippocoon, son of Oebalus by Batia, ii. 21 ; king of Lacedaemon, i. 251 ; his sons, ii. 21, 23 ; he and his sons fight for Neleus against Hercules, i. 251 ; they kill the son of Licymnius, 251 ; they expel Icarius and Tyndareus from Lacedaemon, ii. 23 ; they are killed by Hercules, i. 253, ii. 23

Hippocoöntids, the sons of Hippocoon, kill the son of Licymnius, i. 251, 253. See Hippocoon

Hippocorystes, son of Egyptus, husband of Hyperippe, i. 143

Hippocorystes, son of Hippocoon, ii. 23

Hippocrate, daughter of Thespius, mother of Hippozygus by Hercules, i. 275

Hippodamas, son of Achelous, i. 57 ; father of Euryte, 63

Hippodamas, son of Priam, ii. 49

Hippodamia, daughter of Danaus, wife of Istrus, i. 141

Hippodamia, daughter of Danaus, wife of Diocorystes, i. 141

Hippodamia, daughter of Oenomaus, wooed by Polydectes, i. 155 ; offered as a prize to the victor in a chariot-race, ii. 157, 161 ; her suitors put to death by her father, 159, 161 ; loves Pelops and is won by him, 161, 163 ; persuades Myrtilus to help Pelops in the race, 161

Hippodamia, wooed by Pirithous, ii. 151 ; centaurs attempt to violate her, 151

Hippodice, daughter of Danaus, wife of Idas, i. 143

Hippodochus, suitor of Penelope, ii. 297

Hippodromus, son of Hercules by Anthippe, i. 273

Hippolochus, father of Glaucus, ii. 205

Hippolyte, an Amazon carried off by Theseus, ii. 143 ; also called Glauce and Melanippe, 213 ; daughter of Ares and Otrere, 211 ; mother of Hippolytus, 213 ; killed involuntarily by Penthesilia or by Theseus, 211, 213

Hippolyte, queen of the Amazons, killed by Hercules, i. 205 ; her belt brought by him to Eurystheus, i. 203, 205, 209

Hippolytus, a giant, slain by Hermes, i. 47

Hippolytus, father of Deiphobus, i. 239

Hippolytus, son of Egyptus, husband of Rhode, i. 141

Hippolytus, son of Theseus by the Amazon, ii. 145 ; loved and falsely accused by Phaedra, 145 ; cursed by Theseus, 145 ; dragged to death by his horses, 147 ; raised from the dead by Aesculapius, 17

Hippomachus, suitor of Penelope, ii. 299

Hippomedon, son of Aristomachus or of Talaus, one of the Seven against Thebes, i. 357 ; slain by Ismarus, 369

Hippomedusa, daughter of Danaus, wife of Alcmenor, i. 141

Hippomenes, father of Megareus, ii. 117

Hippomenes, husband of Atalanta, according to Euripides, i. 401, 403

Hipponoe, a Nereid, i. 15

Hipponome, daughter of Menoeceus, wife of Alcaeus, i. 165

Hipponous, father of Periboea, i. 71 ; father of Capaneus, 357

Hipponous, son of Priam and Hecuba, ii. 49

Hippostratus, son of Amarynceus, seduces Periboea, i. 71

Hippotes, son of Phylas, banished for homicide, i. 287

INDEX

INDEX

Idyia, daughter of Ocean, mother of Medea, i. 111

Ilissus, river, Orithyia carried off by Boreas at the, ii. 105

Ilithyia, daughter of Zeus and Hera, i. 15

Ilithyias, the, retard Alcmena's delivery, i. 167

Ilium captured by Hercules, i. 245; founded by Ilus, ii. 39; captured by Hercules, 45; not to be taken without the bones of Pelops, 223, 225; Calchas and others leave their ships at, 243; the sack of, 259, 261; Athena at, propitiated by the Locrians, 267; Ulysses sails from, 281. *See also* Troy

Illyria, traversed by Io, i. 133; Colchians journey to, 117; Hercules journeys through, 221, 223

Illyrians at war with the Encheleans, i. 335; conquered by Cadmus, 335

Illyrius, son of Cadmus and Harmonia, i. 335

Ilus, son of Dardanus, dies childless, ii. 37

Ilus, son of Tros, ii. 37; father of Themiste, 37; wins a prize for wrestling in Phrygia, 37; in obedience to an oracle founds Ilium, 39; receives the Palladium, 39; builds a temple for it, 43; father of Laomedon, 43

Images first invented by Daedalus, i. 121

Imbrus, son of Egyptus, husband of Evippe, i. 141

Imeusimus, son of Icarius, ii. 23

Impiety of Lycaon's sons, i. 389, 391, 395

Inachus, river in Argos i. 129

Inachus, son of Ocean, gives his name to river Inachus, i. 129; the family of, 129, 297; father of Io, 131, and of Argus, according to Asclepiades, 133; testifies that Argos belongs to Hera, 139

Incest of Oeneus with his daughter Gorge, i. 71; of Smyrna with her father Thias, ii. 87

India traversed by Dionysus, i. 331 (cp. 327); pillars set up by him there, 331

Indians, Medus marches against the, i. 125

Indius, two suitors of Penelope, both from Zacynthus, ii. 299

Infertility, human sacrifice to avert, i. 75; of land caused by murder, ii. 55

Ino, second wife of Athamas, plots against her step-children, i. 75; casts herself into the sea, 77; daughter of Cadmus, wife of Athamas, 317; rears Dionysus as a girl, 319; driven mad by Hera, throws her son Melicertes into a boiling cauldron, 319, 321; called Leucothoe as a sea-goddess, 321

Invulnerability of Meleager, i. 65; of Caeneus, ii. 151

Io, daughter of Iasus, Inachus, or Piren, i. 131; seduced by Zeus, 131; turned into a white cow, 133; her wanderings, 133; comes to Egypt and gives birth to Epaphus, 135; finds Epaphus at Byblus, 135; married to Telegonus, 135; called Isis by the Egyptians, 135

Iobates, king of Lycia, receives Proetus from Argos, i. 145; restores him to his own land, 145, 147; sends Bellerophon against the Chimera, 151; orders him to fight the Solymi and Amazons, 153; gives him his daughter Philonoe to wife and bequeaths to him the kingdom, 153

Iobes, son of Hercules by Certhe, i. 273

Iolaus, son of Iphicles, i. 181; charioteer of Hercules, 189; receives Megara in marriage from him, 237

Iolcus, Jason at, i. 67, 93, 95; founded by Cretheus, 85; Pelias, King of, 95; return of the Argonauts to, 121; Jason and Medea expelled from, 123; Peleus purified by Acastus at, ii. 63; laid waste by Peleus, who enters the city between the severed limbs of Astydamia, 73

Iole, daughter of Eurytus, wooed by Hercules, i. 237, 239; taken

INDEX

captive by Hercules, 267 ; Deianira jealous of, 269 ; Hercules enjoins Hyllus to marry, 269, 283

Ion, son of Xuthus, ancestor of the Achaeans, i. 57

Ione, a Nereid, i. 15

Ionian Gulf named after Io, i. 133 ; people of Elephenor cast away in the, ii. 259

Ionian Sea, Hercules drives the kine of Geryon to the, i. 217

Iphianassa, daughter of Proetus, goes mad with her sisters, i. 147

Iphianassa, wife of Endymion, mother of Aetolus, i. 61

Iphicles, son of Amphitryon, hunts the Calydonian boar, i. 67 ; son of Amphitryon and Alcmena, twin brother of Hercules, 175 ; father of Iolaus, 181 ; marries Creon's younger daughter, 181 ; two of his children burnt by Hercules, 183 ; killed in battle, 253

Iphiclus, son of Phylacus, how his virility was restored, i. 89, 91 ; father of Protesilaus. ii. 27, 185

Iphiclus, son of Thestius, i. 63 ; hunts the Calydonian boar, 69 ; in the Argo, 97

Iphidamas, suitor of Penelope, ii. 297

Iphigenia, daughter of Agamemnon and Clytaemnestra, said to have been betrothed to Achilles, ii. 191 ; about to be sacrificed by her father to Artemis, but carried off by Artemis to the Taurians, and appointed her priestess, 191, 193

Iphimedia, daughter of Triops, mother of the Aloads, i. 59

Iphimedon, son of Eurystheus, slain in battle by the Athenians, i. 277

Iphimedusa, daughter of Danaus, wife of Euchenor, i. 141

Iphinoe, daughter of Proetus, goes mad with her sisters, i. 147 ; her death, 149

Iphis, daughter of Thespius, mother of Celeustanor by Hercules, i. 273

Iphis, son of Alector, tells Polynices how to bribe Amphiaraus, i. 353, 355 ; father of Eteoclus, 357 ; father of Evadne, 375

Iphitus gives his bow to Ulysses, ii. 301

Iphitus killed by Copreus, i. 187.

Iphitus, son of Eurytus, supports the claim of Hercules to Iole, i. 239 ; thrown by Hercules from the walls of Tiryns, 239

Iphitus, son of Naubolus, in the Argo, i. 97 ; father of Schedius and Epistrophus, ii. 27

Iris, daughter of Thaumas and Electra, i. 15

Irus, a beggar, Ulysses wrestles with him, ii. 301

Ischys, brother of Caeneus, Coronis cohabits with, ii. 15

Isis identified with Demeter by the Egyptians, i. 135

Islands of the Blest, Achilles in the, ii. 5 ; Telegonus and Penelope sent by Circe to the, 305

Isles of the Blest, Achilles and Medea in the, ii. 217

Ismarus, a city of the Cicones, captured by Ulysses, ii. 281

Ismarus, son of Astacus, slays Hippomedon, i. 369

Ismarus, son of Eumolpus, marries the daughter of Tegyrius, king of Thrace, ii. 109

Ismene, daughter of Asopus, wife of Argus, i. 131

Ismene, daughter of Oedipus, i. 349

Ismenus, river, Amphiaraus flees beside the, i. 371

Ismenus, son of Amphion and Zethus, i. 341

Ismenus, son of Asopus, ii. 51

Isthmian festival, the third, i. 249 ; games instituted by Sisyphus in honour of Melicertes, 321

Isthmus (of Corinth), i. 55 ; the Argo dedicated to Poseidon at the, 121 ; traversed by the Cretan bull, 199, 201 ; cleared of malefactors by Theseus, 245 ; oracle concerning the, 285 ; Sinis at the, ii. 123 ; the goal of the chariot-race for the suitors of Hippodamia, 161

Istrus, son of Egyptus, husband of Hippodamia, i. 141

Italy, named after *italus*, "a bull," i. 217 ; Greeks settle in, ii. 257 ; the Campanians in, 257, 259 ;

INDEX

Campania in, 261; river Navaethus in, 261

Itanus, suitor of Penelope, ii. 297

Ithaca, Ulysses in, i. 177; Ulysses
in sight of, 285; suitors of
Penelope from, 299; Ulysses
returns from Thesprotia to, 303;
Telegonus comes to, 303

Ithacus, suitor of Penelope, ii. 297

Itonus, combat of Hercules with
Cycnus at, i. 263, 265

Itys, son of Tereus and Procne,
ii. 99; killed and served up by
his mother to his father, 101

Ixion, father of Pirithous, i. 67;
attempts to violate Hera, ii. 149;
deluded by a cloud in the likeness of Hera, 149; bound to
a wheel and whirled through the
air, 149

Jason, son of Aeson, hunts the
Calydonian boar, i. 67; son of
Aeson, 93; dwells in Iolcus, 93,
95; sent by Pelias to fetch the
Golden Fleece, 95; admiral of
the Argo, 99; bedded with
Hypsipyle, queen of Lemnos,
99; demands the Golden Fleece
from Aeetes, 109; yokes the
brazen-footed bulls, 109, 111;
swears to make Medea his wife,
111; sows the dragon's teeth,
111; wins the Golden Fleece and
flees with Medea, 113; marries
Medea in Corcyra, 117; on returning to Iolcus surrenders the
Golden Fleece to Pelias, 121;
dedicates the Argo to Poseidon at
Corinth, 121; expelled with
Medea from Iolcus, 123; goes
to Corinth, 123; marries Glauce
and divorces Medea, 123; helps
Peleus to lay waste Iolcus,
ii. 71, 73; sails with Zetes and
Calais, 105, 107

Jesting of women customary at a
sacrifice, i. 117

Jests at the Thesmophoria, i. 37

Jocasta, or Epicasta, daughter of
Menoeceus, wife of Laius, i. 343;
mother of Oedipus, 345; marries
her son unwittingly, and hangs
herself, 349

Justice, daughter of Zeus and
Themis, i. 15

Kibisis (wallet) given to Perseus by
the nymphs, i. 157; Medusa's
head put in it, 159

Kine (cows) of the Sun in Erythia,
i. 43; in Thrinacia, 115; tribute
of, paid by Thebes to Orchomenus, 179; of Hades, 215, 237;
of Geryon, 211; driven away by
Hercules, 215; sacrificed by
Eurystheus to Hera, 219; of
the Sun killed and eaten by the
comrades of Ulysses, ii. 295. *See*
Cow, Cows

Labdacus, son of Polydorus, father
of Laius, i. 335; war of Pandion
with, ii. 99

Labours, the ten, of Hercules,
i. 185-237; completed in eight
years and a month, 219

Labyrinth, constructed by Daedalus, house of the Minotaur,
i. 305, 307; the Minotaur confined
in the, ii. 119, 121; constructed
by Daedalus, 121; penetrated
by Theseus with the help of a
clue, 135, 137

Lacedaemon, Castor and Pollux at,
i. 67; expedition of Hercules
against, 251; allotted to the sons
of Aristodemus, 289; serpent a
symbol of, 291; Hyacinth comes
from, to Athens, ii. 119. *See*
Sparta

Lacedaemon, son of Zeus and
Taygete, ii. 11; the country
named after him, 11; father of
Amyclas and Eurydice, 11

Lacedaemonians help the Dioscuri
to capture Athens, ii. 153; their
muster for the Trojan war, 183

Lachesis, a Fate, i. 15

Laconia, Taenarum in, i. 235

Ladon river, the Cerynitian hind
shot by Hercules at the, i. 191;
father of Metope, ii. 51

Laertes, son of Arcisius, in the
Argo, i. 97; father of Ulysses,
ii. 27, 183; Penelope weaves the
shroud of, 299

INDEX

INDEX

Lyncaeus, son of Hercules by Tiphyse, i. 275

Lynceus, one of Actaeon's dogs, i. 325

Lynceus, son of Aphareus, hunts Calydonian boar, i. 67; in the Argo, 97; his sharp sight, ii. 13; spies Castor in ambush, 33; wounds Pollux, but is killed by him, 33

Lynceus, son of Egyptus, husband of Hypermnestra, i. 139; saved by his wife, 143; reigns over Argos, 145; father of Abas, 145

Lyre, Apollo plays with lyre upside down, i. 31; given by Hermes to Amphion, the stones follow it, 339; made by Hermes out of tortoiseshell and given by him to Apollo, ii. 9

Lyrnessus taken by Achilles, ii. 203

Lyrus, son of Anchises and Aphrodite, dies childless, ii. 37

Lyse, daughter of Thespius, mother of Eumedes by Hercules, i. 273

Lysianassa, daughter of Epaphus, mother of Busiris by Poseidon, i. 225

Lysianassa, a Nereid, i. 15

Lysidice, daughter of Pelops, wife of Mestor, i. 165

Lysidice, daughter of Thespius, mother of Teles by Hercules, i. 273

Lysimache, daughter of Abas, wife of Talaus, i. 91

Lysimache, daughter of Priam, ii. 49

Lysinomus, son of Electryon, i. 165

Lysippe, daughter of Proetus, goes mad, i. 147

Lysippe, daughter of Thespius, mother of Erasippus by Hercules, i. 275

Lysithous, son of Priam, ii. 49

Lytaea, daughter of Hyacinth, slaughtered with her sisters by the Athenians on the grave of Geraestus, ii. 119

Macareus, son of Lycaon, i. 389

Macednus, son of Lycaon, i. 389

Machaereus, a Phocian, said to have slain Neoptolemus at Delphi, ii. 255

Machaon, son of Aesculapius, suitor of Helen, ii. 27; wounded at Troy, 209; slain by Penthesilia, 211

Madness of Athamas, i. 77, 319; of the women of Argos, cured by Melampus, 91; of Talos, 119; of the daughters of Proetus, cured by Melampus, 147, 149; of Hercules, 183, 239; of Actaeon's dogs, 323; of Dionysus, 325; of Lycurgus, 327; of Agave, 331; of the women of Argos, 331; of the pirates, 331; of the matricide Alcmaeon, 383, 387; of the daughters of Cecrops, ii. 91; of Broteas, 157; pretended, of Ulysses, 177; of Ajax, 219; of the matricide Orestes, 271

Maenads tear Orpheus to pieces, i. 19

Maenalus, son of Lycaon, i. 389; instigates his brothers to offer to Zeus human bowels mixed with the sacrifices, 391

Maenalus, father of Atalanta, according to Euripides, i. 401, 403

Maeon, a Theban, escapes from Tydeus, i. 361

Maeonians, Trojan allies, ii. 205

Maera, dog of Icarius, discovers his dead body, ii. 97

Magnes, father of Pierus, i. 19

Magnes, son of Aeolus, i. 57; his sons colonize Seriphus, 81

Magnes, suitor of Penelope, ii. 299

Magnesians, their muster for the Trojan war, ii. 185; drift to Crete and settle there, 259

Maia, daughter of Atlas, one of the Pleiades, ii. 3; bears Hermes to Zeus, 5; shows the infant Hermes to Apollo, 9; receives the infant Arcas from Hermes to bring up in Arcadia, i. 397

Maid, the (Persephone), feats a seed of pomegranate given her by Pluto, i. 39, 41

Maiden, the (Persephone), sends up Alcestis, i. 93. See Persephone

Maidens sent as a propitiation by the Locrians to Athena at Ilium for a thousand years, ii. 267, 269

507

INDEX

INDEX

INDEX

Amymone, a wrecker, i. 143, 145; his sons by Clymene, or Philyra, or Hesione, 145; receives Auge to sell into a foreign land, 257; gives Auge to Teuthras, 257; receives Aerope and Clymene to sell into foreign lands, 309; marries Clymene, 309; father of Oeax and Palamedes, 309; receives Auge to put her to death, 397; gives her to Teuthras, 397; father of Palamedes, ii. 177, 249; demands satisfaction for the death of Palamedes, 249; contrives that the Greek wives should be unfaithful, 249; kindles false lights on Mount Caphereus and lures the Greeks on the breakers, 247, 249

Nauprestides, name given to the daughters of Laomedon, ii. 263

Nausicaa, daughter of Alcinous, king of the Phaeacians, brings Ulysses to her father, ii. 295

Nausimedon, son of Nauplius, i. 145

Nausithoe, a Nereid, i. 15

Navaethus, river of Italy, reason for the name, ii. 261, 263

Naxos, island, the Aloads in, i. 61; Dionysus ferried to, 331; Theseus and Ariadne in, ii. 137

Neaera, daughter of Amphion and Niobe, i. 341

Neaera, daughter of Pereus, wife of Aleus, i. 397

Neaera, wife of Strymon, mother of Evadne, i. 131

Nebrophonus, son of Jason by Hypsipyle, i. 99

Necklace made by Hephaestus and given to Harmonia at marriage, i. 317; taken by Polynices to Argos, 351, 353; given by Polynices to Eriphyle as a bribe, 355; given by Alcmaeon to his wife Arsinoe, 383; coveted by Callirrhoe, 385; dedicated at Delphi, 385, 387

Neleus, son of Poseidon by Tyro, twin brother of Pelias, i. 83; exposed by his mother, 83; quarrels with his brother, is banished and goes to Messene, 85; founds Pylus, 85; father

of Nestor, etc., 85, ii. 183; refuses to purify Hercules, i. 239; slain with his sons by Hercules, 251

Nelo, daughter of Danaus, wife of Menemachus, i. 141

Nemea, Lycurgus at, i. 91; Hercules cuts himself a club at, 183; the lion at, killed by Hercules, 187; the Seven against Thebes at, 357, 359

Nemean games celebrated by the Seven against Thebes in honour of Opheltes (Archemorus), i. 359

Nemesis, turned into a goose, consorts with Zeus, turned into a swan, ii. 25; lays an egg, out of which Helen is hatched, 25

Neomeris, a Nereid, i. 15

Neoptolemus, son of Achilles by Deidamia, formerly called Pyrrhus, ii. 75; fetched from Scyros to Troy by Ulysses and Phoenix, 225; slays many Trojans, 225, 227; kills Telephus, 227; slays Priam, 237; is awarded Andromache, 241; persuaded by Thetis to wait at Troy, 247, and at Tenedos, 251; sets out with Helenus by land for the country of the Molossians, 251; buries Phoenix, 251; conquers the Molossians and reigns as king, 251; gets a son Molossus by Andromache, 251; gives Helenus his mother Deidamia to wife, 251; succeeds to his father's kingdom, 251, 253; carries off Hermione, wife of Orestes, 253; slain by Orestes or by Machaereus at Delphi, 253, 255; said to have rifled and fired the temple in revenge for the death of his father, 255; condemns Ulysses to exile, 305, 307

Nephalion, son of Minos, in Paros, i. 203, 303

Nephele, wife of Athamas, mother of Phrixus and Helle, i. 75; rescues Phrixus from the altar and gives him and Helle a ram with a golden fleece, 75

Nephus, son of Hercules by Praxithea, i. 275

Nereids, offspring of Nereus and

INDEX

reveal Nereus to Hercules, 223 ; at Nysa receive Dionysus, 321 ; changed by Zeus into the Hyades, 321 ; Callisto one of the, according to Hesiod, 395

Nysa, mountain, Typhon at, i. 51 ; in Asia, the nymphs and Dionysus at, 321

Oak, the Golden Fleece nailed to an, i. 77, 95 ; lair of serpents in an, 87 ; sacred, 89 ; of Dodona, 97

Oaths by the Styx, i. 13

Ocaleae, in Boeotia, Alcmena at, i. 181

Ocean, a Titan, son of Sky and Earth, i. 5 ; father of Metis, 9 ; offspring of, 11, 13 ; father of Eurynome, 17 ; father of Triptolemus, according to Pherecydes, 39 ; father of Idyia, 111 ; father of Inachus and of Melia, 129 ; father of Callirrhoe, 211 ; father of Meliboea, 389 ; father of Pleione, ii. 3 ; father of Asopus, 51

Ocean, Pelops goes to the, ii. 163 ; Ulysses wanders about the, 279, 281, 293

Oceanids, offspring of Ocean and Tethys, i. 11

Ocypete, daughter of Danaus, wife of Lampus, i. 143

Ocypete, Ocythoe, or Ocypode, a Harpy, i. 15, 105

Ocytus, father of Guneus, ii. 185

Odius, son of Mecisteus, leader of the Alizones, ii. 205

Oeagrus, father of Linus by the Muse Calliope, i. 17 ; father of Orpheus, 97

Oeax, son of Nauplius, i. 145, 309

Oebalus, according to some, son of Perieres, father of Tyndareus, Hippocoon, and Icarius, ii. 21 ; father of Arene, ii. 13

Oechalia, Hercules at, i. 237, 239 ; captured by Hercules, 265, 267

Oedipus, son of Laius and Jocasta (or Epicasta), exposed on Cithaeron, adopted by Periboea, queen of Corinth, i. 345 ; inquires of the oracle at Delphi concerning his parentage, 345 ; kills his father unwittingly, 345, 347 ; reads the riddle of the Sphinx, 347, 349 ; succeeds to the kingdom of Thebes and marries his mother, 349 ; his children (Eteocles, Polynices, Ismene, Antigone) by Jocasta or by Eurygania, 349 ; banished from Thebes, 351 ; kindly received by Theseus, dies at Colonus in Attica, 351 ; father of Polynices, 357

Oeleus. See Oileus.

Oeme, daughter of Danaus, wife of Arbelus, i. 143

Oeneus, son of Egyptus, husband of Podarce, i. 141

Oeneus, son of Porthaon, king of Calydon, i. 63 ; receives vineplant from Dionysus, 65 ; marries Althaea, 65 ; father of Meleager, 65 ; slays his son Toxeus, 65 ; in sacrificing the first-fruits to the gods he forgets Artemis, 65, 67 ; she sends against him the Calydonian boar, 67 ; he marries Periboea, 71 ; father of Tydeus, 71 ; deposed and killed by the sons of Agrius, 73 (where for Thestius read Agrius) ; feasts with Hercules, 259 ; father of Deianira, 275 ; at Calydon, Alcmaeon to, 383 ; the Aetolian, receives the infant Agamemnon and Menelaus, ii. 169, 171

Oeno, daughter of Anius, one of the Wine-growers, ii. 179, 181

Oenoe, in Argolis, Oeneus buried at, i. 73 ; Cerynitian hind at, 191

Oenomaus, father of Hippodamia, i. 155 ; husband of Sterope, ii. 5 ; king of Pisa, offers the hand of his daughter Hippodamia to the victor in a chariot-race, 157, 161 ; cuts off the heads of unsuccessful suitors, 161 ; dragged to death by his horses or killed by Pelops, 161

Oenone, daughter of river Cebren, wife of Alexander (Paris), ii. 51 ; learns art of prophecy from Rhea, 51 ; warns Paris not to fetch Helen, 51 ; refuses to heal his wound, 51 ; hangs herself, 51

515

INDEX

Oenone, old name of island of Aegina, ii. 53

Oenopion, father of Merope, blinds Orion, and is hidden from Orion by Poseidon in an underground house, i. 33

Oenopion, son of Dionysus by Ariadne, ii. 137

Oestrobles, son of Hercules, by Hesychia, i. 275

Oeta, Mount, Hercules burnt on, i. 269, 271

Ogygia, daughter of Amphion and Niobe, i. 183

Ogygia, the island of Calypso, Ulysses in, ii. 295

Ogygian gate of Thebes, i. 361

Oicles, father of Amphiaraus, i. 67, 97, 353, 357; killed at Ilium, 245; in Arcadia, Alcmaeon repairs to, 383

Oileus, father of the Locrian Ajax, ii. 27, 183

Olenias, brother of Tydeus, murdered by him, i. 73

Olenus, in Achaia, sack of, i. 71; Hercules goes to Dexamenus at 197

Olive, bond of, chosen by Hercules, i. 229

Olive-tree, planted by Athena in the Pandrosium at Athens, ii. 79, 81; Io tethered to, i. 133

Olizonians, their muster for the Trojan war, ii. 185

Oloetrachus, suitor of Penelope, ii. 299

Olympian games celebrated by Hercules, i. 249

Olympus, Hera hung by Zeus from, i. 23, 247; Mount, Ossa piled on, 59; the mares of Diomedes destroyed by wolves at, 203

Olympus, son of Hercules by Euboea, i. 273

Olympusa, daughter of Thespius, mother of Halocrates by Hercules, i. 275

Omargus, one of Actaeon's dogs, i. 325

Omphale, mistress of Hercules, i. 101; daughter of Iardanus (Iardanes), queen of Lydia, buys Hercules as a slave, 241; his servitude with her, 241, 243, 245;

mother of Agelaus by Hercules, 275

Oncaidian gate of Thebes, i. 361

Onchestus, precinct of Poseidon at, i. 179; Megareus at, ii. 117

Onchestus, son of Agrius, escapes from Diomedes to Peloponnese, i. 73

Onesippus, son of Hercules by Chryseis, i. 273

Onites, son of Hercules, i. 275

Opheltes, called Archemorus, son of Lycurgus, i. 91; child of Lycurgus and Eurydice, nursed by Hypsipyle, 357; killed by a serpent, 359; called Archemorus, 359; Nemean games celebrated in his honour, 359

Opis, a Hyperborean maiden, i. 33

Opus, in Locris, Abderus a native of, i. 201; Patroclus at, ii. 77

Oracle at Delphi, i. 27; as to the destruction of the giants, 43; commanding that Athamas should sacrifice his son Phrixus as a remedy for dearth, 75; that Athamas should dwell among wild beasts, 77; that Pelias should beware of the man with one sandal, 95; about the Argo, 97; about the son who would kill his father, 153; as to the sale of Hercules, 241; as to the return of the Heraclids, 283, 285; about the Three-Eyed One, 287, 289; about the foundation of Thebes, 313, 315; that barrenness of land will be cured by putting the king to death, 329; that a father should die by the hand of one of his children, 307; that a father should be killed by his son, 343, 345; that Alcmaeon should depart to Achelous, 383; as to the foundation of Ilium, ii. 37, 39; that Aeacus should pray for Greece, 55; that Oenomaus must die by him who should marry his daughter, 159; that the Mycenaeans should choose a Pelopid for king, 165; that Thyestes should beget a son on his own daughter, 169; about the settlement of a city, 265; about the propitiation of Athena at Ilium,

INDEX

INDEX

Peteos, father of Menestheus, ii. 27

Peucetius, son of Lycaon, i. 389

Phaea, the name of the Crommyon sow and of the old woman who bred it, ii. 129

Phaeacians, Corcyra, the island of the, the Argonauts come to, i. 115 ; the Colchians settle down among the, 117 ; Ulysses cast up on the shore of the, ii. 295; Poseidon turns their ship to stone and envelops their city with a mountain, 297

Phaedimus, son of Amphion and Niobe, i. 341

Phaedra, daughter of Minos by Pasiphae or Crete, i. 303, 307; wife of Theseus, ii. 145 ; loves Hippolytus and falsely accuses him to Theseus, 145 ; hangs herself, 147 ; intervention of Amazons at her marriage, 213

Phaethon, son of Tithonus, father of Astynous, ii. 83

Phalias, son of Hercules by Heliconis, i. 275

Phantes, son of Egyptus, husband of Theano, i. 141

Phantom of Helen carried by Alexander (Paris) to Troy, ii. 175 ; possessed by Menelaus, 279

Phanus, son of Dionysus, in the Argo, i. 97

Pharnace, daughter of Megassares, wife of Sandocus, ii. 83

Phartis, daughter of Danaus, mother of Eurydamas, i. 141

Phasis, river, in Colchis, arrival of the Argonauts at it, i. 109

Phassus, son of Lycaon, i. 389

Phegeus at Psophis purifies Alcmaeon and gives him his daughter Arsinoe to wife, i. 383 ; his sons Pronous and Agenor kill Alcmaeon, 385 ; Phegeus, his wife and sons killed by Alcmaeon's sons, 387

Pheneus, son of Melas, killed by Tydeus, i. 71, 73

Pherae, Admetus at, i. 67; in Thessaly, founded by Pheres, 91 ; Hercules comes from, after saving Alcestis, 239 ; Apollo serves Admetus as a herdsman at, ii. 21

Phereans, their muster for the Trojan war, ii. 185

Phereclus builds the ships for Alexander (Paris), ii. 173

Pherecydes on Orion, i. 31; on Triptolemus, 39; on the homicide of Tydeus, 73; on Hercules and the Argo, 101 ; on Argus, 133 ; on the serpents killed by the infant Hercules, 175 ; on the horn of Amalthea, 257 ; on Thasus, 299, 301 ; on Cadmus and the Sparti, 315; on the necklace of Harmonia, 317 ; on the blindness of Tiresias, 363 ; on Callisto, 395 ; on the father of Telamon, ii. 53

Pheres, father of Admetus, i. 67, ii. 21 ; son of Cretheus, i. 87 ; father of Idomene, 87 ; founds Pherae, 91 ; father of Admetus and Lycurgus, 91 ; father of Periopis, ii. 77

Pheres, son of Jason, murdered by Medea or the Corinthians, i. 123, 125

Pheroetes, suitor of Penelope, ii. 297

Pherusa, a Nereid, i. 15

Phicium, Mount, the Sphinx on, i. 347

Phidippus, son of Thessalus, leader of the Coans against Troy, ii. 185 ; goes to Andros, settles in Cyprus, 259

Philaemon, son of Priam, ii. 49

Philammon, father of Thamyris by a nymph Argiope, i. 19

Philocrates, on the mother of Patroclus, ii. 77

Philoctetes, son of Poeas, suitor of Helen, ii. 27 ; leader of the Olizonians against Troy, 185 ; bitten by a snake in Tenedos, put ashore and abandoned by the Greeks in Lemnos, 195 ; fetched by Ulysses and Diomedes, 223 ; shoots Alexander, 223 ; sails to Mimas, 259 ; goes to Campania in Italy, 257, 259 ; makes war on the Lucanians, 261 ; settles in Crimissa, 261 ; founds a sanctuary of Apollo the Wanderer, and dedicates his bow to him, 261

INDEX

Philodemus, suitor of Penelope, ii. 297

Philoetius helps Ulysses to shoot the suitors, ii. 301

Philolaus, son of Minos, i. 303; in Paros, killed by Hercules, 203, 205

Philomela, daughter of Pandion, ii. 99; seduced by Tereus, 101; turned into a swallow, 101

Philonoe, daughter of Iobates, wife of Bellerophon, i. 153

Philonome, daughter of Tragasus, second wife of Cycnus, falsely accuses her stepson Tenes, ii. 193; buried by Cycnus in the earth, 195

Philyra, mother of Chiron by Cronus, i. 13

Philyra, wife of Nauplius, i. 145

Phineus, son of Belus, brother of Cepheus, i. 137; plots against Perseus, but is turned to stone, 161

Phineus, son of Lycaon, i. 389

Phineus, a blind seer, i. 103, 105; son of Poseidon or Agenor, 105; tormented by the Harpies, delivered by the Argonauts, 105; reveals to them the course of their voyage, 107; misled by his second wife Idaea, he blinds Plexippus and Pandion, the sons of his first wife Cleopatra, ii. 107; punished by the Argonauts, 107

Phlegra, Hercules in the battle of the gods with the giants at, i. 247. See Phlegrae

Phlegrae, giants born at, i. 43. See Phlegra

Phlegyas, son of Ares, slain by Lycus and Nycteus, i. 335, 337; father of Coronis, ii. 13

Phocaea taken by Achilles, ii. 203

Phocian war, the Locrians cease to send suppliants to Troy after the, ii. 269

Phocians, their muster for the Trojan war, ii. 183

Phocis, ruled by Deion, i. 79; Panopeus in, 173; Cadmus journeys through, 315; Oedipus encounters and kills his father in, 345; Daulia in, ii. 101

Phocus, son of Aeacus and Psamathe, ii. 55; murdered by Telamon, 57

Phoebe, a Hamadryad nymph, mother of some of the daughters of Danaus, i. 141

Phoebe, a Titanid, daughter of Sky and Earth, i. 5; wife of Coeus, mother of Asteria and Latona, i. 13

Phoebe, daughter of Leucippus, carried off by the Dioscuri, ii. 13; bears Mnesileus to Pollux, 31

Phoenicia, Agenor reigns in, i. 135, 297; Phoenix settles in, 301; Alexander (Paris) tarries in, ii. 175; Menelaus wanders to, 279

Phoenician woman, wife of Egyptus, mother of seven sons, i. 141

Phoenix, son of Agenor by Telephassa, i. 297; settles in Phoenicia, 301; father of Adonis, according to Hesiod, ii. 85

Phoenix, son of Amyntor, blinded by his father, healed by Chiron, goes with Achilles to Troy, ii. 75; sent as an ambassador to Achilles, 207; sent with Ulysses to Scyros to fetch Neoptolemus, 225; buried by Neoptolemus, 251

Pholoe, Hercules entertained by the centaur Pholus at, i. 191, 193, 195

Pholus, a centaur, son of Silenus, entertains Hercules, i. 191, 193; accidentally killed by an arrow, buried by Hercules, 195

Phorbas, said to be father of Augeas, i. 195

Phorbus, father of Pronoe, i. 61

Phorcides (Phorcids), daughters of Phorcus and Ceto, sisters of the Gorgons, i. 15, 155; have only one eye between the three of them, 155, 157; show Perseus the way to the nymphs, 157

Phorcus, son of Sea (Pontus) and Earth, i. 13; father of the Phorcids (Phorcides) and Gorgons by Ceto, 15, 155; father of Scylla, ii. 293

Phorcys, son of Aretaon, leader of the Phrygians, ii. 205

Phoroneus, father of Apis, i. 61, 129; son of Inachus, king of Peloponnese, 129

523

INDEX

Phrasimus, father of Praxithea by Diogenia, ii. 103

Phrasius, a seer from Cyprus, prescribes human sacrifices as a remedy for dearth, i. 225, 226; himself sacrificed, 227

Phrasius, son of Neleus, i. 85

Phrenius, two suitors of Penelope, both from Zacynthos, ii. 299

Phrixus, son of Athamas, brought by his father to the altar, i. 75; carried on ram with golden fleece to Colchis, 75, 77; marries Chalciope, daughter of Aeetes, 77; father of Argus, 95, 97; his children directed by Phineus, 105

Phrontis, son of Phrixus by Chalciope, i. 77

Phrygia, Cybela in, i. 327; Ilus in, ii. 37

Phrygian prisoner taken by Ulysses, ii. 179

Phrygian woman (Midea), mother of Licymnius, i. 165

Phrygians, Trojan allies, ii. 205

Phthia, concubine of Amyntor, falsely accuses his son Phoenix, ii. 75

Phthia, daughter of Amphion and Niobe, i. 341

Phthia, loved by Apollo, i. 61

Phthia, Deucalion in, i. 53; Peleus in, 67; Eurytion in, 67; Peleus flees to and from, ii. 61, 63; Peleus expelled from, 251

Phthius, son of Lycaon, i. 389

Phylace, Melampus at, i. 89; ships sent from, to the Trojan war, ii. 185

Phylacus, son of Deion by Diomede, i. 79; father of Iphiclus, keeps Melampus in bonds, 89; restores the kine to Neleus, 89, 91

Phylas, king of Ephyra, in Thesprotia, i. 259; father of Astyoche, 277

Phylas, son of Antiochus, father of Hippotes, i. 287

Phyleis, daughter of Thespius, mother of Tigasis by Hercules, i. 273

Phyleus, son of Augeas, bears witness for Hercules against his father, i. 195, 197; expelled

by his father, goes to Dulichium, 197; restored by Hercules, 249; father of Meges, ii. 27, 183

Phyllis, daughter of the king of the Bisaltians, loves Demophon, ii. 263; deserted by him she curses him and kills herself, 265

Phylomache, daughter of Amphion, wife of Pelias, i. 85

Phylonoe, daughter of Tyndareus and Leda, made immortal by Artemis, ii. 23

Phylonomus, son of Electryon by Anaxo, i. 165

Physius, son of Lycaon, i. 389

Pieria, Orpheus buried in, i. 19; Hermes steals the kine of Apollo in, ii. 5, 7

Pieria, wife of Danaus, i. 141

Pieris, an Aetolian slave, mother of Megapenthes by Menelaus, ii. 29, 31

Pierus, son of Magnes, father of Hyacinth by the Muse Clio, i. 19

Pillars set up by Dionysus in India, i. 331; of Hercules, ii. 211, 213

Pindar, on the *kibisis*, i. 157

Pine-bender, name applied to Sinis, ii. 125

Pine-tree, Marsyas hung on a, i. 31

Piras, son of Argus, i. 131

Pirates, Tyrrhenian, their adventure with Dionysus, i. 331, 333

Piren, brother of Bellerophon, accidentally killed by him, i. 149

Pirene, daughter of Danaus, wife of Agaptolemus, i. 141

Pireus, father of Autonoe, i. 277

Pirithous, son of Ixion, hunts the Calydonian boar, i. 67; woos Persephone, 235; seen in Hades by Hercules, who fails to rescue him, 235, 237; father of Polypoetes, ii. 27, 185; aided by Theseus in his war with the centaurs, 145, 149; his marriage with Hippodamia, 151; helps Theseus to carry off Helen, 153; tries to win Persephone to wife, but is detained with Theseus in Hades, 153

Pisa, statue of Hercules made by Daedalus at, i. 243; Oenomaus,

524

INDEX

king of, ii. 157; Pelops returns
to, 163

Pisander, on the mother of Tydeus,
i. 71

Pisander, suitor of Penelope, ii. 297

Pisenor, suitor of Penelope, ii. 297

Pisidice, daughter of Aeolus, wife
of Myrmidon, i. 57

Pisidice, daughter of Nestor, i. 85

Pisidice, daughter of Pelias, i. 85

Pisinoe, one of the Sirens, ii. 291

Pisistratus, son of Nestor, i. 85

Pisus, son of Aphareus, ii. 13

Pittheus, son of Pelops, ii. 115, 163;
at Troezen makes Aegeus lie
with his daughter Aethra, 115;
father of Aethra, 153

Placia, daughter of Otreus, wife of
Laomedon, ii. 43

Plane-tree at Aulis, with an altar
beside it, ii. 185

Plataea, Damasistratus, king of,
i. 347

Plato, son of Lycaon, i. 389

Pleiades, the seven, daughters of
Atlas and Pleione, ii. 3

Pleione, daughter of Ocean, mother
of the Pleiades by Atlas, ii. 3

Pleuron, city in Aetolia, i. 61

Pleuron, son of Aetolus, husband of
Xanthippe, i. 61

Plexaure, a Nereid, i. 15

Plexippus, son of Phineus and
Cleopatra, blinded by his father
on a false accusation, ii. 107

Plexippus, son of Thestius, i. 63

Plisthenes, husband of Aerope,
father of Agamemnon and Menelaus, i. 309

Pluto, son of Cronus and Rhea,
swallowed by Cronus, i. 7; his
helmet, 11; lord of Hades, 11;
sends up Eurydice for Orpheus,
19; carries off Persephone, 35;
gives her a seed of a pomegranate
to eat, 39; sends up the Maid,
39; bids Hercules take Cerberus,
237; Aeacus honoured in the
abode of, ii. 57. See Hades

Podalirius, son of Aesculapius,
suitor of Helen, ii. 27; leader
of the Triccaeans against Troy,
185; heals Philoctetes, 223;
goes to Colophon and helps to
bury Calchas, 243; consults

the oracle at Delphi and settles
in the Carian Chersonese, 265

Podarce, daughter of Danaus, wife
of Oeneus, i. 141

Podarces, afterwards called Priam,
i. 245, 247; son of Laomedon,
ii. 43; called Priam, 45. See
Priam

Podarces, son of Iphiclus, i. 91

Poeas, son of Thaumacus, in the
Argo, i. 97; shoots Talos, 119;
kindles the pyre of Hercules, 271;
Hercules gives him his bow, 271;
father of Philoctetes, ii. 27, 185

Polichus, son of Lycaon, i. 389

Poliporthes, son of Ulysses and
Penelope, ii. 303

Polites, son of Priam and Hecuba,
ii. 49

Pollux, son of Zeus, in the Argo,
i. 97; kills Amycus, king of the
Bebryces, in a boxing match,
103; son of Zeus by Leda, ii. 23;
practises boxing, 31; father of
Mnesileus by Phoebe, 31; kills
Lynceus, 33; carried up to
heaven by Zeus, 33; refuses to
accept immortality while his
brother is dead, 33; alternately
among gods and mortals, 33.
See Castor, Dioscuri

Poltys entertains Hercules at Aenus,
i. 209

Polyanax, king of Melos, ii. 259

Polybotes, a giant, overcome by
Poseidon, i. 47

Polybus, king of Corinth, his
neatherds find the exposed
Oedipus, i. 345

Polybus, two suitors of Penelope,
both from Zacynthos, ii. 299

Polycaste, daughter of Nestor, i. 85

Polyctor, son of Egyptus, husband
of Stygne, i. 141

Polydectes, son of Magnes, colonizes
Seriphus, i. 81; king of Seriphus,
falls in love with Danae, sends
Perseus to fetch the Gorgon's
head, 155; turned to stone by
Perseus, 161

Polydora, daughter of Peleus, wife
of Borus, ii. 61, 63

Polydora, daughter of Perieres, wife
of Peleus, ii. 67

Polydorus, son of Cadmus and

525

INDEX

Harmonia, i. 317 ; becomes king of Thebes, marries Nycteis, 335 ; father of Labdacus, 335

Polydorus, son of Priam and Hecuba, ii. 49

Polydorus, suitor of Penelope, ii. 299

Polygonus, son of Proteus, killed by Hercules, i. 209

Polyidus, son of Coeranus, a diviner, restores Glaucus to life by means of a magic herb, i. 311, 313 ; imparts to him the art of divination, but afterwards deprives him of it, 313 ; departs to Argos, 313

Polyidus, suitor of Penelope, ii. 297

Polylaus, son of Hercules by Eurybia, i. 273

Polymede, daughter of Autolycus, wife of Aeson, mother of Jason, i. 93 ; curses Pelias and hangs herself, 121

Polymedon, son of Priam, ii. 49

Polymele, daughter of Peleus, mother of Patroclus, according to some, ii. 77

Polymnia, a Muse, i. 17

Polynices, son of Oedipus by Jocasta or Eurygania, brother of Eteocles, i. 349 ; agrees with his brother to rule the kingdom alternately for a year, 351 ; banished from Thebes, comes to Argos, 351 ; marries Argia, daughter of Adrastus, 353 ; bribes Eriphyle to persuade Amphiaraus to go to war, 353, 355 ; one of the Seven against Thebes, 357 ; one of the victors in the Nemean games, 359 ; slain in single combat by his brother Eteocles, 369 ; his body buried by Antigone, 373 ; father of Thersander, 379, ii. 187

Polynome, a Nereid, i. 15

Polypemon, father of Sinis by Sylea, ii. 125

Polypemon, a name given to Damastes, ii. 131. *See* Damastes

Polyphemus, a Cyclops, son of Poseidon by the nymph Thoösa, made drunk and blinded by Ulysses, ii. 283

Polyphemus, son of Elatus, in the Argo, i. 99 ; searches for Hylas,

is left behind by the Argonauts in Mysia, 101 ; founds Cius in Mysia, 101

Polyphides, lord of Sicyon, Agamemnon and Menelaus brought by their nurse to, ii. 169, 171

Polyphontes, a Heraclid, king of Messene, i. 291, 293 ; marries Merope, wife of his predecessor, 293 ; killed by Aepytus, son of Merope, 293

Polyphontes, herald of Laius, killed by Oedipus, i. 345, 347

Polypoetes, son of Apollo by Phthia, killed by Aetolus, i. 61

Polypoetes, son of Pirithous, suitor of Helen, ii. 27 ; leader of the Gyrtonians against Troy, 185 ; goes to Colophon and helps to bury Calchas, 243

Polypoetes, son of Ulysses and Callidice, queen of the Thesprotians, ii. 303

Polypoetes, suitor of Penelope, ii. 297

Polyxena, daughter of Priam and Hecuba, ii. 49 ; slaughtered by the Greeks on the grave of Achilles, 239, 241

Polyxenus, king of the Eleans, entrusted by the Taphians with stolen kine, allows Amphitryon to ransom them, i. 169

Polyxenus, son of Agasthenes, suitor of Helen, ii. 27

Polyxo, Naiad nymph, wife of Danaus, i. 141

Polyxo, mother of Antiope by Nycteus, ii. 5

Pomegranate, seed of, eaten by Persephone, i. 39, 41

Pontomedusa, a Nereid, i. 15

Pontus (Sea), i. 13. *See* Sea

Porphyrion, a giant, i. 43 ; attacks Hera, thunderstruck by Zeus and shot by Hercules, 45

Porthaon, son of Agenor, i. 61 ; his children by Euryte, 63

Portheus, father of Echion, ii. 235

Portheus, son of Lycaon, i. 389

Poseidon, son of Cronus and Rhea, i. 7 ; swallowed by Cronus, 7 ; his trident, 11 ; lord of the sea, 11 ; father of Orion, bestows on him the power of striding across

INDEX

Palamedes, 179; ransoms the body of Hector, 211; purifies Penthesilia, 211; the Wooden Horse stationed at the palace of, 233; slain by Neoptolemus, 237; the sisters of, 263

Priest, Chryses, priest (of Apollo), ii. 205; Maro, priest of Apollo, 281

Priestess, Iphigenia, priestess of Artemis among the Taurians, ii. 191, 193, 275

Priesthood of Hera, i. 133; of Athena, 397; of Athena and Poseidon Erechtheus, ii. 101

Procles, twin son of Aristodemus by Argia, i. 287; with his twin brother Eurysthenes he obtains by lot the kingdom of Lacedaemon, 289

Proclia, daughter of Laomedon, wife of Cycnus, ii. 193

Procne, daughter of Pandion by Zeuxippe, wife of Tereus, ii. 99; kills her son Itys, and serves him up to Tereus, 101; pursued by Tereus and turned into a nightingale, 101

Procris, daughter of Thespius, mother of Antileon and Hippeus by Hercules, i. 273

Procris receives a wonderful dog from Minos, i. 173; daughter of Erechtheus by Praxithea, ii. 103; married to Cephalus, 103; plays him false and flees to Minos, 105; has connexion with Minos and receives from him a dog and a dart, 105; killed accidentally by Cephalus, 105

Proetidian gate of Thebes, i. 361

Proetus, twin son of Abas, expelled by his twin brother Acrisius from Argos, i. 145; goes to Iobates in Lycia, 145; marries Antia or Stheneboea, 145; returns and reigns over Tiryns, 147; his daughters go mad, but are cured by Melampus, 147, 149; gives his daughters in marriage, with part of the kingdom, to Melampus and Bias, 149; purifies Bellerophon, 149, 151; sends Bellerophon to Iobates with a treacherous letter, 151; said to have seduced Danae, 155

Promachus, son of Aeson, slain by Pelias, i. 121

Promachus, son of Parthenopaeus, i. 91; one of the Epigoni, 379

Promachus, suitor of Penelope, ii. 299

Prometheus, son of Iapetus and Asia, i. 13; smites the head of Zeus with an axe and lets out Athena, 25; makes men and gives them fire, 51; nailed to Mount Caucasus, but released by Hercules, 53; father of Deucalion, 53; advises Deucalion to construct a chest in the great flood, 55; offers to live immortal that the wounded Chiron may die, 193, 229, 231; released by Hercules, 229; advises him as to the apples of the Hesperides, 231; his prediction as to the son of Zeus by Thetis, ii. 67

Promus, suitor of Penelope, ii. 297

Pronax, son of Talaus by Lysimache, father of Lycurgus, i. 91

Pronoe, daughter of Phorbus, wife of Aetolus, i. 61

Pronomus, suitor of Penelope, ii. 299

Pronous, son of Phegeus, i. 385. *See* Phegeus

Pronous, suitor of Penelope, ii. 299

Prophecy, the art of, bestowed by Apollo on Cassandra, ii. 49; bestowed by Rhea on Oenone, 51. *See* Divination, Soothsaying

Propontis, a Harpy flees by the, i. 105

Protesilaus, son of Iphiclus, suitor of Helen, ii. 27; leads ships from Phylace against Troy, 185; is the first to land, but is killed by Hector, 199; brought up by Hermes from Hades to his wife Laodamia, 199; his people cast away on Pellene, 261

Proteus, king of Egypt, receives Dionysus, i. 327; receives Helen from Hermes to guard, ii. 175; Menelaus discovers her at the court of, 279

Proteus, son of Egyptus, husband of Gorgophone, i. 139

Proteus, son of Poseidon, father of Polygonus and Telegonus, i. 209

Prothous, son of Agrius, i. 73

INDEX

Prothous, son of Lycaon, i. 389

Prothous, son of Tenthredon, leader of the Magnesians against Troy, ii. 185; wrecked at Caphereus, settles with the Magnesians in Crete, 259

Prothous, suitor of Penelope, ii. 297

Proto, a Nereid, i. 15

Protogenia (*not* Protogonia), daughter of Calydon by Aeolia, mother of Oxylus by Ares, i. 61

Protogenia (*not* Protogonia), daughter of Deucalion and Pyrrha, mother of Aethlius by Zeus, i. 57

Psamathe, a Nereid, i. 15; daughter of Nereus, mother of Phocus by Aeacus, ii. 55

Pseras, suitor of Penelope, ii. 297

Psophidians pursue the sons of Alcmaeon, but are put to flight by the Tegeans, i. 387

Psophis, the Erymanthian boar at, i. 191; in Arcadia, Alcmaeon at, 383, 385; the sons of Alcmaeon at, 387

Pteleon, lover of Procris, ii. 105

Pterelaus, son of Taphius, his golden hair, i. 165; made immortal by Poseidon, 165; his golden hair pulled out by his daughter, he dies, 173; his sons claim the kingdom of Mycenae from Electryon, 167; they fight and kill the sons of Electryon, 169

Ptolemaeus, suitor of Penelope, ii. 297

Ptous, son of Athamas by Themisto, i. 77

Purification for homicide, i. 115 (of Argonauts for murder of Apsyrtus), 143 (of Danaids for the murder of their husbands), 151 (of Bellerophon for the murder of his brother), 171 (of Amphitryon for the killing of Electryon), 183 (of Hercules for murder of his children), 187 (of Copreus for the killing of Iphitus), 233 (of Hercules for the slaughter of the centaurs), 239 (of Hercules for the murder of Iphitus), 383 (of Alcmaeon for the murder of his mother Eriphyle), ii. 61 (of Peleus

for murder of Phocus), 63 (of Peleus for the killing of Eurytion), 163 (of Pelops for the murder of Myrtilus), 211 (of Penthesilia for killing of Hippolyte); for madness, i. 149; of Dionysus by Rhea, 327

Pygmalion, king of Cyprus, father of Metharme, ii. 85

Pylades, son of Strophius, brought up with Orestes, ii. 271; goes with Orestes to Mycenae, 271, and to the land of the Taurians, 273, 275; marries Electra, 277

Pylaemenes, son of Bilsates, leader of the Paphlagonians, ii. 205

Pylaemenes, suitor of Penelope, ii. 297

Pylaon, son of Neleus by Chloris, i. 85

Pylarge, daughter of Danaus, wife of Idmon, i. 143

Pylas, king of Megara, receives Pandion and gives him his daughter to wife, ii. 113; slays his father's brother Bias, gives the kingdom to Pandion, and retires to Peloponnese, 113; founds Pylus, 113

Pylia, daughter of Pylas, wife of Pandion, ii. 113

Pylians, Neleus prince of the, i. 239; Hades sides with the, against Hercules, 251; their muster for the Trojan war, ii. 183

Pylius, adoptive father of Hercules at Eleusis, i. 233

Pylus founded by Neleus, i. 85; captured and ravaged by Hercules, 85, 251; Amythaon in, 87; kine of Phylacus brought to, 91; Hermes brings the stolen kine to, ii. 9; founded by Pylas, 113

Pylus, son of Ares, i. 63

Pyraechmes, leader of the Paeonians, ii. 205

Pyramus, river, in Cilicia, i. 301

Pyre of Hercules, i. 271; of Capaneus, 375; of Coronis, ii. 15

Pyrene, mother of Cycnus by Ares, i. 221

Pyrippe, daughter of Thespius, mother of Patroclus by Hercules, i. 275

Pyrrha, daughter of Epimetheus,

529

INDEX

Sacrifice of bulls, i. 89; at marriage, 93; jesting of women at, 117; of a bull to Poseidon, 199, 305

Sacrifices, human, i. 75 (Phrixus), 225 (of strangers, offered by Busiris in Egypt), 367 (Menoeceus), ii. 111 (daughters of Erechtheus), 119 (daughters of Hyacinth), 191 (Iphigenia), 239, 241 (Polyxena), 273 (of strangers, offered by Scythian Taurians)

Sacrifices to Saviour Zeus, i. 185, 187; to heroes, 185; to dead men, 187; to Hercules accompanied with curses, 227; without flutes and garlands to the Graces in Paros, ii. 117; to the souls of the dead, 289

Salaminians, their muster for the Trojan war, ii. 183

Salamis, daughter of Asopus, wife of Cychreus, ii. 59

Salamis, Telamon in, i. 67; island, ravaged by a snake, ii. 59; Cychreus king of, 59; Telamon comes to, and succeeds to the kingdom, 57, 59

Salmoneus, son of Aeolus by Enarete, i. 57; founds Elis, 81; mimics Zeus and is killed by thunderbolt, 81; father of Tyro by Alcidice, 81, 85, 87

Salmydessus, city in Thrace, home of Phineus, i. 103

Same, island, suitors of Penelope from, ii. 297

Samothrace, island, Dardanus leaves, ii. 35

Sandocus, son of Astynous, comes from Syria and founds Celenderis in Cilicia, ii. 83; marries Pharnace and begets Cinyras, 83

Sangarius, the river, father of Hecuba by Metope, ii. 45; Greeks settle on the banks of the, 257

Sao, a Nereid, i. 15

Sarapis, name given to deified Apis, i. 129

Sardinia, forty sons of Hercules by the daughters of Thespius sent to, i. 259

Sardinian Sea, the Argonauts sail through the, i. 115

Sarpedon, son of Poseidon, shot by Hercules, i. 209

Sarpedon, son of Zeus by Europa or Laodamia, i. 299; quarrels with Minos and flies from him, 301; becomes king of Lycia, 303; leader of the Lycians at Troy, ii. 205; killed by Hector, 209

Satyr, that robbed the Arcadians, killed by Argus, i. 131; attempts to force Amymone, 139

Satyrs, attendants of Dionysus, taken prisoners by Lycurgus, but afterwards released, i. 327

Scaea, daughter of Danaus, wife of Daiphron, i. 139

Scaean gate (of Troy), Achilles shot at the, ii. 213, 215

Scaeus, son of Hippocoon, slain by Hercules, ii. 21, 23

Scamander, the river, father of Teucer, ii. 35; father of Callirrhoe, 37, of Strymo, 43; rushes at Achilles, 209; dried up by Hephaestus, 209

Schedius, son of Iphitus, suitor of Helen, ii. 27

Schedius, suitor of Penelope, ii. 297

Schoeneus, father of Atalanta, i. 67, 97; father of Atalanta, according to Hesiod, 401

Schoeneus, son of Athamas, i. 77

Sciron, father of Endeis, ii. 53; son of Pelops or of Poseidon, a malefactor, slain by Theseus, 129

Scironian cliffs, Eurystheus killed at the, i. 277, 279

Scironian rocks, in the Megarian territory, ii. 129

Scylla and Charybdis, the Argo at, i. 115

Scylla, daughter of Crataeis and Trienus or Phorcus, ii. 293; Ulysses sails past her, 293; she gobbles up six of his comrades, 293, 295

Scylla, daughter of Nisus, falls in love with Minos and betrays her father by pulling out his purple hair, ii. 117; drowned by Minos, 117

Scyrius, father of Aegius, according to some, ii. 113

Scyros, Neoptolemus fetched to Troy from, ii. 225

531

INDEX

Scythia, Mount Caucasus in, i. 53; traversed by Io, 133

Scythians, the Taurians part of the, ii. 273

Sea (Pontus) and Earth, their offspring, i. 13, 15

Sea monster, Andromeda exposed to, i. 159; Hesione exposed to, 207

Seal, the Nereid Psamathe turns herself into a, ii. 55

Seasons, daughters of Zeus and Themis, i. 15

Semele, daughter of Cadmus and Harmonia, i. 317; loved by Zeus, 317; gives birth to Dionysus, 319; expires of fright at the thunders of Zeus, 319; wooed by Actaeon, 323; brought up from Hades by Dionysus and named Thyone, 333; ascends with Dionysus to heaven, 333

Seriphus, colonized by the sons of Magnes, i. 81; Polydectes, king of, 155; Danae and Perseus in, 155, 161; Dictys made king of, 161

Serpent, a symbol of Lacedaemon, i. 291; brings dead serpent to life by means of magic herb, 311, 313; coiled about Erichthonius in the chest, ii. 91; portent of the serpent and the sparrows at Aulis, 185

Serpents, sent by Hera to destroy the infant Hercules, i. 175; Cadmus and Harmonia turned into, 335; sea, devour the sons of Laocoon, ii. 233. See Snakes

Servitude, Apollo serves Admetus as a herdsman for a year for the murder of the Cyclopes, i. 91, ii. 19, 21; Hercules condemned to serve Eurystheus twelve years for the murder of his children, i. 185; Hercules condemned to serve three years for the murder of Iphitus, 241; servitude of Hercules with Omphale, 243; Cadmus serves Ares eight years to atone for the slaughter of the Sparti, 317

Seven against Thebes, war of the, i. 355–373

Shape-shifting, of Periclymenus, i. 85, 251; of Nereus, 223; of Thetis, ii. 67

Shell, the spiral, by means of which Minos discovered Daedalus, ii. 141

Shepherd's pipe invented by Hermes, ii. 9; given by him to Apollo, 11

Shield, The, of Hesiod, quoted, i. 157

Shields, invention of, i. 145

Shipbuilder, the first, i. 137

Shirt, the sleeveless and neckless, given by Clytaemnestra to Agamemnon, ii. 269

Shoes not worn by Locrian maidens at Troy, ii. 267, 269

Sicilian Sea, Typhon in the, i. 51

Sicily, thrown on giant Enceladus, i. 45; Hercules in, 217; Camicus in, ii. 141; Greeks settle in, 257; Ulysses wanders to, 279

Sickle, adamantine, given to Cronus by Earth, i. 5; Zeus strikes Typhon down with an, 49; given to Perseus by Hermes, 157

Sicyon, the mad daughters of Proetus driven down to, i. 149; Antiope takes refuge at, 337; captured by Lycus, 337; Agamemnon and Menelaus taken by their nurse to, ii. 169, 171

Side, city, taken by Achilles, ii. 203

Side, wife of Orion, i. 31; rivals Hera in beauty and is cast by her into Hades, 31

Sidero, stepmother of Pelias and Neleus, i. 83; attacked by them, takes refuge in a precinct of Hera, 83; cut down by Pelias, 83, 85

Sidon, Alexander puts in at, ii. 175

Sigeum, Helle drowned near, i. 77

Silenus, father of the centaur Pholus, i. 191

Simoeis, father of Astyoche, ii. 37, and of Hieromneme, 37

Sinis, son of Polypemon and Sylea, called the Pine-bender, killed by Theseus at the Isthmus of Corinth, ii. 123, 125

Sinon lights the beacon to guide the Greeks to Troy, ii. 233, 235

Sipylus, Mount, Niobe turned into a stone at, i. 343

Sipylus, son of Amphion and Niobe, i. 341

Sirens, daughters of Achelous by

INDEX

the Gorgon's hair to turn enemies to flight, i. 253

Sterope, daughter of Pleuron, i. 61

Sterope, daughter of Porthaon, mother of the Sirens, i. 63

Steropes, a Cyclops, i. 5

Stesichorus, as to Gorgophone, ii. 13; in his *Eriphyle* as to the restoration of Lycurgus to life, 17

Stheneboea, daughter of Aphidas, wife of Proetus, i. 397

Stheneboea, daughter of Iobates, wife of Proetus, i. 145, 147; makes love to Bellerophon, and her love being rejected, falsely accuses Bellerophon to Proetus, 151

Sthenelaus, son of Melas, killed by Tydeus, i. 71, 73

Sthenele, daughter of Acastus, mother of Patroclus by Menoetius, ii. 77

Sthenele, daughter of Danaus, wife of Sthenelus, i. 141

Sthenelus, father of Cometes, ii. 249

Sthenelus, son of Androgeus, taken as hostage by Hercules from Paros, i. 205

Sthenelus, son of Capaneus, one of the Epigoni, i. 379; suitor of Helen, ii. 27

Sthenelus, son of Egyptus, husband of Sthenele, i. 141

Sthenelus, son of Perseus, i. 163; marries Nicippe, 167; father of Eurystheus, 167; banishes Amphitryon and seizes the throne of Mycenae and Tiryns, 169, 171

Stheno, a Gorgon, immortal, i. 157

Sting-ray, Ulysses killed by a spear barbed with the spine of a, ii. 303

Stone swallowed by Cronus and afterwards disgorged, i. 9; of Ascalaphus in Hades, 41, 237; of Sisyphus in Hades, 79; persons who see the Gorgons are turned to, 157, 161; vixen and dog turned to, 173; Niobe turned to, 343; serpent at Aulis turned to, ii. 185; ship of the Phaeacians turned by Poseidon to, 297

Stones turned into men and women by Deucalion and Pyrrha,

i. 55; follow Amphion's lyre, 339

Stoning, death by, ii. 179 (Palamedes), 195 (a flute player), 249 (Palamedes)

Strangers sacrificed by Busiris on an altar of Zeus, i. 225; compelled by Syleus to dig his vines, 241, 243; murdered by the Taurians and thrown into the sacred fire, ii. 273

Stratichus, son of Nestor, i. 85

Stratius, suitor of Penelope, ii. 299

Stratobates, son of Electryon, i. 165

Stratonice, daughter of Pleuron, i. 61

Stratonice, daughter of Thespius, mother of Atromus by Hercules, i. 273

Strife throws an apple to be contended for by Hera, Athena, and Aphrodite, ii. 173

Strophades, islands, the Harpies pursued to the, i. 105, 107

Strophius, the Phocian, father of Pylades, brings up Orestes, ii. 271

Strymo, daughter of Scamander, wife of Laomedon, ii. 43

Strymon, river, father of Rhesus by the Muse Euterpe, i. 21; father of Evadne, 131; made unnavigable by Hercules, 217; the Edonians beside the, 327

Stygne, daughter of Danaus, wife of Polyctor, i. 141

Stymphalian lake in Arcadia, the birds at the, shot by Hercules, i. 197, 199

Stymphalus, city in Arcadia, i. 197

Stymphalus, father of Parthenope, i. 277; son of Elatus, 397; king of the Arcadians, treacherously murdered by Pelops, ii. 55

Stymphalus, son of Lycaon, i. 389

Styx, an Oceanid, i. 11; mother of Victory, etc., by Pallas, 13; flows from a rock in Hades, 13; Zeus ordains oaths by the water of, 13; mother of Persephone by Zeus, 17

Suitors of Helen, ii. 27, 29; of Penelope, 297, 299; suitors of Penelope shot by Ulysses, 301

Sun, son of Hyperion, i. 13; Sun's rays restore sight to blind, 33; husband of Rhode, 35; the cows

INDEX

of the, in Erythia, 43 ; forbidden by Zeus to shine, 45 ; father of Aeetes, Circe, and Pasiphae by Perseis, 77 ; father of Augeas, 97, 195 ; the kine of the, in the island of Thrinacia, 115 ; gives a dragon-car to Medea, 123 ; gives Hercules a golden goblet in which to cross the sea, 213, 215, 229 ; father of Pasiphae by Perseis, 303 ; going backward and setting in the east, sign of the, ii. 165 ; father of Circe by Perse, 287 ; Thrinacia, the island of the, 295 ; reports the slaughter of his kine to Zeus, 295

Sunium, a headland of Attica, Menelaus puts in at, ii. 279

Swallow, Philomela turned into a, ii. 101

Swine, Achilles fed on the inwards of wild, ii. 71 ; companions of Ulysses turned by Circe into, 287. *See* Sow

Sword and sandals, tokens of the fatherhood of Aegeus, ii. 115 ; taken up by Theseus, 123

Sylea, daughter of Corinthus, wife of Sinis, ii. 125

Syleus, in Aulis, compels strangers to dig his vines, i. 241, 243 ; killed by Hercules, 243

Symaeans, their muster for the Trojan war, ii. 183, 185

Syria, Mount Casius in, i. 49 ; traversed by Io in search of Epaphus, 135 ; Dionysus roams over, 325, 327 ; Dawn consorts with Cephalus and bears Tithonus in, ii. 83 ; Sandocus migrates from, to Cilicia, 83

Taenarum, in Laconia, the mouth of Hades at, i. 233, 235

Talaemenes, father of Mesthles and Antiphus, ii. 205

Talaus, son of Bias and Pero, i. 91 ; father of Adrastus, 91, 353, 355

Talos, a brazen man, guardian of Crete, killed by Medea, i. 119

Talos, son of Perdix, nephew and pupil of Daedalus, ii. 121 ; his invention, 121, 123 ; murdered by Daedalus, 121

Talthybius, goes with Ulysses to Cinyras, ii. 179 ; goes with Ulysses to Clytaemnestra, 191

Tantalus, father of Niobe, i. 341 ; after the death of her children Niobe goes to him at Sipylus, 343 ; punished in Hades, ii. 155

Tantalus, son of Amphion and Niobe, i. 341

Tantalus, son of Thyestes, former husband of Clytaemnestra, ii. 171 ; slain by Agamemnon, 171

Taphians carry off cattle from Mycenae, i. 169 ; their islands ravaged by Amphitryon, 173. *See* Teleboans

Taphius, son of Poseidon, father of Pterelaus, colonizes Taphos and calls the people Teleboans, i. 165

Taphos, island colonized by Taphius, i. 165 ; could not be taken while Pterelaus lived, 173

Tartarus, a gloomy place in Hades, i. 5, 7, 11 ; father of Typhon, 47 ; father of Echidna, 131 ; Zeus would hurl Apollo to, ii. 19

Tartessus, two pillars set up by Hercules at, i. 211, 213 ; Hercules sails to, in the goblet of the Sun, 215

Taurians, part of the Scythians, ii. 273 ; wooden image of Tauropolus in the land of the, carried off by Orestes, 273, 275

Tauropolus, wooden image of, brought to Athens, ii. 275

Taurus, son of Neleus by Chloris, i. 85

Taygete, daughter of Atlas and Pleione, one of the Pleiades, ii. 3 ; mother of Lacedaemon by Zeus, 11

Tebrus, son of Hippocoon, killed by Hercules, ii. 21, 23

Tegea, Cepheus, king of, i. 253 ; the city defended against enemies by a lock of the Gorgon's hair, 253 ; Auge debauched by Hercules at, 253 ; Arsinoe brought by the sons of Phegeus to, 385 ; sons of Alcmaeon pursued to, 387

Tegeans save the sons of Alcmaeon from the pursuing Psophidians, i. 387

Tegyrius, king of Thrace, gives his

535

INDEX

daughter in marriage to Ismarus, son of Eumolpus, ii. 109 ; plotted against by Eumolpus, 109 ; reconciled to Eumolpus, leaves him the kingdom, 109

Telamon, son of Aeacus, i. 67, ii. 53 ; hunts the Calydonian boar, i. 67 ; in the Argo, 97 ; with Hercules at the capture of Ilium, 245 ; father of Ajax and Teucer, ii. 27, 29 ; murders Phocus, 57 ; expelled from Aegina, 57 ; goes to Salamis, where he succeeds Cychreus in the kingdom, 59 ; father of Ajax by Periboea, 61 ; goes with Hercules to Troy and receives Hesione as a prize, 61 ; has a son Teucer by Hesione, 61

Telchis. *See* Thelxion

Teleboans, the inhabitants of Taphos, i. 165 ; Electryon proposes to make war on them, 169 ; expedition of Amphitryon against the, 171, 173, 175

Teleboas, son of Lycaon, i. 389

Teledice, nymph, wife of Phoroneus, i. 129

Telegonus, king of Egypt, marries Io, i. 135

Telegonus, son of Proteus, killed by Hercules, i. 209

Telegonus, son of Ulysses by Circe, ii. 289 ; sails in search of Ulysses, 303 ; comes to Ithaca and kills Ulysses unwittingly, 303 ; conveys the corpse and Penelope to Circe, 305 ; marries Penelope, 305 ; sent with Penelope to the Islands of the Blest, 305

Telemachus, son of Ulysses and Penelope, ii. 177 ; Ulysses reveals himself to, 299 ; helps Ulysses to shoot the suitors, 301

Teleon, father of Butes, i. 97

Telephassa, wife of Agenor, mother of Europa, Cadmus, Phoenix, and Cilix, i. 297, 299 ; settles in Thrace, 301 ; buried by Cadmus, 313

Telephus, son of Hercules by Auge, i. 277 ; exposed on Mount Parthenius, 255, 397 ; suckled by a doe, 255, 257 ; inquires of the god at Delphi as to his parents, 397 ; adopted by Teuthras, prince of Mysia, and succeeds to the princedom, 397 ; king of the Mysians, chases the Greek invaders, ii. 187 ; wounded by Achilles, 187 ; healed by Achilles with the rust of his spear, 189 ; shows the Greeks the way to Troy, 189 ; father of Eurypylus, 227

Telephus, the hearth of, in Arcadia, Oeneus murdered at, i. 73

Teles, son of Hercules by Lysidice, i. 273

Telesilla, on the death of the children of Niobe, i. 343

Telestas, son of Priam, ii. 49

Teleutagoras, son of Hercules by one of the daughters of Thespius, i. 273

Telmius, suitor of Penelope, ii. 297

Temenus, one of the Heraclids, remonstrates with the oracle, i. 285 ; prepares to invade Peloponnese, 287 ; receives an oracle about a Three-eyed One, 287 ; has Argos allotted to him, 289 ; favouring his daughter and her husband, he is murdered at the instigation of his sons, 291

Ten years' war of Zeus on the Titans, i. 9, 11 ; ten labours of Hercules, 185 ; ten years the period of the Trojan war, ii. 185, 221

Tenedos, Greeks on way to Troy touch at, ii. 193, 195 ; the island formerly called Leucophrys, but named Tenedos after Tenes, 195 ; Philoctetes bitten by a snake in, 195 ; the Greeks sail back to, 231 ; lie off, 233 ; sail back to Troy from, 235 ; Agamemnon touches at, 247 ; Neoptolemus spends two days in, 251

Tenes, son of Cycnus or Apollo, falsely accused by his stepmother and set adrift by his father, ii. 193 ; lands in Tenedos and dwells there, 195 ; repels the Greeks, but is killed by Achilles, 195

Tenos, island, Zetes and Calais killed by Hercules in, ii. 107 ; taken by Achilles, 203 ; Greeks encounter a storm at, 247

INDEX

Tenthredon, father of Prothous, ii. 185

Tereis, mother of Megapenthes by Menelaus, ii. 31

Tereus, son of Ares, a Thracian, ally of Pandion against Labdacus, ii. 99; marries Procne, 99; seduces Philomela, 101; has his dead son Itys served up to him by Procne, 101; pursues Procne and Philomela, 101; turned into a hoopoe, 101

Terpsichore, a Muse, i. 17

Terpsicrate, daughter of Thespius, mother of Euryopes by Hercules, i. 275

Tethys, a Titanid, daughter of Sky and Earth, i. 5; mother of Inachus, 129; mother of Asopus, ii. 51

Teucer, son of the Scamander, king of the Teucrians, ii. 35; gives Dardanus a share of the land and his daughter Batia to wife, 35

Teucer, son of Telamon, suitor of Helen, ii. 27, 29; son of Telamon and Hesione, 61; victor in archery competition, 217

Teucrians named after Teucer, ii. 35

Teutamides, king of Larissa, holds games in honour of his dead father, i. 163

Teuthrania, Teuthras, prince of, i. 257

Teuthras, prince of Teuthrania, marries Auge, i. 257; gives Telephus and is succeeded by him in the princedom, 397

Thadytius, suitor of Penelope, ii. 299

Thalia, a Grace, i. 17

Thalia, a Muse, i. 17; mother of the Corybantes, 21

Thalpius, son of Eurytus, suitor of Helen, ii. 27

Thamyris, his love of Hyacinth, i. 19; a great minstrel, engages in a musical contest with the Muses, 21; is beaten and blinded by them, 21

Thasos, island, conquered by Hercules, who settles the sons of Androgeus in it, i. 209

Thasus, son of Poseidon or of

Cilix, sent out to find Europa, i. 299, 301; settles in Thasos, 301

Thaumacus, father of Poeas, i. 97

Thaumas, son of Sea (Pontus) and Earth, father of Iris and the Harpies by Electra, i. 13, 15

Theano, daughter of Danaus, wife of Phantes, i. 141

Theano (*not* Theanus), wife of Antenor, mother of Archelochus and Acamas, ii. 205

Thebaid, mention of Oeneus and Periboea in the, i. 71

Thebans expose one of their sons every month to the (Teumessian) vixen, i. 171; pay tribute to Erginus, king of Orchomenus, 179; Hercules compels the Minyans to pay double tribute to the, 181; Dionysus proves to the Thebans that he is a god, 331; Lycus chosen commander-in-chief by the, 337; the Sphinx propounds a riddle to the, 347; ambush set for Tydeus by the, 361; armed by Eteocles, 361; Tiresias among the, 361; they seek counsel of Tiresias, 367; defeated by the Argives, abandon the city, 379, 381; found Hestiaea, 381

Thebe, wife of Zethus, gives her name to Thebes, i. 341

Thebes, Iphicles at, i. 67; expedition of Adrastus against, 73; the war of, 75; war of the Epigoni on, 91; Amphitryon and Alcmena go to, 171; three sons of Hercules by daughters of Thespius sent to, 259; founded by Cadmus, 315; Dionysus drives the women mad at, 331; Polydorus king of, 335; Lycus and Nycteus come to, 337; named after Thebe, wife of Zethus, 341; Niobe quits Thebes, 343; Oedipus arrives in, 347; afflicted by the Sphinx, 347; Oedipus expelled from, 351; Polynices banished from, 351; war of the Seven Champions against, 353-373; the seven gates of, 361; Creon succeeds to the kingdom of, 373; captured by the Athenians under

537

INDEX

Thessaly in the great flood, i. 55; inhabited by the Aeolians, 57, 61; Salmoneus at first dwelt in, 81; Pelias dwelt in, 85; Pheres founds Pheræ in, 91; Hercules left behind by the Argonauts at Aphetae in, 101; Phlegyas in, ii. 13; the country of the Pelasgians, 257, 259

Thestalus, son of Hercules by Epicaste, i. 277

Thestius, son of Ares, husband of Eurythemis, i. 63; his children by her, 63; his sons hunt the Calydonian boar, 67, and are killed by Meleager, 69; father of Iphiclus, 97; Tyndareus and Icarius flee to, ii. 23; father of Leda, 23

Thetis, a Nereid, i. 15; saves Hephaestus when he was cast down from heaven, 23; with the Nereids steers the Argo through the Wandering Rocks, 115; daughter of Nereus, Dionysus takes refuge with her in the sea, 327; Zeus and Poseidon rivals for her hand, ii. 67; married by Peleus, 67; her transformations to avoid him, 67; mother of Achilles, 85; tries to make Achilles immortal, 69, 71; departs to the Nereids, 71; entrusts Achilles in female garb to Lycomedes, 73; warns Achilles not to kill Tenes, 195, and not to be the first to land at Troy, 199; persuades Neoptolemus to wait at Troy, 247; buries Ajax in Myconos, 247; advises Neoptolemus to stay in Tenedos, 251

Thettalus, son of Hercules by Chalciope, i. 275, 277

Thia, a Titanid, daughter of Sky and Earth, i. 5; wife of Hyperion, mother of Dawn, Sun, and Moon, 13

Thias, king of Assyria, father of Adonis, according to Panyasis, ii. 87

Thiodamas, father of Hylas, i. 101; a bullock-driver, his encounter with Hercules, 261, 263

Thoas, father of Hypsipyle, saved by her from massacre, i. 99, 359

Thoas, king of the Taurians, Orestes brought before, ii. 275

Thoas, son of Andraemon and Gorge, leader of the Aetolians against Troy, ii. 183; in Aetolia, 307; Ulysses goes to him and marries his daughter, 307

Thoas, son of Dionysus by Ariadne, ii. 137

Thoas, son of Icarius, ii. 23

Thoas, suitor of Penelope, ii. 297

Thoösa, a nymph, mother of Polyphemus by Poseidon, ii. 283

Thoricus, Cephalus at, i. 173

Thrace, Typhon in, i. 51; Lemnian men take captive women from, 99; Salmydessus in, 103; the cows of Geryon disperse in the mountains of, 217; Cadmus and Telephassa settle in, 301; traversed by Dionysus, 331; Tereus in, ii. 99; Eumolpus in, 109

Thracian Bisaltians, ii. 263. See Bisaltians

Thracian people, the Bistones a, i. 201

Thracian Straits, afterwards called the Bosporus, i. 133

Thracians in Thasos, subjugated by Hercules, i. 209; hospitably receive Cadmus, 313; a force of, fights for the Eleusinians against the Athenians, ii. 109, 111; Trojan allies, 205

Thrasymedes, son of Nestor, i. 85

Thrasymedes, suitor of Penelope, ii. 297

Three-eyed One, oracle concerning, i. 287, 289

Threpsippus, son of Hercules by Panope, i. 273

Thriasian plain flooded by Poseidon, ii. 81

Thriasus, suitor of Penelope, ii. 297

Thrinacia, Island of, the kine of the Sun in, i. 115, ii. 295

Thunder and lightning bestowed on Zeus by the Cyclopes, i. 11; Salmoneus's imitation of, 81

Thunderbolt cast by Athena, ii. 247

539

INDEX

213; judge in the competition for the arms of Achilles, 219; many slain by Neoptolemus, 225, 227; drag the Wooden Horse into Troy, 233; slain by the Greeks, 239

Tros, son of Erichthonius, succeeds to the kingdom and calls the country Troy, ii. 37; his children by Callirrhoe, 37

Troy, Rhesus at, i. 21; Hercules at, 23; the war of, 75, 91; Hercules rescues Hesione from a sea monster at, 205, 207; visited by the wrath of Apollo and Poseidon for the faithlessness of Laomedon, 205, 207; named after Tros, ii. 37; besieged, 51; dying Alexander (Paris) carried to, 51; expedition of Hercules against, 61; not to be taken without Achilles, 73; Achilles goes to, 75; Alexander comes with Helen to, 175; Agamemnon musters an army against, 177; to be taken after ten years, 185; Telephus shows the Greeks the way to, 189; the Greeks make sail for, 197; not to be taken without the bow of Hercules, 221, 223; Philoctetes comes to, 223; Helenus leaves, 223; not to be taken while the Palladium was within the walls, 225; the sons of Theseus come to, 237; laid waste by the Greeks, 243; Hermione betrothed to Neoptolemus at, 253; Elephenor dies in, 259; Amphilochus comes later to, 265; the Locrians send maidens to propitiate Athena at, 267. See Ilium

Twins exposed, i. 83 (Pelias and Neleus), 339 (Zethus and Amphion); quarrelling in the womb, 145; Apollo makes the cows of Admetus to bear, ii. 21

Tydeus, son of Oeneus and Periboea or Gorge, i. 71; banished for homicide, 71, 73; marries Deipyle, daughter of Adrastus, 73, **353**; marches against Thebes, 73; killed by Melanippus, 73; father of Diomedes, 73, 379, ii. 27, 183; fights Polynices at Argos, i. 353;

one of the Seven against Thebes, 357; one of the victors in the Nemean games, 359; sent to Eteocles with a message, 359; defeats a Theban ambush, 361; wounded by Melanippus, sucks the brains of his slain foe, 369; Athena in disgust withholds from him the immortality which she had designed for him, 369

Tyndareus, son of Perieres and Gorgophone, i. 79; restored to Lacedaemon by Hercules, 253; son of Perieres or of Oebalus, ii. 13, 21; raised from the dead by Aesculapius, 19; expelled from Lacedaemon by Hippocoon, 23; flies to Thestius and marries Leda, 23; returns and succeeds to the kingdom, 23; his children, 23; exacts an oath from Helen's suitors, 29; gives Helen to Menelaus, 29; procures Penelope for Ulysses, 29; on the translation of the Dioscuri to the gods, he hands over the kingdom of Sparta to Menelaus, 35, **171**; brings back Agamemnon and Menelaus from Aetolia, 171; brings Orestes to trial at the Areopagus, 271

Typhon, a hybrid monster, offspring of Tartarus and Earth, i. 47; brought forth in Cilicia, 47; attacks heaven, 49; pelted with thunderbolts by Zeus, 49; grapples with Zeus, severs his sinews, and deposits him in the Corycian cave, 49; beguiled by the Fates, 51; buried under Mount Etna, 51; begets the Chimera, 151; father of the Nemean lion, 185; begets dog Orthus on Echidna, 211; begets the dragon of the Hesperides, 221; father of the eagle that devoured the liver of Prometheus, 229; father of the Sphinx, 347; father of the Crommyon sow, ii. 129

Tyrannus, son of Pterelaus, i. 165

Tyria, wife of Egyptus, i. 141

Tyro, daughter of Salmoneus and Alcidice, loves river Enipeus, i. 81; mother of twins, Pelias and Neleus, by Poseidon, 83; wife of

INDEX

Victory, born of Pallas and Styx, i. 13

Vine discovered by Dionysus, i. 325; Lycurgus, driven mad by Dionysus, mistakes his son for a branch of a, 327; branch of, given by Dionysus to Icarius, ii. 97

Vine-plant first given by Dionysus to Oeneus, i. 63, 65

Violence, born of Pallas and Styx, i. 13

Vixen ravages the Cadmea, i. 171; sons of Thebans exposed to it monthly, 171; chased by the dog of Cephalus and turned to stone, 173

Vulture tells Melampus how to cure the impotence of Iphiclus, i. 89, 91

Vultures eat the heart of Tityus, i. 29

Wand, golden, given by Apollo to Hermes, ii. 11; of Circe, 287

Wandering Rocks, the Argo at the, i. 115; Ulysses at the, ii. 293

Well of the Fair Dances at Eleusis, i. 37

Wheat given by Demeter to Triptolemus and sown by him over the whole earth, i. 39; parched by women at instigation of Ino, 75

White Isle, Achilles and Patroclus buried together in the, ii. 217

Winds, born of Astraeus and Dawn, i. 13; Aeolus keeper of the, ii. 285

Wine-brewing taught by Dionysus to Icarius, ii. 97

Wine-jar of the centaurs, i. 193

Winged sandals worn by Perseus, i. 157

Winnowing-fan, Hermes at birth placed in a, ii. 5

Wolves, Athamas entertained by, i. 77; feared by the Stymphalian birds, 199; companions of Ulysses turned into, ii. 287

Wooden Horse, invented by Ulysses, ii. 229; constructed by Epeus, 229, 231; dragged by the Trojans into Troy, 233; opened to let out the Greeks, 235

Xanthippe, daughter of Dorus, wife of Pleuron, i. 61

Xanthippus, son of Melas, killed by Tydeus, i. 71, 73

Xanthis, daughter of Thespius, mother of Homolippus by Hercules, i. 273

Xanthus, an immortal horse, given by Poseidon to Peleus, ii. 69

Xenodamus, son of Menelaus by a nymph Cnossia, ii. 31

Xenodice, daughter of Minos, i. 303

Xenodoce (not Xenodice), daughter of Syleus, killed by Hercules, i. 243

Xuthus, son of Hellen by a nymph Orseis, father of Achaeus and Ion, i. 57; father of Diomede, 79; husband of Creusa, ii. 103

Xylophagus, later name for Mount Caphereus, ii. 249

Year, an eternal, equivalent to eight common years, i. 317

Zacynthos, suitors of Penelope from, ii. 297, 299

Zelia, city allied with Troy, ii. 205

Zetes and Calais, sons of Boreas, in the Argo, i. 97; pursue the Harpies and failing to catch them die, 105, ii. 105, 107, or are killed by Hercules, 107

Zethus, son of Zeus by Antiope, twin brother of Amphion, i. 337, 339; pays attention to cattle-breeding, 339; marries Thebe, 341. See Amphion and Zethus

Zeus, son of Cronus and Rhea, i. 7; born in a cave of Dicte in Crete, 7; fed by nymphs, 7; guarded by Curetes, 7, 9; makes war on the Titans, 9, 11; releases the Cyclopes from Tartarus and receives thunder and lightning from them, 11; shuts up the Titans in Tartarus, 11; casts lots with his brothers Poseidon and Pluto for the sovereignty, 11; allotted the dominion of the sky, 11; ordains oaths by the water of Styx, 13; marries Hera, 15; his

544

INDEX

THE LOEB CLASSICAL
LIBRARY

VOLUMES ALREADY PUBLISHED

LATIN AUTHORS

AMMIANUS MARCELLINUS. J. C. Rolfe. 3 Vols.

APULEIUS : THE GOLDEN ASS (METAMORPHOSES). W. Adlington (1566). Revised by S. Gaselee.

ST. AUGUSTINE : CITY OF GOD. 7 Vols. Vol. I. G. E. McCracken. Vol. II. W. M. Green. Vol. III. D. Wiesen. Vol. IV. P. Levine. Vol. V. E. M. Sanford and W. M. Green. Vol. VI. W. C. Greene.

ST. AUGUSTINE, CONFESSIONS OF. W. Watts (1631). 2 Vols.

ST. AUGUSTINE : SELECT LETTERS. J. H. Baxter.

AUSONIUS. H. G. Evelyn White. 2 Vols.

BEDE. J. E. King. 2 Vols.

BOETHIUS : TRACTS AND DE CONSOLATIONE PHILOSOPHIAE. Rev. H. F. Stewart and E. K. Rand.

CAESAR : ALEXANDRIAN, AFRICAN AND SPANISH WARS. A. G. Way.

CAESAR : CIVIL WARS. A. G. Peskett.

CAESAR : GALLIC WAR. H. J. Edwards.

CATO AND VARRO : DE RE RUSTICA. H. B. Ash and W. D. Hooper.

CATULLUS. F. W. Cornish ; TIBULLUS. J. B. Postgate ; and PERVIGILIUM VENERIS. J. W. Mackail.

CELSUS : DE MEDICINA. W. G. Spencer. 3 Vols.

CICERO : BRUTUS AND ORATOR. G. L. Hendrickson and H. M. Hubbell.

CICERO : DE FINIBUS. H. Rackham.

CICERO : DE INVENTIONE, etc. H. M. Hubbell.

CICERO : DE NATURA DEORUM AND ACADEMICA. H. Rackham.

CICERO : DE OFFICIIS. Walter Miller.

CICERO : DE ORATORE, etc. 2 Vols. Vol. I : DE ORATORE, Books I and II. E. W. Sutton and H. Rackham. Vol. II : DE ORATORE, Book III ; DE FATO ; PARADOXA STOICORUM ; DE PARTITIONE ORATORIA. H. Rackham.

CICERO : DE REPUBLICA, DE LEGIBUS, SOMNIUM SCIPIONIS. Clinton W. Keyes.

THE LOEB CLASSICAL LIBRARY

CICERO : DE SENECTUTE, DE AMICITIA, DE DIVINATIONE. W. A. Falconer.

CICERO : IN CATILINAM, PRO MURENA, PRO SULLA, PRO FLACCO. Louis E. Lord.

CICERO : LETTERS TO ATTICUS. E. O. Winstedt. 3 Vols.

CICERO : LETTERS TO HIS FRIENDS. W. Glynn Williams. 3 Vols

CICERO : PHILIPPICS. W. C. A. Ker.

CICERO : PRO ARCHIA, POST REDITUM, DE DOMO, DE HARUSPICUM RESPONSIS, PRO PLANCIO. N. H. Watts.

CICERO : PRO CAECINA, PRO LEGE MANILIA, PRO CLUENTIO, PRO RABIRIO. H. Grose Hodge.

CICERO : PRO CAELIO, DE PROVINCIIS CONSULARIBUS, PRO BALBO. R. Gardner.

CICERO : PRO MILONE, IN PISONEM, PRO SCAURO, PRO FONTEIO, PRO RABIRIO POSTUMO, PRO MARCELLO, PRO LIGARIO, PRO REGE DEIOTARO. N. H. Watts.

CICERO : PRO QUINCTIO, PRO ROSCIO AMERINO, PRO ROSCIO COMOEDO, CONTRA RULLUM. J. H. Freese.

CICERO : PRO SESTIO, IN VATINIUM. R. Gardner.

[CICERO] : RHETORICA AD HERENNIUM. H. Caplan.

CICERO : TUSCULAN DISPUTATIONS. J. E. King.

CICERO : VERRINE ORATIONS. L. H. G. Greenwood. 2 Vols.

CLAUDIAN. M. Platnauer. 2 Vols.

COLUMELLA : DE RE RUSTICA, DE ARBORIBUS. H. B. Ash, E. S. Forster, E. Heffner. 3 Vols.

CURTIUS, Q.: HISTORY OF ALEXANDER. J. C. Rolfe. 2 Vols.

FLORUS. E. S. Forster ; and CORNELIUS NEPOS. J. C. Rolfe.

FRONTINUS : STRATAGEMS AND AQUEDUCTS. C. E. Bennett and M. B. McElwain.

FRONTO : CORRESPONDENCE. C. R. Haines. 2 Vols.

GELLIUS. J. C. Rolfe. 3 Vols.

HORACE : ODES AND EPODES. C. E. Bennett.

HORACE : SATIRES, EPISTLES, ARS POETICA. H. R. Fairclough.

JEROME : SELECT LETTERS. F. A. Wright.

JUVENAL AND PERSIUS. G. G. Ramsay.

LIVY. B. O. Foster, F. G. Moore, Evan T. Sage, A. C. Schlesinger and R. M. Geer (General Index). 14 Vols.

LUCAN. J. D. Duff.

LUCRETIUS. W. H. D. Rouse.

MARTIAL. W. C. A. Ker. 2 Vols.

MINOR LATIN POETS : from PUBLILIUS SYRUS TO RUTILIUS NAMATIANUS, including GRATTIUS, CALPURNIUS SICULUS, NEMESIANUS, AVIANUS, with " Aetna," " Phoenix " and other poems. J. Wight Duff and Arnold M. Duff.

2

THE LOEB CLASSICAL LIBRARY

Ovid : The Art of Love and other Poems. J. H. Mozley.

Ovid : Fasti. Sir James G. Frazer.

Ovid : Heroides and Amores. Grant Showerman.

Ovid : Metamorphoses. F. J. Miller. 2 Vols.

Ovid : Tristia and Ex Ponto. A. L. Wheeler.

Petronius. M. Heseltine ; Seneca : Apocolocyntosis. W. H. D. Rouse.

Phaedrus and Babrius (Greek). B. E. Perry.

Plautus. Paul Nixon. 5 Vols.

Pliny : Letters, Panegyricus. B. Radice. 2 Vols.

Pliny : Natural History. 10 Vols. Vols. I-V and IX. H. Rackham. Vols. VI-VIII. W. H. S. Jones. Vol. X. D. E. Eichholz.

Propertius. H. E. Butler.

Prudentius. H. J. Thomson. 2 Vols.

Quintilian. H. E. Butler. 4 Vols.

Remains of Old Latin. E. H. Warmington. 4 Vols. Vol. I (Ennius and Caecilius). Vol. II (Livius, Naevius, Pacuvius, Accius). Vol. III (Lucilius, Laws of the XII Tables). Vol. IV (Archaic Inscriptions).

Sallust. J. C. Rolfe.

Scriptores Historiae Augustae. D. Magie. 3 Vols.

Seneca : Apocolocyntosis. *Cf.* Petronius.

Seneca : Epistulae Morales. R. M. Gummere. 3 Vols.

Seneca : Moral Essays. J. W. Basore. 3 Vols.

Seneca : Tragedies. F. J. Miller. 2 Vols.

Sidonius : Poems and Letters. W. B. Anderson. 2 Vols.

Silius Italicus. J. D. Duff. 2 Vols.

Statius. J. H. Mozley. 2 Vols.

Suetonius. J. C. Rolfe. 2 Vols.

Tacitus : Agricola and Germania. Maurice Hutton ; Dialogus. Sir Wm. Peterson.

Tacitus : Histories and Annals. C. H. Moore and J. Jackson. 4 Vols.

Terence. John Sargeaunt. 2 Vols.

Tertullian : Apologia and De Spectaculis. T. R. Glover ; Minucius Felix. G. H. Rendall.

Valerius Flaccus. J. H. Mozley.

Varro : De Lingua Latina. R. G. Kent. 2 Vols.

Velleius Paterculus and Res Gestae Divi Augusti. F. W. Shipley.

Virgil. H. R. Fairclough. 2 Vols.

Vitruvius : De Architectura. F. Granger. 2 Vols.

THE LOEB CLASSICAL LIBRARY

ACHILLES TATIUS. S. Gaselee.

AELIAN: ON THE NATURE OF ANIMALS. A. F. Scholfield. 3 Vols.

AENEAS TACTICUS, ASCLEPIODOTUS AND ONASANDER. The Illinois Greek Club.

AESCHINES. C. D. Adams.

AESCHYLUS. H. Weir Smyth. 2 Vols.

ALCIPHRON, AELIAN AND PHILOSTRATUS: LETTERS. A. R. Benner and F. H. Fobes.

APOLLODORUS. Sir James G. Frazer. 2 Vols.

APOLLONIUS RHODIUS. R. C. Seaton.

THE APOSTOLIC FATHERS. Kirsopp Lake. 2 Vols.

APPIAN'S ROMAN HISTORY. Horace White. 4 Vols.

ARATUS. *Cf.* CALLIMACHUS.

ARISTOPHANES. Benjamin Bickley Rogers. 3 Vols. Verse trans.

ARISTOTLE: ART OF RHETORIC. J. H. Freese.

ARISTOTLE: ATHENIAN CONSTITUTION, EUDEMIAN ETHICS, VIRTUES AND VICES. H. Rackham.

ARISTOTLE: THE CATEGORIES. ON INTERPRETATION. H. P. Cooke; PRIOR ANALYTICS. H. Tredennick.

ARISTOTLE: GENERATION OF ANIMALS. A. L. Peck.

ARISTOTLE: HISTORIA ANIMALIUM. A. L. Peck. 3 Vols. Vols. I and II.

ARISTOTLE: METAPHYSICS. H. Tredennick. 2 Vols.

ARISTOTLE: METEOROLOGICA. H. D. P. Lee.

ARISTOTLE: MINOR WORKS. W. S. Hett. "On Colours," "On Things Heard," "Physiognomics," "On Plants," "On Marvellous Things Heard," "Mechanical Problems," "On Indivisible Lines," "Situations and Names of Winds," "On Melissus, Xenophanes, and Gorgias."

ARISTOTLE: NICOMACHEAN ETHICS. H. Rackham.

ARISTOTLE: OECONOMICA AND MAGNA MORALIA. G. C. Armstrong. (With METAPHYSICS, Vol. II.)

ARISTOTLE: ON THE HEAVENS. W. K. C. Guthrie.

ARISTOTLE: ON THE SOUL, PARVA NATURALIA. ON BREATH. W. S. Hett.

ARISTOTLE: PARTS OF ANIMALS. A. L. Peck; MOTION AND PROGRESSION OF ANIMALS. E. S. Forster.

ARISTOTLE: PHYSICS. Rev. P. Wicksteed and F. M. Cornford. 2 Vols.

4

THE LOEB CLASSICAL LIBRARY

ARISTOTLE : POETICS ; LONGINUS ON THE SUBLIME. W. Hamilton Fyfe ; DEMETRIUS ON STYLE. W. Rhys Roberts.

ARISTOTLE : POLITICS. H. Rackham.

ARISTOTLE : POSTERIOR ANALYTICS. H. Tredennick ; TOPICS. E. S. Forster.

ARISTOTLE : PROBLEMS. W. S. Hett. 2 Vols.

ARISTOTLE : RHETORICA AD ALEXANDRUM. H. Rackham. (With PROBLEMS, Vol. II.)

ARISTOTLE : SOPHISTICAL REFUTATIONS. COMING-TO-BE AND PASSING-AWAY. E. S. Forster : ON THE COSMOS. D. J. Furley.

ARRIAN : HISTORY OF ALEXANDER AND INDICA. Rev. E. Iliffe Robson. 2 Vols.

ATHENAEUS : DEIPNOSOPHISTAE. C. B. Gulick. 7 Vols.

BABRIUS AND PHAEDRUS (Latin). B. E. Perry.

ST. BASIL : LETTERS. R. J. Deferrari. 4 Vols.

CALLIMACHUS : FRAGMENTS. C. A. Trypanis.

CALLIMACHUS : HYMNS AND EPIGRAMS, AND LYCOPHRON. A. W. Mair ; ARATUS. G. R. Mair.

CLEMENT OF ALEXANDRIA. Rev. G. W. Butterworth.

COLLUTHUS. *Cf.* OPPIAN.

DAPHNIS AND CHLOE. *Cf.* LONGUS.

DEMOSTHENES I : OLYNTHIACS, PHILIPPICS AND MINOR ORATIONS : I-XVII AND XX. J. H. Vince.

DEMOSTHENES II : DE CORONA AND DE FALSA LEGATIONE, C. A. Vince and J. H. Vince.

DEMOSTHENES III : MEIDIAS, ANDROTION, ARISTOCRATES. TIMOCRATES, ARISTOGEITON. J. H. Vince.

DEMOSTHENES IV-VI : PRIVATE ORATIONS AND IN NEAERAM. A. T. Murray.

DEMOSTHENES VII : FUNERAL SPEECH, EROTIC ESSAY. EXORDIA AND LETTERS. N. W. and N. J. DeWitt.

DIO CASSIUS : ROMAN HISTORY. E. Cary. 9 Vols.

DIO CHRYSOSTOM. 5 Vols. Vols. I and II. J. W. Cohoon. Vol. III. J. W. Cohoon and H. Lamar Crosby. Vols. IV and V. H. Lamar Crosby.

DIODORUS SICULUS. 12 Vols. Vols. I-VI. C. H. Oldfather. Vol. VII. C. L. Sherman. Vol. VIII. C. B. Welles. Vols. IX and X. Russel M. Geer. Vols. XI and XII. F. R. Walton. General Index. Russel M. Geer.

DIOGENES LAERTIUS. R. D. Hicks. 2 Vols.

DIONYSIUS OF HALICARNASSUS : ROMAN ANTIQUITIES. Spelman's translation revised by E. Cary. 7 Vols.

EPICTETUS. W. A. Oldfather. 2 Vols.